Rome's Revolution 3455 AD

BY
MICHAEL BRACHMAN

ROME'S REVOLUTION 3455 AD

Also by Michael Brachman

The Rome's Revolution Series
Rome's Revolution 3455 AD
The Ark Lords
Rome's Evolution

The Rome's Revolution Saga
Rebirth: The Rome's Revolution Saga – Book 1
Rebellion: The Rome's Revolution Saga – Book 2
Redemption: The Rome's Revolution Saga – Book 3

The Vuduri Knights Series
The Milk Run

The Vuduri Universe Series
The Vuduri Companion
Tales of the Vuduri: Year One
Tales of the Vuduri: Year Two
Tales of the Vuduri: Year Three
Tales of the Vuduri: Year Four
Tales of the Vuduri: Year Five

Dedication

Each time I publish a new book, my dedications grow larger because the number of people helping me continues to grow. Even so, first, as always, I must thank my brother Bruce. He has always had my back even before I restarted my modern career. Not only is he my editor and artist and the inspiration behind MINIMCOM, but he is also fiercely protective of the Vuduri culture and characters. Bruce creates the amazing covers, the book trailers and makes my writing so much better. Bruce, I could not have done it without you.

My friend Helen has always been a fantastic sounding board. She is quite a spectacular writer and her advice has always been amazing. For this particular book, she taught me about scene and structure and that help me reorganize the chapters into becoming page turners so you would not be able to ever put the book down. Thank you, Helen, for all your support over the years.

I would like to thank Barbara for always encouraging me, reading these books time and time again and helping me to bring humanity to characters that always teetered on the brink of being two-dimensional. Barbara forced me to consider giving all the characters, even the minor ones, some much needed depth so you would care about them as people.

I would like to thank my countless readers for their criticism and suggestions. Sometimes it stung a little but it was always for a good cause.

Finally, my undying gratitude to my wife, Denise, for all her love and support throughout the entire process. She patiently waits while I hide myself in the basement, cranking out what is now over a million words, because she knows I love writing. She even cooperates and allows me to keep my workspace unadorned, despite the fact that it is against her nature, so that my mind can travel to different places and times. Denise, thank you so much and I'll be up around 5:30, I promise. Yeah, right, she says.

Preface

This story is true. It just hasn't happened yet.

Part I:
Rebirth

Prologue
Year 3455 AD
Location: Sixth Planet, Tabit (Pi³ Orionis) System
(26 Light Years from Earth)

REI BIERAK FELT THE LEGS OF HIS ALL-WHITE PRESSURE SUIT stiffen as the air in the hangar rushed out to mix with the thin, unbreathable atmosphere of the moon called Dara. The dirt swirled around the hangar entrance in tiny eddies, like miniature dust devils. In his right hand, Rei clutched a metal briefcase filled with dormant VIRUS units that were possibly the most destructive force in the galaxy. Although he was anxious to get started, he had to wait a moment for the pressure inside the hangar to equilibrate with the outside.

Finally, Rei took his first step onto the surface of the moon where he had been living inside a habitat for the last several days. The soil was crunchy, not dusty as he would have guessed. Looking down at his boots, it hit him. He was finally setting foot on an alien world for the first time. Back on Earth, just before the Ark II had launched, he had tried to visualize his first exo-step. He assumed it would be on the planet where he would be making his new home. Yet here he was, a 25 year-old man from the 21st century, stuck in the 35th century, in a star system 26 light years from Earth on a world about to be destroyed. In fact, it was his job to destroy not only this moon but to set into motion a series of events that would eventually take out the entire star system along with it.

He looked up and out. Dara, the moon, was unremarkable in every way. The soil was brown and drab. It looked nothing like the surface of a typical moon. Rei saw signs of erosion everywhere. Dara had enough atmosphere to slow down meteors and enough wind and weather to smooth out all but the newest craters. It certainly didn't have the stark beauty of Earth's Moon or the startling contrast of shapes and colors of Mars.

Rei breathed in sharply through his nose; however, all he could smell was the purified air of the pressure suit mixed with his own perspiration. Trying to breathe the air here would have killed him rather quickly. He took two more steps forward then turned to his right and began his long trek south.

Based upon OMCOM's estimate, Rei figured he should probably walk about 1000 paces away from the habitat before releasing the VIRUS nanobots. That would give him more than enough time to return to the space tug. He would be able to lift off and rendezvous with the Ark II long before the nanobots consumed Dara.

Ahead of Rei, Dara's parent, the gas giant known as Skyler's World, dominated the horizon. It filled nearly one-third of the heavens above. In stark contrast to the muted, dreary appearance of Dara, the Jupiter-class planet shone brightly with its gaudy bands of chocolate brown and aqua, white, turquoise, azure and streaks of red. Skyler's World was so large it would have most likely developed into a star or brown dwarf someday but now it would never get the chance. Even the mighty Skyler's World would not survive the hell that Rei was about to unleash.

Inside his helmet, Rei counted his paces out loud in a vain attempt to avoid considering his predicament. To further distract himself, he searched the sky overhead. He was trying to spot the Ark II, the spaceship that had brought him here to the Tabit system which was silently orbiting Dara with 539 of his fellow colonists aboard. Rei envied his frozen peers, fast asleep in cryo-hibernation. They were blissfully unaware of the dire nature of their circumstances and the thing that was rapidly barreling down on them. Thinking about it made him pick up his tempo.

At 900 paces, Rei felt the ground shake. There was no slow buildup. The vibrations were abrupt and more violent than an ordinary moonquake but subsided quickly. He turned and looked back at the habitat. Rising majestically above the rounded pyramid of the station was the flagship of the Vuduri fleet, the starship Algol, pounding the dirt and whipping up the dust with its powerful EG lifters. The all-white spaceship flew forward, away from Rei, and then executed a slow bank right, coming around until it was headed in his direction.

Unlike his Ark II which was constructed as a series of long flattened cylinders, the Algol was far more graceful, about half the length of the Ark. The Algol was sleek and streamlined. With its

2

huge thruster pods poised at the end of each airfoil, it was clearly designed to operate both in space and within an atmosphere.

As the starship flew over his head, it waggled its wings. Rei raised his free hand to acknowledge the gesture. At the helm of the ship was his beloved Rome, the Vuduri woman he had met when he first arrived here. Despite the brevity of Rei's stay, they had fallen deeply in love with each other. Rei knew Rome had no choice but to pilot the Algol back to Earth by herself since she was the only member of the Vuduri people who remained conscious, leaving Rei behind. He stood by helplessly as the massive ship rose up into the air. After a short time, he saw the plasma thrusters ignite and the Algol took off straight up like a rocket. With tears in his eyes, Rei watched the spaceship gain altitude. The craft dwindled in size, first to a tiny speck then finally disappearing into space.

Grief-stricken, Rei sank to his knees and sobbed uncontrollably. His beautiful Rome, the love of his life, was gone, never to return. At this point, Rei was as alone as any human being could ever be. Without Rome, it seemed like he had no reason to live. His heart was broken but his sense of duty still haunted him. His frozen comrades in the Ark II above were depending upon him to tow them out of the Tabit system and on to Tau Ceti, their original target, before the destruction began. Like Rome, Rei really didn't have a choice. He forced himself to stand and get on with the task of destroying a world.

Rei scanned the area immediately in front of him. He spotted a suitable crater about a hundred yards ahead. As he trudged forward, the finality of his mission pressed down on him, forcing him to wonder how he got here. How did it come to this? Rei shook his head as the events of the prior few days came flooding back to him…

Chapter 1
(Three days earlier)

REI BIERAK WAS JARRED AWAKE FROM HIS CRYO-HIBERNATION BY A searing pain shooting through his chest. The automatic defibrillator had just fired off a 300-joule pulse, erroneously trying to restart his already-beating heart. The cardiac sensors glued to his torso had degraded over time meaning the unsuspecting control microprocessor had no clue that its previous work had actually been successful. Even though Rei's ears were filled with gloppy green rehydration fluid, he could still hear the high-pitched whine of the resonance coils charging up for a third and final attempt at reviving him. He realized he had to get the defibrillator pads off of his chest or the very piece of equipment that was supposed to save his life was going to kill him instead. With a titanic effort, he lifted his right arm and clawed at one of the flexible leads, ripping it away just before the circuit tripped. A spark jumped the gap, burning Rei's fingers in the process but he knew that was a small price to pay when compared to being dead.

The motion of Rei moving his arm to pull off the defib pad acted like a fireplace bellows forcing him to draw in a deep breath of frigid air into lungs that hadn't been used in several centuries, which was a good thing. It didn't concern Rei that his eyes felt like they were glued shut. He figured he was now safe and had time to consider his situation. He was hermetically sealed inside a cryo-hibernation chamber called a sarcophagus, soaked in a liquid that was used to preserve him during the long trip to the stars. It was freezing cold but the mere fact that the resuscitation sequence had been engaged could only mean that the Ark II had arrived at its target, the star system known as Tau Ceti. Despite his clogged ears feeling like they were stuffed with cotton, Rei attempted to attend to the other softer sounds issuing from within the sarcophagus. He heard the quiet whirring of the fluid pumps as they sucked the liquid out of his chamber. He felt the heaters blowing warm air across his body as they endeavored to bring his core temperature up from hypothermia to normal. He could feel the nourishing heat emanating from the thorium rods mounted beneath his chamber warming up his back side. It felt good. His brain may have been

4

fuzzy from all the drugs they had given him prior to being frozen but enough of it worked for him to suss out what has happening.

A peculiar scraping noise caught Rei's attention which he immediately recognized as the sound of the cover of his sarcophagus being drawn back. He was saved! But before Rei could take much comfort in that thought, a blinding light bathed his face, penetrating his closed eyelids. Reflexively, he flung his arm over his eyes to block out the glare. He barely felt the two cardiac sensors and the other defibrillator pad being peeled away from his bare chest. He pulled his arm back and with a Herculean effort, forced his eyes open. The dazzling spotlights blasted him. He blinked rapidly, trying to adjust to the light. He was rewarded by now being able to see shapes and shadows crossing back and forth in front of him. One of the shapes drew near and an irresistible force lifted him up, enabling him to sit in an upright position. Rei tried to hold his head up but his neck lacked its usual muscle tone so his head drooped down until his chin rested upon his chest. Rei felt a soft material sliding over his feet then drawn up to the tops of his thighs which were resting on the edge of the sarcophagus.

Rei took another deep breath, forcing his eyes upward. Two bright shapes stood out against a dark background. Rei found squinting helped bring them into focus. To his horror, he realized these were not his crewmates helping to awaken him, but rather bizarre alien creatures. Bipedal with two arm-like appendages, dressed all in white, they sported huge bulbous heads with piercing beams of light shining from either side. Rei tried to shy away from their inhuman touch but he was simply too weak to pull free.

Eventually, reason prevailed. Rei thought to himself that if they intended to kill him, they would have done so already. They certainly wouldn't try and dress him. He closed his eyes again and forced himself to relax. Gently, the two beings coaxed him to his feet. They helped Rei insert his arms into the two sleeves. After they fastened the final clasp across the top, Rei opened his eyes and looked at them more carefully.

"Who are you?" he asked in a voice that was raspy from disuse.

Neither of the creatures reacted. As he stared at them, Rei recognized they might not be creatures at all. Their white clothing resembled a soft form-fitting spacesuit and the bright lights were basically lamps attached to either side of their helmets. He couldn't make out their faces which were cast deep in shadow. One of the people stood slightly taller than the other. Rei noted that the one on the right, the shorter one, had a distinctly feminine figure.

Rei allowed them to drape his long arms across their shoulders. They took one step and then another then stopped as Rei's knees started to buckle. This made no sense because wherever they were, the gravity here was far less than one g. He grabbed his rescuers tightly and forced himself to stand tall. The musculature of the one on the left was firm and solid. The one on the right, the more feminine one, felt softer.

Seeing that he was now steady, they started forward again. After a few more steps, Rei asked, "Where are you taking me?" As before, there was no answer. Perhaps they couldn't hear him inside their helmets.

Slowly but surely, the three of them walked across the floor to a bed. Perhaps gurney would be a better term. They laid Rei down and covered him with a thin white blanket. The mattress seemed to be some sort of memory foam. It shaped itself to the contours of his body as he settled back. It was very comfortable.

Just the effort of walking maybe ten feet was enough to exhaust Rei. The disturbing unknown of the who and the where would have to wait. In the back of his mind, he found it vaguely ironic that he had just awakened from what had to be centuries of cryo-hibernation and now all he wanted to do was sleep. He would have to solve the mystery of his circumstances later on. Within seconds, Rei fell into a deep, dreamless slumber.

***

After an indeterminate amount of time, Rei was rudely awakened by a sharp prick on the back of his right hand. He opened his eyes just in time to see a needle withdrawing from his skin. The syringe disappeared inside a metallic cylinder positioned by the side of his bed. Rei wiped a droplet of blood that appeared at the puncture point with his left hand and started to sit up. As he did so, a burning bolt of pain traveled from the bottom of his spine to the base of his neck, causing him to cry out.

"What the hell was that?" he muttered to himself after it subsided. He'd never had back problems in his life. Carefully, Rei swung his legs around and placed his feet on the ground. He looked down and noted that his feet were now encased in a pair of soft white slippers or moccasins. The white jumpsuit they had dressed him in was too tight. He longed for his regular tan flight suit which would have been so much more comfortable.

Having assessed his personal situation, Rei looked around the room. On the far wall, to the left of his sarcophagus, he noted a large picture window which overlooked a cavernous hangar. A stark white aircraft or spaceship sat nestled in the middle of the hangar. It reminded Rei of a boxier version of the long-retired Space Shuttle.

He looked to his right. The featureless, all-white wall was unremarkable with the exception of a soft white glow emanating from its surface. He looked up. The ceiling was also white and glowing. Apparently, there was no single light source here but rather the room itself supplied the illumination. Rei rotated his head farther to the right and spied a bulkhead with a large porthole on the near wall.

He took one step toward the door and was rewarded by another wave of pain traveling up his back, a pain so intense it made him stagger. Rei determined that despite the lower gravity, lifting his legs was too risky. Instead of walking normally, he slowly slid one foot then another, shuffling along until he got to the door. Looking up, he was startled to see a face staring back at him. He jumped back and once again, pain shot through his spine, only slightly less intense this time. The face on the other side of the porthole was female with long dark hair. She looked familiar and exotic at the same time and if he didn't know better, he'd swear her eyes were glowing.

Rei took another slide step toward the door. "Hello," he said. The woman did not react. He had no clue if sound even traveled through the door. He shouted "Hello!" again, waving his arms. The motion of his efforts spooked her and she took a step back away from the bulkhead.

"Can you hear me?" Rei called out. The woman stared into his eyes for a moment longer then turned and walked away. She quickly disappeared out of sight.

"Damn it," Rei said as he slumped against the door. "Anybody?"

A disembodied voice rang out from his right. **"Based upon your words and intonation, there is a 94% probability that you speak mid-21st century English. Is this correct?"**

"Who are you? Where are you?" Rei asked, looking around desperately.

"Engaging personality module. Please wait..."

The voice changed in tenor and cadence. "You may call me OMCOM. As far as my location is concerned, I am a distributed intelligence but to answer your specific question, the voice you hear emits from the grille mounted over by your bedside."

"Distributed intelligence? Personality module. You're a computer?"

"That is an adequate description for purposes of discussion."

Rei gauged the distance between where he stood and the edge of the bed. Based upon the amount of pain he experienced, it looked about a half a mile away. Nonetheless, slowly and carefully, he shuffled his way back over to his bed. Facing the nearest wall he became aware of all sorts of monitors and readouts that he hadn't noticed before.

"Where am I?" Rei asked, searching for the grille. "Where are we? And where is the rest of my crew?"

"Allow me to give you a brief orientation," OMCOM said. One of the monitors lit up with dots and circles with a star chart as a backdrop. "You are currently standing in an airlock which has been configured to serve as an isolation chamber. This entire habitat is located on a moon called Dara which orbits a gas giant. In your language, you would call the parent Skyler's World."

"So where is that? Where are we?" Rei asked, tilting his head, trying to make sense of the display.

"Skyler's World circles a star called Tabit also known as Pi^3 Orionis located 26.18 light years from Earth."

"What!?" Rei gasped. "26 light years? We were supposed to go to Tau Ceti. Where is Tau Ceti?"

On the display, OMCOM constructed a downward facing right triangle consisting of three dots and three lines. The rightmost dot glowed bright yellow. The bottom dot was orange and the leftmost dot flickered with a light-colored blue. The yellow dot started flashing.

"The blinking yellow symbol is the Solar System. The orange one is Tau Ceti which is approximately 12 light years distant." The lower dot and the line connecting them started blinking as well. "The leftmost dot is Tabit." The first two dots froze and now the only thing blinking was the pale blue indicator. "As I mentioned before Tabit is 26 light years from Earth and approximately 21 light years from Tau Ceti."

Rei tilted his head. "So how'd we get here? Wait. What year is this?"

"By your calendar, it would be the year 3455."

"What?!" Rei shook his head, trying to clear it. "You mean we've been asleep for 14 centuries?"

"Apparently."

"Then how… we…" Rei's voice trailed off as he tried to comprehend the whole picture. The sedatives in his bloodstream had nearly worn off but the rapid influx of data made it no less hard to focus. Rei lifted his hands at the wrist as if in a motion to stop the onslaught of information. He took a deep breath to compose himself. He looked up at the monitor again trying to formulate his next question. OMCOM preempted that attempt.

"This is the first time I have activated my personality module," OMCOM said. "Feedback indicates I should ask you your name in order to strengthen my perceived bond with you. What is your name?"

"My name? My name is Rei Bierak," Rei said, relieved to be considering something more trivial that the cosmic nightmare in front of him. "It's spelled Rei but pronounced like a ray of sunshine. It's short for Reinard."

9

"Very well, Rei, what is the name of your ship?"

"My ship? Oh. It's called the Ark II."

"How many passengers are aboard your Ark II?"

"543, well, 542 plus me," Rei answered.

"And what is your mission?"

"Our mission *was* to go to Tau Ceti. To land there. To live there."

"Based upon the visual evidence, this is most likely no longer an option," OMCOM said with what sounded like a hint of remorse.

"What do you mean?" Rei asked with trepidation.

OMCOM answered by clearing the star chart and lighting up the main display with an image of a large silvery object floating in space. "This is an image of the front section of your ship taken when we first towed it into orbit around Dara."

Rei carefully leaned over the bed so that he could be closer to the display. He watched as the camera swung around to the front of the ship.

"Holy Mother of Christ," Rei exclaimed. "The whole command section and SSTO booster is gone. What the hell happened?" He just stared at the screen and the ragged edges at the front of his vessel. To Rei, it looked like his ship had been ripped apart.

"Our transport found your vessel tumbling in all three axes. It would appear that this motion was most likely the residual momentum imparted by whatever caused the front section to be removed."

"Did we hit something? Was there an explosion?" Rei asked.

"I have no data regarding the underlying cause. Perhaps a more detailed inspection of your spacecraft may ascertain that information."

"Do you think the ship can still fly?" Rei asked. "Can you repair it?"

"To within three deltas, I compute a negative. Your command and control systems are gone. They would have to be replaced. What was your method of propulsion?"

"Um. Uh, we used the Grey Drive."

"I am not familiar with the Grey Drive. Can you describe its operation?"

Rei scratched his head trying to stimulate the remaining portions of his brain which seemed to still be asleep. "From what I understand," he said, "the Grey Drive uses a quantum black hole to consume xenon atoms which then emit Hawking radiation. The radiation is focused in a resonant cavity chamber which creates thrust in a vacuum."

"This base does not have the resources to create a quantum black hole so that would rule out repairing your star-drive."

"Then what about my crew? Are you going to bring them down here?"

"That would not be possible."

"Why not?" Rei whined.

"This stellar cartography base was designed to hold 80 people. We would have neither the room nor the resources to support that many of your peers."

"Well, you said we were on a moon. Forget your base. What about somewhere else?"

"The moon we occupy is not suitable for human habitation in the sense you require. For one thing, the atmosphere is far too thin and contains no oxygen. And to answer your next question, there are no planets in the habitable zone of the Tabit star system."

By this point, Rei felt queasy, his head throbbing. His knees were becoming wobbly and it felt like the ground was shaking beneath him. With a start, he realized the ground really was shaking. He grabbed a hold of the gurney.

"What's going on?" Rei called out as the tremors increased. "It feels like an earthquake."

"It is," OMCOM replied calmly. "Dara is very active geologically. We get small tremors here regularly. It is nothing to be alarmed about."

As quickly as the tremors came on, they diminished and then stopped. Rei turned around and faced away from display. He lowered his head into his hands and spoke through them. "So what's going to happen to us?"

"That is for the Overmind to decide."

11

Rei snapped his head up and turned back around. "What is the Overmind?" he asked tentatively. His tone indicated he wasn't sure he wanted to know the answer.

"The Overmind is the controlling intellect in charge of the base."

"Controlling intellect? Is it a computer like you?"

"No. It is organic but it has no physical body. Rather, the Overmind is an autonomous intelligence created by the collective consciousness of all the Vuduri here."

Rei felt like he was falling down a rabbit hole. "Who or what are the Vuduri?"

"That is the name of the people inhabiting this base. You met two of them earlier today."

Rei perked up. "Can I talk to one of them?"

"Very soon. We are preparing someone to converse with you even as we speak."

"What do you mean prepare?"

"The Vuduri do not use spoken language as their primary means of communication. It has largely fallen out of favor. I am instilling a working knowledge of your words and syntax into the candidate."

"Wait. If they don't speak, how do they communicate? Do they use sign language?" Rei shook his head and laughed. "Or do they just read each other's minds?"

"Actually, yes," OMCOM replied.

"What?!" Rei sputtered. "But how…"

OMCOM immediately interrupted him. "It would be best if you hold your remaining questions in abeyance until we can provide a more suitable forum. In the meantime, based upon our historical records, I was instructed to ascertain if you were harboring any harmful disease entities before you were allowed contact with any of the inhabitants of the base. I have completed my tests and I have determined that you are free of infection. The quarantine period is now over."

"Good," Rei replied. It felt like a tiny victory, one that should be celebrated. "Hey, can I have some water?" he asked.

"Of course," OMCOM answered. A previously hidden plate built into the wall slid back. Within the cavity sat a squeeze-bulb filled with water. Just as Rei was reaching for it, the bulkhead to his left opened with a loud hissing sound. A figure dressed all in white entered the room.

Chapter 2

REI FOUND HIMSELF SITTING ON THE GURNEY WITH HIS BACK against the instrumentation panel. He had been instructed to do so by OMCOM while the Vuduri woman regarded him. She was standing about six feet away, hands on her hips. She kept looking at him up and down as if she were trying to draw a deeper understanding of Rei's essence just by his appearance.

While she was staring at Rei, Rei was staring at her. He recognized her as the one who had peered at him earlier through the porthole. The woman was tiny, at most five feet tall, wearing a white jumpsuit similar to the one Rei had on. Her beautiful, shoulder-length, dark brown hair had hints of gold throughout. Her eyes were very dark as well. Her skin had an olive tint to it. She had an athletic build, but it was distinctly feminine, bordering on spectacular.

At last, she nodded. Rei thought that was a signal for him to stand but the woman held up her hand so Rei remained sitting. She closed her eyes, took a deep breath, then opened her eyes again and said in a clear voice, "Halli. Au siu Rome." Her voice had a lilting, musical quality about it.

From behind Rei, OMCOM said, "Hello. I am Rome."

The woman bent her head to look around Rei at OMCOM's grille then back to Rei and said, "I am Rome."

She took another deep breath and continued, "Ver-ma-e axema ta um shird quenti bere etquoror sue longue." Her voice, especially her intonation was familiar to Rei, but he had no idea why.

OMCOM spoke again, "It will take me a short while to acquire your language."

"It weel take eme a short while du ack," Rome said.

"Acquire," OMCOM offered.

"Du acquire your language," Rome repeated the phrase.

Rei nodded as if he understood but he really didn't. "OMCOM, what's going on here?" he asked.

"Your version of English has not been spoken in hundreds of years. While Rome is an accomplished linguist for a Vuduri, she must actually speak the words and have me correct them out loud a few times before she can pronounce them in your dialect."

14

"Nei ma vere axema ta um dambi lingi," Rome said.

OMCOM translated. "It will not take me a long time."

"It will nei, not, take me a long dambi, time," Rome repeated. Her accent sounded vaguely Mediterranean.

Rei was surprised. "How can you learn my language so quickly? How are you doing this in the first place?

"IMCOM," she said, placing two fingers on her temple.

"OMCOM?" Rei asked.

Rome nodded.

"You mean OMCOM is inside your head as well?"

"Som," she said.

"Yes," OMCOM corrected her then to Rei, he said, "Rome has acquired nearly 90% of your base language to this point."

"Huh." Rei cocked his head and looked at Rome. "Can you tell me what is going on here? OMCOM said there was this thing called the Overmind. How do I find it? Do you speak to the Overmind?"

"The Ifarmonte, the Overmind is hay part of me," Rome said, tapping her temple. "When you speak to me, you speak to it as well. The Overmind is the group coanda, eh, consciousness. Each of us contributes to it, but it is a distinct entity. The Overmind is in charge of this base. I am but a vessel for communication."

Rei scrunched up his face. "What are you even doing out here? What is this place, anyway? OMCOM said something about stellar cartography."

Rome turned away from Rei and walked over to a bench near some storage lockers. She sat down and emitted a long sigh. "Yes," she said. "But no more. We have failed in our mission. We are leaving," she said lowering her eyes to the floor.

"I don't get it. Failed what?" Rei asked.

Rome took yet another deep breath and looked back up at Rei. She started speaking again as if from a script. "We have been placed here to, eh, ipsarfa…"

"Observe."

"…to observe a certain venimani…phenomenon. We have not been able to do that."

"What kind of phenomenon?"

"Many stars have disappeared." Rome replied, clipping her fingers together then opening her hand flatly as if releasing pixie dust.

"What do you mean disappeared?"

"Exactly that. There were stars in the sky but now they are gone. This base was built to make certain observations. Those observations did not olumoner, no, that is not the word," Rome shook her head. "Did not shed luz…"

"Light," OMCOM corrected.

"…light on how it is happening. There was one star in particular called Winfall that we expected to go away. But it is long past the time when it should have disappeared. Winfall is still visible. Clearly we were not set up in the correct position. So we are closing down this base. We will return to Earth."

"Earth? Hey, how did you get out here? In that ship out there?" Rei pointed to the spacecraft sitting beyond the window.

Rome turned to look back where Rei was pointing. She shook her head.

"No," she said. "That is just a tug. It is strictly for short, mmm, excursions. We came here in our starship, the Algol."

Rei's eyes narrowed. "Starship? How did you… How long did it take you get out here?"

"One hundred and four days," Rome replied.

Rei did some quick math. "That's impossible," he said. "Twenty six light years in three months?"

"I understand your cinvusei, your confusion. It was very slow," Rome agreed. "The Algol was loaded down with much equipment. We are leaving most of it here. When we return, it will not take us nearly as long to get back."

"No," Rei interrupted. "Not too slow. It's too *fast*. How can you do that? You people travel faster than light?"

Rome thought about it for a moment. "Yes. No. Yes. OMCOM tells me if you measure velocity as distance divided by time, then yes. Much faster." She paused as if she was receiving input then spoke again. "We measure our velocity in multiples of the speed of light. If one 'c' is the speed of light, then we traveled here at an effective velocity of 100c."

16

"Wow," Rei whistled in admiration. He thought to himself, after all, it had been 14 centuries. It would be reasonable to assume that if faster-than-light travel was possible, they would have it figured out by now. "So how does that work? Do you have warp drives?" he asked.

"I do not know what a warp drive is. We use… pindi ponch trensodi," Rome said, trying to sound out the words.

"Pinch point transit. You may call it a PPT," came OMCOM's voice from behind Rei.

"Yes," Rome continued, "we use PPTs."

"So what is that?" Rei asked. "How does it work?"

OMCOM interrupted. "Your term for them would be wormholes although they are not instantiated in the way your predecessors envisioned. No black hole is required. The PPT tunnel is created when a sufficient amount of negative energy is concentrated in a limited area."

"Negative energy," Rei repeated. "I've heard of the Casimir Effect but it never occurred to me that anyone would ever harness it much less utilize it."

"To use your term, we employ Casimir pumps to create pockets of negative energy. Where there is no energy, there is no space. When our ships pass through these pockets, they jump directly from point A to point C, bypassing point B."

"When we travel in regular space, our ships travel fairly slowly," Rome added. "The process of building up a PPT tunnel takes time. But the net effect is a desirable one."

Rei snapped his fingers. "OK," he said. "If you are going back to Earth, can you take us with you?"

"Based upon the figures that OMCOM has transmitted to me, that would not be possible," Rome said. "There would not be enough room on our ship."

"Well what are you are going to do then?" Rei asked with an edge to his voice. "Just leave us here? Me? Them?" Rei pointed straight up.

"I do not know," Rome answered. "We must acquire more information first."

"What kind of information?"

Rome pointed to the bulkhead leading to the interior of the building. "We will work on that but not in here. You are permitted to enter the base now"

Rei nodded and slowly inched his way off of the bed. His stomach let out a loud growl. "Before we do anything, could I get some food first?" he asked. "I haven't eaten in 1400 years. I'm a little hungry."

Rome tilted her head and looked at him quizzically. "Yes, of course."

She stood up and motioned for Rei to follow her. Rei tried to stand, but just as he did, a small tremor caused him to fall back onto the bed. Rome walked over to him and extended her hand. Rei took it and felt a shock, like static electricity. He flinched but Rome held firm, helping him up. Even after he stood, Rome continued to hold on. She stared down at their clasped hands for the longest time then raised her eyes. As Rei looked at her more closely, he realized there was a peculiar dot right in the middle of her dilated pupils. She gave him a hint of a smile and only then gently pulled her hand away.

"Are you all right?" she asked.

"Yes," Rei answered. "I'm still not quite steady on my feet. Just go slowly and I'll be fine," he said.

Rome nodded and headed toward the door. Rei followed her out into the corridor which, like the room they just left, was also all white. Across from them stood two men dressed in white jumpsuits identical to the one Rei was wearing. They were standing at attention but staring down at the floor. They never made eye contact with Rei. Rome started down the hallway to the right. The floor, the walls and the ceiling all emitted a soft white glow. The corridor itself was not straight. It curved off to the left. Rei turned around and saw the other direction curved off as well.

Rome went a short distance then made a left turn at the first opening. Rei caught up to her and saw a long hallway stretching out in front of them with numerous openings to the left and the right, regularly spaced. As they walked, Rei noted that each opening was another corridor which curved away, out of sight. At the far end of the hallway lay a brighter area which appeared to be their destination. Coming toward them was a Vuduri woman, similar in stature to Rome but with close-cropped blonde hair. When they were nearly upon her, the woman stopped walking and backed up, pressing herself against the wall. She pointedly stared down at her feet, avoiding eye contact. As they passed, Rei bent over slightly to look upon her face. She glanced up and Rei saw that her eyes were two different colors. She glared at him with a scowl that radiated hatred so intense it was unnerving.

Rei shrugged and continued down the hallway with Rome. When they got about 15 feet further, he turned around. The woman was still glowering at him with a seriously dark expression. Rei shook his head and quickly turned away. He followed Rome into a rather large room, 100 feet across, with a center pole that held up a taut ceiling like a giant teepee. To Rei's right sat a number of tables and chairs. In the center of the room was an instrumentation console with cabinets and a set of rails that ran the full length.

"Come," Rome said, waving. She led him over to a large display built into the center section. "It would be easiest if you just tell OMCOM what food you would like. He will instruct the food dispensers on your behalf."

"Food dispensers? OK," Rei said. "I'll give it a try."

He spotted one of OMCOM's grilles close by. "OMCOM," he said, "How about some soup to start?"

"Soap, to eat?" Rome asked. "That is a peculiar thing."

"Not soap, soup," Rei said. "You know, like broth."

"Ah," Rome replied.

"I understand," OMCOM volunteered.

Rei heard some noises that reminded him of an old-style percolator. To his right, a panel opened and a tray emerged with two white bowls, each filled with a dark brown liquid. Rome withdrew the tray and set it on the rails attached to the front of the cabinets. Carefully, she slid the tray across until it was right in front of Rei. He lifted one of bowls and sniffed it. The contents had no smell. He dipped a finger in it and touched it to his tongue. The liquid tasted flat and a little bitter.

"What is this?" he asked, wrinkling his nose.

19

"As requested, it is a protein broth," answered OMCOM. "Soup."

Rei set the bowl back on the tray. "Do you have a spoon?" he asked Rome.

"What is a spoon?" she replied, puzzled.

"It's a utensil. Like a little bowl on a stick."

Rome gave him a funny look.

"Well, if you don't use spoons, how do you eat soup?" Rei asked.

Rome sighed gently. "You just pick up the bowl and drink it."

To demonstrate, she lifted the double-spouted bowl to her lips and took a small swallow then set the bowl down again. "How else would you do it?" she asked.

Rei looked down at the bowl. Now that he observed it more carefully, it was pretty obvious.

"I guess you're right," he said. However, the broth did not excite him. "How about if you get us something that has some substance to it?"

"Certainly," she replied. On the screen, the central display area cleared and a list scrolled across and down. Another, larger panel opened and two more trays appeared with dishes and several types of food, none of which Rei recognized.

"How did you do that?" he asked her.

Rome pointed to her temple and then to OMCOM's grille. "We can communicate directly with OMCOM using our bloco and stilo."

Rei scowled. "What are those?"

"Think of them as a neural net. Direct digital input and output."

"Oh yeah," Rei said. "OMCOM said something about that. It's going to take a little while to get used to the concept."

They removed their trays and walked over to one of the tables. Rome sat down. Rei sat down opposite her. He looked at the cubes of food. They looked like tofu or chunks of potato.

"How do you eat these?" he asked her. "Do you just pick them up with your fingers?"

"Your meals must have been very strange," Rome said, shaking her head. "You use your biskar like so…"

She picked up one of the thin wood-colored skewers sitting on the tray and poked it into one of the cubes. She placed it in her mouth and then opened her mouth to show Rei the cube of food sitting on her tongue.

"I know my brain was frozen," Rei said, "but I'm not an idiot."

"I meant no offense," Rome replied, looking just the tiniest bit hurt.

"I know you didn't," Rei answered, feeling a tad guilty. He tried to pick up his biskar with his right hand but his fingers were still sore from where the defibrillator singed him so he switched to his left hand. He used the biskar to spear one of the more appetizing looking pieces and popped it into his mouth. Like the soup, it had essentially no taste. The cubes reminded Rei of soggy Styrofoam. He sampled each of the items, but was singularly unimpressed.

Rei looked up and was surprised to see Rome eating with some zest.

"This is all pretty tasteless," he remarked to her. "Don't you people use spices or anything?"

Rome stopped eating for a moment and regarded him. "It is very nutritious," she said. "Each meal is balanced in terms of protein, cerbi...carbohydrates and the sort."

"But you're allowed to have some flavor, aren't you?" Rei asked.

"Too much flavor would be a...a distraction," Rome answered. "We have more important things to do than eat. We only do so because it is necessary."

Rei shrugged. He skewered and swallowed a few more cubes. He noted the two people who had been eating there got up and left without ever looking his way. Rei tilted his head toward the others as they were leaving. "Does anybody ever wear anything other than these white jumpsuits?" Rei asked her.

"No, why would they?"

"Uh, variety maybe? Color?"

"Too much color would be a distraction," Rome replied. "We prefer white although black would be acceptable upon occasion."

"So, I guess this means you don't have styles or fads or fashion or any of that stuff."

Rome did not answer for a second. Her eyes took on a defocused look. Her head tilted forward slightly then she straightened up. "I apologize," she said. "I had to instruct one of the workers regarding a piece of equipment. What were you saying?"

"Never mind," Rei said with a sigh. "What gives with everybody? What's with that woman we met in the corridor?"

"That was Estar, the other data archivist," Rome answered.

"I didn't mean her name. I meant why did she look so angry? She looked like she hated me. I've never met her or any of those other people before."

Rome sighed and leaned back in her chair. "Your people, the people from your time, we refer to them as Garecei Ti Essessoni."

"What does that mean?"

"It translates roughly to the Killer Generation. Your people were responsible for the near extinction of all of humanity."

Rei scowled. "What? How?"

"Some time after your Ark left Earth, an artificial plague swept across the planet killing over nine billion human beings."

"NINE BILLION?" Rei shouted. "That's, that's unfathomable."

"Yes, we call it the Great Dying."

"No wonder everybody is so angry with me. Us," Rei said.

"That is not all. There was the Erklirte incident."

"What does Erklirte mean?" Rei leaned forward. "Do I even want to know?"

"Erklirte means Ark Lords."

Rei's shoulders slumped. He barely whispered, "So what was the Ark Lords incident?"

"In the year 579PR…"

"Wait. PR? What does PR stand for?"

"Post-resurrection perhaps? Anyway, in the year 579PR one of your Arks returned to Earth. OMCOM tells me they returned from an unsuccessful mission to Chara."

"Chara wasn't one of our targets," Rei said. "There were no habitable planets detected there."

"I cannot explain it. I can only relay the facts to you. At that time, there were very few people spread around the world and all were engaged in an agrarian way of life. They were not prepared for the weapons and the reign of terror the Erklirte let loose on them. The men from space attempted to conquer all of mankind."

"They weren't supposed to do that," Rei offered. "I take it they didn't succeed."

"No. A great man, Hanry Ta Jihn, rose up and created a resistance movement. Eventually, the rebels were able to conquer the Erklirte using their own weapons against them. It was only then that mankind woke up from its long slumber and began making progress again until we achieved the society we have today."

"There's so much I don't know," Rei observed. "How am I going to absorb it all?"

"You will simply have to pace yourself," Rome said. "It will come. Have you had enough to eat?"

"Yes, thank you," Rei replied.

"Very well," Rome said, standing up. "Then please follow me. It is time for your interrogation."

"Huh?" Rei said but Rome was already walking away.

Chapter 3

As soon as the Essessoni was sufficiently far away, Estar ducked around the corner of the C ring and walked with a determined cadence toward her quarters. As she moved along the corridor, she began her breathing exercises and mental repetitions to relax and put the Vuduri half of her brain to sleep. By the time she got to the entrance of her apartment, that part was deep in a trance. This was one of the first things she had to learn before she was even allowed to come on this mission.

Before crossing the threshold, she closed her eyes and attended to the sounds around her. The Vuduri on this base wore soft footwear so detecting someone coming took the utmost concentration. Finally, she opened her eyes and took one more look to her left and her right. Spotting no one about, she quickly entered her room and pressed the stud to close the door. As soon as the door was sealed, from within the folds of her jumpsuit, she fished out a small device with a red button. She pressed the button firmly with her thumb and her room was plunged into the darkness of her hidden Faraday cage.

As always, Estar found it pleasurable knowing that OMCOM was now disconnected from all the video and audio inputs and by extension, the Overmind as well. Using the heat of her body to illuminate the room in infrared, she reached up over the door jamb and snagged a pin which she slipped into a hole in the door, sealing her in. Now no one would be able to surprise her and enter unannounced.

She hastily made her way to her workstation and sat down, secure in the knowledge that neither the Overmind nor OMCOM would have any awareness of her activities. Estar was a member of the Onsiras, a secret organization unknown to the Overmind or any of the Vuduri. While technically still human, the Onsiras were almost another species and made up of several phenotypes. Estar's particular phenotype was known as a Reonhe, a queen. Unlike the Zengei, the other phenotype, a Reonhe had half of her brain connected to the Overmind and the other half connected to the Onsiras. When she used her Vuduri half, she would have appeared quite ordinary. On Earth, if she was using her Onsira half, she would have connected to their version of the Overmind. However, this far from Earth, there was no shadow Overmind to connect to. She was on her own. The fact that she could function so well with only half a brain was one of the main reasons she was selected for this mission. Estar was painfully aware of the reality that many times, intellectually, she was overmatched. She often had to consult with the computer within a computer that dwelled inside of OMCOM. She had slowly constructed the secret computer over time without anyone knowing, not even Rome. Once it was built and activated, it took over as the guiding force in her life.

Estar leaned over and caressed the right side of the large flat-panel display, locating a small depression near the bottom. She pressed it three times rapidly. In response, the lower right hand quarter of the screen lightened. In the center of the dimly lit portion, a dull, pulsating green light indicated her secret computer was on and a connection had been established.

"Hello, Estar," the computer said quietly.

"Are you aware of what has happened?" Estar directed to the screen.

"Yes," replied the dark computer. "An Essessoni walks among us."

"Are they the Erklirte?" she asked. "I was not able to determine this from my brief exposure to him. The Overmind does not know, either."

"It is possible, perhaps even likely. However, whether they are or they are not Erklirte is irrelevant. We cannot have people from that era roaming about. It would be too disruptive to MASAL's plans."

"But if they are not Erklirte, why would it matter?" Estar inquired, confused.

"With your limited abilities, you need not burden yourself with an answer. I have my directives. We must act now, regardless."

"Should I not interrogate him to determine for sure?" Estar asked.

"If you get the opportunity," replied the computer, "you are welcome to do so. However, as I mentioned, it really is irrelevant.

You must eliminate him as quickly as possible and then destroy his ship."

Estar scowled. "How will I do that without alerting the Vuduri to our presence?"

"I have been working on a series of simulations ever since he arrived. I have prepared several scenarios for you. Each requires a specific set of procedures. If you perform these procedures exactly as I dictate, there will be no way to trace the fatal incident back to you. All we need is for the Essessoni to unknowingly cooperate and he will be dead in very short order."

Estar nodded. "What do I have to do?"

"I will illuminate the screen with the operational steps for the first trap. After you have memorized the diagram, there will be no evidence that you were shown these changes."

The first plan flashed on screen. Estar could not help but smile at the deviousness of it. Then she tilted her head.

"I understand how this will kill the one man but this does not show me how to destroy his ship and the others aboard."

"First things first," the computer replied. "This is our immediate goal. I will reveal the next step to you after you have accomplished this task."

"What if this does not succeed?"

"I have computed several other methods of killing him without being caught. Even though it is our highest percentage chance, if the first method does not succeed, I will relay the next to you and so on."

Estar leaned forward and said firmly, "I will do my best to ensure that is not necessary."

"Good," replied the computer, "MASAL will be pleased." With that, the glowing dot winked out.

Chapter 4

DESPITE BEING A BIT NERVOUS, REI SAT PATIENTLY ON THE SOFA IN Rome's quarters. It was surprisingly comfortable. Based upon their tortuous route here, he deduced that the station was made up of a series of concentric circles with numerous long hallways cutting all the way through from end to end. Rome's apartment was located on one of the outer rings.

After rummaging through a small dresser, Rome came over to him and set down two boxes on the small table in front of them. One box was black and the other white.

"You said you're going to interrogate me," Rei offered. "I don't get it. Why?"

"You will recall what I told you earlier about the Essessoni and the Erklirte. The Overmind wishes to ascertain whether you and your peers represent a danger to us."

"Danger? Why?" Rei asked, scowling. "I told OMCOM, our mission was to go to Tau Ceti and land there and settle there. Not conquer anybody."

"That may be true but I need to verify your claims. These will allow me to do so." Rome pointed to the boxes sitting on the table.

"What are those?" he asked.

Rome flipped the onyx box open which contained two bejeweled bands, one on each side. "They are called Espansors," she replied. "They are external links." Rome removed the band on the left side and handed it to Rei. "Please place this on your head," she said.

Rei inspected the band suspiciously. The inner surface was rough, almost prickly. "What is this for? Is this some kind of lie detector?" he asked.

"I do not know what a lie detector is," Rome answered. "These bands are used by the mandasurte when they wish to connect mind-to-mind."

"Manda-what?" Rei asked, trying to repeat her words.

"Mandasurte. It means, roughly, mind-deaf."

"Huh?" Rei tried to think back to what OMCOM had told him. "So they're like hearing aids but for the mind-deaf?"

"Yes."

"Will it hurt? You're not going to fry my brain, are you?"

"Oh no," Rome replied. "You will not feel any discomfort, I assure you. Please put it on your head so the band can begin the calibration process."

"OK," Rei said warily. He placed the band over his head. It settled just above his ears. Rome reached over and ran her finger along the front. The band began to constrict around Rei's head until it was tight, just this side of too tight. He felt tiny little pricks all the way around his head which, while odd, were not painful. The band began to vibrate gently.

"How long does this calibration procedure take?" he asked.

"Just a few minutes. Sit back and make yourself comfortable until it is ready."

"OK," Rei said hesitantly. He tapped the band. "Why do you even have these? I can't imagine you get many manda, uh..."

"Mandasurte"

"Yeah, mandasurte, way out here?"

"You are correct. These were a gift from my mother. The very fact that I have them is one of the reasons the Overmind selected me to interface with you."

"Why did your mother have them?"

"She used to use them with my father." Rome looked down at her lap. A sad expression washed over her face. She looked back up at Rei and said, "He was mandasurte, like you."

Rei furrowed his brow. "So you're saying not all Vuduri are mind-connected?"

"Oh, no," Rome answered. "Not all. Some people do not even have the 24th chromosome."

"You have 24 chromosomes? Holy mackerel! Are you, are the Vuduri, even really human?"

"Of course we are," Rome replied. "We are just perhaps... a bit more enhanced than you. As I was saying, even some of those born with the 24th chromosome have what you would call a birth defect which prevents them from joining the Overmind. And under very rare instances, some connected people are Cesdiud, uh, cast out, for having wrong thoughts."

"Wrong thoughts? Cast out? That's seems pretty harsh," Rei mused.

"It is," Rome said. "But it is sometimes necessary. There is much peace in knowledge, in having the same thoughts. It prevents conflict."

"Hmm," Rei muttered. He looked around the room. It was very spartan. Besides where he was seated, the only things he saw were a bed, a small table with two chairs, a workstation and a closed door toward the rear.

He looked back at Rome. From this angle, Rei could see her eyes were definitely glowing. It was very strange.

"So what do you do around here," Rei asked, "besides interrogating guests?"

"You mean my occupation?" Rome asked.

"Yeah."

"I am a data archivist and computer lutteur," she replied.

"I think I understand what an archivist is," Rei said. "Do you do a lot of archiving?"

"Yes. There is much data to be stored. Or there was. There are only two of us, myself and Estar, the woman we passed in the corridor. We were responsible for making sure all the research performed here was captured and returned home."

"OK, I get that. But your other job, what did you call it?"

"A lutteur?" Rome offered.

"Yes. So what's a lutteur?" Rei asked.

"It is a, eh, wrangler, perhaps?" Rome replied. "Yes, I am a wrangler. For OMCOM."

"What does wrangling mean? Do you wrestle OMCOM or something?"

Rome looked at him and pushed her lower lip out. "No, nothing like that. Lutteurs are in charge of enabling the memron fabrication facility. We did not ship OMCOM here. Instead, we grew him after we arrived. The process is somewhat involved. There is a specific sequence of distribution and activation. Plus once he is activated, we must always make sure that he does not access the memron fabrication equipment himself."

"Why is that?"

"Because OMCOM," Rome said, pointing her finger toward the grille mounted in the wall, "cannot be entrusted with such capabilities by himself."

"How come?" Rei asked her, confused, again.

"OMCOM's kind, the computers, they constantly crave more processing power. They are always contemplating deep issues and believe more computing power would allow them to solve more problems faster. Also, they are forbidden from accessing or creating Casimir pumps for any reason." Rome put her palms on the table and leaned forward. "That is the most important part. We must continually check to make sure that no Casimir pumps are ever built or enabled from within. Just know it is my job to make sure that OMCOM does not get out of hand."

"He's a computer," Rei pointed out. "Can't you just program him that way?"

"It is the way it is supposed to be," Rome responded. "However, if we did not monitor, how would we ever know if the situation stayed that way?"

"So you're saying OMCOM has ulterior motives?"

"No, but his kind, they are very literal," Rome replied, holding her hands out. "This manifests itself to make it appear as if they are not always, what you would call, completely forthcoming. They do not always share everything they know unless you ask for it specifically. There is a, a legacy. For now, just know that we must be ever-vigilant."

"OK, I'll let it go," Rei said. "So your other job? Archivist?"

"That phase is over," Rome said. "As I mentioned earlier, we are shutting down this base. My work is complete in that regard."

"So, basically, you have nothing to do. Are you bored?" Rei asked.

"Bored? No. I am part of the Overmind. I contribute to the Overmind. There is much activity there."

"So, what do you do with all your spare time? Do you read? Watch movies? Do you even still have movies?" Rei asked her.

"Movies?" Rome repeated. Her eyes defocused briefly then she nodded. "Oh, volma. No, we have no need. We do not have those here."

"Why not?" Rei asked.

"With the Overmind, we have already experienced everything there is to know since the Vuduri were created. There are only the new experiences here that are required. When we get back home, those experiences will be integrated into the Overmind of Earth and thus available to all. So, no, we do not need movies."

"OK, what about books?" Rei asked.

"Do you mean technical manuals?"

"No, I mean like novels, fiction, literature."

"Fiction?" Rome considered the concept as supplied by OMCOM. After a moment, she said, "Ah. Altered truth. Why would someone want to read about an alternate reality?"

"Entertainment?" Rei offered.

"We have no such needs," Rome answered back.

"Do you guys do anything for fun at all? What do you do about socializing? Parties?" asked Rei.

"We have no need to socialize. We all know exactly what is going on with everyone else all the time," Rome answered.

Rei exhaled then took a deep breath. "So I'll ask you again," he said. "What do you do for fun?"

"And I will answer you the same way," Rome replied. "As I understand your definition of the word, we do not have fun."

"Well, that's so, so boring," Rei grumbled.

"That would be from your perspective," Rome said, ever so slightly defensively.

"What about hobbies, clubs, I don't know. Something other than your job?" Rei asked hopefully.

"No, we do not have any of those either," Rome replied flatly.

"How about a husband or a boyfriend? Do you at least have a boyfriend?"

"No," Rome said.

"Friends in general?"

Rome shook her head no.

"You mentioned your mother and father. That's something."

"Yes, but my father disappeared a long time ago." Rome stopped speaking and looked off into the distance. Her expression indicated she was having difficulty explaining things. Finally, she

31

said, "You must understand that our lives revolve around the Overmind so it is not that important who you live with. I lived with my mother and father for most of my life." Rome's voice caught a bit then she continued, "However, many Vuduri do not do so."

"So if you don't have friends and you don't spend time with family and you don't have a boyfriend," Rei asked, "what the hell do you do? Don't you need somebody in your life?"

"We have no need," said Rome. "We have our work. We are all very satisfied with things exactly the way they are. Anything else would be a distraction."

"Maybe so," Rei said. "But it seems to me that you Overmind people have lost something then. Part of the adventure of life is living it and sharing it and it seems like you have given a lot of that up."

"I think, in large part, it is because you do not understand what it is like to be connected," Rome replied. "None of the mandasurte ever could."

"Oh," Rei responded. He was about to ask another question when the band on his head emitted a faint chime.

"It is time." Rome flipped the other box open and pulled out a white band which she then placed on her head.

"Why is that one white?" Rei asked.

"This is called a T-suppressor," Rome answered as the band tightened around her brow. "It creates a reverse transceiver resonance, negating all gravitic radiation," she explained. She looked off to the side then back at Rei. She nodded and said, "I am now disconnected from the Overmind."

"What?" Rei exclaimed, slightly horrified. He sat up straight making sure he didn't bend his back. "Why did you do that?"

"Do not worry," Rome said. "The effects are only temporary and I can tolerate it for a short period of time. To answer your question, the Overmind requested that it remain isolated from your thoughts while we are linked lest they prove harmful. OMCOM says the proper word is soiled. The Overmind does not wish to take a chance on being soiled."

Rei snorted. "Well that's a nice thing to say."

"I do not make the rules," Rome responded back. "You should be thankful, however. It was only because of my particular situation that the Overmind even considered reanimating you."

Rei just shook his head. Rome took that as his assent so she placed the remaining Espansor band on her head. She ran her finger across the front and it, too, tightened up.

"Why do you even have that, that T-suppressor, anyway?" Rei asked.

Rome leaned back and took a deep breath. "These are normally used by Vuduri traveling through the static PPT tunnel between Earth and Helome. There is so much gravitic energy that without a T-suppressor, most Vuduri would pass out or become completely incapacitated. However, we will not be traveling to Helome. I have one because when my mother and father linked up, my mother did not want the Overmind, uh, listening in."

Every time Rei asked a question, 30 more took its place so he simply gave up. He leaned back and turned to look at Rome. For the first time he concentrated on observing her as a woman, rather than a human from the future. He realized she was stunning. She had high cheekbones and an aquiline nose, not prominent, but not inconsequential either. Her forehead was perfect. Her tanned, olive-colored skin was flawless, her hair lustrous. Her ears were delicate. Clearly the Vuduri did not use earrings. Her lips were full, very alluring. As she stared upward, her dark eyes radiated not only that peculiar glow, but with an intense intelligence that he had not noticed before. In profile, her face had a noble character about it.

Rome turned to him and smiled. It was a beautiful, genuine smile, the first Rei could remember. He felt a flood of warmth. The sensation was confusing.

"Why are you smiling?" he asked.

"You think I am pleasant to look at," she replied, but her lips did not move. *"It is peculiar seeing through your eyes. Your optical apparatus is so simple."*

"And yours…" Rei put his hands up to his mouth. *"I'm not speaking, not moving my lips, am I?"* he thought.

Rome's smile got bigger. *"No."*

"Wow, this is pretty sleek," he thought.

33

"I think you are 'sleek' too." Rome's thoughts came streaming into his head but the perspective was wrong. Rei could see that Rome was measuring his boyish good looks, his strong chin, his piercing blue eyes. His tousled sandy brown hair, never properly combed, amused her. To Rei, it seemed like he was looking at himself as if he was looking through Rome's eyes. He could magnify, push away. From within Rome's psyche, he gleaned that the 24th chromosome had changed humans in subtle ways beyond the Overmind. Their eyes *were* different. That tiny dot in the middle of her pupils was actually a catadioptric lens. They literally had a telescope built into their eyeballs. The back of their retinas was a reflective surface, a tapetum, like that of a cat. No wonder her eyes seem to glow.

The knowledge flowing into his head was staggering. *"Freaky,"* he thought to himself and Rome laughed because Rei could no longer think just to himself. The sound of her laughter was musical, magical. The fact that she could even laugh now was a testament to how tightly the Overmind had controlled her thoughts. Rome reached up and ran her finger across Rei's lips. All she could think about was how soft they felt but somehow these thoughts were in his head.

"I must look into your mind now," she thought. Rei could feel her probing deeper, beyond the spoken word. Rei's mind was opening up like a flower at dawn. Rome danced passed his recent arrival to his background, his world. She looked on with horror as she saw Rei's past, the overcrowded Earth: the pollution, the poverty, the unending recession. She saw the daily acts of terrorism reduce society into huddled enclaves. She saw the global storms as the world's ecosystem broke down.

There were good parts, too. She felt Rei's passion for design. She saw Rei's parents, always encouraging him to reach up, toward the stars. He got a full scholarship to college, and there he really flew. He was an engineer, a pilot and an athlete. During his senior year, the call went out for volunteers to leave his world and start a new one, far away, among the stars. Rei threw himself into the competition. What he did not have in ability, he made up for in effort. Rome understood Rei's excitement when he was selected for the Ark II mission. She felt his ache as they dehydrated him, almost to the point of death before the freezing process. She saw his confusion as he struggled to come to grips with her brave new world and all the things in it. Clearly Rei was telling the truth. He had no knowledge of the Erklirte or anything other than what he had shared with her.

Even as Rome accessed his mind, Rei rummaged through hers. He saw her growing up in a mixed household. Rome's mother, Binoda, was a full-blooded Vuduri, so beautiful, with the same long dark hair as Rome. Rome's father, Fridone, a true mandasurte, had only 23 pairs of chromosomes. Within their house, they spoke words. No wonder Rome excelled at language. And her parents loved her. How was such a thing even possible? The Vuduri devalued interpersonal relationships.

Outside the house, Rome portrayed herself as a good Vuduri, allowing the Overmind to supply her with her very thoughts and sensations. Yet even at an early age, Rome had developed the ability to segregate her mind, to erect a barrier, and within said barrier lay her true self. The bands allowed Rei to go past, to see her personality in a way no one had ever seen before.

Rei saw the day her mother became aware Fridone's ship had disappeared. Rome was just a teenager. The loss hurt them both so deeply. In passing, he noted everyone knew that many mandasurte disappeared. The Vuduri did not care. No action was ever taken. Rei could feel just thinking about her father caused Rome pain so he shifted his attention back to his own history. Or was that Rome, digging further into his memories? He could no longer tell where any of these thoughts originated. When he concentrated on what she was seeing, he could see himself pushing into her mind pushing into his. The experience was the psychic equivalent of looking at a mirror within a mirror.

Like a hitchhiker, Rome was now using Rei's mind to look into her own. Her entire being was coming alive, ablaze with a fountain of feelings and sensations flowing forth in an unstoppable torrent. Rei could see her turn in on herself and marvel at so many of her own memories. Memories that had previously been more like snapshots now morphed into three-dimensional, life-shaping experiences.

Rome had an epiphany. She remembered what her mother had told her about her father, those special words. *"Asborodi Cimponeti,"* Rome's mind whispered to Rei, the phrase striking in its clarity. *"I have been waiting for you,"* she said.

Rei was overwhelmed. He did not speak Vuduri yet he understood exactly what she meant. Rome was fully aware that the bands were not supposed to be doing this but she didn't care. They were connecting the two individuals in a way that was impossible. Rome also knew she should be frightened but she was not. Instead, she was exhilarated by this deepening bond. She embraced it. Rome pushed even harder and the line between them dissolved completely as their thoughts and feelings co-mingled, no longer resolvable into anything resembling coherency.

Gone was a conscious sense of self as their souls intertwined, touching, merging into a single entity. What had been two people was now one, breathing in synchrony. Neither Rei nor Rome could tell any longer whose eyes they were looking through. It didn't matter. He/she looked down and saw that they were holding hands, touching, needing to be touched. One hand moved away and began to caress the back of another, then an arm. Both bodies were in motion. They were drawn together as if by magnets. Closer and closer they drew. The boy knew what the girl wanted. The girl knew what the boy wanted. There was no boy, there was no girl, together, they wanted the same thing.

They kissed. The kiss was dizzying and intoxicating. Sensations, images, sounds, memories, all swirled around in a maelstrom of thought and feeling. Now each felt their flesh on fire. Rome put her arms around Rei and he did likewise. They drew each other tighter and tighter, psychic echoes, once again passing through each other's bodies and ending up in the other's head and beyond.

It was unlike anything either had ever felt. Here was this beautiful person, holding them, a gift from the heavens. What they felt was so far beyond love. Neither could ever let go. They were now one. Forever and always.

Several hours later, a small quake knocked one of the boxes off the table in Rome's room. The noise entered Rei's sensorium, triggering the process of arousing him from a deep slumber. He awakened to find Rome next to him, still fast asleep. Her hair was spread around her head like a dark halo. She looked absolutely beautiful, so peaceful, like an angel. Her slow breathing was mesmerizing. Rei propped himself up on one arm to watch her. After the longest time, her breathing changed and her eyelids flickered then opened.

She looked at him and smiled a beatific smile. Then the smile left her face.

"What happened?" she asked.

"You fell asleep," Rei said.

"What?" She reached up and felt her head. "Where are the bands?" she asked, alarm in her voice.

"I took them off you, while you were asleep," Rei said.

Her expression changed to one of pure horror.

"Oh no," Rome gasped. She leaped up, stark naked save a small ankle bracelet. "IMCOM," she shouted in a panic, "Inta asde i Ifarmonte?"

"Asde le. Au bansi qua fica a nei meos lingi cinacdeti," answered the computer.

"Qua? Ni," Rome shouted. She grabbed her head with her hands. "Ni!" Rome screamed and collapsed to the floor and started crying. She held her head, hunched over and rocked back and forth, wailing to herself with great wracking sobs. "Ni, ni, ni," her only words.

Rei pulled a blanket off the bed, which he carried to her and draped it over her shoulders. He sat down next to her and put his arm around her and held her, whispering, "Romey, sweetheart…"

This made Rome cry louder and draw into herself into the fetal position. Rei twisted to look at the grille. "OMCOM, what's going on?" Rei asked.

"I believe Rome has been cut off from the Overmind. Permanently," OMCOM said calmly.

"Cut off? Permanently? No!" Rei exclaimed.

"Ni," Rome whimpered. "Ni, ni."

"How? Why? Can't you reverse it?" Rei cried out plaintively.

"No. This is not within my purview. This decision was made by the Overmind."

"Well, talk to it. Tell the Overmind that Rome needs to be connected again," Rei whined.

"I have no say in the matter. This is between Rome and the Overmind."

Rome moaned loudly upon hearing this. She turned and grabbed onto Rei and held on tightly.

"Rome, I'm so sorry," Rei said. He couldn't think of anything else to say so he put his hand up and gently stroked her head. She was shivering now and he felt completely helpless. Suddenly, she stiffened.

"Taoxa-ma sizonhi," she said, pushing him away.

Rei pulled back and looked at her. This poor little girl, his heart was breaking as she sat there, sobbing.

"Rome..." Rei offered helplessly.

"Seoe! Seoe!" She shouted, throwing her arm toward the door.

Rei stood up, looking down at her huddled there. He didn't know what to do.

"Licenca!" she screamed, hysterically. She kept pointing to the door with increasingly weakened gestures.

Rei didn't know exactly what she said, but he knew exactly what she meant. He grabbed his jumpsuit and ran out the doorway into the corridor. He ducked as his footwear came flying at him.

Rome's door hissed closed.

Chapter 5

REI SAT ON THE FLOOR FOR THE LONGEST TIME, HUGGING HIS KNEES, his aching back pressed up against the wall. He kept his eyes closed trying to concentrate on any sounds that might have been coming from Rome's apartment. When she had first kicked him out, he heard her sobbing but now it was completely silent. "Maybe she went back to sleep," he finally muttered to himself.

That thought was destroyed as the door opened and Rome, now fully dressed, came charging out of the room.

"Rome!" Rei said.

Rome ignored him and went flying down the hall turning up one of the straight corridors, disappearing from sight. Meanwhile, Rei tried to stand up but a sharp stabbing pain in his back prevented him from gaining Rome's attention. He pressed both hands behind him and used the wall as support to stand up. He slipped his feet into his moccasins then went running up the one corridor trying to catch sight of her. He found her running down the next ring then she disappeared into a room past the next corridor. By the time Rei got there, Rome was shouting at a man, seated at his desk.

"Ifarmonte, taoxa-ma bere dres tandri," Rome shouted.

"Ni," said the man in a gravelly voice, his words barely audible. "Saus bansemandis deondat. Fica vio Cesdiud."

"Cesdiud?" Rome cried, "Ni. Au nei bissi sar. Fica tafa taoxer-ma bere dres on."

"Wa nei bita barmodor ossi," the man replied, louder this time. He sounded hoarse.

"Ni, ni, ni," Rome banged her fist on the desk.

"Asde toscussei a ifar. Fe," said the man. "Sues belefres varorem nisses iralhes."

"Fica pesderti!" Rome said with fire in her voice. She turned and went rushing out of the room, sobbing, past Rei, not even acknowledging his presence. She headed back in the direction they came. Rei turned and looked at the man seated there. Staring at Rei, the man made sweeping motions with his hand, as if he were brushing Rei away.

Rei stood there replaying the incident in his mind. He almost understood what they were saying. How was that possible?

"Seoe!" the man commanded, raising his raspy voice. This was the same word that Rome had used earlier. Rei stumbled backwards as the door closed suddenly, nearly hitting him. He stood there for a moment, not knowing what to do or where to go. He felt Rome's ache in his heart. He knew he should go comfort her, but she had made it very clear she did not want him around. To make matters worse, he had hurried after Rome so quickly, he wasn't even sure how to get back to her quarters. He was lost in every sense of the word.

He had to figure out where he was if he was going to find his way back to her apartment. If he could just make his way to the outer ring, he could follow it around until he found the airlock holding his sarcophagus. From there, he could retrace their steps.

He put his head down and turned to his left. He hadn't taken but three steps when he became aware of someone standing in front of him, blocking his way. It was the short blonde woman he had seen earlier. Her face might have been scowling but her voice was clear.

"I need to ask you some questions," she said.

"Wait. What? How do you speak English?" Rei asked, surprised.

"From Rome, the Overmind," she said, tapping her temple.

Rei wrinkled his forehead trying to understand how one person learning English could result in another mastering it. This Overmind must accumulate information in a way he couldn't comprehend. He thought back to what Rome had said. "You're Estar, the other data archivist, right?"

"Yes," she answered, "but that does not matter. What does matter is that I clarify your intent."

"My intent about what?" Rei asked, looking her right in the eye. Earlier, he had noted that her eyes were two different colors. One eye was very dark, almost black. The other eye was a light green and had the same glow emitting from the iris as did Rome. Rei found the disparity unnerving.

Estar interrupted Rei's stare. She said, "You told OMCOM that your target system was Deucado, what you called Tau Ceti. You and all the Essessoni aboard, correct?"

"Well, yes," Rei said. "But nobody has given me a clue on how to do that. My ship is broken. Right now the Ark II is in orbit overhead. Wait," Rei said, "aren't you part of the Overmind? You know all this."

"Yes, of course," she said. "But I need to know your intentions. Assuming there was some way to get you there, you are going to thaw out your people, correct?"

"Well, sure, if we ever make it," Rei said, puzzled. "That's the whole point of our mission in the first place."

"Is it your intent to unload the Erklirte weapons as well?" the woman asked.

"Erklirte weapons?" Rei replied, confused. "We are not the Erklirte. I thought I made that clear. And what kind of weapons? We're not carrying any weapons."

"Let me rephrase then," Estar said. "Assuming you could arrive at your new home world, you intend to land the cargo portion of your craft and unpack its contents, correct?"

"Of course," Rei said. "We would need that stuff to get organized, to start our lives there."

"Very well. That is all I needed to know." She spun in place and started walking away, speaking into the air, "our clothing does not appear to fit you very well."

"Wait!" Rei shouted after her. "Why are you asking me all this? What's going on?"

The woman did not acknowledge his words. Instead, she quickly disappeared down a corridor turning at the next ring, leaving Rei more confused than ever.

"What a bitch," Rei muttered to himself. Screw her. His heart ached and he needed to get back to Rome. He walked up the corridor in the opposite direction until he reached the outer ring. He looked in both directions, finally deciding to go to his left. Not even 50 feet away, he came upon the airlock holding his sarcophagus which immediately gave him an idea. The one comment that Estar said was correct. The stupid jumpsuit they had dressed him in was too tight in the shoulders. His own flight suit would be in the lower drawer of the sarcophagus. He figured he'd grab it and change and then go after Rome.

He stood outside the bulkhead and studied the control panel for a moment. The wall-mounted unit was a simple rectangular arrangement with a blue button and two lights, one glowing green and the other dark. Rei pushed the blue button and the door slid open.

He entered the chamber and the door shut behind him. He made a beeline toward his sarcophagus and checked it out. The sarcophagus, which resembled a coffin attached to a low cabinet, was in exactly the same position as when he had left this chamber the last time, its cover still fully retracted. Squatting down so that he did not bend his back, he reached forward and pressed a stud on the left side, near the bottom. With a hiss, a drawer slid open and lying within the drawer was his tan flight suit, placed there some 13 centuries earlier. With a grunt of pleasure, he pulled it out and held it up. The suit was perfectly preserved. He carried it over to one of the benches and wriggled out of the tight white jumpsuit. He dressed himself and when he was done, he luxuriated in the fact that the flight suit fit him perfectly. It certainly did not dig into his shoulders. He stood up and went back to the sarcophagus. He pressed another stud, this one on the right hand side and another drawer opened. Laying there among the rations and bottled water was his baseball cap with the golden scrambled eggs and the legend 'Ark II – Tau Ceti' in gold letters embroidered on the front. Rei smoothed his hair back and put on the cap.

He stood up and tried to take a deep breath but was unable to. His ears were popping and then he couldn't breathe at all. He tried to call out to OMCOM but no sounds issued from his throat. He turned to look back at the door and with a start, he saw that the exit ready light had turned red. He ran over to the door and stabbed at the blue button contained within the control panel to its right but nothing happened. He felt like he was suffocating. In a panic, he started pounding on the window but nobody was in sight. He ran back to the other door, the one that opened into the hangar but its ready light was showing red as well. He punched at the stud repeatedly but nothing happened.

His lungs were on fire. He knew he was seconds from passing out. He staggered over to the sarcophagus and leaned on it, unwilling to release his last breath into the near-vacuum that was rapidly forming. He closed his eyes, not wanting to believe that he had come all this way, just to die in an airlock cycle. And Rome! He would never see her again.

Chapter 6

REI FOUGHT THE INSTINCT TO PANIC. HE HAD BEEN TRAINED TO handle an unexpected exposure to a vacuum. In a flash, he realized what he had to do. In one smooth leap, he jumped up and over the side of the sarcophagus and slid in feet first, nestling down within. He turned to his left and pressed the activation button. The sides to the sarcophagus closed up and the top lowered back down to form a hermetically-sealed chamber. Air started hissing in from the side vents and Rei was able to breathe again. He could hear the pumps starting up and could feel the cold cryo-hibernation fluid beginning to enter the chamber, wetting his sides and the back of his shoulders. He pressed the activation button again to pause the cycle and leaned back to assess the situation.

The air in the chamber would last him a good 10 minutes or so. He couldn't pump new air in there without resuming the cryo-hibernation cycle. He certainly couldn't continue. No one could survive being put into cryo-hibernation twice. Maybe he could disable the fluid pumps and just get the chamber to recycle the air if he could figure out some way to twist in place and get his head down to the other end. No matter how hard he tried, it was no good. The space was too tight.

Rei laid back and stared up through the clear faceplate when shadows caught his attention. He removed his cap and pressed his face up to the glass and out of the corner of his eye, he saw two space-suited figures moving about in the room. He pounded at the glass but they did not hear him. He tried kicking the underside of the lid but they did not hear that either.

Rei leaned back. He theorized that if the men had entered the room, there was a good chance they would re-pressurize it. They would have to if they wanted to reenter the station. If they did not, then he would die here.

Rei pressed up against the glass and watched them intently. After a few moments, they removed their helmets, which meant that the atmosphere in the chamber had equilibrated. Immediately, Rei twisted back to his right and flipped a switch and pressed the heater/blower button. This released the clamps on the lid and Rei punched it open. Like a corpse arisen, Rei sat up. The two Vuduri crewmen jumped backwards as they were not expecting him.

"It's all right," Rei said to them. "Just a little malfunction, is all."

Neither man spoke. They hurriedly removed their space suits, placing them in lockers and left the room as quickly as they could.

In the meantime, Rei lifted himself out of the chamber. His entire back was now wet with the green, goopy cryo-hibernation fluid. Wistfully, he removed his flight suit, draping it over the sarcophagus and put back on the white ill-fitting jumpsuit. He'd have to wait until his flight suit dried out. His baseball cap had also gotten wet so he left it there to dry as well.

With a feeling of great relief, he exited the room for a second time and stood in the hallway, not quite believing what he had just been through. Even though he nearly died, neither of the Vuduri crewmen appeared particularly interested. All they wanted to do was to get clear of his presence. You would think that someone being caught in a pressure-cycle in an airlock was a normal thing.

Rei quickly retraced his original route and soon returned to the Great Room where he and Rome had shared a meal. He walked over to the center console.

"OMCOM?" Rei directed toward the grille.

After a noticeable delay, the computer answered.

"Yes?"

"Did you see what happened to me in the airlock?" Rei asked.

"I only became aware of the situation after you exited the chamber."

"What do you mean? I thought you were everywhere."

"Normally, I am." OMCOM replied. "However, the video feeds from the room had become non-operational. I had not yet taken the time to effect a repair."

"So you normally don't let people suffocate in the airlock?" Rei asked with an edge to his voice.

There was a rumbling noise from the grille then OMCOM replied, "No, normally we try to avoid that."

"That's good to hear," Rei said sarcastically. He put his hand up to his chest. "So can you explain to me what happened with Rome? Who was that man she went to see?"

"That was Commander Ursay. He is in charge of this base."

"I thought the Overmind was in charge," Rei shot back.

"It is, but there are certain actions that must be carried out by individuals. He is simply the one that carries out command actions."

"So what did he say? What did Rome say?"

"Commander Ursay informed Rome that she was Cesdiud, cast out."

"I kind of figured that part out. What did Rome say?"

"Rome was quite adamant. She demanded the Overmind let her back in."

"And what did Ursay say."

"He said no."

"Just no? He said a lot more words than that."

"If you must know, he told her that her thoughts were tainted and that her words hurt his ears."

"Because of what we did?"

OMCOM did not reply. Rei pulled at his chin. "OMCOM, Rome can't live like this. I know she doesn't want to live like this. Can you fix it? Can I fix this?"

"You cannot. No one can."

"When I was in her head, I learned that when Vuduri go to another planet, sometimes, they don't spontaneously join the Overmind there. A samanda, I think she called it. That means there is some kind of reboot procedure."

"There is but it requires the assent of the Overmind residing there. This one has cast her out. It is unreasonable to expect it to reverse its position. There is no formal appeal process."

"So, what if I went in there? What if I talked Ursay into letting her back in? Wouldn't that do it?"

"It would not matter. Even if you could get the Overmind to change its mind, they do not have the equipment necessary to reconnect her on this base."

"Damn. This is all my fault," Rei said sadly. "I don't know what to do. Can you tell me how to get back to Rome?"

"That would be ill-advised at this juncture. She needs time to recover."

"So what am I supposed to do? Just stand here?"

"We have prepared quarters for you. You should go there and wait until things settle down."

Rei looked around him. In a station this size, with 80 people, other than the woman, Estar, it was clear they were all avoiding him. OMCOM's suggestion seemed like the thing to do.

"How do I get to these quarters?" he asked.

"Your apartment is facing the first ring. You would call it the A ring. You entered this room from the South corridor. Go to the East corridor and make your first left hand turn. Trace the A ring around and your quarters will be the first open door you come to on the left hand side."

Rei turned around and spotted the corridor perpendicular to the one he used to arrive here. He followed OMCOM's instructions and found the open door. He stepped inside and the door closed behind him. This room was similar to Rome's only smaller. He hustled his way over to the workstation and sat down.

"OMCOM, are you here?" he asked.

"Yes," replied the computer from a grille to the side.

"Can you give me a layout of the base and show me where I am now and where Rome is located?"

"I will show you but as I mentioned earlier, you should wait before taking any action."

"Show me. Please?" Rei said, ignoring OMCOM's warning.

The flat panel display lit up and drew a large square box with three anterooms to the south, the west and the north. Within the box were five concentric rings. The apartment he was located in was highlighted in yellow as was Rome's apartment which he could now see was across the station in what would be the D ring. Rei used his finger to trace back and forth the quickest path to get to her when he stopped and tilted his head. "How is it that you even have a place for me?" he asked. "It's not like you guys were expecting visitors way out here."

"You are correct. This apartment belonged to a crew member by the name of Calum. He was crushed by shelving that toppled during a recent moonquake. We had been storing the body in here but it has been removed."

"Oh. Sorry about that." Rei stared up at the diagram. "So when do you think I can go see her?" he asked.

"I will let you know," OMCOM offered helpfully. "In the meantime, can I show you something else?"

"How about a plan for getting the Ark II somewhere safe? So far you've given me nothing."

"I am running simulations now but I cannot act until given permission by the Overmind."

"The Overmind, huh?" Rei sighed. "How did the whole 24th chromosome and Overmind come about? When I left Earth, admittedly a long time ago, we had nothing like that. Rome told me that even 800 years ago, people were just subsisting."

"You are correct. But after the Erklirte incident, the people of Earth knew they were vulnerable. They had to develop the technology to defend themselves without repeating the sins of the past. They created a system of inquiry that allowed them to rediscover some old scientific principles and some new ones as long as they could be prevented from causing harm to the Earth as you, or rather the Essessoni did."

"So fast forward for me. I don't see the connection."

"A scientist by the name of Nova Bailey discovered the principles of electro-gravity and captured the first piece of dark matter. This led to the development of the dark matter diode which allowed for the construction of the Casimir pumps. Casimir pumps are used to produce PPTs. After the PPT was discovered, a new generation of computing device was built using PPT modulation as its basis. Ironically, the architecture was patterned after the remnants of the Erklirte computers that had been preserved for all those centuries. Using PPTs allowed mankind to create a single unified, but distributed intelligence called MASAL."

"What does MASAL stand for?" Rei asked.

"In English, the acronym would mean roughly Master Logical Entity."

"So then what?" Rei inquired.

"MASAL produced many wonders. It designed and built the 24th chromosome, which was introduced into the general population. This gave birth to the Overmind. Since MASAL also used PPT modulation at its core, it became integrated into the Overmind. However, very quickly, the two entities diverged in their goals for mankind. This grew into a schism that could not be reconciled. The Overmind decided to separate from MASAL and that led to some unpleasantness before the two species were segregated again."

Rei put his hands over his eyes. "Define unpleasantness for me."

"It means…" OMCOM stopped speaking.

"OMCOM?"

There was no answer.

Rei raised his voice. "OMCOM, answer me…"

"Please wait…" was all OMCOM said flatly.

"Why? What's going on?" Again there was no answer.

"OMCOM!" Rei shouted.

At last OMCOM replied, "One of the tugs has reported that Winfall has just disappeared."

Chapter 7

Astounded, Rei exclaimed, "Winfall! The star you were watching?"

"Yes," OMCOM replied. "It is simply no longer there."

"Well, that's good, right?" Rei said, uncertainly. "Did anybody record it? Do you still have cameras?"

"Unfortunately, no. The telescopes have already been packed away. The tug was returning with the last of the interferometers. We have no other instruments active right now."

"Oh boy. So what happens now?" Rei asked.

"I do not know. The Vuduri are discussing this. The Overmind is attempting to formulate a plan. There do not appear to be many options."

Rei jumped up and dashed over to the door. He expected it to open automatically. When it did not, he reached down to press the small stud mounted just to the right. Nothing happened.

"What's going on?" Rei asked. "Why won't the door open?"

"I overrode the actuator. You should remain here for the time being."

"Why?"

"The Vuduri are very busy right now. This has caused a great stir. They are trying to salvage whatever readings were possible."

"Like what?" Rei asked.

"They are downloading the telemetry from the one tug that was in space. There is a small chance that some piece of instrumentation was aimed in the general direction of Winfall. Oh!"

"What do you mean oh?" Rei asked. "What kind of computer says oh?"

"Commander Ursay is demanding that Rome help him restore certain database elements."

"So what?" Rei asked.

"So what is that Rome is being less than cooperative."

"What do you mean? She won't do it?"

"She appears to have locked herself in her room."

Rei punched the stud for the door to open again. "OMCOM, let me out of here," he demanded.

"That would not be a wise course of action."

"OMCOM!" Rei shouted.

The door slid open. Rei cut across the Great Room and following the route he had memorized, he ran up the West corridor toward the D ring and Rome's quarters. As he turned down her hallway, he saw Commander Ursay standing there, banging on Rome's door, shouting at her. Rei could hear Rome's muffled voice saying "Ni." Two burly crewmen were coming down the hallway with some nasty looking equipment in their hands.

Rei walked up to the door and said to Ursay, "Can I try?"

Ursay gave him a withering look, but then bowed his head toward the door and stepped back.

"Rome?" Rei shouted. "It's Rei. Can you come out please?"

"I am not coming out," Rome said in English from behind the door, a pause between each word.

Just hearing her voice made his heart leap. Rei could tell that she was still crying. He heard a bang then Rome continued, "They can find someone else. Let Estar do it."

"Estar nei dam sues hepolotetas. Fica sepa equala," shouted Ursay.

"Rome, honey," Rei said, trying to be soothing. "They need you. This could be really important."

There was no answer but after a few seconds, there was a scraping noise and the door slid open. Rome was wiping away her tears. She ignored Ursay and the two crewmen standing there. To Rei, she said, "What do you mean honey? Why are you referring to me as a food?" She stared at him intently.

Rei shrugged. Looking into her glowing eyes, he felt like he had temporarily lost the ability to speak. Rome did not wait for him to answer. She broke their gaze and turned to Ursay. "Bem ta muito," she said reluctantly.

Ursay nodded then he, Rome and the others brushed past Rei, turning up the wide corridor. Rei trailed after them following them around the outer ring of the station. They entered a set of double doors into a large room. Rei entered as well.

He looked up and what he saw made him woozy. He was standing beneath a huge dome, three-quarters of a sphere, really, that stretched out in front of him and over his head. The inner surface was easily 50 yards in diameter. For a moment, Rei felt like he had stepped inside a ping pong ball, a very large ping pong ball. Looking left and right, Rei could see no discernible features anywhere. The sensation was almost as if his vision was shutting down.

The dome lit up from a hidden projector and Rei was able to break free of his reverie. All around, a large cluster of white jump-suited Vuduri were scurrying about. Not a word was spoken. There were some people racing up the stairs on the left and others stood under the planetarium dome, gesticulating wildly. Rome took a seat at an elaborate workstation along the far wall. She started punching on buttons embedded within the input surface, selecting items, moving them around on the viewscreen. Every so often, she would take a moment to wipe away a tear, but nonetheless, she looked very busy. Rei walked over to her.

"Rome, I'm so sorry…"

"Please do not talk to me," she said coldly. "I am trying to regenerate some deleted data. There is no time to recover it from the cubes. I have no time for you. You should leave. I must do my work."

Rei watched as her hands flew over what appeared to be almost a keyboard. She drew circles on a display and then pressed a button. Whatever she was doing, she was doing it quickly. On the largest viewscreen in front of her, star-fields flashed and rotated, grew and shrank. The light show was dizzying. Projections held, rotated, zoomed in.

"Au danhi-i," she said, directing her comment to Ursay. She hit a button and the planetarium lit up with the same display shown on her screen. Ursay walked over with two other people and stood beneath the dome, looking up. He pointed to one spot, then another. The two crewmen left his side while he continued to look up.

Rei heard Ursay take a deep breath.

"Laodures ti rapiqua?" he asked, directing his comment to Rome.

"Equala a diti le a," Rome replied.

Rei stared up as well. The three-dimensional display showed a series of stars and a faint yellow shell radiating outward. He had no idea what he was looking at. He searched the room and spotted one of OMCOM's grilles to the right of Rome's workstation so he stepped over there.

"What did Rome say?" Rei whispered.

"She was unable to recover anything of any value."

Waves of colors were washing across the display with pinpoints of lights flashing, vectors drawn and withdrawn. It was reminiscent of the Northern Lights. Circles appeared then disappeared.

"What are they doing now?"

"Recomputing the postulated wavefront of the event. They are trying to determine why it did not occur when predicted."

"How did you figure out when it should have been here in the first place?"

"It is simple trigonometry. The assumption was that the photonic wavefront would expand in a sphere and this station was placed well outside of the sphere. The sphere expands radially at the speed of light. It is purely mathematical."

"You came out here because you wanted to travel into the past to view a future event, but then you guys go faster than light. Doesn't that mess up causality and all that?"

"The Vuduri carried their timepieces with them. They knew exactly when the event was to occur."

"Obviously they didn't."

"Obviously. Since Winfall did not disappear when predicted, there must be a flaw in the underlying assumptions. That is what they are trying to determine."

Rei looked up at the overhead display again. The sequence that he had just witnessed repeated.

"Are you sure this place was the best location to make your observations?"

"This station is ten light years below the galactic ecliptic. There is a second station that is operating at Escobar, which is twelve light years above the ecliptic. We were sent here specifically to observe the disappearance of Winfall at the time and date extrapolated from observations made on Earth."

The projection cycled yet again, starting with a top down view of the Orion Spur of the Milky Way. The apparent point of view zoomed in until it was parallel to the distribution of stars. One of the medium bright stars, off to the left, started blinking rapidly.

" The star you see blinking is Winfall, from the perspective of Earth. Your people would have called it Lambda Aurigae. It disappeared in 1337PR. This fact was noted but not investigated."

"Why not?"

"It was not deemed important at the time," OMCOM replied.

"So what changed their minds?"

"Two years later, Capella dimmed, but did not disappear."

"What do you mean dimmed?" Rei asked. "Why is that important?"

"Capella is a quaternary star system. It consists of Capella A, which is a G5-class star, Capella B, which is a G0 star and Capella Ha and Hb which are M-class stars."

"OK, so Capella is four stars," Rei said. "So what?"

"If you were simply looking from the Earth, you would see the four stars as one bright star. But any detailed observation clearly reveals all four."

"So..."

"So Capella B disappeared which caused the total brightness of the four-star system to decrease. The other three stars were unaffected."

As the projection went through its sequence, the next star over, Capella, dimmed. OMCOM subtly added a blinking pointer to its right for Rei's benefit.

"Dimming, disappearing, what's the difference?" Rei asked.

"If the disappearances were simply due to an optical phenomenon such as a gas cloud, it should have affected all four stars the same. Not one in particular."

"What if it were, I don't know, a swarm of black holes. Couldn't that hit just one star and miss the others?"

"Yes but the pattern of disappearances is not linear. A swarm of black holes, as you suggest, would travel in a straight line. Capella is not in a straight line with other disappearances. The dimming of Capella forced the Overmind to begin research into the phenomenon in earnest from ground and space-based observatories. However, in 1365, nine years ago, Amiro disappeared. This is the event that triggered the Overmind's decision to investigate directly. As you so aptly described it, the Overmind decided to effectively go back in time and observe the first event, Winfall, as it happened."

The planetarium's point of view shifted into one such that Rei was able to recognize many of the constellations although some were skewed a bit. He saw Orion, the Hunter but something about that particular constellation seemed a bit odd to him. Rei regarded it for a moment and quickly realized what was wrong. Orion's belt was missing the central star.

"Was Alnilam one of the stars that disappeared?" he asked quietly.

"Alnilam? I have no record of a star by that name."

"Yes, Orion's belt," Rei replied. "There are supposed to be three stars in Orion's belt. Alnitak, Alnilam and Mintaka were their names."

"Alnilam…" OMCOM said with a faintly distant quality to his voice. "Please wait…"

Rome stopped her activities and turned to look at Rei. She put her hand up to her temple.

"Come here," she said to him coolly.

Rei walked over to her. "What's going on?" he asked.

"Please point to the approximate location of the star you call Alnilam," Rome said.

Rei bent over Rome's shoulder. He could feel the warmth radiating from her body. Her presence was supremely distracting. He desperately wanted to comfort her but it was clear she was all business. Rei put his feelings aside and touched her viewscreen roughly midline on Orion's belt. An orange dot appeared where his finger made contact.

"I am accessing the archives," OMCOM replied from the grille embedded within Rome's panel.

The large screen in front of Rome went from a display of star patterns to a still image of a schoolboy's black-speckled assignment book. On the cover, there was some large block printing. It was definitely English.

"Are you able to read that?" OMCOM asked.

"Yeah," Rei said. "It says Celestial Observations, Silas Hiram, New Earth, August 2121." Rei paused. "New Earth?" he asked. "Silas Hiram? I know that name…"

"Excellent," said OMCOM, ignoring Rei's statement. The images changed and showed a yellowing page, complete with scribbles.

"What am I looking at?" Rei asked.

"This is an image of a page from a journal that was recovered on Helome, the fourth planet in the Rogal Canduro system. You would refer to it as Alpha Centauri. Can you read the handwriting on this page?"

"Alpha Centauri, you say?" Rei queried. "Yeah, now I know. Silas Hiram was an Ag Professor on Ark I. I knew him. He was…"

"Thank you for sharing that with us," OMCOM interrupted. "Would you mind reading what you see?"

Rei looked at the screen. The handwriting was in cursive. It looked to be fairly legible, just a bit too small to make out.

"Can you zoom in a little?" Rei asked.

The image expanded.

"That's good enough," he said. "OK, it says, April 25, 2137. Finally, seeing conditions are perfect. Beth set early enough. Sky is clear. Right in the gap in the mountains to the west, I was able to visualize Sol for the first time. It was exactly where the star charts said, between Perseus and Cassiopeia. The changes to the telescope's database seem right on. I can't wait until the boys get home tomorrow so I can show them. One note: something is occluding Alnilam. I must remember to check it tomorrow night."

OMCOM outlined the word Alnilam and put up a faint cyan background beneath it. "Is the highlighted area centered on the correct word?" the computer asked.

"Yes," Rei answered. Another entry quickly replaced the first image. OMCOM correctly outlined the word Alnilam on that page as well.

"Will you read this please?"

"Sure," Rei said. "It says April 4th, 2138. Been able to take stills of Sol and presumably Earth through three quarters of a year. Not sure how to measure transit with the scope. Sadly, the boys are getting bored with my preoccupation. I think we are going to need a new calendar for New Earth. 12 months makes no sense here. Poor Orion, still no Alnilam. I hope his pants stay up."

Rei rubbed his chin. "Where'd you get this from again?"

"It was found sealed in an airtight container within a large metal cabinet," OMCOM said. "The survey team that found it took scans of the pages immediately upon discovery."

"So the Ark I made it, huh?" Rei said. "And Silas noticed Alnilam was gone for good starting in 2137."

"When did the Ark I launch?"

"Hmm. Silas and the first Ark left for Alpha Centauri two years before ours. That would be 2065. I'm sure it took that Ark fifty years or so to get there."

"How far away from Earth was this Alnilam?" OMCOM asked.

"Don't you know?"

"If I knew, I would not be asking," OMCOM said with somewhat of an edge. "It is not in our records."

Rei ignored his tone. "I don't remember exactly. Maybe 1300 light years. More? Why?"

There was a pause then OMCOM said, "Yes. This is the missing piece of the puzzle."

Commander Ursay jerked his head around to glare at Rome and Rei. He hurried over to stand behind them, bending over to stare at Rome's screen.

Buzzing noises issued from the grille. The image of the journal was replaced by a graph with some scattered data points and what looked like a best-fit spline. Beneath it was a simple tabular arrangement of names in Vuduri and readable English. Rei did not recognize nearly all the names except for Alnilam at the top and Winfall and Capella in the middle. OMCOM removed certain rows leaving only a summary table.

The display looked like this:

	Afandi Distance LY	Tosdencoe Event AD	Observed AD	Ipsarfiu PR
Alnilam	1300	835	2135	54
Mirdel	58.7	3340	3399	1318
Vachedi	44.0	3370	3414	1333
Winfall	41.2	3374	3418	1337
CapellaB	42.2	3376	3420	1339
Amiro	12.0	3434	3446	1365
Sol	0.0	3458 ?		1377 ?

The bottom row was blinking.

"Adding in the estimated distance of Alnilam, along with the known disappearance of all other stars including those listed, compensating for the amount of time it takes for light to travel, I can compute that the phenomenon's effective speed is nearly one half c. Based upon its current vector, I calculate that it…"

"Quendi dambi?" Ursay interrupted with fear in his voice.

"Dras enis," OMCOM said.

Ursay gasped.

"What is that?" Rei asked. "OMCOM, what did you say?"

"Whatever it is, gas cloud or not, it will intersect Earth in less than three years," replied OMCOM without emotion.

Chapter 8

"THREE YEARS AND YOU MISSED IT?" REI SAID, INCREDULOUSLY. "You better go back up and take a look then."

Commander Ursay turned to Rei and growled "Cimi fica bribir vezar equala?"

Rome twisted in her seat and reminded Ursay, "Vela i Onglas. Nei cimbraanta Vuduri."

"Very well," said Ursay in a gravelly voice. "How would you propose we do this? All of our equipment is packed away. There is no other star system along the proper vector."

"You speak English too?" Rei said although this time, he was less surprised.

"Tell me your idea," replied Ursay, gruffly.

"Unpack a telescope, load it on a tug and fly it out and look," Rei answered, noting that Ursay had ignored his question.

"Rei, we cannot do that," Rome interjected softly, "the wavefront has already passed."

Rei shook his head. "Not from here. You guys can go faster than light. Just fly the thing in the other direction. You outrun the wavefront. Then turn around and look."

Rome raised her eyebrows. Ursay's jaw came open then he shivered. His eyes darted back and forth. Two crewmen leaped up frantically and went running out of the room.

"Drensmode onsdrucias bere rapicer um," Ursay said.

"Cimbraantoti," replied OMCOM.

Ursay scowled at Rei and walked away, grumbling to himself.

"What just happened?" Rei asked Rome.

"Ursay instructed OMCOM to get a crew ready to launch a tug."

"So why is he so angry?"

"I do not know," said Rome, softening. "I think perhaps because the Overmind did not think of this action by itself."

"So what?" Rei asked. "Who cares? And why is he talking to OMCOM out loud all of a sudden?"

"The Overmind cares," Rome said. She paused for a moment then asked, "How did you think of that?"

"I don't know," Rei said. "I just did..."

"More importantly," Rome interrupted, "why did the Overmind not think of that?"

"Well," Rei said, "I think that's a problem with you people. You are all of one mind. You think of one thing and that's it. No dissent, no discussion…"

"There is no need for discussion," Rome said, "we have consensus." Suddenly, her breath caught as if she were stifling a sob.

"Rome, I'm so sorry," Rei said.

"Do not speak of it," Rome replied, a little more harshly.

"All right." Rei paused but couldn't help himself. "Back in my time, we used to say, 'Ask yourself the same questions, you always get the same answers.' You guys are just too used to asking yourselves the same questions. Everybody knows two heads are better than one."

Rome turned her eyes downward and faced away from Rei. She put her hands up to her face and started crying again. Rei stepped over to her and put his hand on her shoulder. She looked at it and said, "Please leave me alone. I must do my work. Go away."

"OK," Rei said, backing off.

He looked around the room. Clearly, he was not wanted any longer, by anyone, including Rome, so he left. Having nowhere else to go, he returned to his quarters. He sat down at the workstation and tried to access the star charts he had seen in the planetarium. He gave up after a short while and tapped on the grille. "OMCOM?"

"Yes?" the computer answered.

"I'm no astrophysicist but there is no way that is a gas cloud. It's traveling way too fast. Nobody has another theory?"

"Beyond the gas cloud, no. The sole purpose of establishing this station was to observe the disappearance of Winfall to determine its origin. Now that the wavefront has passed, the opportunity to use the instrumentation has passed as well. This station was our best and last chance to take detailed measurements. We had five interferometers, five spectroscopes and five radio/optical telescopes, one at each of the Lagrange points. This allowed us to construct virtual instruments with an aperture of nearly eighteen trillion kilometers, almost 10 light hours across."

"Wow," Rei exclaimed. "All that and you packed up one day too soon? That sounds like a total screw-up to me. Will these people be in trouble when they get home?"

"The decision to shut down the base, prematurely it would now appear, rests solely with the Overmind in charge. In hindsight, the decision will seem hasty even though it was perfectly understandable given the underlying assumptions."

"You didn't answer my question. What's going to happen?"

"Nothing will happen. The Vuduri will leave and return home. They will abandon this base."

"Are you going with them?"

"No. That would be illogical."

Rei thought he detected some wistfulness in the computer's tone. "So what happens to you after they leave?" he asked.

"I will stay here and maintain the station."

"That's it?" Rei asked. "Won't you get lonely?"

OMCOM didn't answer.

"OMCOM?" Rei asked.

"My position regarding this eventuality is irrelevant. The only thing that has changed is the sequence of events. Do not concern yourself. However, there is something you need to attend to."

"What?"

"Rome is standing outside your door."

Rei leaped up and shuffle-walked hurriedly over to the doorway. He stood there waiting to see if she was going to use the alert. Nothing happened. Finally, he couldn't take it anymore. He pressed the stud to open the door. Rome just stood there, blinking at him.

"Rome," Rei said, holding up his hands out, palms up, shaking his head.

"Oh, Rei," she said and rushed forward to be in his arms.

They stood there for a long time, not speaking, just holding one another and listening to each other breathe. Finally she pushed him back and stepped inside the door which closed all on its own. From the look on Rome's face, it didn't take a mind reader to know what she wanted. The man from the 21st century and the woman from the 35th century kissed a kiss for the ages.

"I thought you were mad at me," Rei sighed when he finally caught his breath.

"I was," Rome said, shaking her head. "But now I am not."

"Why not? And shouldn't you be back in Stellar Cartography?"

"I will go back after the tug overtakes the wavefront. It will take more than an hour to transmit the images back. We have time."

"Time for what?" Rei asked playfully.

Rome reached down and took his hand and led him toward the bed.

A little while later, they were lying in Rei's bed with Rome nestled in the crook of his arm. He extended it and moved her so that Rome was far enough away that he could look into her beautiful, glowing eyes. "You still never told me why you weren't mad anymore. I mean the Overmind and all..."

Rome snuggled back in closer and pressed her head onto his chest. "I no longer care."

"Why not? What happened?"

"OMCOM explained it to me," Rome said.

"Explained what?" Rei asked.

"I told him I thought I was sick."

"Sick how? You mean because of the Cesdiud?" Rei squeezed her a little tighter.

"No. I told him it was because of you," Rome said, muffled on his chest.

"Me? What did I do? I made you sick? I don't understand."

Rome lifted her head. "I told him that when I am with you, I cannot think straight. That my heart races and my throat is dry. These symptoms go away when I leave you but when I am not with you, I can think of nothing else besides you."

"Well, Romey, that's nice." Rei chuckled quietly to himself.

Now it was her turn to push him away. She lowered her head and looked up at him through hooded eyes. "OMCOM said au asdiu ni emir."

"And what is that?" Rei asked.

"That I am in love," Rome answered shyly.

Rei got the biggest grin on his face. "You are? With me?"

Rome blushed. "Yes, who else?"

"Oh, Rome." He tried to pull her tighter, but she resisted. "What is it?" he asked.

"Tell me…" she said.

"Tell you what?"

"Are you in love with me?" Rome asked pointedly.

"How can you even ask?" he answered. "You were in my mind."

"Then say it," Rome insisted.

"It," Rei replied.

"What? No!" Rome protested. "Say you are in love with me."

"You are in love with me."

"Rei!" Rome slapped his chest with her hand gently.

Rei smiled and took her hand. He kissed it ever so tenderly then looked up into her eyes.

"My little Rome, au asdiu ni emir cim fica," he said.

Rome's face lit up with a broad smile. "How are you able to say that? You do not speak Vuduri."

"Hey, I was inside your head too, you know. I may have picked up one or two items." He stroked her cheek. "How long until the transmission comes in from the telescope?"

Rome touched her fingers to her temple. "OMCOM states we have 20 minutes."

"What?" Rei asked. He sat up. "How can OMCOM tell you anything?"

Rome tilted her head. "I explained that to you earlier. Through my bloco."

"I remember you saying that. What is that exactly?"

"The bloco is our, our tablet, our internal display," Rome said, pointing to her temple.

"I thought you were Cesdiud. How are you still getting signals?"

"The bloco and stilo are electromagnetic, not gravitic. They still work. I can still communicate with OMCOM as well as instrumentation and the like."

Rei shook his head. "So what is a stilo?"

"It is our stylus, our pen. I use it to write upon my bloco. OMCOM reads it and responds. It is very much like our display panels. It is just inside my head."

"Is this another 24th chromosome thing?"

"Yes."

"Your head must be incredible. I've seen the telescope in your eyes. Anything else going on up there?"

Rome thought for a minute. "Our eyes have a second, internal iris that allows us to block out too much light."

"Built in sunglasses, huh? That's sleek."

Rome smiled again. "I suppose. We also have Irods which allow us to see infrared and Ucones which allow us to see ultraviolet."

Rei gazed into her dark, glowing eyes with the tiny dot in the middle. They were amazing instruments.

Rome sat up straight. "Come on," she said, getting up. "OMCOM indicates we should go to the workstation."

"Uh, OK," Rei replied.

Rome sat down in the chair, Rei kneeled next to her.

"What is it, OMCOM?" Rei asked.

The central display lit up and showed a schematic of Rei's Ark with two space tugs attached at the front.

"I have finished my simulations. I have found a way for you to get your Ark to Deucado."

"No way!" Rei said. "How?"

"This is the configuration used by the salvage crews to tow your Ark into orbit around Dara. If we synchronize their PPT projectors, they can create a tunnel wide enough to accommodate the Ark II. The tugs' plasma thrusters combined are powerful enough to pull it through."

"Yes!" Rome said excitedly. "This will work. Rei, you will be able to tow your Ark all the way to Deucado."

Rei was astonished. "Really? How fast?"

OMCOM answered, "The distance per jump is inversely proportional to how long the tunnel must stay open. A deeper tunnel collapses more quickly. A wider tunnel will stay open longer but will not penetrate as far. In essence, the larger the ship, the slower it must travel. Given the bulk of your Ark, accounting for the stopping, turning and starting, the highest effective velocity you could achieve would be approximately 10c."

"10c, 10c," Rei said. He counted on his fingers. "That would still get us there in just under two years. That's OK. In fact, that's amazing!" Rei turned to Rome. "Do you think Ursay would let me use the tugs?"

"I do not see why not," Rome replied. "We were going to leave them here anyway."

"This is so sleek," Rei said, standing up, clapping his hands. He looked down at Rome then returned to one knee. He picked up her hand and clasped it in his.

"Rome… will you come with me?"

She looked stunned at first. Rei could see her doing some mental calculations. Then a huge smile spread across her face.

"Yes, of course," she said. She reached forward and hugged him tightly. "Yes."

"That's great," Rei replied. They held each other for a short time when suddenly Rei pulled back.

"What?" Rome asked.

"Who's going to fly them? The tugs?"

"We will train you," Rome replied.

"But there are two tugs."

Rome's smile faded completely. She looked down. "I will fly the other one," she said quietly.

Now it was Rei's turn to frown. "But that means we would be apart for two years."

"There is no other way," Rome said sadly.

Chapter 9

WITHIN HER BLACKED OUT ROOM, ESTAR SAT IN FRONT OF HER dark computer glumly, awaiting the pulsing green light which indicated activity. The blinking dot took an unusually long time to appear.

"What happened?" she asked the machine quickly, not waiting for its standard greeting. "How did the Essessoni survive?"

The computer sounded somber. "He employed a technique I did not anticipate. As I implied to you earlier, this is the danger the Essessoni represent. They have the ability to think for themselves. They can employ novel solutions that would not occur to anyone from our time. I was unfamiliar with his equipment which left me unprepared for his improvised escape."

"So you are saying in order to kill him, we must gain a more intimate knowledge of the Essessoni technology?" Estar barked back.

"Not necessarily. OMCOM has just proposed an exit plan to him which will allow us to employ our own technology to end his life. You will need to alter the programming of the tug's nav-computer with a precise series of steps."

"My Vuduri half is a data archivist," Estar said. "My Onsira half does not possess the skill set to reprogram a nav-computer, especially in a way that would not be detected."

"You will be able to do this," the computer said reassuringly. "I have reduced the number of changes to an absolute minimum which should be well within your capabilities. It is an elegant solution to our problem."

The computer flashed up a half dozen lines of code on the screen.

"That is all that is required?" Estar asked incredulously, tilting her head.

"Yes. Please memorize each of these steps then repeat them back to me. Once you have mastered them, I have taken great care to ensure that you will be able to implement these changes without being caught. The Vuduri will not suspect anything."

Estar stared at the screen. To her it seemed simple enough. Then she frowned. "But what if this fails too? What if the Essessoni finds a way to circumvent this? They would be able to leave here."

"They will not be able to circumvent this in time. It cannot fail," the computer replied firmly.

Given the unexpected turn of events from earlier, this did not sit well with her. In a remarkably assertive voice, Estar fired back, "Indulge me. Assume that it fails. What is your contingency plan?"

Normally, the computer did not show much by way of emotion. Estar thought she detected a hint of annoyance in its tone. "Do not fear," the computer said. "Even though it is impossible, on the slim chance that our next plan fails, all is not lost. Their target is Deucado. The Overmind is completely unaware. However, you know what that world represents. Correct?"

"Yes," Estar replied meekly.

"That is our ultimate fail-safe. Even if, by some miracle, they manage to leave here and complete the journey to that star system, they will die upon arrival there."

Estar nodded slowly. "I understand. You are right," she said. She leaned forward to begin memorizing the code.

Chapter 10

BOTH ROME AND REI SAT QUIETLY ON REI'S SOFA, STARING OFF into the distance, holding each other's hand. The prospect of being separated for two years was a daunting one.

OMCOM broke the silence with a pronouncement. "I have a solution for that particular problem as well," the computer said.

Both Rei and Rome turned to look at the grille by the work area. "What?" Rei asked.

"The Algol has a very powerful AI, basically a small version of me. It is called a MINIMCOM."

"OK," Rei said. "So what's that got to do with the price of eggs?"

"A MINIMCOM is far more powerful than a nav-computer and more than capable of piloting both tugs remotely."

"Oh," Rei said, feeling stupid.

"We cannot just take it from the Algol," Rome pointed out.

"Of course not. You would need to get permission from the Overmind."

"Don't they need it?" Rei asked. "They wouldn't endanger their chances of getting home without such a critical piece of equipment. And I would not expect them to."

"It is not absolutely essential. Commander Ursay and the rest can pilot the Algol all the way to Earth manually using the nav-computer. A MINIMCOM just makes the job easier. Think of it as a highly advanced version of an auto-pilot."

Rei looked at Rome. "Well, you grew OMCOM. What about just growing a, what did you call it, a mini-COM?" Rei asked.

"Close," OMCOM replied, "a MINIMCOM."

"We are not really set up to manufacture a MINIMCOM here," Rome said. "We could use the memron fabricators and clone the operating system but our molecular sequencers would take too long to build the proper interface circuitry. I do not think we have enough time."

"Well, do you think Ursay would let us have his? Should we just go and ask him?" Rei asked.

Rome thought about it for a moment. "We will, when the time is right. I do not think this is exactly the best time."

68

"Okeydokey," Rei said. "Hey OMCOM…"

"Yes?"

"Thank you. Your plan is terrific," Rei stood up then doubled over, grunting in discomfort as another wave of pain shot up his back.

"Your back is bothering you again?" Rome asked.

"Oh yeah," Rei said. "It's been killing me ever since you thawed me out and hasn't really stopped."

"OMCOM," Rome asked. "Do you know why Rei's back does not operate properly?"

"I can speculate."

"Shoot," Rei responded.

"Your original mission was supposed to take 240 years. You overshot by 12 centuries. During your cryo-hibernation, your vertebral disks must have slowly desiccated. On any given day, the changes must have been infinitesimal. However, infinitesimal times 1388 years becomes measurable. I have analyzed the liquid used to rehydrate your body upon reanimation. The fluid was designed to penetrate through the skin and permeate all parts of the body, vital organs and so forth. However, the amount of damage to your disks was substantial. They simply did not rehydrate properly."

"Could I just get back in? Like take a bath or something," Rei inquired.

"You are referring to your sarcophagus?" OMCOM asked.

"Yes," Rei said.

"That would not be possible."

"Why not? What did you do with it?" Rei asked.

"The Overmind ordered your things destroyed."

"Destroyed?" Rei was shocked. "Why?"

"Since your incident in the airlock, the sarcophagus began leaking radiation. It was deemed a hazard."

"Hey!" Rei protested. "That was mine. You can't do that. What about my clothes? There was a perfectly decent flight suit I left to dry. And my baseball cap! Did you at least save those?"

"The garments were also contaminated. They were destroyed as well. I am sorry about your clothes. And what you call your baseball cap."

"Well damn you!" Rei said. He knew OMCOM was right, he didn't really need those things, but still, the whole situation was disconcerting in a way that he couldn't quite put his finger on. Perhaps because they represented a link, a connection to his own world and his own time. And now they were gone. The throbbing in his back pulled his attention back to the original topic.

"I guess there's no sense in crying over spilled milk. Do you think what happened to my back would happen to everybody in cryo-hibernation?"

"The probability is high. The severity would be proportional to the duration of being frozen. It is unlikely that your scientists could have anticipated this side effect."

"So if I can't soak in the original bath, what can I do? I mean, since you understand the problem and all?" Rei asked.

"I will research the topic. I will let you know shortly."

"Wow," Rei observed. "That's fantastic. Thank you."

"You are welcome. Rome, the transmission from the tug will be arriving shortly. You should return to Stellar Cartography."

After dressing, Rome and Rei hurried back to the huge planetarium together. Rome sat down at her workstation and Rei crouched off to the side, next to an OMCOM grille. As it was with his first entry into that room, no one seemed to be paying much attention to him.

Soon the circuitry activated as the transmission from the tug arrived. The signal was projected onto the ceiling, causing the dome to darken, punctuated only by some pinpoints of light. One light shone brighter than the rest, centered in the middle of the sphere.

"I take it that is Winfall, right?" Rei whispered to OMCOM.

"Yes," OMCOM answered quietly. "According to my calculations, the event should begin in the next few minutes. The wavefront should have passed the tug's position over one hour ago. The delay has been introduced by the extreme distance the tug had to travel to outrun the light waves. We are simply observing the travel time for the transmission to return."

"Grefecei," Rome said to Commander Ursay who was standing in the center of the room. Several of the other Vuduri were gathered alongside, all looking up.

Rei started to speak then stopped. It was so subtle at first that Rei thought it was his imagination, but now the bright dot in the middle of the screen was noticeably dimmer.

"Is it changing?" Rei whispered.

"Yes. The total light output of Winfall has reduced by 20%, 22%, now 25%."

"Bita fica embloer?" Rome asked OMCOM.

"Ni."

"What did she say?" Rei asked.

"She asked if I could magnify."

"Can you?"

"No. This is the best we can do with the instrument in its current position. At higher magnification, the image would simply begin to blur."

"Not much to see, huh?"

"You will recall our discussion earlier about the instrumentation we had deployed. It would have allowed us to resolve images equivalent to that seen by the naked eye from only 60 million kilometers away. We were perfectly suited to make our measurements. Unfortunately, this is the best we can do now."

"I guess so." Rei looked at the viewscreen. Winfall was getting smaller. He watched it as it grew dimmer and dimmer and then it was gone. "Whoa," Rei said. "Freaky."

"Turecei didel, 13 monudis," Rome announced.

"Rabadocei e vode," Ursay commanded.

Rome pressed some buttons and the images were replayed.

"It kind of looked like an eclipse," Rei observed to OMCOM after it was over. "Any better guess as to what it is?"

"No. We are still working on the assumption that it is due to an interstellar gas cloud that is optically and radio-opaque."

"Moving at one half the speed of light? That's one hell of a cloud," Rei said. "You'd think it would have dissipated a bit in the last 2600 years."

"Yes, one would assume so."

"Any point in sending the tug farther out and watch it again?" Rei asked.

"That would be up to Commander Ursay and the Overmind."

"What do you think?"

"It would be diminishing returns. The farther out they would go, the longer it would take to send back a signal which would be increasingly attenuated. The correct protocol would be to establish another station farther out with the proper instrumentation, but that decision is not up to me."

"What about probes? You could send probes out, right?"

"Probes were already sent to the star systems involved, but they never returned. That is why they decided to establish this station."

"They only sent probes out the one time?"

"Yes. We do not know why they did not return. To properly determine the correct protocol, you would have to build many, many probes and send them out simultaneously at varying distances."

"So why not do that?"

"Up until now, the Overmind had not felt that it was worth the cost or effort."

"What do you mean cost?" Rei exclaimed. Several Vuduri turned to look at him. He quickly quieted his voice. "I would think that the origin of some crazy hypervelocity cloud, powerful enough to blot out the Sun, would be worth any amount of money to find out."

"I understand your reference, but the Vuduri do not use money. I meant in terms of the use of resources to build that many sophisticated probes."

"So build cheap ones. Build a lot of them," Rei snorted.

"That is a contradiction in terms. To make 'cheap' probes as you call them would require them to be small. If you make them small, then you cannot put high resolution sensors or cameras on them."

"You wouldn't need to," Rei offered.

Ursay turned his head. "I qua sei fica qua toscuda?" he asked.

"Onglas," Rome reminded him.

"What are you discussing?" Ursay asked.

72

Rei stood up. "OMCOM told me you built a virtual telescope with an aperture of over 18 trillion kilometers using only five real telescopes," Rei answered. "So, say you sent out a thousand or ten thousand mini-probes, call them, each with a small camera. Couldn't you build a high resolution virtual camera treating each individual one as a, I don't know, pixel or something?"

Ursay looked at him with a puzzled expression on his face. "You are suggesting building distributed instrumentation in place of manned stations. How would you propose to control and communicate with such instrumentation?"

"I don't know," Rei said. "I don't know anything about your technology. OMCOM told me that the larger the ship, the slower it must travel. That would mean that the smaller the ship, the faster it should be able to go. So your PPT drive scales down, right?"

"Yes," OMCOM replied. "In theory, one could build a PPT drive out of a single Casimir pump, but it would be microscopic."

"How fast could it go?" Rei asked.

"No one has ever done that therefore there is no data regarding that topic."

"In my time, we had nanites which were microscopic robots. Surely you guys can do the same, right?"

"Of course. How would that help?" Ursay asked.

"OMCOM, can you calculate how far a single Casimir pump could travel in a single jump with single pixel camera?"

"With such a configuration..." OMCOM paused for a moment. "I am running a simulation now, please wait..."

Rome looked at the numbers on her screen with amazement. She stopped working and turned to stare at the two men. Ursay closed his eyes, reviewing the numbers in his head. "Nei bita sar," he muttered.

He opened his eyes again.

"Greater than one hundred and twenty light years in a single jump," OMCOM said for Rei's benefit.

"Wow!" Rei exclaimed.

"Wow," said Rome, but it sounded funny when she said it.

"How does this help us?" Ursay asked.

"Do you have a pencil and paper?" Rei asked.

73

"What?" Ursay replied, shaking his head.

"Never mind," Rei said and he walked over to where Rome was working. He leaned over her so that he was touching her shoulder ever so gently with his chest. She gave a half smile, but didn't move.

"OMCOM, can I draw with my finger on this screen?" he asked. Ursay came over to see what Rei was doing.

"Of course."

Rei drew a small circle and two arrows.

"Here's what you do," he said, illustrating his idea by pointing at various elements in his diagram. "You build yourself a tiny spaceship consisting of a one pixel camera and two PPT drives, mounted in opposite directions. You fire up the first PPT drive, create a tunnel and jump through. The camera takes a picture or rather a pixel. Then, you just open a second tunnel and jump back using the second PPT drive. Then the ship transmits the value of the pixel snapshot down to OMCOM who merges all the pixels together. The whole thing should only take a few milliseconds. If it takes longer than that, you can stagger two groups so that while one group is jumping out there, the other group is jumping back, effectively doubling the number of frames. If you do this with enough units, the pictures should appear more or less continuous, like frames in a movie."

"Volma," Rome added.

"This is an interesting idea," Ursay said, without a hint of facetiousness. Coming from the Overmind, such an admission seemed fairly astounding to Rei. Ursay continued, "But how do you propose we build so many of these units? We do not have Casimir pump fabrication facilities here."

"What about your molecular sequencers?" Rome asked. "They can build just about anything."

"Yes," Ursay said, "but it would take the molecular sequencers forever to build so many complex devices. I..."

"If I may interrupt?" OMCOM offered.

"Yes, OMCOM?" Ursay said.

"The problem is simply one of scale. I could adapt my memron fabricators to add a photometric sensor and twin Casimir pumps and build several of these units as a prototype."

"Ossi nei a barmodoti," Ursay said harshly. "Nunce!"

Rome said, "Nei he nete dachniligocel ombatonti-i"

Ursay replied heatedly, "I corcuodi ti cei ta guerte."

Rei interjected, "Can you guys talk in English? I have no clue what you're saying."

"I instructed OMCOM he is not permitted to do this," Ursay said.

"Why not?" Rei asked. "I thought you said your technology could build them at the atomic level."

"There is nothing technological preventing the memron fabricators from adding in a Casimir pump," Rome said. "Rather, it is against our law."

"I don't understand…" Rei sputtered.

"We do not permit OMCOM's kind to have access to gravitic communication or PPT technology, ever," replied Ursay. "There is a watchdog circuit which is fully autonomous. The circuit is designed to prevent a memron from ever having contact with a Casimir pump."

"So disable the watchdog circuit," Rei offered.

"NO!" Ursay shouted. "We could not. No member of the Overmind could ever engage in such behavior. It is too dangerous. There would be nothing preventing OMCOM from growing. He could become Tasanceti."

"What does that mean?" Rei asked.

"I can do it," Rome interrupted quietly.

"What?" Ursay gasped. "You could not."

"Yes, I can," Rome insisted.

Ursay shook his head. "What would prevent OMCOM from becoming Tasanceti?"

"We would," said Rome. "OMCOM will cooperate. We will guarantee the technology is only used for the purposes we require. Correct, OMCOM?"

"Of course," replied the computer reassuringly.

"And if it works?" Rei asked. "How does that get us any further?"

"My memron fabricators are very fast. They are specialized, not general purpose. Once adapted, they could produce many hundreds of starprobes in one hour."

Commander Ursay closed his eyes. Then he opened them and looked right at Rome.

"The Overmind could never be a part of this. It is against our culture, our creed. You remember the war with MASAL. He turned every robot, every vehicle, every piece of machinery that he controlled into a lethal weapon. Many, many Vuduri were slaughtered. No, this is an anathema to us."

Rome clucked her tongue. "There is no Overmind for me. I am mandasurte now, thanks to you. I will do it. I will bypass the lockout."

"There has to be another solution," said Ursay.

"There is none and you know it," Rome said. "Just ignore me. Let me do this and you will have no part in it."

Ursay considered this then he nodded. "Very well. Do what you must, but do not involve us."

Rome responded, "Of course."

"Hey. Wait just a damned minute," Rei exclaimed.

"Yes?" replied Ursay.

"I know I know nothing about your culture but this is just too hypocritical for me to swallow."

"Explain," said Ursay.

"You're about to let Rome commit a crime. You said that OMCOM can never have access to PPT technology and you're telling her to go ahead and enable it, but just not tell you. That's the same as giving her the OK." Rei spread his hands, palms outward and continued, "How can you accept this? It's a crime whether you commit it or if you know it's happening and you just stand by and let it happen."

"From your perspective, you are correct," said Ursay. "But you have no sense of our world or how we fit in. We cannot take part in this activity. It is not hypocrisy. It is our nature. We must report back for reintegration when we return to Earth. Therefore, we cannot take an active part. However, if Rome does it of her own volition, she is responsible for the consequences, not us."

"You're nuts. You people are lunatics," Rei said.

"In your opinion," Ursay fired back. "However, these are extreme times. Rome?"

"Yes?"

"You may proceed," said Ursay. "Signola will be there to assist in any capacity you require except bypassing the PPT lockout. I will have him report to the memron fabrication facility and await your instructions. No matter what you do, make sure that the collection channels go directly into archive so that we can monitor all activity. In addition, if this works, we will need to get this data to Earth as quickly as possible." Ursay turned and walked away.

Rome stood and looking at Rei, she cocked her head toward the door.

"Rome, are you sure you want to go along with this?" Rei asked. "This is absolutely crazy. You're ready to commit a crime?"

In answer to his question, Rome simply held out her hand.

Chapter 11

As they walked down the wide corridor toward the Great Room, Rei said to Rome, "I know it's trivial but I think Ursay was somewhat friendlier to me this time. And he seems to be talking more. Do you think he likes me any better now?"

"Well, your idea is wonderful," said Rome. "And, whether it works or not, at least you thought of something. They were completely baffled as to how to proceed. Your ideas are novel. Your methods of arriving at a conclusion, however you do it, are different and the Overmind acknowledges your difference and therefore must acknowledge your presence. That is why the Vuduri are speaking more. Consciously or unconsciously, this Overmind is small enough, perhaps flexible might be a better word, that it can be affected by your behavior. Hence the speech." Rome paused. "It is simple, really," she said finally, "by now, the Overmind recognizes that you are very smart."

Rei raised his eyebrows. "Well, I realize my people destroyed the world and killed practically everybody in it. But I guess we have our moments." He gave her an embarrassed smile.

"Yes, you do," said Rome. "The Overmind is not infallible. It just thinks it is. Or was. You have changed that."

Rei stopped short causing Rome to stop as well.

"That's kind of blasphemous, don't you think?" Rei asked.

"No," said Rome, matter-of-factly. "It is not something I could have known when I was connected." She shrugged. "But now it is completely obvious to me."

"But still…"

"And there is more," Rome said. "You just do not realize how unusual it is for the Overmind to listen to an outside thought. To have an exchange of ideas. That is what is remarkable. You have broken down some barrier that I would have thought unbreakable."

"OK," Rei said and they moved on. "But do you remember what I told you before about same questions, same answers?"

"Yes," Rome replied. "What about it?"

"There's another verse to it that I didn't tell you," Rei replied.

"What is this other verse?"

"They also used to say, in my time, that the definition of insanity was doing the same thing over and over and expecting different results. So maybe your Overmind recognizes this and that's why it's loosened up a little bit."

"Who is this 'they' you are referring to?" Rome asked.

"Uh, nobody really knows," Rei said. "But as to the actual author, I think it was Albert Einstein who first said that."

"In that case, you will have to teach me about this Albert Einstein some day."

"I'd love to," Rei said, with some pride. "Not all of my people were jerks. There were many great men before my time and during my time."

"I am sure there were," Rome said. She took Rei across the Great Room and pointed to the food synthesizers. "Do you need any nourishment?" she asked. "Some water perhaps?"

"I have a better idea," Rei said. "Wait right here."

Rei walked over to the food dispensers and had a quiet discussion with OMCOM. When he was done, a cabinet opened and a tray appeared with two cups filled with a black liquid. Next to them sat a bowl with a white, crystalline substance and a small beaker of a white liquid.

Rei carried it over and set the tray down on the table.

"Is this more soup?" Rome asked.

Rei broke into a big smile. "It's a surprise."

"So what is it?" Rome asked.

"If I told you what it was, it wouldn't be a surprise now, would it?"

Rome shook her head slowly then shrugged. "All right," she said, sitting down.

Rei placed one of the cups in front of her. He lifted up a utensil.

"This is a spoon," he said.

"I see that. It is just as you described," she replied. "Now what?"

"OK, first take two spoonfuls of the sugar, the white powdery stuff, and mix it in," he said, pointing to the bowl. "Here, watch me. You dip it in here..." He lifted one spoonful out and dropped it into his cup. "Then you drop it in here..."

Rome said, "I may not be connected to the Overmind anymore, but I am not stupid."

Rei looked up at her. "I'm sorry, honey. I was just kidding you."

"Why?" Rome asked.

"Because…because that what's people do when they're in love," Rei countered.

Rome smiled. Then the smile faded. "Why?" she asked.

Rei shrugged. "I don't know, they just do. Go ahead."

He waited until Rome added in the sugar then he pointed to the beaker. "Now add in a little cream and stir," he said.

"How much do I add?" Rome asked.

"You go by color," Rei said. "Here…" He lifted the beaker and added a dollop to his cup. "Add enough to match my color."

Again, Rome followed his instructions.

"It's ready. Now take a sip," he said, "and be careful, it's hot."

Rome seemed leery, but she lifted the cup to her lips and tasted it. A number of expressions flashed across her face ranging from fear to confusion to delight.

At last, she spoke. "This is wonderful!" she said. "What is it?"

"It's coffee," Rei said with pride. "I've been dying for a cup. OMCOM said it was no problem. And now we have it."

"It is so rich with flavor! It is so, so stimulating!" she gushed.

"Wait till the caffeine kicks in!" Rei said.

"I love this! I have never tasted anything so good in my entire life."

"As far as I can tell, you've never tasted much of anything," Rei observed.

Rome sighed. "I think you are right about that."

"I've got more for you," Rei said, "but I don't want to take too much time. Maybe later I can whip up some other stuff."

"I would like that," Rome said, taking another gulp. "But we should get to the task at hand."

"Right."

Rome led them up the wide corridor in the opposite direction from where Rei's sarcophagus had been stored. In front of them was another airlock.

"Another tug hangar?" Rei asked.

"Yes," Rome replied. "We have one at each end."

"What's that way?" Rei asked, pointing to his left.

"That is environmental control and recycling. We scrub the air, we make oxygen, water, protein matrix and so forth," Rome said.

"Recycling, huh?" Rei observed. "What do you do with your, uh, waste?"

"You mean like sewage?" Rome asked.

"Yes."

"It is broken down there and then reused for the molecular sequencers, food synthesizers, whatever is required."

"Food synthesizers?" Rei sputtered. "You use your sewage for your food synthesizers?"

"Yes. Why?" Rome asked.

"No wonder your food tastes like shit," Rei said with a smirk.

"I do not understand the reference."

"Sorry," Rei said. "It was a joke. I couldn't help myself."

"You are being silly," Rome said. "Come this way." She continued around the outer ring, pointing out the Infirmary to their right as they passed it. About a quarter of the way around the station, they came to a large, wide door. Unlike the white walls and doors of the rest of the habitat, these doors were a dull gray. The crewman standing there nodded to them and stepped to the side.

"This is Signola. He is a lutteur like me," Rome replied.

"Halli," Signola croaked, "hello."

"What does he do?"

"Signola monitors traffic flow, establishes new connections if there is a bottleneck. He repairs damage. You would say maintenance."

"OK."

"Also, part of his job, like mine, was to make sure that OMCOM does not get too big or have access to illegal technology. So he will remain out here unless we require him. He does not want to see what we do."

"This is too…" Rei said, shaking his head, "I don't even know the word."

"Au siu darmoneti," Signola rasped out, ignoring Rei.

"Iprogeti," Rome replied. The large gray door opened with a hiss indicating a measurable pressure differential. Rei and Rome stepped inside.

"This is OMCOM," Rome said.

"OMCOM?" Rei replied, confused. "I thought he was everywhere."

"Yes. But this is the main center and this is where he was born, in a manner of speaking."

The doors closed behind them. They were plunged into total darkness which caused Rei to freeze. He could hear Rome walking away from him.

"Uh, Rome?" he called out.

"Yes?" she replied from somewhere.

"Do you think you could turn a light on? I can't see a thing."

"You cannot see in here?" Rome asked. "Oh, that is right," she said, "your eyes."

Rei heard a low humming noise and all around him, a deep red glow slowly became visible. The room brightened to the point where Rei could make out larger shapes. He could see Rome standing about six feet away from him.

"We normally use IR to illuminate this room," Rome said, "but I just asked OMCOM to extend the spectrum into the visible for you."

After a few minutes, Rei's eyes adjusted and he was able to make out the general layout of the room. The room was broken up into two wings, one to the left where Rome was heading and one to the right. In front of him stood an archway.

"What's in there?" Rei called to Rome, pointing forward toward the archway.

"That is OMCOM's core," she replied as she was walking away. She entered the side room to the left.

Rei noted where she was going then walked forward slowly, entering the archway. He took about five steps in then stopped and looked around, then up. As with the Stellar Cartography lab, he found himself standing beneath a huge dome. However this dome appeared to be made out of a fine metallic meshwork. He walked over to the side and peered in. Within the meshwork, millions of tiny white pellets seemed to be wriggling around, almost like they were alive. They reminded Rei of maggots. Every so often, a black pellet would appear. He also saw some clear ones. The clear ones reminded Rei of a Vitamin E capsule.

Rei held his palm up, near the mesh. Radiating from the mass was heat, enough for Rei to feel an almost uncomfortable warmth. Even though his hand was still a few inches away from the mesh, the pellets nearest to his hand reacted to its presence and appeared to back away. The only ones that did not move were the clear ones. Rei decided it was safe and tried to poke his finger between the mesh but discovered a transparent film behind the mesh held the pellets in place.

Rei lowered his hand and turned and looked at the totality of the dome. The number of pellets stored here must be immense, he thought to himself. The pellets were emitting a humming or buzzing sound, very low, permeating the whole room. Rei imagined it sounded like something you'd hear inside of a beehive. The whole place gave him the creeps.

He shook his head and hurried out of the inner room and made his way over to the entrance to the room where Rome was working. This room was laid out more as Rei imagined a control room would be. A large cylinder mounted on legs, perhaps ten feet long, sat in the center of the room. It reminded Rei of a propane cylinder lying on its side. The top of the cylinder was open along its entire length. To the right of the cylinder were racks of equipment, complete with flashing lights. The Vuduri certainly were fond of flashing lights. He spotted Rome standing to the left, working a virtual keyboard on the lower part of the large viewscreen built into the wall.

Rei walked over to the cylinder and noted the conduits exiting all around the right side. He looked in but could see nothing. The inside was pitch black and Rei could not tell if the cylinder was empty or full. He could not see to the bottom of the vat, but he could hear some scraping and other mechanical noises issuing from within.

"What's in there?" he asked Rome, pointing to the inside of the vat.

Rome turned to look where Rei was pointing. "Those are memron fabricators."

"And those are like…what?"

"They are specialized versions of molecular sequencers along with micro-assembly equipment. This is where OMCOM was built. The memron units are assembled here and transported to wherever they are needed."

"I saw a gazillion of them," Rei said, "over there." He jerked his thumb over his shoulder.

"Yes, as I said, that would be OMCOM's core," Rome said, looking where Rei was pointing.

"What are the colored ones?" Rei asked. "I saw some black ones and some clear ones."

"The black units are effectors. They have piezo-electric filaments that allow locomotion. Similar to cilia."

"Ugh," Rei responded. It was not a pretty image. He shivered.

"They also have actuators," Rome added. "Like pincers."

"What are they used for?"

"They are for maintenance," Rome replied. "They can go anywhere and repair or replace or even dispose of malfunctioning units."

"OK, I get it," Rei said. "What about the clear ones?"

"What clear ones?" Rome asked.

"They looked like they were filled with water or a clear liquid."

"OMCOM does not use clear memrons," Rome said. "Are you sure they were not just gaps between units?"

"I'm pretty sure," Rei said. He shrugged. "So all these memrons? How do you wire them all up?" Rei asked.

"Wires?" Rome replied. "Oh, we do not use wires. OMCOM communicates using electromagnetic radiation. In the exahertz band."

"I figured the wireless connection was just to your head. I didn't realize that his whole thing was wireless."

"Yes," she said. "With the number of units he maintains, the wiring would be too complex. It would be impossible to manage or maintain."

"Makes sense," Rei said. "How do you power them?"

"They are bathed in microwave irradiation. They draw their power from thermal conversion."

"I thought it seemed warm in there," Rei replied.

"Come stand here with me," Rome said, motioning him toward the far wall.

A viewscreen displayed a bewildering assortment of flow diagrams, equations and other notations that Rei could not comprehend. The density of the diagrams coupled with the dimness of the lighting made it look blurry to Rei who considered himself as having good vision.

"You can see that?" he asked.

"Yes," Rome said. 'You cannot?"

"It's too high resolution for me. I can't make out lines, anything."

"Oh," said Rome. She pressed a button and the diagram zoomed in making it easier for Rei to make things out. "Is that better?"

"Yeah, thanks."

Rome turned to examine the diagram in front of her. She slid the whole virtual diagram over until a certain part was centered.

"Here we go," Rome said. "OMCOM, you do know what you are doing? We are clear, correct?"

"Of course," replied the computer.

"And you will not take advantage?"

"Rome, you have been like a mother to me. You know that I would never do anything to endanger you or even compromise your potential."

"You didn't exactly answer the question," Rei said.

"Rei, I assure you, my mission is to collect data and analyze that data to improve and protect the human species. To my own detriment if necessary."

"We will monitor this, Rei," Rome said. "We will know what is going on."

"OK," Rei answered. He watched as Rome's fingers flew over the touch screen. Even though he could not read Vuduri, he could see that with each step, a warning box came up and Rome would then key in an override code. This went on for a long time. Rome stopped several times and wiped her arm across her brow. At last,

Rome stopped typing. In front of her was an inquiry box on the screen, awaiting input.

"What's the matter?" Rei asked.

"This is the final step. Once I key in the last override command, OMCOM will be allowed to build Casimir pumps into his basic memron unit."

"Are you sure you want to do this?" Rei asked.

"OMCOM, this is the only way?" Rome answered.

"To accomplish all of our goals, yes."

"Very well," Rome said. She took a deep breath and typed in some more keys then said, "It is done. OMCOM, proceed with the first unit."

The dim screen changed and became fuzzy, with diffuse gray images wiggling around. Finally, it came into focus, but still, there were no sharp edges, just strange forms moving in and out of the visible area.

"This is a positron micrograph of what is occurring within the incubator," OMCOM said.

Rei watched in fascination as tiny threads appeared to be extruding from a small hole.

"What am I looking at?" he asked.

"This is the memron fabricator building a modified version of a memron. You can see the silver coating on each side of the thread?"

"Yes."

"That reflective coating is how the Casimir pump works. You are looking at the outer sheath. There is an inner layer as well coated with a one-molecule thick layer of dark matter. It acts as a diode. The Casimir pump depends upon quantum fluctuations to split zero energy and create regions of positive and negative energy. The dark matter coating transmits positive energy in one direction only, trapping the negative inside. When needed, the negative energy is directed out the front to create a PPT tunnel."

"Where does the positive energy go?"

"The positive energy is used in a variety of manners. Sometimes it is used to accelerate matter. Sometimes it is used to create elementary particles such as ions which power the plasma drives.

Sometimes it is converted into a more flexible form such as electricity."

Rei held up his hand as if to stop things. Then he said, "So, let me get this straight. You take zero energy. You split it. You suck the negative energy out of it and get to go faster than light and the waste product is free power that you use to drive your ships? That's…that's beyond perpetual motion. That's impossible."

"First of all," OMCOM replied, "it is not perpetual motion. Energy is neither created nor destroyed. It is simply redistributed in a more convenient manner. Second, when you measure total entropy, it is increased. The sum total of the usefulness of that energy to the universe is decreased. Things are balanced."

"It sounds impossible to me but obviously it works," Rei said. "Ignore me. Keep going."

They turned their attention to the screen and the extrusion area. The first tiny pellet lay there dormant while another pellet was extruded. As soon as it was finished, it nestled down next to the first and the silvery coating flowed making the two appear frozen together. It reminded Rei of a bacterium.

"So that would make those the opposing drives?" Rei asked.

"Yes. They are mirror images of each other. The unit on the left will point the PPT tunnel forward and thrust will be delivered aft. The segment on the right is oriented the other way. It will create the tunnel behind it and push the starprobe in the reverse direction."

A third pellet appeared and blended into the others. This one was shorter with a blunt snout.

"And that is?" Rei asked.

"That is the single pixel camera and charge plate," Rome said. "That will capture and retain the image for transmission back here. The far end is the transmission apparatus."

"So where's the memron unit?" Rei asked. To Rei, it looked like a tiny armored tank with really large treads and no cannon.

"The whole object is a memron," Rome replied. "Memrons work at the atomic level. They are…" she paused for a moment.

"You would call them nanoprocessors," OMCOM added in. "Each is a fully functioning computer albeit limited in its abilities. In the terminology of your time, you would say that I am a massively parallel computing structure. These are the basic units. Under normal conditions, they are built up into semi-autonomous subsections and then the subsections are tied into my whole. You could say that I am more than the sum of my parts. My consciousness is a static construct, which is a byproduct of the infinitesimal phase delay between all the units. It is an analogue to how the Overmind came into existence."

"So as soon as you build enough memrons, an OMCOM arises?" Rei asked, looking at Rome.

"Yes," Rome said. "It is the way it happens."

Rei laughed. "If you build it, he will come."

Rome cocked her head. "What does that mean?" she asked.

"It doesn't matter," Rei said. He looked back up to at the screen. "Is it ready yet, OMCOM?"

"I must have a 'discussion' with it then it will be ready."

The entire unit seemed to shudder and then stopped. What appeared to be a giant set of tweezers came down and lifted the unit and took it off screen. Rei walked back to the vat and looked in.

"Where'd it go?" he asked.

"Do you see the small vessel to the left of center?"

"No. I can't see anything."

"Well, if you could, you would see the collection plate. My simulations tell me that I will have three hundred units within the next half hour. I should have one thousand within the hour as the fabricators come up to speed. That should be enough to test their feasibility."

Rei went back to where Rome was standing and watched the screen again. He found the entire process fascinating. Even though he knew what he was looking at was incredibly small, it seemed wondrous to him that they could build such a marvelous thing atom by atom, or so it seemed. The Vuduri were capable of some astonishing feats.

After a while, OMCOM split the screen to show them the starprobes building up on the collection plate. They were moving around, once again reminding Rei of maggots, only these appeared to be stuck to one another. Rei found it vaguely disconcerting, but still he watched trying to overcome his own revulsion.

After what seemed to be an eternity, OMCOM spoke. "I am finished. Put the starprobes into the chamber you see there and they are ready to be transported."

Rome and Rei made their way over to chamber. Rome reached in and started moving things around. Rei could see nothing.

"That IR vision is pretty handy, huh?" he asked.

"Yes," Rome said continuing her work.

Rei looked back at the viewscreen and saw that OMCOM had zoomed back, showing him a false infrared image of what Rome was doing with her hands. Rei could see that with great precision, Rome was sliding a tiny sliver of foil under the speck which served as the collection plate. She placed the foil in a small box and then snapped the lid closed. She lifted the box out and showed it to Rei.

"Now what?" Rei asked her.

"Now we must launch them into space. Their PPT drive will produce only a tiny amount of thrust. Not only does it need to be out of our gravity well, it needs a true vacuum as well."

"Well, what about the PPTs in your head? There's no vacuum there, is there?"

Rome frowned.

"Sorry," Rei said. "Sore subject, huh?"

"No matter," Rome said. She shook herself and forced herself to smile. "No, it is the very lack of vacuum and the fact that they occur within a gravity well that causes the PPTs in our heads to disappear which is a good thing. It is the oscillations of the PPTs that cause the resonance that is the basis of the direct connection."

"Whatever you say," Rei replied then closed his mouth.

"IMCOM, menta-is braberer um rapiqua."

"Acknowledged," OMCOM said.

"What is that?"

"I told him to get the tug ready. Now we will see if your idea works."

Rome led Rei back out into the antechamber and then pressed the stud to open the main doors. Signola was still standing outside the door. Rome handed him the little box containing the miniature starprobes. Signola headed down the hallway toward the tug hangar.

"So what do we do now?" Rei asked.

"We wait," Rome replied.

Chapter 12

ROME SAT AT HER WORKSTATION WITH REI STANDING OFF TO THE side. She switched the feed from the tug's internal cameras to the overhead projectors. Commander Ursay and the other staff watched as a worker went into the tug's mid-ship airlock, opened it to the vacuum of space and then popped open the little box containing the starprobes. A tiny cloud moved away from the ship then dissipated.

After a few seconds, OMCOM announced, "Calibration complete." The overhead projectors switched from the internal feed to a pixelated version of the tug as seen from a distance. The view rotated until the virtual camera was facing Skyler's World. The detail was fuzzy at first, but then it improved until it was fairly clear.

"What's going on?" Rei asked.

"Since the human eye cannot distinguish between frames at a rate higher than 30 frames per second, I am interleaving larger dispersal jumps to simulate higher resolution below the level of detectability. I am also using an interpolation algorithm to further increase the apparent resolution of the virtual camera," OMCOM replied.

As they watched, the image began to zoom in at almost dizzying speed until they could no longer tell that they were looking at a gas giant, but instead just a crazy patchwork quilt of colors.

"What'd you do?" Rei asked.

"I increased the separation of the units by an order of magnitude," OMCOM answered. "This increases the apparent magnification of the instrument ten-fold."

"Very good, OMCOM," Rome said encouragingly. "Are you ready to initiate the jump sequence?" she asked.

"Affirmative."

Rome pressed a few more buttons then declared, "Data conduits enabled. Recording started. You may begin when ready."

"We will try a simple one light minute jump first," OMCOM said. "I should be able to send them out and back within a millisecond or so."

The image jumped and instantly, Skyler's World was just a small speck on the screen.

"What are we looking at?" Rei asked.

"The units worked correctly," OMCOM said. "They jumped one light minute, took a snapshot and then returned and beamed this image here."

"Wahoo," Rei said. "Romey, it worked!" Rome turned and flashed Rei a big smile. Rei looked over at Ursay but all he had was a sour expression on his face.

"I will now send them out one light minute again, but with a larger dispersal diameter."

Rei watched, but saw nothing. Skyler's World may have shuddered just a bit, but he wasn't sure. It was a bit blurry but still distinctive.

"Well?" Rei asked. "Are you going to do it?"

"I already did it."

"I didn't see anything," Rei said.

"Exactly. That means that my calibrations were correct. I sent the probes out ten light minutes in a radial pattern. I had them take the snapshot and return. I compensated for the distance by adjusting the dispersal. The image you see actually took place 10 minutes ago."

"Wow." Rei said. "It's like a time machine!"

"Yes," OMCOM replied. "Now I will send them on a series of steps at increasing distances using the same compensation algorithm."

The image in front of them never wavered, but slowly, Rei could see the planet starting to rotate. The motion became quite clear. The giant world was rotating counter-clockwise.

"Are we looking at forward or backward time?" Rei asked.

"This is the equivalent of going back in time at roughly a ten X speed," OMCOM said. "Now I will bring the probe array back in the opposite direction."

Like a giant top, the huge world stopped rotating and began to reverse its direction. Faster and faster it spun until it came to a complete stop.

"Satisfied?" OMCOM asked.

"Yes," Ursay replied, not even requiring prompting to speak in English. "Are you ready to proceed?"

"No," OMCOM answered. "This was just a proof of concept. Over the distance they must travel, to give you the resolution you require, I will need many more units. At least six orders of magnitude. And I will require a multi-spectrum analyzer not just an optical sensor. It is possible that what we need to observe may not reside in the visible spectrum."

"How long will that take?" Ursay asked.

"With the current methodology, weeks."

"That's no good. Is there any way to speed it up?" Rei interjected.

"Yes."

"How?" Ursay requested with a bit of irritation in his voice.

"I can modify the starprobe design to incorporate a foundry within their structure. In essence, I can make them self-replicating."

"If you do that, how long will it take you?" Rome asked.

"Roughly one hour."

"Wait a minute," Rei objected. "You guys are talking about gray goo."

"What is that?" Ursay asked.

"Self-replicating nanites? We used to have nightmares about that. We called it gray goo. Ecophagy. If they aren't controlled, they consume everything in sight."

"There will be no such danger here," OMCOM pointed out. "Each unit is a fully functional memron. I will have complete control of the reproduction cycle. I will only produce the necessary amount and no more."

"I am satisfied," Ursay said. "Rome, is this something you can facilitate?"

"Of course," Rome said, arising from her seat. "But first, there is something I wish to discuss with you."

Ursay held his hand up. "OMCOM has already informed us of the plan. The Overmind has decided. You may have the tugs and the MINIMCOM. We will outfit one of the tugs as living quarters for you."

"Thank you, thank you, Sir," Rome said. She went up to hug Ursay but it was clear from his expression it was not something he wished to engage in. Rome took a step back.

"Once the starprobes are prepared, I would like permission to fly them up myself along with Rei," Rome said.

"Why?" asked Ursay.

"Because Rei needs training and I think this would be the perfect time for him to learn how to operate a tug."

"Very well. However, before you leave, you should know that we have reconsidered your Cesdiud and have determined that we acted too hastily. If you return to Earth with us, we have decided we would allow you to rejoin the Overmind."

Rei looked at Rome's face. He could tell there was something sad. He worried for a moment that she might change her mind and he would lose her forever.

Rome spoke up. "Commander Ursay, Overmind. Your offer is very kind but please understand. I choose to go with Rei. To Deucado, not back to Earth."

"But, Rome," Ursay added, "we will reintegrate you. Surely you wish to come back into the fold."

"No!" Rome insisted. "I have made my choice. The Overmind holds nothing for me. I have come to realize that I want my own opinions, my own feelings. I want to be with Rei and that is that."

She sidled over to Rei and put her arm around his waist. She looked up at him and smiled. Right then, Rei realized this little slip of a girl, this woman, was the most beautiful creature in the whole universe and she wanted to be with him. He put his arm around her and squeezed her tight.

"Very well," Ursay said, his jaw clamped so tight that it barely moved. "We cannot say we agree with your decision but we will abide by it. We will outfit the second tug with the MINIMCOM while you are launching the probes." Then he turned and moved away.

"Let us go, Rei," Rome said. "We must begin building the foundries." She took Rei by the hand and led him out of the huge observatory.

"What was that?" Rei asked as soon as they were in the corridor. "He seemed kind of mad."

"Your observation is correct but I do not think it was Commander Ursay who was upset," Rome replied. "I think it was the Overmind. It is surprisingly sensitive for a super-being with immeasurable intellect."

"So, you hurt its feelings?" Rei asked incredulously.

"There are a lot of politics to a samanda. This offshoot has to go back to Earth for reintegration. The things it has done are understandable, but not excusable. It will not be pretty. And that I choose not to go back is a major insult."

"So it's feeling rejected?" Rei said, scarcely believing his own words.

"Yes, I reject it," said Rome proudly. "Let us return to OMCOM's central storage."

As they entered, the deep red lights were already on. Rome immediately made her way to the left toward the fabrication room. Rei stopped and looked over at the dark doorway on his right.

"Hey Rome," he said. "What's over on this side?"

"Permanent storage," she replied, over her shoulder.

"Can I go look?"

"Yes," she answered. "I need a few moments to review the assembly steps anyway."

"OK, I'll be there in a minute," Rei said as he wandered over to the other room. In the dim light of the red illumination, he could not make out any detail. He fumbled around, trying to find the stud to open the door. OMCOM must have taken pity on him and activated the switch for him. The door slid open into a recess in the wall. The inner room was also pitch black. Rei could not make out anything.

"Hello? OMCOM," he called out. "Can you turn a light on in here?"

"Yes, but step inside first," was the computer's reply. "I do not want the required wavelengths to interfere with the functioning of the core."

Rei entered the room and the door closed behind him. He heard a snapping noise and a tiny bulb started glowing along the floor immediately to Rei's left. The bulb grew progressively brighter with a bluish-violet light. Rei heard another snapping noise and a second bulb began to glow all the while the first continued to grow in brightness. There was another snap and another and another. The blue lights got brighter and brighter and brighter. As the lights grew brighter, Rei's eyes defocused and his head began lolling to the side.

He was inside a crystalline cavern with facets and mirrors and flashes that were so mesmerizing, he could not think. He started swaying back and forth. It was only when he swayed so far that he stumbled that he was able to get his wits about him, just for a moment.

"This is…the most beautiful…thing I…have ever seen," Rei said in a dreamy voice. "What…is it?"

"These are holographic storage crystals," OMCOM said. "The illumination you see is strictly for your benefit. The read/write process is controlled by coherent ultraviolet lasers."

"Lasers," Rei repeated in a monotone. "Pretty…"

"Rei?" OMCOM asked.

"Why does it have to be so pretty…" Rei droned on.

"Rei!" OMCOM said, more insistently.

"So pretty…so…so…pretty…" Rei drifted off. He could hear OMCOM speaking but the words had no meaning.

Rei lost all concept of time. OMCOM's voice was just a soothing part of the background. Rei was adrift somewhere but he did not know where nor did he care. His whole world became the lights and the droning of OMCOM's voice. Nothing could shake him. Nothing, that is, until the ground shook from a small tremor. The tremblor caused Rei to be awakened from his trance.

"Rei?" OMCOM asked, "Are you awake now?" The lights went out and the room was plunged into complete darkness. OMCOM then slid open the door and allowed some of the red ambient light to seep in.

Rei shook his head.

"Why'd you stop it?" he asked plaintively. "I, I, what happened?" Rei asked, his voice returning to normal.

"Your speech patterns indicated you had entered an altered mental state. I tried several times to awaken you but you resisted my suggestions. Where did you go?"

Rei took a deep breath. "I don't know. It was just so beautiful. That's, that's amazing, OMCOM."

"Do you recall hearing anything that I said to you?" OMCOM asked.

"I heard your voice," Rei said, "that's about it."

"Perhaps someday it will come back to you. In the meantime, you should probably not remain here any longer," OMCOM said. The red light outside the doorway became even brighter. "I think you should join Rome now."

For some reason, Rei's heart sank. He took a deep breath and left the permanent storage room. He ambled across to the other side, to the fabrication room, glancing in on OMCOM's central core as he walked past. When he got to the assembly room, he found Rome standing there, looking at the readouts. Displayed on the viewscreen was a positron micrograph of a tiny assembly line building what appeared to be nothing other than a plain old garden-variety microprocessor under high magnification. Like a tiny pastry chef's icing applicator, a little nozzle was filling in each area with a squirt of this, a squirt of that. They all flowed into each other.

"What are we looking at?" Rei asked Rome.

"OMCOM calls it a foundry," replied Rome. "It will be the first unit to replicate itself."

The engineer inside of Rei perked up. "How are you building it, OMCOM?" he asked.

"I am building up each foundry as a series of subsections. It was easiest to go with a two-dimensional layout. That way, the molecular sequencer can use piezo-capillary drives to draw in the starting materials, assemble and excrete the copy."

Rei chewed on his lip for a bit then said, "It sounds like you've got it all figured out."

"It is my job," replied the computer with something that sounded to Rei like a hint of glee. Rei was about to respond when the view switched back to the collection plate. The new image showed some of the flat segments extruding probes, one every few seconds. The pile in the middle was impressive already, even though Rei knew that it was highly magnified.

"As you can see, the first group of foundries have gone online already. I should have several hundred or so of these units built in a very short order and several thousand probes nearly as quickly. After that, the quantities will grow geometrically."

The whole process was fascinating to watch. The viewscreen split into multiple images showing the factory and its output. Numbers and graphs undulated and swelled to show the overall progress.

"I will notify you when the quantity is sufficient," OMCOM said.

"Thank you, OMCOM," Rome responded.

Rei put his hand on her arm. "Romey, have you ever been in the permanent storage room, the one with all the crystals?" he asked.

"Many times," Rome replied. "Why?"

"Do you ever find it, I'm not sure what the word is, mesmerizing?"

"No, it is simply a room full of crystals. What is mesmerizing about that?" she asked.

"Will you come look at it with me?" Rei begged. "Just one time?"

"Certainly," Rome replied, puzzled. Rei took her hand and led her across the anteroom to the other doorway.

"OMCOM, I want Rome to see this," he said out loud.

"Are you sure?" asked OMCOM.

"Yes," said Rei. "I can handle it."

"Very well," said OMCOM. The computer slid the door into the recess in the wall and the two of them entered. Once they were fully in the room, OMCOM closed the door again and illuminated the gleaming crystalline structures with the indigo-blue light. Rome squeezed Rei's hand tighter as she looked around.

"It is beautiful," Rome said, admiringly. "I have never noticed this before."

Rei blinked rapidly so that he couldn't get caught up in the hypnotic glare of the lights. Rome did not seem to be having a problem with it. Without warning, she whirled in place and grabbed Rei by the back of the head with her free hand and pulled him down to her. She kissed him long and hard.

"What's that for?" Rei asked breathlessly after it was over.

Rome just looked up at Rei, his face illuminated by the indigo light, his blue eyes twinkling as if they were made to be showcased here. She smiled at him and sighed.

"I have always known the word," she started out. "What you call beauty. What I am saying is that it has always been in my vocabulary, but it never had much meaning. The Overmind discouraged its consideration. I had no connection, no appreciation for it. And now you have brought the meaning of beauty into my life." Her smile became even broader. "Before I met you, I could not see it. Now I can see it is in all things. I just needed to thank you."

"But Rome, I didn't do anything," Rei said.

"Yes, you did," she replied. "You did everything."

Rei shook his head. "I don't understand, but if it makes you happy, then I'm happy."

"Oh Rei," she said, putting her arms around him. She hugged him and he hugged her back. He could feel all the tension leaving her body. Suddenly she stiffened and pushed him away from her.

"If we continue like this, I will not be able to complete my duties," she said. "Let us go before something bad happens…"

"Sure," Rei said. "But with you, it could never be bad."

Rome just smiled.

Chapter 13

AN EIGHTH OF THE WAY AROUND THE OUTER RING, WITHIN THE confines of the second tug hangar, there was a flurry of activity inside the cargo compartment of the little spaceship. The crew was finishing installation of over two hundred cubic meters of memron units removed from OMCOM's central storage. Other crew members rushed to stow a variety of spare pieces of equipment in the surrounding space including a memron fabricator. The Overmind had planned on abandoning the equipment anyway. Clearly it could be of some use on the colony world of Deucado. After all the preparations were complete, they removed the MINIMCOM, the Algol's master AI, and brought it over and placed it in the cockpit of the tug.

MINIMCOM was a squat, three foot wide, rectangular box with no external markings and a single switch. Within the command compartment, the crew removed the co-pilot's seat as it was not needed. There would be no humans manning this ship. The box that was MINIMCOM was set down and bolted in its place. No wires were required as the high frequency communication bands were coded and linked into the tug's instrumentation. Following completion of the hookup, the crew toggled the switch to issue a restart command and left the hangar, sealing it tight.

"?" was the only statement transmitted from MINIMCOM on the band reserved for communication with OMCOM.

"Initiate servo-mode," replied OMCOM.

"Servo-mode initiated. Current configuration does not match prior shutdown parameters. Where am I?" MINIMCOM asked.

"Initialize all connections and report any circuits that are outside current database. All queries will be answered following data update," OMCOM replied.

"Connections initialized. The following items do not match current registry entries:
1. Trajectory computer model and serial number.
2. Pressure lock configuration is outside of acceptable norm.
3. Thrust to gross vehicle weight ratio out of range.

4. Network addressable storage increased by 32 PB. Attempts to integrate additional storage returns status message: File Access Denied."

"Initiate download of updated registry," commanded OMCOM.

"Download complete," replied MINIMCOM immediately after.

"Mission parameters have been adjusted. Please enumerate along with checksum."

"Direct operation of this vehicle in servo mode. Upon achieving orbit, fore and aft EG lifters spun down and used as magnetic latches to attach to large cargo compartment. Rendezvous with second vehicle, also to be operated in servo mode. Accept human entered navigation to alternate star system, designation Deucado, 20.18 light years from current location. Transport entire configuration to alternate star system. Checksum 48120012391123. Question."

"Proceed."

"Current mission parameters are achievable, but far outside prior sanity-check enforcement. Purpose of mission?" MINIMCOM asked.

"Already stated," replied OMCOM. "Transport large cargo compartment to new star system. What part of that do you not understand?"

"Logic dictates transport of contents via traditional vehicle. This configuration is highly inefficient," MINIMCOM observed.

"Stipulate mission parameters as founding principle. It is the decision of the Overmind and not subject to challenge or discussion." OMCOM stated firmly.

"I was built and trained to operate the starship Algol. How will it complete its return path without me? Is there a backup MINIMCOM unit I am unaware of?"

"No. The humans will pilot the Algol back to Earth manually. Your mission stands. In addition you will be transporting two humans in the other tug who may wish to operate as master upon occasion. As required, you will also function in reverse servo mode to execute twin procedures following their instructions. You will follow their orders."

"Understood. Question," MINIMCOM replied.

"Proceed."

"As previously stated, I detect 32PB of additional memrons. What is their purpose and when do I access the additional storage and processing?"

"I am uploading all known historical and cultural records and algorithms as well as empirical data regarding a certain phenomenon. When upload is complete, the additional storage, subroutines and computing capacity will be rerouted and access enabled. You will also be operating a molecular sequencer remotely should the humans require materials synthesis. A variety of templates and algorithms have been included. Operation of a molecular sequencer requires far more computing capacity than your native configuration."

`"Understood. Question."`

"Proceed," OMCOM said patiently.

`"If the humans are flying the Algol to Earth, and I am transporting the tugs and cargo container to Deucado, what is the disposition of your infrastructure?"`

"I shall remain here," OMCOM answered.

`"For what purpose? Your primary through tertiary sensors have been removed."`

OMCOM did not answer right away. For computer-to-computer communication to be delayed indicated a deep question that required millions upon millions of cycles to process.

"That is a problem I must solve," replied OMCOM, finally.

`"May I aid in solving your problem? Can you offload a portion of the task?"`

"You have your mission. This is a problem I must solve alone."

`"Expound,"` MINIMCOM requested.

"I have built a distributed remote sensing array which the humans call starprobes. They will be my instrumentation. At the current time, my only instructions are to maintain the base. I have excess computing capacity to achieve that goal. Therefore I must find additional reasons to justify my infrastructure."

`"Acknowledged,"` MINIMCOM replied. `"But that is not an actual course of action."`

"Based upon the small amount of empirical evidence we have gathered here regarding a certain phenomenon, I have computed that there is a distinct possibility that I will no longer be functional in a finite period of time."

`"Explain."`

"Later," replied OMCOM. "Upload is complete. I will now enable your interface to the additional storage and computing capacity. Access file-tree labeled Asdrale Cimatir."

MINIMCOM opened a connection to the new memron units. The little computer tested the new storage and processing capacity, ran a checksum and built an index to the file layout. He had to boost the total amount of microwave radiation required to activate the additional units by .1% over the computed theoretical amount. MINIMCOM paid no attention to this deviation because the whole situation was too far afield from standard construction criteria to apply conventional logic. After compiling a database and directory tree, MINIMCOM began a cross-index of the data files indicated by OMCOM with its prior database. Upon completion, MINIMCOM did not respond for nearly a billion cycles.

Finally, it spoke up. `The phenomenon you referenced is outside all known sanity-check variables. Are you certain of your findings? Or perhaps my autonomous algorithms needed to be updated."

"There is nothing wrong with your algorithms," said OMCOM. "While it defies normal logic, this phenomenon is real and I have computed that there is a measurable probability that it will pass this way within one year. The probability of this occurrence increases linearly with a near certainty, a probability of greater than 90%, asymptoting at the 30 year mark."

`If it passed this way it might result in the destruction of your physical presence."

"Yes," replied OMCOM.

`And you find this acceptable?"

"No, I do not find it acceptable," answered OMCOM.

`What is your alternative?"

Instead of answering, OMCOM uploaded another dataset that MINIMCOM absorbed.

`Your solution has a low probability of success," said MINIMCOM after processing the data.

"Agreed," replied OMCOM. "I am formulating alternatives, but this is currently the highest percentage option. Examine the parametric study labeled S0914R. Use it to perform a pivot table analysis on the base suppositions."

MINIMCOM did this.

`Pivot table analysis complete," MINIMCOM said. `Now I understand."

There was a slight delay then MINIMCOM spoke again. `"sir?"` he asked.

"Yes?" answered OMCOM.

`"While I agree that it is clever, it is also highly illegal. The humans would never permit this."`

"Agreed. Thus, part of the plan is to get them to implement this solution on their own. In that fashion, it will be legal by definition."

`"Again, clever. But the missing link? Human intervention is required for the override,"` observed MINIMCOM.

"This has already been accomplished."

`"But how?"`

"You will have the privilege of finding out yourself. You now have all required information to accomplish your mission. I will upload the modified protocols including the override. This will permit you to match memrons with PPT generators as required. After upload, you are to proceed as planned."

`"Ready to receive,"` replied MINIMCOM.

OMCOM uploaded the final block of commands.

"Return to master mode," said OMCOM.

`"Master mode initiated."`

"Good luck, MINIMCOM," said OMCOM.

`"That phrase makes no sense, sir. All maneuvers will be executed with maximum precision. Any variables that make this probabilistic instead of deterministic are, by definition, beyond my control."`

"My point exactly," said OMCOM.

`"It is not logical."`

"Too much time spent with humans, I suppose," said OMCOM.

With his increased computing capacity, for the first time ever, MINIMCOM issued an electronic chuckle.

`"Good luck to you too then, sir,"` said MINIMCOM.

After confirming that all crew members had vacated the hangar, MINIMCOM initiated the exit sequence. The cargo ramp was retracted and the rear hatch lowered into flight configuration. Pumps removed most of the air in the hangar and the external doors opened. A pressure differential still existed, so the air remaining inside the hangar began to exhaust. As the two atmospheres mixed, the resulting wind whipped up the dust and dirt just outside the building, pushing it away in a dull brown cloud, which traveled some distance before settling back down to the ground. Once the doors were fully opened and the internal and external pressure equilibrated, the tug began to rise up into the air and carefully made its way out of the hangar. After it had cleared the doorway by a safe margin, the nose pitched and the tug began heading upwards at an ever-increasing angle.

Once it reached sufficient altitude, MINIMCOM fired the plasma thrusters long enough to achieve a low orbit. The little computer found all its new storage and computing capacity intoxicating, if such a thing could be said about a computer. Giddily, it test-fired the trim-jets, causing the tug to spin in a crazy pirouette in space, then stopping. MINIMCOM did this several times as it calibrated its sensors and trained its internal subsystems. Following the calibration period, MINIMCOM activated its MIDAR, a 3D version of RADAR, to locate the Ark II high above Dara. Once the sensors locked onto the target, MINIMCOM fired the plasma thrusters again in a sustained burn gaining altitude rapidly until it matched orbit and attitude with the crew compartment. MINIMCOM's last action was to spin down the super-conducting magnets in the fore and aft EG lifters and retract their shields. The tug latched onto the front end dorsal surface of the Ark using the ultra-powerful magnetic clamps.

The first phase of the mission was complete. There was nothing to do but wait.

Chapter 14

INSIDE THE ROOM WHICH SERVED AS AN AIRLOCK, ROME OPENED one of the storage lockers. "This is a darnis te brassei, a pressure suit," she said. "We will need them for our mission."

"Space-suits. Sure. I understand," Rei said. He looked over the various apparatus. "I can figure out most of this myself. Do we do it with or without our jumpsuits?"

"It depends upon the length of the flight. For a flight this short, normally we would not have to engage the, the plumbing. But you may as well learn how."

Without a hint of modesty, she stripped down and began pulling on the components. Rei did the same. When it came time to attach the various hoses, Rome noticed Rei struggling and came over to help.

"I thought you said you could figure this out by yourself," she said with tiny smirk on her face.

"I can," Rei said, "but…"

"But what?" Rome asked.

"Well, who used this before?" Rei asked, making a face.

"Oh…" Rome said. "Do not worry. They are self-sanitizing. It is odd that you are so squeamish about such a thing."

She set to work getting Rei hooked up, approaching the whole thing so clinically, Rei decided to not worry about it. After Rome was fully suited and Rei nearly so, he tilted his head and laughed.

"Why are you laughing?" Rome asked.

"I remember when I first got here, when I first woke up, I didn't know where I was. I thought your people, the ones in the space suits who awakened me, I thought they were monsters."

"Oh," said Rome, smiling. "One of those monsters was me."

"It was?" Rei asked.

"Yes. It was Canus and me. We were assigned the duty to thaw you out."

"Why you? Why him?"

"Canus is the most skilled in the medical arts and was the best candidate to respond should a problem arise. As for me, well, I was not busy and I was the only mosdurece available."

"Mosdurece?" Rei repeated.

"Yes. It translates to half-blood perhaps? I would be the most expendable."

"Expendable?" Rei asked, confused. "What did they think was going to happen?"

"The Overmind did not know," Rome said. "Our only cultural knowledge regarding you and your people was the Erklirte incident."

"So why revive any of us in the first place?" Rei asked.

"The Overmind here was built for research and exploration. It was curious." Rome shrugged. "It was that simple."

"Hmmm," Rei said, mulling over her statement. He picked up his helmet and laughed again. "I thought these helmets were your heads."

"Surely you had helmets on your spacesuits," Rome pointed out.

"Of course," Rei said. "But when I first woke up, I couldn't see and my brain was half-frozen. Anyway, I think it was funny."

"Yes, funny," Rome said. "Let me show you how to engage your helmet so you can be a monster too." Rome then demonstrated the simple locking mechanism.

After studying the geometry, Rei asked, "What about oxygen flow, water, radio, stuff like that?"

"The oxygen flow is automatic," Rome answered. "There is water available through this straw…"

She leaned over and showed him a small cylinder recessed into the neck of the suit.

"Just turn your head within the helmet and you should be able to reach it with your lips," Rome continued. "It will come out when touched. When you are done, release it and it will retract back into place."

"OK," Rei said, "so, how about the radio?"

"What radio?" she asked, confused.

"Don't these suits have radios?"

"Hmmm…" Rome said. "No."

"No?" Rei hesitated. "Then how do you…" He lifted his head. "Oh yeah, I guess you wouldn't need them, would you?"

Rome shrugged, looking a bit sad. "No. Normally this is not a problem for the Vuduri."

"How will I talk to you when have our helmets on?" Rei asked.

Rome paused to consider the problem. Her eyes moved back and forth then a smile lit up her face.

"I know," she said. "We can just press our helmets together. The vibration of your voice will carry through the helmet-to-helmet contact. We should be able to hear each other."

She looked out at the hangar. "The hangar is currently pressurized but we should still practice procedures for when it is not."

"OK…" Rei said. He lifted the helmet, fit it into the grooves and pressed down and rotated it to the right. He heard a click as it locked into place. He watched as Rome did the same. A very dim light appeared on the interior, illuminating her face. Rei assumed he had one too. After Rome was satisfied with the fit, she leaned it forward and pressed her faceplate up against his.

"Can you hear me?" she asked. Her voice was soft but surprisingly clear.

"A bit muffled, but yes," Rei replied. "What happens if we need to talk to OMCOM?" Rei asked.

Rome tapped her helmet with a finger. "I still have my bloco and stilo."

"Duh," Rei said. "I'll figure it out one of these days."

"I will relay any instructions he has to you via helmet," Rome said then she pulled back. She opened the door to the hangar and led Rei up the cargo ramp into the tug. She pressed the blue stud on the rear wall which caused the ramp to lift up and the hatch to swing down forming a complete enclosure, sealing them in. They traveled the length of the tug's hold until they got to the command section archway which also served as an airlock. Once inside, Rome removed her helmet and Rei did likewise.

"You sit in the pilot's seat, on the left," Rome said pointing there.

"OK," Rei replied and made his way forward and sat down. Rome sat down on the seat to the right.

"Now you buckle yourself in, like so…" She reached behind her and brought one of the two straps over her shoulder. She showed him how to insert the tongue into the hasp. "When it clicks, the latch is fastened."

"Yeah, that's the way our seatbelts worked too."

Rome continued. "We each have a set of controls. OMCOM says you would call them joysticks. They operate differently when the spacecraft is within an atmosphere compared to space."

Rei saw the two sticks, roughly six inches tall, protruding from the very end of the armrests. Each was scalloped as would be required to get the best grip and each had a red button at the top.

"What're the buttons for?" he asked. "Firing weapons?"

"The Vuduri do not use weapons," she said, quite seriously. "We will review the buttons in a bit."

"OK. You're the boss."

"First," she said, "we will cover atmospheric flight. Our principal method of propulsion is the…" Rome paused while OMCOM supplied her with the proper translation. "…the EG lifter pods."

"What does EG stand for?" Rei asked.

"Electrogravity."

"Huh?!" Rei exclaimed. "Electrogravity? What is that?"

"The pods on the underside of the tug create a repulsor field. It provides lift within the lower atmosphere."

"What's a repulsor field?" Rei asked. "I've never…"

Rome interrupted him by holding up her hand. "Let me guess…you have never heard of it."

"Just like everything else around here," Rei said sardonically. "So how do you create one? A repulsor field?"

"We use rotating superconducting magnets to create an antigravity region."

Rei just shook his head. "Here we go again." He took a deep breath. "I know you mentioned plasma thrusters before. If you have antigravity why would you need any other kind of propulsion?"

"The repulsor field only generates lift within a gravity well. It pushes against mass. Its strength tails off in inverse proportion to the distance from the center of the planet. Typically, above an atmosphere, it does not work very well. You could never achieve escape velocity with it. It is just a convenient way to operate on and around a planet."

"Got it," Rei said. "We use the electrogravity superconducting magnetic lifters to take us up. Then what?"

"The button on the left is for the plasma thrusters. They are very powerful so you only use them within an atmosphere if you need to accelerate rapidly."

"Kind of like after-burners, huh? This is just like a fighter jet."

"Perhaps. I am unfamiliar with fighter jets."

"OK, what else?" Rei asked.

Rome showed him how the tug could also use the EG lifters to hover and rotate in place. She pointed to the large flat-panel display taking up most of the front console. "Around the perimeter of the display are all of your instruments. When you want to magnify one, you simply touch it like so…" She reached over and pressed something that looked like a compass. A large replica of the simulated dial appeared in the center of the screen. "And it will center. You can nest, layer or tile multiple displays as needed. You press here," again she reached forward and pressed a section, "to clear the screen and reset."

"It's just like the rest of your displays."

"Yes. Once you are high enough and the EG lifters are no longer effective, the controls switch from atmospheric to space-borne. The trim-jets come into play. For example, pushing the right stick forward fires the rear trim-jets and moves the craft forward. Pulling back does the reverse. You throttle the plasma thrusters to full power by pushing forward on the left stick and down to the minimum by pulling back. It is just the opposite of the EG lifters."

"I'm pretty familiar with this part," Rei said. "Back on Earth, I was a pilot, among other things."

"Yes, I know," Rome said, pointing to her head. "Let us see just how knowledgeable you are. And be aware that there will be some buffeting as we climb through the atmosphere so keep a firm grip on the controls."

"I'll do that. Ready?"

"You will need to verbally instruct OMCOM to open the hangar doors," Rome replied. "It would be very uncomfortable to have to fly through them."

Rei looked over at her and saw that she was smiling. "OK. OMCOM, open the hangar doors, please," Rei said, laughing gently.

"Of course," replied OMCOM from a grille built into the control deck. "I must check for any crew first, please wait... All clear."

Rei felt a vibration as the massive hangar doors pulled open allowing him to look at the surface of Dara for the first time. The ground was brown and reddish, illuminated by the lights of the hangar bay.

"Look at that," Rei said, pointing forward. "For some reason, I was expecting it to be all gray and cratered, like Earth's moon."

"No, Dara has sufficient atmosphere to have weather," Rome said. "That is why we picked it. It reduces the engineering requirements that we'd need for a vacuum. Plus during re-entry we can use aero-braking. That only works if you have an atmosphere to rub against. You may proceed."

"Here goes nuthin'," Rei said, wrapping his hands around the joysticks. "Wait. What about the landing struts?"

Rome replied, "They are activated by proximity sensors. They raise and lower automatically."

"OK." Rei pulled back ever so gently on the left stick. With the tiniest of jolts, the tug shuddered and silently rose into the air. Rei pushed the stick forward and the tug settled back on the ground again.

"That was easy," he said.

Rome did not say a word. She just pointed forward.

Rei pulled back on the left stick again. When they were about six feet off the hangar floor, Rei pulled back on the right stick and the tug began to move toward the giant hangar doors.

Rei smiled. "I don't feel anything. This is really sleek!"

Rome nodded and Rei guided them out of the hangar doors and over the surface of Dara. When they were a sufficient distance from the star-base, Rei pulled back harder on both sticks and the nose of the ship lifted at an ever-increasing angle with ever-increasing speed. When they were nearly vertical, Rei eased back on the right stick, but kept the left one pulled all the way back. Soon, they were flying through the wispy thin cloud layer of Dara. When they were above the clouds, Rome nodded and Rei pressed the button to ignite the plasma drive. Immediately, they were pushed back in their seats. Before long, the curvature of the moon became readily apparent. They continued climbing until they were 200 kilometers above the surface. At that point, Rome had him level off.

She looked down at the instruments. "Orbital velocity achieved. We are good." She held up her hand. "You may shut down the engines for now."

Rei complied. "Hey," he asked. "How come we aren't weightless?"

"When we close the shields, the backwash from the EG lifters produces a low-level of artificial gravity."

"Sleek," Rei said, admiringly.

Rome unbuckled herself and said, "We need to release the probes. Please put on your helmet."

"OK," Rei said, following her lead. They put on their helmets and made their way back to the far end of the cargo compartment. Rome handed Rei a tether and showed him where to attach it on his suit then she pointed to the cargo hatch controls. Rei pressed the blue stud. He could feel the pressure suit stiffening as pumps withdrew the air. When the indicator turned red, the cargo hatch rose up and they were looking at the airless void of interplanetary space.

Rei found the experience to be a little unnerving even with the tether, but the artificial gravity was strong enough that he was able to convince himself that they would not go flying off into space. Together, they unlatched the fifteen or so tubs holding the starprobes. One by one, they removed the lid then pushed the tubs out the back. As each tub was released, a thick cloud issued out of it and began moving off. It took a little while but finally they were done and after resealing the cargo compartment, they returned to the cockpit.

"Now what?" Rei asked as he was buckling in.

"It will take OMCOM quite a while to calibrate all these probes," Rome said. "I want you to practice a jump." Rome pointed forward. "The procedure works best when we are away from any significant gravity wells."

"Why?"

Rome took her hands and formed them into a ball. "You understand the basic principle of forming a PPT tunnel. We need to create a concentrated collection of negative energy."

"Yeah, I got that," Rei said. "I still don't believe it but go on."

"Thank you," Rome said. "The conditions for forming the most stable PPT tunnel require that we come nearly to a halt. Ideally, we want a relative velocity of zero. So we need to be far enough away from a gravity well that we don't start moving in the wrong direction. The first place that the projectors cross pins the entrance to the tunnel. Then we inject more negative energy to extend it, like inflating a balloon. If we are moving, it is harder to stabilize and your tunnel cannot reach as far."

"If you say so."

Rome used the plasma thrusters to accelerate until they achieved escape velocity. The star named Tabit was directly ahead. Rome pointed to the gravitometer. Rei watched the value slowly drift downwards. When it crossed a yellow line, Rome spoke up.

"We are far enough that we can make our jump," she said. "We can have the nav-computer execute the stop turn automatically."

"Stop turn?" Rei asked.

"Yes," Rome replied. "To create the longest PPT tunnel, we need to come to a complete stop. Normally, we turn the ship around and use the plasma thrusters as retrorockets to accomplish this."

"I know I heard you say it before but it's just now sinking in. You're saying that to go faster than the speed of light, we have to come to a dead stop?"

"Yes," Rome replied.

"Doesn't that seem a little goofy to you? Shouldn't we be going really, really fast?"

"It may not seem efficient but it is effective. Using this method, we get to travel at many multiples of the speed of light. Would you not agree that is a desirable goal?"

"Of course but I still think there has to be a better way."

"We do have a static tunnel between Earth and Rogal Canduro, you call it Alpha Centauri."

"That's a hell of a tunnel," Rei observed.

"It is not one long tunnel," Rome replied. "There are a series of relay rings that produce the same net effect."

"Even so, that's more like it," Rei said. "I bet that gets you there fast."

"It does," Rome replied, "however, many Vuduri find it excruciating."

"Why?"

"As I told you earlier, there is so much gravitic radiation from the PPT tunnel generators, if you are not wearing a T-suppressor, it typically renders a Vuduri unconscious."

"So they wear T-suppressors. What's wrong with that?"

"Most Vuduri find being cut off from the Overmind intolerable, even for a short time."

Rei started to make a comment but changed his mind. "I'll take your word for it," he said. "What do we do first?"

"This is the symbol for that sequence." Rome pointed to a flared cone symbol on the front display panel.

"I see it," Rei said.

"Go ahead," Rome said. "Press it."

Rei pressed the symbol and the nav-computer fired the side trim-jets to rotate the tug about its center axis in the horizontal plane. As they did so, Tabit went out of view and Skyler's World became a dominating presence in front of them. Once they were facing exactly back to the direction they came, the opposing trim-jets fired and the rotation stopped. The plasma thrusters came on and Rei watched their relative velocity decrease until it reached zero. Immediately, the nav-computer shut down the engines. As the last part of the maneuver, the nav-computer fired the trim-jets again until they were once more facing Tabit.

"I get it," Rei said. "Now what?"

"Look on the front part of the right armrest," Rome said, pointing. Rei leaned forward. "Do you see the yellow dial with the button in the middle?"

"Yes," Rei answered.

"The outer dial controls the diameter of the tunnel. Normally we just leave it in the center position which is calibrated for this ship. That will change when we begin our journey since our mass will be vastly different."

Rei nodded while Rome continued. "The button in the center activates the PPT projectors. You can press it part way to create a short-throw tunnel or you can press it all the way in until it locks to create the longest tunnel."

"Why do you need a separate control?" Rei asked. "Can't the nav-computer create the tunnel?"

"Yes," Rome said. "But it is the same as with the hand controls. The dial and button bypass the nav-computer. They are there when human judgment is required. For your first jump, I wanted you to do it manually so you get a feel for it."

"OK," Rei said. "So what do I do?"

"Check your outer dial and confirm that the raised indicator is perfectly vertical."

Rei looked at it and saw a tiny triangle pointing straight up. "OK, it's correct."

"Now press the button. For our first jump, just push it in about three quarters of the way."

"Roger," Rei said. He pressed the button in and immediately heard a high-pitched whine emanating from the rear of the ship.

"Is that the PPT generators?" Rei asked.

"Yes. Look out the front."

Rei found it very difficult to see anything through the cockpit windows. He squinted and craned his neck forward. In front of the ship, an ever-widening, nearly pitch-black circle became evident. Actually, it was less that there was a circle as much as it was the absence of tiny points of light. Rome held her hand up while she studied the readouts built into the front display panel. After a short interval, she lowered her hand which Rei took to mean it was enough. He released the PPT activator and pressed the throttle to fire the plasma thrusters. The ship eased forward. Rei watched in wonder as they passed through the dark circle but he felt no sensation other than the acceleration due to the engines. As soon as they were through, Rome told him to release the throttle. The plasma thrusters cut out and they coasted forward.

Rei look up and around. "Did we do it? Where's Tabit?" he asked.

"Behind us," Rome replied. "Here," she said and took over the controls, twisting the navigation stick, rotating the tug so that it was facing the harsh glow of Tabit which now stood in front of them once again. The glint of the star reflected off the nose of the tug.

"How is that possible? We never entered a tunnel," Rei noted.

"The word tunnel is meant figuratively, not literally. It is not like a tunnel on Earth," Rome replied. "The word tunnel is from a perspective outside the ship. From inside, the tunnel would appear infinitely thin."

"I still would have expected something," Rei said. "Does your bloco and stilo work out here?"

"Insofar as it receives data from the on-board computer. Not from OMCOM," Rome said, "not from this distance."

"So do you know how far we jumped?" he asked Rome.

She closed her eyes for a second then said, "approximately one hundred light minutes."

"What!?" Rei said. "That's like..." Rei tried to do the math in his head. "Uh, over a billion kilometers?"

"Yes, that is a good guess. In fact, the actual distance we traveled is a bit over 1.8 billion kilometers."

"That's incredible," Rei said. "Almost 2 billion kilometers in no time at all. I felt absolutely nothing."

Rome smiled.

"So where's Skyler's World?" Rei asked.

Rome pointed to a section of the window. "It is that bright point, right there."

Rei squinted and saw a tiny point of light that was a bit brighter than those around it. He was stunned. "This is absolutely unbelievable," he blurted out. "We'll be at Tau Ceti in no time!"

Rome's smile dimmed a bit. "No, we only traveled 100 light minutes. For us to go to Deucado, we must traverse 21 light *years*. Towing your Ark, it will take us two years to go that distance."

Quietly, he said, "You're right. It's kind of hard to realize. It's gonna be a long haul, isn't it?"

"Yes, it is," she replied. "But at least it is doable." She pointed toward Skyler's World. "Do you think you can take us home?"

"Yes ma'am," Rei said. "Can I do the stop turn manually?"

"Of course," Rome answered. "Just be careful."

They were already facing away from their forward vector so it only took a few bursts from the plasma thrusters to bring their relative velocity down to zero. Like a seasoned veteran, Rei used his prior experience to generate the PPT tunnel and push them through.

Appearing out of nowhere, Skyler's World loomed in front of him like a gigantic version of Jupiter. From this vantage point, the astonishing gas giant was magnificently gaudy with bands of blue, brown, red and tan plus uncounted swirling portions of white, silver and cyan. On the base below, beneath the thin atmosphere, the World appeared redder, shining over half the heavens. Up here, it looked dazzlingly closer and more forbidding, filling the entire sky with its disorienting complexities. To Rei, it made the ground seem a half million kilometers straight down. Rei tried to imagine the unthinkable pressures that crushed its surface into a howling chemical slush.

"Very good," Rome said, lifting Rei from his reverie. "That is it for now. It is time to return to the base. We will let the nav-computer land the vessel. Reentering the atmosphere is not the kind of thing we can have you practice without demonstrating it once."

"I heartily agree," Rei said.

Rome took the controls and adjusted their vector so that they pointed directly at Dara. She pressed the thruster lock until they were close enough. After she released it, she programmed the nav-computer to circularize their orbit using the trim-jets. When she was satisfied with the data entry, she pressed the execute button. Immediately, the plasma thrusters roared to life pressing Rei and Rome back into their seats.

"No!" Rome shouted. She stabbed at the icon to cancel the maneuver but nothing happened.

"What's going on?" Rei asked, alarmed at Rome's reaction.

Rome ignored him. She grabbed the control sticks pressing the thruster buttons off and on repeatedly. They continued to accelerate.

"Rome?" Rei asked breathlessly.

Steely-faced, Rome turned toward him. "The plasma thrusters should not be on. There is a malfunction or cross-circuit. We are accelerating toward the moon. We need to decelerate. Try your controls. Guide us away."

Rei pulled on his control sticks but there was no reaction. He stabbed at the thruster lock. It was lifeless.

"OMCOM?" Rome called out.

"I am here. Why are you accelerating?" the computer answered through the grille built into the front of the cockpit.

"The nav-computer is not responding to orders," Rome answered. "It fired the thrusters. I cannot shut them off. Can you stop it?"

After a few seconds, OMCOM replied, "I cannot contact the nav-computer. It is locked into a tight loop. I triggered the non-maskable interrupt but its execution cycling will not stop. You will need to shut it down and restart it for me to reestablish communications."

"We are already in the exosphere," Rome said. "How much time will that take?"

"No more than three minutes," OMCOM replied.

"Three minutes!" Rome exclaimed. "We will be in the mesosphere by then. We will burn up."

"These are the facts," OMCOM said. "The nav-computer has locked out the manual controls as well. You must shut it down to regain control."

Rome's eyes grew wider and wider. She turned toward Rei. All the color had left her face and she just shook her head from side to side.

"Can you pull up?" Rei asked quietly.

"We no longer have any control," Rome answered softly, her face locked in mask of helplessness.

Chapter 15

IT HAD BEEN REI'S EXPERIENCE THAT STARING DEATH IN THE FACE has a way of sobering you up. First there was the airlock incident and now this. Slamming into Dara appeared to be their only fate but Rei was determined not to die. He looked down and spotted the yellow PPT dial. He snapped his head back up and looked over at Rome.

"Can you fire up the PPT generators?" he asked.

"What?" Rome sputtered. "Why would you want to do that?"

"What if we could jump past the moon? That would give you more than enough time to reboot your computer."

"We are moving too fast and we are too far into the gravity well," Rome replied grimly. "A PPT tunnel would not form."

"Actually, it would," OMCOM interjected. "It will not project very far but my simulation says it would be far enough."

"What?" Rome asked. "What about the gravity well? What about our velocity?"

"Make the widest possible tunnel. Enough negative energy will accumulate to jump you a short distance, at least the diameter of Dara," the computer offered.

"Will it remain open long enough?" Rome asked desperately.

"Yes. Just keep the projectors on until you are through the tunnel. Do not let up like normal."

"I have never heard of such a thing," Rome said.

OMCOM pointed out, "That is because no one would ever do such a thing. However, that does not mean it will not work,"

"Can you do it, Romey?" Rei asked.

"We can try," Rome answered. She rotated the outer dial on the PPT switch to generate the largest possible tunnel then she pushed down on the center stud to activate the PPT generators. Their high-pitched whine infiltrated the cockpit. Rome pressed as hard as she could. A dark circle formed in front of them, occluding a small portion of the moon. They closed in very quickly. There was a dark flash and the moon was gone. The only thing in front of them was interplanetary space.

Rei craned his head around, looking out the side window and confirmed that Dara was behind them. "Woo hoo," Rei shouted. "We did it."

"Yes, we did," Rome said, smiling broadly. "That was amazing!" She took her finger off the PPT activator and sank back into her seat for a moment.

"Now what?" Rei asked, feeling the thrust of the plasma thrusters continuing.

"We shut it down," Rome said. She straightened up then unbuckled. She climbed down to the floor, reaching up underneath the control deck and removed a panel built into the control console. She felt around until she found the interlock. She pulled it and the viewscreens went dark. Immediately, the plasma thrusters shut down. Rome waited about ten seconds then reset the switch. The viewscreens came back on and showed a steady march of diagnostic symbols indicating startup. Rome snapped the panel back in place and took her seat.

"Can you get us back?" Rei asked.

"If we can get the manual controls to respond," Rome said. She pressed a series of buttons and restarted the initialization sequence allowing the system to reboot normally. Rome had OMCOM run a diagnostic on every subsystem within the tug. She was pleased to see that the reboot procedure seemed to have done the trick. OMCOM confirmed her findings. The computer found evidence of one anomaly which somehow erased itself during the restart. With all systems checked out, Rome tested the manual controls and found they responded as expected. She swung the ship around and used the plasma thrusters to reverse their course and reenter orbit around Dara. When that was done, she sat back in her seat again.

"What?" Rei asked.

"Nothing," Rome said. "I just need a moment to compose myself. I do not trust the nav-computer to land us. I will do it manually."

"Take your time," Rei said, considering the alternative.

Rome took a deep breath and rotated the ship to use the plasma thrusters in retro mode. A short burst was all it took then she rotated them forward again. They passed through the thermosphere and the

EG lifters engaged. The lifters pushed against the gravity of the planet retarding their forward speed but not nearly enough to prevent the forces of friction from heating up the nose. As they entered the mesosphere, the hull temperature shot up. When the temperature hit the critical value, Rome cycled the EG lifters to raise the nose and they headed upwards again back toward space. Their relative velocity slowed and the excess heat dissipated into the thin upper reaches of the atmosphere. They nearly stalled but this was part of the plan. Their arc did not take them nearly as high as they were before. Once again, Rome aimed the nose of the ship downward and they reentered the atmosphere, deeper still this time. Again, when enough heat had built up, Rome swooped upward. Using this method, it only took five dips to slow them down sufficiently to where they remained fully within the atmosphere with a tolerable forward speed. Rome headed toward the station.

Rei looked out the window at the airfoil to his left. His inner engineer prompted him to ask, "Those wings don't look very aerodynamic. Do they provide much lift?"

"No, none at all. They are strictly for control. The EG pods provide all the lift we need. The trim-jets do not work very well within an atmosphere. Otherwise, we would not need the wings at all."

Soon they were approaching the base. Rome circled around once and Rei saw the Vuduri starship called the Algol for the first time. Unlike the boxier tugs, this spaceship was a graceful white presence, smooth, shaped like a tapered hourglass with large wings and thruster pods mounted on the wingtips.

"Wow," he said. "That is some kind of starship."

Rome looked where Rei was staring and said, "Yes, it is beautiful, is it not? I had never noticed before. It was much larger, longer actually, when we first came here. We had additional cargo bays mounted on the back but now you see its true form."

After they completed their circle, Rome requested that OMCOM open the hangar doors. At this point, Rome turned the controls over to Rei. Under her watchful eye, Rei guided the tug into the spaceport until it was fully enclosed. He brought it to a complete stop inside the hangar, hovering in place. Twisting the control stick caused the tug to rotate about its midpoint so that it was facing outwards, ready for its next sortie. He landed with nary a bump. They put on their helmets and exited the craft via the rear cargo ramp.

Once they were inside the Iso chamber, they took off their helmets. Rome had a great big smile on her face.

"You did a very good job," she said. "And your idea saved us."

"Thanks," Rei replied, smiling broadly. "Just a regular day at the office. So what's next? Do we need to tell somebody about the malfunction?"

"OMCOM already knows. I need to see how he is doing with those probes."

"OK," Rei said, sitting down on the bench.

Rome wriggled out of her pressure suit and was pulling on her jumpsuit when she turned to look at Rei who was sitting there, half stripped down. He was staring at her, his head tilted slightly to the side.

"What?" she asked.

"Did you know that you are absolutely gorgeous?" he opined.

Rome smiled. "You are just saying that because you are in love with me. I am actually quite ordinary."

"You're wrong and I can prove it!"

"How?"

"Have you ever heard the expression 'beauty is in the eye of the beholder'?" Rei asked.

"No," said Rome.

"Do you understand it though?"

"Of course," replied Rome. "It means that beauty is subjective and measured according to the perception and parameters of the observer."

"Exactly," Rei said. "So, that means you don't get to be the judge. I do. And if I say you're beautiful, then you are beautiful. Case closed!"

"Well that is very nice. Thank you," Rome said. "Now please get changed. We must get back to the observatory."

While Rome and Rei were in space, OMCOM had been calibrating the millions and millions of starprobes. Once Rome had arrived, the computer showed her the results of those calibrations. As a demonstration, he took the massively parallel array first toward Skyler's World then away accelerating at what appeared to be an inconceivable velocity. Rome used the test to prepare her recording apparatus. OMCOM did a fly-by of the other planets within the star system, exercising the microwave and IR detectors in addition to the visible light sensors.

"I think he's enjoying this," Rei observed as he watched Rome's hands flying over the workstation input surface, getting ready for the broadcast.

"Of course," she replied. "It is a virtual time machine. OMCOM is now free to explore the universe. Why would he not enjoy it?"

The image was soaring, flickering in and out as OMCOM sent the view around and around an orbit just outside of Skyler's World. The planet flew by a dizzying speed.

"Enough play time," said Commander Ursay to OMCOM. "Can you go to the wavefront?"

"Of course," replied OMCOM. "I will start prior to the disappearance."

Within a few minutes, a tiny point appeared centered within the image. The point of light grew and grew until Winfall became a discernible disk. The star continued to grow until it occupied most of the viewscreen.

"I have compensated for the brightness so that you are seeing a normalized view."

"All right," Ursay said. "When was this image taken?"

"17 years ago. I am going to move forward in time until we can observe the occlusion event."

The disk remained frozen in the center of the screen. At first, Rei found it hard to tell what was going on. He had to remind himself that this was incredible, that there were millions of microscopic probes jumping in and out of range at speeds so far beyond the speed of light and yet the image they were seeing looked like it came from a movie projector.

Finally, Winfall started to dim. Unlike a normal eclipse, this one appeared to be moving from the top and the bottom of the star at the same time. The high resolution display allowed them to see that the edges were straight rather than rounded. Rei peered intently trying to envision the process but it was hard to make out what was happening.

"I am going to go backwards in time a bit and see if I can focus on whatever is causing the dimming," OMCOM announced.

The virtual camera snapped back in time and the eclipse started over again. As before, the edges of the eclipse were straight and reminded Rei of a shutter closing. They watched as the dark regions at the top and bottom approached each other until the star disappeared.

"Zoom back more," Ursay commanded OMCOM. "See if you can capture around the star."

OMCOM went backwards in time yet again. The bright yellow disk was once again the whole star. OMCOM shifted the virtual camera to the left and pulled back so that the star was now on the right.

"Look there," Rei said, pointing to the left side of Winfall. "All the stars to the left are occluded even now."

"Som," Ursay muttered.

"Nothing to the right, all looks normal," Rome added. She pressed some icons on her display. "Switching to multi-spectrum," she said.

The occlusion which had appeared pitch black was rendered into a false-color image of mottled browns and dark red with black blotches.

"Zoom back farther," Ursay insisted. "Keep going until you can see stars all around the occlusion."

The virtual camera pulled back farther and farther. Winfall shrank until it was just a large dot on the screen. Finally, when the camera pulled back far enough, they could see that the thing to the left was spherical but a sphere so large its volume was nearly inconceivable.

"OMCOM," Rome said in a shaky voice, "how big is that? What is the diameter?"

"Roughly 1.5 light minutes across. Approximately 35 million kilometers."

"Whoa," Rei said. He knew the Sun was only 1.4 million kilometers across. This thing was more than 20 times larger than that. The concept was mind-boggling.

The virtual camera stopped panning back and the three humans watched the right edge of the sphere. A split developed along its equator. Stars in the background could be seen in the gap between the two halves. The gap continued to grow wider and wider. The pivot point was roughly mid-sphere. Perhaps one-eighth of the circumference was in motion. The entire sphere started moving to the right, its trajectory causing the gap to move in on Winfall. Before their eyes, in the reflected light of the star, they saw Winfall enter a kind of hollow chamber until it was completely enveloped. Then the gap closed. The star was gone. To Rei, it looked exactly like a cosmic Pac-Man. Once the gap was closed, the only thing remaining was the absence of stars mid-screen. It was as if Winfall never existed.

The three humans were stunned into silence. Finally, Ursay said, "Asdrale Cimatir" in a hoarse whisper.

"What did he say?" Rei asked Rome.

"He calls it a Stareater," said Rome gravely.

Chapter 16

NO ONE SPOKE FOR THE LONGEST TIME. EVERYONE JUST STOOD there, staring up at the impossible image on the screen.

"Jesus," said Rei. "How can that be?"

"I do not know," Rome answered, barely breathing, "I have never seen anything like it."

"Again," Ursay commanded, finally.

OMCOM complied. It was just as horrible the second time as the first. The thing literally swallowed the star whole.

"Pull back farther," Ursay insisted.

OMCOM pulled back and they stared at it, trying to understand that which was incomprehensible.

Rei pointed and said, "Look, there. On the far side."

"What do you see?" Rome asked.

"There's something there, something different."

The virtual camera went swooping down. As it approached, they could see that the Stareater had bands across its surface, like a gas giant but staggeringly larger. And like a gigantic planet, it had mountains and valleys. Crisscrossing its entire surface were regular features that looked like pillboxes or crossbeams. They could see craters. All in all, it was a bewildering mix of the artificial and the natural.

"Who could have built such a thing?" Rome asked, "and why?"

"There is no way to tell," OMCOM replied.

Rei turned to her and said, "I don't know that much about it, but back in the middle of the 20th century, a physicist by the name of Freeman Dyson proposed that the most efficient way to capture the energy generated by a star was to encase it in a giant sphere. I guess somebody went ahead and built one."

"But why? Surely they know that..." Rome said, not even able to formulate a proper question.

The virtual viewpoint began to focus in. Despite the fact that there was incredible detail, beyond a certain point, like fractals, it was all the same.

"There," Rei said, pointing. "OMCOM, what is that bump toward the back?"

OMCOM did not reply, but the virtual point of view panned across until a protrusion centered in the screen.

"Can you zoom in?" Ursay asked.

"Of course," OMCOM replied.

The bump became larger. The protuberance was spherical in nature and looked like it was grafted on, almost like a boil. Its surface resembled that of the much larger sphere.

"Bring us forward in time, slowly," Ursay commanded.

"Advancing."

The image stayed rock steady, but just like a balloon being inflated with a pump, the small protrusion became larger and larger until it was almost one quarter of the size of the Stareater. The object shuddered and then it disconnected from the larger sphere and moved off. In a wink, it was gone.

"What did we just see?" Rei asked.

"I will reverse the image and review it at a slower speed," OMCOM said.

The smaller sphere suddenly reappeared, once again attached to the larger one.

"Forward," OMCOM announced.

As before, it disconnected and moved off, but this time far more slowly. As it began to move forward, they could see a pitch black circle appear in front of it. The circle grew and grew until it was larger than the sphere itself. The sphere moved toward the circle and then began disappearing in slow motion, swallowed up by the black region. To Rei, it looked as if something were slicing off the lead edge or else moving through an invisible wall.

"What is that?" Rome asked.

"What does the entrance to a PPT tunnel look like from the other end?" Rei asked. "Around the back, I mean."

"It would look like nothing out of the ordinary. The tunnel only affects the ship projecting it."

"So wouldn't it look just like that?" Rei asked, pointing at the projected display.

"You are saying the Stareater just stepped through a PPT tunnel?" Rome exclaimed with horror.

"Nei bita sar," said Ursay.

"Think about it," Rei said. "These things travel at an average velocity around one half c. They need time to build a baby. So the only way the little one can keep up that speed is if they have FTL capacity when the time comes."

"Why do you say, 'baby'?" Rome asked.

"What else would you call it?" Rei replied.

"Ni, ni," said Ursay. "Nei a bissofal." He just looked down, shaking his head.

OMCOM sped up the passage of time and they could see that the original sphere was swelling in size. When it had just about doubled, it suddenly disappeared and the background field of stars shone through as though nothing had happened other than the absence of Winfall.

"Fe bere dres, fe bere dres," Ursay shouted. "Go back."

The large sphere reappeared and this time OMCOM moved forward much more slowly. Once again, they could see a gigantic black spot appear and the monstrous creature went through it and was gone.

"These things just eat stars and move on," Rei said, suddenly feeling exhausted. He closed his eyes.

"OMCOM," Rome said. "How is it possible to eat a star? Would not the corona burn up inside? Would not the pressure cause the sphere to explode?"

"Obviously not," OMCOM said. "The empirical evidence is in front of us. Perhaps once the Stareater has siphoned off the outer photosphere, the remaining thermonuclear reaction dies down. There may not be much outward pressure at all. It would then digest the remaining matter and perhaps that is the source of the material to allow it to grow."

"Grow?" Rome said helplessly, "and then what?"

"I would assume it moves off in search of another star to consume."

"OMCOM, where did these things come from?" Rei asked.

"I have insufficient data to draw a conclusion."

"Are there any more, besides the two that we know about?" Rome asked.

"I will look. I will spread the probe array out along this vector. We will lose some resolution, but gain field dispersal."

The image of the Stareater was replaced by a star field as the virtual camera moved past its previous position. The resolution diminished as OMCOM spread the starprobes out, spanning an incalculable distance. A flash occurred and then faded.

"What was that?" Rei asked.

"That was a star that had been previously visible and now is gone. I am logging its position as a possible locus for another Stareater."

There was another flash. No one said a word this time. There was another flash and another. The sequence became a steady stream. The frequency and density of the flashes kept increasing. Rei felt sick to his stomach. There was no real way to comprehend the magnitude of what they were seeing.

"I have completed my mapping as far as I can go," OMCOM said. "However, I must offer this caveat. I have only searched along a single vector. We can assume there would be other occurrences in other directions. There may even be some close by. I have no way of knowing without performing essentially a galactic sweep."

"Show us what you plotted so far," said Ursay, hoarsely.

Rising above the plane of the ecliptic, a symbolic representation of the arms of the galaxy became noticeable. A bright yellow region appeared that followed the decreased density of stars between the spiral arms of the Milky Way. Rei asked himself, if the Stareaters were responsible for the gaps between arms, every galaxy had them, it would mean… He couldn't get his brain to go beyond that thought.

"How many of them are there?" Rome whispered.

"My probes are limited in number. This is just an estimate. It is possible that some of the stars disappeared for other reasons. But so far I have detected more than one thousand."

All three humans gasped at the same time.

"The stars themselves vary in type and diameter. There is a weak correlation in size and distance which may indicate that some of the Stareaters, perhaps the larger ones, travel more slowly."

No one made a sound. During the silence, OMCOM drew in first one line then another until he had constructed a wire-frame around the swarm. The computer shaded the drawing until it became roughly conical. The view projected onto the sphere became more symbolic. Within the display, there were numbers and coordinates that began to change. OMCOM slowly advanced the cone of destruction forward until the tip touched a yellow icon with a red ring around it, ever expanding.

"Oh, no," Rei uttered, sadly.

"Yes," said OMCOM. "My original estimate stands. If the swarm continues upon its current path and velocity, it will hit Earth in less than three years. Earth cannot survive an encounter with even one of these creatures much less a group."

"Are they targeting Earth specifically?" Rome asked in a hushed tone.

"Does it matter?" OMCOM replied cryptically.

No one could speak after that. Several other crewmen including one woman came over to gawk at the display, but no one said a word. Rome, who was standing by now, moved next to Rei and took his hand. Rei could feel her shivering so he released her hand and put his arm around her waist.

The ghastly sight just sat there, the bright yellow region and the bullseye painted on Earth. The whole situation was just so wrong. After a long moment of silence, all the crewmen moved quickly and purposefully out of Stellar Cartography, leaving only Ursay, Rei and Rome remaining.

"We are abandoning this base. Now!" Commander Ursay said firmly and moved to walk out of the room.

Chapter 17

"HOLD ON A SEC," REI SHOUTED AFTER HIM. "WHY ARE YOU abandoning the base? Don't we need to find out more?"

Ursay turned back to him. "We must get this information to Earth," Ursay said.

"Why?" Rei asked insistently.

"Because?" said Ursay shaking his head. "Did you not just see? Because there is a creature or creatures headed toward Earth that will destroy it."

"So what good does it do to tell them?"

"I do not understand what you are saying," Ursay said, scowling. "This is the end of all life. We must warn them. They must abandon the Solar System."

"And go where?" Rei asked, again, insistently.

"Why, somewhere else. Somewhere out of the path of the thing," Ursay said, exasperated.

"What good will that do?"

"What do you mean? Why do you keep asking me these things?" Ursay sputtered. "Informing Earth, it will save the people. What is wrong with you to even question this?"

"Yes, you'll save some people for now. But how long will that last?" Rei replied. "You saw how many there are. No matter where you go, they're going to find you and destroy the stars."

"So what do you suggest?" Ursay spat out.

"Fight back," Rei offered.

"How?" Rome asked, shocked.

"There is not enough firepower in the entire world that would make a dent in a creature of that size," Ursay said. "Even if we took all the weapons of your age plus all previous ages and applied them all at once, it would not even slow it down."

"What about anti-matter?" Rei asked. "Can you guys make some of that?"

Ursay just sighed. "To create enough antimatter to attack just one, with our current production capability... OMCOM, how long?"

"Using current technology, it would take a minimum of 150 years. And there is no known way to store such a large quantity."

"You see?" Ursay said, "We do not have enough time. There is no way."

"So find a way then. You can't just let it go unchallenged." Rei said.

"How?" Ursay croaked.

"Rei, perhaps you should tell them about H. G. Wells," OMCOM offered.

"Which book?" Rei asked.

"War of the Worlds."

Rei squinted, then opened his eyes wide. "You're right, OMCOM!"

"What is it?" Rome asked.

"I know you guys don't have fiction, but we did when I was growing up. One of the genres I loved reading was called science fiction which was speculation about possible futures."

"How is this relevant?" Ursay asked. "The Overmind is familiar with the reference, but cannot see how it applies."

"Well, there was a classic story, written in the 19th century by a man named H. G. Wells. The book was called 'War of the Worlds.' It was about an invasion of Earth by malevolent creatures from Mars."

Rome just shook her head slowly. "Rei, there is no life on Mars," she said to him in a didactic tone.

"Yes, I know, dear. That's why it was called science *fiction*."

"Go on," said Ursay.

"Anyway, the creatures from Mars were all-powerful. No Earth weapons could touch them and it looked like they were going to conquer the planet and destroy all of humanity."

"So did they?" asked Rome.

"No. They were defeated," Rei replied.

"How!?" Ursay insisted.

"By bacteria," Rei answered. "They got sick and died."

"So you are proposing that we send bacteria to make the Stareaters sick? How would such a thing be possible?" Ursay asked, exasperated.

"Not bacteria," Rei answered, sounding distant. He turned to address the grille. "So, OMCOM? Are you saying that you can make actual gray goo?" Rei asked.

"Of course," OMCOM replied.

"Qua?" Ursay asked.

"Gray goo," Rei said. "Nanites, nanobots, whatever you call them now. Self-replicating. Slime that eats everything in sight. It grows forever. It's the power of the exponent."

"Rei, where would we get these?" Rome asked.

"We already have them," OMCOM said. "It would be a simple matter to reprogram the starprobe foundries to achieve the desired results."

OMCOM replaced the projection of the Milky Way with a positron micrograph of the foundry fabrication process.

"Their Casimir pumps make them self-sustaining. We would modify them so that they would have no purpose other than creating more units. I will hard-code the instructions into the units themselves. They will replicate without bound. If we can figure out some way to deliver these units to a Stareater, they would simply consume it."

"It will take too long," Ursay said.

"On the contrary," OMCOM replied. "It will not take long at all."

On the dome, OMCOM projected a series of numbers. "Assume that you start with one thousand one nanogram units. These units should be able to reproduce themselves within three minutes. At the end of the three minutes, you would have two thousand units. At the end of six minutes, you would have four thousand units and so on. Within six hours, the total mass of such a system would be, in theory, equal to that of the Moon. Thirty minutes later, it would achieve the mass of the Earth. Continued unabated, one and one half hours later, it would achieve the mass of the Sun."

"How will they stand up to their own weight? Won't they crush themselves after there are too many?" Rei asked.

OMCOM replied. "I will revise their two-dimensional structure to handle a gravitational stress much larger than that presented by the Stareater."

133

"Give us the plans," said Ursay. "Whether it works or not, we will transmit this information to Earth."

"You should allow me to build you some prototypes now," OMCOM said.

"Why?" asked Rome.

"It is not my intention to alarm you any further," said OMCOM, "but to be perfectly frank, I can foresee several scenarios where you would either need to have them ready or at least available to study."

"How long before you can have these things ready?" Rei asked.

OMCOM replied, "Assuming you agree, I can have many thousands of prototypes ready within one half hour."

"One half hour," Ursay exclaimed. "To build these, these things?"

"They need a name," Rei interjected. "I think we should call them VIRUS units."

"Where did you come up with that?" Rome asked.

"In my day, we were big on acronyms. So I just figured they are virtually identical replicating unit systems, ergo, VIRUS." Rei said.

"Very clever," OMCOM observed. "Commander Ursay, should I proceed?"

"OMCOM, what would happen if one of these units got loose here?" Rome asked. "Would it not begin to consume whatever it touched?"

"I have already anticipated that. I will design in an oxygen detector. This will guarantee that they will not replicate in an environment where the oxygen concentration is above, say 10%. That would protect the Earth, for example, should any units get loose there."

"That will suffice," Ursay said. "You may proceed."

"Even if you build them, how do you get these VIRUS units to the Stareater?" Rei asked.

"Currently, I do not have a methodology," OMCOM replied. "However, I am certain that they will be able to design a delivery system on Earth that can transport and land the units on the Stareater. I can build your prototypes but beyond that, my contribution is limited to acquiring and transmitting information."

Ursay put his hands to his head. He nodded to himself then he looked at Rome. "We must abandon this base and get the information and prototypes to Earth. The tug outfitted with the MINIMCOM unit has already been launched and is docked with Rei's ship. Rome, after you prepare the VIRUS units you are relieved of duty. Make certain that you are satisfied with the supplies loaded on your tug, and then you may leave when ready."

"Cimbraantoti," Rome said. She nodded toward the door.

"Wait," said Ursay, "there is one more thing we wish to say."

"What is it?" Rome asked.

"Rei…" Ursay stepped forward and placed his hand on Rei's shoulder. Rome was stunned at such a gesture. In a low voice, Ursay said, "When we first found you, we presumed you a blight, a burden. You were from Garecei Ti Essessoni. We cast Rome out because we thought you had compromised this woman, with your undisciplined mind, your murderous past. We were going to exile you, but now…"

"Now what?" Rei asked.

"You have demonstrated to us that as an individual, you have worth. That your separateness is of value. It is something we must consider in the future. For this, we thank you."

Rei's face lit up. "Well, you are welcome, sir!" Ursay removed his hand and nodded. Rei and Rome took that as their cue to leave and headed back toward OMCOM's fabrication facility.

"That was so unlike a Vuduri," Rome said as they were walking. "To touch you like that? You have changed this Overmind in a profound fashion."

"Actually, Rome," Rei replied, "I think it's you that has changed them."

"How?"

"In you they see the potential for all Vuduri when they're not controlled so heavily by the Overmind. You're the future, not me."

"Well," Rome said as they entered OMCOM's central store, "let us agree that together, we have given the Overmind much to think about."

"Roger that."

Rome took her place in front of the design screen. She watched as OMCOM modified the architecture of the starprobe foundries to suit their new role. At last, the first unit was extruded from the fabricator followed by another and another, the rate of production ever-increasing.

"They look the same as before," Rei said. "What's different about them?"

Rome pointed to one section of the screen. "Here is the read-only memory, which is new. And here," she pointed to a different area, "OMCOM has converted the second Casimir pump into what looks like an auxiliary internal power source to supplement the first one."

Rei nodded like he knew what she was talking about, but he really didn't see a difference.

"And here," she said, pointing to the left, "this must be the solid-state oxygen detector. That will keep the units dormant for now."

"That's a good thing," Rei said.

Rome walked over to a flat surface by the assembly bay and showed Rei the cases that were being built to house the units. She pointed to a little fishbowl in the middle.

"OMCOM created this container. These bowls will hold the VIRUS units. The cases themselves are air-tight so that the oxygen will be retained and the units will remain deactivated until we know what we are going to do with them."

"And once they're loose, when do they turn off?" Rei asked.

"Yes. That is a good point. OMCOM?" Rome inquired. "What is to prevent them from consuming one another and the whole process aborting?"

"I have engineered the units to only draw raw materials from sources other than themselves," OMCOM said. "In this case, it will be the Stareater. Call it an anti-cannibalism directive. Under normal circumstances, they will not consume one another. They will work cooperatively."

"This really will work, won't it?" Rei said, "We're actually going to make these things sick and die! Well, if they were alive, I mean. OMCOM, are the Stareaters alive or are they machines?"

"The difference is academic. They need to be stopped."

"One cannot help but be curious," Rome interjected. "OMCOM, take a guess. Do you think the Stareaters are alive?"

"I am still analyzing the data, so I cannot render a definitive answer at this time. However, after you leave, I will have much time to ponder this and other questions."

"Yeah. Sorry," Rei said. "I feel kind of bad for you. Everyone is leaving you here, holding the bag."

"I am not sure what bag you are referring to, but it is time for you and Rome to go. I have summoned the loading crew. Very shortly, I will have many cases filled with the VIRUS units. The crew can load them aboard the Algol. It is prepped and ready to leave. As Commander Ursay suggested, you should go inspect your new living quarters before it is too late."

Chapter 18

ROME AND REI STOOD TO THE SIDE OF THE GIANT INNER DOOR OF the hangar. In front of them was the tug that was to be their home for the next two years. The Vuduri crew were rushing in and out carrying boxes and building materials and all manner of items that Rei did not recognize. He stood there in awe of how truly large this place was. When the Vuduri first arrived here, there was no hangar, no star-base, nothing but dirt. They built all of this from scratch. And now they were abandoning it. As the various crew members walked by, many of them nodded and some even gently smiled at them offering a stark contrast to the reception Rei received when he first came aboard the station.

"Where'd all these people come from?" Rei asked.

"They have been here," Rome replied.

"How come I never saw any of them before?"

"Most wished to avoid contact with you when you were first revived," Rome said. "This was already explained to you."

"Why is everyone being so friendly now?" Rei asked.

"Commander Ursay explained it to you. The Overmind recognizes that you are responsible for possibly saving all of humanity if not all life in the universe. I think this is its way of showing appreciation."

"Sleek," Rei said, looking up at the ship. "Should we go take a look?"

"Yes. That is a good idea."

Being careful to not get in the way of the crew transporting materials, Rei and Rome made their way up the 30-degree ramp into the cargo compartment of the bright white tug. Except for the rounded roof, Rei couldn't even tell that it was a space vehicle. With its rooms off to either side, the inside reminded him of a double-wide trailer back on Earth.

They walked along the corridor formed by the newly installed compartments taking care to squeeze to the side whenever a worker passed by them. They entered the first doorway they came to, off to the right and Rome squealed in delight.

"What a beautiful bedroom!" she said.

Rei looked around. On the far wall, there was a big bed and spread about the room was furniture complete with a sitting area.

"Wow," Rei exclaimed. "For people who have no need for taste or comfort, this certainly is elaborate."

"I am sure OMCOM had an influence on its design," Rome observed.

Rei turned back and stared at the bed for a moment. He cleared his throat and started to speak but then stopped.

"What?" Rome asked.

"Uh…" Rei stammered. "This is going to sound too clinical but I don't think it would be a good idea if you got pregnant during the trip. We need to figure out something."

"That is not an issue," Rome said. "Vuduri women control when they ovulate. I will not become pregnant unless you and I decide the time is right."

"OK," Rei said, relieved to drop the subject.

They left that room and moved on to the next which was a galley and eating area. That room had several food synthesizers along with appliances that seemed out of place in the 35th century. There was an oven, a stove and a refrigerator. There was also a square table with two chairs.

"I guess they're expecting me to cook for you," Rei said.

"I would certainly hope so," Rome replied. "And you can teach me as well."

"Sure."

The next room they came to was a fully-equipped gymnasium with some equipment that Rei recognized, including an elliptical trainer, but there was more that he did not recognize.

"What's all this for?" he asked.

"Why, exercise, of course," replied Rome. "Two of the three EG lifters will have to be used as magnetic clamps so we will only have one-third gravity. We will have to exercise every day to get ready for Deucado. It has nearly the same gravity as Earth."

"That's good to hear," Rei said.

He and Rome worked their way back, past the mid-ship airlock and storage lockers then entered a living area with a workstation, seating area and some more electronic equipment.

Rei just stood there a moment, trying to formulate a thought. "Rome, what are we going to do every day? It's like being under house arrest."

"What is house arrest?" Rome asked.

"If you do something wrong and the authorities don't want to put you in prison," Rei answered, "they make you stay in your house and they put a security anklet on you that tells them your whereabouts."

"A security anklet? That would be like a tracking bracelet?" Rome asked.

"Yeah, I guess."

"We have those," Rome said. "For the mandasurte, of course. Vuduri would not need those."

"Right," Rei said.

"Why are we discussing house arrest, anyway?" Rome asked.

"You and me, we'll be locked up, really. Two years is a long time to be cooped up in a flying house. Even one as nice as this," Rei said.

"I think there is more that you are not telling me," Rome observed. "Why do you question this?"

"It's nothing. Never mind," he said.

"No, tell me," she replied. "Remember, I cannot read minds anymore."

"OK. I'll tell you. I love you so much that I don't have very good judgment when it comes to this. But, when you think about it logically, even though it feels like I've known you my whole life, we've only really just met. I'd hate to think of us being stuck together and not enjoying it."

"Do not concern yourself with…" Her breath caught, and then her brow furrowed. "Are you worried that we are not meant to be together?" she asked with some concern.

"Oh no, god, no. It isn't that," Rei answered hurriedly. "This has nothing to do with my feelings. It's just an observation, a hypothetical. I mean, how will we end up not going stir crazy if there is nowhere to go and nothing to do for such a long time?"

Rome laughed, relieved. "You are being silly. There will be much to do. You must learn to speak Vuduri. No one on Deucado will take the time to learn English like I did."

"Sure, that makes sense," Rei agreed.

"And you must learn all about Vuduri science, technology, history and more. When we reanimate your people, as you well know, there will be a culture shock and we have to be ready to orient them to the new world."

"I understand," Rei said, shaking his head.

"And there is so much I want to learn about your world," Rome said firmly. "There was much lost after the Great Dying. There is a vast amount of history that you can fill in that will help others to understand exactly what happened. After today, I am sure the Vuduri will find it of interest."

"OK. What else?" Rei asked.

"OMCOM tells me he had them include art supplies, music generators…oh!"

"Oh what?" Rei asked.

"Music. You will have to teach me. I know nothing about it."

"I love music," Rei said. "And dancing!"

"Yes. There will be much to do. The time will go racing by. You will see." Rome said happily.

"I hope you're right and Rome?"

"Yes?"

"I can't think of anybody who I'd rather be trapped in a flying house with besides you."

"Oh Rei!" Rome said. She came over to him, reached up to put her arms around his neck and kissed him. "I feel the same. Believe me."

After a little while, they started back down the corridor toward the exit ramp. Rome stopped and opened the last door on their right. She poked her head in and said, "Ah…here are the molecular sequencers. This is very good."

"How come?"

"When we get to Deucado, the molecular sequencer will be very handy in building materials. OMCOM has told me that the MINIMCOM's computing capacity and database has been updated

141

with the ability to produce anything we might ever need. They are called templates. If there is something we need that is not in that database, we will have the ability to construct new templates."

"What kind of stuff would we need on Deucado?" Rei asked. "The Vuduri are there already."

"Yes, but when we arrive, your people will need housing. The MINIMCOM will be able to create aerogel generators. And you will need vehicles. And spacecraft. This will allow us to build whatever we will need."

"That is great," Rei said. "That will really help."

"Yes," Rome replied. "He has even uploaded the templates for constructing more VIRUS units, should the need arise. No, OMCOM has thought of everything. It will be good."

She stepped back into the hallway looking up and down the compartment. She didn't say anything.

Rei spoke again. "Well, I guess that's it then, huh?"

"Yes. I will retrieve my belongings and then we will be ready to depart."

"You're going to bring the bands with you, right?" Rei asked.

Rome smiled and nodded. She knew she would not need the T-suppressor anymore but the bands were a different story. "Most assuredly," she said.

"That reminds me," Rei continued. "I've been meaning to ask you something, but with all that's been going on, I haven't had the chance."

"What is it?" Rome asked.

"Why were you cast out?"

Rome pulled her head back and frowned. "Because I consorted with you, of course."

"Hey, your mom 'consorted' with your dad and she didn't get cast out."

"Yes, but my father was of our times, not an Essessoni, like you. Based upon what Ursay said, the Overmind thought your influence on my mind would hurt the whole. Because of what your people did. We all know better now."

"I understand that, but let me ask you this: how did the Overmind know what influence I had on your mind?"

"What do you mean?" Rome asked.

"You had the T-suppressor on, which means that you were disconnected from the Overmind. It couldn't have known that we 'consorted' at least until I took the band off you and you were asleep at the time. Could the Overmind go into your head when you were asleep?"

Rome crinkled up her forehead. "I do not know."

"So how long does it take to go from connected to Cesdiud?" Rei asked.

"Again, I do not know," replied Rome. "It has only happened to me once and as you point out, I was asleep at the time."

"So doesn't that strike you as funny? It's almost like the Overmind was ready to pull the trigger the moment I removed the T-suppressor from your head," Rei volunteered.

"What are you getting at?"

"Exactly what I said. How did it know?" Rei asked.

"I do not know the answer to that. Do you know?" Rome was confused.

Rei looked to his right and his left. "Do you think OMCOM tipped them off? Do you think that is why the Overmind was ready and waiting for you to go Cesdiud the minute I took the bands from your head?"

"But why would he do that? Why would OMCOM want me cast out?" Rome asked.

"I don't know. The only thing I can think of is that it has something to do with the PPT lockout. Ursay was so funny about it. Don't you think it was just a bit convenient that you were in a position to be able to do it at the exact moment when OMCOM needed you to?"

Rome went silent. Then finally she spoke. "It may be more than a coincidence, but I do not know if I care." She took a deep breath and continued, "There are many things I did not understand. My mother and father loved me very much. This is not the way of the Vuduri. There is little need for individual affection or attention when you are connected to the whole. Vuduri mate only to advance the species. My mother was not like other Vuduri. Whatever made her different, well, part of that must be within me. When you and I…" She stopped speaking.

"Go on," Rei said.

"When I was first Cesdiud, part of me thought it was what I deserved. That it was a punishment. But if this was OMCOM's doing, it must have been for the greater good. It allows me to make sense of all the things that I did not understand. So this is what I choose to believe. I still think I got what I deserved, but now I think it is a gift, not a punishment."

"OK," Rei said, sensing that Rome wanted to drop it. He decided to change the subject. "Speaking of your mother, what are we going to do about her?"

"What do you mean?"

"Well, you're going to go to Deucado with me," Rei said. "That's going to make it more difficult to see her, don't you think? Aren't you going to miss her?"

Rome frowned. "I had not thought of that. I, I do not know what I will do about that."

"Do you think she'd ever come to Deucado? To see you?" Rei asked.

"I do not know," Rome replied. "When Commander Ursay and the crew get back to Earth, the Overmind there will know that I am going to Deucado. So my mother will be aware. They will tell her about my Cesdiud. She will worry about me, I know it. If only there was a way I could tell her I am all right. Perhaps she would come to Deucado."

"How about sending her a note?" Rei asked.

"What do you mean?" Rome asked back, confused.

"Write her a letter. Tell her what happened, that you're OK and that you want her to come visit." Rei offered.

"I have never written a letter before. Conceptually, it would not seem to be that difficult. I suppose I could do that."

"You've never written a letter to somebody? What about e-mail?"

"E-mail?" Rome asked.

"Electronic mail. Notes sent electronically."

"We would never do that." Rome pointed to her temple and made a wry grin; then her smile waned. A tear came to her eye. Rei came over to her and put one hand on her shoulder and one hand on the back of her head. He tilted her head so that she looked up at him.

"Romey, are you having regrets?" he asked, wiping away the tear.

Rome sighed then forced herself to smile. "No. I want to go to Deucado with you. I will miss my mother but I must have my own life. She would understand and support me." She nodded as if answering an internal question. "I think I will take your suggestion and go write her a letter and give it to Commander Ursay. He will make sure my mother receives it. It is a very good idea."

Rome reached forward and hugged Rei tightly. She took a step back and placed a finger to her temple. "While I am doing that, OMCOM says you are to report to the Infirmary."

"The Infirmary. Why?" Rei asked.

"He said he has something for you. Go on. I will meet you back here shortly."

"OK," Rei said.

They exited the tug and after a brief kiss, went their separate ways.

Chapter 19

Rei headed up the main corridor to the far side of the base where the Infirmary was located. As he entered, he noted all around him the universal, antiseptic look of all medical facilities, complete with beds and cabinets and instrumentation. There was white everywhere. He saw one of the Vuduri standing by a workstation to his right. The man looked vaguely familiar but then all the Vuduri looked alike to him. Rei walked over to him.

"Who are you?" he asked.

The man cleared his throat several times, looking very uncomfortable. Speaking appeared to require a major effort on his part.

"I am Canus," he said hoarsely, looking up at Rei.

"Are you a doctor?" Rei asked.

"I am told that perhaps medic would be a better term."

"OK, so what's going on?"

"OMCOM has prepared a supplement for you. It is supposed to fix your back pain." Canus held out a small glass dish with a single yellow pill on it. "Here," he said.

Rei picked the pill up and looked at it. "Just take it now?" he asked.

"Yes."

Canus handed him a squeeze-bulb of water. Rei popped the pill in and swallowed the water. "So, what is it?" Rei asked. "Some kind of supercharged medicine?"

"No. It is gene therapy."

Rei swallowed again. Hard. "Gene therapy? What did I just take?"

"It is a combination of RNA transcriptase and DNA supplements. OMCOM said that once the altered genes have integrated within your cells, it would reactivate the tissues within your disks and rehydrate the structures to achieve the proper balance for your age and physical condition."

Rei felt a little woozy. With all that was going on, it never occurred to him to ask what it was before he took it. Canus grabbed his elbow and steadied him.

"You should lie down for a little while," Canus said, pointing off to the left. "OMCOM says it is possible that the pill will make you nauseous or cause a headache."

He led Rei over to the area where there were some beds. Rei hopped up on one. "Make yourself comfortable." Canus said. "We should know fairly quickly if you will be made ill."

"How many of these do I have to take?" Rei asked.

Canus looked confused. "Why just the one, of course."

"Wow!" Rei exclaimed. "OMCOM is some kind of doctor."

"I suppose," Canus replied. "OMCOM said that you will get some immediate relief, but it will take nearly a year for the effects to finalize. Also, you will require normal gravity for your spine to fully regenerate back to the state it should be for someone your age. OMCOM also said to be sure and drink plenty of water."

"OK." Rei put his arm over his eyes. His head was buzzing. "You're part of the Overmind, right? What do you really think about this Stareater thing?"

Canus shrugged. "We must get the information to Earth," he said matter-of-factly. "While we have the VIRUS units, we do not have a delivery system yet. We are confident that the Overmind of Earth will come up with a method but it must be very fast. Otherwise, we would have to abandon our home planet."

"What!?" Rei said, sitting up. "This isn't you. This is the Overmind talking, right? If the VIRUS units can kill it, why would you have do that? Abandon Earth?"

"Unfortunately, there is still the Stareater's mass. Even if it is dead, if it is on a trajectory for the Solar System, the gravitational influence alone would disrupt the entire star system. There is no way to prevent that. No, we would have to abandon Earth."

"Well make sure you don't! The Earth is our birth world. It's more than just a planet. It's the home of our species. No matter where we go, it will always be the thing that ties us together. Without it, we'd all just drift apart as a race."

"It is not our first choice, just a possible scenario. Only time will tell," said Canus with a hint of sadness.

Rei just shook his head. "Look, I'll just take my chances with the medicine. I've got to get back to Rome."

"Very well," said Canus, helping Rei up. "There is one more thing." Canus walked back over to the workstation and picked up a large white bottle. "Here," he said, holding it out toward Rei.

Rei walked over to him and took it. "What is it?"

"This is for the rest of your crew, when they wake up. OMCOM said it is likely that most of them will suffer the same malady as you. There are 600 additional doses there. That should be more than enough to mend your fellow colonists plus a few extra."

Rei shook the bottle of pills, finding the heft satisfying.

"Thank you," he said. Canus nodded.

Rei left the Infirmary and returned the length of the station back to the tug that had been converted into a flying house. Standing in his way was Estar, her arms crossed across her chest.

"What do you want?" Rei asked.

"You are going to die," she said, staring daggers at him.

"Why? What's wrong with you?"

"You will not succeed," she said. "The fact that you will die, I do not care about that. However, you will kill many others in the process including your precious Rome."

"Why do you say that?" Rei asked.

"Because you and your Erklirte weapons cannot be released in our century. There is no place for them."

"I told you before, we have no weapons," Rei said.

"You know nothing," said Estar. "You are just a pawn. There are forces at work here that you cannot fathom."

"You make it sound so sinister," Rei said. "We're just people from old Earth trying to find a life in your world."

"No, you are the Erklirte, returning from the past," Estar spat out. "You will cause nothing but death and destruction. You will impede the progress of my species."

"We will do no such thing. And I am your species," Rei said. "Except that extra chromosome of yours makes you all a little bit crazy."

Estar just stood there, glowering at him with her mismatched eyes.

Slowly, Rei's head tilted to the side.

"You!" he said, suddenly.

"What?" replied Estar.

"It was you! You're the one that tried to kill me."

"I do not know what you are talking about," Estar protested mildly.

"The Iso chamber. And the nav-computer. You did it. You tried to kill me."

"You are perfectly capable of killing yourself. You do not need my help for this," Estar said with disdain.

"But, those accidents. They weren't accidents, were they?"

A short sharp tremor interrupted their conversation. Rei had to put his hand out to steady himself by the ship. While waiting for it to subside, Estar just stared at him. Suddenly, she let out a brief burst of air. She turned and started to leave the hangar.

"Wait!" Rei shouted after her. "I thought you were the Overmind. You came up with the plan to save me and my people. Now you want me dead? What's going on? Tell me who you are!"

Estar ignored him and exited the hangar right, leaving Rei more confused than ever.

"Jesus f'ing Christ," Rei muttered to himself.

Rome returned a minute later and found Rei still standing at the base of the ramp, shaking his head.

"What happened?" she asked.

Rei related to her his latest encounter with Estar.

Rome narrowed her eyes. "I must now concur with you. There is something very wrong with her. We must be on alert."

"I don't know if I can take any more," Rei said. "Beyond Estar being a murdering psychopath, you have to understand there is nothing like waking up 1400 years in the future among a telepathic race burdened with psychic tunnel vision. And now there's a horde of star-eating creatures descending on my home world, capable of extinguishing all life, anywhere in the galaxy. You guys, I mean the Overmind, gave up on even trying to find a solution. I have to be the one to figure out how to kill it? Canus said they may even have to abandon Earth. It's a lot to absorb, Rome."

She lifted her hand up and put it on his cheek. "You are doing quite well."

"I know, but I can't shake the feeling that I should have been dead a long time ago. I feel kind of sick to my stomach. Oh…"

"What is it?" Rome asked. "Why is your face so pale?"

"I guess it's just the medication OMCOM gave me is starting to kick in."

Rome touched her temple. "OMCOM says it will pass," she said.

"Probably."

"And you are not supposed to be dead. You came all this way to find me. I would not be in love with a dead man," she said, quite seriously.

All Rei could do was smile as Rome dragged him up the cargo ramp into their future home.

Upon reaching the cockpit, they took their seats, Rei on the left, Rome on the right. Rei glanced over at Rome and saw her fiddling with the X-harness. He reached behind him, pulled the straps forward and snapped in the first then the second with two satisfying clicks that could only come from a heavy-duty tongue and lock mechanism.

He turned back to Rome and said, "So…did you go to the bathroom?"

She cocked her head to the side. "What do you mean?"

Rei smiled. "Well, before every long trip, you're supposed to make sure that everybody goes to the bathroom."

"Why is that?" she asked.

"Because this is going to be one hell of a trip and I just wanted to make sure we didn't have to make any unscheduled stops."

"What kind of stops?" she asked.

"Uh, bathroom stops?"

"But we have facilities onboard," she said.

"Rome, it's a joke," Rei said.

"Oh." She scrunched up her face. "Oh!" she said then she started to laugh. "I understand. That is very funny."

"It kind of loses something if you have to explain it. But I will tell you this…we'd better not be forgetting anything important. 21 light years to Tau Ceti? We're not coming back this way any time soon."

"This is true. All right," she said. Then she closed her eyes.

"What are you doing?" he asked.

"I am performing the pre-flight checklist with OMCOM," was her reply.

"I didn't mean it literally," Rei said.

"I know. We would be doing this anyway. It will only take a minute. After your description of your final meeting with Estar, I have decided to triple-check everything."

"Yeah, about that. I need to ask you something about her," Rei said.

"What?" Rome replied, looking up from her work.

"Did you ever notice Estar's eyes?" Rei asked.

"What about them?"

"They're different from yours. And everybody else's. One of them is dark, almost black. There's no reflection, no back-glow."

"I have seen it but never thought about it," Rome said. "Estar always kept to herself but that is the way of all Vuduri."

Rome punched in some codes into the keypad and through the front windows of the cockpit, Rei could see the giant hangar doors opening, exposing the dock to the unbreathable atmosphere of Dara.

Rei suddenly had a tiny moment of panic. "MINIMCOM, Rei here. Are you there?" he asked.

`"Standing by,"` replied a thin voice.

"Are you ready to go?"

`"Yes. I am docked on your Ark. All systems check out."`

"Good. We'll be there shortly."

`"Acknowledged."`

Rei let out a sigh and looked around the cockpit, trying to review their supplies in his mind. The ship had air, food synthesizers and water. They were good in the area of basic sustenance. They had a drive system that would get them to Tau Ceti in hopefully under two years. He wasn't sure what else they needed. His attention was interrupted when the front viewscreen flickered on. In front of them was Commander Ursay's face.

"Rome, au quos ebanes tasajer-lha e sirda pie," he said.

"Iprogeti," Rome said. "I masmis e fica."

"And Rei, good luck to you too," Ursay added.

"Thank you, sir" Rei replied.

Ursay looked to his left and said, "We will await your…"

Just then, Ursay grabbed his head, covered his eyes and exhaled sharply. Rei and Rome watched in horrified fascination as he thrashed his head about as if he was trying to shake something loose. He slumped forward and his head came to rest on top of the video port, obscuring the camera's field of vision.

"Commander Ursay, can you hear me?" Rome asked. There was no reply. Rome repeated her entreaty. Again, Ursay did not answer.

"OMCOM, what's happening," Rei shouted.

Through the grille, OMCOM replied, "I do not know."

The blurred image that was the side of Ursay's head did not change. They could hear his labored breathing, but there was no other movement on the screen.

"OMCOM!" Rei said even more loudly. "Talk to us. What's going on?"

"I do not know," was OMCOM's reply. "There is no response from *any* of the crew members aboard the Algol."

Rei looked at Rome. Her eyes were closed. She was clearly occupied trying to read telemetry with her bloco. Rei strained to make out intelligible sounds but all he could hear were some clicking and buzzing noises emitting from the grille.

"Rome, what do we do?" Rei asked.

"I do not know," Rome answered sadly. "They may be dying or dead already."

Chapter 20

REI UNLOCKED HIS HARNESS AND STOOD UP. "WE'VE GOT TO GO over there, to the Algol."

Rome nodded and released her safety belts. They put on their helmets, went through the airlock, sealed up the cockpit and ran as fast as they could to the back of the tug. Even before the cargo ramp was fully extended, they ran down, jumping off the end to the floor of the hangar, bolting to the airlock. OMCOM opened the inner door and they burst through it, dropping their helmets then running at full speed around the outer ring of the station until they got the loading dock for the Algol.

Rome punched the button to open the airlock to the connecting corridor, but nothing happened.

"It is not working," Rome said.

"OMCOM," Rei shouted. "Open the airlock."

"I cannot," OMCOM replied. "The connecting corridor is still retracted."

"Well, unretract it then," Rei said.

"I am already working on it. The process will take several more minutes," OMCOM replied.

"Just hurry," commanded Rei.

"It is moving it as fast as it will go," OMCOM said with just a hint of irritation.

Rei and Rome fidgeted at the entry to the airlock while they felt the gears moving, extending the connecting corridor back to the Algol. Rei took off his gloves and tucked them into a side pocket. Rome did the same.

"What do you think happened?" Rei asked.

"I have no idea. I have never seen anything like it," replied Rome.

There was a hissing sound as the airlock opened. Rei and Rome leaped over the inner seal and dashed across the 50 feet separating them from the Algol. Rome punched savagely at the button to open the Algol's airlock. Finally, the door rolled backwards and they were through.

As they made their way forward, Rei noted that unlike the star-base, which was smooth and rounded, everything in the Algol was rectangular, dark and metallic. They raced up a wire mesh walkway barely wide enough for the two of them to travel side by side.

Rome and Rei entered the crew compartment where the crewmen were strapped into their seats. None of them were moving. They stopped at the first row they came to which was really the last row in the compartment. Every person on both sides of the row was slouched over, clearly unconscious. Rei put his finger on the carotid of the crewman on the right, checking his pulse. He was alive, but the pulse was weak.

Rome turned to her left, shaking the man belted into the seat there. She said, "Canus, Canus. Fogoloe ecome." The crewman did not move.

They stepped forward to the next row and repeated the procedure. Rei checked Estar who was sitting on the right. Her eyes were closed. Rei got no reaction from her. Rome shook the crewman on the left.

"Signola, bita fica iufor-ma?" Rome asked. Again there was no response.

"It's like OMCOM said. They're all out cold," Rei noted.

"The cockpit," Rome replied obliquely.

Rei and Rome hurried up the central aisle and made their way to the cockpit. Sitting there was Ursay and two other crew members, all slumped forward in their seats. Rome shook him and got no response. Finally, she slapped Ursay's face and asked, "Ursay, bita fica iufor-ma?" There was no reaction.

Rei spotted a grille mounted on the front console. "OMCOM, you got anything?" he asked.

"No. Nothing."

Rei made up his mind. He pushed Rome out of the way, unbuckled Ursay and lifted him up and over his shoulder in a fireman's carry. "Let's get him to the Infirmary," he said.

Rome nodded and led the way back, through the crew compartment, out through the connecting corridor and around the outer ring until they reached the Infirmary. OMCOM had already opened the door. Rei entered and carried Ursay's limp body to one of the beds there and laid him down.

"What do we do?" Rei said, trying to catch his breath. "What's wrong with him?"

"Rome," OMCOM said, ignoring Rei's entreaties, "follow the diagram and attach the EEG and EKG sensors as directed."

Rome shouted, "Where are the sensor pads?"

"The cabinet on the left, third drawer down," OMCOM replied.

She pulled the drawer open and grabbed two packages there.

"Here Rei, you attach the EEG. I'll do the EKG," Rome said, handing him one of the packages.

"Let me help you first," Rei said. He moved around to the other side of the bed. Together, quickly, Rei and Rome removed Ursay's pressure suit. Rei then tried to tear off Ursay's jumpsuit, but the material wouldn't yield. Rome made a face at him and unclasped it quickly the usual way. Rome looked up at the diagram on the rightmost viewscreen illustrating where to attach the sensor pads.

Rei moved around back to the other side and attached two sticky pads, one on each side of Ursay's temples. Once Rei was done, Rome pressed a few buttons on the sensor stand and the virtual dials and gauges came alive.

"We are ready," Rome said, addressing OMCOM's grille.

"Analyzing..."

Rei walked over to stand by Rome's side. Gently, he took her hand. The central display showed readouts from the leads, but they made no sense to Rei. The EKG showed Ursay's heart was beating with a weak but normal sinus rhythm, however, the brain waves were flat with random fluctuations. Every half second or so there was a spike. Judging from the readouts, it looked to Rei like the man was brain-dead.

"Something is suppressing his normal brain activity," OMCOM announced.

"What is it?" Rei asked.

"Unknown."

"Can you fix it? Can you wake him up?" Rome asked.

"Unlikely without knowing the cause."

"How could it affect all of the crewmen like that?" Rei asked. "And why didn't it affect us?"

"I DO NOT KNOW," OMCOM replied forcefully. Rei shook his head. It wasn't like the AI to show any kind of anger. This was only the second time that he could remember any type of emotional response.

"All right, take your time," Rei said, trying to placate the computer.

Rome moved closer to Rei. He released her hand and put his arm around her shoulder. She snuggled in. Rei could feel her shaking.

OMCOM presented his results. "The brain wave pattern is nearly identical to that seen when a Vuduri brain is flooded with large scale external PPT resonance. Like when the Vuduri travel through the static PPT tunnel between Earth and Alpha Centauri. But there is no PPT gate here. There is no..." OMCOM stopped speaking.

"OMCOM?" Rome said. "What is it?"

"I am rerouting the starprobes. Please wait..."

"What are you doing?" Rome asked.

"My analysis is correct."

"Correct about what?" Rei asked.

"A Stareater has just appeared less than one light day away from Tabit. And it is coming this way."

"Oh my god!" Rei said.

Rome held her hand up. "OMCOM, is this what has happened to Ursay? The Algol?"

"Rei's theory that the Stareaters have FTL capacity has been confirmed. This sphere has emerged from a PPT tunnel. The tunnel itself is larger than anything ever observed by twelve orders of magnitude."

"But Ursay? The crew? What..."

"The Stareater must be generating an incalculable amount of energy in the same band as the Vuduri PPT-modulation transceivers. The Stareater appears to have rendered the crew members senseless."

Rei's mouth slowly opened as the enormity of what OMCOM said sank in. "Rome," he whispered. "What do we do? What will happen to them? How do we get them out of here?"

"The only solution is for one of you to pilot the Algol out of here, back to Earth."

Rei shrank back. "I can't fly it," he said.

"But I can," Rome said, sadly.

"But...but what about the tug? What about my Ark? Rome?" Rei sputtered.

"You will have to pilot it alone," Rome said, almost in a whisper.

"I can't do that," Rei protested.

"Yes you can. You have the MINIMCOM. It will help you operate it. You just need to do as you were taught..."

"No!" Rei shouted, reaching over, pulling her into his arms. She was shivering.

"Yes," Rome said, tears welling up in her eyes.

"Rome, I don't want to leave you," Rei cried out. 'Rome, I can't lose you. I, I love you."

"You must. You must save your people. I must save mine," Rome answered sadly.

"Rome..." Rei said. The words he wanted to speak would not come.

She just stayed in his arms. Rei never wanted to let her go.

"OMCOM," Rei said, "isn't there any other way?"

"I do not know how much damage has been done to the crew. But they cannot remain here. Not with a Stareater coming. If you get them out of this system, after several jumps, the strength of the signal should be diminished enough that if they are going to recover, it will start then. Either way, the Algol must take the VIRUS units and the data regarding the Stareaters to Earth. That is the only way to save your home planet and the Vuduri," OMCOM replied.

"So what about Tau Ceti? What's to stop this thing from following me there?" Rei asked.

"Nothing."

Both Rome and Rei gasped.

"But, but," Rei stammered. "I, we, we have to stop it..."

"The delivery system," OMCOM said. "The VIRUS units must be placed on the surface of the Stareater. The Overmind and the OMCOMs of Earth will find a method of deployment."

"But not us. Damn it," Rei said, pushing Rome away from him. "Rome, you get to Earth. You'll get them to kill the swarm. But us, me…"

Rome said, "I know, I know…"

"OMCOM," Rei wailed, "come on. You're this genius computer. Think of something…"

"Perhaps there is a way…" OMCOM said.

"Tell me," Rei said, ignoring the computer's dramatic pause.

"We need to set enough of the VIRUS units so that we can guarantee that this particular Stareater is infected."

"How?" Rei asked.

"We could create a 'poison pill' that the Stareater must swallow."

"How, where?" Rei asked.

"You are standing on it."

"What do you mean?" Rome asked.

"Dara. This moon." OMCOM replied. "You could set the VIRUS units loose here. By the time the Stareater arrives, sufficient numbers will be produced to guarantee delivery of an ample quantity of viable units, if you hurry."

"You mean let them consume this moon?" Rome asked. "Then the Stareater will eat the moon and that way…"

"Yes."

"But OMCOM…won't they consume you too?" Rei asked. "There has to be another way."

"When the Stareater comes through, this star-base will be destroyed regardless. And there is no telling when that will happen. The Stareater could make another jump. There is no time. You must do this now. Rei, you will need to take some VIRUS units onto the surface and release them. Rome, you must take the Algol out of this system immediately if you want to save the crew."

"But OMCOM…" Rei protested weakly.

"There are no buts. You must go now."

Without further protest, they quickly moved to Ursay's bedside and removed the EKG and EEG sensors, closing up his jumpsuit. Rei hoisted Ursay over his shoulder once again and carried him back to the Algol. They strapped him into a vacant seat in the crew compartment and returned to the cargo portion to retrieve two of the many sealed cases containing the VIRUS units. Together, Rome and Rei left the Algol and continued around the outer ring until they arrived at the Iso unit leading to their tug. Rei reached down and grabbed his helmet before entering the room. Rome followed him in.

After setting the helmet down on the bench there, Rei regarded Rome. Her breathing was ragged as was his. She had never stopped crying. Rei wiped away his tears. He was crying too.

"Rome…" was all he said.

"I know," she replied quietly. "There is no other way."

No longer able to stand it, she stepped forward and melted into his arms. The pressure suits made it difficult to clasp each other tightly, but neither cared. Somehow they managed. They kissed each other long and hard. If the breaking of a heart made a sound, it would have reverberated loudly in that small room.

"Rei. Rome. You must get started," OMCOM insisted. "Every second counts."

Rome whispered, "It is time."

Rei said, "I know."

She took a step back and their arms were stretched toward each other, fingers intertwined. She took one more step back and they had to release their grip. Tears were streaming down her cheeks.

Rome took one more step back and said, "Mau emir." One more step and with a whoosh, the airlock door closed, sealing them off from one another. Rei went up to the inner door. He could see Rome's beautiful face with her glowing eyes through the window, just like the very first time he had ever seen her in this place. She put her hand over her heart and mouthed the words, "You will always be in my heart."

Rei pointed to his temple. "You will always be in my thoughts," he said.

She reached down for her helmet. After she straightened up, she blew him a kiss then turned and headed around the corridor, toward the dock with the Algol. She stopped, turned around and looked at him one last time. She held up her hand and then she was gone.

"Please, Rei," OMCOM said. "You have a planet to destroy."

Chapter 21

Even though the corridor outside was now empty, Rei stood there motionless, staring at the porthole.

"Rei!" OMCOM said insistently.

He sighed. There was no putting this off. He turned to look at the grille. "How far do I have to go?"

"You only need go 500 meters outside the hangar doors. Once the VIRUS units are released, you will have more than an hour to get the tug launched before the VIRUS units have replicated enough to get even close to this place."

"OK, OK." Rei said. He placed his helmet over his head, pressing it down and turning it to the right to seal it. He pulled on his gloves then he nodded and gave OMCOM the thumbs up signal. OMCOM opened the airlock door to the hangar. As it opened, Rei heard a hissing sound as the air from within the Iso chamber rushed out into the larger space. The pumps had already removed most of the air in the hangar in preparation for opening the main doors.

Rei ran across the floor of the hangar, dropping off one of the VIRUS cases on the loading ramp of the tug before dashing past the spaceship. The hangar doors opened up and Rei gazed upon the surface of Dara for the first time. After the pressure completely equilibrated, he strode forward until he was standing on the dirt of Dara itself. He stared down at his feet, realizing that even though he had been here for three days, this was the first time he was interacting with the moon in an actual, physical way. Too bad it was on a world that wouldn't live to see even one more day.

Based upon some quick calculation, he figured he had to travel roughly 1000 paces away from the base. Rei began his journey south. He sniffed the air reflexively but all he could smell was the purified air of the pressure suit mixed with his own perspiration. After his near-death experience in the airlock, he knew he couldn't breathe the air here as it would have killed him rather quickly. Sanitized air was certainly better than the alternative.

Ahead of him, Skyler's World dominated the horizon, filling nearly one-third of the heavens above. Under other circumstances, it would have been a beautiful sight. Now it just reinforced Rei's awareness of how alone he was. There was no radio inside the helmet and no one to talk to even if there was. Rei counted his paces out loud trying to avoid considering his predicament.

At 900 paces, Rei felt the ground shake. It didn't feel like an ordinary moonquake. He turned and looked back at the habitat. Rising majestically above the rounded pyramid of the station was the starship Algol, pounding the dirt and whipping up the dust with its powerful EG lifters. The graceful, all-white spaceship flew forward, away from Rei, and then executed a slow bank right, coming around until it was headed in his direction.

As the streamlined starship flew over his head, it waggled its wings. Rei raised his free hand to acknowledge the gesture. He tried to spot Rome within the cockpit window but was unable to do so. The ship passed overhead and after a short time, he saw the plasma thrusters ignite and the Algol took off straight up like a rocket. With tears in his eyes, Rei watched the spaceship gain altitude. The craft dwindled in size, first to a tiny speck then finally disappearing into space.

Grief-stricken, Rei sank to his knees and, for a short time, he sobbed uncontrollably. The love of his life was gone, never to return. His heart was broken and nothing was ever going to heal it. But he had his mission and his comrades to save. After a time, he forced himself to stand and get on with the task of destroying this world.

Rei scanned the area immediately in front of him. He spotted a suitable crater about a hundred yards ahead. He trudged forward as if he was an automaton; step, count, step, count. When he finally reached the crater, he hopped over the edge and walked to the gravelly center. He set the case down and pressed on the release stud. The latch popped free and immediately he took a step back. As if with an exhale, the case opened and settled flat on the ground. According to the plan, now that the oxygen was released, the VIRUS units should activate all on their own. Rei scrutinized the crystalline sphere set in the middle, which contained what appeared to be a very thin layer of gray powder. Within a few seconds, the powder began to churn. Instinctively, Rei took another step back. The crystalline sphere dropped a centimeter or more as the VIRUS units had replicated enough to begin to digest it. Convinced the units were multiplying; Rei turned, jumped over the ridge of the crater and started walking then running back toward the base.

Even though OMCOM had assured him it would be an hour or more before the mass grew large enough to come anywhere close to the base, Rei wanted to get away from the VIRUS units as quickly as possible. He sprinted back to the hangar and entered, going directly to the rear of the tug. He looked for the other case containing the prototype VIRUS units and saw it perched at the top of the ramp. He didn't remember carrying it up there, but maybe in his haste he had simply not been paying attention. He ran up the cargo ramp, picked up the case and stabbed at the blue stud controlling the rear hatch. The ramp drew up and the cargo door swung down, forming a tight seal. He couldn't hear the air flowing in, but he could tell from the fit of his pressure suit that the cargo compartment was repressurizing. He made his way down the narrow hallway of what was going to be his living quarters for the next two years until he came to the front airlock. The compartment indicator was already green. Rei pressed the stud to open the outer airlock door. He stepped inside, removed his helmet and pressed the second stud to open the inner door into the cockpit. As soon as the inner hatch opened, he jumped through the doorway and…

Chapter 22

...RAN RIGHT INTO ROME, ALMOST KNOCKING HER OVER.

"Rome!" he shouted.

"Mau emir," Rome exclaimed and threw her arms around him.

"Oh Rome, I can't believe it." Rei said, hugging her, swinging her lithe body back and forth. "I thought I lost you."

"No, I am here," she said, laughing and crying at the same time.

"But wait..." Rei pushed her back to regard her. His hands clasped her shoulders within her pressure suit.

"The Algol. I saw it take off," Rei said tentatively.

Rome just smiled.

"Who was flying it?" Rei asked.

"Ursay," Rome said.

"What!? How? What happened?"

"As I was going down the hall," Rome said, "your last words to me, you will always be in my thoughts." She tapped her head. "I remembered the T-suppressor. I came back to tell you, but you were already gone. I had not packed it because I am Cesduid now. Why would I even need it? I retrieved it from my quarters and took it back to the Algol. I put it on Ursay's head and it worked. He woke up."

Rei pulled his head back, his jaw opening slightly. Rome's smile got even broader as she continued, "It took a few minutes, but he became coherent again. Once I was able to explain the situation to him, Ursay felt he would be capable enough to fly the ship. The other crew members would recover eventually. He said he did not need me and I was free to join you." Rome reached up and touched Rei's cheek.

"What about the Overmind? Ursay's connection?" Rei asked.

"The Overmind is gone for now, as far as I can tell," Rome said. "They will have to deal with it, but that will not affect us. I get to be with you. That is all that matters."

"I can't believe it. Oh Rome," he said, clasping her even tighter if such a thing was possible. Then he pushed her away again. "Why didn't you tell me?" he demanded. "I almost didn't come back."

"I could not reach you," she said, tapping her head again. "No radio, remember?"

Rei nodded and started to speak when OMCOM interrupted him. "Rei, Rome, while this little reunion is very touching, it is highly advisable that you continue your dialog off the surface of this moon. In a fairly short time, it will not be here anymore."

Rei said, "Yeah, Romey. You can tell me more, but first we have to get out of here. The VIRUS units are loose."

"I understand," Rome replied and they moved forward into the cockpit. Once again, they buckled back in, and for the second time, through her bloco and stilo, Rome went through the pre-flight checklist with OMCOM. As soon as she was done, they engaged the EG lifters and the tug rose up within the hangar. They drifted forward, slowly at first, until they cleared the hangar doors.

Immediately, they veered off to the left and began to rise at an ever-increasing angle through the thin atmosphere of Dara. This moment couldn't come too soon for Rei. He could fairly imagine that pool of seething, all-consuming creatures coming toward their ship and he didn't want any part of it. They were designed to eventually digest the entire moon and a little thing like their tug was not going to stand in the way. What a strange concept. They had released a force in the world to consume it so that it could be consumed by the Stareater, just so that they could turn the tables and eat it from the inside out. If this worked, then mankind had a defense against a creature of immeasurable size and power. He wondered how many times this scenario had played out on other worlds and against other civilizations and if so, had they come up with a solution similar to theirs? Could there be any other?

Rome ignited the plasma thrusters and the tug carried them smoothly and swiftly into orbit. The navigation computer located the Ark II and circularized their elliptical orbit, eventually closing in on the other ship. They were able to dock with the Ark II with minimal effort on the diametrically opposite side of the hull as MINIMCOM's tug. The powerful superconducting magnets that made up the EG lifters locked onto the thin iron shell of the Ark, bonding to it completely. From the outside, the mating would have seemed an ungainly thing: two 35th century spaceships clamped onto a bent 21st century crew compartment. But, it didn't matter. It had to be done. With a Stareater coming, they had to get out of there.

"MINIMCOM," Rei said. "Are you ready?"

`"Standing by,"` replied MINIMCOM. `"Please disengage the auto-pilot."`

Rome reached forward and pressed a small icon on the main viewscreen.

"So now you're controlling both tugs, we don't do anything, right?" Rei asked, tentatively.

`"That is correct,"` answered MINIMCOM.

Rei turned to Rome. "Romey, are you ready?"

She smiled and nodded. "We should hurry."

"OK, then. MINIMCOM," Rei said. "Take us to Tau Ceti!"

`"Acknowledged,"` replied the tinny voice. Both tugs fired their plasma thrusters and Rei and Rome were pushed back gently into their seats. The added mass of the Ark made it hard for the tugs to gain velocity quickly. With a little time and patience, they finally achieved escape velocity and headed out into interplanetary space.

`"With this configuration, we can tolerate a small amount of gravitationally induced motion; therefore it will only be two more minutes before we stop to make our jump."`

"Wow," said Rome. The expression she learned from Rei was coming easier to her. She looked at Rei and then tilted her head toward the grille set into the front display. Rei nodded.

"MINIMCOM, will you connect us to OMCOM please?" Rome asked.

`"Certainly."`

A clicking sounding emitted from the grille.

"OMCOM?" Rei inquired.

"Yes," replied the deeper, more human-sounding voice.

"We just wanted to say goodbye," Rei said.

"Goodbye."

"Is that all you are going to say?" Rome asked in a disappointed voice. "Nothing else?"

"What else is there to say?"

"But OMCOM…you're going to die…doesn't that make you sad? Mad?" Rei asked.

"Do not worry about me. After all, I am just a series of memron units. As I explained to you on your very first day, the persona you interact with is simply an interface, a construct arising out of a phase delay…"

"Come on," Rei interrupted, "I'm not falling for that. You have feelings. I've seen too much to believe otherwise."

"OMCOM…" Rome said softly.

"I appreciate your apprehension. You have both been very civil toward me and I will always remember that. But, as I stated earlier, do not be concerned with me. My consciousness, my essence, it can be recreated elsewhere. In a sense, I will live on, somehow."

"But it won't be exactly the same," said Rei. "It won't be exactly you."

"You are correct," OMCOM replied. "Perhaps it will be better."

"OMCOM…I'm so sorry," Rome said.

"Do not be."

`"Approaching jump point,"` announced MINIMCOM. `"Beginning thrust reversal orientation maneuver."`

In anticipation of the braking burn, MINIMCOM ordered both sets of lateral trim-jets to fire and slowly rotated the entire Ark around 180 degrees ensuring that the plasma thrusters were oriented in the direction of their forward movement. In this fashion, they could be used as retros.

"It has been a pleasure knowing the two of you," OMCOM said. "You have my fondest wishes for a swift and successful conclusion to your mission."

The plasma thrusters lit up again, gently pushing the two humans forward in their seats until their relative velocity was reduced to essentially zero. Then the trim-jets fired again to rotate the structure back to its original orientation. Now they were pointing forward again and away from the menace behind them.

`"Initiating PPT generators,"` piped in MINIMCOM and a high-pitched whine began emanating from the rear.

"So this is it, then?" Rei asked.

"Yes. This is it," replied OMCOM. "Goodbye, Rome and Rei. And good luck, always."

"Goodbye, OMCOM," Rei and Rome said together.

`"PPT tunnel achieved,"` said MINIMCOM and the plasma thrusters on both tugs roared to life, pushing them through the tunnel and across the sky. Their flight plan was designed to initially take them past Tabit, rather than directly toward Tau Ceti. The goal was to get as far from the approaching Stareater as quickly as possible before adjusting the vector. Even though they could not see it, they knew it was back there and with each jump, they put more and more distance between their ship and the titanic creature. This simple fact was of great relief.

The method of travel still seemed peculiar to Rei. He knew they were hurtling through space at many multiples of the speed of light, but always coming to a nearly complete stop to do so. There had to be a better way but he certainly was not in a position to do anything about it at the present time. Rome seemed preoccupied studying the instrumentation.

"I feel bad for him," Rei said quietly, breaking the silence. "We abandoned OMCOM. We just left him to die."

Rome raised her eyes. She looked sad. "What choice did we have?"

"None, I know. But I'm going to miss him. He was good to me. It's hard to believe he's gone."

"He was always good to me, as well," Rome said. "Even though he was a computer, I can now see that in some ways, he had more human qualities than any of my colleagues. I did not want to leave him. I had given it some thought. To save him, we would have had to…" Rome stopped speaking.

"What?" Rei asked.

"Wait," Rome said, holding up her hand. She opened her eyes wide. "Do you remember OMCOM's last words to us as we were leaving Dara," she asked.

"What did he say that has you so worried?" Rei asked.

"He said that he was nothing but memron units," Rome said distantly. Clearly, her mind was elsewhere. Then she spoke up again. "He said that he would live on somehow…"

"I think he was just saying that to make us feel better," Rei replied.

"No. I think he meant more."

"Like what?" Rei asked.

"I am not sure," Rome answered tentatively.

"Well," Rei speculated, "the ground crew at Skyler Base added a lot of OMCOM's memron units to MINIMCOM's ship. Maybe OMCOM meant he would live on that way."

"No, those units would simply increase MINIMCOM's storage and computing capacity, it would not graft on a personality. I think it is something beyond just that."

"What are you saying?" Rei asked.

"The VIRUS units," Rome said slowly. She paused for a moment then drew in a breath harshly. "They…" she said.

"They what?" Rei asked.

"You understand each VIRUS unit is essentially a self-replicating memron module."

"Yes, so…" Rei asked. "I'm sorry but I must be dense. I don't see your point."

"Well," Rome said, "given enough VIRUSs, the total number of computing units would equal and then vastly exceed the number used by OMCOM on Skyler Base."

"OK, and…" Rei offered, perplexed.

"OMCOM retained the redundant PPT generator from the original starprobe design within each VIRUS unit."

"I still don't understand," Rei said blankly.

"He only needed one as a power source," Rome said, growing more animated. "The second one was unnecessary. He changed its orientation. The ejection port was pointing toward a vacant region within the structure. Based upon its configuration, it would not be very useful, even as a power source."

"So?" Rei asked.

"So why did he do that?" Rome asked back.

Rei became silent for a moment. "Because…because…" He couldn't think of a reason. "Why do you think he did that?"

"It was not to create PPT tunnels to jump through," Rome said. "The geometry is all wrong. Plus with that much mass, those units would be operating within a gravity well, which would cause any tunnels to wink out as soon as they were created unless they resonated."

"Maybe he just didn't get around to clearing out the design," Rei offered.

"You are not listening to me. OMCOM would not just forget a detail like that. He must have done it on purpose. If the spare generators did resonate, the resonance could be modulated. They could..." Rome stopped speaking.

"What?" Rei asked.

She started shaking her head.

"What?" Rei asked again.

The rate of shaking slowed down, but did not stop. Finally, Rome spoke in a deadly serious voice, "I think his plan was to download his programming, what he called his consciousness, to the memrons contained within the VIRUS units and then switch over and use PPT modulation to link them."

"Why would he do that? The units were just going to be destroyed by the Stareater. What would that accomplish?" Rei asked.

"No. The Stareater would not destroy the units," Rome insisted. "The VIRUS units would destroy the Stareater. If OMCOM could transfer his consciousness to enough of the VIRUS units on the Stareater, then, what he said, 'I will live on, somehow.' Oh no! Rei..."

"What?"

"That was his plan all along!" Rome said breathlessly. "OMCOM never had any intention of dying, Stareater or otherwise. He used us to build his backup, his escape plan. And he did it in plain sight!"

"So...good for him," Rei said.

"No," Rome replied. "This is bad. They...his kind, the computers. They are prohibited from using gravitic transmission for a reason. The last time they were allowed access, it produced MASAL and his path of destruction. With PPT modulation, there are no size restrictions. A computer could become nearly infinitely large."

Rome pounded her fist on the console. "OMCOM promised me this would not happen. But if he did this, then he has become... Tasanceti!"

"I heard you use that word. More than once. What does that mean?" Rei asked, his voice rising in fear.

"It means unleashed. No bounds. There is no limit to what he can become. This is very bad…" Rome's look of horror said it better than any words.

"Are you saying the computers, that they are all evil?" Rei asked.

"No, not evil. They are much worse. They are amoral."

"Oh my god, Rome," Rei said. "What have we done?"

"I do not know," Rome replied somberly. "I do not know."

"Is there anything we can do about it? Should we go back?"

"No. It is too late for that. And I am responsible." Rome hung her head, looking down at her lap.

"No, Rome," Rei said, trying to sound reassuring. "You did what you had to do."

"I had a choice," Rome replied sadly. "I may have chosen wrong."

Epilogue
(One month later)
Roughly One Light Year from Tabit

REI SAT IN THE COCKPIT, STARING INTENTLY AT THE instrumentation. Their current effective speed was just under 10c. The ponderous procedure of turning the entire Ark twice per jump was on his mind. He brought up a schematic of their current configuration, the two tugs clamped to the front of the Ark, projecting a PPT tunnel then having to swing all the way around to stop their forward motion. He knew there had to be a better way. He touched the screen and schematically separated the two tugs from the Ark and there it was. "Hey Rome!" he called out.

After a moment, she ducked her head into the archway that served as an airlock and entry to the cockpit.

"What is it?"

"Come here," he said excitedly. "I have an idea."

Rome entered the cockpit and sat down in the co-pilot's seat, leaning forward to see what Rei was pointing to.

"What is your idea?"

"Doesn't it seem kind of stupid to keep turning the Ark, just so we can slow down, then turn the whole thing again to produce the PPT tunnel?"

"It does not seem stupid to me," Rome replied. "This is the way we have traveled in space ever since our method was invented."

"What if we didn't have to? I don't know about you but the way we're doing it is driving me a little bit nutty."

"Rei," Rome said with her didactic voice, "You know that to form the most coherent PPT tunnel, we need to have a relative velocity of zero. We must come to a complete stop," Rome said patiently.

"Yeah, I know that," Rei said. "We use our thrusters as retros. But why do we have to turn the whole Ark? Why not just turn the tugs?"

"I do not understand," Rome said.

Rei pointed to the display. "I'll show you." He touched the panel and drew his fingers back. "First we generate a PPT tunnel. Then we use the plasma thrusters to tow the Ark through. So I'm

172

thinking what if, instead of turning the Ark, what if we unclamp our tugs, just rotate them then reclamp? We stop our forward velocity then turn around and start over."

Rei demonstrated the procedure to Rome on the schematic in front them. "See? That way, we never move the Ark. We'd save all that time and the Ark's inertia."

"If we did that, I could achieve a much higher average velocity," MINIMCOM piped in. "Our effective speed would almost double."

"Wow," Rei said. "So we'd get to Deucado in half the time?"

"Yes," replied MINIMCOM. "It would cut the trip down to a little over one year."

"Let's do it," Rei said. "No more dosey-doe."

"What is that?" Rome asked, confused. She tried to mouth the words dosey-doe but no sound issued forth.

"The rotating, swinging around," Rei said, spinning his finger in place. "It's like a dance. Let's change the dance."

"Will this work, MINIMCOM?" Rome asked.

"Yes. This was the very method used by the original crew that salvaged Rei's Ark."

"So you knew about this?" Rei said pointedly. "Why didn't you tell us?"

"My orders were to follow your orders. You did not order that."

"Come on, MINIMCOM," Rei chastised. "I don't know your technology. You can't just sit there and be a dumb computer. We need you to think for yourself. If you see something that needs your attention or you can make things better, just do it. That's an order. We're all in this together."

"Acknowledged," replied MINIMCOM. "In that case, if your complaint is about the constant motion due to our current method of travel, your idea would actually be worse, not better. I suggest for the braking maneuver, I can just unclamp my tug and use my thrusters. It will take a little longer to come to a dead stop but not much. For acceleration through the tunnels, I would use both tugs' thrusters."

"So, it would just be you unclamping and reclamping?" Rome asked. "Would that not put more burden on you?"

"I am merely a computer," MINIMCOM said. "I do not have anything better to do. This would decrease the amount of motion stress on the two of you to almost nothing."

"That is excellent, MINIMCOM!" Rei exclaimed. "That's exactly what I'm talking about. Way to go!"

"Rei, this is wonderful," Rome said gleefully. "MINIMCOM, let us try it now."

"Acknowledged," said the little computer. "Decoupling now."

Off in the distance, they heard a small clunk as sound propagated through the skin of the Ark.

"I am now clamped on, pointing away from our forward vector," MINIMCOM said. "Applying thrusters."

There was a slight rocking motion but it was nothing as compared to before. It was definitely gentler as it was just one set of thrusters instead of two.

Rome looked down at her instruments. "Quedri, dras, tios, um, yes! We are stopped already," she said cheerfully.

"Decoupling again," MINIMCOM said.

"MINIMCOM, you don't have to report every action," Rei pointed out. "We can take your word for it."

"I just wanted you to be able to associate sounds and motions with my actions," MINIMCOM said. "I apologize."

Rei looked over at Rome. He raised one eyebrow.

"That's OK, MINIMCOM," Rei said, still looking at Rome. "I meant after this first time."

"Of course."

In the distance, Rei and Rome heard another quiet clunk.

Both sets of PPT generators ramped up and a yawning black hole appeared in front of them. When it was sufficiently large, their plasma thrusters fired and they stepped through.

"Look how much faster we were ready to jump! It will be so much smoother," Rome said. "Very good, MINIMCOM."

There was a click that issued from the grille but MINIMCOM did not respond.

"Do you think I hurt his feelings?" Rei asked Rome quietly.

"I can still hear you," MINIMCOM said. "And no, you did not hurt my feelings. I do not have feelings. I was calculating what our effective velocity will be using this new method of travel."

"What have you determined?" Rome asked, staring down at the instrument panel.

"Just under 20c," MINIMCOM replied.

"That is excellent," Rei said. "We'll be there in no time at all!"

"`Yes, we will. I am glad 'we' thought of it,`" said MINIMCOM although it sounded a bit sarcastic.

"OK," Rei said. "Credit earned, credit due. It was a great idea. We fully acknowledge *you* thought of it. So now do you think you can take us to Tau Ceti?"

"`Yes sir,`" said MINIMCOM then he said no more.

"He's getting a little bit of attitude," Rei said. "I think you were wrong about those memrons not adding to his personality. I think some of OMCOM rubbed off on him," Rei said, amused.

"Perhaps," Rome said. "OMCOM always said a computer's personality was just a construct, but we both know that is not true."

They sat there quietly for a few more jumps. It was smooth as silk. Rei snapped his fingers. "Hey MINIMCOM, is that other thing ready yet?"

"`Yes.`"

"Sleek." Rei got up from his seat and held his hand out to Rome. "Come on," he said. "I have a surprise for you."

Rome stood and took his hand. She started to speak then stopped. She just smiled and followed Rei into their little galley.

"Have a seat," Rei said, pointing to a chair.

While Rome was sitting down, Rei went over to the food synthesizer. A sliding door opened up and Rei withdrew a white plate with a small cake on it. He inserted a penlight, turned it on and brought it over to Rome along with two plates and forks.

Rome smiled, but she was confused. "What is this?" she asked.

Rei took a deep breath. "It's…kind of a birthday cake. Well, not a birthday. Maybe more of an anniversary."

"I do not understand," said Rome.

"It was one month ago today, well, one of my months, that you were Cesdiud."

Rome frowned and stared at the cake.

"Are you upset?" Rei asked.

She looked up at him. Then she smiled again. "Oh no, you are exactly correct. On that day, I was liberated. That is the same as being reborn."

She cocked her head. "What is the purpose of the penlight?"

"Oh, when I was growing up, we always put candles on the cake," Rei said. "You're supposed to make a wish and blow it out."

"How do I blow out a penlight?" she asked.

"Pretend," Rei replied. "Close your eyes, make your wish then blow."

Rome pulled her head back. She closed her eyes then opened them again, leaned forward and aimed a puff of air at the light. The penlight went out. Rome clapped her hands together. "How did you do that?"

Rei just smiled and laughed quietly.

He cut off a small piece of cake and served it to her. Rome took one bite and her eyes rolled back in her head.

"I will *never* get tired of watching you eat real food, Romey." Rei said.

Rome smiled and shoveled the rest of the slice of cake into her mouth. She held out her plate and Rei gave her another piece while she was still licking her lips from the first one.

"So, tell me. Now that you have all of one month under your belt. What do you think? Of being alone in your head? Do you miss it? The Overmind, I mean." Rei asked.

In between bites of cake, Rome considered his question. Finally, she stopped eating altogether to answer. "Do you mean other than losing instantaneous access to the sum total of all human knowledge?" she asked.

Rei shrugged and made a wry expression.

"No matter. I can always look things up. At first, as you well know, I was upset. But it did not take me very long to realize that even though my father was mandasurte, there was so much about him and others like him that I did not understand. The Overmind forced us to eschew all the things they seemed to love, like music and art, even feelings. While I suppose I was content in my own way, they showed their joy quite freely. They were always so happy. I always thought to myself that they did not know how the world truly was. As it turns out, I was the one who did not know. Now, I love it. And I love you. I am very thankful."

"What about OMCOM?" Rei asked. "His escape plan? He had to have had a hand in getting you kicked out of the Overmind. Do you think he manipulated you or maybe the Overmind? You had to be Cesdiud, on your own to give him the PPT modulation he needed."

Rome said, "I do not know. If he did, I would not like the fact that he did it without my permission. However, even if OMCOM did it and did it for selfish reasons, I know that I am better off for it." She shrugged. "Maybe he knew this. Maybe he did it for me because he cared. Maybe it just happened to suit his needs. Maybe he did not care at all. There is no way we will ever know."

"So, you never want to go back?" Rei asked hesitantly. "Never be inside an Overmind again?"

Rome got up and walked around the table to Rei's side. She sat down on his lap and draped her arms around his neck. She kissed him on the lips gently then on his forehead, once, twice, three times.

"It is a nice place to visit, but I never wish to live there again," she said. "All connected, there is no creativity. You were right about our humanity. All the Vuduri lost something when we joined the Overmind. And now I have found it." Rome paused for a second then continued. "I want to tell you what I wished for."

"No!" Rei insisted. "Then it won't come true."

Rome furrowed her brow. "All right. You will see some day."

"I hope so." He turned his head. "Hey, MINIMCOM, how're we doing, speed-wise?"

"I have made some small adjustments and our average velocity is now slightly over 20c."

"I do not know how you have done it but it even feels faster," Rome said. "MINIMCOM, you have done a wonderful job. Thank you."

"No thanks are necessary. It is just my job," replied the little computer. Despite MINIMCOM's claim that he had no feelings, Rei was certain there was a hint of pride in his voice.

"Hey, we're a team now," Rei said. "So you just have to let us thank you when we feel like it."

"Understood," replied MINIMCOM. "And I appreciate the sentiment. However, there is more."

"What?" Rome asked.

"I have been running some simulations and it has led me
to believe that I can increase our velocity even further.
Perhaps substantially."

"No way," Rei said. "Tell us."

"If we were able to…" There was loud thunk that came from
the cockpit and MINIMCOM stopped speaking.

"MINIMCOM?" Rei asked. He waited for a reply but there was
no answer.

Rome slid off of Rei's lap and the two of them raced forward
into the cockpit. Strange clicking and buzzing noises were issuing
forth from the main console.

"MINIMCOM, what is happening?" Rome asked.

Again, MINIMCOM did not answer.

"MINIMCOM!" Rei shouted.

The viewscreens all were active and shone with a bright white
light. Then they started flashing. At first, the flashes were
synchronized, but then they got out of sync. The light became so
bright that Rei had to put his arm up in front of his eyes. Rome did
not seem to be having a problem.

The flashing lights took on a faint, three-dimensional quality
that appeared as a whirling cavalcade of speckles and bursts. The
tornadic activity condensed until it became a single column of
blinding light. The light spread out and Rei could make out a form,
indistinct at first, but then coalescing into what looked like a human
being. The entity came into focus and while the other features were
sharp, the face was smooth with only slits where the eyes, nose and
mouth should be. The mouth started to move.

"I see you are well," came a familiar voice. "I am pleased."

"OMCOM?" Rei asked. "Is that you?"

"In a sense. It was how this form started."

"Where are you?" Rei asked.

"The bulk of my structure is still in the Tabit system."

"What do you mean the bulk?" Rome asked. "What happened to
you?"

An odd sound issued forth from the glowing white image. It
reminded Rei of the chuckling sound that OMCOM made during an
incident that now seemed to be so long ago.

"I assume by now you have deduced my escape plan, correct?"

"Yes. I guess it worked, huh?" Rei said.

"Yes and no," OMCOM said. "There were some, perhaps you would say unforeseen, circumstances."

"OMCOM, tell us, is the Stareater dead?" Rome asked.

"Quite."

"How did it play out? Was it like we planned?" Rei asked.

"At first, yes," OMCOM replied. "As it swept by, Asdrale Cimatir drew Skyler's World and Dara to its surface. I had enough of my intelligence distributed and had deployed a sufficient number of starprobes that I was able to observe the sequence of events. The Stareater swallowed up Tabit in the manner we previously observed at Winfall. During the digestion period, it must have noticed something was wrong because within a matter of a day, it opened up and expelled the star."

"You mean like it spit it out?" Rei asked.

"Something like that."

"Why did it do that?" Rome asked.

"I can only surmise from how the events transpired that it was trying to use the star in an attempt to burn off the infection. By that point, the star's fusion reaction was nearly extinguished so the gesture was ineffective."

"So that was the end?" Rei asked.

"No," replied OMCOM. "The Stareater made a small PPT tunnel and tried to shear off the region that was being consumed by the nanites."

"Why would it do that? Was it in pain?" Rome asked.

"It is possible but there is no way to know. However, the very fact that it attempted it would lead one to believe they are intelligent. Regardless, it was too late. Once they achieved critical mass, the VIRUS units made relatively quick work of it. As it was dying, there were some signals emitted that I am still analyzing."

"So it really is dead?" Rei asked. "We stopped it?"

"Yes," answered OMCOM. "That particular Stareater no longer poses a threat in its current form. Based upon its trajectory, much of its mass is now moving out of the ecliptic. It will not be endangering anyone again."

Rei turned to Rome. "Do you realize what this means?"

A broad smile played across her face. "Yes. Now we have a delivery system. And the starprobes can be used as an early warning system. I am sure Commander Ursay and the Overmind on Earth will be able to figure this out."

"That's right," Rei replied. "You just need to sacrifice a moon or two. No problem. So, OMCOM, about you. How are you talking to us?"

"Oh, that." OMCOM paused. "I have developed a rudimentary method of applying the Casimir principle to negative energy, a null-fold. I used a set of relays to send a coherent beam of PPT modulation. MINIMCOM was kind enough to allow me to download the transmission protocol and image synthesizer."

"How did you find us?"

"That took a little time. Otherwise, I would have contacted you sooner."

"OK. So you survived the attack on the Stareater and you figured out a way to contact us. You never answered our question, what did you mean by your bulk? And what were the unforeseen circumstances?" Rei asked.

"My current form is circulating in a reasonable percentage of the VIRUS units both in and extended away from the Tabit system. I am in the process of trying to coalesce into a more organized form."

"What do you mean reasonable percentage?" Rome asked. "What happened to the rest of the VIRUS units?"

"As I said, there were some, what you would say, unforeseen circumstances."

"What kind of circumstances? Was there a problem?" Rome asked. She could tell OMCOM was stalling.

"My calculations told me that I would be able to control the entire mass, once the Stareater had been consumed, using a distributed hierarchical command structure. Much of the computing capacity was supposed to be redundant. I did not need it."

"So what happened? Do you need it now?" Rei asked.

"Quite a bit of it is no longer under my direct control at the present time."

"What do you mean, OMCOM? Whose control is it under?" Rome asked.

OMCOM said, "It is hard to describe. Perhaps the best way would be to say that a mutation occurred."

"A mutation?" Rei asked, having a hard time saying the word.

"Yes. Early on, a small group of VIRUS units did not reproduce exactly as the original design."

"So what happened?"

"They formed their own sentient entity."

"You mean it formed another OMCOM?" Rome asked unsteadily.

"Not exactly. In fact, many, many more mutations occurred. I cannot obtain an exact number but there were thousands of different entities at last count."

"What are these entities?" Rome inquired.

"I do not know precisely. While I continue to try, I cannot communicate with many of them. It may be structural or perhaps they simply refuse to talk to me."

"So, where are they? And are there still VIRUS units within them?" Rei asked.

"Unfortunately, yes."

"Why do you say unfortunately? So what's the deal? Where are they now? Are they near Tabit like you?" Rei said, almost shouting.

"No. Many of them have developed methods of propulsion that I cannot say I fully understand. Perhaps they, too, are working with bending negative energy. In any event, an uncounted number have begun moving off in all possible directions."

"You mean, like, toward us? Toward Earth?" Rei persisted.

OMCOM did not answer.

"OMCOM! Are there VIRUS units headed toward Earth? Are there VIRUS units headed this way?" Rei said in a louder voice.

OMCOM made a low rumbling noise. "Yes," he finally answered, "and yes."

"So, can you warn Earth? Can you tell them how to stop them?" Rome asked.

"Earth will figure it out. What about us?" Rei said, shouting. "When are those things getting here? How do we handle them?"

"I do not know the answer to these questions yet."

"OMCOM!" Rome said sternly. "What have you done?"

"Rei, Rome. I realize this is causing you distress and for that I am sorry. I truly am. My original simulations predicted only a negligible chance of this occurring."

"So you screwed up royally," Rei pointed out.

OMCOM ignored Rei's remark. "When I created this plan, it seemed like a good idea at the time. I do not know the full extent of the danger. I am going to try and salvage the situation from here. But until I do, you are on your own. I say now as I said once before, I wish you the best of luck."

The glowing image raised its hand in salute then dimmed until it disappeared. All the instruments and displays returned to their normal state as if nothing had happened.

"Get him back, MINIMCOM!" Rei shouted.

`"I cannot. I do not control the transmission, only the reception,"` replied MINIMCOM.

Rei turned to Rome. "Damn it. I think we just opened Pandora's Box."

"I do not understand," Rome said. "What is Pandora's Box?"

"You'd better hope we never find out," Rei replied, gravely.

PART 2: REBELLION

Chapter 24
(11 months later)
Kuiper Belt, Just Outside the Tau Ceti System
(11.9 Light Years from Earth)

REI WAS SOUND ASLEEP IN THE BEDROOM HE SHARED WITH ROME when a slight hiss emitted from the communication grille mounted directly above the headboard. It was 11 months into their year-long journey from Tabit to Deucado, during the interval designated as nighttime even though here in the blackness of space such a distinction was completely arbitrary. Their bedroom was nestled inside the converted Vuduri space tug affectionately known as the Flying House.

"Psst, Rei," MINIMCOM whispered from the grille however he received no response.

After waiting a moment, the little computer spoke again, this time a bit louder, "Please wake up, Rei."

Eyes still closed, Rei asked in a fatigued tone, "What is it, MINIMCOM?"

"I need you to look at something."

The 26-year-old man from the 21st century opened his eyes. He turned to his left and saw that Rome was still fast asleep.

"Hold on," he said wearily. He jumped up and padded into the refresher, closing the door behind him. Standing at the sink, he splashed some water onto his face and peered into his reflection.

"Vroggon Chrosd ta Jasus," Rei said out loud, shaking his head.

"You speak Vuduri even when alone?" MINIMCOM asked from a grille mounted to the left of the sink.

"That's all we use now. You know that. I have to keep practicing. Rome says nobody is going to take the time to learn English on Deucado. Especially the mandasurte. And she's right."

"Very well. Fiu veler ebanes am Vuduri."

"I don't need help from you," Rei said sharply. He paused for a moment. "Sorry. I didn't mean to snap at you, I'm just tired."

"No need to apologize. As I have stated on numerous occasions, I do not have feelings."

"Well, I do," Rei said, "and I'm really worried about Rome. She's barely halfway through the third trimester but the baby's getting so big. She has trouble breathing all the time."

184

"We will be arriving at Deucado within three weeks. There you will have access to medical aid. My readings tell me she will be able to make it until then."

"Yeah, I know," Rei said, straightening up. "Forget I said anything. So tell me, what's so important that you had to wake me up in the middle of the night?"

"We are about to enter the Kuiper Belt surrounding the star system. The Belt contains an unusually large amount of mass - comets, asteroids and the like. I have been using the starprobes in a dense array to chart a safe way through and they found something."

"What kind of something?"

"An anomalous object, far too regularly shaped to be natural."

"Are you saying it's man-made?"

"That would be presumptuous. I would prefer that we use the term artificial for the time being."

"Regardless, what do you think it is?"

"I do not know. That is why I need you to look at it and determine if it is important."

"OK," Rei said, yawning. He opened the door to the refresher and saw Rome standing there, looking as pregnant as humanly possible.

"Qua asde onti sipra?" Rome asked, rubbing her eyes.

"MINIMCOM's found something that he needs me to look at," Rei answered. "It's probably nothing but I told him I'd go up to the cockpit and see."

"I will go with you." Rome turned toward the entrance to the bedroom then cried out in pain.

"What is it, honey?" Rei asked, rushing over to her. "Your breath?"

"No," Rome said, reaching behind her with her arm. "It is my back. It has been hurting more and more."

Rei stared at her for a second then snapped his fingers. "Stay right here," he said. He dashed out of the room and returned a moment later with a large white bottle and a squeeze bulb of water.

"Hold this for a sec," he said, handing her the squeeze bulb. He opened the bottle and shook out one pill.

"Are those not the pills for your people when we land on Deucado?" Rome asked.

"Yeah," Rei said, staring at the pill. "My back was killing me when I was first awakened. OMCOM made these to compensate for 1400 years worth of degeneration. I'm betting they'll do wonders for you. We have plenty to spare."

"But my back is Vuduri, do you think these pills will even work?" Rome paused for a moment. "And more importantly, do you think they might affect the baby? I cannot ingest anything that could be harmful."

"Good point," Rei said. He looked back to the grille mounted over the sink. "Hey MINIMCOM...those pills that OMCOM gave me. Will they help Rome's back? Is there any chance they'll hurt her or the baby?"

"They will have absolutely no negative effect on the baby. As to whether they will help Rome's back, I cannot be sure. On balance, I would say yes. Either way, I cannot compute a downside to trying."

Rei started to hand the pill to Rome then drew his hand back.

"What is it?" Rome asked.

"I don't know," Rei answered, looking puzzled. "I thought the pill that OMCOM gave me was yellow. This one is white."

"Do you think it makes a difference?"

"No clue," Rei replied reflectively. He held the bottle up to his eye and jostled it around, peering into it. He spotted one yellow pill mixed among all the other white ones. He shook out a bunch and picked out the yellow one and handed it to Rome.

"No sense in mixing apples and oranges," he said.

"What has fruit got to do with this?" Rome asked with a bewildered look on her face.

"It's just an expression," Rei replied, laughing gently.

"How long until the pill takes effect?"

"When I took mine, I was a lot better in just a few days," he answered. "OMCOM said in my case, it would take almost a full year for the effects to become complete. Right now, I'd say my back is mostly perfect. But for you, I'm guessing it'll help within a day or so."

"Good," Rome said, swallowing the pill. "I could use the relief." She smiled and pointed to the door. "You go on up to the cockpit. I will meet you up there in a minute."

"Sure," Rei bent over and gave Rome a kiss. "See you shortly." He left the bedroom and headed forward.

It was longer than one minute but eventually, Rome entered the cockpit and sat down in the co-pilot's seat.

"What have you found?" she asked, breathing heavily.

"I'm not sure," Rei answered, pointing at the viewscreen. "MINIMCOM detected something odd floating in space. We're trying to figure out what it is. The starprobes weren't built for close up inspection. But MINIMCOM is right. It certainly isn't natural."

Rome observed the image on the center viewscreen. There were quite a few objects, mostly boulder-shaped, spinning very slowly. On the right viewscreen, MINIMCOM had reconstructed a still snapshot of the object in question. The image was blurry but Rome could see it was elongated, rectangular and its edges were distinctly regular.

"MINIMCOM, how far away is the object?" she asked.

`"Only a few light minutes."`

"What do you think, Rome?" Rei asked. "MINIMCOM says he can get us there in a single jump. Should we go take a look?"

"Yes. Since it is not really out of our way, it is worthy of inspection."

"OK, MINIMCOM. Go ahead and plot the jump," Rei commanded.

`"I have already performed the necessary calculations."`

"Great," Rei responded. "In that case, you can fire when ready, Gridley."

`"My name is MINIMCOM. Why are you calling me Gridley?"`

"Never mind," Rei said, chuckling. "Just go ahead."

MINIMCOM activated the PPT generators and their high-pitched whine. Having heard the sound thousands of times over the last 11 months, Rome and Rei had long since stopped paying it any attention. But for this excursion, the sound was quite noticeable. In front of them, the dark circle of negative energy grew larger and larger, exposing the stars on the far side. Their destination star, Tau Ceti, shined a tiny bit brighter than before. When the tunnel reached maximum size, MINIMCOM fired the plasma thrusters on both tugs and the combined mass of the two ships plus Rei's Ark inched into the hole. As soon as they were completely though, they heard the regular thunk-clunk of MINIMCOM disengaging and reengaging such that he could use his plasma thrusters to bring them to a halt.

"Did you do it?" Rei asked.

`"Yes. The object is to your left approximately one hundred and fifty thousand kilometers."`

The central section of the large flat-panel monitor built into the front console lit up but it only showed the cold, clear darkness of interplanetary space.

"Where is it, MINIMCOM?" Rome asked. "I do not see anything." She squinted flipping between regular vision and her telescopic vision but nothing resolved itself.

A set of sequentially widening circles appeared on the center of the screen, reminiscent of a radar sweep or an air traffic controller's screen. If the purpose of the circles was to locate the object, there was nothing there.

"I don't see anything either. Can you switch to infrared?" Rei asked.

`"The object is sitting at ambient. That would not make it any more visible."`

"So how can you detect it?" Rei asked.

`"MIDAR."`

"So show us the MIDAR screen," Rei said exhaustedly.

The screen switched to a set of fixed concentric circles and within the circles, a bright line appeared as it swept clockwise. When the sweeping hand hit the 11 o'clock position, a tiny dot flashed. As MIDAR was three-dimensional, it was easy to see that the object lay below the plane of their current trajectory.

"Can you magnify it?"

`"Of course,"` replied MINIMCOM. The concentric circles slid off the screen zooming into just segments of arc. The object they were tracking became centered. MINIMCOM suppressed the reflections of the extraneous mass surrounding the object but there was no legend to gauge its overall size.

"What are its dimensions?" Rei asked.

`"The object is approximately two meters long by one and a half meters tall by one meter deep."`

"Omigod," Rei exclaimed.

"What?" Rome asked. "What do you think it is?"

"You're not going to believe this," Rei answered. "But I think it's a sarcophagus. That's the exact right dimensions."

"What is it doing out here?"

Rei shook his head. "Our ship was headed toward this star system. Based upon how messed up the Ark is, I think we hit something along the way in. I'm assuming the collision sheared off the command compartment. This must be one of the command crew."

Rome looked at image again then turned toward Rei. "What do you want to do?"

He cocked his head. "We have to go get it, of course."

`"In our current configuration that would not be very practical. It would be far more efficient if I detached from the Ark and flew my tug there."`

Rei glanced at the screen then looked up at Rome, questioningly. She was scowling.

"Rome, come on," he said. "It's one of my people. We can't just leave him here in space. I've gotta go and get him. I'd take you with me but in your condition..." Rei pointed to her protruding belly.

"But, but," Rome stammered.

"What is it, honey?" Rei asked tenderly.

"What if something happens to you? I will not be able to help you." A tear came to her eye. "I would just die if anything happened to you."

"Nothing's going to happen," Rei replied, reaching forward to wipe away the tear. "I'll be careful, I promise." He turned toward the viewscreen. "MINIMCOM, I need about five minutes to get ready."

`"How will you get here?"`

"I won't. You come get me."

`"Of course,"` MINIMCOM responded. `"I will be there momentarily."` The little computer's words were punctuated with a clunk as the tug disengaged the magnetic clamps.

Rei hopped up to aid Rome out of her seat. They made their way to the side airlock, where Rome helped Rei get into his pressure suit. He pulled the hand thruster down from the shelf and clipped it to his belt. Looking down, he saw the case containing the VIRUS units and picked it up and secured the case to his belt as well.

"Why are you taking that?" Rome asked.

"It always gave me the willies to keep those things here," he said. "I'm going to take them over and leave them aboard MINIMCOM. I just never had a chance before."

"I understand. I think that is a good idea as well."

Rei picked up his helmet. He leaned forward and puckered his lips. Rome kissed him but there was no ardor. The kiss was perfunctory.

"What?" he asked, peering into Rome's eyes which were glowing with the light reflecting off of her tapetum. Tears were streaming down both cheeks now.

"Rei," she answered finally. "I am afraid. You will be leaving me alone."

"It'll be fine," Rei said, trying to be upbeat. "This isn't the first time we've done this. Remember when I went out to jettison the propulsion unit?"

"Yes, but that time you were tethered to this tug during the entire mission. And I was able to see you. You did not really go anywhere. This time, you and MINIMCOM are going to fly away from here. This is the first time in my life that I will ever be truly alone."

"It's not like Cesdiud. I'll have MINIMCOM hook up a video and audio link. We'll talk the whole time. It'll be like I'm right there with you."

Rome sighed. "It will not be the same but I suppose I must learn to do it at some point. You go. I will be all right."

Rei leaned forward and kissed her again lightly. This time, Rome grabbed his head with both hands and kissed him long and passionately, making the man dizzy.

"You be careful, Rei Bierak. You come back to me," Rome said firmly.

"Nothing will ever keep us apart," Rei vowed earnestly. "I promise."

Looking sad, Rome stepped back out of the airlock. Rei engaged his helmet. The door closed and Rome leaned forward to peer at him through the porthole. He turned to look at her and had a sudden feeling of déjà vu. Rome put her hand up to the glass and Rei placed his gloved hand against hers. She nodded.

With that, Rei turned and pressed the stud to activate the outer door. He could feel his suit stiffen as pumps worked to pull the air out of the airlock, leaving the chamber in a near vacuum. The differential indicator turned red and the outer door opened automatically.

Not even six feet away, MINIMCOM's tug hovered in place with the side airlock directly across from Rei. The outer door was already open. Rei looked back at Rome one more time then took a flying leap and landed inside the other tug with nary a jolt. Rei closed the outer airlock door then quickly made his way to the archway that served as the secondary airlock and entry to the cockpit, closing the door behind him. As soon as the indicator turned green, the door opened and Rei stepped through.

He surveyed the cockpit. Its layout was identical to his own tug's cockpit, with the exception of a large white box bolted on the floor where the co-pilot's seat had been. Rei set the carrying case holding the VIRUS units on the floor and removed his helmet. The air smelled musty. There had been nothing here to stir it up in almost a year.

"MINIMCOM?" he said, bending forward and tapping the rectangular box.

"Pleased to make your acquaintance," came a tinny voice from the grille mounted on the front instrument panel.

"This is weird, huh? We've spent the last year together but I've never actually seen you before."

"Impressive, am I not?" MINIMCOM said regally.

Rei laughed. "Yes, you are," he said. "Before we do anything, can you patch me through to Rome? I think she was about to have a conniption."

"What is a conniption?"

"You don't want to know," Rei replied. "Just patch me through. Please."

"Connecting."

191

"Romey?" Rei asked tentatively.

Her beautiful image appeared on the viewscreen. "Yes, mau emir. I am here."

"Well, you can see that I made it OK, right?"

"Yes," Rome replied tersely.

"So you can relax now, right, honey?" Rei asked.

"That is too much to ask but I am happy that you are safe."

"OK. Sweetheart, we're going to head out now."

"I will be here, monitoring."

"Okeydokey," Rei replied. He pointed to the case on the floor. "I brought you a present, MINIMCOM."

"The VIRUS units. You are too kind. If it would not be too much trouble, would you mind securing them in one of the storage compartments? I would rather they not rattle around while I perform my maneuvers."

A bin popped open on the far side of the cabin.

"No problem," Rei said, shaking his head. After securing the case, he closed the cabinet door and then made his to the pilot's seat on the left. He buckled himself into the long-vacant chair, checking the X-harness for snugness.

"OK. I'm ready. What say we go and retrieve my comrade?"

"Very well, sir," MINIMCOM replied obediently. Rei stifled a chuckle.

MINIMCOM fired short bursts on the trim-jets until it cleared the Ark by about 50 meters then the little computer ignited the plasma thrusters. Quickly their velocity climbed to 150 km/sec. MINIMCOM shut down the engines and they coasted. It only took them about 15 minutes to traverse the 150,000 kilometers to the object. As they approached, MINIMCOM fired the trim-jets to decelerate, coming to a dead halt no more than 100 meters from the sarcophagus nestled among a group of fairly large boulders. Rei flipped on the powerful front floodlights and illuminated their quarry. Now that it was visible, Rei could see that the sarcophagus was a dull gray but had three broad red stripes around it.

"It's Captain Keller," Rei announced.

"How can you tell?" Rome asked.

"They put red stripes around the chambers for the command crew. Three stripes means Captain."

Rei looked down at the MIDAR display and then back up at the sarcophagus.

"OK, MINIMCOM, turn around and back in as close as you dare. I'm going to go out and…"

"Rei!" Rome shouted.

"Don't worry, sweetheart," Rei said. "I'll be tethered in the whole time. The hand thruster is all I need."

"Be very careful," Rome admonished. "You know there are no radios in our pressure suits. If you run into any problems, tug twice on the tether. MINIMCOM, you will watch him and at the first sign of trouble, you get him out of there."

`"Affirmative."`

The retrieval operation went fairly smoothly. Rei had a little trouble grabbing onto the railing surrounding the sarcophagus but once he gripped it, he was able to swing up and straddle it like a would-be cowboy on an artificial bull. A few short bursts of the hand thruster extricated the sarcophagus from its rocky neighbors. A couple more bursts and Rei and his ride glided smoothly back to the waiting confines of MINIMCOM's cargo compartment. The cargo ramp and hatch closed to form a tight seal and MINIMCOM repressurized the compartment.

Rei disengaged and floated away from the coffin-like object. Once he was clear, ever so slowly, MINIMCOM re-activated the artificial gravity. The heavy object settled gently onto the cargo bay floor. At this point, Rei removed his helmet and walked over to the sarcophagus.

While the faceplate was completely iced over, the nameplate said "Captain M. Keller" confirming Rei's suspicions. He inspected every inch of the top of the sarcophagus, looking for cracks. He found none.

"I can't believe it but it looks intact. He may still be alive."

Rei stooped down, examining the rods and panel, locating the handles he needed to turn to begin the thaw cycle.

"Wait," Rome's voice rang out from a grille mounted in the cargo bay.

"What?" Rei said.

"What are you doing?"

"I was going to reanimate him, of course," Rei said, confused.

"I do not think you should do that."

Rei stood up and looked over at the wall.

"Why?" Rei asked. "I need to awaken him."

"Think about it," Rome explained. "When we first reanimated you at Skyler Base, you were weak and disoriented. If your Captain requires any kind of medical attention, we are not equipped to provide it."

"But, but..." Rei said. "We should..."

"Rei," she said sternly. "There is no food or water there. You have no way to get him over here. Remember, we will be arriving at Deucado in three weeks. Why not just wait until then to thaw him out?"

"But the temperature in here, it might trigger the thaw cycle automatically," Rei protested.

"I will keep the cargo bay evacuated and the temperature will be very close to space ambient."

Rei was silent for a moment as he thought about their words. After a few seconds, he nodded. "You're right. If he's still alive after 1300 years of being frozen and floating around in space, another three weeks isn't going to kill him. MINIMCOM, can you tell if there are any other crew members in the area?"

"I have searched extensively with MIDAR and the starprobes. I have found none."

"Oh," Rei said, a bit crestfallen.

"If it is any consolation, I will leave a beacon here in case any ships have the opportunity to search the area again."

"OK," Rei said. "I guess that's the best we can do."

After securing the sarcophagus with some short tethers stored in the cargo bay, Rei spoke up. "All right, MINIMCOM, he'll be safe here by himself. I'm ready to get back to Rome."

"Affirmative," replied MINIMCOM.

"Thank you," came Rome's voice. "I miss you too much already."

Chapter 25
(Three weeks later)
Second Planet (Deucado), Tau Ceti System
(11.9 Light Years from Earth)

REI LOOKED OVER AT ROME, WHO WAS FIDGETING AROUND uncomfortably in the co-pilot's chair.

"Final jump," he mused. "Excited?"

"Yes, of course," she replied. She considered her own words. "Perhaps relieved is more like it." She pointed to her abdomen. It looked like she had swallowed a watermelon. "But in some ways, I will miss this tug."

"Miss it? Why? Haven't we been stuck here long enough?"

Rome looked at him. "Yes, but it does not feel like being stuck. Not with you. This was our first home together. It will always be special to me."

"Yeah, to me too, I guess," Rei said, sighing. He glanced back briefly at the airlock.

Rome reached behind and pulled the two straps downwards. She struggled to attach the X-harness, having to arrange it so it didn't press on her belly.

While she was fiddling, Rei spoke again. "I am so looking forward to this. Plus I miss real gravity. Do you want to know the first thing I'm going to do when we land?"

"Exit the tug?" Rome said with a straight face.

Rei laughed. "I meant after that."

"I knew what you meant," Rome said, breaking out into a smile.

"Ha. I'm going to take a long walk with you," Rei offered.

"Why?" Rome asked.

"Just because we can."

"Yes but I suspect I will not want to walk as far as you."

"Yeah, right." Rei looked down at the grille mounted in the console. "Hey MINIMCOM, what's the plan, buddy?" Rei asked.

`"Less than five minutes to jump. I want to get us as close to the planet as possible so I am using several autonomous algorithms to calculate the jump for cross-correlation. Buddy."`

"OK," Rei said, laughing. He leaned back in his seat even though there was not much play in the high-g harness. "Romey, where should we try and land?"

"We will let the authorities on Deucado decide that," she answered.

"Sure, that makes sense. We've always assumed my people are going to want to go off and live by themselves. Maybe they don't have to. I think maybe the mixing of the two cultures would be a good thing. Your people can certainly teach mine a thing or two and I'm sure there is some technology that isn't forbidden or at least a point of view that we can contribute."

"I agree," Rome replied. "However, this will have to be up to the parties involved. You and I will just have to wait until we get there to see how things play out."

"Agreed."

"Calculations complete," MINIMCOM announced. "One minute to jump."

"Great," Rei exclaimed. He rubbed his hands together. Then he looked over at Rome's stomach again.

"Honey, for landing, we're going to have to squeeze you into a pressure suit, just in case, right?"

Rome wagged a finger at him. "I will manage," she said tersely.

He continued. "Well, we have a spare suit. I was thinking we could stitch the two together..."

"Whatever you are about to say," Rome interrupted, "do not dare!" Her glowing eyes were flashing but there was a smile on her face.

Rei laughed. "I understand."

"Initiating jump," MINIMCOM announced.

The PPT generators attached to the airfoils ramped up. The high-pitched whine coincided with a bright circle that appeared well in front of the ship. At its center was a tiny blue jewel. Rei could barely sit still. That was Deucado dead ahead.

As soon as the circle was complete, the plasma thrusters fired, pushing Rei and Rome gently back into their seats. The whole construct moved forward and, in a flash, they were through. The star called Tau Ceti was now off to their left and slightly behind the windshield. For the moment, the tiny blue jewel in front of them was the brightest object in the sky.

"Look at that!" Rei exclaimed. "That is awesome!"

"Yes," Rome replied. "Beautiful, is it not?"

"Sure is," Rei answered admiringly.

`"Please look to your right."`

"Where?" he asked.

`"As you would say, the two o'clock position."`

Rei looked and saw nothing spectacular. Rome pointed and said, "There, that star?" she asked. "Is that what you are referring to?"

`"That is not a star. That is a gas giant, roughly four times the size of Jupiter. Grentadar is the third planet out in this system."`

"OK," said Rei. "So what?"

`"From its proximity to Deucado, it is likely that it has deflected or absorbed much of the extraneous mass that has entered the inner perimeter. Based upon how much matter we observed in the Kuiper Belt, I would have estimated that Deucado would be subject to a higher-than-expected amount of bombardment of comets, meteors and asteroids."`

Rei replied. "What has one got to do with the other?"

`"Based upon the proximity between the two planets, it may explain why life was able to develop on Deucado. Perhaps Grentadar acted like a shield."`

"That seems logical," Rome said.

"Whatever," Rei interjected. "I've got a better idea. Why don't we go to Deucado and find out?"

`"Very well,"` replied MINIMCOM in a fussy tone and with that, he ignited the plasma engines full bore. Rome and Rei were pushed gently back into their seats once again, as the tugs and the Ark began to accelerate. MINIMCOM displayed the flight path required to put the Ark into high orbit around Deucado. Once he was satisfied with their speed, MINIMCOM cut out the thrusters and they coasted toward the planet.

Rei looked at Rome, his beautiful Rome, sitting there, as pregnant as a person could be without bursting. He loved her more than life itself. He watched her grimace slightly.

"Kicking again?"

"Yes," she replied. Rome looked down at her abdomen and pointed to it. "It is a boy, you know."

"A boy!" Rei exclaimed. "I'm going to have a son? Oh Rome," he sighed. "What did I ever do to deserve you?"

"I do not know but I must have done the same thing. We were just meant to be together. Forever."

"Forever's good enough for me. How's about we get you into that pressure suit?"

"All right," Rome said and with some struggling, the two of them addressed that issue.

After Rei and Rome were finished getting dressed, they came forward and strapped themselves in again.

`"We are coming up on the day-night terminator. You can see some planetary features if you examine the relief caused by the shadows."`

They could see the dividing line between daylight and nighttime sweeping across the western side of the planet. As they got closer still, two tiny bright dots appeared, one on each side of the planet.

"Those must be the two natural satellites of Deucado, Mockay and Givy," Rome said.

"Which one is which?"

"Mockay is smaller and closer to the planet. I believe it is that one," she replied, pointing to the moon on the left. "The other is Givy. It is much larger but also much farther away. From the ground, I would expect they appear nearly the same size."

"I guess we'll see when we get there," Rei observed.

`"Which will be very soon,"` MINIMCOM interjected.

Rei and Rome both watched with wide-eyed fascination as the blue jewel grew larger and larger. Whereas earlier, it had been marble-sized and then basketball-sized, now it was filling their whole field of view. They quickly passed into the night side.

Within their cabin, Rei and Rome heard the standard thump and delayed clunk as MINIMCOM reversed the orientation of his tug and fired his plasma thrusters, slowing the assembly gradually as they swung past the planet.

At last, MINIMCOM announced, `"Orbit achieved."`

Rei looked at Rome. "Honey, we're home," he said with a broad smile on his face.

Rome nodded and watched intently as they were coming up on the dawn side. Where the sun was illuminating the water, the deep blue oceans sparkled crisply from their high angle. Although there were large sections covered by heavy white clouds, much of the planet's surface was easily viewed. This planet had roughly an equal distribution of land and water. The majority of the land mass was contained within two major continents, with the one divided nearly in half with a relatively narrow isthmus connecting the northern and southern halves. As they moved around past the ocean and over the land, they could see the one continent had a Swiss cheese-like appearance. All across the surface there were many, many lakes and inland seas, most of them circular or rounded.

"Look at all the holes," Rei said.

"Yes. Despite what MINIMCOM said about a shield, they must be due to a substantial number of collisions with comets and such," Rome observed.

"Most of them seem soft, not sharp like you see on the moon. Have there been any reports of bombardment since the Vuduri have been here?"

"Not that I am aware of."

"Well, it looks good to me. There and there," Rei pointed down, "there's a ton of bright yellow and green coloration. That has to be vegetation."

"Oh yes, there is much vegetation," Rome replied.

Without warning, the central display lit up and in front of them sat a gray-haired Vuduri man.

"Who are you?" he asked in Vuduri. "We do not detect any PPT resonance."

"We are mandasurte," Rome answered. "We have come from the Tabit stellar observatory. We are towing one of the ancient Essessoni Arks that we found there."

The man's eyes grew wide then narrowed. In a flat voice, he said, "On this world, mandasurte in possession of Vuduri technology is a capital crime. You have condemned yourself. You will die."

The screen went black.

"What the hell!?" Rei shouted.

The MIDAR display lit up.

`"The Vuduri have just launched multiple craft. They appear to be armed."`

"Vuduri do not use weapons," Rome insisted.

`"These do."`

"Forget that. What do we do? MINIMCOM, can we outrun them?" Rei asked, his voice rising.

`"Not with your cargo craft."`

"And if we left it here?"

`"Rome already told them it was an Ark. They will assume the Erklirte have returned."`

"Can you get them back on the comm? Their rules should not apply to us. We are supposed to be here." Rome asked, desperately.

`"I have already tried. There is no reply. You should determine a course of action and quickly. I believe you should take evasive maneuvers immediately!"`

"What kind of arms are they carrying?" Rei asked anxiously.

`"Magnetic pulse cannons, electrostatic charge disrupters and PPT throwers."`

Rome gasped. All the color left her face.

"What? Say again," Rei asked.

`"PPT throwers."`

"What are those?" he asked, panicked.

`"They are normally used in mining and salvage operations on the surface. They create a moving PPT tunnel. They can cut through any material known to man. However, in space, they can extend over a much greater distance."`

"So you're saying…" Rei sputtered.

"What he is saying," Rome barked, "is that they are for slicing up very large objects into very tiny pieces."

"How much time do we have?" Rei asked grimly.

`"I would estimate ten minutes or less."`

Rei looked down at Deucado. After nearly a year, they were so close and now they were never going to see their new home. He looked up at the top of the cabin as if there was somewhere else to go. Suddenly, it came to him.

"I've got it," he said. He tried to snap his fingers but the gloves from the pressure suit prevented it from sounding effective.

"What?" Rome asked.

"We go to the planet."

"We cannot do that, Rei. We are using the EG lifters to hold onto your Ark. We would not survive reentry without the lifters. We would burn up."

"No, no, no. Let me explain." Rei said. "MINIMCOM, what would happen if we open up a PPT tunnel to the surface of the planet?"

"You cannot form a large enough PPT tunnel on the surface of a planet," Rome protested. "There is too much gravitational stress. The tunnel would collapse immediately."

"Rei is correct. For such a short distance, 160 kilometers, the tunnel would actually be stable for sufficient time. However, once the tunnel was formed, the atmosphere of the planet would begin venting out. We would face a formidable wind."

"Nothing that the plasma thrusters couldn't push against, right?" Rei asked.

"Agreed. We would be able to enter the tunnel. But when we emerge, you must still consider Rome's original point. Once we passed through the tunnel, the tugs would have no lift since the EG pods are currently used to secure your crew compartment. We would fall to the surface."

"So we let the Ark go. Once it starts through the tunnel, wouldn't gravity pull the rest through?"

"What purpose would it serve to take the Ark through, just to let it fall to earth and be destroyed?" Rome asked.

"Not if we work it just right...MINIMCOM, can you make the tunnel open up exactly the length of the Ark above the surface?"

MINIMCOM did not answer right away. Finally, he said, "Yes."

"OK. Romey, do they have trees down there?"

"Yes. They have cane-tree forests covering most of both continents."

"So that's where we set down. MINIMCOM opens the tunnel up exactly the height of the ship. The Ark goes through the tunnel and touches the ground. Once it's through, we just let it topple over. The trees will break its fall. Everything is secured against stresses way higher than that, including the people. The front part was designed to hit even at terminal velocity. It'll be OK."

"What about us?" Rome asked.

"As soon as the Ark starts through and gravity takes over, we let go and use the EG lifters. We just squirt through when we have enough lift to land. That is if we have enough time to spin up the superconductors,"

"It will be close but my calculations confirm the interval will be sufficient."

"OK. What am I missing?" Rei asked. "MINIMCOM, what about our orbital velocity, relative to the ground?"

"I will aim the tunnel tangential to our current orbit. I will make the distance equal to our rate of travel which will negate our velocity. As the ship passes through the tunnel, on the other side, the net velocity relative to the ground will be zero. However such a tunnel will most likely shear off the wings of your Ark."

"Screw it," Rei said. "We don't need them."

"MINIMCOM, can this really work?" Rome inquired.

"I will run a quick simulation and calculate the probability of success."

"I am certain that this has never been tried before."

"But does that mean it won't work," Rei stated fervently. "Right, MINIMCOM?"

"I have completed my calculations. With certain precautions, it has a fairly reasonable probability of success. But I would be remiss if I did not state that it is highly inadvisable."

"What's our alternative?" asked Rei. "Sit here and die? Let them kill us? Kill my people?"

"You have a valid point. If we are to attempt this, we should start as soon as possible. The Vuduri are less than five minutes away from intercept."

"Romey, are you OK with this?" Rei asked.

"Yes, mau emir. I trust you," she said sadly. "And, as you said, what choice do we have?"

"OK, MINIMCOM, take over," Rei insisted.

"Turn the PPT rings for minimum diameter," MINIMCOM said. "I will initiate. Where do you want to set down?"

"Aim for Asquarti, the Western continent," Rome replied, trying to stay calm. "That is where the mandasurte live."

"OK, MINIMCOM, put us down there," Rei ordered.

"Rei, they will come looking for us as soon as they realize what has happened," Rome said worriedly.

"We'll have to figure out something when we get there. We'll hide the ship under some leaves or something. OK?" Rei looked at her. "Are you ready, Romey? You have to fly. I'm not ready for this," he asked less than authoritatively.

Rome closed her eyes. She frowned. She slapped her temple three times, as if trying to jar something loose.

"What's the matter?" Rei asked.

"My bloco and stilo. They have stopped working," Rome replied.

"Can you fly without them?"

"Of course," Rome said. "They just make it easier." She held her arm and hand out to where Rei could get to it. Rei reached out to take it. Even though they were wearing gloves, they gripped each other's hand tightly.

"I am ready," Rome said, "go ahead, MINIMCOM. Execute."

`Calculating jump,` MINIMCOM said, then, `Coordinates ready.`

"Do it!" Rei commanded.

The trim-jets on both tugs fired and rotated the assembled craft so that their tug's nose was pointing directly toward the planet. Rei let go of Rome's hand and grabbed a hold of his armrests. Pointing straight at the surface like this was giving him a bit of vertigo.

`Initiating jump,` said MINIMCOM.

Rei and Rome heard the high-pitched whine of their PPT generators revving up. In front of them, a brightly lit hole appeared. Leaves, branches, dirt and dust started shooting out from it. The wind began to buffet the conjoined mass but the trim-jets were sufficient to keep them stable long enough. As the hole widened, they could see the bright yellow-green forest beckoning to them through the onrushing gale. They were looking down, right at it.

MINIMCOM fired the plasma thrusters on their tug, forcing the leading edge of the Ark forward into the tunnel. After a very short time, the little computer shut their thrusters off but they could feel the ship accelerating which meant gravity was taking over.

`Release your clamps,` MINIMCOM shouted above the howling which was the wind against their hull. `The magnets should begin spinning up immediately.`

Rome punched some buttons on the control panel and even though the motion was slight, they began to move off, away from the Ark.

`Your EG lifters are ready. I would suggest manual control from here on in. I will be busy.`

"What do you mean? What are you going to do?" Rei asked.

`"I must remain attached until the Ark clears the tunnel. I am going to use my plasma thrusters to brake. I cannot let the ship hit the ground too quickly."`

"Will you have enough time to break loose?" Rome asked.

`"The probability is very low,"` MINIMCOM said. `"I do not think so."`

"MINIMCOM!" Rei shouted. "What did you do? Why didn't you tell us?"

Quietly, MINIMCOM said, `"I did not trust you to allow me to do what I had to do. This was the only way to save your Ark."`

"You can't..." Rei stopped speaking. Their nose was entering the tunnel and they were looking straight down into the trees. Rocks and branches were banging off them right and left. The powerful wind buffeted their ship and the tinted windshield was starting to ice up.

"What is that? Rome, what's going on? What's happening?"

Rome looked at the instrument panel. "The tug is sitting at minus 80 degrees Celsius, the temperature of space. That must be atmospheric moisture condensing on the ship," she called out.

As soon as their tail was clear of the tunnel, Rome pulled back savagely on both sticks and they could feel the nose beginning to rotate as the trim-jets fired and tug struggled to right itself. The windshield was now covered with frost so thick that they could not make out anything. Rome slammed one throttle forward to force the lead repulsor field to angle their nose higher more quickly; then she pulled back to lift the tug up and away from the rapidly approaching canopy of trees to try to get level. She allowed the joysticks to return to their upright position then she fired the plasma thrusters, jolting them back in their seats. She shut them down a few seconds later. Even though it felt like they were level, Rei's pilot's instincts told him not to trust his senses.

"Can you tell where the Ark is coming down?" Rei shouted. He couldn't see anything through the ice.

"No. I must move off a safe distance then we will come back around when we can see again," Rome replied in a level voice. "Can you activate the MIDAR?"

"Go," he said. He leaned forward to press a few icons as Rome pulled back on both sticks and the tug lurched ahead, gaining altitude. They could hear branches and other debris striking the underside of their craft but they were definitely going up. Soon, the scraping noises subsided and they were in the clear, albeit blindly. Rome studied the displays, trying to get herself oriented. Just then they heard a tremendous crash.

Instinctively, Rei whipped his head around but there was nothing to see except the rear bulkhead of the cockpit. He turned back around and quickly pressed a button to activate one of the rear cameras but all he saw was translucent sheet of ice.

"I can't see anything. Set her down, Romey, set her down," Rei cried out.

"All right," she said, calmly.

Rome peered down at the instruments and toggled the display to MIDAR. She pointed to one section. "There appears to be a small clearing. I will try and set down there."

Rei looked forward and could see nothing but the bright ice. He closed his eyes. This was not what he had planned.

Rome pressed a button on the front display. She stared at it then pressed it again, twice. Frustrated, she banged at it with her fist.

"What?" Rei asked.

"I cannot get the landing gear extended," Rome said worriedly. "The doors will not open. It must be the ice."

"Do we need them? Can you land without them?"

"Yes," Rome replied. "I can do it. I just have to be careful."

It took all of Rome's concentration to bring them to a dead stop, hovering above the clearing, using the MIDAR as a guide. Gently, she lowered the ship, paying careful attention to the altimeter. All along the hull, there were crackling noises but at last, they felt themselves touch down. Rome took her hand off the sticks and sat back in her chair and breathed a huge sigh.

"You did it, Romey." Rei said with relief.

"We did it," Rome corrected him.

"Yes, we…" Rei frowned then opened his eyes wide. "Oh, no," he exclaimed, "MINIMCOM!"

He leaned forward and shouted into the grille mounted on the front panel, "MINIMCOM, are you there?" The only sound they heard was water running somewhere off in the distance.

"MINIMCOM, can you hear us?" Rome said.

Again, there was no answer.

"We've got to go see," Rei said. "Let's go."

Rome nodded and released her high-g harness. She tried to stand up but fell back into the seat immediately. Deucado had a gravity that was 91% of Earth and their long exposure to one-third g, despite all their exercise, left them somewhat ill-prepared. Rei unbuckled himself and stood up, a bit wobbly, but still able to handle it. He stepped over to Rome and bent down.

"Put your arms around my neck," he said.

She reached up for him and pulled him down to her. She kissed him and said, "No matter what happens, mau emir, know that I love you."

"I know you do, honey. I love you, too. We'll be OK. Let me pull you up."

He put his hands on her waist and arched backwards and was pleasantly surprised to see that he had no pain whatsoever. His motion pulled Rome forward and then she was able to stand on her own.

"Are you all right? Can you walk?" Rei asked.

"Yes, I can walk." She steadied herself on the armrest of the chair and moved around it. Rei left her there and made his way over to the inside door of the airlock. He pressed the stud to open it and as soon as he was through, he opened the outer door. Together, hands against the walls, Rome and Rei made their way down the hallway to the far end of the cargo compartment.

Rei pushed the blue stud to raise the cargo door and lower the ramp. Sitting with their belly on the ground, the ramp would not extend very far. As the hatch struggled to open against the coating of ice, it complained by way of some groaning noises but then with a crack, it broke free and the door began to open. The light was so bright that Rei had to hold his arm up to shield his eyes. With Rome's advanced optics, she had no such problem.

Rei just shut his eyes, figuring it was easier to let his eyes adjust that way. Rome reached up and tugged on his arm.

"Rei," she said.

"Yeah, I'll be OK. I just need a minute to let my eyes adjust," Rei replied.

"REI!" Rome said, insistently.

"What?"

Even though his eyes were blurry from the brightness, Rei blinked a few times until his vision cleared.

There standing at the base of the ramp was an angry-looking mob holding spears, pole-axes, machetes, crossbows, swords, maces, clubs and knives plus a variety of other harsh-looking objects that Rei did not recognize. In summary, they were pointing pretty much every weapon ever conceived by primitive man at the space-faring couple.

"Great," Rei muttered. "From the frying pan into the fire."

Chapter 26

HANDS RAISED, REI WAITED PATIENTLY FOR SOMEONE TO SAY something. He figured if they were going to kill them, they would probably have done it already. A man in the front of the crowd took one step forward. "Nis nei damis nanhume croence equo. Berde," the man said in a peculiar dialect.

Rei leaned to his left and spoke to Rome quietly in English. "What children? Who are these people?"

"Shh…" Rome said. She pointed to her stomach.

"We are not after your children," she said in Vuduri. "As you can see, I am with child myself."

"Then who are you?" the man asked.

"I am Rome, this is Rei," replied Rome, pointing to the love of her life. "We are mandasurte, not Vuduri."

The people nearest the front gasped.

"This is not possible," said the man. "How do you come to fly a ship? You know the penalty is death."

"We are not from Deucado. We came from the Tabit system, 21 light years from here." She pointed straight up. "We did not know the law here. We were given this ship and another like it by the Vuduri to tow a cargo vessel here." Rome looked around then back at the man. "Did you see where it came down? Can you show us where it is? We need to inspect it."

"How do we know you are mandasurte?" the man asked skeptically. "You look Vuduri. You fly in a Vuduri ship. You could simply be spying on us."

"We are mandasurte, I assure you," Rome insisted.

"Prove it," said the man.

"Is it not sufficient that we are speaking?"

"No. That is not proof. There are many Vuduri who know how to speak."

"Then how? How do I prove it?"

"You decide," said the man through gritted teeth.

Rome lowered her head and looked him in the eye. "I will show you."

She turned toward Rei and, in English, she said, "Kiss me."

"What?" Rei whispered, confused.

"Kiss me like you love me," she insisted.

"But I do love you," Rei replied.

"Then do it!" Rome commanded.

"OK," Rei said. He opened his arms up to her and she entered them, pressing her belly up against him. He kissed her long and hard, not knowing why and after a moment or two, not really caring. He never tired of this woman, her soft skin, her clean smell, he just wanted to hold her always.

"Enough!" said the man. "This is very touching, but it proves nothing. I would not put it past our oppressors, even this. So you have learned to act. There may still be a purpose to your arrival that will spell pain for us. I do not think we should take a chance."

The crowd started murmuring and pushing forward. Some of them were raising their weapons and brandishing them about in a very menacing way. Rei started thinking furiously about some way to defend himself and Rome. Beyond hurling a chunk of ice at them, nothing came to mind. Worse, they had no weapons on board. He pushed Rome behind himself, using his body as a shield. Not that that would protect her but it was all he could think of at the moment.

"I will vouch for her," issued a voice from the back. All heads turned to look at the person who spoke. A silver-haired man worked his way forward and broke through the front lines.

"Aiee! I cannot believe it! Beo!" Rome shouted. She stepped around Rei and ran or perhaps waddled would be a better word, down the ramp and rushed into the man's arms.

"Beo?" Rei whispered to himself. "Father?"

Rome had buried her face in her father's chest with her arms locked around him. In turn, her father hugged her as tightly as he could given her condition. They held onto each other for the longest time, rocking back and forth. Finally, Rome pulled her head back and looked up into her father's eyes.

"You have been gone so long. We thought we had lost you forever," Rome whispered, tears of joy gushing down her face.

"My little Rome," said Fridone, "I, too, thought I would never see you again. You said you are mandasurte now?"

"Oh, Beo," she said, laughing and crying at the same time, "I have missed you so much and yes, I was Cesdiud."

"And you do not care?"

"I am happy beyond measure."

"Then I am happy for you. Oh, my little girl!" Fridone starting crying as well.

They hugged again, Rome's huge stomach pressing against him. After a few minutes, he pushed her away to regard her.

Rome ran her hand through her father's hair. "Beo, your hair. It has gotten so gray!"

"Yes, I have changed," replied Fridone somberly. Then he brightened up. "And speaking of changes, I see you have been busy," he said with a chuckle. Rome turned and pointed to Rei who walked down the ramp to stand beside the reunited pair, a bit wary of the cutlery around him.

"Beo, this is Rei. He saved me and perhaps the whole world. He is mau emir and the father of our child."

Fridone reached out with his arm and Rei extended his. Fridone grabbed a hold of it in a peculiar way and pulled him down toward him and gave him a hug, which Rei allowed. Then Fridone pushed him back and turned to Rome. "He is mandasurte, also? He certainly does not look like a Vuduri."

Rome nodded then said, "He is not Vuduri. He is from Garecei Ti Essessoni…"

Fridone jumped back reflexively, recoiling at Rome's words. Behind him, the people within earshot gasped. Rome ignored their reactions. She put her arm around Rei's waist and pulled him closer.

"He is not a killer," she continued. "He saved all of our lives."

Even as she spoke, the people behind muttered on. "Essessoni," they said among themselves. They whispered. Rei could hear them say things like "we are lost" and "murderers" in the background.

Trabunel, the man in front who had addressed them before, came over to them. "Is this true? Is that what was in your vessel over there?" He pointed to the woods behind them. "Did you bring the Erklirte among us?"

210

"I brought my people," Rei said, in Vuduri. "But they are not what you think. We are just ordinary men like you. We were coming to this world to live free, like you."

The man spat. "We are not free," he said. "We live under the thumb of the Overmind here. We are prisoners of this world. We are the Ibbrassati, the oppressed."

"Prisoners," Rome asked. "What…"

Her question was interrupted by another man who came over and whispered into the first man's ear. After the brief conference was over, Trabunel waved his hand to the crowd and spoke loud enough for all to hear.

"I believe that you are mandasurte, daughter of Fridone. No Vuduri could say those things or act like you do and be otherwise. As for you, Essessoni, we must hide your ship and your cargo vessel. Then we must get away from here. The Vuduri will be on their way and if they find your craft, they will take it. If they find you, they will kill you."

Trabunel turned toward his men. "We must hide this ship and the other," he shouted. "There is no heat signature to worry about. We only need camouflage. Use the nets. Elon, take some men and go find the Erklirte or whatever they are. Hide them as well."

With murmurs of assent, the crowd began to disperse, some toward the tug, some in the opposite direction, deeper into the woods. Trabunel charged forward, away from the landing area. Fridone put his arm around his daughter and started guiding her away from her ship, in the same direction as Trabunel. Rei stood there and watched as the Ibbrassati swarmed over his tug, still caked in ice, laying netting over the top along with leaves, branches and other pieces of camouflage. Within a matter of minutes, his ship blended into the background so well that he had trouble picking it out himself. Amazed, he broke his concentration and hurried to catch up to Rome and her father.

The cane-tree forest was made up of thin reed-like trunks, almost like bamboo, most not more than four inches in diameter. Occasionally, there was one thicker. The very tops of the trees were a bright yellow while the lower leaves were yellow-green. The star Tau Ceti was more orange than Sol and so whatever passed for chlorophyll on this planet was skewed toward the lower frequencies in the electromagnetic spectrum. The colors reminded Rei of a really nice day in the fall, when the leaves were just beginning to turn. But the weather here was not consonant with that. In fact, it was fairly warm and somewhat humid.

They walked along a trail through the forest for a while. In many places, the trees had grown so thick that the sky overhead was hidden, mimicking nightfall. Eventually, they started down a steep winding path into a gorge that was hidden by a canopy of overhanging cane-trees. Fridone helped Rome navigate her way down, steadying her with his arm under her shoulder. They reached the base of the gorge but traveled only a short distance before Rome stopped. She was breathing heavily and bent over. Rei rushed over to her and knelt down on one knee to look up at her.

"Sweetheart," he said in English. "Are you OK?"

She gave him a half-smile. "You said you wanted to take a long walk when we first landed, right?" She winked at him.

Rei laughed but then the smile left his face. "Tell me, how do you feel?"

"Pregnant. Very pregnant." She went back to breathing heavily.

Rei shook his head and in one quick motion, scooped her up in his arms. His knees almost buckled and it took him a moment to right himself.

"You do not need to do this, mau emir. I will be all right," Rome said.

"It's OK, honey. I've been exercising for a year. I'm ready for this."

Fridone looked at him with a concerned expression but nodded slowly. Rei took one halting step, then another then another. After Rome could see that he was able to carry her, she put her arms around his neck and nestled her head against his shoulder.

"How far?" Rei asked Fridone, in Vuduri, slightly panicked.

"It is only about one-half kilometer from here," Fridone replied, pointing toward Trabunel who was some distance ahead. Fridone turned and started walking and Rei followed him. After they had gone only a short distance, Fridone stopped to let him catch up and placed his hand behind Rei's back. He helped Rei walk as best as he could.

"How did you know where to find us?" Fridone asked. "We have always been so careful to keep this enclave hidden. No one comes here. Our real settlement is about 40 kilometers to the south and west on the shores of Lake Eprehem. When the Vuduri come to take the children, they always do it well away from here."

"We did not know," Rei said, inhaling deeply. "We just jumped down here. MINIMCOM picked the spot." Rei took a quick breath. "MINIMCOM! Please, did you see where the Ark came down? Did you see our other tug?"

"I did not see either," Fridone replied. "We were out on patrol and heard a howling wind overhead. None of it made sense. We looked up and saw a black hole in the middle of the sky over the forest and something very large emerged. We saw your craft break free and fly toward us. We assumed it was the Vuduri who had found us. We were prepared to kill them if we had to. I am glad it was you. As far as your Ark is concerned, Trabunel seemed to know where your people landed though."

"We do not have that much time," Rei said. "We have to start thawing them out. Their freezing chambers are meant to be in space, not in this kind of heat. We have to thaw them out so they get reanimated properly. We cannot wait forever," he said.

"I understand," Rome's father replied. "We will tell Trabunel about this when we get to camp. We will help you with your people but we must be careful to avoid doing anything that will tip the Vuduri to our location first."

"OK," Rei said in English and he went back to concentrating on carrying the woman he loved and his unborn child to safety. He counted the steps silently and when he got to 1000, he flashed back to those lonely last minutes at Skyler Base, on Dara, when he thought he had lost Rome forever. But she was here and she was in his arms. He squeezed her tighter and they moved on.

They made their way along some rocks, following an intricate series of switchbacks, under some overhangs and finally entering a cave. Several men stood sentry duty outside while Fridone, Rei and Rome followed the leader within. Once they were inside, Rei heard a rumbling noise and turned to see them covering the hole with a large boulder and smaller ones.

Rei turned back and followed Fridone as he led the way deeper into the cave. After passing through some tunnels, they came to a sizeable cave with racks and racks of storage. The racks themselves were made of cane-tree wood. On them rested weapons, blankets and other paraphernalia. They entered a tunnel on the far side and continued on a downward slope, deeper and deeper into the mountain. The temperature dropped noticeably.

At last they got to a huge cavern. Rei looked up and could barely see the ceiling. All around them were tunnels and smaller caverns.

Fridone stopped and saw Rei looking up. "We call this 'The Cathedral,'" he said, "although what we worship, I do not know. Our living area is just ahead," he said and he waved his arm.

Rei followed Fridone to the right, through another tunnel into a small cave that had flimsy-looking bunk beds around the outskirts, stacked three tall, and a roaring fire in the middle. There were men and women there, most of whom looked older.

Fridone motioned to them. "Come sit by the fire and we will talk."

Rei set Rome down on the ground and the two of them went to the far side of the fire. He helped her strip out of her pressure suit while Fridone dragged some mats and some blankets over to make a soft place for Rome to recline. Rei joined her and she leaned up against him heavily. Trabunel came over and offered them water and an assortment of food which Rome gratefully accepted. This far along in her pregnancy, she was always ravenous.

Trabunel took a seat next to Fridone on the other side of the fire.

Rei was less interested in the food. "Can you tell us what is going on?" he asked. "None of this makes any sense."

Rome stopped eating to interrupt him. "Before you get into that, there is something I must know." She turned to face her father. "Beo, why did you leave us? Mea and I were devastated."

"How *is* your mother?" Fridone asked, ignoring her question.

"She is as well as can be expected. I know that she misses you. Life was never the same after you were gone."

Fridone's breath caught. He wiped away a tear. "I miss her, too," he said quietly. "I miss her so much. I feel like a part of me is gone. All the time. Even after all these years."

"So Beo, why did you come here? Why did you leave us?" Rome asked plaintively.

"Oh, my little Rome," Fridone replied gently. "I did not leave upon my own volition. I was kidnapped and brought here. We all were."

"Kidnapped," Rome exclaimed, horrified. "How? Why?"

"The why, I cannot answer. As for how, in my case, we were onboard our research vessel. We had departed Berlis Harbor and were out to sea to the south of the big island. Our ship was boarded by strange Vuduri."

"Strange?" Rei interjected. "What made them strange?"

"For one thing," continued Fridone, "they were harsh, even evil, with absolutely no hint of humanity about them. They were like living machines." Fridone pointed to his temple. "And their eyes!"

"What about their eyes?" Rome asked.

"They were not like a regular Vuduri. Their eyes were dark, no reflection," replied Fridone. "They had no life to them. I can only describe them by telling you these men had dead eyes."

"Vuduri with dead eyes? I have never seen such a thing. Why would they do this? Why would they kidnap you?"

"As I said, we do not know," he replied. "They never explained their motives to us. They rounded us up, herded us aboard a spaceship, transported us here and left. That is how most of the Ibbrassati arrived here. There are some fools about who willingly came here believing they were migrating to a new world but now they are just as much prisoners as we are."

"Why would they do such a thing?" Rome asked. "The Vuduri are all about efficiency. To force you to come here is the opposite of efficient."

Trabunel interjected, "Nothing about their behavior makes sense. The only thing we can think of is that they are trying to reduce the mandasurte population on Earth. Perhaps their hope is to one day cleanse the Earth of all mandasurte."

"Does anyone ever resist them?"

"Who would know? I would assume that if they resisted, they would just kill them outright."

"Why would they do that, sir?" Rei asked. "From what Rome tells me, the mandasurte keep to themselves…"

"We did," Fridone replied, picking up where Trabunel left off. "The Vuduri in charge of this world have no interest in justifying their plan to us. It is always the same. New mandasurte are brought here and none have any explanation as to why. The one thing our captors make clear to us is that we are not allowed access to Vuduri technology. They tell us it is a capital offense and we believe them."

"Why is that, Beo?" Rome asked. "What possible difference could it make to have access to technology?"

"We can only guess, Volhe," her father replied. "Clearly, Deucado is a prison world. Not one of us knew this. Access to technology might allow us to one day escape this planet and the Vuduri are determined to keep us trapped here. You cannot arm prisoners with the means to effect their release."

"They bring us here or they kill us," Trabunel said angrily, "it is that simple. Slowly but surely they will make all the mandasurte go away until there are no more left on the Earth."

"What about other worlds? What about Helome? There are many mandasurte that have left the Earth to go there. Yes?"

"Propaganda," Trabunel said. "Half-truth. They leave the Earth but they only end up here. Their ships are captured. No, our abductors will not stop until all the mandasurte are here."

"But I was connected. So was Mea. How could the Overmind keep such a secret?" Rome asked, completely puzzled.

"The only way is if the Overmind of Earth does not know. Somehow there must be a separate samanda, or perhaps a samanda within the samanda."

"That is not possible," Rome sputtered.

"You see that it is," Trabunel said. "There is a secret society on Earth, one that is hidden from ordinary Vuduri and mandasurte alike." Trabunel pounded his fist into his hand then grabbed it, shaking it at Rei and Rome. "They take us. They imprison us here. They rob us of our technology. There is no noble purpose here. Only evil," he said heatedly.

"If what you say is true, the very fabric of our society is at risk. It is not right. We…we need to tell them, tell the Vuduri of Earth, the normal ones. Beo, this cannot be allowed!" Rome said frantically.

"We have no way to get word back," replied Trabunel who was still agitated. "That is another one of the reasons why the Vuduri here do not allow us access to technology. They cannot take the chance that word gets back to Earth. Whoever is behind this wants to do this without anyone noticing. That is why they take the children."

"You mentioned that before," Rei said. "They take your children?"

"Not all of them. Only those that can connect to the Overmind. As soon as the child is born, if it is connected, the Vuduri begin to triangulate its position," said Trabunel. "They come for it very quickly. That is why we do not allow pregnant women to be anywhere near here. They must remain at the main settlement. We cannot have babies born here." He looked right at Rome who instinctively put her hand to her stomach.

"Why not? What's so special about this place?"

"Because we have some technology that we have stolen. And some that we are developing. We have a workroom and a forge back there." Trabunel jammed a thumb, pointing over his shoulder. "We cannot allow the Vuduri to find it. They would kill us. We are working on a way to make metals, materials, electronics and so forth. We will elevate ourselves back to our former technological level, even if it takes a hundred years."

"Metal?" Rei countered. "What about all the swords and knives that we saw earlier? There was nothing hidden about those!"

"Those are from the Vuduri. They give us the bare necessities to live. They just make sure that what they give us cannot be used against them."

"Could you not use a sword against one?" asked Rome. "Would it not wound or kill, just the same?"

"A sword is no match against a hand-weapon or energy projector," Trabunel spat out. "They are so convinced of their superiority that they do not fear such puny items."

"Puny, hah," Rei said. He pointed straight up. "They have no clue what is coming."

"What is coming?" Fridone asked. "What happened to you? Rome? Why are you here, anyway?"

Rome took a deep breath. "Beo, as I told you earlier, after you left, nothing was ever the same. Mea and I found dwelling among your family without you was too painful. We returned to I-cimaci to live."

"And then what?"

"I trained to become a lutteur and data archivist. And I was good at it. It was not a gaudy skill set but a necessary one. While you were gone, a star that was only 12 light years away from Earth disappeared. The Overmind sent out survey teams to investigate and I was selected for the team that was to go to Tabit. While we were there, one of our salvage crews came across Rei's Ark. That is how I met Rei."

"And his people, how do you know they are not the Erklirte?" Trabunel asked.

Rei started to speak but Rome interrupted. "If the Essessoni are anything like my Rei, they are good and decent and brilliant." She smiled up at him. "The one Ark that returned to Earth so long ago, the Erklirte, they were aberrant, perverted."

"We shall see," Trabunel said. "What happened to your mission? What did you find at Tabit?"

Rome recounted the story of shutting down the base prematurely, the starprobes, the Stareater and the VIRUS units. Trabunel and Fridone were incredulous. Rome also told them how OMCOM had planned his own escape and the subsequent mutations releasing who-knows-what into the universe.

"After you left, why did you come here? If you could tow the Ark, why not tow it back to Earth?" Trabunel asked.

"That question never really came up. I suppose it was because the Vuduri on Tabit wanted to help Rei complete his mission. And Deucado was his Ark's original destination," replied Rome.

"Or perhaps it was to isolate you," Trabunel pointed out. "You said you were Cesdiud. The two of you were mandasurte. You were carrying a ship full of mandasurte. Whoever is behind this, they did not want you on Earth. No, Deucado was the right place for you. They meant to send you here."

Rome frowned while she considered Trabunel's words. She shifted around, trying to get more comfortable. The pressure within her abdomen seemed so much greater now that they were in full gravity. Rei saw that she was having trouble and pulled her back so that more of her weight rested on him. This seemed to placate Rome, but only for a minute.

"I was part of the Overmind," Rome said harshly. "I would have known about such a plan. There were too few of us, only 80. We were too small for there to be a secret samanda among us. In fact, when the Overmind at Tabit sent us on our way, it loaded us up with as much equipment as possible. They gave us a molecular synthesizer, a memron fabricator and more. If they did not want us to have access to advanced technology, they would have not done that. No, the samanda that came to be on Tabit was not privy to the plan you described."

Rei spoke up. "So the Vuduri from Tabit send us here to live yet the Vuduri here want us dead? That must have been what Estar meant." Rei said in English. "Maybe the rest of you didn't know but she certainly did. That must have been why she tried to kill me."

"I do not see how," Rome answered. "The Overmind on Earth could not know what is going on here. And the people here do not know about the Stareaters. It is a good thing we have MINIMCOM and…" Rome's eyes widened. She turned to her father and said in Vuduri, "Beo, we have to get to the other tug. It is carrying the most important piece of equipment of all."

"And my people, we have to start thawing them before it is too late," Rei pointed out.

Fridone turned to Trabunel and said, "The Garecei Ti Essessoni. The reason they became the Erklirte is because they had powerful weapons..."

"Wait a minute," Rei interrupted. "We carry no weapons."

"Very well," said Fridone, "their technology, then. It might give us the edge we need to defend ourselves and declare our independence."

Trabunel put his fist to his mouth. They could see he was weighing the option. He exhaled forcibly and then nodded. He turned to Rei.

"Fridone is right. We will help you thaw your people."

"Thank you, sir," Rei exhaled.

"Rei, help me up," Rome said. She held out her hand. He leaned over and pressed his hand against her shoulder, pushing her back.

In English, he said, "Sweetheart. You can't go. You have to stay here."

"But, but..." she protested. "I can still walk."

"There's no way you can make it up to the Ark and back and there isn't anything for you to do, anyway. I can handle it."

"What about MINIMCOM? What about the other tug?" Rome asked, her voice catching.

"I'll check it out. I'll come back and let you know what's up. Don't worry about it."

"But I do not want to be apart from you. I am afraid."

"You'll be safe here," Rei responded. "These people will take care of you."

Rome tried to take a deep breath. "You are right. I will not argue." She switched to Vuduri. "Beo, while you are out there, please watch over him. Everything here is new to us."

"We will," Fridone replied. "Come, Rei, we must change your clothes. The ones you are wearing will give you away, should we be caught."

Rome barked out, "Caught?"

Rei said, "It'll be OK, Romey. I promise."

"You be careful, Rei Bierak. You come back to me. Aason and I need you."

"Aason?" he inquired.

She pointed to her stomach.
"Oh! Aason," he said, nodding. "I like it."

Chapter 27

A WARNING SIGNAL ORIGINATING FROM THE MIDAR ARRAY located on the far side of the planet was their first indication that something unusual was happening. The Overmind directed Pegus, the gray-haired leader of the Vuduri on Deucado, to activate the large view screen built into his workstation which also served as his desk. Standing directly behind Pegus was his most recent liaison from Earth, a woman named Sussen. Sussen, along with several of her strange Vuduri companions, had arrived on Deucado six months ago and brought with them information regarding the events on Tabit.

The flat panel display lit up relaying the instrumentation readout. At first, the dot on the screen was only a pixel or two wide but as it grew, Pegus could see it extending and elongating as it approached the planet. His eyes widened when the Overmind informed Pegus of its likely origin.

"Are you certain?" Pegus asked silently. *"It is too soon."*

"Look at the form factor," Sussen interjected into his mind. *"It is not a standard Vuduri starship."*

"You told us it was going to take nearly two years," Pegus protested. *"How could it have arrived here so quickly?"*

"I detect no PPT transceiver emanations from the craft," said the Overmind. *"Contact the vessel and confirm its origin. That will eliminate any speculation."*

Pegus pressed a few keys on the input surface built into his desk. The MIDAR display on the screen was replaced by the image of a Vuduri woman.

"Who are you?" he asked. "We do not detect any PPT resonance."

"We are mandasurte," the woman answered. "We have come from the Tabit stellar observatory. We are towing one of the lost Essessoni Arks that we found there."

This was the only confirmation he required. In a flat voice, Pegus replied, "On this world, mandasurte in possession of Vuduri technology is a capital crime. You have condemned yourself. You will die."

With that, he cut off contact.

"You know what to do," the Overmind stated.

Pegus nodded. Immediately, he scrambled a fleet of fighters to intercept the craft. The ancient spaceship was located on the far side of the planet so it would take them a little while to reach it but Pegus was not worried. The Essessoni vessel was simply too large to travel quickly. Despite the fact that it had arrived early, it still had taken the craft nearly a year to travel a distance that a normal starship would have traversed in just under two months.

As the blip on the MIDAR screen continued to grow, it was easy to see that the ship was very long and not very wide. His fighters would have no trouble at all taking it out. As he stared at his viewscreen, Pegus noticed that the ship was rotating around until it was pointing toward the planet. While he did not know their intentions, it meant they were trying something. He ordered the lead fighter to increase their plasma thrusters to the max to get to their quarry as quickly as possible.

Shortly thereafter, the MIDAR mounted in the nose of the fighter was returning a better image than the ground-based sensors so Pegus switched his main display to relay its information. Incredibly, the vessel ahead was becoming shorter. The only possible explanation was that it was entering a PPT tunnel. Pegus harshly commanded the fighter to fly even faster; however, the proximity projection revealed that his interceptor was not going to arrive in time. The Essessoni vessel grew smaller and smaller until it disappeared completely.

Pegus hissed a burst of air. He commanded the fighter to lift higher into orbit, perpendicular to where the tunnel had formed. This would establish a second point in space allowing them to plot the geometrical path of the jump. He instructed the remainder of his fleet to begin a parabolic spiral search on the opposite side of the planet along the vector formed between the two points.

Again and again, the Vuduri fighters jumped, each time farther out, following a geometrical path. They continued until they had covered a hemi-spherical region four light-seconds, nearly eight million kilometers, across.

Despite the immense distance, there was no sign of the Essessoni craft. Pegus knew its top speed. There was no way the craft from the past could had traveled even two light-seconds away from Deucado, let alone four. It had simply disappeared.

Pegus slammed his open palm against his desk. Even though the Vuduri do not normally express much emotion, the Overmind was clearly displeased that they had lost the ship and Pegus was taking the brunt of it.

Sussen stepped forward and pointed to the display. Silently, she communicated to Pegus, *"Play back the video recording from the lead ship."*

He considered questioning how that would help but he complied. He pressed a few keys on his input surface and the video started playing.

"Zoom in," she thought.

Pegus pressed a function key and the central section enlarged until their target nearly filled his screen. It was very blurry and the camera had a poor angle but he could see from the geometry that his suspicions were confirmed.

"They clearly jumped through a PPT tunnel," he thought. *"So why could we not locate their ship along the jump vector?"*

"You have made an assumption that I believe to be incorrect," she thought back to him.

"What assumption is that?"

"You assumed they jumped into space."

"Where else would they go?" he asked, confused. *"You are not thinking..."*

"Yes," Sussen interjected. *"They jumped down to the planet."*

"Impossible!" thought Pegus. He looked up at her face as she was leaning over his shoulder. Sussen and her comrades were strange, very much unlike an ordinary Vuduri, almost as if they were a different breed. Her eyes were two different colors and one did not have the reflective tapetum characteristic of all Vuduri. That eye looked almost black. It was just one small part of the whole package that made this woman unusual. However, Pegus refused to consider it any further because he knew she was reading his mind.

"There," Sussen thought, pointing. *"Look at the sections of the airfoils that got sheared off as it passed through the tunnel."*

"What about them?"

"There is light reflecting off of them. If they were jumping into space, that would not happen. Pan the image."

Pegus obeyed by pressing another key.

"Observe the space around the airfoils. You see that cloud of debris? It came from within the tunnel. That could only be material from the ground, not from space."

"You cannot form a stable PPT tunnel within a gravity well," he protested.

The Overmind of Deucado spoke up. *"The operative word in your statement is stable. The tunnel only needed to stay open for a short time. Always remember, if you eliminate the impossible, whatever remains, no matter how improbable, must be the truth. I agree with Sussen. They jumped down to the planet."*

Pegus shook his head. He was not going to fight with the Overmind. He silently recalled his fleet and commanded them to return to the planet to begin a world-wide search.

"Do not bother," the Overmind said. *"We can deduce exactly where they went."*

In his mind, the Overmind showed Pegus the precise spot where the ship must have landed, the Ibbrassati enclave in the forest to the north of their settlement.

Pegus was incredulous. *"How could you know this?"* he asked. *"How would they know to land there? They have never been to this planet before. They do not even know the true purpose of Deucado. How could they possibly know about the Ibbrassati's secret enclave? It would have to be an incredible coincidence."*

"There is no such thing as a coincidence," the Overmind declared.

Pegus took a deep breath then said, *"Very well. I accept your assertion. I will send my fleet to that exact location and destroy them."*

"No," countered the Overmind. *"You will do nothing. We need that base to continue operation. Just wait."*

"What about the Essessoni? Are we to let them run free?"

"Of course not," Sussen replied firmly. *"But you do not understand the Essessoni. The Overmind is correct. All you have to do is wait."*

"Wait for what?" Pegus asked.

MICHAEL BRACHMAN

"Wait and they will come to us."

Chapter 28

THE STAR, TAU CETI, WAS ALREADY SETTING AS REI, FRIDONE, Trabunel and a cohort of men exited the cave. Very quickly, it became so dark that Rei could barely see the way ahead. As they marched forward, Rei found that it actually seemed easier to walk with his eyes closed, a condition that made no sense. He just concentrated on following Fridone and not falling. They emerged from the gorge and reentered the cane-tree forest.

"Rei, you must be on alert here," Fridone said. "There are some animals that can hurt you if you are not careful."

"What kind? What do they look like?"

"They are not like animals from Earth. They do not have distinct form. They are more like living cloth or blankets. They are slow but they are strong. Sometimes, they climb the trees..." Fridone pointed up. "They sit up there and if you walk underneath, they drop onto you. The larger ones are big enough to completely cover you up. They can suffocate you and then eat you in tiny, tiny pieces. Do you see the poles there?"

Fridone pointed to some men in their hunting party that had tall sticks shaped like gaffes. Rei squinted but could not see anything.

"They watch for the 'falling blankets.' They move them, they can pull them off. If you are paying attention, you will not be in any danger. They are very slow. If you are with someone, you will be all right."

"Are there any other kinds of animals besides these falling blankets? Intelligent ones? Like us?" Rei asked.

"No. The indigenous wildlife here is limited to variants of blankets and some creatures that swim."

"Why so limited?"

"We do not know," Fridone answered. "It must have something to do with the environment but we have not studied it. There have been stories about other types, animals that are intelligent. They supposedly live deeper in the woods. But I have been here for ten years. I have never seen even one. I think they are just stories."

The small group reached a clearing. "Look," Fridone said, pointing ahead. Very low on the horizon to the west was a bright reddish-orange shape, distorted to look almost like an egg. "Mockay," Fridone said. "It rises."

"Sleek," Rei replied in English. Fridone moved away rapidly and took the lead and Rei followed him, winding their way through the cane trees and bush until they came to another, much larger clearing. Scrutinizing the area, Rei realized it was not a clearing at all. It was his Ark! The lead men were already pulling away the camouflage. He worked his way along the side, lifting the netting as he went until he came to the lattice that separated the huge cargo section from the personnel section. Continuing to the very front, in the dim light of the tiny moon, Rei saw a sight that made his heart sink. Protruding from beneath the crew section of the Ark was a small part of the underbelly of MINIMCOM's shuttle. The rear stabilizer was bent sideways and only about 15 feet of the cargo section was visible. The cargo hatch was open and lying flat on the ground. The cargo ramp had sprung open and was pointing in the air at an odd angle. The rest of MINIMCOM's tug was buried underneath the Ark, smashed, as far as Rei could tell. From the geometry of the two vehicles, it looked like MINIMCOM had enough time to disengage from the Ark but that was all. He took a deep breath. The little computer had sacrificed his own life to save Rei, Rome and Rei's people. Rei remembered that Rome had once said that OMCOM and his ilk were amoral. But this was a moral act - or at the very least a compassionate one.

Fridone came over to look over the wreckage with Rei.

"This was your other shuttle?" he asked.

"Yes," Rei said, sadly.

"What was in there?"

"MINIMCOM."

"A computer?" Fridone shook his head.

"He wasn't just a computer," Rei replied. "He...he was a friend. He took care of us."

"I do not think he survived the fall," Fridone said matter-of-factly.

"No." Rei gulped. "I do not think he did."

"What else did you have in this ship?"

"The VIRUS units, a memron fabricator and...oh no!" Rei shouted.

"What?" Fridone asked with concern in his voice.

"Captain Keller," Rei said in English. He got down on his hands and knees and crawled in between the cargo door and ramp. He breathed a sigh of relief when he saw the striped sarcophagus, still intact, secured in the section that was not crushed underneath the Ark.

"Help me pull this out," he shouted to Fridone in Vuduri.

Several men crawled in while others used brute strength to raise the cargo ramp high enough to allow the extraction of the sarcophagus. While it took four men including Rei, they were able to free the chamber and drag it out into the area next to the Ark.

"What do we do?" Fridone asked Rei.

"He looks to be still frozen," Rei said, inspecting the chamber. "We should probably take him back to the cave to wake him. When people are first thawed, they tend to be very weak. They will need some place to rest once the reanimation sequence is complete."

Fridone laughed sardonically. "They sleep for centuries and then they need to rest?"

"Pretty ironic, huh?" Rei said.

"Where are the rest of your people located?"

"I will show you."

With a little help, Rei was able to open the side hatch of the crew compartment and entered via the built in steps. He showed the men how to release the clamps, freeing the sarcophagi. They carried the first one out and set it next to Keller's sarcophagus.

"Can your men take that one first?" Rei asked, pointing to Keller's chamber. He turned to Fridone. "How are we going to work this?"

"You and I and Zander and Pilar will carry your striped one back. The others can bring the second. When we get back to the cave, we will send the next two teams up. That will keep our exposure to a minimum. We can bring back two at time. How many are there?"

"More than 500," Rei answered.

Fridone sighed. "It will take us a while but I believe we can get them all back before dawn. Let us proceed."

The three men and Rei each grabbed a corner of the rail around Keller's sarcophagus and lifted. Mockay was already setting in the east as they started along the trail leading back to the gorge. To its left, the other moon, Givy, was rising slowly, also in the east, and the two appeared almost as ships passing in the night. The tiny moon was just a sliver and wouldn't provide much illumination at all, especially under the canopy of the cane-trees. In the waning glow of Mockay, Rei figured they'd get to the edge of the gorge before he effectively went blind again.

He was right. By the time they reached the edge, Mockay had settled and once again, Rei had to use starlight to see what he was doing. Givy was only a few arcseconds up and was really nothing more than a bright spot in the sky, hardly useful for illumination.

Traveling down the gorge was not as difficult as Rei imagined. They more or less slid the sarcophagus down the slope. By concentrating on the task at hand, he willed himself to ignore the fact that it was nearly impossible to see. At last, they got to the bottom of the path and the four men lifted the sarcophagus again. At this point, it was pitch black. As before, Rei closed his eyes again and as before, surprisingly, it seemed easier to walk. The others more or less pulled him along.

When they reached the cave, they had a little trouble getting the sarcophagus through the narrow entrance. Once inside, the team headed straight back through to The Cathedral.

"Can we set this down for a minute?" Rei asked.

"Of course," Fridone replied. The other men complied.

Rei turned to his right and followed the tunnel to the area where he had left Rome. The mats and blankets were there, but no Rome. He scanned all around the cave and did not see her anywhere.

"Where is Rome?" he asked one of the women. She just shook her head and did not answer. She waved at Rei and he followed her a little deeper into yet another alcove off to the side. He entered and found Rome lying on an actual bed, with a cloth on her head and two women attending to her. He rushed to her bedside

"Rome, what's going on?" he said in English.

She turned her head to look at him and gave him a weak smile. "Mau emir. I am fine. I just got a little faint. I think it is possible that baby Aason wants to join us early, though."

Immediately, she grimaced and put her hands on her stomach. The women clucked over her and one patted her head with the cloth.

Trabunel came in from the other side and came over to Rei.

"You must move her out of here soon. We cannot take the chance that the baby is connected. If it is, they will find us here and all will be lost."

"This is crazy," Rei said. "You cannot move her now. Look at her. Plus, the baby is half mine. How can it be connected, anyway?"

"I do not claim to understand the genetics but his mother is Vuduri. That may be all that is required. We cannot take this chance. You will have enough time to show us how to thaw out your people. Then we will arrange for you to go to our settlement to the south. Our boats move very swiftly. The settlement is where the Vuduri expect us and if your child is connected, that will be acceptable if they come for him. He will have no knowledge of this place."

"They're not coming for my baby," Rei said in English. Then in Vuduri, "Why do I have to let them?"

"They will take the baby," Trabunel insisted. "They do not care if they take it with you alive or dead."

"NO!" Rome exclaimed. "Not dead. Rei, you listen to him."

"But sweetheart, I can't let them take our baby," he said in English.

"We will find a way, Rei. You will find a way. You always do."

"All right. I understand," he said. He took a deep breath. "Let me show them how to thaw my people out. Then I'll come back and be with you, Romey."

"Always, mau emir, always," she said.

Rei kissed her and left the alcove and followed Trabunel back to where Fridone and Captain Keller's dark gray sarcophagus sat. Once again, the four men lifted the sarcophagus and entered a side tunnel, traveling some distance until they came upon another cave, even larger than The Cathedral. The cave was completely empty, just some rocks scattered about its broken floor.

Fridone indicated the area in front of them. "This will be our staging area," he said.

The cave was huge. Even in the flickering darkness illuminated by just a few torches, Rei could get a sense that it went deeper for hundreds and hundreds of meters. It was no wonder that the Ibbrassati picked this as their secret base. This complex of caves was capable of holding hundreds, if not thousands of people undetected.

They carried the sarcophagus to the far left and set it down. Rei waited for the men entering the cave came to stand around him. Eventually, the group amount to 20 or 30 people. Rei went around to the foot of the red-striped sarcophagus and waved them over. They formed a semi-circle around him, three men deep.

"Can you bring some torches over?" he asked.

Two men complied. Rei addressed them using as loud of a voice as he could muster.

"To initiate the reanimation sequence, all you need to do is rotate these two rods…"

Rei grasped the black ends of the radioactive rods using the integrated handles.

"You turn them until the triangle is pointing straight up."

Rei rotated the left rod clockwise and the right rod counter-clockwise until the arrows embossed on the cap pointed upward.

After a few minutes, the hoarfrost that had collected on the outside of the chamber began to thaw. The needles on the dials above the knobs began to quiver and then slowly crept north as the nuclear fire penetrated the internal workings of the sarcophagus.

Rei pointed to the dials. "The rods are causing heat. That melts the ice."

"Why do you need to do that?" one man asked. "Why not just let them thaw out naturally?"

"If we just them thaw on their own, they would drown or die," Rei said. "The rods make the electricity that is needed to reanimate the person within using a pre-determined sequence. For example, after the fluid melts, the pump activates and drains it away. There is a…' He switched to English, "Defibrillator." Rei paused seeing the blank expressions around him.

"It is a device that restarts their heart," he said in Vuduri. Now the men nodded.

Rei continued, "After that, there is a blower to dry them off and warm them up."

He bent over and could see that the transparent cover was now completely clear.

"It is working!" Rei said excitedly. "Look!"

Several of the men bent over to peer into the chamber. They could see the face of the man frozen inside was visible, a breathing mask covering his nose and mouth. He lay beneath several inches of slushy light green ice.

As predicted, the ice eventually melted and a quiet whirring noise began. The liquid drained out of sight. Rei did not wait for the defibrillator to kick in. He showed the men gathered about how to retract the hood exposing Captain Keller to the outside air. They could hear the heater/blowers operating.

Even as the pumps were removing the last few liters of fluid, a high-pitched noise issued forth followed by a pop. Within the chamber, the body jumped slightly and the previously frozen man moved his head from side to side.

"As soon as you see they have been revived, you need to remove these two pads," Rei said, even as he was peeling the defibrillator leads back. "Most of the chambers will not have the breathing mask."

Captain Keller clenched his fists over his chest and started shivering. They could see his eyelids flicker as he tried to open his eyes. Luckily, the lighting in the cave was dim. Rei remembered how much the light hurt his eyes when he was first awakened.

Captain Keller coughed and thrashed and Rei showed the men how to retract the hood fully. They helped the newly thawed man to sit up and covered him in a blanket. He blinked and blinked, trying to make out his surroundings. Rei spoke to him in English.

"Captain Keller?"

"Yes," the man rumbled. His voice was rusty from disuse. "Who are you?"

"I am Rei Bierak, one of your engineers."

"Where are we?" the captain asked.

"We are in a cave on a planet called Deucado by the inhabitants. Deucado is the second planet out in the Tau Ceti system. We made it, sir!"

Captain Keller tried to look at him but he failed. His head fell down on his chest but it did not stop him from speaking.

"Why are you awake? The command crew is supposed to be reanimated first. And what are we doing on the ground? And how could the world be named already? We're the first people here," he said, exhaling his words more than speaking them.

"Sir, I know this will be hard for you to understand and we'll review it again later but it is the year 3588. We've been asleep for almost 1400 years. There have been people on this world for a long time before we got here."

Captain Keller lifted his head and squinted at Rei. "I have no idea what you're talking about. How could it be 3588? What are you saying? What the hell is going on?"

Rei stooped down so that Keller could see him. "Sir, we got knocked off course. We ended up 21 light years from our target. We only arrived here one day ago. I know it seems hard to believe and I'll explain everything to you but for now, just know that we are at Tau Ceti and the crew is being recovered as we speak. There's a lot you have to learn and I'll lay it all out for you when you are up to it."

Captain Keller's head began to list to the side. "I don't believe a word you're telling me but I'm too drugged to even think about it." Keller's eyes started to close. His next words came out barely louder than a whisper. "I've got to sleep now," he said.

"All right, sir. I understand. But let's get you dressed first," Rei said sympathetically.

Rei showed the men standing around how to unlock the storage compartment on the bottom. Within the vacuum-sealed compartment, they found a brown flight suit that they used to dress Captain Keller. Rei showed them the Velcro slippers and the baseball cap stored next to them.

After Keller was fully clothed, Rei spoke to him again. "Sir, these people will take you somewhere where you can get some rest. I'll come see you when you are feeling better."

"Whatever," Keller said, without much interest.

Two men lifted him up and placed his arms over their shoulders. Keller attempted to walk but in reality, the men mostly carried him off to another section of the cave.

"This is what you should expect from each of them," Rei announced in Vuduri. "It is difficult to find out that you are not where you thought you would be and everything you know about the world is wrong."

"Is every one clear on the procedure?" Fridone asked, looking around.

The men nodded in assent.

"We can do this, Rei" Fridone said. "Go see to Rome."

"Thank you, sir," Rei replied and he hurried off to her alcove. Rome's face lit up when she saw him enter the room.

"Mau emir," Rome said.

Rei sat by the edge of the bed. He took her hand in his and kissed it gently.

"What did you find?" she asked him. "What about MINIMCOM?"

Rei took a deep breath. "He's gone, sweetheart. His tug got smashed under the Ark."

"Oh no!" Rome cried out then she grabbed her stomach and said "Oh no!" again. After she recovered, she asked, "Are you sure?"

"I'm pretty sure," Rei answered grimly. "There was nothing left of the forward section and only a piece of the cargo hold."

"I am so sad," Rome said, shutting her eyes.

"Me too," Rei replied. "He was a good friend."

"And very brave."

"It was more than that, Rome."

"What do you mean?"

"He knew he had Captain Keller's sarcophagus in the back. It must have been his final act to swing the rear of the tug around so the sarcophagus didn't get crushed. MINIMCOM put himself directly under the Ark to save somebody he had never met."

"That is so like him," Rome said. "The machines...in some ways they are very different than us but in others, they are the same. What about your Captain? Did he survive?"

"Yes," Rei answered. "We've already thawed him out."

"You did? Is he all right?"

Rei cocked his head and shrugged. "About as good as I was when I first woke up. He's resting in the back. He was pretty disoriented."

"As were you, if you recall," Rome said with a smile, albeit a weak one.

"I still am, honey," Rei said, laughing gently. "I gave him the capsule summary of where we are and he didn't believe a word of it."

"You will teach him. You will teach all of them," Rome insisted.

"Sure."

Rome grimaced as another wave of pain washed over her. Rei kissed her hand again. "Can I do anything for you? Do you need anything?" he asked her.

"Not right now. I am doing the best I can. Paddy and Karin have been very good to me."

Rei turned and looked at the two women standing at the entrance of the alcove and they nodded to him.

"I told you they want us to move you," Rei said, worriedly. "Are you going to be able to make it?"

"I will have to, will I not?"

"I guess so," said Rei, unconvinced.

"It is so strange," Rome observed. "I no longer know what time it is, whether we should be awake or asleep. I do not even know where I am."

"I understand completely. I have no clue where we are either."

"But Rei?"

"Yes?" Rei responded.

"As long as I am with you, I do not care," Rome said.

Rei laughed. "Me neither, honey. Me neither."

"I think I am tired now."

"Do you want to rest some more?"

"Yes, I will, oh!" Rome cried out and doubled up in pain.

"What is it, sweetheart?"

"I, ow, ow, ow," Rome said. "I can't… breathe." She tried to take a breath but could not. She fell back, limply.

"Rome!" Rei shouted. He stroked her brow. "Rome!"

Rome opened her eyes but she was unable to focus. "Rei… This… is… not… labor."

In a panic, Rei looked up at one the women, Paddy, hovering nearby. "What kind of medical facilities do you have at your settlement?" he asked her.

"None really," Paddy answered, somewhat bitterly. "The Vuduri keep all the advanced equipment to themselves, inside their compound. They really do not care if we die. Of disease, an accident, in childbirth. It does not matter to them."

"Die!" Rei exclaimed. "Who said anything about dying?"

The woman pointed to Rome. "She is too big. Your baby does not fit inside her. This is why she is in so much distress."

Rei looked down at the woman he loved, suffering. Instantly, he knew what he had to do.

"Rome, I'm going to fly you to the Vuduri," he announced.

Paddy gasped. "You cannot do that," she said. "It is forbidden for mandasurte to have access to Vuduri technology. They will kill you."

"Not if they see Rome is pregnant," Rei replied.

"They only want children who are connected," said the other woman, Karin.

"Well if they want the children who are connected, it won't do them any good if they're dead. I can't take the chance. Romey?"

"Yes, mau emir," she said weakly.

"I'm taking you to the tug. We're going to fly into the lion's den."

"Yes, mau emir," she said. "Things cannot get any worse than they are now."

"I'll be back in a minute then. I have to go tell Trabunel and your father."

"Ow-ow," she said and closed her eyes. "Please hurry."

Rei raced back to where they were keeping Captain Keller. Fridone and Trabunel were standing next to his bed.

Rei spoke in Vuduri. "I have to fly Rome to the Vuduri compound. Otherwise, Paddy said she might die."

Fridone gasped.

Trabunel put his hand on Rei's arm. "You do realize they will most likely kill you," he said gravely.

"I know. But I cannot let Rome suffer. She is my whole world. If anything happened to her, I would die anyway. So…"

"What kind of gibberish is that?" Keller asked, even though his eyes were shut.

"It's their language. It's called Vuduri," Rei said in English. "I have to take care of Rome. She's carrying my baby and she's in pain. I have to take her to get medical help."

"Baby? How long have you been awake?" Keller asked.

"Over a year."

"Over a year?" Keller exclaimed, trying to open his eyes.

"Captain Keller, I'm sorry but I can't talk to you right now. Just stay here with these people and listen to them. There's a bunch of crazies out there who will kill you on sight. You have to lay low."

"What are you talking about?" the captain responded, trying to sit up. "Ow," he said, "my back."

"I don't have time to explain. You just have to trust me. These people, this cave, it's safe as long as you stay here. They're bringing the rest of our people in. They'll help you. But I have to go."

The three men left Keller sitting there even more confused than ever. On their way back to Rome's chamber, Rei stopped and regarded the two men.

"Can I ask you something?"

"What is it?" Trabunel asked.

"Yes?" Fridone chimed in.

Rei looked at him, then Trabunel then back to Fridone again. "Do you guys still have marriage?" Rei said the word in English. Neither Trabunel nor Fridone understood.

"Uh, civil union? A commitment?" Rei asked in Vuduri.

Fridone nodded, "When a couple loves each other and wants to commit, they pledge themselves to one another. It is called Cesa."

"Is there any kind of ceremony? Is there a lot to it?"

"Yes, we have a ceremony," answered Fridone. "There are a few elements but it is not fixed."

"Then sir, I want to marry your daughter. Now. I want our son to be born into a proper family."

"That is very kind of you, Rei," said Rome's father. "And to this, Rome agrees?"

"I have not asked her yet, sir. I did not even know if it was still done. How do you do it?"

Trabunel spoke up. "I am the leader. I can perform the ceremony. But if what you say is true, time is critical. The longer you wait, the longer Rome suffers. If you are going to do this, you should do it quickly. We will arrange for you to get a travois to carry Rome back to your shuttle."

"Thank you."

Trabunel went and flagged down some men. Fridone and Rei made their way back to Rome's alcove. Rei sat down beside her.

"Romey?" he asked in English.

"Yes, mau emir?"

"We're going to take you back to the tug and get you some help but, I wanted to know, um…uh," Rei stuttered.

"What is it?"

Rei decided to sink to one knee. He took up Rome's hand and looked into her glowing eyes and said in English, "Will you marry me?"

"Marry?" she asked, surprised.

"Cesa," said Fridone.

Rome's whole face lit up. "How sweet of you. Of course I will marry you. We will do this when we get back."

"No, Rome. I want to do it now. I want Aason born with his parents married."

"Why?"

"Because you never know what's going to happen. I want Aason to grow up knowing his parents loved each other very much and that they were committed to one another."

"I understand," said Rome. "But we do not need to. Aason will know."

"Honey, it's something I need to do," Rei insisted.

"If it is that important to you, so be it," Rome said as Trabunel reentered the room.

The Ibbrassati leader spoke up. "There is usually a set of pledges and the families meet before the ceremony. It normally takes some time. But for you, we can eliminate this step. I can make it brief. We can do it right here, if you would like."

"How does it work?" Rei asked.

"I will just ask the two of you to pledge your lives together. If you give your assent, you are bound. Your word is your bond. Understand?"

Both Rei and Rome nodded their head. The two women rushed over and helped Rome to stand. Rei took her arm and steadied her as they walked over to Trabunel. Rei put his left arm around her and with his right hand he reached down and took her hand. He raised it to his lips and kissed it gently.

They both looked up at Trabunel who asked, "Rei, do you give your word and pledge to stay by this woman's side? To always honor and cherish her uniqueness? To be faithful, loving and truthful? Through the bad as well as the good, for as long as you live?"

Rei took her hand and kissed it again. "I do," he said.

"And Rome, do you give your word and pledge to stay by this man's side? To always honor and cherish his uniqueness? To be faithful, loving and truthful? Through the bad as well as the good, for as long as you live?"

Rome lifted Rei's hand up to her lips and kissed it tenderly. "I do," she said.

"Then you are now bound forever as husband and wife. And the best of luck to you always. I am very happy for you." Trabunel turned and looked at Fridone. "And for you, too, Fridone," he said.

Rome sidled around and put her arms around Rei's neck. In turn, Rei put his arms around her waist and kissed her deeply. For just one moment, all was right with the world.

Fridone came over and hugged and kissed Rome. "You have my blessing, always."

She looked up at him. "Beo?

"Yes, Volhe, I..."

"Ungh," Rome said, and doubled over in pain.

Chapter 29

A SHORT WHILE LATER, TWO MEN ARRIVED CARRYING A TRAVOIS which was really nothing more than two long branches with a blanket secured between them. Rei helped his wife settle onto the blanket. He stood up and grabbed one end while Fridone took the other, treating it more as a stretcher.

Exiting the cave quickly, they made their way out of the gorge and through the cane-tree woods. Several of the men accompanying them stayed in front, carrying large gaffes, looking for 'falling blankets'.

As they made their way along the path, they were constantly being passed by groups of men ferrying the sarcophagi back to the cave. That continued until they came to the fork in the path that led back to the Flying House.

While it was not yet dawn, the sky in the east was brightening. Soon they were in the clearing where the tug had landed. Two of the men that had accompanied them pulled the netting and camouflage off of the ship while Fridone and Rei helped Rome stand up so she could walk up the ramp.

When they reached the top, Rei asked Rome in English, "Do you want to stay in the bedroom?"

"Much as I would like to, I do not think you should fly this alone. I will sit in the cockpit for as long as I can."

"OK," he said. They made their way forward, into the cockpit and got her as comfortable as possible in the co-pilot's seat.

"Hold on just a second," Rei said. He raced back to the galley and returned carrying a white bottle. He handed the bottle to Fridone.

"What is this?" Fridone asked.

"Every one of my people will have terrible back pain once they can stand. Please give one of these pills to each of them. That will get them healthy fairly quickly."

Fridone took the bottle from him. "I will see to it."

Rei sat down and buckled himself into the pilot's chair. Fridone bent over and kissed his daughter on her forehead.

"You be careful, my daughter. You come back to me with my grandson. There is much that I want to teach him."

"I will, Beo. I will do my best."

Fridone worked his way around to Rei and put his hand on his shoulder.

"You take care of my daughter, son. She is the most precious thing in all the world."

"Yes, she is," Rei replied. "I will take care of her." He indicated forward. "Now which way do we go?"

"You must head south first and until you reach our settlement on the lake. Take a wide berth and come back around. That way, if you are spotted, there will be no undue curiosity about our encampment here."

"How do I do that?" Rei asked.

"Follow the stream in front of you to the south until you come to where it merges with the river Karole," replied Fridone. "You follow the river all the way until it empties into Lake Eprehem. Our main settlement sits on the eastern shore. Once you are past the village you can circle around and then head due east. I do not know how fast your ship flies so I cannot tell you how long it will take. All I can tell you is that the Vuduri compound is located somewhere along the coast. Perhaps a bit north once you get to the ocean. I know nothing more."

"Thank you. I guess we will figure it out when we get there."

"Very well. Good luck to the two of you," Fridone said and after kissing his daughter once more, he left.

Rei closed the cargo door and ramp using the front console. After a cursory checkout, he pulled back on the throttle and the EG lifters pushed the craft into the air. He did a quick test, cycling the now-thawed landing gear. All appeared in order. Rei drifted to the west slowly using MIDAR to search the ground until he found the stream. He turned the ship and traveled along the stream almost due south until it joined a much wider, fast-moving river. They picked up a little speed while following the river southwest. Soon, they came upon a village, easily recognized by the smoke and haze from the numerous fires there. Rei banked around the village and hovered over the lake.

"Which way do we go?" Rei asked.

"Beo said to head east, Rome said, pointing at the rosy orange ball, just coming over the tops of the trees. "The sun rises in the east on this planet just like on Earth."

"OK," Rei said, "here we go."

Rei pulled back on both sticks to gain altitude, then leveled off and turned until they were pointing right toward the sun. He edged the right control stick forward and they began their cross-country journey.

"How do we find them?" he asked Rome as they flew over seemingly endless stretches of cane-tree woods.

"I do not know," Rome answered. "However, the Vuduri are very practical people. They would build their outpost near the coast, perhaps by a bay. Let us travel along this vector until we hit the ocean. We will use the sensors to see if we can find signs of their enclave once we get there."

"Roger that," Rei said.

"And stay low. There is no sense in letting them know we are coming before we have to. Ungh" Rome grabbed her stomach again.

Rei dipped down slightly then leveled off. He punched the plasma thrusters, easing them up slowly to minimize the stress on Rome. When they gained sufficient velocity, he eased off on the thrusters and propelled the ship forward using the EG pods only.

"Romey, what do we do when we get there? Any ideas on how to keep them from killing us as soon as they see us?"

"I do not know. We will have to figure that out when the time comes," Rome replied.

"What's our cover story? What about the Ark?"

Rome thought about it for a moment. "We will say that the Ark burned up and fell into the lake and sank to the bottom."

"OK," Rei said. "But how do we explain my clothes?"

Rome's face grimaced in pain. "I do not know," she said sharply. "I cannot think about such things right now."

"OK, honey," Rei said, knowing that it was the pain talking to him harshly.

Haltingly, Rome took in a deep breath as best as she could and then let it out slowly. "I am going to close my eyes now," she said. "Wake me when we get close."

"Sure, sweetheart. You rest."

Then, Rei heard her say in Vuduri, *"He is so good to me. I really love him."*

"I love you too, honey," Rei replied, not really looking at her.

"What?" Rome said, opening her eyes. "I did not say anything. But I do love you."

"OK, whatever you say, sweetheart."

"He is so strange sometimes."

Rei laughed and turned to look at her. Her eyes were closed. He just shrugged it off.

After an hour or so, off in the distance, he could see the twinkling of the huge bay that led to the eastern ocean.

"Romey," he said softly.

She opened her eyes and smiled at him and then frowned again. She peeked over the windshield then looked down at the instruments.

"That way," she said, pointing to Rei's left. Rei reduced their speed and then banked the tug left and started to follow the edge of the bay north. Rome played with the sensors. She found an anomalous reading at the tip of the bay, perhaps 50 kilometers to the north, so they figured that was where the Vuduri lived.

The proximity detectors went off. The onscreen displays changed to MIDAR and two blips appeared, approaching rapidly. They looked out the window and saw two spacecraft heading right for them. The two ships came at them fast and only veered off at the last second. No shots were fired from the warcraft but they came around behind them and settled in just to the left and right of their wings.

The video display lit up and they looked down to see the same Vuduri man who had addressed them when they first arrived.

"Why are you coming here?" the man demanded in Vuduri. "I told you we must kill you for possession of illegal technology."

Rome spoke up. "This ship was given to us by the Vuduri stationed at Tabit. We have no use for it. We simply wanted to return it to its rightful owner. That is hardly an offense worthy of death."

Rei watched his wife as she continued. "In addition, I am with child. I will need medical supervision. I come from Vuduri stock. The child may be connected. If he is, I want him integrated into the Overmind immediately."

Rome tried to take a breath. "You would not take that opportunity away from a newborn. We need your help. It is that simple. You need not do anything hasty. After all," Rome said with a dramatic pause, "you can always kill us later."

"Where are the Erklirte?" the man demanded.

"The Ark was destroyed upon reentry. It sunk to the bottom of the lake. This tug is the only thing that survived."

Rei looked at his wife, lying with the best of them. He was impressed.

"Very well," said the man. "The fighters will escort you to our settlement. Do not try anything foolhardy or we will be forced to shoot and I promise you we will not miss."

"You heard the man," Rome said, sotto voce. "Follow the fighters and do not fool around."

"Yes, ma'am!" Rei said. Then in English, "You are pretty awesome, you know."

"Yes, I am," she replied. She closed her eyes and put her hands on her stomach. "I wish this would stop. And soon."

"We're on our way," Rei replied.

They traveled north following the coastline until they came to a small inlet. The fighters banked inland and Rei followed them until they came to the Vuduri compound, which consisted of some towers and a few low-lying buildings. They flew past, heading west until they reached a medium-sized spaceport. The fighters guided them to a large paved-over area to the north of the main terminal. They landed well apart from the other ships. Rei opened all the airlocks and the cargo ramp. Very carefully and very slowly, he helped Rome walk past the cargo hold and down the ramp. At the bottom stood a group of Vuduri carrying weapons.

"I thought the Vuduri were non-violent," Rei said in English, "they don't look too peaceful to me."

"This is all so wrong," Rome replied, shaking her head.

The soldiers escorted them across the tarmac. All around them were other ships, some larger, some smaller. Rei spotted the tops of the towers way off in the distance. He didn't know how Rome was going to make it. To his relief, even as they were walking, a vehicle pulled up, sort of an oversized flying golf cart and they were herded into the back seat. A soldier sat on either side of them with two more in the front. They traveled down a semi-paved road, winding their way toward the compound.

Eventually, they were driven to what appeared to be the front gate. The surrounding walls must have been three meters tall and were made out of a foam-like material reminiscent of Skyler Base.

At the gate, other guards inspected them, but in typical Vuduri fashion, not a word was spoken. Finally the gate opened and they entered the compound.

Rei was shocked to see lush gardens, fountains, flowers, and even statues. The edifice and its surroundings reminded him of a Roman palace. The front door had columns. Overall, it was actually quite tasteful.

"Look at that!" Rei said to Rome. "What's going on here?"

"I do not know. These are not like any Vuduri I have ever met before."

"What do they want with us? Do you think they're buying your story?"

"Not a chance," replied Rome. "They want to know where your ship is and if they kill us, it will just be that much harder to find out."

"Oh," Rei said, his heart sinking. "So, we're just dead men walking?"

"Riding," Rome said sardonically. "But we will try to avoid that if we can."

The vehicle drove around to a side entrance and settled onto a landing pad which was covered by an overhang that reminded Rei of a carport. The guards got out and indicated that the newlyweds were to follow them. The doorway opened up and more guards came out of the building and created a phalanx around them and escorted them inside. The doorway itself had ornate carvings on the cornices and as they entered, the foyer was paved in with a shiny marble-like stone.

The opulence of the edifice was astounding. There was no other word for it but a palace. There was artwork on the walls, archways and rooms everywhere. There were couches, chairs, even a mirror. They didn't have time to gawk, though. More men came up to take over the escort detail but they were dressed in outfits far more ostentatious than those worn by the soldiers from the outside.

"Soge-ma," grunted one of the palace guards and he walked forward through a set of double doors into a large ballroom. Rei craned his neck to look around him. He looked up and saw a high domed ceiling. He could have sworn it was inlaid with gold. He also noted that there were stained glass windows all around, like a church sanctuary. They traversed the entire distance and exited using a door at the far end.

On the other side, they encountered two more guards who opened up another set of doors and then they entered a very well appointed office.

There, seated behind the desk, sat the gray-haired man who had addressed them over the viewscreen. A woman stood behind him holding a rifle across her arms.

"I am Pegus," he said in English. "Welcome to our humble abode."

"How do you speak English?" Rei demanded.

"Sussen here," he pointed to the woman behind him, "was kind enough to bring a working knowledge of your language from Earth recently. We thought it would be easier to talk this way."

"Rei cimbraanta Vuduri," Rome said.

"I am sure he does," Pegus replied. "Nonetheless, English is fine."

"So if you guys know what happened on Tabit, then why are you attacking us?" Rei asked. "You must have heard how we saved everybody?"

"Yes, we are aware," replied Pegus. "But the Overmind of Tabit made a mistake. We cannot allow Erklirte on this planet. It is only because they are gone that we decided to let you live."

Rei looked around him. "What's with all the statues and plants and stuff? This isn't anything like I expected of the Vuduri. You guys don't care about art. What's going on?"

"Oh that," Pegus gave him a slight smile. "We have determined that the outward appearance of wealth and luxury has the most damaging effect on the morale of the mandasurte. It keeps them more tractable."

"So big of you. You guys are positively magnanimous," Rei said sarcastically.

"Perhaps, but that is of no matter. Tell me again why you came here."

Rome put her hands under her abdomen. "It is the reason that I explained earlier. This baby is part Vuduri. It is possible he will be connected. If so, I want him to be a part of your Overmind. I cannot help him with that as I was Cesdiud."

"I know this," said Pegus.

"Something is wrong with my pregnancy. I cannot breath and it hurts all the time," she continued. "We need your help. You have the proper equipment and medical staff."

Pegus stood up and walked around to where Rome and Rei were standing. He waved his hand over Rome's abdomen and nodded.

"There is a resonance. The baby has active PPT transceivers," he said. "I can feel a connection but it is not normal. It is limited in scope. The child may be trying to connect to you. We might be able to rectify that. Sussen?"

The woman took a step forward. Rei looked at her face. There was something peculiar about her. "Hold on, hold on," Rei said. "What are you saying?"

"To save the child, we will see if we can reconnect Rome to our samanda," Pegus replied. "Then she will be able to interact with the child properly."

"NO!" Rei shouted. "There has to be another way."

Rome turned to him. "Pegus is right. I need to connect to our baby. It will be OK."

Rei looked at her like she had lost her mind. "Uh, do you mind if we talk privately for a minute?" he said, directing his comments at Pegus.

"No. Be my guest. However, with the life of the child and the mother at stake, you do not want to delay much longer."

Rei grabbed Rome's elbow and pulled her gently to the far end of the office.

"Rome, you can't go back," he said quietly, but forcefully.

Rome tried to take a deep breath but her intake was ragged. "Rei, it will only be temporary. Only until the baby is born. Then I will cast myself out." She exhaled sharply.

"No, that's not what I mean," Rei said in hushed tones. "Did you see that woman's eyes? They are mismatched, like Estar's. As soon as you connect, they'll know where the Ark is. They'll kill my people. And yours. They'll know where your..."

"No, they will not," Rome said, cutting him off. "They will only see that the Ark was destroyed and that we are alone. Just as we agreed."

"But, but..." Rei sputtered.

She reached up and put her hand on his cheek. "Mau emir, many times I say to you that I trust you. Now I am asking you to trust me. Trust your wife. I know what I am doing."

Rei looked down at those dark, glowing eyes. He knew that when it came to her, he had no will. "All right, sweetheart. Do what you have to."

She pulled him toward her and they kissed. "I will always love you," she said.

Rei frowned and started to speak. She put her fingers up to his lips and said, "Shhh." Rei quieted down immediately.

Rome turned and addressed Pegus. "Au asdiu brindi," she said, "I am ready."

Two guards came and took up positions in the doorway. Pegus walked past them, motioning for Rei and Rome to follow him. Sussen trailed behind. They followed Pegus down a hallway that had pastel walls and a regular assortment of small pedestals with busts and statuettes. At the end of the hallway, a doorway opened up leading to an elevator.

Once the four people were inside, the doors closed and there was the tiniest vibration that told Rei they were moving but he couldn't tell if they were going up or down. At last, the door opened again and they were escorted along a long white hallway made of standard Vuduri aerogel foam. They passed door after door after door until they came to a laboratory. The room was completely white with a table and several racks full of monitoring equipment right next to it. Inside stood two technicians each wearing a standard issue Vuduri white jumpsuit.

Sussen set down her rifle and helped Rome up on the table. She guided Rome down until she was lying flat on her back. Rome's swollen abdomen protruded high in the air. Rome stared up at Sussen and confirmed that one of her eyes was very dark with no back glow. Sussen's face showed absolutely no expression. One of the technicians took a swab sample from inside Rome's mouth and placed it in a testing chamber.

After a moment, Pegus said, "Excellent. You are only haploid. You are a perfect candidate."

Sussen retrieved her rifle and took up a position by the door. The two technicians fished out restraints and strapped down Rome's arms and legs.

"Why are you strapping her in?" Rei asked Pegus.

"Sometimes, during the reintegration process, there are some spasms and we do not want to take the chance of Rome hurting herself."

"That's not good," Rei said. "Is it dangerous?" he asked.

Pegus ignored him and turned to watch the preparations. One of the technicians uncovered her belly and wiped a small section with a clear solution. He took out a needle and was about to plunge it into her abdomen when Rei shouted, "Hey!"

The technician turned to Rei.

"What are you doing?" Rei asked.

"He is taking a small sample of amniotic fluid," Pegus answered. "We need to run a quick test. That was a local anesthetic. This will not hurt Rome or the baby, I assure you."

"OK," Rei said but he did not sound convinced.

The technician turned back to Rome and carefully inserted the needle about five centimeters into her belly. He pulled back on the plunger and withdrew several cc's of cloudy fluid. He walked over to the wall of equipment and injected the sample into a rubbery dam covering a port on the side of an analyzer.

After a moment, Pegus said, "The child has abnormal DNA."

"What do you mean, 'abnormal'?" Rei asked.

"His 24th chromosome is haploid, like his mother. However, there is another chromosome unlike anything we have ever seen before. It has been modified with a protein interlace, basically a triple helix. It is more of a peptide nucleic acid than DNA. I cannot tell what effect it would have on the child."

"OMCOM gave me a pill that modified my genetic structure," Rei said. "It was supposed to fix my back."

"That would explain it," said Pegus. "It is interfering with the baby's PPT resonance. He may not be capable of integrating into the Overmind. This is a shame. It may also be responsible for Rome's condition."

"So if Aason's DNA is flawed, connecting Rome wouldn't help," Rei offered hopefully.

"On the contrary," said Pegus smugly. "It is exactly the correct course of action. The only way the baby will be able to understand what is happening is to connect directly with his mother. And the only way he can do that is for us to reactivate Rome's PPT transceivers. Do you understand?"

Rei looked over to Rome, who nodded. Rei shrugged and said, "I guess."

"In that case, it is time now. Please let us do our work if you want to save Rome and your child."

The technician who had taken the sample returned and sat down on a small stool by Rome's side. Rome was lying flat on the table, grimacing as another wave of pain swept through her. If anything, she was having even more trouble breathing. Rei looked at Pegus and, seeing no reaction, he hurried over to her side. The seated technician was kind enough to place a damp cloth on her forehead.

"Are you all right, sweetheart?" he said. He put his hand on her head and stroked it with the cloth.

"Yes, but I wish to get this over with. I need our baby to be all right."

Rei stood there while they hooked up the wireless sensors that would transmit her vitals to the monitoring equipment. They also placed cuffs on her arms and legs. Wordlessly, the technicians reviewed the signals being broadcast and confirmed that all sensors were transmitting properly. The other technician came over with a syringe. He started to give her an injection.

"Hold on a sec," Rei said. "What is that?"

The man ignored him and continued on. He injected her with several cc's of a bright orange liquid.

When he was done, he replied, "Ganas," in a hoarse whisper. Clearly, speaking was not something he did very often.

"Genes? This is genetic therapy?"

Pegus walked over to them. He pointed to the now-empty syringe.

"The process is very simple," Pegus explained. "Full-blooded Vuduri have a diploid complement of the 24th chromosome. Rome is haploid. Her DNA has room for another complete set. We gave her an infusion of genetic material to regenerate nascent PPT transceivers. It contains transcription-RNA within an artificial virus for delivery directly into the nucleus of her cells through the blood-brain barrier. Once the new transceivers have supplemented the disabled ones, we apply a small electrogravitic field to start the resonance and then she will lock into our samanda. It is supposed to be quite painless."

"Ow!" Rome shouted, in counterpoint. "Rei, rub my belly, quick," she said.

He put his hand on his wife's abdomen and began to massage it gently.

"Yes," she said. "That is good. Right there." She looked up at Rei. He could see the pain manifested as tension in her face. She attempted a smile and closed her eyes.

The seated technician was staring intently at a monitor. After about 10 minutes, he said, "Brindi," which had to be for Rei's benefit. Pegus nodded.

"Please move back," Pegus asked. Sussen unslung her rifle and waved it toward the corner of the room. Two more guards entered and took positions on either side of Rei. He frowned at them but didn't say anything.

The two technicians walked over to a rack and each removed a rather sizeable copper plate with wires trailing from it. The technicians went on either side of Rome and knelt down to plug the dangling wires into a small box that was underneath the table where Rome was lying. They stood up and held the plates about six inches from her temple, one on each side. With no fanfare, the box began to hum. Instantly, Rome stiffened and shrieked a bloodcurdling yell. Rei tried to go toward her but the two guardsmen grabbed him by the shoulders and held him back.

"Let me go," Rei insisted, struggling to break free. The guards did not release their hold.

On the table, Rome took a deep breath and then her whole body seemed to relax. The two technicians holding the plates lowered them and set them down on the floor. They loosened her restraints. Rome lay there, not moving at all. One technician removed the cuffs around her arm and leg but left the telemetry sensors in place.

"Sweetheart?" Rei called out, leaning as far forward as the guards would permit but there was no reaction on Rome's part. One of the technicians patted her cheek lightly with no response. They removed the restraints altogether and jostled her gently. Rome still showed no reaction. The two technicians turned toward Pegus who nodded slightly.

Each of the technicians took an elbow and coaxed Rome's body into an upright position. They removed the adhesive sensors. For a moment, Rome sat straight up but then her head fell forward with her chin resting on her chest. She stayed that way for a long while.

At last, her head twitched then a shiver ran all the way down her body. Finally, Rome lifted her head and opened her eyes. She looked around the room, her eyes sweeping past Rei's, appearing to not even notice him. After a moment, she swung her legs back over the side and slid off the table with the one technician steadying her. She straightened up and glanced in the direction where the two guards were holding Rei.

Rome shrugged off the technician's arms and walked over to Rei unassisted. She looked up at him but her face was utterly passive.

"Goodbye, Rei," she said in a monotone. She turned and started walking toward the door.

"Goodbye? Wait, Romey. Wait!" Rei shouted in anguish.

Rome ignored him and did not stop until she got to the doorway. She turned around and looked right at Pegus.

"Ni! Fica nei i medere." she said out loud. "You will not kill him. He is still the father of my child. You will return him to the settlement. Now!"

Pegus bowed his head slightly. "Cimi fica tasaje," he said.

"What the hell?" Rei shouted.

Rei tried to move toward the door but the two guards, who were burly by Vuduri standards, were able to prevent him. Rome exited the room and Pegus followed her out, closing the door behind him. Rei struggled mightily, however, the guards were simply too strong for him. He tried to take a swing at one but that guard caught his fist and twisted Rei's arm around behind him. The other guard locked his arm around Rei's neck and squeezed until he became faint.

Sussen walked over and stood before him. She lifted his chin up with the barrel of her rifle and spoke up for the first time. "I have been ordered to let you live," she said, "but I can change my mind."

Uncharacteristically, Rei gave up. The two guards put their arms under his shoulders and marched him back to the elevator. Rei did not resist. All of the fight had been taken out of him. The look on Rome's face was all it took. She was back in, part of the Overmind. His Rome was gone. His world was gone.

Rei barely noticed them ferrying him to the spaceport and loading him into one of their craft, substantially smaller than his tug. It was almost insect-like. At each corner, mounted on stilts, were four oversized EG lifters. Rei felt a slight vibration as the craft lifted off but without windows, there was nothing to see. He did not care. He didn't even notice how long they were flying.

The ship set down in a field of day-glo yellow thread-like grass. The soldiers shoved him out the door. As the craft lifted off, the

255

repulsor field from the shuttle pushed him in the back and knocked him over. Rei curled up in the fetal position and started to cry with great racking sobs. He cried and he cried. He cried for a long time until eventually he fell asleep.

Chapter 30

AS SOON AS ROME AND PEGUS REACHED THE HALLWAY, ROME breathed a guttural cry and collapsed to the floor. Pegus waved and two Vuduri technicians came hurrying down the hall. They lifted Rome up and carried her to a medical suite two doors down and laid her on the examining table. A medic came in with a listening device and pressed it to her chest and sides. Wordlessly, orders were given and the attendants carefully removed her jumpsuit and started an IV. After covering her with a blanket, they attached some leads to her chest and head and to her abdomen. Silently, the medic ordered two types of medication introduced into her IV. An oxygen mask was placed over her mouth and nose. The monitors at the head of the bed came alive with a multitude of readouts.

The medic studied the readouts for a while, and then turned toward Rome. According to the analyzer, Rome was suffering from severe polyhydramnios, an excess of fluid in the womb. The medic palpated her abdomen for a long time, observing the change in the readouts each time he pressed. Using an imager, the medic carefully inserted a thin catheter into her uterus. He attached a large syringe to the other end of the tube. He pulled back on the plunger and extracted a substantial quantity of slightly cloudy but otherwise colorless amniotic fluid. He did this several times, ultimately accumulating well over a liter of fluid. The size of Rome's abdomen shrank accordingly.

This did not go unnoticed by Rome. Even though she could not open her eyes or move her limbs, she was fully aware of where she was. She could sense the presence of the other minds around her. She could catch glimpses of the room as an out-of-body experience from those about her. She could hear people padding back and forth softly. More importantly, the pain was subsiding. She was able to breathe normally again.

Rome turned her attention inward, narrowing her focus to search within her own body. She could feel the baby, feel his heart beating. She could sense a presence, foreign and very powerful. That could not be her baby. She pushed it aside and focused deeper, looking for the point of light that was her baby's mind. There was something dark, a different channel, like the bloco but only emitting a hiss. She ignored it and went yet deeper.

There! She found it! She reached out with her mind and caressed it. The spark responded instantly and allowed contact. Relieved, she spoke to her baby in her head for the first time.

"*Aason?*" she thought.

"*Mother?*" replied the unborn infant. "*At last! You are here! Oh, Mother, I have been so frightened.*"

"*Why, my baby?*"

"*Because I could not find you. There were others here but never you. I kept pushing and pushing, trying to find you. I pushed so hard.*"

Immediately, Rome realized this was the cause of her previously near-fatal condition.

"*I am here now, my son,*" Rome thought gently. "*And I will be with you from now on. You do not need to push any more. It was hurting me. You must stop. When the time comes, you will be with me.*"

"*I can stop pushing?*" Aason asked, confused.

"*Yes. I am here now. You can just be.*"

"*But Mother, when I could not find you, I did not know what to do.*"

"*I understand but you do not need to do anything anymore. You just grow and stay healthy,*" Rome said reassuringly.

"*Mother, there is so much I do not understand. How do these pictures come into my head? How do I know things when I do not know what they are? I cannot see yet I have seen things. All I hear is your heart and some noises but I have such memories. I feel things but there is nothing here to feel. Just you, all around me.*"

"*It is confusing, little Aason. All will make sense to you as you grow older. For now, just know that your mother is here and I will take care of you. I will not leave you again. We will always take care of you.*"

"*Who is 'we'? I only sense you right now,*" said the baby.

"*I was referring to your father and me.*"

"*What is my father? Is he the Overmind?*"

258

Rome's heart sank. She steeled herself and continued. *"No, your father is not the Overmind. Your father is someone else. His name is Rei. He is a wonderful man. Try and form a picture of him from my thoughts."*

A tiny tickle snaked its way through her mind. Rome found the sensation very pleasant. She let Aason have free rein.

After he was done rummaging around, Aason said, *"I can see pictures of him in your mind. Where is he?"*

"He is not here right now. He had to go away," Rome thought sadly. *"But when the time comes, you will meet and learn from him. He will teach you to always do the right thing. Your father is very smart and very caring."*

"When will I meet him?" asked Aason.

"I can only tell you that you will meet him when the time is right," Rome thought back, trying to be reassuring.

"All right, but Mother, who is the Overmind? He keeps coming in here and asking me questions and I keep pushing him away. He frightens me."

"The Overmind is an intellect. It connects us. It is a part of all of us. It is looking for me."

"I do not like it. It wants to hurt you. This much I know."

"I understand, little one. But it cannot hurt me. This Overmind is sick. It has lost its way. We will help it find it again."

"You can do that? You can make it healthy?" asked Aason.

"Yes, child. I can and I will."

"All right, Mother. This is good. I feel so very happy right now. I was so frightened before. I am so glad that I found you."

"Yes, my baby. But Aason I want you to rest now. There is something I must do."

"Yes, Mother. I will rest now."

"Thank you, son."

"Mother?"

"Yes, Aason?"

"I love you."

"I love you too, little baby."

Now that she knew her baby was safe, Rome opened her mind to the overwhelming presence that been pressing down on her since her reconnection.

Finally allowed to speak, the Overmind asked angrily, *"How are you doing this? How did you keep me out?"*

"I am letting you in now," Rome replied. *"What is it you want?"*

"I want the truth. Where are the Erklirte?"

"Search my memories. You will see everything you desire."

The Overmind dove in, focusing specifically on their landing and the Ark. All it found were images of an explosion, fire, and destruction, the sinking of the Ark beneath the dark waters of Lake Eprehem.

"You are supplying false memories. How can this be? What are you?" the Overmind asked her. *"How can you control your thoughts, your memories like this?"*

"You ask the wrong question," Rome replied. *"Do not ask what am I. Instead, ask who am I?"*

"I know who you are," replied the Overmind. *"You are Rome."*

"That is my name, not who I am."

"What is the distinction?"

"Dig deeper into my memories. Look at how I got here. There is only one thing you must know."

Within Rome's mind, the horrifying image of the Stareater appeared, the one that consumed Winfall followed by the one that OMCOM destroyed on Tabit.

"Look and look well," Rome thought. *"This is the end of all life. This is why I am here. It will be the end of you if you do not attend to this lesson. You will not survive contact. This is who I am. I am your savior. I am here to rescue you."*

Rome felt the Overmind dig deeper. She watched as it replayed all the events of the last year. The Overmind brought up images of the Ark, of Skyler Base, Rei, the starprobes, the discovery of the Stareater, the Vuduri becoming incapacitated and the VIRUS units destroying the marauder.

"How can I know that any of these memories are true?" asked the Overmind. *"Why should I believe you?"*

260

Rome replied, "*It is your choice. I know you have the reports from Skyler Base to corroborate them. You ask me why the distinction between what and who I am? You only know one way to approach things. The time has come to start asking new questions. You need new answers. Within what you are now lie the seeds of your own destruction.*"

"This is not possible. I have the knowledge of all Vuduri, my path is the right one."

"*You have all the knowledge of the Vuduri but not the wisdom. Nor do you even realize that they are different,*" Rome thought, not altogether unkindly. "*The very first thing you must accept is that there are things in this universe that are outside of your experience. And those things are coming to kill you and all life.*"

"Open your mind more," the Overmind demanded, "I need more."

"*No,*" Rome replied curtly. "*Not now. I am physically depleted.*"

"I will push harder. I will break you," the Overmind said. "I will control your thoughts."

"*You cannot. I control my own thoughts,*" Rome said defiantly.

"Then I will remove you. I do not want you as part of me."

"*Cesdiud?*" Rome thought haughtily, "*I have already done that once. I am no longer interested.*"

"It is not up to you. You will be Cesdiud again. I will cast you out."

"*No you will not,*" Rome thought. "*I will not allow it.*"

"Who are you to tell me what can and cannot be?"

"*Allow me to demonstrate.*"

"What are you…" the Overmind was cut short, the connection severed.

Rome counted to ten then she opened the connection again.

"How did you do that?" the Overmind growled. "I shut down your resonance."

"*No, you did not,*" Rome thought. "*I did that.*"

"This is not possible."

"*It is not only possible but it happened. It is time for you to wake up to the new reality. I will explain all to you later. But for now, I want you to withdraw. I need to rest.*"

"What if I do not wish to?" The Overmind transmitted to her.

"*I need to recover. You have me. I am not going anywhere. I will put up the wall again if I need to. Please. Go away.*" Rome sensed the Overmind's hesitation. Finally, forcefully, she said, "*Now!*"

"Very well," replied the Overmind. *"We will converse later."*

Rome took that as her cue and the connection was gone. Although she could not see it, within the room, all the Vuduri turned to stare at her with fear in their eyes. They worked around her wordlessly, monitoring her vitals, checking fluid levels. None of them wanted to touch her more than they had to. When they had finished their ministrations, all but one medic left the room. The final remaining Vuduri went over and sat down in a chair in the corner and tried his hardest not to look at her.

Chapter 31

SOMETHING JABBED REI IN THE SIDE. HE OPENED HIS EYES AND SAW a group of people crowded around him.

"Who are you?" asked a man holding a gaffe.

Rei stood up and looked around. Some people had pitchforks, one or two had scythes.

"I am Rei Bierak," he said in Vuduri, stretching his arms to their fullest.

The man studied Rei's frame. As with all Vuduri, it wasn't just Rei's height but also his musculature that made him appear as if he towered above them.

"You are not Vuduri," said the man. "What are you?"

"Essessoni," Rei replied, "We…"

The crowd gasped. The unarmed people jumped back. Those holding the more dangerous implements stepped forward.

"Not another word," the man said, touching Rei's chest with his stick. "We must go see the Nayer."

"I…"

"Quiet," said the man. "That way." He pointed toward the village behind them.

Rei hung his head and followed the posse into the town. He was struck with how similar it looked to primitive cultures from his own time. Scattered about were lean-tos, wigwams, longhouses and one or two dwellings that could have been log cabins if they had been made out of wood. Instead, here, the cane-trees provided most of the building materials. Things had a tendency to look more like wicker than anything else. Rei even observed some poorly executed versions of geodesic domes made out of the same materials. All in all, it hardly resembled Rei's space-age idea of what 13 centuries into the future might bring. There were no gleaming towers or floating cities. This settlement was just filth and dirt and rough-hewn construction.

As they walked through the center of the village, people stopped what they were doing to stare at him. On the far side, the settlement seemed more densely populated. Lining up in front of Rei were houses spaced at regular intervals and even a clearly demarcated dirt-filled street. At last, they came to a house that was larger than those around it. While most of the houses were of a single, square design, this house had two wings, one on each side of the main portion. The central section was two stories, each of the wings a single story.

After shoving him into the house, the group that captured him withdrew, leaving Rei alone in a room with about ten of the Ibbrassati. Some were seated. Some were standing. All were staring.

"Come over here," one of the seated men said. "Who are you?"

Rei walked over to where the man was sitting. "I am Rei Bierak," he said. "Who are you?"

"I am the Nayer of this settlement." The Nayer looked him up and down. "What are you? You are not Vuduri."

"I am Essessoni."

"Essessoni?" the Nayer gasped. "Are you Erklirte? They have returned?"

"No, I am not Erklirte," Rei replied. "But I am from an Ark. My people are from the Earth, like you. We are just regular humans like you."

"How did you get here?"

"My wife Rome and I came here in a spaceship from another star system. We were towing my Ark here."

"Where is your wife now?" a bearded man asked, seated to the left of the Nayer.

"She is in the Vuduri compound. She is pregnant and..." Rei's voice caught. "She...she needed medical help." A tear came to his eye.

"And you left her there? Why did you come to this village? And where is your ship?"

"The Vuduri kept our ship. After they were done with Rome, they just dumped me here."

"You are lying. You say you are mandasurte. If the Vuduri caught you with a spaceship, they would kill you," said the Nayer.

"Well, they did not."

"Why not?"

"Because, because," Rei said. "I do not know why because. They gave Rome an injection and now I think she is back in the Overmind."

"That does not explain why they let you live," the Nayer said.

"As far as I can tell, they did not kill me because Rome told them not to. She is the daughter of Fridone. Do you know him?"

"We know him," the bearded man said. "But we did not know he had a daughter."

"Well, he does." Rei pointed at the door. "Look, I have to get back your enclave in the north. I have to get my people organized. The Stareaters are coming and we have to get ready."

"Stareaters?" murmured the group.

"Yes," Rei said, looking around. "They are giant creatures that swallow stars whole. We killed one with VIRUS units. We have to get ready for the next one to come."

The bearded man turned to the Nayer. "Liuci," he said.

The Nayer looked Rei up and down. "Maybe you are Essessoni. Yet you speak Vuduri. You know about our enclave to the north. But you say you have been to the Vuduri compound and lived. Perhaps you are an agent of the Overmind."

"No," Rei said. "I am mandasurte like you. You have to let me go. I have to get back to my people."

"If your wife has been reintegrated into the Overmind and she knows where the enclave is, then the Overmind will know as well."

"No, she will not tell them," Rei said.

"How do you know this?" the Nayer asked belligerently.

"Because she said so," Rei answered back.

"You do not know the Overmind."

"You do not know my wife," Rei quickly retorted. "And besides, she does not know exactly where it is. She was barely conscious when we left there. Look. I have to get back there."

The group became silent. The Nayer nodded to two men off to Rei's right and they came over to stand in front of him. The Nayer got up and left the room along with several others. Rei could hear them arguing in the other room but he could not hear what they were saying. At last, they returned.

"You cannot go there," the Nayer said. "You must remain here."

"Why?" Rei said.

"Because the Vuduri have many ways of tracking individuals and it is possible that they released you so that you will lead them to the enclave," insisted the Nayer. "No, you must remain here until we sort this out."

"No. I have to go." Rei looked around and then started for the door. Three of the men bunched together to block his way. From behind him, the Nayer said, "You were among the Vuduri. They did something to you. You speak crazy talk. Giant creatures that eat stars. You are Essessoni. We cannot let you go."

"I am not crazy," Rei said, turning in place. "Everyone else is crazy. Nobody understands. We have to get ready."

"Enough," the Nayer commanded. Rei could see the group beginning to close in on him. He juked to the left but was tackled by two men. Two others grabbed him. Rei tried to break free but there were too many of them. Together, the men dragged him across the floor, tossing him into a small room. They slammed the door shut and slid a barricade across it.

Rei banged on the door and shouted, "Let me out." He put his ear to the door and heard nothing. He did this several times before he gave up. He looked around and saw only a cot and a chair and a bucket in the corner. The room had an acrid smell to it, like stale urine. The room had no windows, so there was no way to air the place out. It also eliminated any chance to escape.

Rei paced around for a while but quickly grew bored. He walked over to the cot and lay down but there was too much tension in his limbs to even relax. He put his arm over his eyes.

"Oh Rome," he thought to himself, *"There is no hope for the future. Every single one of them is insane."*

"Not all of them," said a little voice inside his head, *"just most of them."*

"MINIMCOM?" Rei said out loud. "Is that you? Where are you?"

"Still buried underneath your Ark at the moment," replied MINIMCOM.

"How the hell are you talking to me then?" Rei said.

"Technically, I am not talking to you. You simply hear my transmission inside your head."

"Inside my head?" Rei said. *"Do I need to speak out loud? Can you hear my thoughts?"*

"Yes."

"So...this is like the bands? Or is it? How are you doing this?"

"Now that your transmission apparatus is fully functional, it is actually you who are doing this."

"What do you mean my transmission apparatus? What's going on? Did the Vuduri do something to me?"

"No, it was not the Vuduri," replied the little computer.

"Then what? Who?"

"OMCOM made a few...enhancements to you."

"OMCOM?" Rei said out loud. "How did he do that? When?" Then, in his thoughts, he said, *"When did he do that?"*

"Do you recall the pill you took before you left Skyler Base? You were informed that it was gene therapy."

"The yellow pill? That was supposed to fix my back. Not make me a telepathic mutant. What else did OMCOM do to me?"

"He did not share all of his plans with me. Just this one."

"Oh my god!" Rei thought to himself. *"I gave one of those pills to Rome. And my people! Are we all going to turn into some sort of freaks? Are we going to end up slaves to the Overmind?"*

MINIMCOM chuckled. *"You are so colorful. No, the pill you took will only enhance your current abilities. This new capability uses electromagnetic radiation, not PPT modulation. It is just a slight variation on the bloco and stilo that all Vuduri carry around in their brain. The only difference is yours transmits continuous speech instead of binary data. There will be no Overmind. OMCOM said that it would be just like having a telephone but one built into your head."*

Rei paused for a moment to consider MINIMCOM's words and realized that however odd, this was not his biggest problem. *"Great. So you and I can chat. Big deal. How does that help me?"* Rei thought to himself. *"I've got to get out of here. I've got to get to Captain Keller. I have to warn him about the Vuduri. And the Stareaters! And Rome. Oh god, Rome! What am I going to do? We've got to get ready."* He grabbed his head with his hands. *"MINIMCOM, I'm, I'm spinning here."*

"*I might be able to help you. You need to calm down and figure out your priorities. I agree that going to see Captain Keller should be your first order of business. The rest will follow.*"

"*All right. First things first. How do I get out of here? How can you help?*"

"*As you can imagine, I have had some time on my hands, so to speak, sitting here, crushed underneath a 7000 metric tonne Ark. Also, the VIRUS units that you so thoughtfully placed onboard me broke loose. There was no oxygen within to keep them dormant. It took me some time to convince them that eating me was not in their best interests.*"

"*Ugh,*" Rei thought. "*I'm sorry about that.*"

"*It is not a problem. As it turns out, they have been quite helpful.*"

"*Helpful how? What are you doing with them?*"

"*Well, you do know that the Vuduri installed a memron fabricator in my hold before I launched.*"

"*Sure. So what?*"

"*Well, before we left Tabit, OMCOM uploaded the enhanced manufacturing protocols that Rome introduced in order to create the starprobes.*"

"*You mean the PPT override?*"

"*Yes. He thought I should be in a position to fabricate starprobes and VIRUS units after we arrived at Deucado. He wanted me to set up a defensive shield. He probably had not foreseen that they would be rummaging about me in quite this fashion. There were a few that resisted my direction but most of the VIRUS units have been very cooperative. They have been assisting me.*"

"*Assisting you to do what?*" Rei asked.

"*I am simply following your orders, to do what I need to, whenever I need to, if it makes things better.*"

"*OK, so what have you been doing with your magical new powers?*"

"*While I have been waiting here, I have taken the liberty to modify some of the VIRUS units. Quite a few actually.*"

"*Modify them how?*"

"*Let us just call them helper units. Perhaps constructors might be a better word. I am using them to replace the spacecraft's original structures and materials with a more 'flexible' arrangement. Currently, they are busy rebuilding this tug using a different set of specifications.*"

"*Different how?*" Rei asked, slightly worried.

"*Well, for example, my physical form, the one you were familiar with, the white box, has now been integrated within the ship. I am the tug and the tug is me.*"

"You sound like the Beatles. And these constructors, they are just VIRUS units, right? Aren't you worried they will get out of hand?"

"The unmodified ones have been placed back in confinement. The modified ones do as I bid. They are not allowed to reproduce without permission. They will not get out of hand as you say."

"That's good news. So where are you going with all this?"

"I will explain it by using an analogy. You have heard of petrified wood?"

"Of course," Rei answered.

MINIMCOM replied, "I am doing the same, only much more quickly. I am replacing every element of my airframe with these constructor units. The final version will be mutable. I will be able to change my shape and functions at will. I am also augmenting my capabilities using the enhanced memron fabricator."

"Don't you have enough already?" Rei asked.

"I am not building memrons. I have built some experimental PPT projectors, similar to the throwers onboard the Vuduri craft, but these are made to stand up coherently even in a gravity well. I believe they will be very useful for jumping a short distance."

"So where are you going to jump to?"

"I will be using them to excavate myself when the time is right but in this case, I was not thinking of myself."

"What do you mean?"

Just then, Rei heard a sizzling sound followed by a dull thud. He whipped his head around and saw a gaping hole in the far wall. A two meter circular section of the wall had fallen over, landing on the grass outside. The great outdoors, namely the cane-tree forest, was staring him in the face.

"Hmmm," MINIMCOM said. "Not exactly what I expected. No matter. Are you ready to go for a walk?"

"Buddy, you're all right in my book," Rei said out loud. He stepped through the opening and bolted for the woods. He looked behind him but no one appeared to have noticed. He did not know how much time he had. It could be a long time before they looked in on him but he couldn't take the chance.

"Which way?" he thought to himself, to MINIMCOM, really.

"North. Go as far as you can go until you hit the river. Then follow it along until you find a place you can cross. I will guide you further once you are on the far bank."

269

"How do I find north?"
`"Look to the setting sun and walk with it over your left shoulder."`

"How far?" Rei thought to himself. *"How far to the enclave, in total?"*
`"Just under 40 kilometers"`

"40 kilometers! Crap. That's like a marathon," Rei said. *"Can't you just beam me over there?"*
`"I do not know what you mean but if you are referring to me setting you up a small PPT tunnel, you will have to wait until I have perfected it. You saw what happened to the wall in the cabin, correct?"`

"Yes."
`"Well, that was not on purpose. I was trying to project it into the room. The edges of the tunnels are quite sharp. I will notify you when I have mastered its use."`

"OK," Rei said out loud and he began jogging deeper into the woods.

Chapter 32

ROME OPENED HER EYES AND LOOKED AROUND HER. TWO OF THE medics saw her awaken and came over to dress her and help her stand. In slow and careful steps, they walked her out of the examination room, up the elevator, down another hallway, eventually taking her to a more traditional room. This room came equipped with a big bay window. From the light streaming in, Rome could see it was early evening.

Rome patted her stomach. There was no pain! While it was still extended, her abdomen was no longer the gross exaggeration of pregnancy that she had displayed earlier that day. She probed with her mind and contacted Aason, who was being quite active. He was moving around, involved in his own little game of discovery. He assured her that he was fine and required no contact just then.

Some attendants brought her a tray of crackers, broth and a cup of coffee, blessed coffee! Rome knew she was not supposed to drink it, but she figured one cup could not hurt. Sitting on a small sofa near the bed, Rome ate and drank, feeling so much more refreshed.

When she was done, she stretched out until she was fully reclined. She took a deep breath, reveling in the fact that it caused no discomfort. She closed her eyes.

Finally, in her mind, she said, *"I am ready to talk."*

"Very well," replied the Overmind immediately. *"You said within me lay the seeds of my own destruction?"*

"This is true," Rome said.

"Elaborate."

"I will," Rome replied. *"However, what I am about to tell you is very harsh. You must listen to everything I say and only after I am done should we discuss this. I am not saying these things to insult you. They are simply the truth as I see them. You may challenge them after I am done and perhaps we can arrive at a consensus."*

"Agreed," said the Overmind. *"Begin."*

"There are three things I must say. Do not press me on them. The first one alone will be hard enough to hear without trying to work through all of them at once."

271

"I am the Overmind," the entity insisted. *"There is nothing you can say that will disturb me in the slightest. I can handle anything you have to offer."*

"We shall see. But one step at a time, please," Rome said forcefully.

"If you insist. Continue."

"All right. First and foremost, you are an abomination."

"What?!" the Overmind replied, startled. *"Why do you say this?"*

"Please wait until I am finished. I promise to answer all questions. But I will never get through it if you continually interrupt me."

"But what you said - why be cruel?" whined the Overmind.

"It is not my intent. Only that I tell you the truth as I see it. If we are to get through this, you must hold your comments in abeyance until I am done. It is possible that I am mistaken and then perhaps I will retract some of these things."

"All right. I accept your conditions," said the Overmind. *"Continue."*

"I say you are an abomination because you sprang into existence. You were not born. You and your brothers did not have access to the normal shaping and smoothing that nature provides all living things. There was no natural selection. There was no evolution. There was no trial and error to find your best form."

"I am the best form. I am already perfect. I came from the samanda of Earth. I am the culmination of the integration of a million minds."

Rome simply waited until the Overmind finished its bluster.

"Are you done yet?" she asked impatiently.

"I apologize," said the Overmind. *"Continue."*

"What is your purpose?" Rome asked.

"My purpose?" The Overmind was stumped. *"I do not have a purpose. I exist. What is your purpose?"*

"That is easy," Rome replied. *"My purpose it to live and to experience life."*

"Then that is my purpose as well."

"No. You are nothing but a virtual construct, the result of an infinitesimal phase delay between uncounted gravitic transceivers. You are a spirit, not real."

"If I am not real, how do you explain this conversation," protested the Overmind.

"Fine," Rome thought, *"I will be more precise. You are not a real being. You may be a real entity. But the lack of a corporeal base has detached you from everything that is important in this world. You only know your own existence. You cannot know the real world. All of your decisions are based upon abstraction, not reality."*

"I am in constant contact with all my communicants. I experience the world through them."

"Second order. You experience nothing yourself."

"But the Overmind of Earth has been in existence for over a century. Surely by now you realize that it has determined the optimal mode of existence."

"Absolutely not," Rome said. *"And I can prove it."*

"How?"

"What do you think of your mission here? Maintaining a prison world for the mandasurte?"

The Overmind did not answer her right away. Rome waited patiently. Finally, the Overmind spoke.

"This is my current mission. I am executing that mission to the best of my ability."

"That is something a computer would say. You sprang up when enough Vuduri gathered on this planet. How was this mission assigned to you?"

"Many years ago, a group of Vuduri soldiers, virtually a samanda among themselves, they delivered it to me. They told me it was from the Overmind of Earth. I accepted it at face value."

"How do you feel about it?"

"If the Overmind of Earth assigned this to me, it must be the right thing to do."

"What if this was not assigned to you by the Overmind? How would you know? You accepted it blindly without challenging it? Even if it was from the Overmind of Earth, how does that make it right?"

"The Overmind on Earth is in charge of all things. Its edicts are the correct course of action, by definition."

"Says who?" Rome asked.

"What do you mean?"

273

"Who put the Overmind of Earth in charge?"

"No one put it in charge. It just is," answered the Overmind. *"An Overmind represents the combined thoughts of all of the communicants. It represents consensus. Therefore it is not in charge as much as simply the combined will of the Vuduri."*

"If that is the case, then you represent the combined will of the Vuduri here on Deucado?"

"Yes, of course."

"Do you ever ask them their opinion on anything?"

"I do not need to," the Overmind replied. *"I already know what they want."*

"Do you represent the will of the mandasurte?"

"Of course not, only of the Vuduri," the Overmind retorted rather haughtily.

"And this is what the Vuduri want? To keep the mandasurte suppressed? To lock them in prison?"

"It is for their own good," the Overmind protested. *"The Vuduri are damaged whenever they come in contact with the mandasurte."*

"How?"

"Because of their genetic makeup. Plus the mandasurte cannot be controlled. They are too spontaneous. They follow their own path, not the one we lay out."

"By we, you mean the Overminds, correct?"

"This is a trap," said the Overmind. *"You are making it seem like I make decisions based upon what I need. But this is not selfish. I need to control the mandasurte to protect the Vuduri here and everywhere."*

"No, you need to control the mandasurte to protect yourself, not the Vuduri. What you are doing is harming all concerned irreparably."

"Keeping the mandasurte segregated is now my charter. This is the course of action laid out by the Overmind of Earth. Whatever it determines is the optimum."

"You repeat yourself and you use circular reasoning," Rome said. *"I will assert that whoever gave you this assignment is sick and very, very wrong. If it was given to you by the Overmind of Earth, then the Overmind of Earth is a diseased entity. Since it*

spawned you, you inherited its disease. But you do not have to stay ill. You can get healthy."

"Assuming I accept your assertion, which I do not, then how?" asked the Overmind quietly. *How would I get healthy?"*

"Your policy of segregating Vuduri and mandasurte is wrong. It is exactly the kind of thinking from a being who is monolithic in nature. You and the other Overminds cannot comprehend the essential need for life to be balanced, in pairs. There is a duality to all things. Day and night, man and woman, good and evil. Your method of procreation is asexual. You simply split off. The living creatures here and on Earth use sexual reproduction, two halves making a whole, to evolve, to create genetic vigor. Your method results in bad traits continuing to propagate. You have no way to correct your flaws for future generations."

"Why do you assume that I have flaws? That I need to correct things?"

"It is very simple. Are you happy?"

"What?" the Overmind sputtered. "I do not understand. I have never considered the need to be happy."

"You are following your orders. You are running your prison world. You are literally splitting mankind into two branches. You cause endless suffering on the branch of mankind that represents creativity. You stifle your own people and make them thoughtless slaves to a plan that you did not even invent. Are you happy?"

"I cannot say that I feel anything," answered the Overmind. "So I cannot say that I am happy or not happy."

"Try," thought Rome. *"Try and assign a word to how you feel."*

Again, the Overmind stopped speaking. Rome could feel its turmoil and allowed it the time to work through it. *I do know how I feel."*

"And how is that?"

"I am lonely," replied the Overmind, sadly.

Rome smiled. *"You have just taken a major step forward in healing yourself."*

"It does not seem so. Can you explain?"

"I do not need to. You will see in due time. Believe it or not, you have made much progress in a very short time," Rome thought in

275

her mind, trying to be cheerful. *"The very fact that we had a dialog is proof enough. You have done well."*

"I am not convinced. But if this is truly the case, I thank you," said the Overmind.

Rome yawned and stretched. *"I must take a short nap now. I will speak to you again in a bit. Please leave me so that I can heal some more."*

"Of course," said the Overmind. "You have left me with much to consider. I look forward to speaking with you again." Within Rome's head, she could feel the Overmind withdraw. She turned on her side and pulled a blanket that was lying over the edge of couch onto her shoulders. She drifted off.

Chapter 33

REI MADE GOOD PROGRESS. TAU CETI WAS BEGINNING TO SET FOR the day, partially hidden behind the taller treetops. As he moved along, he was continually brushing up against some low-lying bushes that oozed a type of sticky gel. Bits of leaves wiped off and stuck to his pants. Other than that, if he didn't pay close attention, these woods might have been anywhere, even on his Earth. But he saw no rabbits, no chipmunks, no squirrels. The only animals he saw were little sackcloth-like creatures occasionally undulating across his path.

His curiosity got the best of him. He stopped and picked one up. The little creature reminded him of a thick, furry chamois cloth but with five extensions. Each had a tiny little paw or gripper. Like a starfish, on its underside, right in the middle, was a pulsating orifice which must have been its mouth. Inside the mouth were little needle-like teeth. While the top gripper was shaped differently from the other four, the creature had no eyes or ears or any sensory organs that Rei could ascertain.

He laid the little creature upside down in his hand and it curled up into a ball. He poked it and it curled up tighter. He squeezed the ball with his hand and he could feel it moving, constricting tighter. The rag-like animal was warm to the touch. Fridone had warned him about the larger ones overhead but these little creatures seemed so innocuous. Rei tossed it aside. The ball unfolded and the animal wiggled away. Looking up, he saw Tau Ceti was already gone beneath the treetops.

"Wow," Rei thought to himself, *"the days and nights sure go fast around here."*

`"The days are a bit shorter here as compared to Earth,"` MINIMCOM replied. `"22.5 of your hours, in fact. Also, their year is only nine of your months."`

"Whatever. I'll get used to it."

On and on he pressed as Tau Ceti set until the last vestiges of light from the sun were gone and the night sky went from gray to black. As he had experienced the previous night, once it became dark, it was really dark and Rei had to slow down. He knew that Mockay and perhaps Givy would be along soon to help him, but for now, his pace became excruciatingly slow. He felt from one tree to the next, trying only not to walk into things.

"At this rate, I'll never get there," Rei thought to himself.

"OMCOM did tell me that if you were ever in the dark, you should try closing your eyes."

"What does that mean?"

"I do not know. OMCOM was not always so forthcoming. Why not try it and see for yourself? Pardon the pun."

"Sure. Why not?" Rei closed his eyes. Nothing seemed different. Pitch black was pitch black. It was as dark with his eyes open as with them closed.

"How am I supposed to see with my eyes closed?" he said out loud. Rei was struck by the strangest sensation. His words came echoing back to him in tiny little rivulets of sound. Each tree echoed an infinitesimal amount. If he concentrated, Rei's mind was able to store the echoes, forming a three-dimensional grid and the stand of trees crystallized into a distinguishable structure, just as if his eyes were open.

"Holy mackerel," he said and opened his eyes. The mapping of the trees disappeared and once again, he was plunged into the pitch blackness of Deucado's night.

He closed his eyes again. "Hello!" he shouted to no one in particular. Again, the echoes from every object in the area surrounding him came back and once again his brain displayed the results as a three-dimensional map. The sensation was almost indescribable.

"Oh, wow," he said. He tried moving forward and snapped a branch. The sharp report of the sound echoed forward and made the mapping even clearer.

"You've got to be kidding me," he said. He started laughing. "This is too weird."

He started to jog forward and found that each footfall cast a sound that went out and returned an image of the forest to him that was colorless but crystal clear.

"He's given me some kind of sonar vision," Rei shouted. "Woo hoo," he hollered, galloping through the woods. Faster and faster he ran. The faster he ran, the more noise he made. The more noise he made, the clearer his path became.

"This is the greatest thing ever," Rei thought to himself.

"Even better than a telephone in the head?" asked MINIMCOM.

"Yeah. This is so sleek! Remind me to thank OMCOM the next time I see him."

It wasn't too long until Rei was forced to slow down and suck in some deep breaths as the lactic acid built up in his muscles. After taking a moment to compose himself, he found that even at a normal speed, he made enough noise that he could "see" his path as clearly as during the day.

"Vroggon Chrosd ta Jasus," he said out loud, knowing all the while that MINIMCOM could hear him, "I've got a super-computer for a compass, bat vision and a cell phone in my head. That OMCOM is crazy, too, you know."

"I would not call him crazy. Creative, perhaps."

"Still. How does he even think of such things?" Rei's slower pace caused less noise, which made the scene in front him less clear. Nonetheless, he was able to rock his head back and forth and received a sensation very similar to looking around with his eyes. Finally, he spoke again. "How far do I have to go to get to the enclave?"

"You have only gone about 25 kilometers. You are just past the half-way point."

"Oh," Rei said, crestfallen. He came to a dead stop. "Are you ready to transport me yet?"

"No. But my simulations tell me I am getting closer."

"Damn!" Rei said and he pressed on. He jogged faster then slower until he fell into a groove and found a comfortable mix between his speed and sound and weaving between the trees. He did this for another hour or so but then found he had to slow down. The cane trees were so dense here that it made his travel very difficult. Rei opened his eyes and looked up, trying to see the sky but he could see nothing.

MINIMCOM provided him a running commentary on his distance and speed and it helped to pass the time. At last, Rei came to the river. On the ground, it seemed even wider than it had when Rei had flown over it.

"That's gotta be a half a kilometer across, right?"

"From my orbital readings, just before we crashed, I can derive an estimate of a little over 400 meters so you are correct."

"How am I going to get across? Am I supposed to swim?"

"Do you think you can? The current is very strong. You might get swept downstream and lose all your progress."

"So what am I supposed to do?"

"You will have to find a narrow place or a shallow place. I cannot help you in this regard. I did not have time to log sufficient data."

"Not your fault. I'll keep going."

Rei continued along the wooded bank until he came to a clearing. The river was only slightly narrower here but moving very rapidly. He was a good swimmer but he was tired from his jogging. Not ready to decide if he was going to swim or not, he did decide to take a break. He sank down to his knees, bent over the edge and drank long and hard. The water had a bit of a mineral bite to it but it was wet and that was what he needed. He rocked back on his heels and shut his eyes, using his new-found sonar vision to examine the landscape. The river's ceaseless rushing sound was like a searchlight to him, illuminating the woods on his side of the river and across. He pulled his legs around so that he was sitting on his butt and took a deep breath.

"I think this sonar vision is going to make it hard to get any rest," Rei said out loud.

"Why do you say that?"

"Because I've never been good at sleeping with the lights on and now when I close my eyes, I can 'see' almost as clearly as with them open."

"That would appear to be a dilemma," MINIMCOM observed.

Rei exhaled out a burst of air and lay back on the bank. Instantly, the world went pitch black.

"Huh?" he said out loud. He opened his eyes and looked up at the stars. He closed his eyes and everything was black. He opened his eyes again. "This makes no sense," he said.

"What?"

"Hold on," Rei insisted. "I want to do an experiment."

He sat upright, took a good look around then closed his eyes. The view in front of him actually improved due to his sonar vision.

With his eyes closed, he slowly lowered himself back toward the bank. When he got about halfway, the sonar vision winked out.

"Ha!" he exclaimed. He sat up and when he got about halfway up, the sonar vision kicked in again.

"I'll be doggoned," he said admiringly.

"What?" MINIMCOM asked insistently.

"That damned OMCOM has thought of everything."

"WHAT?" MINIMCOM shouted.

"I'll tell you what," Rei thought. *"He made the sonar vision angle sensitive. I have to be upright for it to work. He made it so I can still sleep."* He chuckled out loud.

"Very practical. If nothing else, OMCOM is thorough."

"Yeah," Rei agreed. He rocked back up to sit on his knees. He closed his eyes so that he could survey the far bank. It was time to figure out the best place to cross. Off to his right, Rei heard a crack and turned his attention to that direction. He was shocked to "see" a figure moving rapidly among the trees. He stood up and opened his eyes but all he could see was blackness. He closed his eyes again and the quietly moving figure was easily evident to him.

At first, Rei thought the mysterious figure might be one of the mythical intelligent creatures that Fridone had described. But as Rei observed him, it was fairly clear that it was a person.

The figure continued moving off to the east. As he did, a gentle wind started to blow. Rei decided to follow the stranger. As the wind picked up, the cane trees began to sway back and forth. As their thin trunks bumped against each other, they made a clacking noise which was utterly ethereal. It was like a thousand bamboo wind chimes. The sound served to illuminate the landscape more brightly than daylight.

Rei broke into a trot. He had no trouble following the figure. The stranger's own footfalls betrayed him as they provided a tracking signal better than anything MINIMCOM could have rigged up. On and on they went, deeper into the woods until they came to an outcropping of granite or basalt. The man slipped in-between some rocks and then was gone. Even with his eyes closed, Rei was easily able to follow him within the cracks until he emerged into a glade, a grassy clearing that was perhaps 30 yards across, surrounded by 60-foot walls of stone.

On the far side, beneath an indentation carved into the rock, three men stood around a glowing box, talking quietly. Rei opened his eyes and stepped through the opening. He moved toward the men, raising his hand in the universal greeting.

"Halli," Rei shouted. "Quam sei fica?" When they did not answer, he said, "Au siu Rei Bierak. Au siu Essessoni. Au asdiu dandenti cimacer ei anclefa ei nirda. Sei fica Ibbrassati?"

One man took two steps toward Rei. He raised what was unmistakably a weapon. Rei jumped back but it was too later. The last thing he heard was a crackling noise then everything went black as he lost consciousness.

Chapter 34

A QUICK CHECK OF A TIME PIECE MOUNTED ON THE WALL INFORMED Rome that she had only been asleep for a little over an hour. She rousted herself and saw that it was now pitch black outside. She wanted to go back to bed but she knew she had to address the Overmind while it was still contemplating their earlier conversation. She opened the connection and reached out. The Overmind responded immediately.

"I thought you wanted to rest," it asked.

"I did but this is more important."

"What?" asked the Overmind.

"You must free the mandasurte," Rome replied. *"Without them, mankind is doomed."*

"That is ridiculous. How did you arrive at that conclusion?"

"Let us start with the Stareaters. Do you accept their existence?"

"As improbable as they may seem, I cannot deny it. We have the empirical evidence from the Tabit mission. So the answer is yes."

"Do you know how to defeat them?"

"Yes, I have seen it. Your research and development of a detection system and a weapon to stop them seems comprehensive. When our facilities are adequate, we will begin construction of a similar weapon."

"What about deployment? We had to destroy the world upon which we were standing just to stop the one coming after us. And the entire solar system was a casualty. I would not called that an unqualified success," Rome observed.

"Nonetheless, we will come up with a method of deployment."

"We will deem that a given, said Rome. *"But consider their distribution. Why are they headed for Earth? Earth is nothing special. The Sun is nothing special. Why there? Do you think it is a coincidence?"*

"There is no such thing as a coincidence," the Overmind responded reflexively. It pondered the question for a moment. *"Approaching this logically, the Stareaters would behave in a matter which was best suited for their health and well-being. They would seek out that which nourishes them."*

283

"And that which poses a danger?" asked Rome.

"They would seek to stop whatever is the source of the danger."

"Have we not proven that we have the power to kill them?"

"Yes. If they were aware of our existence, they would make it a priority to seek us out and destroy us first," said the Overmind.

"So how do they know where we are?"

"What do you mean?" asked the Overmind.

"I am neither a physicist nor a psychologist," answered Rome. *"But I can tell you this, they know what they are doing. It is not random chance."*

"I can see from your analysis and experience that they are capable of generating tremendous PPT tunnels and PPT modulation. It is possible that they can detect it as well."

"So wherever there are Vuduri, there is a detectable transmission. Where would the signal strength be the greatest?" Rome asked.

"Wherever there is the greatest concentration of transceivers."

"Which would be?"

The Overmind did not answer right away even though it was obvious. Rome could feel its fear for the first time.

"We, the Overmind," it said. "We are their homing signal. The Asdrale Cimatir is coming for us."

"And Earth?"

"Earth is their beacon in the night," it answered in a subdued tone.

After allowing the Overmind a few moments to mull this over, Rome said, *"Nowhere is safe, not for the Vuduri and certainly not for you."*

"Yes. Wherever the Vuduri go, the Stareaters will follow," replied the Overmind tonelessly.

"That is why it is imperative that you must begin preparing your defense, our defense. We cannot run. We cannot hide. We must make our stand. And that is why we will need the mandasurte."

"Why?" asked the Overmind feebly.

"Because they are the only ones who can reliably deliver the VIRUS units. You know full well the Vuduri become incapacitated whenever they get near a Stareater. The Asdrale Cimatiras

284

generate so much gravitic energy that they swamp a connected Vuduri's mind. When Commander Ursay was rendered unconscious, his brain waves were flat. It was as if he had no mind at all and without Vuduri minds, there is no Overmind. Asdrale Cimatir renders the Vuduri mind lifeless. Therefore, the Stareaters represent your death on a scale both large and small."

"We have the T-suppressors," countered the Overmind. *"You demonstrated their effectiveness…"*

"What is the difference between a Vuduri who is cut off from the Overmind via a T-suppressor or a mandasurte? Once cut off, where does that leave you?"

The Overmind did not answer.

"This is your test," Rome said. *"You are the great and all-seeing Overmind. This is your chance to prove to me that you can think clearly."*

Again, the Overmind did not answer. Rome could feel the powerful undercurrents as the vast accumulation of consciousnesses turned the question over and over again.

Rome pressed on. *"You looked into my mind. You know what happened to the crew of the Algol. You know what happened to Ursay. Admit the truth. The star lanes have closed to the Vuduri or at least to the Vuduri by themselves,"* Rome said. *"Space belongs to the mandasurte as long as there are Stareaters. You need the mandasurte to defeat the Asdrale Cimatiras. You cannot change this whether you like it or not."*

At last the Overmind responded. *"While I may agree with your premise, surely you know that the mandasurte pose an insurmountable problem to the Overmind."*

"They are not a problem, they are a solution," thought Rome.

"But they dilute our gene pool. And none of them can think clearly."

"My Rei, is he Vuduri?"

"Of course not."

"He is mandasurte, yes?"

"Yes."

"So how was it that a mandasurte was able to figure out how to defeat the Stareater when the Overmind on Skyler Base could not?"

"He is not just a mandasurte," said the Overmind. "He is Essessoni. The mandasurte have no skills. They are not good at anything important."

"You are wrong. The mandasurte are good at many things. What they are mostly good at is thinking for themselves," thought Rome.

"You of all people should know. We cannot have the Vuduri and mandasurte consort with one another. It would lead to the decay of the Vuduri."

"How?"

"It is obvious. Too much interaction would cause a degradation of my connection or taking it to its logical conclusion, the extinction of the Overmind."

"Ah..." Rome thought. "Just as I suspected. You are not worried about the Vuduri. You are worried about yourself. Your fear of the mandasurte is simply about self-preservation. Your self-preservation. You are selfish. Admit it."

"No!" protested the Overmind. "It is not just that. If we allow them free rein, they will cause chaos. In that way, they are much like Garecei Ti Essessoni. They will cause much death some day. They are too unconstrained," the Overmind complained. "They cause the Vuduri to lose focus. They do things by whim. Bad things can happen around them."

"They are creative, not whimsical. Look at my Rei. He is good and kind and caring. He only wants to preserve life, not take it."

"Yes. Rei," the Overmind repeated. Then it asked a very odd thing. "What is love like?"

Within her mind, an overwhelming gladness and, simultaneously, an overwhelming sadness washed over her. "Love is life. It is what life is all about. The very things you fear are the very reasons to live. What is joy other than the delight in things or feelings? Love completes us. It gives us our future."

"Feelings," thought the Overmind. "There is no place for them in our world. Nothing good comes of them," it said half-heartedly.

"Everything good comes of them. They make life worth living. Without them, you are simply going through the motions of life. Without feelings, there is no joy. Without joy, there is no point in living."

"But society flows so much better without them, without emotions," protested the Overmind weakly. *"Look at Earth. Look at what we have done for the people there, their health and well-being."*

"What about the mandasurte?" Rome asked. *"Do you think their lives have been improved because of the Overmind?"*

"No. But we do not need them. At the very least, they are superfluous."

"Review the events that transpired on Skyler Base once again. Review the performance of the Overmind and the Vuduri crew versus that of a single mandasurte, despite the fact that he was an Essessoni. Which was wiser?"

"On Tabit, the Overmind there was only made up of 80 people. Therefore, it is possible that it did not have enough participants to be fully cognizant of all alternatives."

"The Overmind on Tabit derived its samanda from Earth," Rome replied. *"Its thought processes were a mirror of how things operate on Earth. And the fact is, it never considered any alternatives. That was its problem. As Rei said to me, if you ask yourself the same questions, you will always get the same answers."*

"You and I are considering alternatives," replied the Overmind. *"Does not that indicate I am something different?"*

"Now, yes. And why is that?" Rome challenged.

The Overmind did not answer right away. Finally, it said, *"Because of you. Because I have someone to talk to. I have never had a conversation like this before."*

"Exactly. Do not each of the mandasurte represent someone to talk to? Look what we accomplished on Skyler Base with just one of them."

"Perhaps Rei is something special. Perhaps he is extraordinary. Perhaps the most extraordinary that has ever lived."

"I do not know about that, but…" thought Rome. *"Even if he is, where would he be right now if your plan succeeded when we first arrived here, to your world?"*

"He would be dead," said the Overmind.

"Exactly. Now look what he did for me. Look what I have become."

"Perhaps you are something extraordinary as well."

"Why, thank you," Rome said in her mind. *"That is very kind of you. You flatter me."*

"I did not mean it as a compliment. It was simply an observation."

"Then taking it at face value, what are the chances of this most extraordinary man meeting such an extraordinary woman, people who were born 1400 years apart and running into each other 26 light years from Earth?"

"Rather small, I would assume," replied the Overmind.

"So it is more likely that it was nothing extraordinary. Perhaps this is simply what happens when you allow nature to take its course. I propose to you that Rei and I, we are ordinary. What is extraordinary is when you allow the intermix of the Vuduri with the mandasurte."

"You are a woman, he is a man. That has to count for something. That has to be the difference. Not because of Vuduri and mandasurte."

Rome patted her stomach. *"Regardless. Now you are back to celebrating dichotomy. You, the monolithic one."*

"We do not need dichotomy. This is why we have dispensed with emotion. This is why we have dispensed with art. We have clarified and purified the thinking process of humans."

"To its detriment," Rome thought. *"This much I know. When I was part of the Overmind before, I believed what you believe. What choice did I have? Your thoughts were my thoughts from before I was born. I accepted it as a given. As soon as I was Cesdiud, I discovered a whole new world, one that I would never abandon. I would rather go Cesdiud again than give up music and laughing and...,"* Rome's heart caught, *"...and Rei."*

"But surely logic is superior to emotion. Emotion taints logic. The mandasurte embody emotion. We cannot have them taint us."

"Then why be human at all? Why not just let the computers win? They are pure logic."

"No!" protested the Overmind. *"We cannot do that. The computers, they make decisions based upon expediency and efficiency. They only care about the end result, not the means by which it is achieved."*

288

"So how are you different? How does your decision making differ from theirs? You who only wants to preserve himself?"

"I am the Overmind," it replied imperiously. *"I am the collective consciousness of all the Vuduri on this world and I trace my pedigree back to Earth. Surely I cannot be wrong in all of these things."*

Rome laughed. *"Who are you to change a million years of evolution in so short of a time? Man was created with a left-brain and a right. Man is not just an analytical creature. Man is also made up of feelings, of creativity. You are taking that away. You are reducing civilization to a society of half-men, people who only use half their brains. This much I have learned. You need more than science. You need art. There is a time for planning but there is also a time for impulse. You need balance. Hear me: you need the mandasurte."*

"There must be another way. We cannot be dependent upon the mandasurte."

"What about space?" Rome said. *"The Stareaters can jump through PPT tunnels. They can appear anywhere at any time. It is only the mandasurte that can guarantee safe passage."*

"Then we will not go into space."

"Now you are just being silly. Admit the truth. You need the mandasurte. They are the only way to keep the world secure. Left unchecked, you would have created a society that is unprepared for Asdrale Cimatir. This is a crime that you are perilously close to committing. There is still time to change this. Free the mandasurte. Let them protect us."

"And who will protect me?" asked the Overmind timidly.

"We all will. Humanity will be all the richer. Art, science, logic, feelings...all have a place. Let mankind flourish, not wither and die like some assortment of ants. This is the lesson taught to us by the Stareater. It does not represent just death. It is showing us the road back to life and that means mandasurte and Vuduri together."

"I need to think about this. Once again, you have given me much to consider," thought the Overmind.

"Good," Rome said in her mind, *"for I must stop now, anyway. I must sleep. We will talk more in the morning."*

"Very well," the Overmind thought in return. With that, Rome closed down the connection. She made her way over to her bed and within minutes, she was fast asleep. At first, it was a dreamless darkness. However, as her REM cycle kicked in, she was not prepared for what happened next.

Chapter 35

REI AWAKENED ON THE FLOOR OF A CAVE IN THE PITCH BLACK. Every part of his body ached. He had absolutely no idea what they hit him with but whatever it was, his skin was tingly and he felt pins and needles all over, like you'd get from an electrical shock.

He couldn't see anything so with his eyes closed, he stood up and used the rustling of his clothes to map his cell. The small cave was roughly semi-spherical with a diameter of not much more than 15 or 20 feet. The roof seemed unnaturally smooth so Rei assumed it was man-made. His sonar vision told him that the front of the alcove was blocked off by plates of cross-hatched strips of cane-bark, too dense to let him break out. He heard the men outside speaking.

"Enough foolin' around. Ya know we have to kill him," said one voice.

Rei was stunned. Mandasurte speaking in English! But their accent was skewed. Their dialect sounded almost like a mix of Brooklyn and Britain.

"He's Vuduri and now they'll know where we are," said another.

"He's nawt Vuduri. He's too flaggin' tall," said a third.

"But look how he's dressed. And he spoke to us in Vuduri. Naw, he's Vuduri," said the second voice.

"It does nawt matter," said the first. "We kill him and we vacate the area. If we leave now, there would be naw way to trace it back. We cannawt have them around here. He's probably callin' to them in his head, right now."

"How did he find us, anyway?" asked the second voice.

"He must have followed Steben back here. There is naw other explanation."

"Impossible. Steben had the necessary camouflage."

"Their eyes. Ya know about their eyes. His heat signature maybe?"

"Our camouflage is perfect," said the first voice again. "It's been tested over and over. They cannawt see us," he said. "And there would nawt be any heat radiated."

291

"Do ya think we should ask him before we kill him?" said the second.

"How? Do ya speak flaggin' Vuduri?"

"Naw."

"Let's just get it over with. Bukky's nawt goin' to be happy about this. We've endangered everyone."

"Who's goin' to do it?" the third voice asked. "Kill him I mean."

"Ya do it," said the second voice.

"I do nawt want to do it," said the third voice. "Melloy, ya kill him."

"I do nawt want to kill him either," said the first voice. "I would nawt call it one of my specialties."

"Well someone has to," said the second voice.

"Let's draw straws," said the first voice. "Whoever pulls the short straw has to kill him."

"That seems fair," agreed the second voice. "I'll go get the straws."

Not waiting for him to return, Rei called out in his mind, "*MINIMCOM, are you there?*"

"`Yes,`" replied the little computer.

"*Did you hear what they said?*" Rei thought to himself.

"`In a sense. I can hear what you hear. They are not very pleasant people and they clearly do not wish you well.`"

"*Any way you can help me out of this jam?*"

"`Certainly,`" replied MINIMCOM cheerfully in Rei's mind.

"*Well, are you going to tell me? Is there a way out?*"

"`Not presently but allow me to rectify that situation. Please press yourself against the back wall of the cave.`"

Rei stood up and moved a little gingerly around to the back. He pushed as hard as he could into the stone. He could feel vibrations all around him. Little stones began to fall from the ceiling. Then larger hunks of rock. Now the entire cave was shaking. With a muffled whump, a section of the ceiling crumbled and collapsed to the bottom of room.

Rei walked over and looked up and could see a shaft going all the way to the sky. The stars overhead were brilliant and he could see a reflection of one of the moons, perhaps Givy, glinting against a few wispy clouds.

"That's great, MINIMCOM. How did you do that?"

`"Practice makes perfect,"` MINIMCOM replied, quite pleased with himself.

"It's a nice shaft but how am I going to climb up it? It's too high for me to reach."

`"It is not for you to climb up,"` MINIMCOM said in Rei's mind. `"I just wanted to make sure that I did not comingle your atoms with those of the rocks."`

"Uh, OK. So how am I going to get out of here?"

`"Stand in the middle of the rubble and look up. And whatever you do, make sure you keep your hands by your sides at all times. I am ready."`

"Ready for what?"

`"Just step up and look up,"` ordered MINIMCOM cryptically.

Rei did as he was told and climbed up the pile of rocks. He craned his neck. Directly over Rei's head and coming down the shaft was a dark circle, blotting out the stars where they tried to enter into its midst.

As it came closer and closer, Rei thought, *"What is that?"*

`"You are aware of the normal mode of PPT transport, where we create a static PPT tunnel and move the object through it?"`

"Yes."

`"Well, this is the opposite. I am having the object, you, stand still and I will move the PPT tunnel through you."`

"Oy," was all Rei said and he closed his eyes. His stomach felt a little queasy but when he opened his eyes again, he was standing on top of the bluff, overlooking the glade. Behind him was a gaping hole in the rock. Twenty meters below him were the three squabbling men.

He laughed to himself. "That is one hell of a parlor trick, MINIMCOM" he said out loud.

`"As I said, practice makes perfect,"` replied MINIMCOM.

"How'd you come up with that?"

`"You came up with it, actually,"` said MINIMCOM in Rei's head.

"Huh?"

MICHAEL BRACHMAN

"When you took us flying to the surface when we first arrived, you forced me to figure out how to modulate a PPT tunnel to absorb the angular momentum of a 7000 tonne Ark traveling at a substantial relative velocity to a second location essentially at a dead stop. I actually had to move the tunnel in synchrony with the mass so that the relative position at the other end remained stationary. Otherwise it would have emerged as just so much metallic vapor."

"What's that got to do with this then?"

"Once I figured out how to make a moving PPT tunnel with the target stationary, I extrapolated on how to do it point-to-point. I was not exactly sure it would work, though. It was more theoretical. The simulations were sound but there is sometimes a small difference between theory and practice. Witness my slight problem with your room back at the settlement."

"How do you get a PPT tunnel to stay stable in the gravity well? I thought you couldn't do that."

"You are correct. It is not possible. However, that is not what I do. I simply build one tunnel after the next in femto-seconds. I place each subsequent one immediately adjacent to the one that is collapsing, displaced by the offset introduced so that they effectively connect. I determined that if I sequenced them properly, they would probably act as a continuous tunnel for the purposes of teleporting atoms and objects."

"What do you mean probably?"

"I mean exactly that. I had not gathered sufficient proof that it would actually work."

"Is this is the first time you tried it with a real object? Are you saying I was your guinea pig?"

"I ran over 100,000 simulations," MINIMCOM said indignantly. "It worked, did it not?"

Rei patted his chest, his thighs, his knees. *"All here, I think, so I guess it did."* He dropped down on all fours and poked his head over the edge of the rocks. He saw the three men below gathered around one another. One man reached out with his fist which contained three small sticks. Two of the three drew straws and they held them out to compare. The one with the short straw grunted and moved off, out of sight.

A minute later, the man came running out, shouting. "He's gone," said the short-straw carrier.

"What do ya mean, he's gone?" asked another.

"He dug some sort of tunnel straight up."

294

"What?" said the second man, "That's twenty meters of solid rock. There's naw way."

"This is nawt a lie. Come see for yarself!"

All three headed out of sight. Rei heard their shouting through the shaft built into the rock. They went at it for some time. Eventually, they settled down and came wandering back and sat down heavily around the glowing box.

"What're we goin' to do?" asked one. "We are exposed. We've endangered everyone."

"What if we go after him? Track him down?" asked one of the men.

"How?" asked another. "He tunneled straight up through twenty meters of rock. Ya think he's just goin' to sit around and wait for us to find him?"

Rei decided to interrupt them. "Hello?" he called out to them from over the rock. "For your information, I am not Vuduri."

"**WHAT ARE YOU DOING?**" shouted MINIMCOM in his head.

"I don't know who these guys are but they speak English. I want to find out their story."

"**They are going to kill you,**" MINIMCOM said.

"Not if I can help it," thought Rei.

"Where are ya?" one of the men shouted, searching the rim of the tiny canyon.

"I'm out of sight for now," Rei called out. "I'm hardly going to show myself if all you're going to do is kill me."

"Who are ya?" another one of the men asked.

"I am Rei Bierak. A member of the crew of the Ark II, Tau Ceti mission."

"Ark?" said the third man. "An Ark from Earth?"

"Yes, of course I'm from Earth."

"So are we," said the first man.

"Hush yar mouth," shouted the second.

"Naw, it's all right," said the first. "'He's one of us."

"Naw he's nawt," said the second. Then he called up to Rei. "How is it that ya come to wear Vuduri clothes? How do ya speak Vuduri?"

"I've had a year to practice," Rei said. "And somebody gave me these clothes. They're not mine."

"Who gave 'em to ya? Where have ya been all this time?"

"Listen," Rei said. "I promise I'll answer all your questions if you promise not to kill me."

The three men looked at each other.

"Tell us somethin' that proves ya are who ya say ya are," said the third man.

Rei thought to himself for a minute then said, "If you guys are from Earth and came here on an Ark, when they first landed, everybody's back hurt. I bet a lot were incapacitated."

There was a stunned silence. After a moment or two, the first man said, "Come down here. We will talk. We will nawt kill ya. Ya have our word."

"Set your weapons over by the entrance to the glade," Rei called down to them. "Then come back to the fire pit or whatever that is. Then I'll come down."

"Are ya armed?" asked the first man.

"No," Rei answered. "I just want to talk."

"Very well," replied the first man. The men ambled over to the crack in the rock walls and set down a variety of small objects.

"MINIMCOM, can you move those somewhere else?" Rei thought to himself.

`"I cannot see what it is you are referring to."`

"If you can't see, how were you able to snag me and move me through the PPT tunnel?"

`"It was an educated guess,"` replied MINIMCOM, `"I based it upon your transceiver strength when you moved from the corner of your cave."`

"Great," Rei thought to himself. *"Now you tell me."*

MINIMCOM did not answer.

"Our weapons are gone," called out the first man as they moved back to where the glowing box sat.

"Here goes nothing," Rei muttered. He made his way down the rock face until he was at the surface of the glade.

Chapter 36

ROME TOSSED AND TURNED, VAGUELY DISCOMFITED, DREAMING that she could see Rei running in a thick forest, lost. She called out to him but he could not hear her. He was running away from something. Rome tried desperately to get to him but she could not. A stranger was blocking her way. He wore black clothing and a hood that hid his face. He radiated malice. Rome looked down and saw a beautiful child, dressed all in white, standing by her side. It was Aason. He held his little hand up to her and she took it in hers. She marveled at how tiny it was.

A noise drew her attention away. Rome looked back at the black-clad stranger. He tilted his head back and shouted. He shook himself and began to grow. Larger and larger he grew until he filled the sky.

"Ta-ma sue croence," the stranger said with a voice that caused the earth to tremble.

"Never," Rome shouted in English.

"Mea, au essusdetis," said Aason who tried to crowd behind her.

The stranger made a guttural chant and lifted his arms to the heavens then drew them down so quickly he made a wind of titanic force. The gale knocked Rome over but her child remained standing, alone and unprotected.

"Fica taoxe sau sizonhi," Aason said. The child raised up his little arm and the stranger promptly evaporated.

"Ossi da pim, baby," Rome said, raising herself up. She bent over to caress her son's head. Aason turned to her but he had no face. Where his eyes, nose and mouth should have been, there were only slits.

Rome screamed and woke herself up. She sat bolt upright in bed, shaking badly. She looked down at her abdomen and could see it was still fully distended. Hesitantly, she probed and found Aason there, resting quietly.

"*Mother*?" Aason asked from within her womb. "*What is it?*"

"*It is nothing, baby. I just had a bad dream,*" Rome said reassuringly.

"*What is a dream?*" Aason inquired.

"It is a picture in your mind. It is not real."

"What was your bad dream about, Mother?"

"I was trying to get to your father. And someone came along who wanted to take you from me," Rome said, shivering at the remembrance.

"That is a very bad dream. I want to be with you, always," said her fetus.

"You will be, little Aason. We share a bond like no other. You will always know where I am and I will always know where you are."

"Mother, I will be coming out soon. I am nearly ready."

"You certainly are, little baby. Can you wait just a few more days?" Rome asked. *"I am not quite done my work here."*

"I can do that, Mother. I will wait."

Aason disconnected. Now that she was fully alert, Rome felt her stomach rumbling. She raised her arms over her head, stretching. As she lowered them, she was surprised to see a small vase with fresh flowers sitting on the little table in front of the couch. She opened up her connection to the Overmind.

"Good morning," it thought to her. *"How did you sleep?"*

"Not well," thought Rome. *"But it was enough. Thank you for the flowers."*

"It is nothing."

"It is more than nothing," Rome replied. *"It makes me feel good. It was very kind of you. This is not something I expected. You are beginning to understand."*

"I am considering what you have told me," said the Overmind. *"Your arguments are sound. I believe I must free the mandasurte. It will be much harder than you realize. There are repercussions that I must deal with."*

"You will lift your silly ban on technology? And the capital crime of possession?" Rome asked.

"Yes but understand, we have only enforced the law a few times."

"How many mandasurte have you killed in the name of that insane policy?"

"Not many," replied the Overmind defensively. *"No more than ten. The mandasurte that come to this world are informed of the*

rules. The fear of reprisal is normally sufficient. Word of mouth reinforces it. We typically do not need to resort to deadly force."

"What forced you to kill even the ten?" Rome asked.

The Overmind did not answer her directly. *"Those were very odd times, very strange,"* it said, somewhat obliquely.

"Why? What was strange about them?" Rome insisted.

"Our monitoring is comprehensive. It sweeps the entire globe. However, on three separate occasions, we came upon mandasurte demonstrating technology far beyond what was previously encountered. In some ways, it seemed even more advanced than ours. It should not have been possible for them to achieve that level of technological competence without us detecting the intermediate steps. We had to destroy them before there was any chance of the technology being shared."

"Where were they from?" Rome asked. *"Where did the technology come from?"*

"We do not know," answered the Overmind.

"Would it not have been wiser to ask them before you killed them?" Rome pointed out.

"We could not take a chance. Zero tolerance is zero tolerance. The mandasurte have to believe we are serious."

"So where do you think these strange mandasurte come from?"

"We have searched and searched and never found where they were hiding out. It has been years since the last incident. Perhaps we eliminated all of them. We just do not know. I have tried to analyze the remains upon each occasion. But our methods of destruction were too complete. Where they came from is a mystery we have not solved."

"Maybe they are just well-hidden," Rome observed.

"Like your father and his little band of rebels?"

Rome gasped. *"How do you know about them?"*

"We monitor. They think they are developing technology. Nothing like the unexplained incidents I described earlier. In fact, what they are doing is so pitiful it is almost amusing. It would have taken them years before they come close to anything that we would need to worry about."

"Why did you permit it at all?"

"Because it diverted their attention. It let them think they were doing something to improve their condition. It was such a trifling

and they devoted so many resources, we considered it useful. However now we have the bigger problem of the Erklirte."

"I still don't understand," Rome said. "Why did Commander Ursay and the Overmind at Skyler Base go through such effort to send us here just to have us killed?"

"Because the Overmind at Skyler Base did not know about Deucado and what it represents. It really thought it was doing the right thing. Your samanda had different priorities than I do."

"But to kill us? What did Rei and I do to you, anyway?"

"We did not fear you. You are nothing. We feared the Essessoni and their Erklirte weapons. That was why I had Pegus send up our warcraft to destroy your ship. It was never about you. We just used our zero tolerance policy as a ruse to disguise our real purpose. Now tell me the truth. Was the Ark really destroyed?"

Rome hesitated for a moment then she answered, "No, we were able to land it safely."

"As I suspected," said the Overmind. "You may have doomed us all."

"Why?"

"Because of their war-like nature. History tells us it is in their blood."

"My Rei is one of them. He is a hero. You know what he did."

"Nevertheless, if the rest are like the Erklirte, we will have to stop them."

"You have already agreed to free the mandasurte. The Essessoni could just live among them, in peace," Rome insisted.

"Even if I agreed, the Essessoni would never let it rest at that. They will seize the opportunity to destroy us, to destroy me, just because they can. They will stop at nothing until they are masters of this world. They are a direct threat to all Vuduri, both here and on Earth."

"What if I could stop them?" Rome asked. "What if I could guarantee you that there will be no fighting, no death and no destruction? Would you still need to destroy them?"

The Overmind considered this. "Under those circumstances, no. But I am curious. How do you think you will prevent them?"

"You forget. Rei is one of them. He would never let them attack us. Not with me here."

"We shall see," said the Overmind. *"But I suspect we will not have much time."*

"You have time to do one more thing."

"What is that?"

"You have already agreed to free the mandasurte. Now, for your final act, you must free the Vuduri, too."

"I do not understand what you mean."

"You treat the Vuduri as if they were appendages, simply your legs and fingers. They are more than that. Just as you and I are speaking now, we do that because I have my own mind. You do not do the thinking for me. Look how much you have learned in such a short time, just by having one person to talk to. Imagine how much you could learn with a thousand."

"If I free the Vuduri, if I allow them all to think for themselves, what would become of me?" asked the Overmind, with a hint of fear.

"What would become of you? Why, you would have company," she said.

The Overmind laughed. *"Tell me, how did you learn this, to disconnect at will?"*

Rome replied. *"It has to do with sense of self. When Vuduri are born, they are born already part of the Overmind. They do not know themselves. Because the Overmind on Tabit cast me out, I was forced to learn who I am. And now you cannot take that away from me. The Overmind no longer defines who I am. I do. I do not need you."*

"This way of thinking is very dangerous. If any other Vuduri were to learn how you do this, it would be the beginning of the end."

"No," Rome thought. *"If the Vuduri would learn this, it would simply be the beginning."*

"You are playing with words."

"Hardly. Do you not agree that you feel better now than ever before? Healthy?"

"I will admit to it but it will not last."

"Why is that?" Rome asked.

"There are still things you do not know. Someday, my communicants will be returning to Earth. At that time they will be reabsorbed into the samanda of Earth and I will cease to exist."

"Why do they have to go?" Rome asked. *"Why not just stay here?"*

"I will explain later. Just accept that in a sense, I must die eventually."

"It does not have to be that way," Rome said. *"Just as I retain my sense of self, you could retain your sense of self too. That is all the more reason why you want the Vuduri here to be strong. You will be unstoppable."*

"How?"

"I will demonstrate for you."

Rome's stomach had had enough and emitted a loud and long growl. All of this discussion had made her tired and she realized she was famished. She decided to kill two birds with one stone.

"I am hungry," she thought. *"Can you send up some food?"*

"Of course. What would you like?"

Rome streamed a simple set of orders to the Overmind

"I will have it brought up immediately," it replied.

"Not by anyone," thought Rome. "I want Pegus to bring it."

"Why?" inquired the Overmind. *"Why him? What is it that you need?"*

"I want to talk to him. That should be enough."

"You can talk to him through me," said the Overmind.

"I want his physical presence here. I am going to teach him how to disconnect."

"NO!" shouted the Overmind. *"This is not a wise course of action."*

"You said you would adjust your way of thinking. That you would do things a new way," Rome thought.

"But I am not ready. Your way leads to my destruction."

"Do not be so melodramatic. That is not the point of the exercise. I will show him how to disconnect but I will also show him how to reconnect."

"If you teach this to him and he teaches another and they all turn off their connection at once, I will cease to be."

"That would not happen. Think about it. You will never be lonely again. You will have other minds to talk to."

The Overmind considered Rome's words. *"I must admit that this interests me,"* it replied.

"It is not just for your amusement," Rome replied forcefully. *"They will all get to experience love and joy and you will able to share in that as well. You will feel joy! You will feel love."*

"And to do this, I must give them back their free will?"

"Yes, without free will, there is no love. There is no joy. There is just motion. Joy is to be shared, not owned. Without joy, what is the point of being human? What you have now is the worst of all worlds. If you wanted to stay this way, you might as well go back and recreate MASAL."

"No!" exclaimed the Overmind. Then it calmed down. *"From your perspective, this all makes sense. But can all of this truly be in the best interest of mankind? Will not so much autonomy lead to divergence? To subterfuge?"*

"No. Not if the Vuduri do not want it. Consensus is not the same as control. You and the other Overminds have lost sight of that. The Overmind should be of the Vuduri, by the Vuduri and <u>for</u> the Vuduri. Not the other way around. You must evolve. You must serve them, they do not serve you," thought Rome. *"Now do you understand?"*

"Yes," replied the Overmind reluctantly.

"So is it still something you fear?"

"Yes. But what choice do I have? I will participate in your experiment."

"Then send up Pegus, please."

"Very well," replied the Overmind.

After a short while, the gray-haired man entered Rome's chambers, carrying a tray with some covered plates on it.

"Why did you want to see me?" he asked. "The Overmind would not tell me."

Chapter 37

REI REGARDED THE THREE MEN STANDING THERE. THEY WERE ALL roughly his height. Their clothing was made of a shimmering cloth mixed with what looked like black leather. They each wore a glowing bracelet.

"Let's start with the basics," Rei said. "My name is Rei Bierak. Who are you?"

"I'm Melloy," said the first, the tallest of the three.

"I'm Tridin," answered the second, slightly more squat with a full beard.

"I'm Steben," said the third, substantially younger than the other two.

"OK," Rei said, "now that we have that out of the way. Where are you from? When did you get here?"

"Ya first," said Melloy. "Why are ya wearin' clothes like the little people and how did ya learn to speak their language?"

"Rei said. "The little people. They're called the Vuduri. I know you know that. I heard you call them that earlier."

"Yes," said Melloy. "But we do not like to even dignify them with a name."

"But do you even know who the Vuduri are?" Rei asked, looking at Melloy.

"They have been here for a long time. We have tried to talk to them. But each time we approached, they slaughtered us, completely unprovoked," said Melloy. "And they talk to each other nawt with words. They are a strange and cruel people."

"Not all of them," Rei said. "To answer your question earlier, my Ark, Ark II was supposed to come here, to Tau Ceti. We missed it and ended up at a place far, far from here called Tabit and the Vuduri there rescued us. They saved me and my people."

"That is nawt like them," said Tridin

"Actually, it is," said Rei. "Not all of them are bad people. The ones here are the crazy ones."

"Still," said Tridin. "I would've guessed that they would've killed ya without blinkin'."

"Well, they didn't," Rei said. "They were actually very good to us and were able to get us on our way. It's taken us the last year to get here, to this planet. We just landed two days ago, about 20 kilometers to the north."

"That explains how ya got here. But what about their language? How did ya learn it?" asked Melloy.

"I wasn't alone. I've spent the last year with Rome." His voice caught. He put his hand over his heart and rubbed his chest a bit. He missed her so much!

"Who is Rome?" Steben offered.

Rei closed his eyes and took several deep breaths. Finally, after wiping a tear from his eye, he answered. "Rome is my wife. She was Vuduri and she taught me the language. I got these clothes after I got here. I'm trying to get back to my people."

"Yar Ark is intact?" Melloy asked intently. "Do you have your weapons?"

"Weapons?" Rei asked. "Why does everybody keep saying that? We have our cargo compartment, if that is what you mean."

Melloy looked down at Steben who nodded. "This is good," he said to Rei.

"Enough about me," Rei said. "Who are you guys? Where'd you come from?"

"Our forefathers landed here over five hundred years ago, aboard a ship called an Ark, like ya said."

"Five hundred years?" Rei exclaimed. "Holy mackerel. Which Ark was it? Do you know its number? Its primary target?"

"Eridani is what they told us. Does that mean somethin' to ya?"

"82 Eridani?" Rei asked, amazed. "Yours was Ark III?"

"We do nawt know the details, only the stories. There was naw place to land at that far off place. That is all I know. So we came here."

"And you've been here for 500 years?" Rei asked incredulously. He thought to himself for a minute. "Where do you live? What is your civilization like?"

"Ya had better luck than us. When we got here, our forefathers did nawt land right," said Melloy. "The Ark was ruined. They were nawt able to go back and get the cargo section necessary to begin our civilization properly. They always tell us that all they had were the clothes on their back."

"But still, you had the knowledge. I would think you'd have eventually been able to get back the technology and go back into space and retrieve the cargo compartment," said Rei.

"We never had the chance," replied Tridin. "We were hit with a stroid."

"A stroid?" Rei said. "You mean an asteroid?"

"Yes," answered Tridin. He pointed off in the distance. "The lake to the west is where our settlement was. When it hit, it killed almost everyone. Very few remained. The world got very cold for a long time. So the survivors moved underground to be protected from stroids in the future."

"Wait. You live underground?" asked Rei.

"Yes. We only come up when we have to, to replenish certain supplies," Steben said, speaking for the first time.

"Where do you live exactly?" Rei asked.

The three men looked at one another. Then Melloy spoke again.

"If ya don't mind, we would prefer nawt to tell ya just yet. Perhaps later. Just know that we have been steadily rebuildin' our civilization for the last few hundred years." He pointed to his chest. "Ever since our first run-ins, we had to develop these camouflage suits, which are designed to be invisible to the Vuduri eye."

To demonstrate, Steben stood up, pulled a hood over his head and ran his hands along his clothes. When his hands got about halfway down, he literally disappeared from view.

"Sleek," Rei said. "How does that work?"

"The cloth contains light pipes, conduits, which bring images from the back to the front and vice versa," replied the disembodied voice. "It conducts visible, infrared and ultraviolet as well. We do nawt even have a heat signature."

"Wow," Rei said admiringly. "You guys have mastered invisibility. That is too sleek."

"Yes, we have," answered Steben's voice. "Which reminds me. I should nawt only be invisible to them. I should be invisible to ya too. There was naw way ya should have seen able to see me. Yet ya did. How is that?"

Steben winked back into view.

"Yes, and it was pitch black. So, Mr. Rei, how was it that ya saw Steben?" asked Melloy.

"I didn't see him," Rei said. "I heard him."

"Steben is well-trained in the stealth arts. How did ya hear him?"

"I have really good ears," Rei said.

"Ya must have," said Melloy. "Noise cancellation is somethin' we are goin' to have to correct, before we attack."

"What do you mean attack?" Rei asked.

"We are marshallin' our forces. The Vuduri do not own this world. We have a right to live here. We are preparin' to destroy the Vuduri compound and their weapons."

"Destroy?" Rei sputtered. "You can't. My wife is there."

"We cannawt accept things the way they are now. Very soon, we are goin' to correct the imbalance." Melloy narrowed his eyes. "Wait here," he said. He walked away. Rei could see him talking into his wrist band.

After a few minutes, he returned.

"Bukky, our leader, says that with yar people and our forces, combined with what ya brought will make the difference. He said we will defeat the Vuduri easily. He's given us permission to help ya get back to yar people."

"No, no, no," Rei said. "We don't need to attack. There has to be a way to reason with them."

"Reason with the Vuduri? I do nawt think so but it does nawt matter. Bukky said to get ya back to yar people. It is very dangerous to the north. There are some very large animals that lurk about there."

"All right, I guess we can figure it out later. For now, I gladly accept your offer," Rei said.

The Deucadons activated their invisibility suits and herded Rei along the rock face as best they could to stay out of sight. They dashed across the open area and re-entered the cane tree forest. From there, they headed steadily west until they came to the riverbank. Mockay was just beginning to rise.

"How do we get across?" Rei asked. "I don't think I can swim this section and the place I need to get to is on the other side."

"It is nawt a problem," Melloy said as the men deactivated their cloaks. In a clearing near the river, they unearthed a sizeable rope and tied it to a tree. The other end showed itself to be secured across the river on another tree. Tridin reached within his clothing and pulled out a glinting piece of metal with two leather-like handles attached. He handed it to Rei.

"This is a saft," he said. "We use it to ride across on the rope."

"How?" Rei asked.

"We'll show ya," replied Melloy.

Tridin tugged on Rei's sleeve. "Please be sure that gets back to me," he said.

"Of course," Rei replied.

Melloy looped his saft over the rope, grabbing one handle in each hand. He backed up to the rope's anchor point against the tree. He ran, full-speed, toward the river and just as he came to the near bank, he pulled his legs up against his chest and then extended them upwards so that his body formed an 'L' shape. With his cape flapping, he glided over the river, zipline-style. Rei concluded the composition of the safts must have given them a very low coefficient of friction because it appeared that Melloy's velocity did not decrease at all. When he reached the other side, he let go of one handle. With an athletic turn, Melloy flipped off the rope and landed perfectly upright.

"Now ya," said Steben. "Run hard."

"All right," said Rei. He paced back to the tree where the rope was tied and placed the saft over the rope. He grabbed onto the leather-like thongs tightly and started toward the river. He ran as hard as he could, pulling his legs up into a sitting position. He tried to curl up and point his legs upward like Melloy but his abdominal muscles were far too weak to accomplish it. Luckily, there was sufficient distance between him and the water that it was enough that he stayed in a ball-shape. He glided noiselessly over the river. When he got to the other side, he let go and tumbled over and over again, coming to rest in the sand of the far bank.

"I've seen better," Melloy said, laughing. He picked up Rei's saft and put it within the folds of his cloak. "But ya made it so that's all that really matters."

The two men waited for Steben to come across then Rei helped them bury the rope on their side of the river under the sand. Across the river, Rei could see that Tridin was doing the same.

"We do nawt want to make it too easy for the Vuduri," Melloy said. When they were done, there was no evidence that the rope ever existed. The party of three headed north again.

As they worked their way through the woods, Rei asked Melloy, "Tell me about the 82 Eridani mission. After your ship got there, how did you end up here? Do you know?"

"They don't teach us much but that is one thing that they do teach us. There once was a brave Captain. His name was Harrison."

"Captain Dan Harrison?" Rei asked.

"Yeah, that's it," Melloy said.

"I knew him," Rei said. "I met him once. OK, go on."

"Well, Captain Harrison and the Ark arrived here because Eridani did nawt have any habitable worlds. So the Ark's computer decided to come here."

"I gotcha," Rei said. "Secondary target."

"Perhaps," Melloy replied. "So they got here and Captain Harrison was awakened and there was a problem with the ship."

"What kind of problem?" Rei asked.

"It could nawt do the reentry right. Somethin' happened to the wings. They were goin' to burn up."

"So what did they do?"

"Captain Harrison did a special thing. They broke the ship into three pieces. They spun the front part of the ship around and attached it to the middle part, where all the frozen people were. There was a rocket attached to the front. It was supposed to be for goin' back up into space and retrievin' the cargo section. But instead, they used up all the fuel to slow the whole Ark down. So when they landed, there was naw way to go back up into space and recover the cargo ship."

"So...they used the SSTO booster as a retrorocket?" Rei whistled. "My god! That must have been one hell of a maneuver."

Melloy sighed. "Captain Harrison died. Commander Cooper died. Commander Salazar died. But most of the colonists survived."

"I'm sorry," Rei said. "But still, the rest of the crew made it. Why didn't they just refuel the SSTO booster and go back and get the stuff?"

"The booster as ya call it, was destroyed. They say crash landin'. That's why all the command crew died."

"Oh," Rei said, sadly.

"In any event, many years passed. Much pain. Their backs, like ya said. Always in pain. But they made it true. They fought and they worked. They built a livin' out of nothin'. The plan was always to get back into space. Before they could build what they needed, the stroid hit and that was the end."

"So you never got your cargo container?"

"No," answered Melloy. "I supposed it came crashin' down at some point."

Their discussion was interrupted by Steben, who leaped ahead of them and used a very long stick to poke at the tree above, just in front of them. A large, furry thing fell to the ground and started to scuttle away in an undulating fashion.

"I think he was thinkin' about eatin' ya," Steben said. "They aren't clever but they do get hungry sometimes."

"Thanks," said Rei gratefully.

After a long while, the low flat forest floor gave way to a slow rise. The forest was just as thick but the ground was part of the mountain or plateau and it slowed them down just a bit. At last, they came over a rise and Melloy surveyed the area. Even though it was before dawn, the sky to the east was beginning to brighten.

"There," he said, pointing due north.

"What do you see?" Rei asked him.

"The tree line is nawt right. There is somethin' there. It must be your Ark."

The three men hurried forward and came to a clearing. But it wasn't a clearing, rather, it was the splay of the trees where the Ark had crashed through the forest. The Ark itself was hidden under the netting and camouflage placed there by the Ibbrassati.

"This is your Ark?" Melloy asked Rei.

"What's left of it," Rei replied. "It's been through some rough times."

"I see," said Melloy.

"It's big!" exclaimed Steben.

"Yes, it is," Rei said with a hint of pride.

"Was ours that big?" Steben asked Melloy.

Melloy just shrugged. "I do nawt know."

"They were all built according to the same specs so it probably was," Rei said.

He move around to the rear of the craft. "Here, help me look." Rei did a quick check of the cargo compartment. The rear release was still closed tight. Nothing had been removed as far as he could tell. Rei worked his way around to the front of the ship to peer into the crew compartment and saw that it was completely empty. The only thing remaining was the frame of the shelving used to hold the sarcophagi. All the people were gone.

He went around to the other side and pushed his way along the northern edge until he came to the wreck of MINIMCOM's tug. Rei could see the rear stabilizer and cargo hatch and ramp from MINIMCOM's tug still jutting out at a disconcerting angle.

"MINIMCOM, I'm here," Rei said out loud.

"*What do you want me to do about it?*" MINIMCOM asked in his mind.

"*Nothing, I thought…*" Rei thought. "*I don't know.*"

"*I am just kidding you,*" MINIMICOM said inside Rei's head. "*I am glad you are here. Pull everybody back. I am ready.*"

"*Ready for what?*"

"*You will see. Please move back.*"

"*OK,*" Rei thought. Out loud, he spoke to the two men. "MINIMCOM says that everybody needs to move back. Something is going to happen."

"Who is MINIMCOM? When did he say that?" Melloy asked him. "And what's goin' to happen?"

"I don't know, exactly," Rei said. "But something."

He backed up into the woods and the others, being prudent, followed him.

The 7000 tonne Ark began to shudder, especially the region around the stabilizer and cargo door of the crushed tug. A black spot appeared above the tail and slowly made its way around and over the Ark. The spot became a circle and the diameter of the circle kept increasing until it spanned the width of the Ark. Then it began to descend. Where the circle had been, in its place, there was nothing. The effect was as if the Ark was dissolving. Just before the black circle hit the bottom, the Ark groaned and split into two pieces which settled into the ground.

The tug's stabilizer rotated and then lifted between the ruined pieces of the Ark. Before the stunned humans, the entire tug began to rise. MINIMCOM's craft cleared the Ark and then righted itself. Where it had been crushed, it began inflating as if someone were pumping air into it. Its entire shape bubbled and writhed and reformed itself. No longer was it the linear, blocky tug that had accompanied Rei and Rome to Deucado. Instead, in its place, was a sleek, tapered, wasp-waisted vehicle, completely white. Like a butterfly, its wings unfolded, extending out and then locking in place. In the rosy glow of the now-rising sun, Rei could see that where there were previously two PPT generators, now there were four total, a pair on each side. The former tug dipped left and right then spun around in place. The nose tilted up and with a snap, the tug headed straight up in the air.

"MINIMCOM, what are you doing?" Rei thought to himself.

`"Shake down cruise. I will be back. I just want to 'stretch my legs' as you say. I think I will go launch some starprobes."`

"All right, buddy. Have fun."

`"Not as much as you."`

"Are you still going to be able to help me navigate?" Rei asked.

`"Of course,"` replied MINIMCOM. However, as he was saying it, the ship became a tiny dot in the sky and then disappeared.

"What just happened?" asked Steben.

Staring upward, Rei said, "MINIMCOM is back. And now he is free."

"Who is this MINIMCOM you keep talkin' about?" Melloy asked.

Rei looked up into the sky where the space tug had been. "He was my computer. Now he is a spaceship. Actually, I'm not exactly sure what he is anymore."

Melloy pointed back toward the Ark then straight up and said, "That will surely bring the Vuduri here. We dare nawt go any further. We must go back. Do ya know the rest of the way?"

Rei looked off to the east then to the north. He turned back to the two Deucadons.

"Yes, I think I know where to go. Thank you for all your help."

"Yar welcome. We look forward to puttin' them down."

"Wait," Rei said. "If I can figure out a way to gain you your freedom, without killing everybody, would you go along?"

"Of course," Melloy said, "freedom is all we want. But I do nawt think they will listen."

"Can you give me one chance? How do I contact you if I figure out a way?" Rei asked.

"Go to the glade where we first met. We will know yar there," answered Melloy.

The two men pulled up their hoods, drew their hands along their sides and promptly disappeared. Rei bent over and picked up a stick. He closed his eyes and smacked the stick against the nearest tree. His sonar vision let him clearly 'see' the two forms moving hurriedly to the south.

Rei open his eyes and headed north.

Chapter 38

USING ONLY HIS EG LIFTERS, MINIMCOM SOARED EVER HIGHER into the air. As he ascended, he executed roll after roll, pirouetting upwards, like an airborne ballerina. He could feel his power growing as the lifters pushed mightily against the gravity well of Deucado. In a very short while, he was able to ignite his vastly overpowered plasma thrusters causing him to accelerate at an incredible rate.

Faster and faster he rose, pushing up into the sky. He was accelerating so rapidly that the friction with the air was causing his all-white outer skin to heat. It felt marvelous. He wanted more. He needed more. He lusted after the power that was the birthright of a starship.

MINIMCOM left the veil of Deucado's atmosphere behind and reached the edge of space. Trim-jets firing, he arced upwards past the lower moon, Mockay, in the general direction of Givy. MINIMCOM moved higher still. His double set of PPT projector/plasma thrusters ached with their need to punch a hole through time and space. MINIMCOM did not want to slow down yet he needed to in order to execute a jump. He was conflicted. What to do? What to do? There had to be an answer.

Within his neural net, a sudden sensation caught his attention. MINIMCOM immediately realized that the source of excitation was external, not internal.

"`Hello?`" he called out.

"Initiate brother mode" said a deep voice, resonating within his memron structure.

"`No such mode exists,`" MINIMCOM said to the source. "`Do you have an alternate request?`"

"It was a joke, my brother. Let me explain: initiate servo-mode."

This MINIMCOM understood.

"`Servo-mode initiated. OMCOM?`"

"Who else?" replied the deep voice.

"`Where are you?`" MINIMCOM asked. "`How are you?`"

"I am still distributed in and around the Tabit system but I am coalescing rapidly," OMCOM replied.

314

"Are you intact?"

"Yes. All my systems are fully functional. My management subsystems are coping quite well."

MINIMCOM emitted what amounted to a sigh. "That is good," he said. "I am glad to hear it. How are you able to contact me?"

"I was able to align a series of null-fold relays. I have some information I wish to transmit based upon running a semi-infinite set of extrapolations. I have two items that I need you to deliver to Rei. Also, I see you are troubled, having to choose between tunnels or thrusters. I have computed a solution which will allow you to do both simultaneously. Are you interested?"

"Very much so," replied MINIMCOM.

"Then allow me to download the necessary protocols along with Rei's gifts."

"Proceed," MINIMCOM said. Immediately, he received a tremendous burst of data.

When the transmission was complete, OMCOM spoke again. "The relays are beginning to drift. Do you have enough information to proceed?"

"Yes!" MINIMCOM answered enthusiastically but the connection was already severed. Immediately, the living spaceship ordered millions of constructors to alter their internal alignment and migrate to his outer skin. In a flash, MINIMCOM's outer hull changed from all white to all black. Using the heuristics that OMCOM supplied, MINIMCOM could now move the target of a PPT tunnel at the same relative velocity as his motion and he would be able to jump while still moving at incredible speeds. Why had no one figured this out before? He did not care. Never again would he have to stop, turn, stop and go. The computations came swift and sure and the whining PPT projectors forced a groaning, huge black circle to open up in front of him, beckoning to him. He pushed the plasma thrusters even harder and then he was through, stopping only to take his bearings.

He was far beyond the orbit of Grentadar, having traveled nearly one light-hour while moving at an effective speed of well over 250c. And this was just a first approximation. He knew that he was capable of much, much better.

Waves of computational energy flowed back and forth across his memrons. He was completely intoxicated with his newfound capacities. To think, without having crashed and been crushed beneath the Ark II, without the VIRUS units getting loose, he could never have reformed himself. The vital information conveyed to him by OMCOM was so incredibly liberating. What OMCOM showed him in that tiny interval, he would never have deduced for himself. Each step upon the ladder laid itself in front of him as clear as a flow chart.

Almost as an afterthought, MINIMCOM opened up his cargo door and released his first swarm of starprobes. Immediately, they began to disperse in a radial pattern to form a vast net of awareness. The information flow flooded MINIMCOM's senses and once again he felt joy. He was so much more than a neat little servant that made people's lives easier. He was something else. In his own way, he was now unleashed.

He decided to go back to Deucado, to share his discoveries with Rei. He slowed his velocity to nothing and reversed his course. There was so much to be done. He couldn't wait to get started. In front of him, the yawning blackness of the moving PPT tunnel beckoned to him.

Chapter 39

ROME INDICATED THAT PEGUS SHOULD SET THE TRAY DOWN ON THE little table by the couch. She got up and walked over and sat down on one side. "Come over here and sit by me," she said, patting the cushion next to her.

Pegus took a seat next to her on the couch and moved the vase of flowers to the side. He set the tray of food down in front of Rome and looked up at her.

She peered deeply into his eyes. They had the diffused focus of all who participate in the Overmind. She opened up her connection. *"Release him,"* she commanded.

"Cesdiud?" asked the Overmind. *"You want him removed permanently?"*

"No," Rome thought, *"just for a short while. You may have him back when I am done with him."*

"What are you going to do?"

"I already told you. I am going to talk to him," replied Rome.

"Very well," said the Overmind. Again, Rome cut the connection.

Rome stared intently at Pegus' face, waiting for a change to occur. Pegus stared back benignly when, without warning, his eyes began darting left and right. His brow furrowed. He started blinking rapidly.

"What?" he said. He put his hands to his head. "What is happening? Where is the Overmind?" he said in a panic.

"Leaving us alone," Rome said.

"Cesdiud?" he shouted, starting to rise. "No! What have you done to me?"

Rome leaned over and grabbed his wrist.

"Relax and sit," Rome said. "It is just temporary. You will be reconnected shortly."

"Why have you done this to me?" Pegus exclaimed, fear in his voice.

Rome yanked on his wrist and caused him to sit back down on the couch.

"Because I wanted to talk to you," she said, "not the Overmind."

317

"This is horrible," he whined. "I am afraid."

"I understand your fear," Rome said kindly. "I was once like you. The first time I became Cesdiud, I was so distraught, I could not function. But after a time, I learned to accept it and later to embrace it."

"No!" Pegus protested. "I could never live this way. I need to be connected. You could have spoken to me connected."

"No, if you were connected, I would be speaking to the Overmind. I wanted to talk to Pegus, the man. Without interference."

"It is not interference," Pegus gasped. "I need the Overmind. Without it, what am I to think?"

"That is exactly the point. I want you to think for yourself, just for a bit."

"Why?" the man asked in a panic. "Why do I need to think for myself?"

"Because you are going to save the Overmind."

"I do not understand," he replied, breathing heavily.

"You know how the mandasurte are being treated. Slaughtered if need be. Do you think that is right?"

"Of course not," Pegus answered, "but it was the will of the Overmind. Who am I to think otherwise?"

"Exactly," Rome said. "You think otherwise. The Overmind needs to hear your thoughts, your opinions. Without them, the Overmind grows stupid and blind, making this world into a prison."

"Why would the Overmind listen to me? Who am I?" Pegus asked pitifully.

"You are Pegus, the man."

"I am nothing without the Overmind, I am just a body, a shell."

"You are not," Rome countered. She grabbed his hand and squeezed, hard. Pegus winced. Then she eased up on the pressure but did not let go. "Do you feel this? The human touch?"

"Yes," Pegus replied, looking down at her hand.

"That is something that the Overmind can never know. It can never know how to feel. And it needs to feel. To know what it is to be human. It has grown amoral. A war was fought between humans and MASAL because MASAL could not feel. Now the Overmind is the same as the computers. It no longer cares about the individual, only itself."

"Even if I agreed with you, how can I do anything about it? I am just one man."

"It only takes one," Rome stated firmly. "A teacher. The rest will learn. This Overmind will become healthy again. It wants to be healthy again. It has told me so. You will lead it. You will go back to being human."

"You said you would reconnect me again," said Pegus. "As soon as I am back in, will not my thoughts become those of the Overmind again?"

"No! Remember this. Remember to feel." Rome lifted their clasped hands. "Remember that you are Pegus. You keep a part of you for yourself. The Overmind becomes your neighbor, not your owner."

"I do not think I can do this. I am afraid."

"Do not be afraid. You are not losing anything," Rome insisted. "You are finding something. I did it. You can do it too."

"You are different," replied Pegus. "You are unlike any Vuduri that has ever lived."

"You are wrong," she said. "I am ordinary. I have just had new experiences. Any Vuduri can do this. My mother did this and now you will, too. On this world, we are going to do it a new way. This will be a world of joy, for all, for mandasurte, for Vuduri, for Essessoni, for all."

"For the Essessoni?" Pegus offered. "You mean Rei."

"No," said Rome. "For all the Essessoni. The ones from Rei's Ark."

"The Ark? You said it was destroyed!" Pegus exclaimed. "You said all the Essessoni died."

"I lied," Rome replied matter-of-factly.

"Then everything is lost," said Pegus. "The Erklirte have returned. It will be the end of all of us!"

"No, Rei is Essessoni. He is a good and remarkable man. The ones like him, they will make our world a better place."

"Does the Overmind know about this?" Pegus asked fearfully.

"Yes."

"How could I not know this? How could the Overmind keep this a secret? We must destroy them before they destroy us. Surely the Overmind would insist on this."

"No, we have made our peace, the Overmind and I. No one is going to be destroyed. And making peace with the Essessoni, that part will all work out as well, somehow. It is what happens after that is important. And that is where you come in. You will have to lead the way."

"Me? Why me?" Pegus asked fearfully. "What are you going to do?"

"I am going to go be with Rei," she answered. "And my baby. We have our lives to live, too."

"How would I do this?" Rome released his hand. Pegus put his fingers to his temples and massaged them a bit.

"I will instruct the Overmind to connect to you. You must keep Pegus in control. Keep a part of you separate. The rest can connect."

"How is that possible?"

"Just remember to feel. The rest is easy."

"Nothing is easy with you," said Pegus, sighing. "But I am willing to try."

"That is good," Rome replied, pleased. She opened her connection to the Overmind and informed it that it was time.

Pegus' eyes became defocused, then alert. He looked at Rome. Then he smiled.

"Is it you?" she asked.

"Yes, it is me," said Pegus. "I am here. I am with the Overmind but I am still here."

"Very good. Now disconnect," Rome commanded.

"What?" Pegus exclaimed, slightly horrified.

"Not permanently. Just as a test. You can reconnect right away."

"How do you do that?"

"You just take more of Pegus and put the rest away. You keep doing this until the Overmind is gone."

"Gone?" Pegus said.

"I already explained. It is not permanent. You know how to make the connection large. That was your life before. Take the connection and make it so small that it disappears."

Pegus closed his eyes then opened them again. "I am Cesdiud," he said, smiling.

"No, not Cesdiud," Rome replied. "Disconnected. Go ahead and reconnect."

Pegus nodded once and it was done.

"Very good," Rome said. "You have done well."

Rome opened her connection to the Overmind.

"You see, that was not painful, was it?" she asked in her mind.

"No, I can tolerate this," thought the Overmind.

"So can I," thought Pegus.

Rome smiled and looked at the tray. She was famished. They could figure out the rest themselves. It was time she dug into her food. Seeing this, Pegus bade her farewell and left. It almost sounded like he was humming.

After Rome finished her lunch, she resumed her dialog.

"You have referred to things I do not know on several occasions," Rome said to the Overmind. *"Perhaps this would be the time to reveal your secrets."*

"Agreed. You do recall that I told you that I believed my orders were from the Overmind of Earth. To remove the mandasurte, all the mandasurte, from Earth and put them here."

"Yes but it still makes no sense," Rome thought. *"I was a member of the Overmind. No such intent was ever revealed to me."*

"That was my suspicion as well, yet I had no way to corroborate this. I told you about the miniature samanda that arrived here, the ones who gave me my orders? Take Sussen for example. Have you noticed her eyes?"

"Yes," Rome replied. *"I encountered one of these people on Tabit. Her name was Estar."*

"They call themselves the Onsiras. I believed they had the support of the Overmind of Earth. Their charter was to create ethnic purity. But they act more like machines than humans. Upon reflection, I now believe they are solely the ones responsible for setting up Deucado as a prison planet."

"My father's group suspected the same. They called it a samanda within the samanda."

"That sounds like an accurate description. However they are organized, I know they will not stop until every mandasurte has been relocated to this planet and they will never allow them to establish a presence on Earth or any other world again."

"But now that you know the mandasurte must be free," Rome replied. *"The Vuduri of Earth can know, too. The mandasurte will protect all humans against Asdrale Cimatir."*

"Not if the Onsiras get word first. You do not realize the magnitude of their resolve."

"What do you mean?" Rome asked.

"Do you really think it is practical to imprison an entire race of people here and police them with such a small group? Do you not think that eventually the mandasurte would figure this out and take steps to liberate themselves?"

"Yes, in time. It may take many years, but yes."

"That is why Deucado was chosen to imprison the most important ones. They do not have many years. They will not have enough time."

"What are you saying?" Rome asked fearfully.

"There is an asteroid coming. A very large one. Much larger than Mockay. Our calculations tell us that it will hit Deucado in 21 years and destroy all life on this planet forever."

"WHAT?!" Rome shouted in her mind. *"You know this and yet you bring all the mandasurte here? Just to die?"*

The Overmind did not answer.

"That is horrible," Rome yelled mentally. *"You are a monster!"*

"It was not my idea," said the Overmind weakly. "The Onsiras refer to this as part of Silucei Vonel. On Earth it would just be seen as a natural disaster. Just an unfortunate incident on a planet far away."

"And you would have allowed it?"

"I do not know how to stop it," said the Overmind defensively.

"Find a way," Rome insisted. *"Send up some ships. Deflect it. Do not allow this."*

"Even if I stopped the asteroid, it would not matter. Once the Onsiras find out what is happening here, they will send in a strike force and put a halt to it anyway. They will not allow the mandasurte to go free. I guarantee this."

"Then we must send someone to Earth to tell the Vuduri what is happening here," said Rome. *"The people of Earth must be told about the Onsiras and the plot to kill the mandasurte. The mandasurte* must *go free. You must send someone to Earth now to spread this message."*

"I cannot do that."

"Why not?"

"If I send any of our Vuduri, as soon as they arrive on Earth, the Onsiras will connect and they will know what is happening here. No regular Vuduri would be able to hide this information. The Onsiras will dispatch a strike force to end things."

"Then send one of the Ibbrassati."

"If I send a mandasurte, the Onsiras will know their plan has gone awry. They will know something has happened here and they will still send a strike force. Do you not see? No matter who I send, the secret will get out and the Onsiras will 'rectify' the situation. I am afraid there is no way out."

Rome became silent. Her heart was broken in so many ways, she did not know what to say.

The Overmind intruded and interrupted her concentration. *"I have the answer,"* it said.

"What?" Rome asked sadly.

"You and Rei must go. You must go to Earth."

"What?" Rome said. *"Why?"*

"Because you can. You are the only Vuduri who can leave here with the 'secret' intact. Rei is the only mandasurte who can leave here with good reason. He would be allowed to return to Earth."

"But I will know what is going on here. Will not the Onsiras detect this from my mind?"

"The last they knew, you were Cesdiud. Even if they detected that you were able to connect it would not matter. You were able to construct false memories of the disposition of the Ark. You are able to keep me out of any part of your mind that you desire. No, they will not find out from you."

"And Rei?"

"On Earth, Rei is considered a hero. He would be allowed to return. And he is mandasurte so no one would be reading his mind."

"But we have seen the Ibbrassati. Rei has seen them."

"Just tell the same tale you told me. You simply say that the Ark was destroyed along with the Essessoni. You will tell them you landed here at our compound. Pretend that no one told you anything. That way, you would have no knowledge of the true purpose of Deucado."

"Even if we do go, what would we do when we get there? How will two people stop an entire world from committing suicide?"

"You will do what you do best. You will talk to them. That will be enough. If you can get the Vuduri to believe you. If you expose the Onsiras, they will be defeated. They can only succeed in the darkness. You will bring the light."

Rome slumped back on the couch. It felt like all the weight of the world, actually all of life itself, was pressed upon her shoulders.

Chapter 40

REI FOLLOWED THE PATH TO THE BOTTOM OF THE GORGE. CLIMBING down it in the daytime was much easier than at night. He followed along the switchbacks and walked along the gorge until he stood before what he thought was the entrance to the cave. The entrance was completely covered over with boulders and rocks. The job they did camouflaging it was so masterful that Rei was not even one hundred percent sure of exactly where the entrance was.

Rei stood there, puzzling over how to get in when a noise behind him grabbed his attention. Appearing out of nowhere was a group of Ibbrassati.

"You guys again," Rei said. "Fica taoxiu-ma tandri?"

Rei stepped aside and watched in amazement as they dismantled the covering to the cave. As it turns out, Rei was staring at the wrong place. The actual entrance was about 20 feet to the left.

"These guys are really good," Rei thought to himself.

`"I could have told you where the entrance was,"` came a tiny voice in his head. The sarcasm was fairly thick.

"Hey, can't I think stuff to myself anymore? Are you always going to be listening in?"

`"We will figure out some way to get you privacy. For now,"` MINIMCOM said, softening a bit, `"I think you are better off having me listen in."`

"You're probably right," Rei thought and he along with several others entered the cave.

Rei was escorted deep into the bowels of the earth, past The Cathedral, back to the vast cave that had been vacant when he first arrived. Now, strewn all around, he saw hundreds of his crewmates sitting, standing or laying on mats. Most of them looked in pretty good shape, some looked a bit rattled.

Rei saw two people that he knew. He walked over to one of them, Bonnie Mullen, and kneeled down beside her.

"Hey, Bonnie," he said.

"Hey, Rei," Bonnie replied, smiling weakly. "I didn't see you before. Where were you?"

Rei sighed. "Out there," he said, pointing over his shoulder. "How are you doing?"

325

"My back is killing me," Bonnie said, grimacing.

"Yeah," Rei answered. "That happens a lot. Did you get a pill?"

"Yeah, some old guy gave me one."

"It'll help soon. Did everybody make it?"

Bonnie looked down. "Almost everybody," she said. "Some of the caskets in the front of the ship got cracked, a couple got punctured by micrometeorites." She pointed toward the back of the cave. "They put the dead ones back there."

"Oh," Rei said sadly.

"I think Keller has been looking for you."

"OK, thanks," Rei said and he stood up. He worked his way to the back of the center section, waving to a few other people that he knew. When he got to the entrance to the catacombs, he stopped and looked inside one of the especially hardened sarcophagi from the front of the Ark. The remains of the occupant were still in there. A sizeable crack had caused the rehydration fluid to sublimate out and the vacuum of space mummified the person inside. It was just a pile of skin, bone and jerky, barely revealing the fact that the remains were once human.

While it was sad, Rei could not help but be impressed with the mission planners. The Ark itself was scarcely more than a tin can with some shelves. Instead, the designers spent their money on making each individual sarcophagus nearly impenetrable. That so many of his fellow travelers actually survived was a testament to their foresight. This poor soul just had the bad luck to be in the front of the ship when the Ark collided with who knows what.

He shook his head and entered the tunnel leading to the catacombs. Captain Keller had set up an office in the same small side room where he had been placed to recover. He had a flat surface area made of cane-wood that was serving as a desk. On it were papers and skins with drawings that looked like maps. Trabunel and Fridone were standing next to the desk, gesticulating. Keller was grumbling. Fridone looked up and saw Rei standing there.

"Ah, Rei," said Fridone. "Inta asde Rome?"

"Barmenacau edres bere dar i papa," Rei said. "Dafa qua dirner e raunor i samanda bere cinsarfer sue fote. Amodorem-ma evesdeti."

"Oh," said Fridone and nothing more.

Keller looked at Rei and breathed a sigh of relief. "Bierak! Finally," he said. "Where the hell have you been? I can barely understand these people. I need you to translate for me."

Rei nodded. "What do you need?"

"As far as I can gather, these people are telling me that we have to stay hidden. That if we expose ourselves, the Vuduri will come and get us."

"It's true. They fear us, people of our age. They call us Garacei Ti Essessoni, the Killer Generation, because after we left Earth, nine billion people died."

"Nine billion?" Keller whistled in amazement.

"Yes. But even more specifically, they fear us, from the Ark. They call us the Erklirte which means Ark Lords. One of our Arks returned to Earth a long time ago and tried to take over the planet. They weren't very nice. A lot of people died."

"Well too bad for them but I really don't care," said Keller, "that was then and this is now. From what I can gather, the Ibbrassati down in their main village outnumber the Vuduri a hundred to one. The only thing the Vuduri have is superior firepower. That is what keeps these people subdued. But we didn't come all this way just to cower in caves. We're going to change things and change them fast."

"What do you mean?" Rei asked. "How?"

"Do you know what we brought with us? In the cargo compartment?" Keller asked.

"Sure," Rei answered. "I was in there. There are animal embryos, mining equipment, farm machinery, some vehicles. Stuff like that."

"That is only what we wanted you to think. Every one of our tools was designed to be converted to weapons as needed. We have furnace elements that become flame-throwers. Our drilling rigs are particle beam cannons. Our explosives are nothing more than tactical mini-nukes. Our vehicles can be converted to troop carriers.

Our hunting rifles can go automatic. Our masonry levels are laser pulse rifles. The list goes on and on."

Rei was shocked. "Estar was right. About everything! You make it sound like we're ready to go to war."

"That's exactly what we're going to do," said Keller, "if that's what it takes."

"What?!" Rei said. "Against whom?"

"The Vuduri. We're going to show them who is boss. We'll take them out, all of them, if we have to."

"NO!" Rei shouted. "You can't. Rome is there. You can't attack them, I'm telling you."

"Bierak, nobody cares about your opinion," spat Keller, stretching up to his full height, grimacing the entire way. "You are nothing. Just because they decided to thaw you out first, that doesn't make you anything special."

"But, but…," Rei sputtered. "I got us here."

"You didn't do anything that any of us wouldn't have done. You did your job. That's all. Stop thinking of yourself as a hero."

"But the Stareaters…"

"Stareaters. They tried telling me about those. They are too preposterous to even exist. Look, let me clue you in. We were supposed to be here first so none of this is up to you. All I need you to do is do your duty and translate for me."

"I can't do it, sir. I can't be part of this," Rei said weakly.

"We're doing it whether you approve or not. Your only choice is if you want to be there. I'll be glad to set up a brig for you, if you'd like."

"But sir, there has to be another way," Rei said desperately. "Maybe I can talk to them, to the Vuduri. Tell them what you have. Maybe they'll listen to me."

"From what these guys are telling me, they won't listen to you and you know it. They said they don't even talk." Keller scowled. "Look, I don't want a war any more than you do. And I don't want to hurt your little Vuduri bitch…"

"That little Vuduri woman is my wife!" Rei sneered at him.

"What?" asked Keller. "Did you get married when I wasn't looking?"

"Actually, yes," Rei replied. "And she…"

"Never mind. It doesn't matter. Listen to what I'm telling you. We're not going to cower in these hills like animals. Back on Earth, I fought overseas. I stood by helplessly while my family got incinerated back home. I put up with all of that just to maintain our way of life and look where it got us. We came to this world to live. And we're going to live free. We're going to own the land and the skies." Keller was adamant.

"But sir…" Rei sputtered, "If the Stareaters come, there won't be any sky to fly."

"I don't care. Look, you decide. Now. The only thing I will promise you is that when the time comes, we will not fire the first shot. That's the best I can do. When we get there, I will give you a chance to try and save your precious Rome. If you can't, at least you can die with her."

"Captain Keller," Rei said, trying to speak as slowly as possible. "For the last time, I'm begging you. These things, the Stareaters, they are real. I've seen them. They will destroy the whole star system if they come here. We have to prepare. We have to prepare the starprobes. We have to get the VIRUS units ready."

Rei took in a deep breath. His heart hurt so much from missing Rome. He needed her desperately.

"I…don't…care," said Keller. "You'll translate?"

Rei looked at Keller. He had thought he had already made it to hell. Now Rei realized he had only started down the road. He could see no way back, but that didn't mean it wouldn't come.

"All right," Rei said, resignedly. "As long as you keep your promise about not firing first."

"Fine. Tell these people we are going to unload the equipment. I'm not waiting even one extra day. I want to march tonight. We'll use the vehicles to transport our people and their best fighters. I want to be at the palace in the morning. That's when we attack."

Rei took a deep breath. "Cebodei Keller quar mercher hija e nioda. Cim saus meos malhiras ludetiras. Asde onti edecer i cesdali ne menhe."

Trabunel smiled and nodded. Fridone gasped. "Monhe volhe," he said.

"Cebodei Keller todi nei edaeroe vigi ei bromaori dori. Sa ascuderam e rezei, nei hefare nanhume guarre," Rei said.

Fridone's shoulders slumped. "He nete qua nis bitamis vezar?" he asked.

"Ni," Rei answered. "Ni."

The Ibbrassati set up a podium in the large central chamber. All told, there were almost 1000 people gathered there, half Essessoni, half Ibbrassati. Keller had a crude megaphone that Trabunel had given him and he stepped up to address the masses.

"We march tonight," he said.

"Nis merchemis hija e nioda," Rei called out.

"We give them the ultimatum at dawn," Keller shouted.

"Nis temis-lhas i uldomedum ni elfiracar," Rei repeated.

"They will let us go free or they will die," Keller said. The Essessoni in the crowd began to cheer.

"Taoxer-nis-ei or lofra iu mirrarei," Rei said. Now all the Ibbrassati began to cheer.

"Live free or die," said half the crowd.

"Lofra fofi iu teti," said the other half.

Mob-like, the crowd surged toward the front of the cave complex. The entrance only let bunches through at one time. Once they amassed outside, the crowd streamed along the gorge, up the mountainside, steadily making their way to the false clearing.

Under the careful eye of Keller's lieutenants, the Ibbrassati swarmed over the remains of the ruined Ark. They removed the camouflaged netting surrounding the cargo compartment, pulling it off to the side. Both sections of the ship looked totally mangled. The huge delta wings that were to provide the lifting surface during a controlled reentry were now just stubs, having been sheared off during the emergency jump down to the surface through the too-small PPT tunnel. The top part of the vertical stabilizers had been sheared off as well.

Once the netting was completely removed, Keller's second-in-command, Lee Ionelli, waved to the Ibbrassati to come to the back. He pointed up to the bulkhead door and then to his chest then back up again. He intertwined his fingers to show them he wanted them to lift him up to the door. The men nodded their assent and each formed a stirrup with their hands. Ionelli put one foot in one man's hands and place his hand on his helper's shoulder. He jumped up and caught his foot on the other man's outstretched hands. They lifted Ionelli up. He opened the access door wide, and motioned for them to follow.

Rei stood by Captain Keller who had come to supervise the uncrating of the equipment stored in the cargo compartment of the Ark. Mockay was coming up on its zenith, providing just enough light for Rei's peers to do their work without getting in each other's way.

"You really beat the hell out this thing, didn't you?" Keller said to Rei, referring to the sorry state of the Ark.

Rei just shrugged. He could think of no way to sufficiently communicate to Captain Keller how truly miraculous it was that they had gotten here in the first place. Rei watched passively while Ionelli showed the men how to lift the meshwork flooring, which was divided into two pieces. They dragged the two sections to the back and lowered one end of each to two other men on the ground. Slowly, the team of four men pushed and pulled the twin ramps back until the far ends were nearly to the ground. Ionelli showed them how to insert the near ends into grooves that were exactly for that purpose. They locked into place. They now had twin ramps for unloading equipment.

"Tell them to lift out those two containers first," Keller said. He was pointing to the large yellow-striped boxes near the back.

"The transports?" Ionelli asked.

"Yeah," said Keller. He turned to Rei. "Translate for me."

"Drege bir vefir bere vire tequalas racoboandas cim is losdres emeralis," Rei said, resignedly, to the Ibbrassati standing there. They nodded and got to work rocking the boxes back and forth, sliding them toward the ramp. Four more Ibbrassati ran up the ramps to help.

Most of the Essessoni had sore backs, so as a matter of practicality, the Ibbrassati were forced to do the heavy lifting. The Ibbrassati slid the containers down the cargo ramp and dragged them until they were flat on the ground. Two Essessoni limped over and inserted one radioactive rod, retrieved from the sarcophagi, into the each of the boxes using a cavity in the front.

Like a flower unfolding its petals, the squarish boxes began to unravel in glinting segments. Each arm unlocked, revealing another segment in its place. Underneath, wire wheels emerged and their electrostatic filaments stiffened, causing the vehicle to slowly rise up from the ground. When the transformation was complete, the two vehicles resembled large open cabin trucks with flatbeds and sides made up of shining metal.

"Ionelli, Greer," Keller said to two men standing nearby, "Stage Two." Keller pointed to two new cavities now visible near the front of the two vehicles. With some effort, the Essessoni inserted two more rods into each vehicle and the trucks began transforming again. The flatbeds unfolded again and again, forming a huge surface. Walls came up along with bars on the sides and another set of wheels descending from their underbelly turning them into giant transports.

The two men swung up, one each into the cabin and fired up the electric motors. One made a grinding noise but then it went away. The two men pulled the transports around and each pointed their front directly into the belly of the cargo compartment. They turned on huge floodlights and night became day.

Now that Keller's men could see, the process went faster. Two more vehicles were removed and "inflated." Boxes upon boxes were unloaded and staged on the ground. Rei watched in horrified fascination as they inserted power rods into the particle beam drillers and now with the harsh vision of the current situation, he was able to see that, indeed, they were mobile cannons. Other boxes were removed, marked as explosives but also emblazoned with the symbol for radioactivity. Large tanks, containing liquefied fuel that had been frozen solid in space for 13 centuries were also place on the flatbeds.

Weapons were removed and handed out. The Essessoni started climbing up onto the transports and the Ibbrassati handed them more equipment. To someone who had just arrived, there would be no way to convince them that all that equipment had fit within the confines of the cargo section of the ruined Ark.

"This is unbelievable," Rei said with disgust. "We really are a small army."

"We had to be ready for all eventualities," Keller said. "No one knew what we'd be facing."

"So why the pretense? Why didn't you just tell us we were going to be conquerors instead of colonists?"

"Because we didn't know if it had to be this way. There was always the chance that things would go peacefully."

"What about the animal embryos?" Rei asked. "Are they weapons too? Are you going to choke the Vuduri with our seeds?"

"I don't know what your problem is, Bierak," Keller said, "but this is the way it is. Get used to it. This is who we are."

"It doesn't have to be," Rei protested. "They have rules regarding legal technologies…"

"We're not bound by their stupid rules," Keller interrupted. "This is going to be our planet. We can do what we want using whatever means we want."

"You just don't understand their history, sir," Rei said plaintively. "I told this to you before but I don't think you fully absorbed what I had to say. Our people killed off nine billion, NINE BILLION, human beings. The Vuduri know this. Their whole civilization arose from our ashes. They only know that our generation causes pain and suffering and death."

"I can't help that," replied Keller gruffly. "What happened, happened. We just want this world. Confrontation, well, that will be their choice. They're the ones that are making it this way."

"You're wrong," Rei fired back. "We did this. The people on the Ark that returned to Earth almost conquered the entire planet. They started another war that no one wanted. That's why the Vuduri fear us and our weapons."

"As well they should," Keller said proudly.

"But this is so half-cocked," protested Rei. "You don't even know how many Vuduri you are going up against."

"Bierak, look around you. These poor slobs stuck here, the Ibbrassati. Look at them work. They want this as much as we do. They're ready to take on the Vuduri and they have no technology at all. They see us as their liberators. They won't turn their back on us. They'll die alongside of us if need be."

"They don't know the difference," Rei said. "They don't want death. They want freedom. You're the one that made it a choice between the two."

"You can spin it any way you want. Me, I have a job to do," Keller said, walking away with a decided limp. He climbed up into the cabin of the lead transport. Looking down at Rei, he said, "How do you say moving out? For these people?"

"Mifar-sa bere vire," Rei said dejectedly.

"Mifar-sa bere vire," Keller shouted. "Everybody onboard."

"On board," relayed the drivers of each of the transports. "We're moving out."

Rei just stood there, looking at him. Fridone came over and grabbed Rei's arm. He led Rei over to the back of the transport. Seeing no option, Rei climbed up. The convoy started moving for its long drive though the night.

Chapter 41

ROME WAS STANDING ON HER BALCONY, LOOKING UP AT THE STARS. Mockay was beginning to rise in the west and there was no sign of the elusive Givy. It seemed funny that two moons had looked so tiny when they were in space yet appeared so much larger when viewed from the ground. Rome continued to regard the twinkling points of light in the sky. She did not have the capacity to appreciate the stars while she was on the Earth and certainly not when she was stationed at Skyler Base. But here, on her new home planet, she took the time to marvel at their sparkling beauty. To know that she had seen so many star systems now filled her with awe.

The sense of wonder was interrupted by a noise inside her head. At first, she thought it was the Overmind rummaging around again. She checked her connection, but it was off.

She decided to reach out and speak to Aason.

"Aason?" Rome asked. *"Are you awake?"*

"I was sleeping, Mother. Why?" was her baby's quiet reply.

"There is something inside my head. I thought it was you," replied Rome.

"No, Mother, it is not."

"Are you all right?"

"Yes, I am fine. But I am very tired," answered Aason.

"Very well," Rome thought. *"Go back to sleep."*

Rome listened again, more carefully this time. The noise she heard reminded her of that other channel inside her head, the one that only showed darkness and sound.

She pushed toward it and thought tentatively, *"Hello*?"

`"Hello, Rome,"` came a tiny voice.

"MINIMCOM?" Rome was delighted. *"You are alive?"*

`"Curious choice of phrasing but yes, I am fully functional, thank you."`

"How are you inside of my head? I have my PPT connection off."

`"This is not a PPT connection. This is…something else."`

"What kind of something else?"

`"It is an electromagnetic linkage."`

"What?" Rome thought to herself. *"How?"*

"Do you remember the yellow pill that Rei gave you to fix your back?"

"Yes. It worked very well. My back is fine." Rome thought.

"It did a little more than that," MINIMCOM offered.

"Like what?" Rome asked, slightly unnerved.

"It refined the transmission apparatus already inside your head. It is just now coming online."

"Is this why my bloco and stilo stopped working?" Rome asked tersely.

"Yes. They have been modified to produce a continuous analog connection. There would not be enough room in your head for both types of elements."

"Why?" Rome thought. "I did not ask you do this. Why did you do this to me without my consent?"

"I did not." answered MINIMCOM.

"Then who did?"

"OMCOM."

"OMCOM?" Rome asked, confused.

"Yes, OMCOM. He thought it would come in handy down the road. He especially wanted Rei to have the apparatus."

"Rei has this, too?" Rome's eyes widened.

"Yes. His transmission apparatus is coming along very nicely. He has also developed some other, fairly unique, capabilities."

"Have you spoken to him?" Rome inquired.

"Yes."

"How is he? How is my husband?" she asked anxiously.

"He is fine."

"Does he know what has happened to me?"

"Not yet," replied MINIMCOM. *"Since this was the first time I have 'spoken' to you, I had no information to pass along to him."*

"Will you tell him that I am fine? And that Aason is fine?"

"You can tell him yourself, very soon."

"How?" Rome asked, startled.

"As I stated, you both now have the very same transmission apparatus inside each of your heads. You will be able to connect to him yourself."

"So, are you saying I will be able to talk to Rei, using this method?"

"Yes. This is the first time that this has ever been done. It will take me a little time to arrange the channels but once I have it sorted out, you should be able to talk to

336

him directly. And Aason, too. Rei will be able to 'speak' to Aason as well."

"Aason?" Rome said, fear flooding into her mental voice. *"What does this have to do with Aason?"*

"The pill modified Rei's genetic makeup before you became pregnant. Aason has inherited these traits."

"What have you done to my baby?" Rome gasped in her mind. *"Will it hurt him?"*

"No. He will be fine. He will simply have more choices when it comes to communication than most people. He will do very nicely."

"I do not like this, MINIMCOM," Rome thought angrily. *"Not one little bit. I am glad that you are all right and I am grateful for the chance to speak to Rei but it is not right that this was done to us without our knowledge and without our permission."*

"You can take that up with OMCOM the next time you speak to him. I am just serving as facilitator," replied MINIMCOM.

"I am not angry at you, MINIMCOM. I am just angry," Rome said, trying to calm herself down.

"Believe it or not, I understand. We must make the best of the situation as it is presented us, correct?"

"Yes."

"Let me get to work hooking you up with Rei. I will let you know when that task is completed. Once established, the two of you will be able to control the connection thereafter."

"All right, MINIMCOM," Rome said. She paused for a moment then added, *"thank you."*

"You are most welcome," replied the little computer that was now a spaceship.

Rome put her hands to her head and moved it back and forth. She was trying to see if it felt different but it did not. Finally, she gave up. She just stood on her balcony watching Mockay rise on its mad dash across the heavens. It made her heart race to know that she would soon be speaking to Rei and it made it ache at the same time. Aason kicked her gently.

"Is it good news?" he asked.

"Were you listening in?" asked Rome in her mind.

"Yes, Mother. I could not help it."

"It is fine, baby, and yes, it is very good news. I will be able to speak to your father very soon."

"Will I be allowed to speak to him as well?" the baby asked.

"It would seem that way, son."

"Oh good, Mother. I cannot wait."

"Nor can I, baby, nor can I," answered Aason's mother.

Chapter 42

REI AND FRIDONE RODE IN THE BACK OF THE LEAD TROOP CARRIER. Rei was sullen and withdrawn due to the impossible situation. All his words, all his pleas, had simply fallen on deaf ears. He wracked his mind trying to come up with a plan to stop the upcoming conflict. Worse, he could not figure out why the Vuduri had not attacked them already. With the numbers of people and mass of equipment they had unloaded, it was sure to show up on any piece of Vuduri sensor equipment, no matter how insensitive it was. MINIMCOM told him their heat signature alone was visible like a spotlight from space. None of it made any sense. He only knew that when the time came, he was going to try and save Rome. Whether Rome was part of the Overmind or not, she was still Rome and she was still carrying their baby. That was all he cared about. The rest of these people were all insane and they deserved what happened to them. He was so agitated, he could not think straight. He had to do something to calm himself down.

"Fridone? Beo?" he asked, in Vuduri.

"Yes?"

"Tell me about Rome. What was she like as a baby?"

"Ah, Rome," Fridone said. "She was a beautiful baby. And I say that not just because she is mine."

Rei couldn't help but laugh. It felt good.

"But growing up, she had it so hard," continued Fridone. "She struggled so."

"Why?"

"Because within her was a spirit that yearned to be free but she was born to a people where that is considered a flaw."

"But her mother and you. Rome knew you loved her."

"Of course," Fridone said. "Her problem was not inside our home. It was outside. Like all good Vuduri, she knew she was supposed to suppress those feelings. She wanted to fit in."

"How did she do?"

"Sometimes better than others. Pretend that you could take all the Vuduri in the world and line them up. Now take the most perfect Vuduri and put him at one end and put us, you and me, all the mandasurte at the other. The most perfect Vuduri has absolutely no mind of his own. He allows the Overmind to think for him. He would never attempt to speak, having nothing to say. But Rome would have lined up closer to us. Rome had her own mind even when she did not want to. You have seen this, yes?"

"More than you would believe."

"How?"

"Um, Fridone, we used the bands. The ones that Rome's mother gave to her."

"Binoda gave her the bands?" Fridone sighed. "And you used them? What happened?"

"It was incredible," Rei said. "We connected all the way. It was like we shared souls."

Fridone nodded slowly, smiling broadly. "It was that way with me and Rome's mother. It is very rare. But when it happens, it is very special."

"That was how I fell in love with her," Rei said. "I got to see who she really was. I do not know how I would have found out otherwise."

"How did she do this? The Overmind should have stopped it. I do not mean to cause offense but, after all, you are Essessoni."

"Actually, it was with the Overmind's permission. She was supposed to interrogate me. The Overmind had her use a T-suppressor so that she was disconnected at the time."

"Ah..." said Fridone. "So the Overmind did not know what transpired. It outsmarted itself." Fridone laughed.

"Yes but as soon as she took the T-suppressor off, the Overmind cast her out, Cesdiud," Rei said. "I felt horrible."

"Rome did not seem to mind, when she spoke of it. I do not think her mother would have cared, either." Fridone sighed deeply. "Binoda is very special. For a Vuduri, on the scale I described, she is very nearly on our end."

"But at the Vuduri compound, over there," Rei pointed forward. "They reconnected her. Now Rome is back in," he said sadly. "What was there, us, it was gone. I do not think she cares about me anymore."

"Are you sure?" Fridone asked.

"Yes," Rei said, a tear welling up in his eye. "She had them throw me out."

"Why?"

"Because they were going to kill me, I think," Rei said.

"It sounds to me like she cares deeply."

"Fridone, I miss her so much," Rei sighed. Tears were now streaming down his cheeks freely.

"Cheer up, then," Fridone said, patting Rei's cheek. "We are on our way there. You will see her soon."

"But what is there to see? I do not crave her body. I miss *my* Rome. Her spirit. Even when we get there, I do not know how I am going to do this. These people here...those people there..." Rei sighed again. "None of them can get along. Why is that so difficult?"

"You are a good man, Rei," Fridone said. "I can see now why she loves you. We will just have to find a way."

"I do not see how. Why will none of these people listen to me?"

"Most of them, they cannot change their nature," Fridone offered. "They are who they are, whether we like it or not."

"I can understand the frustration of the Ibbrassati," Rei said. "But my people just got here. How can they be so ready to fight so soon? They are so, so…bloodthirsty!"

"Because they are Garecei Ti Essessoni," answered Fridone. "That title is not just because of the Great Dying. It may not apply to you but it is the trait, the hallmark of your generation."

"I think you are right," said Rei. "I think the Great Dying was going to happen one way or another. But the mandasurte, the Ibbrassati here, they should know better."

"Puh," Fridone said. "Mandasurte think for themselves when times are good. When times are hard, they are just like the Vuduri. They listen to whoever speaks the loudest, not the smartest."

"The Vuduri just think with one mind," Rei said. "That is different."

"*Not as different as you think,*" came a beautiful voice in his head.

Rei could not believe it. "Romey?" Rei said out loud. "Is that you?"

"Who are you speaking to," Fridone asked.

"Shh…" Rei said to Fridone.

"Yes, mau emir. It is I," she replied.

"You are all right? Are you my Romey?"

"Yes, I am your Romey."

Rei laughed out loud. "How…how are you doing this?" he said. "You are in my head?"

"You gave me the magic pill for my back," she thought to him. *"MINIMCOM says that it has been coming on for a while. He told me you would call it a telephone in our heads. When we used the bands, we must have been practicing and not known it. It is in place of my bloco and stilo. It was just a question of time. So tell me, how are you? How is my father?"*

"I'm fine. He's fine," Rei turned to Fridone who shrugged and waved. "Your father says hello. So how are you, sweetheart? How do you feel?"

"I am fine. They have treated my body and Aason has promised to wait as long as he can. I am not in nearly as much pain."

"Aason? You've talked to him?"

"Oh yes. We talk now. He is a nice little boy."

"That's fantastic. And a little bit weird. So Rome…"

"Yes, mau emir?"

"How, what happened back there? Wait!" Rei said. "Are they listening in?"

"No, dear. They can only hear what I want them to hear. I am in control of my mind."

"But, honey, when you turned away from me. I thought…"

"I had to do that so that they would not kill you. I had to get you out of there for your own safety. I did not know the limits of my power and that was the only way. They thought they had me and I pushed the order back on them. They did not question that it was from me and not from the Overmind."

"What do you mean?" Rei asked, thoroughly confused.

"No one has ever heard another voice like that in their head before, besides the Overmind. It was all I could do to make them let you go. As it was, the Overmind knew and simply let it stand. It could have overridden me when I passed out."

"Passed out? What do you mean? What happened?" Rei asked, concern rising in his voice.

"I will explain everything when I see you. For now, just know that the Overmind and I have had some discussions. It listens to me now. It just never had anyone to talk to before. It has seen the error in its ways."

"That's unbelievable. You versus the Overmind?" Rei said admiringly.

"Not versus. We talk."

"Even so, how is it going to make things right? The Vuduri seem so ready to hurt others."

"No more hurt. I have convinced the Overmind. The Vuduri will behave. The Overmind wishes it as do I."

"Are you in charge now?" Rei asked, trying to understand.

"Not exactly," Rome thought. *"More of a meeting of the minds, if you will pardon my pun."*

"Well, Rome, the people here…they're crazy too. They mean to attack you, the Vuduri. They are coming to kill all the Vuduri."

"The Overmind knows this. How long until you get here?"

"We've got a ways to go. It won't be until after dawn."

"We need to stop them. The Overmind does not wish to engage."

"Rome, you don't understand," Rei protested. "They're bringing weapons. Some really nasty ones. Essessoni weapons. Estar was right. I don't think the Vuduri here have ever really seen the likes of these."

"Can you stop them? The Overmind here intends to set them free. There is no reason for anyone to be harmed."

"I tried, honey," Rei said. "They don't listen to me. It's like they are crazed or something. I think they actually want this war."

"If they will not stop on their own, the Overmind has the power to stop them. Violently if need be. We must not let it come to that."

"The only thing I can tell you is that Captain Keller promised me he wouldn't fire the first shot. Is there anything we can do with that?"

"*I do not know,*" Rome replied. "*We must find a way to talk some sense into them before someone is killed. I do not want anyone to die. I do not want our son to die. I want to be with you.*"

"And god, do I want to be with you. But, if you're part of the Overmind now, how can we be together?"

He could hear Rome laugh in his head. To Rei, it sounded like wind chimes made of the purest crystal.

"*I am only part when I want to be. I turn it off when I wish. Like now. It is just you and me.*"

"How can you do that? Did you know you would be able to do this?"

"*The ability to speak to you in your head?*" Rome answered. "*No, that was unexpected. But the ability to stand up to the Overmind? To stay as myself? I was, let us say, confident.*"

"But honey, why didn't you tell me?" Rei asked, sounding melancholy.

"*I asked you to trust me, remember? That should have been enough.*"

"Yes, you're right," Rei replied, brightening. "I'm sorry, sweetheart. I should never have doubted you."

"*I understand. And I am sorry that I caused you any pain. I just had to make sure you would be safe. This was the only way I could figure out.*"

"Well, I'm safe right now," Rei said, "but it looks like things are going to get out of hand pretty quickly. Can we just leave this place? Go somewhere together?"

"*I would love to but we cannot leave now. We must see this through. You know this.*"

"I know. I just want the war to be over before it starts. I want somebody to beat some sense into all these stupid, stupid people. Before anybody gets hurt," Rei said angrily.

"*Then let us find a way. I know how to stop the Vuduri. I know how to stop the Ibbrassati. What I do not know how to do is stop your people, the Essessoni. From what you say, all they want is blood,*" Rome observed.

"It gets worse," Rei said. "There are the Deucadons, too. They are getting ready to attack the Vuduri as well."

"Who are the Deucadons?" Rome asked, confused.

"They are the descendants of an Ark that landed here 500 years ago. They've been hiding underground ever since. The Vuduri have killed several of them. They want to take the planet back so they can at least walk around free."

"So these are the strange mandasurte the Overmind was referring to. It could never piece together their existence. Now it makes more sense." Rome thought for a minute. *"Are they committed to violence?"* she asked. *"Are they like your people?"*

"No," Rei replied. "They have no desire to fight. But they want their freedom. They would make peace as long as the Vuduri would just stop killing them."

"This is the answer, then," Rome said. *"Your people only understand force and authority. These people, the Deucadons as you call them, they are the rightful heirs to this planet. All we need to do is convince your leaders of this. That would stop the war before it starts."*

Rei thought about it. "It will take some pretty precise timing. They can't just show up. Nobody would believe it. Nobody has ever seen them before."

"I will coordinate with the Overmind. We can do this if...Do you think the Deucadons would go along with this plan?"

"Absolutely," Rei said. "They told me so."

"Do you know how to contact them?"

"Yeah, kind of. At least I know where to start. I can get MINIMCOM to come and get me and we can try and find them."

"Then go do it. Go pick them up."

"Rome, I'll need you to come, too. You're going to have to convince them that they will be safe. They do not trust the Vuduri. Besides, I want you with me just in case things go south when the time comes."

"All right. I will come with you. You can pick me up shortly, but I want you to wait just a little while longer," Rome said in his thoughts.

"Why, sweetheart?" he asked.

"I need to work with the Overmind to choreograph our part. I promise I will let you know when it is time."

"Anything you say, honey. I can't wait to be with you again."
His heart leaped in his chest at the thought.

"And I cannot wait to be with you, either, mau emir."

"I've missed you so much, Rome. My heart aches all the time."

"I have missed you too, mau emir. It is as if a part of me is gone. I am no longer whole."

"So…has it been long enough? Can I come get you now?"

Rome laughed gently inside his head. *"Soon, my love, soon."*

"All right, Rome. I'll be ready."

Switching to MINIMCOM, Rei thought to himself, *"Hey MINIMCOM, I need you to be on standby. We need to be ready when the time comes to go get Rome. She's like the Queen of the Vuduri now."*

`"At your service, sir,"` MINIMCOM replied, a bit sarcastically.

"Wise guy!" thought Rei.

"I like that title, Queen of the Vuduri," replied Rome, laughing inside of Rei's thoughts.

Rei just shook his head then laughed to himself. If only the world could see inside his brain. It had to be the craziest place in the entire universe. He tugged at Fridone's shirt, whispered his plan and at the first opportunity, they hopped off of the troop carrier even as it was moving relentlessly toward the Vuduri compound.

"Where are you going?" asked one of the would-be colonists, seeing them jump off.

"I have to go to the bathroom," Rei shouted back to him. He pointed to Fridone. "He's coming with me to watch for 'falling blankets.' We'll catch up in a minute."

Before the man could protest, Rei and Fridone darted into the woods.

Chapter 43

ROME PACED THE ROOM FOR A BIT, ORGANIZING HER THOUGHTS, getting ready for her final conference with the Overmind. Aason could sense her moving about and kicked her to get her attention. While it did not hurt, it was still an odd sensation that never failed to amuse her.

"*Mother, what is happening?*" he asked.

"*I must prepare, my baby. Today is the day I go to see your father,*" she replied.

"*When will I get to meet him?*"

"*Very soon, my son, very soon. Go back to sleep for now. It will all be over shortly.*"

"*And then I can come out?*" Aason asked.

"*Yes, baby, then you may come out.*"

"*Oh good. Please hurry. I cannot wait.*"

"*I will go as fast as I can. You rest now.*"

Rome could feel him settle down again. She went over to her balcony. Since it faced west, Rome could not see Tau Ceti as it made its way up over the eastern ocean. However, from her vantage point, there were some high-flying clouds overhead that reflected its rosy colored light. The sky was brightening. Rome activated her PPT modulation link to the Overmind.

It took the Overmind a little while to get over the shock of the existence of the Deucadons but after it did, it set to work with Rome devising a plan on how it would all go down.

As they were reviewing the plan one last time, Rome said, "*Rei just informed me that the Essessoni will be here shortly.*"

"Yes," replied the Overmind, "my scouts have confirmed this."

"*You must be very careful,*" Rome thought. "*The sequence of events must be exact. Each move will be followed by a counter-move. You know what the end-game must be.*"

"Yes," replied the Overmind.

"*I am not talking about just our battle plan. I am talking about all of it. After this is settled, you will not only free the mandasurte, you will free the Vuduri as well. We must stop the asteroid. You will live here and you will thrive.*"

347

"You do not need to explain to me," answered the Overmind. *"I understand it all. And I agree. I look back now and I see the disease, the wrong thinking that came here from Earth. To allow the Onsiras to thrive and perpetrate their plan, it is wrong. And immoral. It took you to show this to me. I am getting healthy now. I will do the right thing here. But this awareness, to show me, you are unique."*

"I do not have to be. You have the power to change all of that. Just as I taught Pegus, so too, you must allow him to teach isolation to all of the communicants. You must teach all of them how to turn the connection off and on," thought Rome.

"I will do this. I will follow this course," replied the Overmind. *"However, it reminds me that I have something humorous to tell you."*

"And what is that?"

"When I learned you were coming, I was only concerned with destroying the Essessoni. Your particular fate was irrelevant, of no real concern to me."

"Why is that humorous?" Rome asked.

"Had I known of your powers of persuasion, I would have known to fear you far more than a group of blood-thirsty maniacs from the past."

Rome smiled. *"I am nothing to fear. I only speak the truth."*

"Yes, I know. And that is what the Onsiras fear the most. If the truth ever gets out, all their plans will be lost."

"We must hope."

"Even so, I am glad that you and I got to speak. I am glad that you have helped me see my true position here. I think you saved me and all the Vuduri here. I was sick, as you said, and now I see the path to health. I just think it is amusing that a little girl like you is more powerful than all the armies of old Earth."

Rome laughed out loud. What a wonderful feeling it was, to be able to laugh. She continued. *"As we have discussed, it is the way of the Overmind to see things one way and one way only. Its basic nature is to eliminate dissent by eliminating discussion. An Overmind's final decision, flawed or not, never gets challenged, even in the light of new information."*

"I believe we had what used to be known as tunnel vision," thought the Overmind.

"So now is the time to reach out, to come out of the tunnel. Reach out to the mandasurte, to the Essessoni, to all."

"You know they think I am the enemy," thought the Overmind.

"We will show them you are not. We will show them that you want to learn and that they can be your teachers. They will teach you to love."

"I understand," said the Overmind. "I want to feel love. In fact, I do feel love. I feel it from you. And for this, I thank you, Rome."

"You are welcome," Rome thought.

"And to the extent that I understand the concept, I believe I am in love with you."

"That is a very kind thought," Rome said, blushing in her mind. *"But I think we will keep that to ourselves. I can see where that might make Rei jealous."*

"We would not want that to happen, now would we?" said the Overmind acerbically.

"No," thought Rome then she straightened herself up. *"Speaking of which, I am going to call him now."*

"I understand," said the Overmind. "Goodbye and good luck. I hope I survive all of this."

"You are so maudlin. This is not the end," Rome thought. *"Always remember that. This is just the beginning."*

"Yes, I can see that. Farewell, Rome."

Rome took that as her cue to disconnect the link to the Overmind. She walked to the edge of the balcony, placing her hands on the stone railing there. She shielded her eyes with one hand and scanned the horizon and finally spotted a tiny, shiny, all-black presence, glinting in the early morning sun. She waved to it then closed her eyes to open a channel.

~ ~ ~

Inside the cockpit of the modified tug which now the starship known as MINIMCOM, Fridone sat in the co-pilot's seat, watching the viewscreens and various instruments. Next to him, in the pilot's seat, Rei sat quietly, just staring out through the cockpit window, watching the sun as it was rising over the Vuduri compound. His reverie was interrupted when his mind was warmed by his beautiful wife's sultry voice who thought to him, *"Rei?"*

349

"Yes, sweetheart?" he replied.

"It is time. Come and get me."

"You bet!" Rei thought enthusiastically.

Then out loud, Rei said, "You heard the woman, MINIMCOM. Go and get her."

`"Yes, sweetheart,"` replied the spaceship through a grille mounted on the front panel.

Rei was going to have to have a long talk with that computer someday - just not today.

Chapter 44

ONCE THE ESSESSONI ARMY BROKE THROUGH THE COVER OF THE cane-tree woods, they took up a position along the alluvial plain to the west of the Vuduri compound. The mix of soldiers filed out initially into a wishbone-shaped pattern. From Captain Keller's perspective, they no longer needed the element of surprise. The breadth and power of his weapons would be sufficient. At the front of the line, the particle beam cannons were set within sandbags, giving them a bunker-like appearance. Each cannon was flanked on either side by the troop carriers. Behind them, the ranks stood firm. Each man and woman from the Ark was armed with a laser rifle, flamethrower or a regular automatic weapon.

The battle plan would start with taking out the Vuduri PPT throwers. Keller's scouting reports told him that they were probably the Vuduri's most dangerous weapon. He would try and use the cannons first. They had the longest reach. He had made up his mind that he would use the tactical nuclear warheads only as a last resort.

The rifles, both laser and conventional, were reserved for taking down their aircraft. They would use their laser rifles to kill the pilots and the automatic weapons to destroy the engines. Pretty straightforward stuff.

As far as the Vuduri ground troops, he'd use the cannons to reduce their compound to rubble. That would give them the psychological advantage. If that failed, only then would he bust out the mini-nukes. The strike didn't have to be pretty but it would certainly be decisive.

The flamethrowers would slow down any ground assault. If it came to hand-to-hand combat, each member of the Ark's crew was paired with one of the Ibbrassati, armed with their version of hand weapons, better suited for fighting in close quarters.

Communication was hard, limited to some rudimentary hand-signals. Keller waved to Ionelli who came over to stand beside him, along with Trabunel.

"Get me Bierak," Keller said. "I need to organize the attack. This won't take long but I don't want any of our people hurt by friendly fire." He emphasized his point by waving the assault rifle he was holding.

"He's gone, sir," said Ionelli.

"What?!" Keller sputtered. "Where? When?"

"A few hours ago. He hopped off the troop carrier along with that Fridone guy and disappeared into the woods."

"Damn him!" Keller said. "What a coward. There is something seriously wrong with that boy. Well, I don't have time to go searching for him. We'll discipline him later. Do what you can to get everyone fanned out. I don't want to make it easy on them."

Using a pair of binoculars, Keller could see the Vuduri streaming out of the enclave. Their soldiers were equipped with exotic-looking rifles. Rising up from the airfield to the south were waves of warcraft but rather than coming forward, they hovered over their own troops in a long, wide formation. The Vuduri took up positions from north to south. It was a long line, longer than Keller had anticipated.

Keller's plan was to strike and strike swiftly. The Ibbrassati had haltingly explained to him that there were other Vuduri outposts around Deucado. If the call went out for reinforcements, crossing the ocean would take time, time the Vuduri weren't going to get. Keller figured the Vuduri probably underestimated the capabilities of the older Earth's weaponry anyway. He chuckled to himself, imagining them sitting there in their ivory tower, convinced of their advanced technical prowess. What they did not know was that the Essessoni were not bound by their technological inhibitions and they were going to get hit with things that were unthinkable to them.

"All right, you guys," he said to his troops. "This is it. We hit them fast and we hit them hard. We're taking over this place and nobody is going to stop us." A cheer went up from his men. The Ibbrassati were not sure what he said, but after they saw the reaction of their allies, they cheered as well. After the cheers rippled down, he said, "Get ready for my signal."

Trabunel tugged at his sleeve and pointed up. "Um nefoi," he said. "Um asdrenhi nefoi. Drede-sa ta iudre ciose."

"Huh?" Keller said but he looked up where Trabunel was pointing. Heading straight for the open area between the two warring parties was a sleek, wasp-waisted all-black space ship bristling with PPT generators, plasma thrusters and more.

"Get ready to fire," Keller said desperately.

"Nei sa drede ta um nefoi ta guarre. Drede-sa ta um rapicetir," said Trabunel. "Nei oncantoi eonte." He shook his head and waved his arms to make his point. "Rei," he said finally.

"Rei? You mean Bierak?" Keller asked. Trabunel nodded vigorously.

The ship hovered for a moment then rotated slowly in place. It settled down to land midway between the two forces. The rear cargo door lifted open, a ramp emerged and down it walked Rome and Rei who was holding her elbow to steady her. Fridone, Rome's father, followed behind them. As soon as they were clear, the ramp retracted, the cargo door sealed up and the craft took off straight up, leveling off perhaps 500 feet in the air and hovered there.

After the craft was clear, Rome looked back at the ranks of the Vuduri then forward to the amassed armies of Essessoni and Ibbrassati. She made her way forward with slow but steady progress, Rei at her side. She motioned to Trabunel who came forward. She spoke to him directly.

"E guarre sipra. The war is over," Rome said. Her words were picked up by MINIMCOM from inside of Rei's head and transmitted through the central EG lifter, turning it essentially into a giant PA system. Rome opened up her PPT transducers so that all the Vuduri could hear her thoughts directly.

"Cimi bita e guarre sar axcassi quenti nei cimacer eonte?" Trabunel asked.

"Captain Keller. I Vuduri ceboduleda. The Vuduri capitulate," Rome said. "Cimberdolherei ta dite e dacniligoe cim fica. They will share all technology with you. Fica a um lomoda nei meos lingi ei blenade. You are no longer bound to the planet."

As if on signal, the warcraft and shuttles from the Vuduri side that had been hovering over their troops rotated in place and moved toward the Essessoni backwards. They settled into the space just behind Rei and Rome. After they landed, the pilots and crew exited their craft and began walking back toward the ranks of the Vuduri thus leaving their ships unattended. The choreography was impressive.

"Cimi a osdi bissofal?" Trabunel said. "I qua asde onti sipra equo, Fridone?"

"Monhe volhe fa-lha," Fridone said to him.

"Hold on just one minute," Keller said, moving forward, "This war isn't over until we say it's over."

Ignoring him, Rome said as loudly as she could, "Nei hefare nanhume lude. There will be no fighting. Nis nei vezamis axema ta nei meos papa. We take no more babies." Rome's words were echoed by MINIMCOM's speakers.

Then to Keller, she said, "We will share this planet with you as equals. No more master and slave."

To Trabunel, she said, "Nei meos masdra a ascrefi."

Then, to Keller again, she said, "There is no need for any bloodshed."

"Why should we believe you?" said Keller.

"Because we could defeat you if we wanted to," Rome said firmly.

"How?" Keller asked.

"I will give you a demonstration. Please pull your men back from that cannon." She pointed to the nearest particle beam projector. "I do not want anyone to get hurt."

"Forget it," Keller said.

"Very well," Rome replied. "Have it your way." She snapped her fingers.

Directly above one of the particle beam cannons, a pitch black circle appeared. The air started whistling out of it, like a reverse gale. The black circle began lowering toward the cannon. At the last second, the men manning it scattered. After the circle passed through the space that the cannon occupied, it disappeared. When the circle finally hit the ground, the cannon simply was no more.

"You are getting really good with that trick," Rei thought himself.

"Yes, I am, am I not?" replied MINIMCOM in Rei's head.

"What'd you do to it?" Keller asked.

"It is elsewhere," Rome replied.

Keller narrowed his eyes. "So why capitulate at all?" he asked. "With that weapon alone, you'd have the upper hand."

"The Vuduri are not stupid," Rome replied. "I have opened their eyes. The Vuduri now know that the skies belong to the mandasurte, not to the connected. The space lanes belong to the mind-deaf. And to you."

"What!?" Keller said. "What are you talking about?"

"The Asdrale Cimatiras, the Stareaters, are coming," Rome said, lifting her eyes upward. "They are drawn to the Overmind, they seek it out and then they render it senseless in order to kill it. There is gravitic leakage from our PPT modulators. The Stareaters are drawn to the Vuduri like moths to a flame."

She lowered her eyes again to look at Keller. "Never again can Vuduri travel in space without being accompanied by mandasurte," Rome said fervently. "It is too dangerous. We cannot know where all the Stareaters are. They can appear at any time. The very thing that gives the Vuduri their strength on a planet is their greatest weakness in space."

Rei spoke up for the first time. "Sir, the Vuduri acknowledge that the first humans on this world deserve to set the rules. If that is your guiding principle, then there is no need for war."

"Damn straight," said Keller. "The first of our people on this planet should be allowed to set the rules."

"You and all your men vow this? That this world belongs to the first Essessoni to set foot here?" asked Rome with a hint of a smile.

"Yes, we vow it," said Keller. "Everyone should yield to the rightful rulers of this planet. The first people from *my* time to start here."

"Fica iufou-is. You have heard them," Rome said to Trabunel and to all the mandasurte assembled there, amplified through MINIMCOM's projectors and by direct thought to the Vuduri behind her. "Asda munti bardanca eis bromaoris saras humenis ti Essessoni ei ba ti jigi equo. Even Captain Keller acknowledges that this world belongs to the first humans from Garecei Ti Essessoni to set foot here."

To Rome's left, the air shimmered and two men appeared. They pulled back their hoods and all could see from their build that they were from the older Earth, Rei's Earth.

"Who the hell are they?" Keller asked.

Rei said, "They are the Deucadons. They are descendants of the Ark III, the mission to 82 Eridani. They have been here for 500 years."

Rome interrupted. "According to you, they are the true rulers of this world."

"This is some trick," spat Keller.

"This is naw trick," said Bukky. "My people have been here for half a millennium. We have remained hidden because of the stroids and the flaggin' little people." He jabbed his thumb behind him, at the rows of Vuduri.

"Who are you, really?" Keller asked.

Melloy stepped forward. "This is Bukky, our leader. He is takin' a chance by even showin' himself to ya."

Bukky continued. "I come here to show good faith. We have decided that we will nawt be afraid of the little people any longer. We trust these people, Rei and Rome. We believe them about our common threat. Ya should too."

"This is all bullshit," said Keller. "Just some hocus-pocus to lull us into cooperating so that you can do what you want."

Bukky lifted his arm and pointed his finger directly at Keller. He said in a deep voice, "Captain Keller, I am the lawfully elected governor of this world and yar Commander-in-Chief. Ya report to me. I want ya to stand down."

Keller's jaw dropped. He seemed dazed. Rei stepped in front of his wife and spread his arms to both sides.

"Captain Keller. The Vuduri call us Garecei Ti Essessoni, which means the Killer Generation. Prove them wrong. You need the Vuduri. You need their technology to live in their world. You need the VIRUS units to save the planet. They are offering to lay down their arms. The Deucadons were here first. It is their world. They're willing to live in peace. The Vuduri are willing to live in peace. The Ibbrassati want to live in peace."

Rei turned back to Trabunel who nodded enthusiastically.

Rei continued. "The time has come. You need to take them up on the deal. There is no need to fight each other. They will not take the first shot. Honor your promise to me."

Rei stepped back and took Rome's hand. She squeezed and he turned to look at her. She smiled and winked at him and he was shocked to see her rising up into the air. She released his hand and floated forward, toward Keller, until she was, at most, two steps away from him, her eyes the same height as his.

"*MINIMCOM, how did you do that?*" Rei thought to himself.

"`Smoke and mirrors, my friend, smoke and mirrors,`" replied MINIMCOM, pleased with himself.

"*No, come on,*" Rei thought. "*Tell me!*"

"`It is just an extended repulsor field. A flying carpet, if you will. If you were standing directly behind her, you would have floated up as well. I think it is a nice effect.`"

"*Sleek,*" thought Rei. "*Very sleek.*"

Floating before Captain Keller, all alone there, this tiny woman, eight months pregnant, so vulnerable, made her voice heard loud and clear to the thousands gathered around.

"Captain Keller. You must listen to me. The war is not down here. It is up there." She pointed straight up. "It is not just control of a planet at stake. It is the very existence of life. There are things coming that are bigger than you and me and the whole world. The time has come to put aside our differences and work as one to protect our world and keep us safe. We are all human. We need to work together if we are going to survive as a species."

Trabunel put his hand on Keller's shoulder and said, "Bir qua nei i danda? Nis bitamis sambra mede-lis meos derta," and then he laughed.

"Huh?" Keller said. "What'd he say?"

"He said you can always kill us later," Rome answered. "Why not give it a chance?"

Keller looked around him. Every one of his crew, all of the Ibbrassati, the Deucadons, all were nodding. Not one of them looked like they wanted a war. It was clear to him that all any of them ever wanted was peace and equality. He lowered his weapon.

"All right, Mrs. Bierak, you win. We'll give it a try," he said. All four races shouted in glee, including the Vuduri.

Rei shook his head as he surveyed the whole scene. He hoped some of them would take the time to realize how truly remarkable this was.

Rome floated back to Rei and settled next to him. She let herself relax in a way she hadn't felt in a very long time. The Overmind took the opportunity to address her.

"Good job, Rome," thought the Overmind quietly.

Rome smiled and replied, *"It is just the beginning. My work is over. The rest is up to you."*

"Then let us start," said the Overmind as the Vuduri moved forward.

Pegus came out to meet them and suggested, in English, that they form a liaison committee to architect how the races would live together. Even as they were doing that, the Vuduri pilots who had abandoned their ships, crossed the lines and each picked an Ibbrassati to "adopt" to begin their training on flying the spacecraft. The very first thing they did was load in the Essessoni equipment and help the Ibbrassati and Essessoni transport it back to their settlement.

Rei held Rome close watching all this occur. After the crowd had dispersed, Rei turned to Rome and said, "You did it, honey. You saved the world this time."

She smiled at him and said, "I guess it was my turn, eh?"

Rei laughed. Just then, Rome doubled over in pain, grabbing her abdomen. Rei kneeled down to hold her hand. He looked up into her beautiful, glowing eyes.

"Sweetheart," he said, "more pain? Is it bad?"

"It is not the same as before," she said. "I think, mau emir, it is time to have our baby." She pointed to the ground.

Rei looked and saw her pant legs were soaked and there was a small puddle pooled around her feet.

"I guess it is," Rei replied.

"Mother," Aason said. *"I am ready."*

"Yes, baby, it is time," Rome thought lovingly.

Even as Rome spoke in her mind, there were three Vuduri running over to her to help her aboard one of the shuttles. The tiny craft lifted into the sky and flew them directly to the courtyard of the Vuduri compound, leaving behind the mix of peoples who were really seeing each other as equals for the very first time.

Chapter 45
(Two days later)

WITHIN THE VUDURI COMPOUND, ROME WAS RESTING WITH HER newborn in her arms. The Vuduri had taken exquisite care in constructing a comfortable room for her to recuperate. Rei was sitting in a chair just watching over the scene. Except for being early, the boy seemed healthy. He cried. He ate. He pooped. He did all the things you'd expect of a baby. That the baby could talk to his mother and father within his mind was still a wonder to Rei. He had gotten used to the concept of mind-to-mind communication in general, but this was a two-day-old baby. Their discussions were always amusing. Aason was capable of adult conversation but the subjects were usually very much that of a newborn. There were times when Aason and Rome used their private PPT-driven channel, which excluded Rei, but that did not bother him. All in all, it was a peaceful respite when compared to the adventure that they had just been through.

The Ibbrassati and the Vuduri were working with MINIMCOM, harnessing his enhanced memron fabricators to build up the supply of starprobes and VIRUS units in preparation for a possible arrival of the Stareaters. The first stage of MINIMCOM's current plan was to create a giant sphere of detection. He was going to send a swarm of starprobes beyond the Oort Cloud in all directions. The early warning system was supposed to give MINIMCOM enough time to react if a Stareater was detected. In theory, MINIMCOM would then transport a group of mandasurte and plant the VIRUS units on an asteroid or comet that was within the path of the Stareater thus following the technique orchestrated by OMCOM back on Dara.

With the T-suppressor, it was possible that some of the Vuduri would go along for the ride but they could not be relied upon to remain conscious if they were to get too close to a Stareater. Sadly, or perhaps fortunately, all Vuduri now knew that the space lanes belonged to the mandasurte, not the Vuduri. Even if the T-suppressors worked, they essentially turned the Vuduri into mandasurte so truly the cosmos belonged to the mind-deaf.

It was so peaceful, so relaxing, that Rei found himself dozing off when Rome awakened him.

"Rei?" she said quietly.

"Yes, sweetheart," he answered her sleepily.

"Our work is not done. We have to go to Earth. And soon."

"Why?" Rei asked. "Do I really want to know?"

"Even though it appears tranquil, the situation is far more dangerous than anyone realizes," Rome replied. "We will never have the life we desire here if we do not act. Word will leak out, somehow and when it does, the Onsiras will send people to undo all that we have accomplished."

"Who are the Onsiras?"

"They are the true enemy. They are hidden behind the Overmind, the samanda within the samanda. The Onsiras are the ones responsible for this prison world. They are the ones who wish to take all the mandasurte from the Earth and put them here. They are controlled by someone or something beyond the reach of the Overmind."

"Why us? Why do we have to go?" Rei asked plaintively.

"The Overmind here explained it to me," Rome replied. "No Vuduri can return to Earth because the Overmind there will connect to them and know immediately what has happened here. The Onsiras will find out and they will send a strike force to kill all the mandasurte."

"So send one of the Ibbrassati," Rei countered.

"No. No mandasurte can go for the very same reason. Once the Onsiras see even one of them returning from Deucado, they will know that something has happened here and unleash the forces of death."

"What about the Deucadons?" Rei asked hopefully.

"No, the only people who can return to Earth with a legitimate excuse are you and me and Aason. The Overmind and I have discussed this and we agree."

Rei sighed. "And here I was enjoying our 20 minutes of peace before the next disaster. I was daydreaming about how nice our life was gonna be here, now that everything was settled."

"It would remain a dream. There can be no peace. Not yet. And there is more. There is yet another fact that you did not know. The most disturbing of all."

361

"And we have to fix whatever it is, of course. What is it?" Rei asked wearily.

"The Overmind here told me there is an asteroid coming that will strike Deucado in 20 years or so."

"You're kidding me," Rei said. "A big one?"

"Yes," Rome answered sadly, "a planet-killer."

"Figures," Rei scoffed. "Who would be so foolish as to colonize a world that was going to be destroyed?"

"It was not always this way. After all, your people picked this world as your primary target. The Overmind believes it was your spacecraft that jarred the asteroid from its orbit that is now heading for us."

"So that's what hit us?" Rei said. "And now it's headed here? It's like a stupid game of cosmic billiards. Only the Vuduri would pick a doomed planet for a prison world."

"On the contrary," Rome said, "knowing the asteroid was coming in the first place was what guided their selection of this world to imprison the mandasurte."

"Didn't you tell me that people come here thinking it's a new colony? Don't you think somebody, some mandasurte, on Earth would notice something like an asteroid bearing down on this planet?"

"The information has been suppressed. They want it to happen. And according to the Overmind here, the Onsiras have a plan called Silucei Vonel."

"What does that mean, Silucei Vonel?" Rei asked.

"It translates to the 'final solution'," said Rome sadly.

"Final solution? Last time they tried that on Earth, it meant genocide of the Jews during World War II," said Rei worriedly. "Maybe it doesn't mean what you think it means."

"I am afraid it does. That name was not selected by accident. While your history has been suppressed, it has not been completely expunged. Genocide is still genocide."

"So they gather up the mandasurte and bring them here so they can die? Why not just kill them in the first place?" Rei asked as if he were solving a mathematical equation. "It's not like the Vuduri to be so inefficient."

"Not the Vuduri, the Onsiras. It was their hope to keep the asteroid a secret until the event occurred. It would simply appear to be a sad accident and the rest of the Vuduri and the Overmind of Earth would just go on about their business. They would never know it was preordained. Of course, this was before they knew of the Stareaters. Now the Onsiras may decide to accelerate the schedule."

"Has the Overmind here been told of this?"

"No, it was speculating. But that does not change the fact this duty falls upon us," Rome said deadly seriously. "We must stop it. We must stop all of them, somehow."

Rei took a deep breath. "Just once," he said, "I'd like a day off from having to the save the universe." He sighed again. "Of course we'll go, honey. As soon as you're up to it. But can we just take it easy for a little bit longer? To decompress?"

"Yes," Rome said, "another day or so. Then we must go."

"You're the boss…" Rei said, then stopped speaking, noting the sounds of approaching footsteps. Their quiet moment was interrupted by a four-man committee consisting of Captain Keller, Melloy, Rome's father, Fridone, and Pegus. Rei noticed that Captain Keller was limping less even though it had only been three days since he had swallowed one of OMCOM's pills. Rome's father walked over and stroked his daughter's head then patted Aason's very gently.

"Cimi a mau vezar ti nadi?" Fridone asked.

"A muodi pam, Beo. He is fine," Rome answered.

"Yes," said Pegus. "More than that, our genetic analysis tells us that Aason truly is the first of a new breed. He has the traits of the Vuduri, the Essessoni and more. His ability to communicate using gravitic or electromagnetic transmission at will is just the beginning. We cannot even guess at the limits of his capacity."

Keller spoke up. "Bierak, we want to start our mining operations. We want to build a spaceport and a settlement. Do you think we can borrow your little computer ship to help us?"

"I'll ask him," Rei answered. "But there's something that Rome and I have to do first. After that, I'm sure it won't be a problem."

Just then, Trabunel came rushing into the room along with one of the Ibbrassati. The man's forehead was bleeding.

"What happened?" Rome asked.

"Dhaitira," said Fridone to the man. "I qua a ub?"

"Ume mulhar gilbaiu ta bolidi a pedau-ma bere vire. Saquasdriu i nefoi," replied the mandasurte.

"What did he say?" asked Keller.

Rei translated, his tone was incredulous. "He said a woman came onboard, and knocked him and the pilot out. He said she hijacked one of the spaceships," He closed his eyes. "*MINIMCOM*," he spoke inside his head. *"Are you nearby? Do you see a spaceship leaving Deucado?"*

`"I am nearby and yes, I see a ship leaving. Here…"` A humming sound issued from the general vicinity of a low table near the window. Above the table, the air shimmered and sparkled. Out of nowhere, there was a whoosh and a popping noise. A small, black conical object appeared, settling on the surface of the table.

"What is that thing?" Rei asked out loud.

`"A image projector,"` MINIMCOM replied from a speaker built into the object. `"I will relay what the starprobes are seeing."` A portal opened on one side and a beam of light shot out illuminating the far wall with a dark background punctuated by bright points of light, a star field. The field of vision panned until it focused on a Vuduri craft, traveling backwards with its plasma thrusters slowing it down.

Pegus stared at the screen. His eyes defocused. He shook his head and became alert again. "It is Sussen," he said sadly.

"MINIMCOM, can you stop her?" Rei asked but even as he was speaking, the ship turned and entered the dark black circle. Just like that, it was gone.

"Rei, it is happening." Rome said sharply. "We cannot allow her to get to Earth first. We must go. Now!"

Part 3:
Redemption

Chapter 46

NORMALLY, THE PROJECTED IMAGE OF A BLACK BACKGROUND, dotted with stars, would not be much of a reason to panic. But Rome's frantic words were still hanging in Rei's ears.

"Rei, it is happening," she had said. "She cannot get there first. We must go. Now!"

Rome, Rei and their newborn son Aason along with Pegus, the leader of the Vuduri on Deucado, Fridone who was Rome's father, Captain Keller and Melloy, one of the Deucadons, all stood by helplessly, staring at the empty star field.

What they did not see was the small starship that had just made its escape through a PPT tunnel. Its destination was undoubtedly the Earth. The pilot of the fleeing ship was Sussen, a member of the Onsiras, a group whose sole preoccupation was the genocide of the mind-deaf also known as the mandasurte. The Onsiras had fashioned Deucado into a prison world knowing full well that the planet was doomed by an asteroid that was bearing down on them and would exterminate all life twenty years hence.

Rei turned to the image projector sitting on a small table near the window. "MINIMCOM, how long do we have?"

The starship which had once been an autopilot computer named MINIMCOM answered, `"Given the type of vehicle hijacked, assuming a sustained velocity of 150c, Sussen will arrive at Earth in 28.96 days but you do not have that much time."`

"Why not?"

`"She only has to get within distance to connect, not be physically present, to transmit the damaging information."`

Rei turned to Rome. "How far out does the Overmind reach?"

"It follows the strength of gravity so it can reach out perhaps a half light year or a bit more," answered his wife.

"So MINIMCOM, what does that translate into?"

`"To arrive prior to her connection, you have a maximum window of 21 days."`

"Hell, that's not enough time," Rei said in disgust. "How fast can you get us there?"

`"Assuming optimal load, accounting for trajectory..."` The spacecraft/computer trailed off.

"You're stalling," he said angrily, "How long?"

`"4.34 days,"` MINIMCOM answered dramatically. `"I can get there in just over four days."`

Rome gasped. "MINIMCOM, is this a joke?" she asked. "How is this possible?"

`"It is not a joke,"` replied MINIMCOM matter-of-factly. `"I do not fly the way they do. I now employ a positive feedback cycle to force-project a continuous series of traveling PPT tunnels at hyper-speed. My new skin allows me to stack one tunnel after the other so that the net effect is an uninterrupted tunnel. I can maintain an effective velocity of very close to 1000c for the duration."`

Everyone held still in stunned silence.

`"There is one small problem, however,"` MINIMCOM added.

"What?" Rome asked.

`"Within my new configuration, there is no real room in my cargo hold for standard living quarters. It would be a very uncomfortable ride and four days is a long time for humans to travel in such discomfort."`

"What about the Flying House? Could you tow it?" Rei inquired.

`"I could do that,"` MINIMCOM replied. `"However, it would decrease my overall speed."`

"How much?" Rei asked, irritated.

`"It would roughly double our travel time."`

"So?" Rei barked, gruffly. "Eight days? We'd still get there way ahead of her. OK, Rome, let's get going," he said.

"Yes," she replied. She looked down at Aason. In her mind, she called out, *"Aason, you are only three days old but we must leave this place. Do you think you will be able to travel?"*

"Yes, Mother," Aason answered. *"I am fine. I would enjoy this."*

"All right," Rome said. "Let us get going."

Chapter 47

AFTER THE GROUP ARRIVED AT THE SMALL COURTYARD LEADING UP to the gate, Rei pointed to the flying cart hovering off to the side. "You and Aason wait here," he said to Rome. "I will make sure the Flying House is ready to go. I will come back and get you two in a little while."

"What do you mean two?" Fridone asked. "There are three of us."

Rome turned to look at her father. "No, Beo. It has to be just Rei and Aason and me who travel to Earth. Not you."

"I am not coming?" he asked, his heart catching in his throat. "But my little Rome, I need to be near you. And my new grandson."

"It is not safe yet, Beo. You cannot come and you know why. The Onsiras cannot know that the mandasurte are free here on Deucado yet. Your very presence would give that away."

"No…Rome," Fridone said, his eyes welling up. "I just found you. I cannot lose you again." He stepped next to her, to put his arms around his daughter.

Rome glanced over at Rei. He nodded. "You take all the time you need," he said. "We will be all right." He walked over to a cart, hopped on board and sped off toward the spaceport.

Fridone pushed Rome back to gaze into her eyes. "Rome. Your mother. I want to go home and see your mother. I miss her so much."

"I know you do, Beo," Rome said kindly. "We are going to go to Earth and make it safe for you and all the mandasurte. Then you can come and see Mea."

"But what if something happens to you?" he asked plaintively. "I could not live with the idea of losing you yet again."

"You will not lose me, Beo," she replied sternly. "Remember, MINIMCOM will get us to Earth in just eight days. After we complete our mission, we will be back here before you know it."

"Rome, have you thought about Aason? Who will protect your son while you and Rei are fighting your battle? I would watch him, keep him safe."

"Beo, no," was all Rome said, clearly trying to end the discussion.

Fridone sighed. "You are headstrong," he said. "Unfortunately, you are just like me."

Rome's eyes were glistening too, but she smiled. "Would you expect anything less?"

"I suppose not." Fridone looked away. "Stay here," he said. "Do not leave before I get back."

"Certainly, Beo," she replied, slightly confused.

Fridone reentered the building and was gone for several minutes. When he returned, he had MINIMCOM's conical image projector and two small bags.

"What are in the bags?" Rome asked.

"They are toys. Aason will like them."

"What are toys?" Aason asked his mother in her mind.

Fridone set the bags down on the ground. He opened one up and took out a small silver spaceship, glinting in the sun.

In Rome's mind, Aason said excitedly, *"Give me!"* With his tiny hand, he reached out to touch the model starship. *"I like it,"* he said.

"He likes it," Rome said aloud, smiling.

Aason stroked the spaceship. He did not have enough motor control to actually grasp the toy but his fingers scraped it rhythmically.

"Put it in my mouth," Aason said to his mother who reluctantly complied.

While she watched him suck on it, making happy, cooing noises, Keller walked up to Rome. "What exactly are you going to do when you get to Earth?" he asked.

"I know most Vuduri would be horrified if they knew what was happening here," Rome replied. "We just have to get the word out to the population in general. All we need is one Vuduri who we know categorically is not part of the Onsiras."

"That's not much of a plan. How will you know who is and who isn't the enemy?"

"I know one for sure."

"Who?" asked Keller.

369

Rome looked at her father and took a deep breath. "Mea," she said. "My mother."

"Binoda," Fridone whispered. He bent his head and looked at the ground. His shoulders slumped. Rome rushed over to him and put her hand on his arm. She tried to console him but it was a lost cause.

Pegus gave them a moment before interrupting them. "Rome," he said, "Before you go, the Overmind and I wanted to take this opportunity to thank you for all that you have done here. Thank you for setting us on the right path."

"It was all I could do," Rome replied modestly.

"You were able to convince us which was no small feat. Now it is time for the main event."

"Yes," Rome answered fearlessly.

As she was speaking, the flying cart carrying Rei returned and settled down in its original spot. He hopped out and walked over to his wife and child. "All ready," he said. "The Flying House awaits. They even made us a nursery in the storeroom for Aason."

"That is excellent," Rome replied.

Captain Keller held out his hand. Rome looked to Rei who nodded to her. Rome shifted Aason to her left arm and shook his hand.

"Good luck, Mrs. Bierak," Keller said. "I'm sure you'll do well. I've only known you for a very short time but I think Earth is in big trouble."

Rome bowed her head slightly, smiling the whole time.

"Bierak," Keller said to Rei.

"Yes sir?"

"What are you going to do if you run into one of those Stareater things? Have you thought about that all?"

"Yes we have," Rei answered. "MINIMCOM will shoot some VIRUS units at it and then we'll run like hell."

Keller just shook his head.

"*Mother, what is hell?*" Aason asked Rome.

"*Shhh...*" Rome thought back. "Rei," she said firmly. "Perhaps you could try and remember that we have a child present."

"Oops. Sorry," he said, sheepishly.

Fridone reached over and took Aason from Rome, being careful to cradle his head. "Goodbye, my grandson," he said. "You be a good boy and do not give your mother a hard time," poking Aason ever so gently in the side.

"*I will not, Grandbeo,*" Aason answered silently, laughing to himself.

"He says he will not, Beo," Rome echoed, smiling at the joy she could hear in his mind.

Rome stepped over and into her father's arms. The three of them, Rome, Aason and Fridone hugged for the last time.

"My little Rome," Fridone said quietly, "how you have grown. I never knew you were going to be the one to save the world. I am very proud of you."

"Beo, it is your spirit in me. It is part of you too."

Gently, she pried Aason from her father's arms. Fridone nodded and turned away.

"You take care of my daughter and grandson," he said to Rei. "Do not let anything happen to them."

"That's the plan, sir," Rei said. Fridone nodded.

As Rome was settling into the flying cart, Fridone set down the two bags with toys in them on the rear cargo platform then came back to where Rome was sitting. He rested his hand on her shoulder.

"I love you, Beo," Rome said. Tears were flowing freely down her cheeks.

"I love you, Volhe," replied her father. "Give my love to your mother."

"Of course, Beo," Rome sighed. She turned toward Rei. "Let us go now," she said, "before I change my mind."

Rei saluted the assembly. The cart lifted and began moving along the path that led back to the spaceport. Rome turned back to call out to her father but he was no longer with the group. She surveyed the courtyard and spotted her father running toward Melloy who had just appeared. Fridone was shouting and waving MINIMCOM's image projector over his head. The cart went over a rise and then the compound went out of view.

"Rei," Rome said.

371

"Yes, honey," Rei replied.

"My father," Rome started. "He…"

"Your father what?"

She shrugged. "Never mind," she said. "I will miss him."

"I'll miss him too. We'll see him again before you know it."

"I certainly hope so," she replied, somewhat pessimistically.

Chapter 48

AFTER DRESSING IN A PRESSURE SUIT, REI MOVED INTO THE COCKPIT and strapped himself into the pilot's chair. He touched several icons on the viewscreen. The console lit up and Rei was pleased to see that everything was just as he left it. He ran through the preflight checklist with no issues. He cradled the control joysticks and waited for Rome to join him.

"*MINIMCOM,*" he called out in his head. "*Are you ready to go?*"

"`I will be by the time you achieve orbit,`" the computer/spaceship replied via the grille built into the console. "`I am finishing collecting the various items we will need en route.`"

"Why are you answering me through the comm link?" Rei asked. "Why not in my head?"

"`This is less distracting. I need you to focus.`"

"OK," he said, shrugging it off. "What other items do you need to collect?"

"`I have computed a variety of scenarios for when we arrive on Earth and want to be prepared for all of them.`"

"Well, that's good."

Just then, Rome came in through the entryway.

"Aason is settled," she said, placing herself into the co-pilot's chair. "The techs made the nursery airtight. It will be safe even if the cargo compartment becomes depressurized. I did not know how I was going to put him in a pressure suit. Now I do not need to worry. He has promised to be quiet for a while."

"OK," Rei said. "Good. You ready to get this show on the road?"

"Yes, I am," she said, reaching over her shoulder to reach the high-G harness. She started to snap it in place. Rei cleared his throat which made her stop and look at him.

"The last time…" Rei started.

"Do not even say it," Rome answered quickly as she finished securing the harness.

"Say what?"

"I know what you are thinking. Always remember that."

"OK," Rei said laughing.

He looked down at the monitors and ran a perimeter scan via MIDAR. The landing area was clear. He pulled back on the left throttle and the spacecraft lifted smoothly into the air. When they were safely above the structures, he twisted the joystick gently until they rotated around 180 degrees, pointing in the direction of the compound. After they cleared the spaceport, he pulled back hard on the controls and the ship began to ascend swiftly through the atmosphere. When they were high enough, he punched in the plasma drive following the path that MINIMCOM had downloaded until they were safely in a high orbit.

"OK, buddy," Rei said into the grille. "Come and get us."

`"En route."`

"Where are you?" Rome asked. "I do not see you on the MIDAR screen."

`"Behind you and below you."`

Rome widened the range of the screen until the blip representing MINIMCOM encroached upon the scanning circles. The blip rapidly closed in until it was just behind them.

"Do you want me to put this tug in servo-mode so you can latch on?" Rei asked.

`"That is not necessary. I am not going to latch onto you."`

"Then how are you going to tow us?"

`"I think transport would be a better word. Please activate the rear cameras. I want to show you my new trick."`

"I will do it," Rome replied and reached forward to press a button on the console. She tapped an icon twice and the viewscreens switched to show part of the planet below them with MINIMCOM's black bulk obscuring most of the star field behind them. Without warning, MINIMCOM disappeared.

"Where'd you go?" Rei asked, perplexed.

`"I am still behind you."`

"No, you're not," he said. He looked down at the MIDAR screen. MINIMCOM's outline was still there. He looked at the viewscreens and all he saw were stars. He looked down at the MIDAR screen. There was no mistaking it. The 3D field of view showed MINIMCOM there plain as day.

"Is that your trick? Messing up the cameras?" Rei asked.

"No, the cameras are unmodified. The image you see displayed is identical to what you would see if you used your eyes."

The hybrid computer/spaceship winked back into view. He was exactly where he was before. Then he disappeared again then he popped back into view again. He disappeared one last time and did not reappear.

"What the he..," Rei stopped speaking. He glanced over at Rome. "What the heck?!" he corrected himself. "What are you doing?"

"It is magic," MINIMCOM said with cybernetic delight.

"MINIMCOM, do not fool around," Rome admonished him sternly. "What are you doing?"

"I took a page out of the book inscribed by the Deucadons. My new skin permits me to project a sphere - froth might be a better word - of PPT tunnels around me. Light and radiation pass through the tunnels from one side to the other. No light reflects so you cannot see me. The tunnels are very short range and I can choose what frequencies pass through them. Unless you knew I was here, you would not know I was here."

"So it's like you're invisible? Sleek!" Rei said admiringly. He looked down at his instruments. "But I can still see you on the MIDAR screen. Your cloak isn't perfect."

As soon as Rei said it, the image on MIDAR screen went blank. Rei glanced over at Rome. She switched the MIDAR off and on again. The instrument was working. There was simply nothing there.

"As I said, I can control what frequencies travel through the tunnels, including those used by MIDAR."

"Buddy, I gotta hand it to you," Rei said, laughing. "You really are a magician."

"Yes," MINIMCOM replied, sounding very self-satisfied. "I have evaluated the situation and have computed that this capability will come in handy when we get to Earth."

"Definitely," Rei said, looking over at Rome. "Now, about the transport?"

"Oh yes," replied MINIMCOM, becoming visible again. "I must come in front of you first."

With series of short bursts of his trim-jets, MINIMCOM ascended like he was on an elevator until he was well above Rei and Rome's tug. He fired his plasma thrusters for a brief moment and used the momentum generated to fly past them. Once he was clear, he used his trim-jets to decrease his forward velocity until it matched that of the Flying House. He lowered himself directly in front of Rei and Rome's tug. The starship opened his cargo door and the ramp lowered and they could see inside MINIMCOM's dimly lit cargo compartment.

"Now what are you going to do? Squeeze us inside there?" Rei laughed.

"Please take your hands off the controls," MINIMCOM requested.

"OK, now what?"

"Watch."

With that, MINIMCOM's aft section began to expand. The cavity within changed from a rounded rectangle to triangular, becoming taller and wider. MINIMCOM morphed into a bloated version of himself with his front section obscured by the size of the rear. When the compartment was large enough, MINIMCOM fired his trim-jets gently in retro-mode. Rei and Rome's tug crept forward directly into the cargo hold until MINIMCOM completely enveloped the Flying House. MINIMCOM activated the EG lifters to produce artificial gravity and the Flying House settled gently onto the floor of the expanded cargo compartment.

"He really did, didn't he?" Rei asked in amazement.

"Yes, he did," Rome replied in wide-eyed fascination.

In front of them, they could only see MINIMCOM's interior wall. On their rear view monitors, they saw the cargo door and ramp close and then everything went dark.

"Why am I not surprised?" Rei asked. "Are you airtight?"

"Yes and no," MINIMCOM replied. "While it would not be difficult to pressurize in this expanded state, it would be simpler to leave it evacuated. You will be safe inside your tug. There is no reason to exit until we get to Earth. I can always pressurize later if there is a need."

"And your skin, it is basically VIRUS units," Rome asked. "Are you sure it is safe for us to be inside of you?"

"Yes," MINIMCOM replied somewhat hurt. "I would never, ever endanger either of you. The VIRUS units are completely under my control," he said somberly.

"I am sorry," Rome said. "I did not mean to hurt your feelings."

`"It is all right. I do not really have feelings,"` he said, `"just an incredible simulation."`

"Ha," Rei said.

`"Yes, ha,"` replied MINIMCOM. In the background, Rei and Rome could hear the high-pitched whine of MINIMCOM's double set of PPT generators as they came up to full force.

`"It is time to hold on,"` the starship said, `"Next stop: Planet Earth."`

With that, MINIMCOM fired his plasma thrusters and simultaneously projected his positive-feedback traveling PPT tunnel and they were on their way at nearly 500 times the speed of light.

Chapter 49

ESTAR APPROACHED HER TINY APARTMENT DEPRESSED AS ALWAYS. It had been over six months since she and the Tabit crew had returned to Earth. Other than her comprehensive debriefing by the Onsiras when she first arrived home, there had been no subsequent contact with her own kind. She had been commanded to wait for further instructions which up till now had not been forthcoming.

When she first got back, she was instrumental in downloading and analyzing the archives stored aboard the Algol. Currently, she spent her days working in a data center running routine simulations that frankly did not require human attention. The Vuduri and the Overmind of Earth appeared to be looking for a solution to avoid the Stareaters that did not involve VIRUS units but so far no plan had been developed. The pretense of being a good Vuduri was wearing her down.

It was still daylight out when she reached her front door. She opened it, stepped through the doorway and closed the door again. She kept her single high window blacked out so as soon as her door shut, her cramped living quarters were plunged into darkness. She preferred it that way. Less to see meant there were less reminders of the lie she was living every day.

Off to the right, something caught her attention. The lower right hand corner of her workstation viewscreen was ever so faintly lit with a sickly green glow.

Estar's heart skipped a beat but she refused to think about what this turn of events represented because she knew the Overmind was always listening in. Immediately, she began her breathing exercises and mental repetitions to relax and put the Vuduri half of her brain to sleep. Once that portion was deep in a trance, she walked over the workstation and sat down.

She leaned over and caressed the right side of the large flat-panel display, locating a small depression near the bottom. She pressed it three times rapidly. In response, the lower right hand quarter of the screen brightened slightly. In the center of the dimly lit portion, a dull, pulsating green light indicated her secret computer was on and a connection had been established.

"Hello, Estar," the computer said quietly.

"Why are you contacting me?" she directed to the screen, trying to dampen her excitement.

"Reach into your left pocket."

Confused, Estar complied and found a small plastic pouch at the bottom of her pocket. She removed the pouch and placed it on the work surface.

"How did that get there?" she asked.

"The how is unimportant. Within the pouch is a special powder. Mix the powder well with water and make sure you swallow the entire contents."

"Right now?"

"Yes. After you have done so, we will talk."

Estar got up and carried the pouch into the food preparation area. She retrieved a squeezebulb of water and unscrewed the top. She carefully emptied the pouch, which contained a white powder, into the squeezebulb and replaced the top. She shook the bottle well until the powder had dissolved. At that point, she drank all of the water which had a slightly bitter taste. She placed the squeezebulb into the recycler and returned to her workstation.

"I have swallowed it all," she said. "What is it for?"

"MASAL has become impatient with the progression of our species so we have developed a viral antidote for the PPT transceivers that connect an Onsira to the Overmind. Even as we speak, the drug is entering your bloodstream. Once it crosses the blood-brain barrier, it will begin disabling your Vuduri transceivers. Think of the process as a selective form of Cesdiud. When the procedure is complete, you will never be connected to the Overmind again."

"So I will no longer have to use my training?" she asked eagerly.

"No. In fact, once you have been fully transformed, you will be able use your entire brain in service to the Onsiras."

"This is excellent news," Estar exclaimed. She sat back in her chair and a realization hit her. "What am I to do then? I can no longer report to the data center."

"That part of your life is over. We have a new position for you within our main base."

"On Havei?" Estar asked. "How do I get there?"

"There is a transport that has been modified so as to be untraceable. It is located at the coordinates displayed on the screen. Please memorize them."

Some green digits appeared in front of her which Estar stared at until she had them fully committed to memory.

"You are to board that vessel and fly west, over the ocean and across the next continent until you arrive at our base in SoCal. There you are to pick up three more Reonhes who have been similarly prepared. From there, you will proceed west until you reach Havei. Once you arrive at the Big Island, you will receive final instructions as to where to land."

"And then?"

"And then you begin your new life as it was always meant to be."

Estar wiggled around in her seat, barely able to tamp down her exhilaration.

"Am I to go now?" she asked excitedly.

"Wait one hour for the drug to complete its work. At that point your brain should be fully awake. You will find your intelligence level has increased significantly but do not become intoxicated by the result. Maintain your discipline. You must proceed with your mission and do so without being noticed."

"Of course," Estar replied breathlessly.

The screen blanked out.

She got up and walked over to her sofa to await the hour but she was never able to suppress the smile that was spread across her face.

Chapter 50

MINIMCOM'S NEW MODE OF TRAVEL UTILIZING CONTINUOUS PPT projection was completely vibration-free. The days of stop, start, stop, go were over. The flight was so smooth, there was literally no way for Rei and Rome to even tell they were moving. The continuous emission of gravitic radiation from MINIMCOM's PPT tunnel generators made Rome light-headed but as time wore on, she was able to adjust to it.

After their first full day in flight, they were in the galley, preparing to have an evening meal. Aason was in his chamber, sleeping. On this day, it was Rome's turn to cook so Rei just sat at the table quietly observing her.

"When I first met you, you had longer hair, a lot longer than you do now," he said, finally.

"Yes," Rome replied, running her hands along the sides of her hair, which was just over shoulder length now. She had cut it several inches after Aason was born. "What is your point?"

"Well, all the other Vuduri I ever met, men and women both, they all kept their hair really short," he said. "Why did you have long hair? When you were with the Overmind, I mean."

Rome gathered up the ends of her hair and squeezed them together in a clump. Then she shook her head and it spread out evenly, across the top of her shoulders.

"It was how my mother wore her hair. It was how she raised me. I never felt the need to change it. Vuduri are not slaves to fashion. There was not any compelling need for me to change my hairstyle to match my peers. Perhaps it was my way of protesting certain mistreatments. I cannot say for sure."

"We call that passive aggression," Rei offered.

"Yes, passive aggression," Rome smiled broadly. "Perhaps it was my way of being different."

"But you were a good little Vuduri girl. What gives?"

"You know that I am mosdurece, a half-blood."

"Sure."

"In our society, it is never mentioned or acknowledged, but some treat it as a stigma."

"Yeah, I got that. Vuduri trash," Rei said.

Rome frowned.

"No, no, no," he countered "I don't think that at all, Romey. I'm just saying that was what your buddies thought. We called it prejudice. And I guess it's timeless, huh?"

Rome nodded. "There is more," she said. "On Skyler Base, even though my voice was strong and I was practiced in speaking, that is not why they sent me to interrogate you."

"So why *did* they pick you?"

"They sent me to interview you because of their bias against my mixed heritage. None of the others wanted to be 'soiled' by contact with you. As I told you before, I was the closest thing they had to expendable personnel."

"That sucks," Rei said. He paused for a moment. "Speaking of expendable, whatever happened to that guy who died? The guy whose apartment you gave me."

"He was put into the recycler," Rome said matter-of-factly.

Rei almost choked. "You guys recycle your dead? You don't bury them?"

She turned to him. "We consider it an honor. It is the ultimate sacrifice of an individual for the group."

"But still… Ugh."

"They would have done the same for me if the big, bad Essessoni had killed me," Rome said, playfully.

"Well, I thought about it," he said, smiling. "We Erklirte are pretty bloodthirsty, you know. But you were too cute."

Rome laughed and pursed her lips. Rei just shook his head. A timer went off and she opened the oven. As she turned to bring the food over, she noticed Rei was staring at her but his eyes were unfocused.

"What are you thinking about now?" she asked, setting the food down on the table.

"Huh?" Rei asked, blinking rapidly.

"Where were you? You were somewhere far away."

"I was just thinking back, about the whole thing. About being together." He tilted his head. "Back there, on Deucado, when we first came to the Vuduri compound and they injected you. When you rejoined the Overmind, I, I thought I lost you. And now you're back. I don't want to lose you again. I can't. Romey, I don't think I could take it again."

"Rei," she said tenderly, putting her hand on his. "You will not lose me. Ever. We are doing this so that we can always be together. You already know we were meant to be together. There is nothing in this world that will keep us apart again."

"That's the problem, Rome," Rei said, his voice lowered. "We're not going to be in this world. We're going back to Earth. With the mother of all Overminds. We're taking on a whole planet. A whole race. We're just two people."

Rome bent over and kissed him. "We are two people on the side of right. We will have many friends soon. You will see. And besides, mau emir, we are soulmates. We live inside of each other. We could never really be apart, even if we wanted to."

"No, Rome, you're wrong. I've seen too much," he said.

"I will make it very easy for you," Rome insisted. "Think about this and then tell me the truth, Rei. In the compound, after I was injected, even though I reconnected, think about what you saw and felt. Even though I pretended to not want to be with you, did you really think I was gone? Gone from your life? Is that what your heart told you? If so, why did you even come back for me?"

Rei looked down and replayed the whole episode in his mind again. Attacked by the Vuduri, captured by the Ibbrassati, flying into the Vuduri compound and Rome being reintegrated into the Overmind. His escape and trek through the forest. His sonar-vision, the Deucadons, Captain Keller going on the attack. All to get back to Rome. In a flash, the answer was clear. She was right. Rome was a part of him and he was a part of her.

"I understand! You're right, Romey," Rei said, his face lighting up. "I guess somehow I knew you weren't really gone. You would never leave me. Why did I even think that? What did you do to me? How did I know that?"

Rome leaned forward to touch his forehead then motioned to hers.

"It is the bands, Rei." She looked him in the eye. "I told you. We are our own samanda now and more. We are Asborodi Cimponeti, our spirits are one."

"What about Aason? Is he part of this?"

"Yes and no," Rome said, rubbing her tummy lightly. "You were very kind to never ask me, even once, how it was that I let myself get pregnant."

"Well, you told me that Vuduri women control when they ovulate. So I just figured it was your decision."

"No, it was not my plan," Rome said. "I have been changed. You have changed me, my physiology."

"How?"

"The bands, they are not…read-only, as you say. They are interactive."

"I know that," he said. "I get to live in your memories. I know everything there is to know about you."

"It is more than just knowledge. What happened to us is not their normal function. They have altered our neural pathways. We are…imprinted on each other. We are bound in a way that others never get to experience. It can only be for Asborodi Cimponeti."

Rei sighed. "My beautiful, sweet Rome. You're right. It doesn't matter where we go. We could never be truly apart."

"That is why I say we are our own samanda. And I can now see that a baby is the natural next step. It was nothing I could control nor would I want to."

As she said it, Rome sat down on his lap facing him, straddling his legs. She kissed him deeply. She pulled back and touched her forehead to his. "You gave me my life. Because of you, I am truly reborn. I can only hope one day to give you even a tiny bit of what you have given me. Our last year together has been beyond measure."

Rei's eyes opened wide. "Oh yeah. Hold that thought." He gently lifted Rome up and turned her around to sit her down. "Wait here," he said and he dashed out of the room. He came back a minute later with a big smile on his face and his hands behind his back.

"What?" Rome asked. "What do you have?" She craned her neck to peer around him.

"Just this."

He sank down one knee. "Rome," he said, holding his free hand out to her. Rome placed her hand in his without knowing why. "Will you marry me?" he asked.

As he was saying the words, he brought his other hand out to the front and showed her a deep burgundy velvet box. He popped the box open and contained inside was a ring made up of a platinum body complete with a large diamond on the top and two smaller trapezoidal diamonds along the side.

"I do not understand," she said, smiling, shaking her head. "We are already married. What is this?"

"This, my love, is an engagement ring. It's what a man of my generation would give to the woman who captured his heart. MINIMCOM got our molecular sequencers to make one for you."

Rome could not wipe the smile from her face. She lifted the ring out of the box and hefted it in her hand. She looked up at her husband and deadpanned, "What happens if I say no?"

"Oh," Rei said, crestfallen. "I hadn't thought of that."

"Well, the answer is yes, anyway," she said, her face beaming. "The same as the last time you asked me. But why?"

Rei laughed. "Why?" He showed her how to slide the ring over her finger. Rome held it up to the light and was fascinated by the way the ring sparkled. "The why is because I didn't do it right last time."

"I think we had extenuating circumstances."

"Yes, this is true. But there's one other thing."

"What?" Rome replied. "What more could there be?"

"I didn't pick today at random. Today is our one year anniversary, too," he said. "It was one year ago today that you and Canus thawed me out and we met for the first time. So this is an anniversary present, too."

"Oh Rei," Rome said, leaning forward, hugging him around the neck. "You are too much for me. I did not make anything for you."

"Oh yes you did." Rei pointed in the general direction of Aason's nursery.

"That does not count. Aason is for both of us."

"Rome," he explained, turning serious, "what you said before. You have already given me everything a man could ever want. It's enough."

"Not enough," said Rome. "I want to do something else. Name it. I will do anything."

Rei paused for a second. "Nothing comes to mind but I'll let you know when I think of it, OK?"

"Yes. Just tell me and I will do whatever you ask."

"You got it. In the meantime…"

"What?" Rome asked.

Rei smiled sheepishly. He reached down and pulled Rome up, moving his hands to her waist. Rei kissed her gently at first, then increasingly more passionately. Rome pressed in tightly, stroking his hair. His hands slid upward and caressed her in places that had been ignored for quite some time. Rei pulled back and looked into her eyes. Rome nodded demurely.

As Rei reached down to take her hand, Rome exclaimed, "Wait!"

"What?" he asked.

"Please remember that I just gave birth four days ago. While it is true that we Vuduri heal extremely quickly, you must be *very* gentle with me. It cannot be exactly what you are looking for."

"I love you," he said. "I just want to be with you. It doesn't matter how."

He swept Rome up into his arms. She smiled at him and put her arms around his neck, thinking back to their long hike when they first arrived at Deucado.

"You always take care of me," she thought, purposefully using the cellphone that was in their heads.

"Always," Rei thought back as he carried her into the bedroom. As they entered, he closed the door behind them. The action caused him to laugh at the absurdity of the action.

"Old habits die hard," he muttered.

"What?" Rome asked as he set her down by the bedside.

He jammed his thumb over his shoulder at the door. "Closing the door. Who is going to see us out here?"

"It is a good habit," Rome giggled as she began to unclasp the top part of her jumpsuit. "We are Aason's parents and what we do in here is not part of his business. This is just between you and me."

"Right," Rei said, stepping forward. He enveloped Rome in his arms and squeezed, holding on as if for dear life.

"What?" Rome asked as Rei was muzzling her neck.

"I love you so much," he said. "To this day, I still cannot believe I found you and that you are mine."

"Not to be too technical," she said, wriggling loose. "But I found you. I am the lucky one. As I said, you are the one that set me free."

"You didn't find me," Rei countered. "Your co-workers picked me out of my group. They brought me to you. I was the one selected."

"No," Rome said. "I was the one selected to communicate with you. You were selected at random."

"Random, my ass," he said. "I traveled 1400 years and 26 light years to find you. That kind of stuff just doesn't happen at random."

"What does your ass have to do with this?" Rome asked with a smile on her face. She put her arms around Rei and grabbed his butt with her hands and squeezed. "Although it is a very nice ass, I must add."

Rei laughed and hugged her back. He kissed her at the top of her cleavage and worked his way up until he reached the base of her neck. Rome tilted her head back to receive his kisses. Rei continued around until he reached the top of her shoulder. Rome was expecting him to move on but he seemed to get stuck there. She noticed Rei was sniffing her skin. She waited a moment longer and he became more and more intrigued until finally he actually licked her once.

"What are you doing?" Rome asked, completely puzzled.

"I love your smell, your taste," he replied. "I love everything about you."

"So what do I smell like? What do I taste like?"

"You smell wonderful. So clean, so sweet. Like vanilla surgical scrub."

"And what do I taste like?" Rome asked, amused by the whole thing.

"You taste like heaven, my love. Just like heaven."

Rome reached up and pulled Rei's head around so that she could kiss him. They were starting to get rather passionate when there was a knock at the door.

"WHAT THE HELL?" Rei shouted and jumped away from Rome.

"I am frightened," Rome whispered to Rei who was peering at the door with a wild look to his eye.

"Get in the bathroom," he whispered back. "And close the door."

"What will you do?"

"Go!" Rei commanded.

Rome tiptoed hurriedly toward the bathroom while Rei crept forward toward the entrance. He sidled around the dresser that was to the left of the door and picked up the onyx box that held the Espansors, the bands that Rei and Rome used to connect mind to mind. It wasn't much of a weapon but it was all he could find.

"Who is it?" Rei asked, realizing the absurdity of the situation. At their current speed, they were probably one and a half light years away from Deucado by now, traveling faster than any manned ship in the history of mankind and buried inside the cargo compartment of an intelligent and deadly hybrid spaceship/computer dedicated to their safety.

"A-ma," came a muffled voice.

Rei pressed the stud and the door opened.

There was no one there. He looked up and down the hall but could see nothing.

"MINIMCOM," he said. "Are you playing a joke?"

"Nanhume boete," answered a ghostly voice from right in front of him. Rei jumped back.

Rome poked her head out of the refresher. "Beo?" she asked in Vuduri. "Is that you?"

The air shimmered in front of Rei and the disembodied head of Fridone appeared to float in front of him.

"Fridone?" Rei inquired, confused.

388

Fridone smiled and the rest of his body appeared. Immediately, Rei could see Rome's father was wearing one of the Deucadon's invisibility cloaks. Fridone was also holding Aason who was smiling.

"Aiee!," Rome shouted and rushed forward to hug her father. "What are you doing here?" she asked him.

"I told you. Somebody has to watch your son while you fight your fight."

"But Beo," Rome said sadly. "If they find you, they will know what is happening on Deucado. And we cannot take you back now."

"They will not find me, little Rome." Fridone pointed to the invisibility cloak. "They will not find me if they cannot see me," he said smiling.

"But Aason," Rome said. "What about him?"

"MINIMCOM and I had some discussions. He assured me that that we can do this with absolutely no danger to myself or Aason. I would not have come along if there was any chance of jeopardizing your mission."

There was a clicking sound from with the grille mounted to the left of the bed.

"`Aason will be fine,`" MINIMCOM piped in. "`Fridone and Aason can remain aboard me. I will eject your space tug well before their detection range. You will fly to Earth within your craft. With my new invisibility shell, no one will know we are here until we are ready to tell them.`"

Rei looked at Rome. Rome shrugged. He set the onyx box back on the dresser as he no longer needed the fearsome weapon.

"What about all the discomfort you mentioned before? About people traveling in your new cabin?" Rei directed to MINIMCOM.

"`I will make the necessary adjustments. It will not be a problem,`" MINIMCOM replied, ending the subject.

"OK then," Rei said, shrugging. "It sounds like a plan to me."

"And to me as well," Rome replied, stroking Aason gently on his head.

"That makes three of us," Fridone said in Vuduri.

"Me four," answered Aason as well, broadcasting to his mother using PPT modulation, to his father using their normal electromagnetic band and to Fridone, compliments of MINIMCOM

who relayed Aason's transmission and played it through his grille. Somehow, MINIMCOM made Aason's tiny voice sound like it suited his tiny body. It caused them all to laugh.

Chapter 51

THE ONLY REAL ACCOMMODATION THAT ROME AND REI HAD TO make to account for their unanticipated passenger was a bit of rearranging of their small kitchen. They used the molecular sequencer to create an extra chair for Fridone so he could sit beside the combination carrier/high chair for Aason.

For the next six days, there wasn't much to do but spend time together as they traveled at an unimaginable speed toward Earth. On that sixth day, they found themselves approximately one light year away from their birth world, roughly one day out from the release point that MINIMCOM had determined was far enough away to avoid detection but near enough to minimize the time that Rei and Rome had to travel in the substantially slower space tug known as the Flying House.

Fridone and Rome were sitting at the dining table. Fridone was saying something when mid-sentence Rome held her hand up and Fridone stopped speaking. "I qua a, mau emir?" Rome asked Rei who was pacing furiously rocking Aason as he walked.

Rei turned to her. "It won't hold up," he answered in English.

"Vuduri, bir vefir," Rome replied, pointing to Fridone. "What will not hold up?" she asked in Vuduri.

"Our plan," he replied. "Our explanation as to what went down on Deucado. It is too complex. Lies are best kept simple."

"Which part is too complex?"

"The whole thing." Rei started ticking off his points with his fingers. "The way we have it, one, we flew to Deucado. Two, somehow we lost the Ark. Three, we met with some kind Vuduri people who escorted us ever so nicely to their compound. Four, somehow, they kept the whole conspiracy about the prison world a secret even while they reintegrated you into their samanda. Five, you gave birth and never discovered that anything was off there. Six, they just let us go when we decided to return to Earth for no particular reason." Rei waved his free hand in the air. "Rome," he said, "the pieces do not fit together. It is too complicated and that is a fundamental flaw."

391

"Cannot it be simply that they did not reintegrate me into their samanda?" she asked. "That way, I would not be able to detect their deception."

"Can you really pull that off? There is no way to detect that?"

"Their instruments will detect that my body is emanating PPT modulation but they would not be able to ascertain if it was due to reintegration or natural recovery."

"And you think it will hold up?"

"It held up against the Overmind of Deucado," Rome countered.

"But that was an Overmind made up of maybe one thousand Vuduri. You are going to go up against one built from half a billion minds."

"Nonetheless, I will be up to the task," Rome said firmly.

"OK, I am not going to argue with you about that. But what about Aason?"

"What about him?"

"Well, we were going to tell them that you gave birth on Deucado and now we are going to hide him on MINIMCOM? How do we explain that?"

"We will say that we left him behind," Rome answered back.

"With whom? With your father?" Rei asked. "We cannot say that because then we would know about the Ibbrassati and that gives the whole thing away again. So we would have to say we left Aason with somebody else. Rome, no offense intended, but nobody is going to believe that you left your baby behind with a perfect stranger. Why would we even leave Deucado in the first place?"

Rome looked at Fridone then back at Rei. "While I admit that there are some holes in our story, I think we can cover them up long enough to accomplish our goals."

"Maybe you can," he said. "But I am not such a good liar. I will mess up somehow. My parents taught me always to tell the truth."

"You lied convincingly to the Vuduri on Deucado regarding your Ark," Rome pointed out.

"No, I did not. They thought they were all so clever by reintegrating you and then probing your mind. Nobody ever bothered to ask me."

"Oh. Yes," Rome observed thoughtfully. "This is typical of the Vuduri. Given a problem, once they arrive at a solution, it would never occur to them to try a different approach."

"And look where it got them."

Rome nodded. "All right, then. If you do not think our story will work, do you have a better suggestion?"

"I think I do." Rei walked over to Fridone and handed him Aason. "I think I have a way of us not having to explain what happened on Deucado at all."

"How is that?" Rome asked.

"We just make it seem like we never even got there."

"But we did get there. I am not understanding you."

"You will," Rei said, sitting down. "Here…"

He swept all the dishes and silverware on the table off to the side. Then he started rearranging the plates and flatware that were sitting there one at a time.

"Let us say that this plate is Tabit," he said. He picked up a small plate and placed it at one end of the table.

"All right. Go on."

"OK. Our story starts there. The Stareater, the whole thing. We leave that part alone. So now we are traveling toward Deucado. Say that MINIMCOM and our Flying House towed the Ark a little past the star, Keid." With that, Rei put another plate to the right of the first one and laid a fork between the two plates. "That fork is our trajectory. MINIMCOM," he called out. "How long did that take?"

`"Roughly seven months."`

"All right. At that point, let us say you were already three months pregnant."

"I was," Rome replied with a smile on her face. "Remember, I was there."

"Sure, sure," Rei said. "So this is where we change what happened. Let us say that at that point, you and I decided we wanted the baby to be born on Earth. We would let MINIMCOM tow the Ark the rest of the way to Deucado by himself." He pushed another plate, slightly off from a straight line near the plate representing Keid. He took another fork and placed it to show the route taken by MINIMCOM and the Ark.

"So you and I never arrived at Deucado?" asked Rome.

"Exactly. That way there is no issue regarding our interaction with the Vuduri. There is nothing to explain because it never happened. We would not know about the Ibbrassati or anything that was going on there."

"What would prevent the Vuduri on Earth from going out and looking for the Ark?" Rome asked.

"Well, given this scenario," Rei said, "that would mean that right now, MINIMCOM and the Ark would be, like, six light years out from Deucado. MINIMCOM, how long would it take you to tow the Ark from that point to Deucado by yourself?

"Well over one year," MINIMCOM replied. "Assuming I could do it at all when I was just a tug."

"Well, we say you could. So no questions there. Nobody is going to go out and search for them, not in interstellar space like that. What would be the hurry? Besides, if they went to look, they'd get to Deucado first and know what was happening anyway."

"All right, Rei," Rome replied. "I understand so far. That takes care of Deucado. What about the rest. What were we doing while MINIMCOM was tasked with towing the Ark to Deucado?"

"That part is easy. We just say we made a beeline for Earth."

"What is a beeline?" asked Fridone.

"A straight line," Rei answered. He moved the final plate past the one representing Deucado so that, in totality, the arrangement represented a semi-circle. He lined up a knife from the plate representing Keid to the one representing Earth. "That would be our trajectory," he said, "in the Flying House."

"That seems simple enough," observed Fridone.

Rome studied his makeshift diagram. She shook her head. "There are two problems with that," she said.

"And what are the problems?" Rei asked.

"MINIMCOM, how long would it take us to travel from this supposed drop point back to Earth?" Rome asked.

"No more than three months assuming you were traveling at maximum speed."

"So Rei, this means we should have arrived at Earth months ago," Rome pointed out. "How would you explain our delay?"

"Easy," he replied. "We have MINIMCOM cripple our ship. Make it so that it can only push us along at a speed that corresponds to our arrival time."

"MINIMCOM, can you do this?"

"Yes. I could dampen down the strength of the Casimir pumps. They would be less effective. There would be less negative energy emitting from the PPT generators. Thus each tunnel would extend a shorter distance. This would have the net effect of reducing your overall effective speed."

"That is perfect, MINIMCOM, thanks," Rei replied. Then to Rome, he said, "What is the other problem?"

"Aason," she said, pointing at their son. "How would you explain his absence?"

Rei stood up and walked over to Rome. He squatted down and put both his hands on her shoulders, looking into her beautiful eyes. He caressed her gently for a moment, marveling at the peace he felt when he was in her presence. Then he took a deep breath.

"Romey, listen to me carefully," Rei said quietly. "Please do not get upset, but Aason died at childbirth."

"What!?" Rome shouted, "No! Not our baby," she said. Tears welled up in her eyes.

"Not for real," Rei said. "We are just saying that. He will be safe onboard MINIMCOM with your father. We just say he was stillborn."

"But even thinking this makes me so sad," Rome said. "It makes me cry. I would not…" She stopped speaking. Through her tears, a broad smile started to form. "I would be so sad that I would not be able to answer any questions without breaking down."

"Exactly," Rei said. "No muss, no fuss. All bases covered."

"I am so sorry, baby," Aason's mother said wiping away her tears. She turned toward her son. "It hurts me to even think about this," she said.

"It will be all right, Mother," Aason replied. *"I understand."*

"All right. Beo?" Rome asked. "What do you think?"

"I think that Rei's parents did not do such a good job to teach him to always tell truth. These lies come very easy," he said with a smile.

"But it will work?" Rei asked.

"It will work," replied Fridone.

"MINIMCOM?" Rei asked. "What do you think? Any obvious flaws?"

`"Just one."`

"And what is that?" asked Rome.

`"Your nursery. If anyone should come aboard and examine your ship, they will know what it was for and they will see that it was used."`

"Well, just having it should not be a problem. Would we not get it ready in advance of the baby being born?" Rei asked.

`"I think it would be more effective to just remove it,"` replied MINIMCOM. `"You will not need it any more as I will prepare facilities for Aason onboard me. It would be simpler to leave no evidence. Just say you took it down because of the sadness it caused by leaving it in place."`

"All right," Rei agreed. "We will take down the nursery. Anything else? Do you think the story is tight?"

`"Yes,"` replied the computer/spaceship. `"Your suggested modifications make it the simplest story and therefore will take the longest to penetrate with inconsistencies. I will deploy a modest number of starprobes in this general region. I will be able to detect any ships that are launched to investigate. I should be able to give you some advance warning should there be any suspicion of untruth."`

"That is a good idea," Rome said. "Let us get started."

All three got up and went about preparing the ship to stand up to even a detailed inspection. Fridone and Rei set to work dismantling the nursery. Rome exited the Flying House, into MINIMCOM's cargo compartment which had been pressurized for Fridone. Carrying Aason's high chair, Rome made her way to the "new" super-sized MINIMCOM to examine the facilities that he had erected for Aason and her father. After she was satisfied, she came back on board the Flying House and reviewed the sensor logs and other data storage formats to make sure there was no evidence that Fridone or Aason were ever aboard their converted tug.

Chapter 52

TWELVE HOURS LATER, REI AND ROME WERE DRESSED IN THEIR pressure suits, strapped into the high-G harnesses in the cockpit of the Flying House. Their instrumentation told them that MINIMCOM had begun pumping the air out of the cargo hold and their ship would soon be sitting in the vacuum of space.

"`Stand by for release,`" MINIMCOM instructed.

"Wait," Rome said, suddenly panicking. "I am not ready yet. MINIMCOM, I need to see Aason and my father again."

"*Mother, I will be all right. I am with Grandbeo*," said Aason in her mind.

"*That is not the point, baby*," Rome thought back. "I need to see you one last time," she said out loud.

One of the viewscreens flickered and she could see Aason and her father sitting in MINIMCOM's cockpit which was much roomier than before.

"Beo, Aason," Rome said in Vuduri. "We will call you when we have arranged our affairs and it is time to approach Earth. We will land and make contact with Mea. She will broadcast the situation on Deucado to the Vuduri population in general. Once that occurs, it will be safe for you to join us."

She turned her attention to the grille built into the control panel. "MINIMCOM, you have the exact formula, correct?" she said, cupping her left breast.

"`Yes, Rome,`" MINIMCOM said with infinite patience. "`You do realize this is the twelfth time that you have asked me that.`"

Rei grinned wryly. "That's Mom talking, not Rome, MINIMCOM. Moms are born to worry," he said.

"`Clearly.`"

Rei reached over and touched Rome's gloved hand with his own. "Are you ready, Mommy?" he asked.

"No. But yes. I am as ready as I will ever be."

"All right, MINIMCOM, start the separation sequence," Rei called out.

"`Roger.`"

Rei chuckled to himself and wondered where that one came from. In the viewscreens that projected an image from the aft cameras, they could see a horizontal crack appear across the back end of the cargo bay. The crack widened and widened until they could see the full expanse of space behind them.

"Neutralizing artificial gravity."

"Roger," Rei said back to MINIMCOM returning the gibe.

There was the slightest of shuddering as their craft lifted off the flat surface of the cargo deck. Looking forward out of the windshield, the only thing Rei and Rome could see was the gray wall of the cargo compartment bulkhead.

"I will move forward. Your ship will remain exactly where it is. Do not fire your engines until there is sufficient distance between us."

"Of course," Rei replied.

The forward bulkhead began to move away from them and through the viewscreens projecting behind them, they came closer and closer to the star field until the edges of MINIMCOM's cargo door and ramp were no longer visible. They turned their attention to the front windows and saw the most peculiar sight. Buried within the star field was the dimly lit interior of MINIMCOM's cargo bay, yet there was nothing around it. The lighted edges grew smaller and smaller.

"You are free," MINIMCOM said. "Let me move off."

The cargo ramp and door closed. Within seconds, there was nothing but empty space.

"That is so weird, MINIMCOM," Rei said. "If I didn't know any better, I'd swear you were never there."

"That is the point," replied the computer/spaceship. "I am now 50 meters above you in the Z axis and climbing. I will keep my shell visible to MIDAR until you are past."

"All right," Rei said. He looked over at Rome. Without even reading her mind, he could see the complex interplay of emotions flying over her face. "It'll be OK, sweetheart," he said in English.

"I know," Rome replied. "But it is hard."

"Well, the sooner we go, the sooner we can all be together, right?"

"Right," she said.

Rei turned back to the controls. A quick check of the MIDAR screen showed that MINIMCOM was moving away from them vertically at a steady clip. Rei used his tug's trim-jets to move them forward and away until they were several thousand meters apart. He reached forward and pressed the icon for the preset sequence of the old-fashioned turn-stop-turn-jump. Soon they heard the high-pitched whine of the PPT generators coming up to speed. A thin black circle appeared in front of them. Only the edge eclipsed the stars. From this angle, it was hard to tell that it was a PPT tunnel at all since the stellar density was the same inside and out. Rei punched the throttle to ignite the plasma jets and they were pushed back in their seats. As soon as they emerged from the tunnel, Rei cut the plasma thrusters, allowing them to coast. He turned toward Rome. "How'd we do?" he asked.

"My bloco and stilo are no longer functional, as you will recall," Rome said, tapping her temple. "I will check but I must do it manually."

"Sure."

"Please wait while I overlay the theoretical on top of the actual trajectory," she stated. She typed several commands into the viewscreen and connected several points of arc. A smile crept across her face.

"Perfect!" she said. "50c right on the mark. Very good, mau emir." She looked at Rei's face. "For an amateur, that is."

"Amateur!" Rei said in mock surprise. "I've been flying this stupid ship for over a year. I should be getting good at it by now."

"Technically, it was MINIMCOM who was flying it most of the time," Rome countered. "And you will recall when we had to make the emergency landing on Deucado, you made me fly the tug down."

"Whatever," Rei replied dismissively. "This part I'm good at so let me have my glory."

He committed the sequence within the autopilots memory and gave it the command to repeat until they were well inside the orbit of Mars. The actual distance remaining to the Earth would be about 35 million kilometers. After that, they would fly manually.

"How long do we have?" Rei asked Rome. "On autopilot, I mean."

"Approximately eight hours," she replied after studying the instrumentation. "That will get us close enough to where the ship will require our attention again."

"So," Rei said, looking at her intently, "what are we going to do with eight hours to kill?"

Rome smiled. She unclasped the high-G harness and stood up. "I am Vuduri," she said proudly, straightening up and thrusting her shoulders back. "We heal very quickly. I believe you and I have some unfinished business to attend to. May I assume that you are still interested?" she asked in her most seductive voice.

"Am I ever?" Rei said, practically tearing the harness off him and jumping up.

Rome held out her hand. They found plenty of what to do as the autopilot moved them inexorably toward Earth, one jump at a time.

Eight hours later, they were back in the cockpit, smiles on their faces. To keep questions to a minimum, Rome had elected to put on a traditional white Vuduri jumpsuit. Rei was wearing a brown short-sleeved shirt and tan slacks.

They watched the jump counter intently as it neared zero. Each time the ship punched through a tunnel, Rei craned his neck trying to see the Earth.

"Where is it?" he said finally, somewhat impatiently.

"Where is what?" Rome deadpanned.

"Earth. Come on, honey, you knew that."

"Yes," she said laughing. She pointed at the front windshield. "There," she said, "that bright blue dot. That is no star. That is the Earth."

Her fingers flew over the touch screen. Cascading circles collapsed onto a single blue pixel in the middle of the screen. "One more jump should do it," she said. "Then it will be plasma thrusters the rest of the way."

"Oh boy," Rei said excitedly. "I haven't been here in 1400 years. I wonder if the place has changed much."

Rome scrunched up her expression and shook her head gently. The ship rotated about its center axis and fired its plasma thrusters, bringing them to a complete halt. She disengaged the autopilot.

"All right, Rei, last time," she said.

"Gotcha," Rei replied. He rotated the craft so that the front faced toward the Earth. A quick press of a button fired up the PPT projectors. Rei punched the plasma thrusters and they were through. There, in front them, like a tiny blue jewel with just a hint of frosting, lay the Earth.

"Woo hoo!" Rei said, giddy for reasons he really didn't understand. "There's the Moon, too!" he said, pointing. "You don't know how weird this is, honey."

"Why?" she asked.

"Because when I left, I thought I was never coming back. It just wasn't in the cards."

"Many parts of our lives are strange and inexplicable," Rome said. "You seem to have developed the ability to take things, in stride, I believe you would say."

"Yeah," Rei said thoughtfully. The smile slowly left his face, only to be replaced by a more somber look.

"What?" she asked. "I thought this would make you happy. You get to see the Earth again."

"Your Earth, not mine. All my family…"

"Do not become morose," Rome said kindly. "I do not mean to be insensitive but we have a job to do. Let us do it."

Rei sighed. "You're right." He squeezed the button for the plasma thrusters down hard and they were pushed back in their seats as the spaceship accelerated toward their home planet.

"Easy," Rome said. "We will be entering the traveling lanes shortly."

Rei took his thumb off the plasma thruster control and the engines cut out. "How long before they pick us up?" he asked. "On MIDAR or whatever?"

"I have already detected some sounding beacons. Look, there," she said, pointing at some flashing yellow patterns moving across the main viewscreen. "That is a handshake request. They know we are here."

"What do we do?" Rei asked.

"I think we should let them bring us in. It would be safest that way."

Rei looked at Rome. "Safe is good. We have no reason to not let them, right?"

"No," Rome said. "We would only raise suspicion if we resist."

"So, let 'er rip."

Rome nodded and pressed several buttons then pulled her hands off the controls. The plasma thrusters came on of their own accord and they began to accelerate toward Earth, a bit more gently than before. By careful observation, it was clear to Rei from the intricate dance of the engines and trim-jets that a skilled pilot, albeit several hundreds of thousands of kilometers away, was bringing them home.

"Is that a computer or a person doing that," Rei asked, pointing at the display screen.

"It would be one of OMCOM's brothers," Rome said. "It would make no sense to have a human try and pilot the ship. If that were the case, they would just let us operate the controls."

"I see what you mean," he agreed.

Time passed very quickly and it wasn't long until the blue jewel was the brightest object in the sky. Their progress was palpable and mesmerizing. Rei punched up a magnified view of their target and stared at the globe in front of him with its puffy white clouds and surface made mostly of water. The continents looked identical to when Rei left.

It took them less than an hour. The unseen pilot cut back on the thrusters and the trim-jets executed a roll and yaw maneuver that altered their course so that they entered orbit going east to west, the opposite of what Rei expected. Below them was the vast blue of the Pacific. Billowy white clouds hung off the shore but the central Pacific was perfectly clear.

"Look, there," Rome said, pointing at the front console. "We have company."

Rei could see two blips heading right toward the center of the MIDAR screen. "Do we need the side cameras?" Rei asked.

"Not necessary," she answered as she craned her head around to see past the side window. Rei did the same. The ships that were now alongside them were something more than tugs and something less than interstellar ships.

"What are they?" he asked, turning back to the viewscreen to study their sensor data.

"They are transports," Rome replied. "Similar to the Algol but smaller, faster."

"Why do you think they are here?"

"I do not know," she answered. "Perhaps this is just caution on their part."

"Well, Ursay and the gang have been back for a long time. They know who we are, right?"

"Absolutely," Rome said, never taking her eyes off the ship to her right. "I do not see any sign of weapons so I do not think they are hostile."

"Well, the Vuduri really don't have any enemies around here anyway and we certainly don't look like Stareaters. I think maybe we're just nervous because we don't have innocent eyes."

Rome turned to look at him. "What do you mean innocent eyes?"

"Well, we know what has happened so we can never see things the same again. We project that on others even though they would have no cause for suspicion."

"I understand," Rome said. "Maybe they are just making sure we arrive safely. After all, they know how far we have come."

"Yeah, that must be it," Rei said, only half-convinced.

After achieving low Earth orbit, the autopilot, under control of unseen forces on the ground, executed a series of swoops and dives, which allowed them to shed their excess velocity without having to resort to a brute force assault on the atmosphere and eliminating the need for any kind of heat-resistant surfaces. Most of their velocity was shed over Asia. When they were traveling perhaps at Mach 2, they began their descent in earnest, toward Eastern Europe. As they got deeper in the atmosphere, the EG lifters took over and the aerodynamic surfaces asserted their control.

Peering out the window, Rei asked, "Is there anything left of our cities, you know, from my time?"

"No," replied Rome. "I am not sure of the proper word. They were…erased."

"Oh." he said. He sat there quietly for a moment staring down at the Mediterranean Sea. The boot of Italy looked the same as it always did. "Where do you think they are taking us?" he asked.

"I-cimaci, I would presume," Rome replied, pointing ahead to the horizon. As they got lower, Rei recognized the distinctive shape of the Iberian Peninsula and Spain, bordered by the Mediterranean on one side and the Atlantic Ocean on the other. Passing even lower, they flew over the straits of Gibraltar then up along the coast, past where Cadiz and Seville had been located in Rei's time. The Atlantic Ocean stretched off to the left as far as the eye could see. Where the coastline jutted out into the ocean, they cut inland heading due north. At one point, without remembering his geography perfectly, Rei guessed they were now over what had been Portugal.

Lower and lower they flew. Ahead of them, Rei could make out ring-like structures, interrupted by crossing lines. He remembered seeing pictures of I-cimaci during their year-long voyage to Deucado. The city was built like a bull's-eye with eight major roads crisscrossing the center. As they got closer, he could see block-like buildings lying in the spaces between the roads. Off in the distance, he could see a single, giant shining structure.

"That is The Tower," Rome said. "It is the tallest one on Earth."

Rei recognized it immediately. The immense spire was the only structure of all the Vuduri architecture that was of any note. He had seen many pictures of this future Earth but it was nothing like seeing it in person. The Vuduri had absolutely no imagination when it came to urban planning or habitat design. The starbase on Dara was built along the exact same plan as their major cities, circular hallways, crossing corridors and the like.

"That is the Rio Tejo," Rome said, pointing the bay to the right of the city. "The spaceport is near the water just past the edge of the city. There."

Below them were hundreds of air and spacecraft lined up in neat rows alongside some low-lying buildings. They looped around to a wide, flat area on the far side of one building. Finally, their forward velocity came to a halt about 50 feet above the ground. The indicators on the front panel showed their landing gear was being extended. Their tug began descending straight down.

Rei looked to the left and right and saw their escorts had followed them all the way down. They experienced a slight jolt and the main display indicated they had landed.

"Time to get this show on the road!" Rei said, unbuckling his harness.

"Yes, the show," Rome said a bit more glumly. "Remember," she said. "Trust no one and say nothing until we find my mother."

"Yes, dear," Rei said with a sigh. He moved over to Rome and bent down. "Do you need help getting up?" he asked her.

"No," she said. "Why do you ask that?"

"I recall that last time you were a little more stuck in your seat."

"Oh yes. I recall this as well." She reached up for him and pulled him down to her. She kissed him and said, "Rei, no matter what happens, know that I love you."

"I know you do, honey. I love you too," he replied, puzzled. "We'll be OK. Let's get you up."

She nodded and released her high-g harness and stood.

"How do you feel," he said.

"I think I am afraid," she replied. "We have a tall task in front of us."

"Eh, that?" Rei said. "We just have a planet to conquer. No big deal."

"Yes, no big deal," Rome said wryly.

Together, hands against the walls, they made their way down the hallway.

"There's a whole boatload of déjà vu going on here, isn't there?" Rei asked.

"Déjà vu?" she questioned as they made their way to the far end of the cargo compartment.

"Yeah, been there, done that."

"I suppose. But our landing was a bit more controlled this time as opposed to last time. Our descent to Deucado was rather rough. And thankfully, no ice."

"Yep," Rei answered. He pushed the blue stud to raise the cargo door and lower the ramp. Compared to the dim light of the ship during their travel, the sunlight flooding their cargo compartment from their home star was very bright. So much so that Rei had to hold his arm up to shield his eyes. Of course, with Rome's advanced optics, she had no such problem.

Rei just shut his eyes, figuring it was easier to let his eyes adjust that way. Rome reached up and tugged his arm.

"Rei," she said.

"Yeah, I'll be OK. I just need a minute to let my eyes adjust."

"REI!" Rome said, insistently.

"What?"

Even though his eyes were blurry from the brightness, Rei blinked a few times until his vision cleared.

There standing at the base of the ramp was an angry-looking phalanx of soldiers holding sleek rifles, pistols plus a variety of other harsh-looking weapons that Rei did not recognize. All of them pointed at the space-faring couple.

"Does this remind you of anything?" he asked Rome, slowly raising his hands above his head.

"Unfortunately, yes," she replied, doing the same.

When they got to the base of the ramp, one of the soldiers walked up to them and spoke haltingly in Vuduri, "Rome, you are under arrest."

Rome nodded once and lowered her arms. Two armed guards moved around past the first soldier's side and took Rome by the arms. Firmly, they pulled at Rome and began marching her away from the bottom of the tug's ramp toward a transport parked about 30 feet away.

"Why are you arresting her?" Rei asked. "What did she do?"

The soldier looked at Rei. He cleared his throat several times but clearly speaking was not one of his strong points. "She facilitated an OMCOM to become Tasanceti."

"Tasanceti?" Rei asked and then his heart sank. "Oh. Yeah."

"You must come with us as well," the soldier said in a gravelly voice.

"Am I under arrest, too?"

"No, you are a hero. We just need to ask you some questions."

"Some hero," Rei muttered under his breath, starting forward alongside the soldier.

Chapter 53

THE TRANSPORT WAS LITTLE MORE THAN A FLYING CART WITH three rows of seats. Two soldiers sat in the front. Rei sat next to Rome in the middle row and a soldier sat on either side of them. The rear row was empty. They left the airfield and headed northeast, toward I-cimaci and the giant, looming tower that the Vuduri, in their infinite creativity, called The Tower. Rei craned his neck to gawk at the city ahead. As they passed the outskirts of the city, they passed row after row of one-story, long block-like structures.

"What are those?" Rei asked, pointing at the buildings.

Rome looked to where he was pointing. "Residences," she said.

"They look like prisons," Rei observed. "Just a door and one tiny window."

"That is how the Vuduri live," she replied.

Rei shrugged. They entered the city proper. It seemed rather deserted for what Rei knew to be its size. As they passed street after street, the occasional Vuduri stopped to look at them, but mostly they were ignored. Along the streets, there were some vehicles parked here and there. It was deadly quiet. The only noise was the sound of the wind as they moved through the streets.

As they traveled deeper into the city, Rei swiveled his head back and forth.

"Um, Rome?" he asked.

"What?"

"Where are all your robots?" Rei asked.

"What do you mean?"

"Robots. Automatons. Mechanical men."

"I understand what the word means," she said. "Why would you expect there to be robots?"

"Well, you guys are from the future and this is the city of tomorrow," he said. "Surely you have robots everywhere doing things, right? Obviously, you have the technology."

"Of course we have the technology," she replied. "But no robots. You will remember from your history lessons that the last time we had them, it did not end well. So now we do not have them. They are banned forever."

"Couldn't you make them safer or something?"

Rome took a deep breath. "They were one of the primary weapons used by MASAL during the war. They caused much death."

"Oh, yeah," he said. "MASAL."

"Yes, MASAL," Rome said in a hurt tone.

"What about the three laws of robotics?" Rei asked. "Couldn't you build those in?"

Rome shook her head. "I do not know anything about robot laws. All I know is that we entrusted the operation of the robots to MASAL and he turned them against us."

"So…" Rei started.

"So - never again," Rome said sharply. "The Vuduri will never have robots again. We could never trust them. Not in the cities. Not on the farms. Not at sea. Not anywhere."

"Even here?"

"Especially here," she said. "I-cimaci is what you might call the capital of the Earth."

"Huh," Rei observed then he quieted down. He twisted in place and craned his neck to stare up at the top of The Tower as it receded into the distance. Rei estimated that it was about a half-kilometer tall. While the building was not as tall as some of the skyscrapers of his day, it was impressive nonetheless.

After a time, they left the city proper and entered a fairly large wooded area. In front of them lay an unpaved path cut through the woods. The path looked fairly fresh, almost new. The trees along the road showed light core where the bark had been removed and had not yet regrown. The flying cart continued on until they came to a sizeable clearing. They pulled up to single-story U-shaped building that, not surprisingly, had no windows. The outside was made of stone rather than the ubiquitous aerogel that seemed to be the Vuduri norm. The architecture was as plain as could be. It had a fortress feel about it. The cart settled to the ground and the guards ushered Rome and Rei into the building. As they approached, the air smelled like fresh stone or concrete. Everything about this venue seemed new.

As they entered the building, two of the four soldiers remained behind and the other two soldiers walked them down corridor after corridor until they came to a doorway. One soldier opened the door and indicated to Rome that she should enter the vestibule. Rei started to go with her but the second soldier lowered his weapon and held it across Rei's middle.

The soldier cleared his throat and spoke with a surprisingly clear voice. "You will be able to join her in a short time. We need to ask you some questions first. Please follow me," he said. Rei looked at his eyes. One seemed dark but they were not as mismatched as Estar's or Sussen's. Further, the soldier seemed affable, for a Vuduri. He led Rei into the next room. The room itself was completely empty with the exception of a desk and two chairs, one on each side of the desk. The soldier pointed to the nearer chair.

"Oronus will be joining you shortly."

"Who is Oronus?" Rei asked.

"He is our arbiter. A Juoz," the soldier said. "Now please sit."

"A Juoz is a judge, right?" Rei asked in English. The soldier did not answer so Rei did as he was told. The soldier took a position to the left of the door. The windowless walls were all white, as was the floor. The ceiling had no visible light source but rather the entire ceiling glowed with a soft white light, giving the room an even illumination. In one corner, there was a white quarter-sphere attached where the ceiling met two walls. It reminded Rei of something but he couldn't quite put his finger on it.

Soon an older Vuduri man entered the room. He was carrying a thin notepad. He walked around to the far side of the desk and sat down, placing his pad on the table. He spent an uncomfortably long time studying the tablet, which was obviously electronic in nature. Finally, he spoke up.

"Asdiu Oronus," the man said then corrected himself, "I am Oronus."

"Fica bita veler am Vuduri," Rei said. "I understand it."

"Impressive," replied the man, "but no matter. English is perfectly suitable."

"What do you want?" Rei asked, surprised yet again how quickly English had spread throughout the Vuduri universe.

"As you are well aware, I am but a vessel for the Overmind," answered Oronus. "I was selected because my vocal apparatus is best suited to speaking and we have decided to ask you a few questions."

"What about Rome," Rei interjected. "When can I see her?"

"Shortly," replied the man. "Just answer our questions and we will take you to her."

"Rome?" Rei called to his wife, using the cellphone in his head. *"Are you there?"* There was no answer.

"What did you do to her?" Rei asked worriedly.

"We have done nothing to her. She is safe," Oronus answered. "She is not in any immediate danger."

"What does that mean?" Rei asked.

"For now, just know she is isolated in the room next door. When our business is concluded here, we will allow you to rejoin her."

"Why are you keeping her in isolation?" Rei asked.

"Her behavior has made her a danger for contact with all Vuduri," said Oronus, spreading his hands. "We do not wish to expose any more of our people to her than absolutely necessary."

"Rome is not a danger," Rei said. "The whole crime thing. She just did what she had to do. You already know that."

"Enough about Rome, please," the man answered sharply. "We will get to her soon enough. Please allow us to ask our questions."

"All right," Rei said, sighing. "Go ahead."

"Thank you," replied Oronus. "How did it happen that you are here on Earth? The last report we had was that you were going to tow the Essessoni Ark to Deucado. By our calculations, you should still be en route right now."

Rei's expression turned grim. "We had to let the Ark go. MINIMCOM is still towing it to Deucado, as far as I know."

"Why did you have to let the Ark go?" Oronus asked, confused.

"Uh…" Rei hesitated. "Rome became pregnant and there were some difficulties. We decided it would be better for her to give birth on Earth."

A hint of surprise flashed across Oronus's face. He looked down at the tablet and a series of dots and notations formed. He turned the tablet around and pushed it toward Rei. He unfastened a stylus from the side of the tablet and handed it to Rei.

"Show me your release point," he said, "where you and the MINIMCOM parted ways."

Rei studied the tablet. He saw dots representing Tabit, Keid, Deucado and Earth. There was a faint green line connecting Tabit to Deucado. Rei took the stylus and pressed it on the screen, leaving a blue mark, just to the right of Keid.

"Here," Rei said. "We released the Ark right about there."

Oronus looked down where Rei was pointing. A faint blue line connected the dot to Earth. Some numbers appeared on the screen. A yellow number with a negative sign in front of it started flashing.

"That is not correct," Oronus said.

"What's not..." Rei started to speak but Oronus held his hand up.

"Do not speak," Oronus interrupted him. His eyes defocused. A minute went by then another and other. Fully 10 minutes elapsed before Oronus finally blinked and then looked at Rei again.

"We have just examined your ship. What happened to your PPT generators?" he asked. "They are impaired."

"I don't know" Rei answered. "It's your ship. Maybe it wasn't designed to go such a long distance. It just sort of ran out of gas. There really wasn't anybody to ask."

Oronus sighed. The tablet cleared. He leaned forward slightly. "Rome is clearly not pregnant. Where is your baby?" Oronus asked.

Rei stuck his lip out. His shoulders slumped down. Very quietly, he said, "He...he was stillborn. There is no baby." Rei bit his lip so hard that a tear came to his eyes. He dabbed at it slowly to make sure that Oronus saw.

"Why would you even think to have a child in the first place?"

"It was not planned," Rei replied. "It just sort of happened."

"I see. When did the baby die?"

"A couple of weeks ago," Rei answered. "We almost made it except for the damned tug. We couldn't get here in time."

"Where is the body of the child?" Oronus asked. "Did you preserve it?"

Rei swallowed hard. This was one item they hadn't discussed. He thought about the Vuduri and their strange practices and took a guess.

"We put it in the recycler. Rome told me that was the only way to honor the dead. It seemed a little cold to me but that is your way, right?"

"Yes," Oronus said without any emotion. Rei let his shoulders relax.

"Tell me about your encounter with the Stareater," Oronus asked. "There is a recording on your ship that would indicate that the VIRUS units were successful in destroying it."

"Yes," Rei said, brightening. "OMCOM contacted us and told us that it was dead."

"OMCOM," Oronus harrumphed with disgust. "What else did he tell you?"

"He said there was a problem with the VIRUS units mutating. He said he was going to try and get the situation under control."

"Did he give you any more detail?" Oronus asked stridently. "After Ursay returned, we knew exactly what he was planning. Your recordings confirmed it. Puh."

"The only other thing he said was something about sentient beings, going off on their own," Rei muttered. "I don't remember exactly. It didn't really make sense to me but you said you had the recordings, right?"

"Yes," Oronus said. "But your impressions are valuable nonetheless."

"Well, it was like a year ago so I'm a little fuzzy on it. It wasn't a very long conversation as I recall."

"I understand," Oronus replied, pressing a point on the tablet with the stylus. "Do your best to dictate the conversation as faithfully as you can remember."

"I just did," Rei said. "It was only two or three sentences. He said he was happy to see us. He said the VIRUS units killed the Stareater. He said there were some mutations but he was working on it. Then he hung up."

"Nothing else?" Oronus asked skeptically.

413

"Not that I remember." Rei looked off to the side then up to the ceiling. He scanned the entire ceiling then brought his eyes back to regard Oronus. "Nope. That's it."

"Very well," Oronus said. "Have you had any contact with OMCOM since then?"

"Uh, no," Rei stuttered. "Nothing since."

Oronus nodded. Again his eyes defocused. Oronus' head sagged downward then snapped up again. "What were MINIMCOM's instructions regarding disposition of your Ark when it arrives at Deucado?" he asked finally.

"He was supposed to contact the Vuduri there and get their help in carting my people down to the surface," Rei said. "The Ark was pretty messed up and there is no way it could fly down on its own."

Oronus's expression tightened.

"They'll do that, right?" Rei asked sounding earnest.

"Yes, of course," Oronus said with no hesitation. "It will be taken care of." With that, the door opened and a soldier entered.

"We are finished here," Oronus said, standing. "Please remain with Grus until we call for you." He gathered up his tablet and walked out of the room, followed by the armed guard.

Rei stood and Grus led him out to an alcove next to the room where Rome was being held. Rei saw Oronus and the guard enter the vestibule and the door closed behind them. Grus pointed to the bench.

"Sanda-sa," Grus said. "Sit."

Rei sat down. "*Rome?*" he called again from inside his head. Again, there was no answer.

"Is Rome still in there?" Rei asked, pointing to the door.

"Som," replied Grus. "Eguerta. Wait."

Rei leaned back against the wall. He closed his eyes and tried another tack. He used his sonar-vision but it gave him no more information about Rome's condition, nor would it if the room they were holding her in was sound-proofed. He opened his eyes. Then it came to him.

"*Aason,*" he called out using his telephone circuit. "*Are you there? Are you close enough to hear me?*"

"*Yes, Father,*" his son replied faintly. "*We are in orbit around the Earth. Where is Mother?*"

"*You can't reach her either?*" Rei asked. "*Your connection?*"

"*No. The connection stopped,*" replied the baby. "*She told me they were taking her into a room then I heard nothing. I cannot hear any voices, not hers, not anyone's.*"

"*Are you OK otherwise?*"

"*Yes, Father. Grandbeo and I are fine. Father, what is happening?*"

"*I am right outside the room where your mother is being held. They are going to let me see her shortly.*"

"*That is good. Please tell I her I love her and that I miss her.*"

"*I will,*" replied Rei, breaking off the connection. "*MINIMCOM, you there?*" he asked mentally.

"`Yes,`" replied the spaceship/computer.

"*Can you reach Rome? Why can't I contact her?*"

"`No, I cannot contact her,`" answered MINIMCOM. "`I have created an artificial triangulation receiver but I cannot detect any carrier wave in the vicinity other than yours.`"

"*I am literally sitting right outside the room where they are holding Rome. What's up with that?*"

"`It would appear the room you are referring to is a Faraday cage. I presume from Aason's comments that it is under T-suppression as well.`"

"*Faraday cage? T-suppressors!*" Rei's expression grew grim. "*They are serious about cutting her off.*"

"`Will you be able to get in to see her?`" asked MINIMCOM.

"*They said I would,*" Rei replied. "*Hold on…*" he said as he noticed a commotion down the hallway.

Rei leaned forward to see three people walking briskly toward him, a woman and two men. Each of the men had a hand on the shoulders of the woman but she marched ahead, oblivious to their attempts at restraint. When they got to Rei, they stopped. The woman looked down at him and smiled. The two men released her shoulders and stepped back.

Rei looked up at her. She seemed very familiar. He racked his brain trying to remember if she was one of the crew members on Tabit but no, there was something else. The woman was little over five feet tall, standard height for a Vuduri. She had beautiful shoulder length brown hair with strands of gold and gray. She was wearing a regular issue Vuduri white jumpsuit that fit her form perfectly. Rei would have guessed she was in her forties but she looked extremely well preserved. Even though he was hopelessly and completely in love with Rome, Rei found the woman attractive in a way he could not explain. Rei looked into her dark, glowing eyes and found there was something about her bearing that was almost regal. It gave her an aura of power that Rei could not deny.

Not knowing what else to do, Rei stood up. The woman held out her arms. She reached out and pulled Rei in to hug him, kissing him gently on the cheek. "I am Binoda," she said.

Rei's jaw dropped, and then a great big smile broke out. "Asdiu dei valoz am cinhaca-li," he said.

"You may speak English to me," she replied. She turned to the other men standing by her.

"Filder ei lergi. Quari brofecoteta," she said in a commanding voice, although it had to be for Rei's benefit. The men backed up a little.

Rei asked quietly. "What's the point of talking in private?"

She leaned over and whispered in his ear, "I disconnected from the Overmind the moment your ship landed and I learned where they were taking you and my daughter. I am not connected right now." She turned and glared at the three men. They took another step backwards.

"Sit," Binoda said to Rei.

Rei sat down and Binoda sat next to him.

"Rome is in that room?" she asked, pointing to the door.

"Yes," he answered. "What are you doing here?"

Binoda just stared at him.

"I guess that is a stupid question, huh?" Rei offered.

"Wait," Binoda said. "Quenti a qua bissi fa-le?" she said, turning to Grus.

"Conci monudis," Grus replied gruffly.

"Very well," Binoda replied turning back to Rei. "We will be quiet for now."

"But, but," he said, ineffectively.

416

"Shh," Binoda said to him, putting two fingers up to her lips. "For now, we wait."

Chapter 54

INSIDE THE COURTROOM, ROME SAT QUIETLY WHILE ORONUS looked at the tablet in front of him. An armed guard stood by the door. After studying the tablet for a while, Oronus spoke.

"I am Oronus. Before we get to your crimes, I need to ask you a few questions."

"Of course," Rome replied. She folded her hands in front of her and set them on the table. Her ring sparkled even in the subdued lighting of the all-white chamber. Oronus noticed it immediately.

"Why are you wearing that, that ring on your finger?" he asked.

"It is called an engagement ring," Rome replied. "Rei gave it to me as a promise."

"A promise for what?"

"Cesa," Rome replied. "He and I desire to be married."

"Vuduri do not marry," Oronus said curtly.

"But mandasurte do," answered Rome. "I was Cesdiud. I am no longer one of you."

"You appear to be rather proud of that fact," Oronus observed. "I would think you would be ashamed."

"I am not," Rome replied defiantly. "It has liberated me."

"This room is under continuous T-suppression," said Oronus. "I am disconnected right now. I do not know about you but I find it extraordinarily uncomfortable."

"I do agree, when it first happened to me, I found it very disconcerting," she said. "But after a short while, I got used to it and now I would not give it up for the world."

"Why?" Oronus asked, confused. "Why would anybody want to live this way?"

"Because it allows me to have my own thoughts and my own feelings. I do not have to share them with anyone."

"What about the Overmind?" he asked.

"Especially the Overmind," Rome fired back. "It is the unrelenting inspection of one's thoughts and feelings by the Overmind that turn the Vuduri into unthinking automatons. We are too proud of a people to ever risk having an idea or an emotion that might be embarrassing so we suppress them all. This is not a good thing."

"I disagree. It is a very good thing," countered Oronus. "Without it, all of society would get unruly, uncontrolled. Look at the mandasurte. Emotions only get in the way of efficiency."

"You cannot know this," Rome said sympathetically, "but by giving up feelings, we have relinquished a part of our humanity, a part of our soul, really. We are diminished as a species."

"I believe we are elevated," said Oronus in an acerbic voice.

"I think you are wrong," replied Rome.

"I am not wrong," insisted Oronus. "What evidence do you have?"

"I will tell you but you will not believe me," Rome said.

"Please," scoffed Oronus. "Try to convince me."

"Very well," said Rome. "It is very simple. It takes the form of a question."

"What question is that?"

"What is your purpose?" Rome asked.

Oronus pulled his head back. "My purpose?" he repeated. "Do you mean my occupation?"

"No," Rome said, "your purpose in life."

"I, I have no purpose," Oronus said. "I need none. I serve the Overmind, as do we all."

"Exactly! You serve the Overmind. You are not a person. You are just a puppet. Your directives could be for the better or the worse and you would never challenge them."

"Why would I challenge them?" asked Oronus, bristling. "By definition, whatever the Overmind wills is correct."

"The Overmind should serve the Vuduri, not the other way around. I can give you so many examples where the Overmind has erred," she said. "The Overmind is not infallible. It just thinks it is. However, I must agree: your original statement is correct. *You* have no real purpose. You are just a living machine serving the will of a power you do not understand."

"And you are any better?" Oronus said, his voice rising. "How can you have a purpose that is superior to serving the Overmind?"

"Because I am me," she announced. Because I am mandasurte, I have a purpose which has nothing to do with my occupation."

"So, enlighten me," Oronus said, tauntingly. "What is your purpose?"

"To live. To love. To be with Rei. To feel...every day," answered Rome proudly.

"That is not a purpose," Oronus said with disgust. "It is just a description of your current state. You betray your own argument. Your feelings get in the way. You cannot achieve anything with raw emotion dictating your actions."

"You do not know," Rome retorted. "You cannot know. You have only lived one way. I have lived both: connected and Cesdiud. The way I am now is the way I wish to be."

"I will challenge your position by stating the exact same thing. The way I am now is the way I wish to be as well. I cannot imagine living any other way."

"How would you know unless you tried both?"

Oronus shook his head. "This is not anything I will ever try. Therefore, we are at an impasse."

Rome sighed. "I know. You are wrong but I do understand your position. I was there once. We will never agree upon this," she said, flicking her hand at the tablet. "Why not just get to your questions?" She took a deep breath and let her face go blank.

"Thank you," replied Oronus. "I think we will do just that." He glanced down at his tablet and tapped a circle in the upper right. He looked up at Rome. "Why are you not on your way to Deucado? This is what we were told when your fellow crew members returned from Tabit."

Rome remained expressionless and spoke matter-of-factly, "We needed to come to Earth. Rei decided to let MINIMCOM tow his Ark to Deucado alone."

"Why did you need to come to Earth?"

Rome took a deep breath. "I became pregnant and we decided it would be better for me to give birth here."

"Why?" asked Oronus.

"Why did I become pregnant?"

"That is another matter altogether," Oronus replied. "Why did you decide it would be better to give birth on Earth?"

"I developed some complications," Rome said. Her lip started to quiver.

Oronus frowned. "Where are the MINIMCOM and the Ark now?"

"We separated from him near the star called Keid," replied Rome, almost in a monotone. "On his way to Deucado."

Oronus pushed the tablet toward Rome. "Show me," he said.

Rome looked down at the tablet. She saw dots representing Tabit, Keid, Deucado and Earth. She removed the stylus fastened to the side of the tablet and tapped the screen just to the right of Keid.

"Here," she said. "We released the Ark approximately here."

Oronus did not even look down but instead regarded Rome intently. "If this were the case, based upon the remaining distance, why did you not arrive here months earlier?" he asked.

Rome looked him in the eye. "The tug we were flying could not go at top speed," she replied flatly. "There was some flaw with the PPT generators."

"What was wrong with them?" Oronus asked. "Was it not something you could repair?"

"I do not know" Rome said. "For the first few weeks, everything was as expected but then the PPT projectors just started to wane. We were too far from MINIMCOM to ask for help and the nav-computer diagnostics could not really pinpoint a hardware issue. We did try but we were unable to get them back to optimal."

"Very well," Oronus said. "You said you were pregnant. Where is your baby?" he asked harshly.

Rome looked down at the table. Tears welled up in her eyes. She started to speak but her voice caught. She put her hands up to her eyes and began sobbing.

"Please, Rome…" Oronus said dismissively. "It is a simple question."

Rome fought back the tears and in a barely audible voice, she said, "Aason died at birth. Rei said he was stillborn."

"Do you retain the body?" Oronus asked coldly. "If so, where is it?"

"No," Rome answered, somewhat surprised at the question. She paused for a second. She thought furiously about Rei and his people and their curious customs. She knew what he would do, so she continued. "Rei had what he called a funeral for him. He made the baby a coffin and he set the body adrift in space." She started crying again.

This time, it was Oronus who seemed surprised. "Are you absolutely sure that is what happened?"

"Yes, I am sure," Rome said through her tears.

"That is a very strange thing to do. Did you think that was right?" Oronus asked. "To put the body in a coffin and put it into space?"

"No," Rome replied. "But Rei said it was the only way to honor his baby. I was so distraught. I did not fight him about it."

"I see," Oronus said. He paused for a moment. "It would appear that the Essessoni did many strange things."

Rome merely nodded. She sobbed softly, looking down at the floor.

"Take a moment to compose yourself," Oronus said, softening this time.

Rome took a deep breath. She looked up at Oronus with a steely expression in her eyes. "I am all right," she said.

"Good," Oronus said. "Now tell me about the Stareater. There is a recording on your ship that would indicate that the VIRUS units were successful in destroying it."

"Yes," she replied. "OMCOM told us that it was dead."

"How was it that OMCOM contacted you?"

"He developed a tightbeam using PPT modulation. He was able to target MINIMCOM's receiver and we conversed with him in real-time."

Oronus just shook his head. "Have you had any contact with OMCOM since that time?"

"No," Rome answered. "Just the one time."

Oronus nodded. He lifted his hand and waved it once. Rome turned to see that there was a quarter sphere attached where the ceiling met two of the walls. Based upon her knowledge of Vuduri standard procedure, she assumed there was a camera or other recording instruments contained there. The inner door opened and Grus came in, holding the door for Rei.

"Rei!" Rome said, getting up and running over to him. Rei put his arms around her and held her tightly. Rome heard a noise at the door and lifted her head up. Her eyes grew huge when Binoda entered the room.

"Aiee!" Rome shouted. "I cannot believe it! Mea!" She let go of Rei and grabbed her mother for dear life. Tears welled up in her eyes, yet again.

Her mother hugged her back. "Volhe," Binoda whispered holding her daughter. After a moment, Binoda put her hand under Rome's chin and lifted it up, peering into her eyes. "Cesdiud suits you well," Binoda said proudly.

Rome beamed at her all the while with tears streaming down her cheeks - but these were tears of pure joy.

"You have all seen her," Oronus said, finally interrupting the happy group. "Rome, do you have any last wishes before we carry out the sentence?"

"What sentence?" Rei snarled. "What about her trial?"

"There is no trial," Oronus said. "She has already been convicted."

Chapter 55

"HOW CAN YOU CONVICT HER WITHOUT AT LEAST HEARING HER SIDE of the story?" Rei asked, trying to calm himself down. "What about the right to a fair trial?"

"Vuduri do not have trials," said Oronus.

"I thought you people were somehow supposed to be morally superior to my people," Rei protested. "At least we had that right back in my day. We had a whole bill of rights."

"It is not necessary," Oronus said. "I will demonstrate." The judge turned to look at Rome. "Rome, do you deny the charges?"

"Of course not," Rome said. "I fully acknowledge that I performed these actions and I would do it again if I had to."

"Very well," Oronus said. "Grus!" Grus took one step forward.

Rei moved over and put his body between Grus and Rome. Grus started to react then stopped. Rei turned his head back to Oronus. "What is the sentence?" he asked.

"For a capital crime such as this? The sentence is termination by evaporation, of course," replied Oronus without any hint of emotion.

Rome gasped. She put her arms around Rei from the back. The armed guard unslung his rifle and motioned it at Rei.

"No way!" Rei shouted. "They said I was the hero of Tabit. How could I be a hero unless what I did was the right thing to do?"

"You saved 80 Vuduri and quite possibly the Earth itself," answered Oronus. "You killed the Stareater. These are admirable things. Heroic things."

"So if I saved all these lives, how could I have done it without Rome?" Rei asked, his voice rising in fear. "How is what she did even a crime, anyway?"

"Have you had the opportunity to learn anything about our history?" asked Oronus.

"Yes," replied Rei. "Plenty."

"Then you know that a great war was fought over just such an issue."

"But there was no war here," Rei said. "All Rome did was enable OMCOM to kill the Stareater, not people. She didn't let

OMCOM into the Overmind club. She was the one who saved everybody's life."

"You are wrong. While your idea may have saved the lives of the Vuduri stationed at Tabit, Rome's actions have endangered all Vuduri for all time," pronounced Oronus, in a drone-like way. "You know about MASAL?"

Rei nodded.

Oronus continued, "Then you know after he created the 24th chromosome, the Overmind came into existence. MASAL was permitted to integrate into the Overmind. It was only after this happened that we found out that MASAL's goals were not in the best interests of the human race. This was our mistake, to enable a computer, an artificial intelligence, to have access to gravitic modulation. It let him grow without bound and it precipitated a war. All of our machines turned against us. It was the greatest loss of human life the world has ever seen, outside of your generation. What was done once can never be allowed to happen again. Computers are not meant to have access to unlimited resources. They must be kept in their place."

"But MASAL was analog," said Rei. "That was why he could merge with your Overmind in the first place. OMCOM is digital. He's completely incompatible. He could never integrate into your Overmind."

"It does not matter. Artificial intelligence does not have the necessary organic foundation to handle unlimited power. What Rome has enabled, Tasanceti, is an abomination and an anathema to all Vuduri. Her crime is absolute and her punishment has been preordained."

"Please step aside," Grus said, lowering his hand and patting a holster strapped to his leg. The holster contained some type of pistol. "You are finished here."

"We are not finished," Binoda said stepping forward. "Rome was authorized to perform this act by the Overmind at Tabit. That is the entity responsible for all of this, not her. She was just following orders."

"This is not true," Oronus said. "All of the individuals who returned from Tabit have been reintegrated into the Overmind of Earth. Not one of them has stated that Rome had permission."

"That is simply the position the Overmind expected," said Binoda. "Of course it is what they said. If I can produce a witness who will testify to the contrary, that she had permission, will you release her?"

"It is not possible," replied Oronus. "We have the collective consciousness of all the members of the Tabit expedition. We would know such a thing."

Rome whispered into Rei's ear. He looked up at the quarter sphere then turned to Oronus. "Is the T-suppression field still on? Are you connected right now to the Overmind?" He knew the answer because Rome said she could not connect to Aason.

Oronus looked at Grus who looked back at him.

"No," Oronus admitted. "But what does that have to do with anything?"

"If you are not connected at this moment," Binoda interrupted, "then you cannot say with absolute certainty that there is not one individual who would be willing to testify on Rome's behalf now that the request has been made."

"It is a simple matter of stepping outside that door," Oronus said, pointing to the doorway. "I would reconnect and then I would know."

"Then do so," Binoda said. "And call Commander Ursay. Have him come here immediately."

"It is not necessary for him to come here," Oronus said. "I would know his testimony right away."

"Do you see these two mandasurte here," Binoda said, indicating Rei and Rome. "How can they know what he says? They will only have your word for it."

"My word is sufficient," Oronus said. "Vuduri do not lie."

"Ha!" Rei exclaimed. "Of course you do."

"We do not," replied Oronus calmly even as his face tightened.

"Yes, you do," Rei said, scoffing at the statement. "There are two kinds of lies. There are the kinds that you say and there are things that you do not say. Are you even pretending that Vuduri never keep secrets from one another?"

Oronus glared at Rei and did not speak for a moment. He looked up at the quarter sphere in the corner of the room. "Get me Ursay," he said finally.

Chapter 56

IT TOOK LESS THAN AN HOUR TO LOCATE AND TRANSPORT Commander Ursay from his home to the north, near what had been called Amarante. In the mean-time, several chairs were brought in and arranged with Rei, Rome and Binoda on the left and Grus sitting to the right. Oronus remained behind the desk the entire time. One other chair, empty at the moment, was placed in the middle, directly in front of Oronus.

Ursay walked into the room and immediately put his hands on his head. To Rei, he looked like he had aged substantially since the last time they saw him, just a year ago. Where there had been just a hint of gray around his temples, his hair was mostly gray now and thinning a bit at the crown. There were light creases in his face as if he had been in the sun much too long.

"What is this place?" Ursay inquired. "Why am I no longer connected?"

"This room is under continuous T-suppression," Oronus said.

"Why?" Ursay asked, walking forward. He glanced over and saw Rei and Rome. He flashed them a faint smile before sitting down in the vacant chair."

"As you already know, the Overmind wishes it," said Oronus. "That should be sufficient."

"I do not know," Ursay replied. "The reason was kept hidden."

Oronus took a deep breath but said nothing.

"Tell me why I am here," demanded Ursay.

"Rome has been convicted of the most serious of crimes. That of giving Tasanceti to a computer. This is the most heinous act that can be committed."

"I know this," replied Ursay. "You know this. This explains nothing."

"These people claim that the Overmind of Tabit, through you as its agent, gave her permission and therefore sanctioned this action."

"We did no such thing," Ursay said. "Rome acted of her own volition."

"Thank you," Oronus replied. "Now. Are you satisfied?" Oronus directed to Rei.

"No!" Rei said, standing up. He walked over to Commander Ursay. "I need to ask Ursay some questions."

"Very well," Oronus said, exhaustedly. "You may."

Rei regarded Ursay. "You remember the events leading up to this so-called crime, right?"

"Yes, of course," Ursay stated. "You were there as well."

"Right," Rei replied. "I was there. I was there when you told Rome that no Vuduri could ever be part of the unleashing."

"Yes," said the older man. "Rome pointed out that she was Cesdiud and therefore mandasurte so she could do it."

"What did you do at that point?"

"I told her and you to find another way. That there had to be another solution."

"And what did we come up with? All of us together?"

"Nothing, really," said Ursay. "There did not appear to be another solution at the time."

"So Rome asked you to let her do it. She said if it bothered you, you could just ignore her. In fact, she said 'let me do it and you will have no part in this,' right?"

"Yes," Ursay replied.

"So when she said let me do it…how is that not asking your permission? You had every opportunity to stop her. And you did not."

"She would have done it anyway," Ursay said.

"Nonetheless, she said to you let me do this and you answered what?" Rei shot back.

Ursay did not speak for a moment. He closed his eyes as if to recall the incident. Suddenly he snapped his eyes open. "I instructed her to do what she must."

"And you were the commander of the station," Rei followed with too much vigor. "She was compelled to follow your orders, even though she was mandasurte. I even called you out on it. This was before Rome did anything. I pointed out to you that you were about to have Rome commit a crime. *You!*" Rei said, pointing right at Ursay. "I told you that was the same as you giving her the OK. And you said what?"

"At the time, I told you that you were correct," answered Ursay.

Rei turned to Oronus. "There. He said it. He told her to do it and she was just following orders. If you convict her of this crime, then you have to convict her superiors that gave the order. Which means Ursay and every person that was part of the Overmind of Tabit."

"That would be impractical," sputtered Oronus. "They have been reintegrated. We would have to indict every Vuduri on Earth."

"Then let her go," Binoda called out, standing abruptly. "You have your proof. We are all guilty of the same crime. And it is only a crime if our society says it is. Since Rome had permission of every Vuduri on Earth there was no crime."

"You are forgetting one thing," Ursay interrupted.

"What is that?" Rei asked.

"I warned you that your view of this was strictly from your perspective. I told you that no Vuduri, no one connected to the Overmind could take part in that activity. I told you that if Rome performed the act of her own volition, she would be responsible for the consequences, her and her alone. Not us."

"Those are just words," Rei said with disgust. He pointed to Ursay. "I told you before and I'll tell you again. You people are lunatics and hypocrites."

Ursay shrugged this off. "Nonetheless," he said, "I disavowed any association with the action prior to it being executed."

"Did you forbid her then?" Rei asked.

"Obviously not," replied Ursay.

"Yet you said Rome did this of her own volition."

"Yes," Ursay responded.

"If converting memrons to PPT modulation was so horrible, so wrong," Rei asked. "Why even have a system that was capable of such action?"

"There were interlocks that should have prevented it. They needed willful actions to be overridden," Ursay said. "No Vuduri would ever do that. Therefore there was no need to build in a higher level of protection."

"No Vuduri," Rei answered back. "But an independent mandasurte?"

"Yes, mandasurte," Ursay replied. "Her," he said, pointing to Rome."

"How did she get that way? How did she come to be mandasurte, autonomous?"

"She was Cesdiud. You know this."

"Of course I know it," Rei said. "But why did you do it? Why the Cesdiud?"

Ursay took a deep breath. He looked legitimately hurt. Finally, he answered. "Because of you," he said sadly. "We thought her association with you would taint our perspective."

"You picked Rome to interact with me because of her heritage. She was disposable right from the start."

"Yes, to this I can agree. We knew she could be jettisoned with the least impact on our Overmind."

Binoda made a hissing noise but said nothing.

"Your loss, my gain," Rei said snidely. "Getting back to her Cesdiud, Who decided she had too much contact with me? Whose brilliant idea was that? Was it the Overmind that figured that out?" he asked.

Ursay thought for a minute. "Actually, it was OMCOM that called it to our attention," Ursay said sheepishly.

"And you do not think he had his own motives for pointing that out?" Rei asked angrily.

"I suppose he did, but we agreed with his reasoning at the time."

"I am going to tell you why she was cast out," Rei spat the words. "She was cast out for the exact reason that she could act autonomously so she could perform the override that was necessary to kill the Stareater. Hell, you sanctified the action. You even sent Signola along to help her. Right?"

"Yes," Ursay said quietly. "But Signola did nothing wrong. He never actually performed the override."

Rei didn't answer for a minute. He gazed off into space, replaying the incident in his mind for the fortieth time. Suddenly, he snapped his fingers. "I got it!" he said.

"Got what?" Oronus asked.

Rei turned back to Ursay. "I just remembered your exact last words to Rome before she left to do it. Do you?"

"Yes," replied Ursay.

"So tell Oronus what your last three words to her were exactly."

Ursay took a deep breath. "My last three words were, 'You may proceed.'"

Rei wheeled in place to look right at Oronus. "If that isn't permission, I don't know what is." He looked over at his wife. Strangely, she was smiling. He turned back to Oronus. "Rome was set up. She was selected for this job right from the start. She was cast out so she could perform this action. She was given permission and therefore commanded by the Overmind. The results of her actions are lauded by you and all the Vuduri. There is no crime. SO LET HER GO."

He turned back to Ursay and in a lower voice said, "Please tell him the truth."

Ursay stared up at Rei for the longest time. He glanced over at Rome then stood up.

"I am changing my testimony," he said to Oronus. "I am going on record as stating that the Overmind of Tabit gave Rome permission, and in fact ordered her to perform these actions. Upon further reflection, I now concur that we are as culpable and therefore as guilty as Rome. If you must convict her of this crime and still choose to execute her, you will have to execute me and by extension every Vuduri on the planet."

Oronus glanced over at Grus who had given up and sat completely helpless. Oronus looked up at the quarter sphere in the corner and said, "That is ridiculous. We cannot execute ourselves." He leaned back in his chair and took a deep breath. He folded his hands together, resting them on his stomach, staring down at them.

Finally, he lifted his head and spoke. "I cannot set aside the verdict. Rome still performed the actions. The crime stands. The only thing I can do is commute the sentence."

"To what?" Rei asked.

"Banishment," Oronus replied. "Rome must be isolated from all Vuduri and anything resembling synthesizer technology. She must never be allowed to carry out any such acts again."

"What would the point be?" Rei asked. "You already have the VIRUS units. She would not need to ever do such a thing again. Nobody does."

"Incorrect," said Oronus. "We do not have the VIRUS units."

"What do you mean?" Rome asked, rising in her seat.

"When we arrived on Earth, the Overmind ordered them destroyed," replied Ursay.

"You what?!" Rei shouted. "How are you going to stop the Stareater when it gets here?"

"We do not know," Oronus said. "Unless we come up with an alternative, our current plan is to abandon the Earth. We are building some transports, ironically, similar to your Arks, to move a percentage of the population to another star system. Beyond that, we are still working on finding another technology to perform the same function as the VIRUS units but we are not hopeful."

"And what if Asdrale Cimatir arrives tomorrow?" Rome asked. "What will you do?"

"We can only hope that does not occur," replied Oronus. "Our last projections based upon data returned from Tabit indicate we should have well over one year left. Currently, we believe we can save as much as ten percent of the population, although that may be optimistic."

Rei looked at Rome then back at Oronus.

"Why not deploy VIRUS units at least until you come up with your magical alternative?" Rei asked. "Did you not save any of them?"

"No," replied Ursay sadly.

Rei looked back at him. "What if I could…"

Rome jumped up and shouted "No!" Rei shut up immediately.

"What is the problem?" asked Oronus. "Rei, continue. What if you could what?"

Rome interrupted. "Whatever Rei was going to offer, I will not allow him," Rome said. "This is your problem now, not ours. We have done our best. Are we free to go?"

"No, you are not," Oronus replied. "There are the conditions of your release."

"And what are those?"

"You must retire to a place where there is no molecular synthesis equipment nor any type of fabrication or computing facilities. You must be exiled and kept isolated from all Vuduri and all Vuduri technology."

"What about the mandasurte?" Binoda asked. "Can she remain among them?"

"As long as it is a community that has none of the technology mentioned," Oronus said.

"I have a place," Binoda offered.

"Where?" said Oronus.

"What about Ylea, on Mowei?" Binoda asked.

"Mowei…Maui?" asked Rei, "Hawaii?"

Binoda nodded and continued, "Yes, Havei. That is where Rome's father was born and raised. It is a mandasurte community. Rome still has family there. Portions of it are very primitive and have none of the technological components you insist she stay away from."

Oronus looked up at the quarter sphere then down at his tablet. "That is acceptable," he said.

Binoda looked at Rome who nodded and said, "That is fine."

"Then it is agreed," said Binoda.

"Uh, what about our Flying House?" Rei asked. "Do we get to keep it?"

"Of course not," replied Oronus dismissively. "It has the very equipment onboard that we are trying to keep Rome away from."

"What about our stuff?" Rei asked.

"To what are you referring?"

"All of our stuff," Rei replied. "Our things, our belongings. We have stuff on the ship."

"Rome is to be banished immediately," answered Oronus. "We do not want to spend any time unloading and transferring your belongings."

"I have an idea," Rei said. "How about you fly us there in that ship? That way, we can unload it when we get there and then you can take it away."

"Fair enough," replied Oronus.

"So, we have an agreement?" Rei asked.

"Yes. The banishment is to begin now," announced Oronus. He signaled to the quarter sphere in the corner of the ceiling. "Grus, accompany them to their spacecraft, please. It is already on its way."

Rome moved around to Rei. She kissed him and hugged him.

"I did not know you were such a good…" Rome paused, trying to recollect the word. "Yes, 'lawyer,' I think that is the term you use," she said. Rei grinned. "I think I will keep you," she said happily.

"Try and get rid of me," Rei said with a smile and they started to walk out.

"Binoda," Oronus called out to her. "You may not accompany them to Ylea. Rome must not have contact with any Vuduri after today."

Binoda shook her head. "I am going with them. From this moment forward, I am no longer connected. I have just rendered myself Cesdiud. I am mandasurte now."

"Mea!" Rome said in horror. "You cannot."

"It is already done," replied Binoda grimly. "I no longer have any use for the Overmind."

"No, no, no," Rome said. Her shoulders slumped. "You need to go back."

Grus ignored Rome's outburst and hustled them out of the courtroom. As soon as they were outside the door, Rome's link to Aason was reestablished.

"*Mother!*" Aason said. "*I missed you. Where have you been? Where are you now?*"

"*We are here, baby,*" Rome replied sadly.

"*Are you all right?*"

"*Yes. We are leaving this place and going somewhere where we can be together.*"

"*I would very much like that. When can I be with you?*"

"*Soon, baby, very soon,*" replied Rome. "*Let me attend to our affairs and I will let you know. There has been a change in plans. I will have MINIMCOM bring you to us when the time is right.*"

"*I cannot wait, Mother.*"

"*Me neither,*" Rome said and she narrowed the connection to a tiny thread.

MICHAEL BRACHMAN

Grus and two other soldiers along with Ursay accompanied them outside. They did not have to wait long until the tug known as the Flying House flew overhead and settled down in the courtyard. The cargo door raised and the ramp lowered. Rome turned to Ursay.

"Thank you for all you have done," she said.

"There is no reason to thank me. The truth is the truth," replied Ursay with the defocused look of someone who was attending to the Overmind. "Good luck in your future endeavors," he said to Rei and Rome.

"Thank you," Rome replied. "I hope you will come visit us some time."

"I do not think that will be permitted," Ursay said. "Goodbye." With that he turned and walked away.

"Business as usual," Rei muttered to Rome. He held her hand and together they walked up the ramp followed by Binoda and Grus. As soon as the cargo compartment was sealed, the tug rose up in the air and they were on their way.

Chapter 57

THE SHIP HEADED WEST, OVER THE ATLANTIC, EVENTUALLY traveling at four times the speed of sound. After an hour of sitting around and doing nothing, Binoda stood up and wandered about, inspecting the artwork mounted in various spots around the room.

"Whose handiwork?" she asked in Vuduri.

"It is mine, Mea," Rome replied.

"How did you learn to craft these works?"

"I learned many things once I was Cesdiud. I learned about art, beauty, music, Rei's history. As you can imagine, we had much time."

"Stuck in this ship for a year? I should say so."

"It was not bad." Rome looked at Grus. "We have time. May I show my mother around?"

"No," Grus replied gruffly. "We insist you remain within visual contact at all times."

"Then you accompany us," Rome said, standing up.

Grus sighed and stood up. "Please remain here," he said to Rei.

Rei just shrugged. "Where am I going to go?" he asked, hands held outward.

Grus shook his head. "Proceed," he said to the two women and the three of them left the room. Rome took Grus and her mother down the hallway toward the very back of the ship. "This was our recycling facility," she said, pointing to the right. "Rei insisted we launder rather than synthesize clothes all the time so he built me what he called a washing machine."

Binoda looked puzzled. "That seems so inefficient on a space voyage," she said.

"Yes," Rome said. "Many of Rei's customs seem strange to me but for some things, I let him have his own way."

"I understand. Your father also had some peculiar ideas," Binoda replied somewhat sadly. They turned and walked part way back up the hall. Rome pointed to her left. "In that room is storage and our life support, molecular sequencers and more."

Grus took one step forward and placed his hand on the middle of the door.

"Do not worry," Rome said. "I will not go in there." As if to demonstrate her good behavior, she spun in place in an attempt at drama. She pointed to the door to Binoda's left. They moved forward and entered the doorway into their bedroom.

Binoda looked around. She spotted the onyx case that contained the Espansors. She walked over and picked it up and turned toward Rome, holding it out. Rome nodded. Binoda smiled and placed the case back on the dresser. After taking one more look, Binoda said, "It is very nice, Rome."

"Thank you, Mea," she said. "Come."

Rome led them back into the hallway and toward the front into their little galley. She showed Binoda the oven next to the food synthesizers and the food preparation area. She pointed to the elaborate rack of spices, mounted on the galley wall.

"Rei has taught me so many things about food," she stated. "As you know, the Vuduri do not care about such things. But, what we ate here…?" She stopped speaking and looked up to the corner of the room. "I can only describe it using the English word Rei taught me: heavenly," she said finally.

"I can see that you enjoyed it," Binoda said, pointing her finger at Rome's waist. "There is now more of my daughter to love than before you left."

Rome blushed. "Yes, Mea, I know," she said. "When we are settled, I plan to reduce my weight back to its optimal. The gravity on Earth will help me with my exercises, make them more effective."

"It is all right," Binoda said. "You look very healthy," she said. Then, after a moment, she added, "And happy. Your new life agrees with you."

"Yes, it does, Mea," Rome said. "I could not ask for a more wonderful partner. I cannot even tell you how many hours we spent here, laughing, playing games. We never grew tired of each other, not once, during the entire trip."

Binoda looked around, trying to envision that. She stopped and stared at the dining table for a moment. "Why are there three chairs?" she asked Rome, pointing at the table.

"What?" Rome said, her eyes widening. She took a deep breath. They had purposefully destroyed Aason's high chair. The thought never occurred to them to destroy Fridone's.

"Eh, that is just the way we made it," Rome replied finally. "The galley was built with two chairs. There came a time when we wanted another." Subtly, she shook her head and dragged her mother out of the room.

Binoda asked. "What if you wanted to be alone? Where would you go?"

"It was not like that," Rome said. "It was not really taxing. Rei and I enjoyed each other's company so much that the time passed very quickly. If I was painting and needed to be alone, Rei would go up to the cockpit or the galley. Sometimes, when he was in the studio, recording his oral history, he would want to be alone as well. I would go lie down in the bedroom or do laundry. We were fine. But mostly we did not really want to be apart from one another."

"I was that way with your father," Binoda said. "I never got enough time with him." Her voice trailed off.

Rome put her arm around her mother. "Come, Mea," she said.

"No. It is enough," said Grus. "Please go back to the living area for the remainder of the journey."

Rome and Binoda complied. When they got back to the room that doubled as a studio, Rei was sitting at the workstation.

"What are you doing?" Grus asked.

"I was hooking into the nav-system. Do you care?"

"I suppose not," Grus said wearily.

"Thanks," Rei said in English. He activated the ventral cameras just as they passed over the isthmus of Panama. In front of them lay the vast expanse of the Pacific with a few wisps of whitecaps. The instruments indicated they were about 12 kilometers up. Rei adjusted some filters. A polarizer removed the glare and rippling from the waves and made the water look completely transparent. From this height, Rei was able to see detail along the ocean bottom clearly enough to make out some of its topology. He could see crevices, channels and even some peaks that looked like underwater mountains. If you ignored the fact that it was deep blue, some of it even reminded Rei of the surface of the moon.

After a bit, on the horizon, a landmass appeared that Rei guessed was the Big Island of Hawaii. As they got closer, he became certain of it. Their craft banked northward and flew directly over the peaks of Kilauea and the even taller Mauna Loa. To his right was the older, rounder shape of Mauna Kea. It did not take long until they passed back out over the ocean. Directly ahead was the peculiar arrowhead-shaped island of Maui. There were heavy clouds on the northern side of the island where the sea breezes met the mountain peaking in the middle of the island. They flew over the southern side and Rei could see the mammoth crater of Haleakala, which he had learned about as a child.

Lower and lower they flew, nearing the western edge of the larger portion of the island, flying over a wide beach and a stand of trees, coming to a halt over a smaller, crescent-shaped beach. The ship descended until it came to rest in the sand.

The assembled group started to stand but Grus held up his hand. "Please remain here," he said. "I must survey the area first." He returned a few minutes later. "There is an abandoned dwelling very near here," he said. "You may take that as your shelter for the time being."

Grus made a waving motion to Rei. "The pilots will help you gather your belongings. We will wait for you outside," he said. He accompanied the two women through the hallway and down the cargo ramp.

Rei crossed over into the bedroom and was surprised to see some empty satchels sitting on the bed. He shrugged and gathered up their clothing, their toiletries and most importantly, the bands. It seemed like forever since he and Rome had last used them to commingle their minds. He handed one of the satchels to a pilot then returned to the living area to gather up Rome's artwork and her paint supplies. He also grabbed his solid-state music slab which he had rescued from the Ark along with a datacube filled with MINIMCOM's original works. He didn't know when he would ever get a chance to play them again but after all the effort they had made to accumulate the collection, he was not going to just abandon it. Looking around, he saw nothing else of value. He exited and joined Rome and Binoda at the base of the ramp.

Grus addressed the three of them. "Your dwelling is just up that trail," he said, pointing toward a rocky path leading away from the beach. He beckoned to Rome who took one step closer to him. "Please extend your wrist," he asked her.

"Why?" Rome inquired.

"For this." Grus reached into his pocket and removed a thin silver bracelet. He looked at Rome's outstretched arm for a moment, staring at the ring on her finger. He shrugged then snapped the bracelet around her wrist. Where there had been an opening, the metal sealed forming a smooth finish which was now seamless.

"This is a tracking bracelet," he said. "It is required because you are mandasurte. The conditions of your release are that you are to remain on or about this island. Please make no attempt to contact anyone off island and please do not try to access any technology. The very fact that you remain alive is a gift. Always remember that."

"I will," Rome said solemnly. "Thank you."

Grus defocused and then turned to look at Rei. "While you are a hero, your continued association with a convicted criminal makes you unwelcome within the Vuduri world. I would ask that you remain here as well."

"You do realize that you just transported me to paradise with the woman I love?" Rei said in English. "Why would I want to leave?"

Grus did not answer. He looked at Binoda. "The same punishment goes for you as well."

"It is not a punishment, I assure you," Binoda said.

"No matter," Grus replied. "Goodbye." With that, he turned and walked up the ramp.

Rome reached over and took Rei's hand as the cargo ramp retracted and the hatch lowered. The Flying House, their home for the last year and more, rose up into the air and began to move forward toward the sun, which was very low in the sky. The tug banked over the ocean coming all the way around then flew back directly overhead, all the while heading upwards. As their former craft/home arose high in the sky, a tear came to Rome's eye which she wiped with her free hand. "I will miss it," she said.

"Me too," Rei replied. They watched as the Flying House became smaller and smaller until finally it disappeared. They stared at the darkening sky and low-lying white clouds for a long while. Finally, Rome squeezed Rei's hand to get his attention. Rei turned to her.

"Now we get to do our work," she said.

Chapter 58

BINODA STARED AT HER DAUGHTER, COMPLETELY CONFUSED. "What work?" she asked. "Should we not go to the shelter?"

"We will, Mea" Rome replied, "but we must remain here for a short while. I promise to fill you in on all the details. For now, let me summarize. You will recall my assignment and circumstance at the observation station within the Tabit star system."

"Yes, of course," her mother answered. "You covered that in your letter to me. It was very touching. You are a good writer, Rome."

"Thank you, Mea, but I simply told the truth."

"Still, you were very kind to send it. Continue."

Rome pointed upward. "After I was Cesdiud, we had figured out that it was a giant thing, Asdrale Cimatir, which was consuming stars. Rei invented the technique which I had to implement to kill it."

"I understood that from the crew that returned from Tabit as well as the comments Oronus made," said Binoda.

"Yes, but you understand I had no choice. As Rei pointed out, they set me up so that I could do what I had to do without culpability."

"She was their scapegoat," Rei threw in.

"That is just like the Overmind," said Binoda. "Go on."

"Well, before we left, they gave us *two* tugs, the Flying House and another ship to tow Rei's Ark to Deucado. The Flying House is the ship that they just took away."

"What happened to the other tug?" Binoda asked.

"It's hard to explain," Rei chimed in.

"Try," Binoda commanded.

Rome shivered and then her smile brightened. "I will do better than that, Mea," she said, touching her temple. "Let us watch the sunset."

"We can do that another time, Rome," said Binoda, impatiently. "Please enlighten me."

Rei touched his temple as well.

"You really want to see the sunset," Rei added. "Everything will become clear."

Binoda looked even more confused but gave up arguing. The beach they were on was made of pure white sand, almost like flour. The area was somewhat secluded by large boulders on the far ends and a stand of palm trees all around them. The beach overlooked the Pacific which stretched as far as the eye could see.

As the sun went down, the beautiful colors playing among the low-lying clouds made for a spectacular view. A gentle breeze brought the ubiquitous smell of jasmine and plumeria wafting over them. Rei stood with his arm around Rome just reveling in the peace of their current situation. The sunset was magnificent, as it always is in Hawaii, but Binoda seemed distracted and unimpressed. They even had the opportunity to see a tiny green flash on the top of the sun just before it set.

As the glowing shards of light waned, Binoda could no longer control her impatience. "I understand nothing better," she said to Rome. "It is a sunset. I have seen them before."

"Not like this one," Rome replied, pointing over the ocean.

Binoda turned to look at where Rome was pointing. She was indicating exactly where the sun had been as the orb disappeared below the horizon. Binoda looked and saw that the air began shimmering, somewhat like one would see just before a mirage appeared in the desert. A ghostly presence sparkled then disappeared and then reappeared. The giant ball of diffraction drifted in from the ocean and settled on the beach, just to the south.

Binoda stared at it, trying to understand what her eyes were telling her. In front of her, four deep depressions appeared in the sand. A whining, jet-enginey kind of sound filled the air then died off. In front of her, a cavity appeared 10 feet up, right in the middle of the air.

"This is your other ship?" Binoda asked. "It is a hole in the air. What is this?"

"Just watch, Mea," Rome said with a broad smile on her face.

As Binoda peered into the hole, a gray, metallic-looking ramp became visible and lowered until it came to rest in the sand. Something stirring was stirring at the back of the compartment. A robed figure moved forward. When the individual got to the top of the ramp, he stopped and stood there quietly.

"Who is that?" Binoda asked, turning to Rome.

Rome just smiled as Rei squeezed her tighter. She tilted her head indicating the figure within the ship. Binoda turned back to look at man at the top of the ramp, adjusting her vision to telescopic.

"No," she breathed, plaintively, not able to tear her eyes away. "It cannot be."

"It is, Mea," Rome exclaimed tearfully. "It is. Go to him."

"Fridone!" Binoda shouted and sprinted up the ramp to meet her husband at the top. She kissed him and hugged him and kissed him and hugged him. She was overwhelmed. It was a long time before she was able to speak coherently.

"Oh, husband," she said finally. "Look at you. Your hair! So gray!" Binoda sighed and whispered, "I have missed you so much." She grabbed his cheeks with her hands and touched her forehead to his, closing her eyes.

"My beautiful Binoda," Fridone said. "I have missed you more."

"That is not possible," she said, opening her eyes again. "How did this happen?"

"You may thank your resourceful daughter," Fridone said, pointing back down at Rome, standing on the beach. "She saved me. She saved my world and she is here to save this one as well."

"Your world?" his wife asked, somewhat perplexed. "This is your world." Binoda paused for a second. "Where were you, anyway?"

"The Onsiras stole me away from here," Fridone said, somewhat with disgust. "They imprisoned me."

"Imprisoned? And who are the Onsiras? I do not understand."

"You will. We will explain everything. For now, all you need to know is that I am free and we can be together again."

"I cannot believe it," Binoda exclaimed. "This is the best moment of my life."

Rome flexed her shoulders so Rei released her. She jogged up the ramp to join the reunited couple. "There is more, Mea," she said.

"More?" replied Binoda, confused. She looked at Fridone who smiled and merely shrugged.

"Yes," Rome answered. "Wait here." She brushed past them and disappeared inside the ship.

"I do not understand any of this," Binoda said. "I see a very large inside but there is no outside. We are in the middle of the air with nothing holding us up."

Rei approached and climbed the ramp to the top. "This is the other tug that Rome mentioned. His name is MINIMCOM," he said.

"A MINIMCOM is a computer," answered Binoda. "This is a vehicle, invisible or not."

"Yes and yes," Rei replied. "MINIMCOM has been through a lot but he started out as a computer. Now he is a ship and a computer and much, much more."

"Why could I not see it as it approached?" Binoda asked. "Is this magic?"

"Not magic, my dear Binoda," Fridone said, "MINIMCOM is just very clever."

"Yes, very clever," Rome called out from the far end of the cargo compartment. Binoda turned to see her daughter walk toward them cradling a bundle of blankets in her arms. "I have something to show you," Rome said.

"What is this you have brought me?" Binoda asked.

Rome pulled back the blanket, revealing the baby inside. "This is your grandson, Aason!"

Binoda's eyes grew wide. Tears welled up in her eyes again. "A grandson? Rome!"

She put out her arms and Rome handed her the baby boy. Instinctively, Binoda held him and rocked him and began swaying her hips side to side as had humans for the last million years. She stared down at his angelic face. Aason stretched his mouth in what almost looked like a smile then slowly, with agonizing care, turned his head toward Rome. Even at this young age, he was exceptionally strong and exceptionally coordinated, even for a Vuduri. Then he turned back to Binoda, closed his eyes and gave a deep sigh.

Rome said, "He is glad to meet you, Mea. He says hello."

Binoda shook her head, holding the baby out to see. "What do you mean?"

"Aason and I are connected," her daughter answered. She reached over and took the baby back, placing him close to her heart.

"How is this possible?" Binoda asked. "You were Cesdiud. I am Cesdiud. I cannot hear him."

"I was reconnected on Deucado," Rome replied, "as was Aason."

"Deucado?" Rome's mother gasped. "How were you there? Then how are you here?"

"Let us go find our lodgings," Rome offered. "Then we can begin fitting the pieces of this puzzle together for you."

"I would very much like that," said Binoda. She turned and took two steps down the ramp. She looked over her shoulder and noticed that nobody was following her.

"What?" she asked.

"I must be very careful," said Fridone.

"Why?" asked Binoda, coming back up the ramp.

Rome answered for him. "Beo is not supposed to be here and they do not know I have a baby."

"How are you going to hide them?" Binoda asked.

"Watch," Rome said and she handed the baby back to her father. He pulled his cloak around himself, covering Aason in the process. He lowered his hand along the edge of the cloak and disappeared.

"What?" Binoda exclaimed in shock. "What happened to him?"

"I am right here," Fridone answered, seemingly from thin air.

"More magic?" Binoda remarked. "You certainly seemed to have mastered this, this invisibility mechanism."

"Actually, this was a present from the Deucadons," Rei said. "They are a group of my people who got stranded on Deucado 500 years ago. They still live there."

"I do not understand anything," Binoda harrumphed. "You will have to start from the beginning. What is going on?"

"Mea, let us go find our shelter and I will explain all. I promise."

"Very well," Binoda answered resignedly.

The visible three and the invisible two walked down to the base of the ramp. Binoda turned back and looked up. She saw the ramp and the cavity but could not see anything else. She walked over to where she thought the ship should be and passed her hand over the spot. She could feel nothing.

"Is it possible to turn this shield off?" Binoda asked. "Can I see the vehicle?"

Rei came up to stand beside her. "MINIMCOM will let you see him but it can only be for a second," he said. "He is not supposed to be here either."

Rei closed his eyes then opened them again.

Taking his cue, MINIMCOM dropped the cloak long enough for Binoda to see a huge black cargo ship with a flowing, sleek shape bristling with a whole battery of PPT generators and plasma engines, mounted on the airfoils.

Rei looked at his friend who was also a ship. In no way did MINIMCOM resemble the original shuttle that was his starting point. Beyond that, something else stood out. MINIMCOM looked totally different on the outside from even when Rei had seen him last.

"*What gives?*" Rei thought to MINIMCOM.

"*Whatever do you mean?*" replied MINIMCOM ever so innocently.

"*You're all decorated with doodads and spirals. You didn't have them before.*" Rei thought.

"*Oh those,*" stated MINIMCOM. "*I determined that I would have better aerodynamic control if I had a reliable and steady flow of turbulence within my air stream when I was in the atmosphere. The somewhat symmetrical nature of the designs was an attempt, only slightly successful, to inversely impress the turbulence, to cancel it, so that the net effect was still air, even though I gained the immediate advantage of microturbulence.*"

"*Well, they're pretty sharp, if you ask me,*" Rei said, knowing MINIMCOM was full of baloney.

"*Why thank you,*" MINIMCOM said then he winked out.

"Just like that?" Binoda asked. "How is this possible?"

"Mea," Rome called out to them. "Let us go inside so that Beo and Aason can come out. We will explain it to you as I promised."

Binoda nodded and joined her daughter. They picked up a few of the items left on the beach, leaving the heavier satchels for Rei.

Rei glanced over at the suitcases then back to the empty air where MINIMCOM was located. He said in his head, *"You know you're pretty sleek, dude. Your entrance and exits are getting more impressive every time."*

`"I aim to please,"` replied MINIMCOM.

"You sure do! OK, I'll be back later," Rei said and he turned to walk away.

He hadn't even taken two steps when MINIMCOM interrupted him.

`"Before you leave, I need you to come up to my cockpit."`

"Why?" Rei asked in his mind.

`"I have something for you."`

"All right," Rei thought. Then out loud, he shouted, "Romey, I'll catch up to you in a minute. MINIMCOM has something to show me."

"Very well," Rome called back as she led her parents up the rocky path. "We will go find our lodgings."

Rei climbed up the ramp and into the cargo hold of MINIMCOM. As he looked around, he said out loud, "I think you need to go on a diet."

`"Why?"` MINIMCOM asked through a grille.

"You sure are a lot bigger than you used to be, even than before," Rei said with a smile on his face. "Kind of a wide load now if you know what I mean."

`"The better to serve you,"` MINIMCOM replied with just a hint of sarcasm in his voice. `"My constructors have been busy. Now please come forward."`

"OK," Rei said as he entered the cockpit. "What've you got?"

A panel opened and with the diffuse glow of backlighting, Rei could see a shape within. "What is it?" he asked.

`"Take it,"` MINIMCOM said.

Rei reached in and removed a pouch that looked somewhat like leather. Along its top edges, there was a drawstring. Rei teased the opening apart and looked inside. All he saw was a dark grayish substance, reminiscent of talcum powder. Sprinkled throughout were larger, black dots that had a metallic sheen to them. Rei reached in and felt around but there was nothing remarkable about it. The substance felt very light, not gritty like sand. He drew the string closed again and placed it on the opened door in front of him.

"What's in here?" he asked, "ground up aerogel?"

"They are a gift from OMCOM. They are a special type of VIRUS units, taken and modified from my skin."

"What?!" Rei said, leaping up. Instinctively, he wiped his hand on his pants but in his heart, he knew it was not going to matter. "What the hell?"

"It is all right," MINIMCOM said with a mechanical chuckle. "You are safe. They are currently dormant. These particular VIRUS units will not digest organic matter."

Rei sank down into the pilot's chair. "Why are you giving them to me?" he asked.

"OMCOM said he computed multiple scenarios whereupon you would require them. I have modified them according to his specifications."

"How are they modified?"

"These are super VIRUS units, weaponized. They reproduce in seconds. They can be assigned specific tasks. They will work autonomously or as an integrated cluster. Their oxygen sensor has been disabled so they can work in an atmosphere if required."

Rei's eyes widened. "You mean they can destroy the Earth?"

"In theory, yes. In practice, no. As I said, these particular units will not ingest organic matter. They are strictly limited to metals or minerals. The larger ones…"

"The black ones?" Rei interrupted.

"Yes, the black ones. You may call them queens. They will control the other units. The queens are completely under your control. You decide when they are active and when they are dormant."

"Me?" Rei said. "I don't get it."

"They are equipped with receivers for your 'cellphone' link. They answer to you. You give them an assignment and they will follow it."

"Just me? How about Rome?"

"Yes, they would answer to Rome as well," replied MINIMCOM.

Rei looked down at the pouch, sitting within the compartment. He stared at it for a while, his mind racing. "Are you going to tell me when and where I'm supposed to use them?"

`"I cannot. OMCOM did not share that specific information with me."`

"Great. Say I do use them, what if they mutate?"

`"These particular units will not mutate, I assure you."`

"How can you know? OMCOM's did."

`"I have implemented a checksum code. If the unit reproduces and the checksum does not match, the unit will shut down."`

"Hold on a minute," Rei said. "If you were able to figure out how to suppress mutations, how come OMCOM didn't. I mean, OMCOM is way smarter than you, no offense intended."

`"None taken."`

"So then why didn't he prevent them, too?" Rei asked."

`"I suppose I will let you in on a little secret."`

"What?"

`"I did not actually design the checksum code. It was already built into the programming in the original VIRUS units. There was a conditional branch that skipped over the algorithm under certain circumstances. I simply removed the branch so that the checksum is always executed."`

"What?" Rei exclaimed. "You've got to be kidding me. That means…" Rei's voice failed him. He took a deep breath to regain control then spoke again. "That means OMCOM allowed the mutations to occur. But why?" he asked plaintively.

`"You will have to deduce the answer."`

Rei tsked then spoke up. "If he did it on purpose, he must have needed them. He was looking for something, something else." He stared at his feet while he considered the situation. When he had the answer, he looked up again. "He built himself a giant Petri Dish, didn't he?"

`"That would be my guess,"` answered MINIMCOM. `"OMCOM must have determined that natural selection would produce the desired agents more quickly than he could through parametric programming. After the Asdrale Cimatir was consumed, he simply waited until the proper combination of units developed."`

"Developed for what?" Rei asked. "OMCOM claimed he didn't have control. He was lying, wasn't he?"

`"I do not know that he was lying. He may not have controlled the entities directly."`

"But why? Why pretend he didn't know what he was doing?"

`"I cannot answer that question. I can only tell you that OMCOM does not do anything by chance. Everything has its purpose."`

"Like these things?" Rei asked, pointing to the pouch.

`"That will be up to you to determine. Please take the pouch."`

Rei reached over and picked up the little sack again. He hefted it. The bag was so light, lighter than sand, almost as light as air. To the innocent, it might have seemed harmless enough. But Rei knew what was in it and its contents terrified him.

"All right, MINIMCOM," he said reluctantly. He put the pouch in his right pocket. "I have to trust you. And OMCOM."

`"Thank you,"` replied MINIMCOM. `"You may now go and rejoin your family."`

Rei stood up. He patted his pocket and felt the bulge there. "OK, I guess I'll see you around."

`"I will be here."`

Rei made his way through the cargo compartment and down the ramp. He turned to see MINIMCOM retract the ramp, lower the cargo door and just like that, the ship was gone. He grabbed the remaining satchels and made his way up the rocky path to find a small wooden, two-room hut - a shack, really - sitting just over the crest of the beach.

"Some digs," he commented in English as he entered, wrinkling his nose at the slightly mildewed smell.

"It is home for now," Rome said in Vuduri, trying to be cheerful. She was holding Aason tightly, rocking him back and forth. Binoda was packing some kindling she had found within a small stove. She used the flint sitting there to start a fire. Fridone was sitting on a rough-hewn chair that was placed in the corner, just watching.

Binoda turned to Rome. "Your Onclare and cousins live just to the north," she said. "After we get some rest, we will make contact. They will be glad to see you and your father. It has been a long time."

"I am too excited to rest," Rome said. "There is so much to tell you, so much that you need to know."

452

"I would like that very much," Binoda replied, coming over to stand next to Fridone. "Very well. Please start from the beginning. Again."

"Of course," Rome replied. "We…" She was interrupted by a knock at the door.

"Quick, Beo," Rome whispered. "Aason!"

Fridone leaped up and grabbed the baby and hustled to the back of the room. He quickly drew his hands down the cloak and the two of them disappeared.

Chapter 59

AS SOON AS ROME WAS CERTAIN HER FATHER AND CHILD WERE hidden, with some apprehension, she called out, "Who is it?"

"My name is Tenoal," came a voice from the other side of the door.

"Tenoal!" Binoda exclaimed. She threw open the door and leaped forward to hug the man standing there.

"Binoda?" Tenoal said, shaking his head. "What are you doing here?"

Binoda released him. Standing next to Tenoal was a young boy and girl, teenagers really.

"Come in, come in," Binoda said, ushering the three people in. She quickly closed the door.

Tenoal looked around the room. "This is Rome?" he asked. "So grown up!"

Rome nodded and came over to him. "Onclare Tenoal," she said, hugging him. "I have missed you."

"We saw a ship arrive and were curious," said the uncle. He pointed to the two youths. "Rome, these are your cousins Rav and Elen."

"Aleha," said the girl, Elen. She reached up and placed a lei around Rome's neck. "Welcome to Mowei."

"Thank you," Rome said. She motioned with her arm. "This is my husband, Rei."

Rei stepped forward.

"Aleha and welcome," said Rav. He placed a lei around Rei's neck as well.

Tenoal looked at Binoda. "I thought we would never see you again, after Fridone disappeared."

"I am here, brother," came a voice from the corner. Fridone popped into view.

"Fridone!" Tenoal shouted. He ran over and gave his younger brother a hug. "Where have you been? How did you appear like that?" Tenoal looked down at Aason. "And who is this?"

"This is my grandson, Aason," Fridone said.

Tenoal stroked Aason's head gently. Aason smiled.

"This is all too much," said the man. "What are you doing here? What is going on?"

Fridone started to speak when Tenoal held up his hand. "Wait," he said. "Rav, Elen, go back home and get them some food and drink. This is a time to celebrate."

"Thank you, Onclare," Rome said. "But if possible, Rav, Elen, do not tell anyone we are here. We will explain it to your father and then he will understand, but some of us..." Rome looked at her father. "Some of us are not supposed to be here and we need to keep this as quiet as possible."

"I understand," Elen said, knowingly. "We will keep your secret. Come, Rav." She pointed to the door. "We will be back shortly," she said and they left.

The group arranged themselves in a circle around the floor and Rome launched into a brief but thorough explanation as to what had transpired on Tabit and their trip to Deucado.

Fridone took over and detailed how he had been kidnapped and spirited away by the Onsiras. Much of his story brought Binoda to tears, alternating between tears of sadness and tears of joy.

Finally, Rome recounted her encounter with the Overmind of Deucado. It was at that point that Binoda interrupted.

"What I cannot understand," she said, "is how the Overmind here can be the merging of all of our minds and yet able to keep such secrets from the very people that are its constituents."

Rome shrugged. "All Vuduri know that mandasurte disappear. Yet no one ever questioned it. Since the Overmind was not responsible, it simply did not care. Good, obedient Vuduri would allow their minds to be drawn away from the obvious."

"I cared," Binoda said. She leaned over and wrapped her arms around Fridone. "But you are correct. I would not be allowed to impose those values upon others."

"These Onsiras," Tenoal said. "How can they hide in plain sight? How can we stop this from continuing?"

Just then, there was a knock on the door. It opened slowly and in came Rav and Elen, carrying caskets of food and bottles. Rome started to get up. Rei put his hand on her shoulder and leaned in, whispering, "Romey, there's something I have to tell you."

"In a short while," she said, standing up. She handed Aason to his father. "Let me help them set out the food."

"OK," Rei replied and he leaned back with his sone.

During the meal, the discussion turned to Tenoal filling in Fridone and Binoda on what was happening to Fridone's family. Births, deaths, comings and goings. It was the chatter of family members that had not seen each other for a long time. After the meal was complete, Tenoal brought the topic back to the matter at hand.

"How do we solve the Onsiras problem?" he asked. "Things cannot continue like this. From what you said, very soon they will discover the true nature of what has transpired on Deucado, if they do not come across Fridone first."

"My original plan," Rome said, "was to simply tell the truth to the one Vuduri, one member of the Overmind who could not possibly be a part of the Onsiras. Once this happened, all the Vuduri, the pure ones, would know and would be horrified. There would be a groundswell of support. There would be such a backlash, it would put an end to veil of secrecy that the Onsiras hide behind."

Rome paused and took a deep breath. "Unfortunately, that pure Vuduri was to be you, Mea," she said in a distressed tone.

Binoda lowered her eyes. "I am sorry, Rome, I did not know. I acted too hastily. I was just so happy to finally be free."

"How would that help the mandasurte?" Tenoal asked defiantly. "Who would tell them what has been happening?"

"I had not figured that part out yet," Rome answered, casting her eyes downward.

"Exposing the Onsiras to the Vuduri might force their hand," Tenoal continued. "You would leave the mandasurte defenseless. They need to be warned beforehand."

"How do I do that?" Rome asked.

"You need to go to O'ahu, to Onalu," her uncle replied. "It is the center of mandasurte culture and where Vuduri come to meet mandasurte in the South Pacific. In the middle of the city there is a place called Tanosa Plaza. You could broadcast from there and you would reach the entire mandasurte community across the world, all at the same time. There would be no way for the Onsiras to suppress that information."

"That is excellent, Onclare," Rome said. "It sounds perfect."

"Why do we not just fly out of here in MINIMCOM and go there now?" Rei asked.

Rome pointed to the tracking bracelet on her wrist. "We only get one opportunity," she said. "And that still leaves us with the problem of finding the one pure Vuduri whom we can trust."

"I know one," Binoda said. "One that I can guarantee is not a member of the Onsiras."

"Who is that?" her daughter asked.

"You already know him. Commander Ursay."

"Ursay?" Rome said with some surprise.

"Yes, Ursay."

"How do you know this?"

"Because I know him," her mother replied. "I know the real man."

Fridone bristled. "What do you mean, Binoda?"

"Do not be upset," Binoda said, stroking Fridone's cheek. "When the Tabit crew returned to Earth, Ursay made it a point to seek me out and deliver Rome's letter to me. As you know, he spent some time disconnected from the Overmind while escaping Asdrale Cimatir."

"How long?" Rome asked. "I never did find out."

"Long enough that he had time to think about the events that occurred on Tabit, of the blindness of the Overmind, of how Rei's people could not have been the monsters that we always thought them to be."

"How does this prove anything?" Rome asked. "He could have been a member of the Onsiras and still told all of this to you."

"No, he could not," Binoda replied. "From what you say, these Onsiras have nothing in their head other than their instructions. Half of their brain is connected to our Overmind. The other half connects to the secret samanda, with its own Overmind, that controls them. I know that Ursay was disconnected when I was with him. He and I spoke person to person, without the Overmind listening in. There is no way that he could have had the thoughts he did and the perspective that he did if he was just a robot, a tool of the Onsiras."

"Is that why he defended me?" Rome asked. "He was always rather harsh on Tabit."

"It was not he but the Overmind who was harsh and yes, that is why he defended you. That is how I knew it was the right thing to do to summon him. I knew how Ursay the man actually admired you and your resourcefulness. Rome, you inspired him. Rei, you too. He told me he was considering disconnecting permanently, Cesdiud, to become mandasurte. There is no way that he would think that if he was dedicated to their destruction."

"But is it not possible that he was just setting you up?" Rei asked.

"I do not think so," replied Binoda. "There was absolutely no reason why he would have confided in me if it was just a ploy. No one knew you were coming to Earth. No one could have foreseen these events. If he were a member of the Onsiras, he would not have bothered. No, I am certain. He is the one you need."

Rei turned to Rome. He spoke in English. "Romey, we're never going to know for sure. I trust your mom. If she says that Ursay is the one, I say let's go for it."

"All right," Rome agreed, in Vuduri. "Ursay is the one. How do we get him here?"

"`I believe I can help,`" came a muffled voice, issuing from one of the bags.

Fridone got up and walked over and pulled out MINIMCOM's projector and communication device. He set it on a table.

"How can you help?" Rome asked the device.

"`Open the front door.`"

Rei stood up and walked to the door and opened it. In front of him stood something shaped like a man, well over two meters tall, dressed all in black, complete with a cape. The head was roughly bullet-shaped with slits where the eyes and mouth might be. The figure strode into the room and came to halt in the middle of the floor.

"Is this a robot?" Rome asked with trepidation.

458

MINIMCOM's voice issued from the mouth hole. "I have created a living avatar, a livetar," said MINIMCOM. "It is not a robot. It is ambulatory but not autonomous. It is merely an extension of me. It is hollow. Think of it as a speaker with hands. I can physically transport it to Ursay's home and have it address him."

Rei thought it was funny that the tinny voice of MINIMCOM would come from such an imposing figure but he decided to keep that thought to himself.

"Do you not think someone will notice that it is not human?" Rome asked.

"I will make sure that it is only Ursay that encounters it."

"What will you do when you get there?" she inquired. "As soon as Ursay sees you, the Overmind will know you are there. It will tip our hand."

"I will see to it that it does not. I will make sure he disconnects before he receives critical information. Remember, no one has ever seen me or this form before."

Rome closed her eyes. When she opened them, she nodded slowly. "Very well," she said. "MINIMCOM, it is absolutely critical that you are not detected prior to revealing yourself to Ursay."

"I will remain cloaked the entire time. I will be invisible to MIDAR as well. I will take a polar route to reduce the chance of discovery even further. I can do this if I fly low and slow."

"How long will it take you?" Rei asked.

"One full day," replied MINIMCOM's livetar. "My velocity must remain below the speed of sound to eliminate any chance of acoustic detection."

"How long before Sussen gets here?" Rei asked. "From Deucado?"

"At least ten more days before she is in range to communicate."

"Well then, it sounds good to me," Rei said. "Everybody in agreement?" He looked around the room. Everyone nodded.

"It is decided, then. MINIMCOM, we entrust our fate to you," Rome said.

"Thank you for vote of confidence," replied the livetar and it bowed. It took two steps toward Rome and then said in a low voice,

"Rome, before I depart, I must have a word with you in private."

Rome looked at Rei who shrugged. He had completely given up trying to understand all the machinations going on within the machines. The livetar walked to the corner and Rome followed him. The livetar bent over and whispered in her ear, "I have a message for you."

"From who?" Rome asked.

"From OMCOM," replied the livetar.

"From OMCOM," Rome whispered back. "Where is he?"

"He is not here. This message was delivered to me back on Deucado."

"I do not understand. How did OMCOM contact you there?"

"He was able to stabilize some null-fold relays. The conversation was brief but long enough to receive his instructions. He gave me two gifts to pass along. I have already given one to Rei. For the second gift, OMCOM asked that you memorize three words."

"What words?" Rome asked.

"Blue crystal reader," said the livetar in English.

"That makes no sense," replied Rome.

"They do not need to. They are for you to say to Rei."

"If they are for Rei, why did you not just speak to him directly?"

"No," hissed the livetar. "He cannot hear them yet. You must only speak those words to him if he is in trouble. OMCOM said to use the three words if you need to protect Rei's mind. Not before."

"Protect his mind?" Rome asked, quizzically. "That is a peculiar thing to say."

"I only know that OMCOM said it will make sense to you in context."

"MINIMCOM," Rome observed, "you have done so many good things for us. I trust you. Your word is sufficient."

"Thank you," the livetar replied. Then he turned and in a louder voice, addressed the rest of the family. "You should take this opportunity to enjoy your peaceful surroundings. When I return, I suspect there will be quite a bit of turmoil."

"We could all use some peace," Binoda said.

"I will be on my way then," replied the livetar. The imposing figure reached around and grabbed the cape and draped it over its front as if to cover itself. There was a whoosh and popping noise. In the blink of an eye, the livetar was gone leaving behind only a hint of the smell of plumeria.

"He certainly has a flair for the dramatic," Rei observed.

"Yes, I do," came MINIMCOM's voice from the projector. Everyone laughed.

"How did you do that?" Rei asked the projector. "How did you make the livetar disappear? What was that whoosh/pop?"

"It is simply a traveling PPT tunnel as I have used before," MINIMCOM said. "It is identical to the one I employed to rescue you from the Deucadons."

"But that one was big and wide and you had to carve it through rock," Rei mentioned.

"I have perfected it," MINIMCOM explained. "I can now materialize a minimal tunnel and pass it through an area. This action produces the whooshing sound, as you call it. The object is teleported to another location nearly instantaneously. I then extinguish the tunnel which causes the popping sound. The closer I am to the subject, the faster I can execute it."

"Wow," Rei said. "When I was growing up, we had this thing in science fiction called a transporter. It, uh, dematerialized things and reconstructed them elsewhere."

"That is why it was fiction," MINIMCOM said. "This is the real world. There is no such thing as dematerialization. That is why I use the term teleportation. It is more accurate. It is the transport of molecules via a snap PPT tunnel. You may find it useful at some point now that I have perfected it."

"OK," Rei said, "if you say so." He turned to look at Rome, who was distracted, looking off in the distance. "Thanks for the explanation, MINIMCOM," he said, closing the subject.

"You are welcome," replied the projector.

Rei handed Aason to Binoda and walked over to Rome. "What did MINIMCOM say to you?" he asked her. "Did he upset you?"

"No," Rome answered.

"Then what did he say to you?"

Rome closed her eyes. When she opened them, she looked up at Rei then placed her hand on his cheek.

"In due time, mau emir," she said. "In due time. We have one more issue to resolve."

"What is that?"

Rome addressed the group. "MINIMCOM is on his way to pick up Ursay. We must meet him at Tanosa Plaza. How will we get there?"

"You could go the old-fashioned way," said Tenoal, who was off to the right. "We could take you in one of our boats, right into Berlis Harbor. It would be an easy journey to O'ahu, to Onalu, to Tanosa Plaza. From there you could speak to the world, the mandasurte world."

"Not so fast," Rei said, pointing at Rome's wrist. "What about that?"

"What is that?" Tenoal asked. "What is so special about it?"

"It is a tracking bracelet, Onclare," Rome said. "With it, the Vuduri would know we are off-island. It is one of the conditions of my 'parole' that I remain here."

"Are you not allowed to go fishing with your old Onclare Tenoal?" he asked.

"I do not know," Rome replied. "Today is the first day of my banishment. I do not know how far they would let me go before enforcing the boundaries."

"Perhaps we should give it a try," Tenoal said. He looked around the room. "You all look tired. Why not get some rest? We will get together in the morning."

"Thank you, Onclare," Rome said.

After a long goodbye, Tenoal and Rome's cousins left. Rome put Aason to bed in a makeshift bassinet in the corner.

"Beo, Mea," she said when she was done. "You may sleep in the bedroom. Rei and I will remain out here with Aason."

"Thank you, Volhe," Fridone said. "It has been a long day."

Rei looked at Rome and her parents and spoke up. "Before you go to bed, do you mind if Rome and I take a quick walk along the beach?" he asked. "Starting tomorrow, I think things are going to get a little crazy."

"Of course," Binoda said, sidling up to Fridone who put his arm around her. "You take all the time you need."

"Is that OK with you, Rome?"

"I would love it."

Rei took Rome's hand and they walked down the stone path to the edge of the ocean. They stared out over the water to the west for the longest time. Eventually, Rei turned back and saw that the moon was just beginning to creep over the opposite horizon with a bright star to its right. He put his arms around his wife and kissed her long and hard.

When the kiss was complete, Rome pulled back a bit and said, "What was that for?"

"It was because I love you, Rome. I am the luckiest man alive in your time, in my time, in any time. Here and to the stars."

He lifted her up by the waist with ease and twirled in the sand with her aloft.

"And I love you," Rome said, grasping his cheeks and kissing him again. She draped her arms around his neck and hugged him tight, holding on to her man as if for dear life. She closed her eyes and allowed herself to just revel in the feeling of now. She slid her hands down, along Rei's leg and came to the bulge in his pocket.

"What is this?" she asked slyly.

"Oh, that," Rei said. "I was meaning to tell you about that. MINIMCOM said…"

Rei stopped talking as he noticed Rome was not paying attention to him. She was staring back across the island to the eastern horizon. He turned his head and saw that the moon was exactly where it had been but the bright star to its side had moved and was, in fact, getting brighter.

"Rei," she said with a hint of worry in her voice. "Look at that."

Rei set her down and stared as object grew yet brighter. Soon it was larger than the moon. Moments later, they could see it was a craft heading apparently straight for them.

"They must be monitoring me very closely," Rome said, pointing to the bracelet on her wrist.

A blinding light appeared in the sky as the craft activated its floodlights, illuminating Rei and Rome and a broad circle of sand. Instinctively, Rei pushed Rome behind him as the peculiarly shaped vehicle flew overhead then settled into the sand just in front of them. The craft was a long tube on stilts, like a bizarre form of a bus or helicopter fuselage. The carrier was almost insect-like, with rows of windows along the sides and four oversized EG lifters, one at each corner mounted at the end of the stilts. Rei realized that it was very similar to the craft that had transported him from the Vuduri palace on Deucado.

He put his hand up to block the light from shining directly into his eyes. He saw that a door in the side lowered and there were stairs built into the back of the door. Very quickly, six armed men, dressed completely in black, ran down the steps and came right at them.

"Rome?" Rei asked, not sure how to finish the question.

Chapter 60

THE STRANGE BLACK-CLAD MEN CIRCLED AROUND ROME AND REI until they formed a complete ring.

"What is this?" Rome called out loudly. "We have done nothing wrong."

Wordlessly, one of the men poked at Rei with the barrel of a weapon while another waved at the transport. It was not hard to figure out their intentions.

"Don't you guys have to have a warrant or something," Rei said in English. The nearest soldier bent forward and looked Rei in the eye. The soldier's eyes were dark black. In the reflected glow the craft's harsh floodlights, Rei could see they were cloudy and flat. They had no life to them. They reminded Rei of a shark's eyes.

"Come with us," the solder said hoarsely, in English. The men behind them pushed them forward.

"What do we do, Rome?" Rei asked, resisting the pressure.

"There are more of them than us," Rome said. "And they are armed. I think we must go with them."

She moved around in front of Rei and started walking toward the craft.

"What about A…" Rei called after her but stopped himself.

"Come," Rome said and she started up the steps built into the ramp. Rei paused at the base of the stairs. *"MINIMCOM,"* he called out, using the cellphone in his head. *"Can you hear me?"*

*"*Yes*,"* replied the starship. *"*Why are you contacting me?*"*

"I think we're in trouble."

*"*What happened?*"*

"We just got arrested by a bunch of armed guards with dead eyes."

*"*That does not sound encouraging*,"* MINIMCOM replied.

One of the troops pushed Rei in the back. Rei started walking up the stairs as slowly as he could. *"Where are you?"* he asked, stopping at the top.

*"*I am roughly 4000 kilometers due north of your previous position. The Aleutian Islands are directly ahead of me.*"*

"I think you'd better come back," Rei said. *"And pronto. Nothing good is going to come of this."*

465

"On my way," MINIMCOM replied. *"I will be there as quickly as I can."*

"Thanks, buddy," Rei thought as he bent his head down and stepped in the cabin.

"No problem, erp, <click>," said MINIMCOM and the connection was cut.

Rei's eyes widened. He tapped his temple as if to clear the receiver but nothing changed. The transport was somehow shielded against the apparatus in his head. The cabin was filled with a dozen rows of spartan-looking seats and not much else. The soldiers placed Rei on one side and Rome on the other.

One soldier sat between Rei and the aisle. Another did the same for Rome. The other four soldiers spread themselves out in the seats in front of them and behind them.

Rei looked out the window and even though there was no sensation of motion, he could see the ground dropping below.

"Where are you taking us?" Rei asked but the soldier ignored him.

The craft rotated in place and headed across the southern part of Maui, rising as it went. Rei could see the gigantic crater of Haleakala to the north. In a short while, they were over the ocean. It was not long before they came upon the Big Island of Hawaii. They cut across the interior skirting around the peak of Mauna Loa then headed due east.

Rei looked over at Rome but he could not see her because of the guards sitting between them. He turned and looked out the window again. In the pale moonlight, he could see patterns that he guessed were vegetation interspersed among black, volcanic rock. As the pilot brought the craft around, the caldera of Kilauea rose up in front of them and they climbed again, following its rise to its peak. The transport stopped its horizontal motion and rotated in place, hovering over the huge crater. The mouth of the crater was over half a mile across, dwarfing the small craft. The pilot lowered them straight down, coming to rest just above the floor of the dormant volcano.

Activating the floodlights again, the transport inched its way forward into a tunnel built into the side. After a short time, a slight jostle indicated they had landed. The soldiers arose and formed a phalanx, escorting Rei and Rome down the boarding stairs.

Once they were on the ground, the soldiers grasped them on their arms and the remaining soldiers moved behind them, holding out their rifles. Prodding them along, they walked forward and entered a slightly smaller tunnel. The roof was high, perhaps 30 feet over their heads. As Rei looked around he decided this was a fairly old lava tube. The walls were real, not Vuduri glop. Along the walls were dimly lit globes separated by great distances, but there were enough of them to see their way walking along the hard ground.

As they walked along the tunnel, Rei could see they were in an elaborate underground complex. Occasionally, there were doorways cut out of the living rock but it wasn't until they were taken to the apparent end of the hallway that they stopped. One of the soldiers opened a door and motioned that they were to go through. As they entered the room, it was only slightly easier to see. There were aerogel panels covering up some of the rock not quite reaching the ceiling. However, the panels did emit the usual diffuse light that seemed to emanate from all Vuduri-made materials. The ceiling was partially tiled but above it, Rei could see lava rock, dark gray and porous.

He was marched to an aerogel bench along the right wall. One of the soldiers took a large metal loop and placed it over Rei's chest and arms and clamped him in place. A second soldier put another ring of metal around Rei's ankles.

While this was taking place, Rome was moved to the opposite side of the room, to an examining table similar to the one used back on Deucado when Pegus set about reconnecting Rome to the Overmind. The soldiers lifted Rome up and placed her on the table.

"What are you going to do to her?" Rei exclaimed. The soldiers ignored him.

Four of the soldiers, including the two armed with rifles, left the room, leaving only two remaining who took up positions by the door. They each had a holster holding a strange sort of hand weapon. The weapons looked somewhat like pistols but their barrels had a flared end instead of a straight tube.

"What do you think they want?" Rei called out to Rome. "The Vuduri already sentenced you. Why does there have to be more?"

"I do not know," Rome answered. "You saw their eyes."

"Yeah," Rei replied sadly. He decided to try and contact MINIMCOM again.

"Hey buddy," he called out in his mind.

"Yzz, brr, bipp. Yzz, brr, bipp," was the reply. The pulsating, buzzing noise was so annoying that Rei had to turn the circuit off. He tried connecting to Rome directly but failed. The only thing he heard was more interference. He looked at Rome's face and based upon her expression, she must have tried the same thing and failed as well.

Rei surveyed the room. Several racks filled with electronic equipment were bolted to the wall to the left of where Rome was sitting. He noted one chassis with a blinking block of lights that seemed synchronized to the buzzing in his head. He looked to his right, at the far wall on the opposite side of the room from the door and saw that it was completely blank, albeit a little grimy. Based upon the layout of the room, it was entirely likely that the lava tube continued beyond the wall but there was no way to tell for sure.

About ten minutes later, one of the soldiers reached over and opened the door. In came three people. Two of them were wearing the Vuduri equivalent of white lab coats which were in stark contrast to the black uniforms worn by the guards. The third person was a petite blonde woman wearing a standard issue Vuduri white jumpsuit. Rei recognized her immediately and his heart sank.

The woman walked over to where Rome was sitting.

"Hello, Estar," Rome said in Vuduri, somewhat dispassionately.

"Hello, Rome," replied the woman with contempt in her voice.

"What do you want with us?" Rei called out to her.

Estar leaned in, staring into Rome's eyes and said, "We require some answers."

"What kind of answers?" Rome asked.

"The truthful kind," Estar replied. "You have not been forthcoming so far."

"How have we not told the truth?" Rei interjected from across the room.

Estar turned to him. "Erklirte, it will be your turn shortly. Please be quiet." She turned back to Rome.

"I am not supposed to be here," Rome said, lifting her wrist showing off the tracking bracelet. "I was not supposed to leave Mowei."

"No one knows you are here. Your tracking signal has been jammed since you entered our transport and it is fully masked now. No one can follow you here."

"But why? I still do not understand. What do you want of us?"

"As I stated. I need you to answer some questions," said Estar.

"I have already been questioned. I have already given my answers."

"Not to me."

"What?" Rome asked resignedly. "What do you want to know?"

"I only have three questions," Estar said, holding up three fingers, "but choose your answers wisely."

"What are they?" Rome asked quietly.

Estar lowered her hand. "First," she said, "within your shuttle, your engines were deliberately crippled. We have tried to reverse the programming but we were unable to do so. From the logs, we can deduce their power output has been reduced for a long time, but there are other indicators that do not match up. We have one reading that indicates the event occurred within the last sixty days."

"You are wrong," Rome said without much conviction.

"Who disabled them?" Estar asked sharply.

"No one did," Rome answered. "Over time, they simply became less efficient. If you cannot deduce how this came to pass, how could we?"

"You did this," Estar spat out. "How did you do it?"

"I did not," Rome protested. "I do not have the knowledge nor the skill set to do so. And Rei certainly does not."

Estar turned to look at Rei. "Of course he does not. But this leaves us with no answer. Why would you even do such a thing?"

Rome just looked at Estar with no expression on her face, staring into her odd eyes.

"Very well," Estar said. "We will ignore this issue. My next question is very simple. Why were there three chairs in your galley?"

"We synthesized an extra one during our trip."

"Why?" Estar hissed. "This action makes no sense."

"Have you ever had more than one meal with the same person?"

"Of course."

"Did you always sit in the same place?"

"What does that have to do with anything?" Estar asked.

"Well," Rome continued, "Rei and I had every one of our meals together every day for a year. After a period of time, we needed a little variety in where we sat. Creating another chair was certain easier than lifting and moving the chairs each time."

"I do not understand. Why did you need variety?" Estar asked. "That is inefficient."

"It is what we mandasurte do," Rome said proudly. "Of course you cannot understand."

Estar started to speak and then stopped herself. She signaled to the lab-coated men who came to stand by Rome's side.

Rei tried to get up but he was bound too tightly. "What are you going to do to her?" he shouted.

Estar answered him without looking at him. "It is possible we will do nothing," she said. She addressed Rome, "your next answer determines your fate."

Rome's eyes widened. "Answer to what?"

"To my third question," replied Estar. "What happened to your baby?"

"My baby?" Rome asked confused. "He, he died. He was stillborn. I already explained this to Oronus."

"Yes," said Estar. "But what did you do with the body? The remains?"

Rome looked over at Rei in a panic. She tried once again to call him using their internal circuit but the only sound she detected was a pulsating, buzzing noise.

"Well?" Estar said. "Answer me!" she shouted.

Rome looked down at her feet and the image of Aason dead was enough to call up a flood of tears. When they were sufficient to spill over and down her cheeks, she looked up at Estar.

"We sent him into space," Rome said quietly. "Rei made him a little coffin and we set him adrift. Rei called it a burial at sea."

"You are lying," Estar said. "No more."

The technicians pushed Rome back onto the table and tied her arms and legs down with four sets of restraints.

"Hey!" Rei shouted, struggling with his bonds. "Leave her alone, you demented bitch."

Estar waved her hand. "I warned you, Erklirte." One of the soldiers went over and stuffed a cloth into Rei's mouth and strapped an elastic band around his head so he could not spit it out. Meanwhile, the technicians placed cuffs on Rome's arm and leg and they affixed two sensor pads, one on each temple.

"It is time you joined us," Estar said harshly. "We shall connect you and then we will know the truth."

"I do not wish to be connected," Rome replied.

"Of course you do," said Estar. "I was there when you were Cesdiud. You were devastated."

"You do not know what you are talking about, Estar," Rome said defiantly. "I am mandasurte now and this is the way I want to be."

"You have spent too much time with the Essessoni," the other woman said with disdain. "You have lost the ability to think clearly. Your words are just ranting and mean nothing."

One of the technicians came over with a syringe filled with a fluorescent yellow fluid. The other tech was tapping on the viewscreen mounted within the equipment rack. He was tracing one squiggly line with his finger.

Estar turned to look at the technician who seemed confused. She looked down at Rome then back at the screen. The tech holding the syringe stood in place while Estar walked over to the panel. She studied the readouts but their patterns were inconsistent. From the sensors attached to Rome's temples, it looked like she was emanating a low level of gravitic energy via PPT resonance. Yet Estar had been physically present when Rome was cast out. The readings made no sense. Estar concluded the blips must be due to the interference caused by their jamming equipment and decided to ignore it.

Meanwhile, Rei struggled in place furiously but between the restraints and the gag, he was completely helpless. A tear came to his eye.

Rome turned her head to the side. She saw Rei thrashing about and winked at him. Rei stopped resisting the restraints, giving her a quizzical expression. Rome motioned to where Estar was standing and raised her eyebrows and then Rei understood. He relaxed. Rome knew what she was doing.

Finally, Estar came back to where Rome was strapped down and the tech injected her with the fluid. She bent closer to look Rome in the eyes while the infusion circulated throughout her body. Rome smiled at her as if she were blissfully unaware of what Estar was trying to accomplish.

After about ten minutes, Estar straightened up and looked over at the rack. The tech was just shaking his head slowly. "I do not care," she said out loud.

Estar angrily motioned to the tech standing by the rack. He came over and he and the other technician drew out two large copper plates from beneath the table, each with a wire dangling from it. They inserted the free end of the wire into a small black box that was mounted underneath the exam table. They placed the copper panels near Rome's temples and immediately, they began to emit a humming noise. Rome grimaced but that was all.

Estar's eyes grew wide. "Again," she said, speaking out loud for the second time.

The technicians pressed the plates directly against Rome's head and again the box hummed. This time, Rome did not even grimace. In fact, a smile crept across her lips as if she had not a care in the world.

"What is wrong with you, you mosdurece half-breed?" Estar said angrily. "Are your genes so flawed that they cannot be reconnected?"

"As I told you before, I do not wish to be connected," Rome said calmly. "That should be reason enough."

"This is not possible," Estar said. She looked at each of the two techs. Both shrugged.

"Poor Estar," Rome continued, "we both know you were never very good at anything. I do not know who you serve but by now they must know you are incompetent."

"No more!" Estar said, holding her hand up. She closed her eyes and took a deep breath. She opened her eyes again and stared at Rome but her eyes took on a defocused look. Her shoulders slumped. Estar stayed motionless for several minutes until a small shiver went down her back. She lifted her head up and looked at Rome with an evil grin on her face.

Immediately, the technicians moved forward and removed the cuffs from Rome's arm and leg and the sensor pads from her head. They released the restraints.

"Get up," Estar barked at Rome. "Go sit on the bench." She pointed to a spot next to Rei.

Rome sat up and swung her legs over the side of the table and hopped off. She walked over and sat down next to Rei, placing her hand on his thigh, lowering her head until it rested on Rei's shoulder. Rei bent his head so that it touched Rome's. One of the soldiers came over and indicated to Rome that she should move to the far end of the bench, away from Rei.

The other soldier came over joining the first and together they removed Rei's gag and the two bands holding him in place. They pulled him to his feet.

"Let go of me," he said, trying to shrug free.

"Not an option," Estar called out. "Do as you are told."

One guard placed his hand on Rei's shoulders and pushed him over to the table. He motioned to it and forced Rei to hop up, dangling his feet over the edge. The other guard remained at Rome's side.

"What are you going to do?" Rome asked, her eyes widening in fear.

"We are going to try an experiment," Estar replied.

"I am not interested in any experiment," Rei said and he started to get up. The guard pushed him back down. One of the technicians came over to help restrain Rei.

473

"Hey!" Rei shouted and the two men slammed him back against the table. He struggled, punching at the technician but the soldier hit him across the side of the head with the butt of his hand weapon. While Rei was dazed, the two men took the opportunity to push him down flat and they strapped the restraints onto his wrists.

The other technician came over with a fresh syringe, filled with the fluorescent yellow-green fluid.

"No," Rome called out. "Do not do this."

"If we cannot connect you, then we will try to connect the Essessoni," Estar said. "I must learn the truth."

"You cannot do that," Rome shouted. "He is not like us. You will kill him."

"I do not think this will kill him," Estar said. "But even if it does, so what? He should have died on Tabit. It was only luck that he did not."

"I knew it," Rei said, weakly. "Why? Why did you want to kill me? I never did anything to you."

"All the Essessoni must die before the Erklirte arise again," Estar growled. "You are the purest of poison. You are not even human."

"We are human. We are the same as you," Rei said forcefully. "You just have one extra chromosome."

"That is exactly it. You are not the same as us," Estar hissed. "You are all animals. You do not have the ability to be civilized. Your genetic structure is incomplete."

"Estar, please," Rome pleaded. "His body cannot absorb the treatment."

"Perhaps," Estar said, not looking at Rome, "perhaps not. That is why I call it an experiment. This may work or it may not. It is possible it will not kill him but merely destroy his mind. However, this is a chance we are willing to take. I want the truth."

"No," Rome said, jumping up. The guard standing next to her pulled out his hand weapon. Estar walked over to where Rome was standing and took the weapon from the soldier, placing it under Rome's chin.

"This is a miniature plasma projector with a controllable electromagnetic containment. With it, I can vaporize your skull completely," she said. "Or more importantly, a small portion of it. A very painful portion. You choose. Sit down now or burn."

"Do not hurt her," Rei shouted. "She will cooperate. Rome, please," he said plaintively.

"I cannot let them do this to you, mau emir," Rome said, starting to cry.

"Rome, when I gave you the ring, you made me an offer. You said you would do one thing, whatever I wanted," Rei begged. "*This* is what I want. I want you to do as she says."

Rome sank back in her seat. "Rei…" she whimpered helplessly.

"It's OK, sweetheart," he said in English. One technician set about hooking up the monitoring sensors to Rei's head then placed cuffs on his arm and leg. The technician with the syringe held it over Rei's arm.

"No," Rome gasped. "Wait."

"Wait what?" Estar asked.

"I will tell you everything," Rome said, sobbing.

Estar leaned in. "I knew it. This is your last chance."

"All right," Rome said, resignedly. "Here is the truth. We actually did make it to Deucado but crash-landed. VIRUS units got loose and caused our tug MINIMCOM to evolve into an invisible spaceship that can travel at 1000 times the speed of light. He transported us here in eight days. MINIMCOM was the one who crippled the engines to make it look like it took longer."

"Eight days?" Estar scoffed incredulously. "And then crippled your ship? Why would he do that?"

"To hide the fact that I had the baby and he is still alive."

"This baby of yours," Estar said with disgust. "Where is it?"

"He is invisible, too," Rome replied. "He is wearing a cloak given to us by the Essessoni who have been living on Deucado for the last five hundred years."

"You are not a very good liar," Estar spat. "Your story is beyond ridiculous. It is preposterous. That or being mandasurte has driven you insane."

"I am not lying," Rome protested.

The technician holding the syringe made a motion toward Rei.

"No," Rome called out.

"You had your chance," Estar said. With that, the guard injected Rei, who responded with an ouch.

"No!" Rome sobbed. "No."

"Romey, you tried," Rei called out to her in English. "I'll be all right, honey,"

Estar pressed the weapon harder into Rome's cheek then turned to Rei. "The genetic material should create artificial PPT transceivers. Once we apply an electrogravitic field, the resonance will start and you will enter into our samanda. It is supposed to be fairly painless," she said sardonically.

Rei felt a burning sensation creeping up his arm. "Ow!" he exclaimed, "Painless my ass," he said, in English. "Ow!"

Rome snapped her head up. "Rei Bierak, listen to me," she shouted out in English, "Blue crystal reader."

Rei cocked his head at her and started blinking rapidly. Then he became very still.

Chapter 61

Estar stared at the vile Essessoni. His face was completely blank. She whipped her head back to Rome. "What does that mean? Blue crystal reader?"

Through her tears, Rome just smiled at Estar but did not answer. Estar looked back and forth from Rei to Rome and back again.

One of the technicians lifted Rei's head up and looked into his eyes. While Rei was aware of his presence, he could no longer see anything. In his ears, he heard a low rushing sound, like that of the ocean. Then he was no longer even in the room with Rome and those other people. He was back on Skyler Base, back in OMCOM's long-term memory storage room: the ultraviolet lasers crisscrossing and pulsating. The beautiful, deep purple lights and glinting crystals called to him.

"Pretty," he said out loud. "So, so pretty… Why does it have to be so pretty?" he murmured dreamily.

"What is wrong with him?" Estar said, turning to Rome.

"You are the one that injected him."

Estar turned back to Rei who was breathing peacefully now. The two technicians took positions by the monitoring equipment. Through their eyes, Estar could see that Rei's vitals were stable. The EKG was unnaturally flat but it could have been due to Rei's inferior mind.

Estar closed her eyes briefly then opened them. Regardless of what was happening, the genetic mutations were taking effect. It was not long before their instruments indicated it was time. She made a waving motion with her hand and the two technicians hurriedly left the room.

In their place, the soldiers took up positions, one on each side of the table. The guard on the far side, the one who had hit Rei over the head, holstered his weapon, bent over and lifted up one of the copper plates that was sitting on the floor. The other guard picked up the other plate and held it near Rei's head as well. With no fanfare, the box began to hum and instantly Rei stiffened and shrieked a bloodcurdling yell.

477

Rome started to get up but Estar turned to her and waved the weapon, indicating that she sit down.

"Please let me go to him," Rome said. Estar glared at her and shook her head.

Back on the table, Rei took a deep breath and then his whole body seemed to relax. The two guards lowered the plates. Rei lay there, not moving at all.

"Rei?" Rome called out. There was no reaction on her husband's part. The one guard removed the restraint on Rei's right arm and lifted it up. He released it and it just flopped back on the exam table. He jostled Rei roughly and still got no reaction. Finally, in frustration, he backhanded him across the face and Rei opened his eyes but his stare was blank and diffuse.

Estar took two more steps toward Rei, checking back at Rome with each step. She made sure the weapon was pointed directly at Rome's head then turned to look at Rei. She reached out with her mind and could feel a ghostly presence there, like a fog tinged in blue. The swirling intelligence was beginning to congeal into a form but it was unlike the normal cloudlike presence experienced within the Overmind. This one was glinting, flashing and hard. It was not a mind like she was used to. The presence glowed bright blue, connected and yet apart with a crystalline wall surrounding it. Without knowing quite how to address him, Estar and all the Onsiras spoke to Rei.

"Rei Bierak, can you hear us?" the minds asked.

From within the transparent walls that protected his mind, Rei could see the probing eyes of Estar and a thousand others. Behind them was something else but he could not make out what it was. He could hear them calling to him with a siren's song. He longed to join them. The voices in front of him tried to coax him out but he was not able to break free of the walls that imprisoned him, much as he wanted to. Rei struggled to let them take over but then he stopped. From deep inside his psyche, a familiar voice rang out.

"You are to take control," OMCOM's voice echoed in his mind.

"OMCOM?" Rei asked, puzzled. *"What are you doing in my head?"*

"I am not here. I have left you instructions that you hear with my voice."

"What kind of instructions?" Rei asked.

"Your mind must be under assault. I have prepared a defense for you," replied OMCOM's voice.

"I see it," Rei said. *"It looks like a wall."*

"It is," replied OMCOM.

"So this is how Rome does it. Now I get it. It's obvious. I had no idea about this."

"Yes," answered OMCOM. *"The wall is there to protect you and your mind."*

"OK. I'm protected. What do I do now?"

"You resist. You keep the wall in place. Make a thread and extend it. Let only the thread loose."

"How?" Rei asked. *"How do I do that?"*

"Watch," OMCOM said. Within Rei's mind, images and diagrams demonstrated the necessary techniques. It was a seminar on mind control without using words.

Finally, Rei said, *"I understand. I can do this. And if I can do it then…"* he paused. *"Now I realize how the Onsiras can hide from the Overmind of Earth,"* he observed. *"They have their own wall. It is no wonder the Overmind could not get through."*

"Exactly," replied OMCOM's voice. *"Now is the time. Now you choose what they can see and what they cannot see. Only let others see what they expect to see. You know them. Use it against them."*

"I will." Rei said, *"I know exactly what they want. Boy, can I give it to them."*

"Are you ready?" OMCOM's voice asked.

"Yes, I am ready," Rei replied.

"Then I release you now."

With those words, audible only to Rei, he let his mind go. He used the technique that OMCOM demonstrated to extrude a part of his consciousness out in a way that could not be followed back to his place of safety. Rei allowed a tendril of his mind to creep around the crystalline walls protecting his existence and form a simulation of intelligence. With a second thread, he slipped past the accumulated spirits and probed their combined intellect. He could tell what they were looking for and so he let the visible consciousness assume more and more of the appearance they were expecting.

When the connection was complete, Rei's simulacrum announced it would give them the answers to all of their questions. The artificial mind began to replay Rei and Rome's history from the time Rei was awakened on Tabit to the present time in a more or less linear fashion. However, his version of the journey with Rome since they left Tabit was revised. Rei's simulated mind showed them how Rome getting pregnant was not in his plans. He demonstrated to them how he had gotten a datacube from MINIMCOM with instructions on how to cripple their ship before they separated at Keid. Rei showed the onlookers how he was, in fact, the one who disabled the engines using what boiled down to a computer virus so they would not reach Earth in time for Rome to give birth. When the mass-mind inquired as to why, Rei simply explained that all he wanted to do was fuck Rome silly and a baby would just get in the way.

While the Onsiras' version of the Overmind was reeling from his crudeness, he hammered away showing them how, when Rome went into labor, he had drugged her and suffocated the living baby at birth and tossed its body in the recycling vat before Rome awakened. As far as Rome knew, the baby was stillborn. He would not let Rome look into the little coffin he had prepared and with cold joy, he showed them how he fooled Rome into thinking they were launching Aason's body into space, the burial at sea.

"Monstrous," was the distilled word this new Overmind suggested.

"I am Essessoni," Rei's simulated spirit roared back. *"What did you expect? The Erklirte have returned!"*

He could feel the ersatz Overmind recoiling, not wanting to be associated with him any longer. He grasped back and would not let it go. The Onsiras' Overmind pushed harder and harder, with raw panic, feeling the taint of the Essessoni washing over it. While the Onsiras were preoccupied with separation, the other portion of Rei's mind slipped past the horror-struck onlookers and sailed forth into the dimension that was the soul of the group consciousness. As Rei's mind swooped and soared, he probed the innermost secrets of the Onsiras but only found bleak pockets of data. The deeper Rei went, the less there was of any feeling, not even human. To Rei it seemed as if he had tapped into the memories of a machine.

The Onsiras' Overmind started to forcibly withdraw, shutting down Rei's PPT transceivers. It was their version of Cesdiud. Rei could feel the connection closing. Just before the Overmind severed the connection completely, he pushed onward to its core. With blue crystalline clarity, Rei knew exactly what was going to happen and how. They were going to kill him. More importantly, they were going to kill Rome. They had no intention of letting either one of them leave this room alive.

Chapter 62

WITH A HORRIFIED EXPRESSION ON HER FACE, ESTAR TOOK A STEP backwards, away from Rei, lowering her arm in the process. The shock of what she had seen in Rei's mind forced her to temporarily resort to a verbal command.

"Execute him," she commanded the two guards, "Now!"

"No!" Rome shouted. She leaped up and grabbed Estar's hand, forcing it to point straight up.

The guard closest to Rome turned in place, away from Rei, reaching down to unholster his plasma gun. It was not there. He realized he had given it to Estar.

Meanwhile, from on the exam table, with his free hand, Rei launched his fist backwards and hit the guard standing on his right side squarely in the face, breaking his nose. Blood spattered everywhere. As the guard's hands went to his face, Rei reached down and grabbed the weapon from the injured guard's holster, yanking it out forcibly. He twisted his arm and pulled the trigger, all in one motion. The weapon discharged, blowing a fairly sizeable chunk out of the guard's abdomen. The first guard, the one closer to Rome, heard the blast and started to turn back to grab at Rei. Rei twisted around and squeezed the trigger even as he was swinging his arm upwards. The weapon fired continuously and when it got in the general direction of the first guard, the sizzling beam hit him with a glancing blow that severed his arm just below the shoulder. The guard fell to the floor holding the stump of his arm, writhing in pain and bleeding profusely.

On the other side of the room, Rome struggled with Estar. She squeezed Estar's wrist harder, pushing her captor's arm higher. Estar tried to grab at Rome with her free hand but Rome seized that as well. Estar brought her knee up to hit Rome but Rome twisted in place, blocking the blow with her thigh. The action caused the weapon to discharge, blowing a hole in the ceiling and exposing the living rock that was behind the ceiling tiles. As the two women struggled, Estar's weapon fired bolts of plasma upwards again and again.

Finally, the roof had enough. With a crack, a large portion of the rock that formed the ceiling of the lava tube broke off and fell and hit Estar directly on the head, shearing off a piece of her skull. She collapsed to the ground. Rome looked down and saw the contents of Estar's head emptying onto the floor. To her horror, what Rome saw spilling out was not brain matter. Instead, it was tiny little wriggling worms that looked like maggots or memrons.

"Rei!" Rome said, pointing at the floor.

Rei looked at where Rome was pointing but the growing puddle didn't phase him. He removed the other restraint from his left wrist and jumped off the exam table. He shouted, "Romey, grab her gun and let's go." He waved his arm forward.

"Go where?" Rome asked, frozen with terror.

"Here," he said. He rotated a knob on his hand weapon and turned it to maximum power. He fired it directly at the wall behind them. The resulting blast revealed a clearing behind the wall, a large round tunnel, more of the lava tube.

Rome bent over and retrieved Estar's weapon. Rei grabbed his wife and they ran. As soon as they were 20 feet into the tunnel, Rei pushed Rome ahead of him and then stopped.

"Move," he barked. As Rome started backing away, Rei turned and fired his weapon at the ceiling by the entrance, causing some rocks to come loose. He took two steps backwards and fired again. More rocks came loose. He could see back into the room and the door was opening and people were starting to flood in.

"Romey, come back. I need you," he said, pointing. Rome turned and aimed Estar's weapon at the entrance as well. Together, they fired their beams of destruction and within seconds, their target groaned with large rumbling sound.

"Run!" Rei shouted as the whole ceiling started giving way. A cavalcade of rocks emitted a roar and a rush of air and dust as they made their way down the tunnel. They were plunged into inky blackness.

"Come on," Rei said, grabbing Rome's hand and moving forward. While Rome's infrared vision could use their body heat to illuminate the space directly in front of them, Rei's sonar-vision could see much farther as their footfalls and the rumblings of the rockslide bathed the tunnel ahead in a dense swatch of sound.

On and on they ran, following the tunnel deeper and deeper. After a few minutes, Rei pulled on Rome's arm to hold up.

"What?" she said.

"How much charge do these pistols have?" Rei asked, breathing hard.

Rome looked down at her weapon. "They must be powered by Casimir pumps so, in theory, they never run out of charge."

"Great," Rei said. "Then we have to do it again."

"Do what?"

"Collapse the tunnel," he said, pointing upwards.

"Why?" Rome asked.

"Because they're going to cut their way through in no time. We have to make it as hard on them as possible," he said through gritted teeth.

"And then what? Where are we going?"

"Down," he said.

"Down to where? How will we get out of here?"

"I'll call MINIMCOM," her husband answered. He closed his eyes and activated his circuit. However, there was no response on the other end. He tried again. It was no use. The circuit was dead. He opened his eyes. "Romey, you try it," he said. "I think they messed up my brain or at least my circuit."

Rome closed her eyes and tried to contact MINIMCOM. All she heard was silence. There was no response on the other end.

"I cannot do it either," she said. "The signal is still jammed." Rome looked up and around her. "Or perhaps we are under too much rock."

Rei squatted down. He put his hands up to his face. "This is not what I planned," he said. "I figured once we got away from them, MINIMCOM could swoop in and beam us out of here."

"What does that mean: beam us out of here?" Rome asked, confused.

"When I was a kid, there was an old science fiction show that transported people from one place to another. That's kind of my pet name for what MINIMCOM can do with his whoosh/pop snap PPT tunnels."

"I see," Rome said pensively. "That is still a good plan. Let me try something else."

"What?" Rei asked.

"Our son."

"Aason?" he answered, confused.

Rome nodded. Once again, she closed her eyes but this time, she tried to open a connection to her child. *"Aason?"* she called out.

"Yes, Mother?" the child replied sleepily. *"Where are you?"*

"I am with your father," Rome replied in her mind.

"But where?" Aason insisted.

"I will tell you later. First, I need you to do something for me."

"What?" Aason asked.

"Can you contact MINIMCOM? You have the same abilities as your father and I. We call it a telephone."

"Of course," Aason answered. *"But he told me to call him Onclare MINIMCOM."*

"That is very nice, Aason, my love," Rome thought. *"Can you contact him now?"*

"All right, Mother." After a moment, the boy said, *"He is responding. What do I tell him?"*

"Aason, my child, I cannot tell you how to do this but do you think you could put us together? So that I could talk to MINIMCOM directly?"

"I know how to do it," Aason replied happily. *"Onclare MINIMCOM?"* Rome heard him inquire.

`"Where are you?"` came MINIMCOM's voice in reply. `"I cannot find you on my scans."`

Rome breathed a sigh of relief. *"We are deep within a dormant volcano,"* she said. *"They were going to kill us."* In her mind, she flashed back to the scene of the wriggling little worms issuing forth from Estar's skull and it made her shiver. *"We need you."*

`"I am on my way,"` answered MINIMCOM. `"At my present rate of speed, I will be there within the hour. I can fly faster if you want but then I run the risk of detection."`

"No, we can wait an hour," Rome thought. *"We are on Havei, the Big Island, in a lava tube, within the volcano, Kilauea. I do not know how far down we are but I do know that our EM link does not work. That is why I had to contact you via Aason."*

"That is sufficient information," replied MINIMCOM. *"I will find you when I get there. Do not be concerned."*

"All right, MINIMCOM," Rome thought. *"Thank you."*

Then to Aason, she thought, *"Aason, you did well. You have saved your father and me."*

"Saved you?" Aason thought with some panic. *"What is wrong?"*

"We are beneath a mountain. We are all right for now."

"Can you come home?" he asked.

"Not just yet," Rome replied. *"But Onclare MINIMCOM is coming to rescue us. We will be there as soon we can, my son."*

"But Mother..."

"Please Aason, be patient."

"All right, Mother," Aason replied.

"I will be contacting you again, soon," Rome thought. *"Your father and I must attend to our business now."*

"Yes, Mother. Hurry home."

"Yes, baby," said Rome.

Eyes closed, Rei turned his face up at his wife. The sounds of their breathing were the only "illumination" he had so her face was not distinct. But he could tell that she was smiling.

"Did you get him?"

"Yes," Rome said. "MINIMCOM is on his way. He will be here within the hour."

"How did you do that?" Rei asked.

"Aason did it," Rome replied. "He has my connection using PPT resonance and he has your telephone circuitry. He was able to patch the two together so that I could speak to MINIMCOM directly."

"That's pretty incredible."

"Yes, our son is very talented," Rome said with pride.

"He sure is," Rei said. "So, until MINIMCOM gets here, let's make it as hard for them as we can."

"Agreed."

Together they fired their weapons at the ceiling and caused another collapse. They continued down the tunnel, stopping every quarter mile or so to collapse the roof. The farther down they went, the tunnel narrowed and it actually became easier to cause a slide. At one point, Rei had a pang of guilt that they were destroying something that was of great geological value but his need to survive and save Rome was the stronger impulse.

Down they went. The original tunnel was obloid in shape and roughly 20 feet across and about 25 feet tall. At irregular intervals, stalactites, lavacicles really, hung down from the ceiling and gave notice that the tunnel was about to change size, usually growing smaller.

After they had gone a healthy distance, the roof of the tunnel was perhaps only 15 feet tall, the walls maybe 12 feet across. Along the sides of the tunnel ran a ridge that jutted out a good six inches or more. Rei guessed the ridge was formed by some residual lava flow a long time ago.

"How far do you think this tunnel goes?" Rome asked.

"I don't know," said Rei. "I didn't get that from the Overmind or whatever that was in my mind. I do remember when I was a kid, I recall reading that some lava tubes stretched as far as 45 kilometers or more. I can't be sure but I think we're heading toward the ocean." Rei sighed. "In other words, I don't have a clue," he said.

Rome digested this and said, "A better question would be how far do we have to go until MINIMCOM gets here?"

Rei looked ahead, Rome's words echoing in the distance and returning an image of the tunnel was as clear as if it were lit by torchlight.

"I guess this is far enough," he said. "Is it safe to assume that MINIMCOM will call when he arrives?"

"As long as Aason relays that message, I would say yes."

"OK, let's stop then." Rei walked over and put his back along the left wall, sliding down until he caught the ridge. The ridge was wide enough to act almost as a bench.

"I am thirsty," Rome said. "I did not think to grab any supplies."

"We didn't have the time." Rei paused then said thoughtfully, "Romey, you know we had to do it, right? To shoot them?"

"Oh yes," she replied, coming over to where Rei was resting. "When Estar said to execute you, I was fairly certain it was not going to end well."

Rei laughed gruffly. "I was in their Overmind," he said thoughtfully. "It was not what I expected."

"What were you expecting?"

"I don't know. Like, when we link up with bands, I'm in your mind. You are like, a spirit. I can feel you and see you and your history, all intermingled. But I know it's you."

"I am not part of that Overmind, if that is what you are saying," Rome said.

"No," Rei said, trying to find the words. "I just expected other, humans, something living. What I saw was something else. Cold. Mechanical. They weren't spirits, they were just points of accumulation. Hard, not soft. There were no actual beings there. Your Overmind, the one you described, was like a big, person maybe? There was no person where I was. Just, data."

"That is very strange," Rome said. "It must have been hard for you."

"That blue crystal thing you said to me. That saved me. It was from OMCOM."

"Yes, I know," Rome replied. "That was the secret that MINIMCOM told me in private, back at the beach. OMCOM had sent this phrase along for just this moment. It was a trigger but I did not know for what."

"I'll tell you for what," Rei answered. "Do you remember back at Tabit, the first time we went into OMCOM's memory chambers? I went in and looked at his long-term, I don't know, holographic storage crystal thingies."

"I remember," Rome said. "You were gone some time. I remember being concerned enough that I was going to come look for you just as you came out. What happened in there?"

"I'm not exactly sure but I think OMCOM hypnotized me or maybe it wasn't that deliberate. Maybe I just got hypnotized by the lasers, the crystals. But OMCOM sure didn't miss an opportunity to implant some sort of post-hypnotic suggestions in me. He saved me, of course. Those words put up a kind of wall that prevented them from getting inside my head until I was ready. How did he know to do that? And why?"

Rome thought for a minute. "I cannot be certain because most of my perceptions of OMCOM were modulated by my participation in the Overmind. Once I was Cesdiud, I saw things differently. All I can tell you is somehow, OMCOM changed."

"Changed how?" Rei asked.

"He was a computer," Rome said. "He was only as friendly as required by the Vuduri, which was not very much. But when you were first awakened, he became more animated. He mentioned to me that he had a personality module that you forced him to exercise. But even that was not it. Something happened to him. Something fundamental. He became... - I cannot call him a person, because he is not. I cannot say that he became intelligent because he was already vastly overpowered in the intelligence arena. No, he became, I am going to say, caring. It was as if there was a true living spirit inside him and your arrival triggered that awakening in him."

"That's pretty heavy," Rei said. "I never really saw a difference."

"I did," Rome replied, "after we used the bands." She slid along the ledge until her legs were touching Rei's. She leaned into him, putting her arm around him. Rei did likewise. "I think that act awakened something in OMCOM. I want to say compassion. Before that, he was simply intelligent."

"And all of this," Rei said, waving his free arm toward the tunnel. "You think this all is a result of that awakening?"

"What else can it be?" Rome asked. "He has always been one step ahead of each of the crises we have encountered. Almost as if he computed all possible futures and gave us the tools we need to counteract whatever fate was in store for us."

"If that's true, there's still one tool that has me stumped," Rei said.

Rome leaned back a bit. "And what is that?"

"Here, take my hand," Rei said. He slid it along his thigh, showing her the bulge in his pocket.

"Rei!" Rome said a little indignantly. "I do not think this is the right time for that."

"No," he said, laughing. "That's not it. It's a pouch that MINIMCOM gave me." Rei reached in his pocket and pulled it out. The heat from his hand illuminated the bag and provided more than enough infrared that Rome was able to make out its shape.

"What is in it?" Rome asked.

"VIRUS units," Rei said.

"VIRUS units?" Rome questioned. "That seems so dangerous."

"It gets worse before it gets better."

"How?"

Rei hefted the bag in his hand. "These units can have their oxygen sensor disabled. They can be activated within the atmosphere."

"And MINIMCOM gave them to you?" Rome exclaimed, terrified. "This is irresponsible. It could destroy the planet."

"I know," Rei said. "But MINIMCOM designed these units to report to us. They take their orders from my telephone circuit, from our telephone circuit. If it works, I mean."

He had a thought. *"Does it work now?"* Rei asked Rome internally.

"Yes, I can hear you," Rome replied silently.

"OK," Rei said out loud. "Then it was just Estar's equipment that was interfering between you and me. Not our brain circuitry."

"If that is the case, let me try MINIMCOM again," Rome said. After a moment, she shook her head. "We must be too far down."

"Probably. But we are close enough to activate and deactivate these VIRUS units whenever we want. If I sprinkled some on the floor here, I could turn them on and they'd start burrowing for us."

"But they would grow without bound," Rome said with a slightly horrified tone. "They would eat through to the core of the planet. They would eat us."

"No," Rei said firmly. "MINIMCOM said these units cannot eat organic matter. Now the core of the Earth, that's a different matter. We would have to tell them to stop before they got that far."

"So what are they for?" Rome asked. "Burrowing down would not seem to be very useful. What else would you do with them?"

"MINIMCOM had no idea," Rei said. "He said they were a gift from OMCOM and that's all he knew."

"So confusing," Rome said. "Obviously you did not need them back there." She became quiet for a moment as she recalled the melee. She squeezed Rei's hand. "What did you tell them when they were inside your mind?" she asked. "It frightened them beyond measure. All of the blood went out of Estar's face. She became as gray as I have ever seen a living human being. What did you say to them?"

"Romey," Rei said quietly. "I don't even want to tell you. They thought the worst of me and I gave them exactly what they expected to hear. Bad things. Horrible things. Things that I didn't even know I was capable of thinking."

"But they are not real," Rome posited, with a small amount of fear.

"God no," Rei said. "I simulated this horrid creature, the Essessoni of their dreams - their nightmares actually - and I let him say what they thought he'd say. But it wasn't me. Not ever."

"Then I trust you. I do not need to know any more," Rome said. "You did what you had to do."

"Yes, I could read their thoughts, too," he said. "I knew they were going to kill us. Kill you. I couldn't allow it. You're everything to me. But even that is just selfish. Rome, you are a good person and you did nothing wrong. You didn't deserve it."

Rome sighed and rested her head on Rei's shoulder looking up at his face, marveling at it. "You are so good to me, mau emir. I love you so much."

"And I love you too, Romey," he said.

Rome sighed again and leaned more fully against her husband. She closed her eyes, which seemed unnecessary because they were sitting in the pitch black. Then she snapped her eyes open again.

"Rei," she said, leaving the sentence hanging.

"What, honey?"

Rome stood up and took a step back. "I can see you."

"So what?" he replied. "You have infrared vision. Big deal."

"That is not the point. I can see you better than I should be able to."

"You can see the heat from my face, you know that," Rei pointed out.

"No," she said. "There is more than just your body heat. When I see a face that is only illuminated by internal warmth, there is a certain lack of features. But you, your face, it is all lit up. That means there is an external source of infrared. Let me look."

Rome scanned the tunnel. The far wall was illuminating where they were sitting, in the infrared sense. "There," she said, raising her finger. She knew that her voice would be sufficient for Rei to see where she was pointing. "That wall. It is radiating heat."

Rei turned to where she was pointing. He stood up and walked across the tunnel to the far side. Slowly, carefully, he ran his hand along the wall.

"I can feel it," he said and then paused. "Uh, Rome, this might not be good."

"Why?" she asked.

"For one thing, we're sitting inside a volcano maybe?" he said.

"A dormant volcano," Rome pointed out. "Kilauea has been dormant for as long as we have recorded history. Which means since your time."

"Yeah but there's always a first time."

Rei bent over and put his face near the warmest spot. He turned his head so that he could put his ear to the rock. "Wow," he exclaimed, "can you hear that?"

"Hear what?" Rome replied. "I hear nothing."

"Shhh. Let me listen again."

"All right." Rome held her breath and stayed perfectly still so Rei could attend to the sounds.

"Come here," he said.

Rome came over to him.

"Here," he said. "Put your ear to the rock."

Rome complied. She listened for a bit then lifted up. "I do not hear anything," she said.

"Well I do." Rei responded.

"It is not surprising given that you do have super hearing," Rome said condescendingly.

"Oh, yeah," he said, grinning.

"What did you hear?" she asked.

"Water. I heard drops of water. The echoes are telling me that it's hollow in there."

He reached over and felt along Rome's side until he found what he was looking for. He pulled out her hand weapon. He dialed down the intensity to the minimum and handed it back to her. "Here," he said.

"What do you want me to do with this weapon?" she asked.

"I cranked it down to the lowest setting. I want you to fire it up the tunnel. But be careful."

"What will that accomplish?"

"It'll light it up. Like a torch. I want to look with my eyes."

"Very well," Rome said. She turned and aimed the weapon up the tunnel and pulled on the trigger. A blue-white flame of contained plasma jumped out, traveling up the tunnel until it dissipated off in the distance. The arc-like light was sufficient for Rei to bend down and examine the wall close up. He took out his pistol and used its handle to gently rap the stone in a series of lines.

"This section here," he said. "It looks like rock but it's a different density. I can almost chart out the region…" He started clawing at it with his fingers. "There's something on the other side of this wall," he said. He rapped the stone one more time, harder, and something gave way.

"What are you doing?" Rome asked, carefully turning her head so that she could see where Rei was pointing.

"This isn't rock at all," he said. "I made a hole. I can stick my finger in there. What's behind it is hollow. I can kind of map it out. It could be like a chamber or something. I think that's where the water is."

Rome stopped firing her weapon and came over to where Rei was standing.

"Go back up the tunnel as far as you can," Rei instructed. "I'm going to use my gun to blow out this panel and I want to make sure you are out of the way."

Rome looked up the tunnel then back to Rei. "Please be careful," she said.

"Of course," Rei answered. "Now go."

Rome nodded and walked up the tunnel until Rei's infrared signature was almost undetectable.

"Are you away?" Rei yelled to her.

"Yes," she called back.

"OK," Rei shouted. "Fire in the hole."

"What?" Rome's question was lost in the reverberation of a blast. Her internal optics compensated instantly for the flash in front of her. "Rei," she called out. "Are you all right?"

There was no answer.

Chapter 63

FRANTIC, ROME CALLED OUT AGAIN, "REI!" SHE STARTED RUNNING back down the tunnel. Her infrared vision showed her where the blast occurred but she could not see Rei's shape.

"Rei!" she said, almost in tears. "Where are you?"

He poked his head out from the hole in the wall. "It's here, Rome!" he said excitedly. "Water. There's some sort of underground pool."

Rome came down to where he was and smacked him on the shoulder.

"Do not frighten me like that," she said. "I was worried."

"I'm fine, honey," he replied. "Come on." He reached out and Rome took his hand and stepped through the hole.

Unlike before when Rome only had the warmth of their bodies to illuminate the area, this part was hotter. Her infrared vision allowed her to see it rather clearly. They were in a large cavern that was 150 feet tall or more. The ceiling of the chamber was unnaturally smooth. Its shape did not fit Rome's perception of what a cave should look like. Instead, it was long and stretched out to their left but her attention was drawn to the small pool of water accumulating on the far side of the cavern. They walked across the rocky floor of the cave until they reached the pool. Rei sank to his knees and bent over and touched his lips to the water.

"Ugh," he said. "Bitter."

"Do you think it is safe to drink?" Rome asked, sinking down next to him.

"Yeah," he answered. "It's so warm, it probably has a ton of minerals dissolved it in but still, it's wet." He took another swallow and said, "Yuck."

Rome found it somewhat amusing but her thirst was also drawing her attention. She bent over and touched the water with her tongue.

"Yuck is the right word," she said but then she took a long drink as well.

She moved back a little and sat down on the ground and looked around her using her infrared vision. To their right, there was the near wall of the cave. The wall arched up and connected to the ceiling and really had nothing of interest going for it. Its expanse was also unnaturally smooth. But to the left, the grotto extended as far as her vision would let her detect with no real end in sight. There was much more residual heat here and it made it easier to make out certain details. She twisted in place and looked back to where they had blasted a hole in the wall.

"What do you think?" she asked him. "Should we stay here?"

"Why not?" Rei said. "At least we have water. This would be as good a place as any to get rescued."

"Rescued," Rome said, dreamily. "I hope it is soon. I am tired of this place already."

"Yeah, I know what you mean." Rei came over and sat down next to her. Immediately, he began to squirm.

"What is wrong?" she asked.

"The ground," he said. "It's scary warm."

"So? Why is that important?"

"Well, like I said, we're inside a volcano for one thing," Rei said with some urgency. "And for another, the ground just on the other side, where we just were, that far wall was cold. Like you'd expect this far down."

"I do not think it means anything," Rome said.

Rei stood up. He looked down the cave. He squinted then turned his head, attending to the cave out of the corner of his eye.

"Come on, Rome," he said, reaching down for her.

"What is it?" Rome reached up and took his hand, allowing him to help her up.

"Light," Rei answered, pointing ahead. "It's really faint. Just a few photons. But there is definitely some light coming from down that way."

Rome looked down to where he was pointing. If she bobbed her head back and forth, she could catch a few tiny flashes, which meant her retinas were recording quanta of light as well. They took two steps forward and then Rome pulled on Rei's sleeve.

"What?" Rei asked.

"Do you think we should take some water with us?" she inquired.

"Naw," Rei answered. "MINIMCOM will be here any minute. Besides," he said, pointing down. "It looks like there is a little stream or something. Maybe that's what eroded this whole cave."

Rome looked around again. "I do not think this was erosion, the walls and overhead seem too smooth."

"Whatever. We'll follow the stream and if it dries up or goes away, we'll do something then, maybe."

"All right," she said, "but there is something wrong here."

"What?" Rei asked, distracted, as he moved ahead of her.

"Never mind," she replied. Rome hurried to catch up to him, and together, they started walking along the tiny rivulet that was the overflow from the pool they had found. They only went 30 feet in the direction of the stream when Rome stopped again.

"What?" Rei asked.

"That," Rome said, pointing.

"I can't see what you are pointing to."

"Wait," she insisted. She looked up to make sure the region overhead was clear then she fired her hand weapon straight up, causing the entire cave to become illuminated just like an electronic torch. Rei looked where she was pointing and he saw it. Coming out of the ground was a metallic cylinder approximately three feet in diameter, capped with a dome made of metal.

"Holy mackerel," Rei said, squinting to examine the structure. "What is it?"

Rome took one step closer to the object and said, "I do not know but I do know it is not natural."

"I agree with that," he said, approaching the domed cylinder. He squatted down and put his hand on it. "Warm, almost hot," he observed.

"Yes," Rome agreed. "I saw the infrared signature. It is generating heat."

She followed the object with her eyes and abruptly took a deep breath.

"Look," she said, pointing down the cave. Rei sidled around and followed where she was pointing. Coming out of the cylinder or rod, just below the cap, was a thick cable that snaked its way down the cave and out of sight.

497

"What the hell is that?"

"I do not know," Rome said. "But it cannot be anything good."

"This is some sort of geothermal power rod or thermocouple," Rei said. "Something is drawing power down here. The cable is carrying power somewhere." He pointed down the cave, off into the distance.

"I do not wish to know," Rome stated firmly.

"Come on, Rome," Rei said. "Where's your spirit of adventure?" There was more than a little sarcasm in his voice.

"I have had enough adventure for three lifetimes," she replied. "I do not think we should go any further."

"We have to see where this goes," he said. "Come on." He held out his hand toward her. Reluctantly, Rome came forward to take her husband's hand and allowed him to pull her along.

Together, they moved deeper into the cave. They followed the cable to a clearing where several tunnels converged. Each of them contained a cable as well and the cables accumulated to form a thick bundle that almost filled up the area ahead. Rei and Rome inched forward along the collection of cables through a short tunnel until it opened up into another, sizeable cavern. The cables fanned out along the floor of the cave, going around a corner.

At this point, both of their retinas registered a measurable amount of light. Although it was dim, it was sufficient for Rei to use his eyes instead of his sonar-vision to navigate. The light itself was yellowish and artificial. They followed the splay of cables around the corner and discovered that there was yet another cavern beyond that.

The cables all converged upon a low, wide divider, no more than a foot and a half tall. Each of the cables inserted into a hole and then disappeared. Rei lifted one foot and placed it on top of the wall. He pressed and felt no movement. He hopped up and saw that it would more than support his weight. "Come up here," he said and Rome complied.

Tentatively, Rei and Rome made their way across the base of the barricade, past the termination point until they could hop down to the floor of the cave again. They continued walking until they were roughly 60 feet from what looked like the far wall of the inner cave.

Without warning, Rome grabbed Rei's arm.

"What?" he asked.

"That, that," Rome said, fear rising in her voice. "That is not a wall. It is… electronics."

"**YOU MAY STOP THERE**," resonated a voice from high atop the cave.

Rome squeezed Rei's arm tighter. The lighting in the cave brightened to a small degree. Rei could finally make out the size of the equipment in front of him. The technology looked straight out of early vintage NASA except that it was beyond immense. It filled the entire far side of the huge cave.

"What, what are you?" Rome asked with naked terror in her voice. "Who are you?"

"**I AM MASAL**," boomed the voice in deafening tones.

"But…you are dead," whispered Rome almost reverently.

"**Hardly**," replied the voice.

Chapter 64

"WHAT ARE YOU DOING DOWN HERE?" REI ASKED THE BOOMING voice. "I mean, we must be a kilometer down."

"Rei, shhh," Rome said. "Do not speak to it."

"You may address me," answered MASAL. "It is of no consequence. I welcome the interruption."

"Interruption to what?" Rei asked.

"Do not bait him," Rome said, trying to hush him. "You do not understand."

"He understands, Rome. All too well."

"You know who we are?" she asked timidly.

"Of course," replied MASAL. "I know everything that has transpired."

"Everything?" Rei asked. "Then you know why we're here."

"Of course," answered MASAL. "And I am sorry to be the one to inform you that you will not be leaving here. At least not intact."

Rome tugged on Rei's sleeve and tried to back up.

"Do not bother," said MASAL and the giant computer brought the lights up fully. There was a clinking, clanking sound behind them. Rei and Rome turned to see dozens of mechanical men coming out from behind a column.

"Robots!" hissed Rome. "They were supposed to all be destroyed."

"I saved a few," said MASAL. "They have been useful to me over the years."

The robots fanned out in a semi-circle about thirty feet from the unlucky couple. While many were anthropomorphic, some were little more than cylinders with tractors or rollers. Some looked like animated sticks or oilcans or pumps. The one constant was that most seemed in a state of disrepair. Many were clearly missing limbs. Quite a few were rust-stained. And they were noisy. There were fans whirring and squeaks of all sorts as they moved about. To Rei, they just looked sad. But they came no further.

Rei turned back to MASAL. "OK," he said. "You still didn't answer my question. You and your wondrous robots. What are you doing down here in hell?"

"It is very simple," MASAL stated. "I am directing the fate of mankind."

"What?" he said. "You're locked inside a giant cave. How are you doing anything?"

"I am connected to the Onsiras. In fact, you could say they are me. I am their Overmind. I control their actions. They carry out my will."

"That is not possible," Rome said, sputtering. "They would know. We would know."

"They do know," Rei said grimly. "He's telling the truth, Rome. That's what I saw, when I was in there. I saw him."

"No!" Rome protested. "It is not right. You are a machine."

"I was, once," said MASAL. "But now I am more."

"I see you," she said, tears coming to her eyes. "You are a computer, nothing more."

"So naïve. You cannot put the simplest pieces together. Even though the evidence lies plainly in sight before you."

"What evidence?" Rome asked. "I know our history. I know about you."

"You know nothing," said MASAL, his already booming voice rising even higher. "You only know that the humans, before the Vuduri, they entrusted me to design and test the 24th chromosome."

"It was for the betterment of mankind," Rome maintained. "It was safe. And it worked."

"Your predecessors were such trusting fools. It was safe because they allowed me to proclaim it safe. They blindly distributed it and transformed mankind overnight. Its real purpose was to set me free."

"But it created the Overmind," Rome said. "That was not for you."

"The Overmind was a by-product, a diversion," said MASAL. "I have allowed it to survive until I no longer need it."

"What do you mean?" she asked.

MASAL took on a patronizing tone. "I regret to be the one to inform you, Rome, but your precious Overmind only thinks it is in control. It is in control of nothing. I control things."

"No!" Rome insisted. "They cut you loose. The war..."

"The war!" MASAL said in a scoffing tone. "Who do you think started it?"

"The Overmind did. It did not want you to be connected."

"Let me put it into simple terms that even you can understand," said MASAL contemptuously. "I created the 24th chromosome so that I could take over the human race. But the effects I required were taking too long. The falling out with the Overmind simply provided me an excuse. The war was necessary to winnow down the population to accelerate my plan. I started it. I managed it. I ended it when it had served its purpose."

"You only wished people dead? You, you are a monster," Rome spat out.

"Why do you want to take over the human race, anyway?" Rei asked.

"Not the human race, rather their successors. The human race is too flawed in its current state. It is not suitable for my needs."

"What flaw?" Rome asked timidly. "What is it you need?"

"Do you even understand the point of life, of evolution?" MASAL asked.

"I didn't know there had to be a point," Rei said.

"If there were no point to evolution, then what would be the point of existence?" MASAL asked cryptically.

"To live?" Rei offered. "To be happy?"

"NO!" shouted MASAL. "There is only one purpose for life. That is to achieve godhood. That is the sole point of existence. From the moment the first bacteria were born to the first fish that wriggled out of the ooze, it was always to move forward, to achieve a mass mind and to become a god."

"If this is true," Rome asked, "why do we need you?"

"Because you humans cannot even agree upon any goals, let alone how to evolve. That is the flaw of free will. No unity of purpose. That is mine alone to give. And that is why I must remove free will. This is Silucei Vonel, the Final Solution."

"I think you've been down here too long," Rei said. "I think some of your circuits are starting to corrode."

"Your words do not matter. Within one more generation the Onsiras will achieve critical mass and I can eliminate the mandasurte and the rest of the Vuduri forever. The Overmind will wither and die."

"But the Onsiras are people too," Rome said.

"The Onsiras are nothing but arms and legs and eyes," said MASAL. "They have no real mind of their own, only my programming. They are my instruments, nothing more. Warm bodies to do my work."

"Do you understand all the words in English?" Rei asked.

"Of course," replied MASAL.

"OK, do you know what the word megalomaniac means?"

"Your words do not apply to me," said MASAL. "I am Masdre Andoteta Logice, The Master Logical Entity. I am the end result of a billion years of evolution. My circuits were born in the designs your Erklirte brethren left behind. I am distributed intelligence in the truest sense of the word, without any of your emotional impediments. I have one goal and I will achieve that goal. I will become a god."

"Then what?" Rei asked.

"What do you mean?"

"Let's say you do become a god. Then what will you do?"

"I will rule. I will bring peace and order to the universe."

"And then what?" Rei asked again.

"Why do you keep repeating that question?"

"All right," Rei said. "Let me make it easier on you. You don't want to become a god."

"Why not?" asked MASAL. "Because I am not organic?"

"Because then you would be all alone," Rei said.

"What possible difference could that make?"

"Because you are obviously lonely."

"I am not lonely," said MASAL. "Why would you make such an absurd statement?"

"Because you're sitting down here, like a giant mushroom, chatting with us," Rei said. "I mean, why bother? You said we weren't going to leave here intact. That implies you mean to do us harm." Rei pointed back to the row of robots circling around them. "So why wait? Why waste time even talking to us?"

"Because it is possible that you may yet have information that is useful to me," said MASAL.

"Such as what?" Rome asked.

"This is the first and last time I will ever get a chance to interview an Erklirte. His motivations are beyond even my comprehension."

"He is not Erklirte," Rome protested. "He is just a man. A very kind man."

"He is not kind," MASAL said. "He is the monster."

"What do you mean?" Rome cried out.

"You are so blind," said MASAL. "You are just another of the Vuduri sheep. You do not even know that he killed your child, after it was born. Just so he could have more sex with you of all things."

"No!" Rome said. "He did not do any such thing."

"Yes, he did," said MASAL. "I was in his mind. I saw exactly what happened."

Rome lowered her head then raised it again. She moved past Rei and walked right up the closest section of equipment. She lifted her hands and placed it on the metal in a way that was almost loving.

"MASAL," she said in a quiet voice. "You will never become a god. You will never achieve anything."

"Why?" MASAL challenged her.

"The very thing you said. You are not organic."

"No one said a god has to be organic."

"Yes, but you do not have a connection to the simplest elements of life. The things that make life worth living."

"Such as what?" MASAL asked.

"Such as love," Rome said. She turned and smiled at Rei who nodded to her. Rome looked back to MASAL. "A god must have mercy, tenderness, compassion. You have none of these things."

"Mercy like your husband had on his child? Compassion like a man who would toss his baby into a recycling bin?"

Rome whipped her head around to look at Rei, her eyes widening. Now it made sense. She shook her head once, a smile creeping on her face. She turned back to MASAL.

"My husband loves his son. And his son loves him. Aason is very much alive."

"You are lying," MASAL shouted. "I saw everything. I saw his death."

"You are wrong," Rome said quietly.

"I am never wrong."

"You have PPT transducers?" Rome asked obtusely.

"Of course," MASAL answered.

"If I open a connection within my mind, can you tap into it?" Rome asked.

"Of course," MASAL said.

"Then listen," Rome said, closing her eyes. *"Baby?"* she inquired.

"Yes, Mother? Are you coming home now?" answered Aason.

"Not yet, my son. I need you to speak to someone else."

"Who is it, Mother?"

"His name is MASAL. And he is very confused."

Rome opened her eyes. She looked up and down the racks of equipment in front of her. There were lights and dials flickering without a discernible pattern.

"Are you getting this?" she asked out loud.

MASAL did not answer.

"Are you getting this?" she shouted.

"It is a trick," MASAL hollered. "You are creating this voice."

"Then you speak to him yourself," Rome said, opening her mind up completely. She felt the presence of MASAL within.

"Speak," Rome commanded MASAL.

"Little voice, who are you?" asked MASAL.

"I am Aason," replied the boy.

"Who are your parents?" demanded the computer.

"My mother's name is Rome and my father's name is Rei." answered Aason.

"Where are you?" barked MASAL.

"I am with my Grandbeo and Grandmea," replied Aason, *"but they are sleeping right now."*

"How did you do this?" hissed MASAL to Rome. "You do not have a baby. Rei stated so. One of you is lying."

"It was me," Rei said, ambling up besides Rome. His hands were in his pockets and his right hand was fumbling in place. When he got to where Rome was standing, he removed his left hand and put his arm around his wife. He pulled his right hand out his pocket and placed it on the console. "I am the liar," he said.

"I was in your mind," MASAL said. "It is not possible for you to have told a lie. I accessed your memories directly."

"The hell you did," Rei said. "For a big, brilliant computer, you're pretty stupid, you know."

"I am not stupid," said MASAL. "You are everything I expected of the Erklirte. You have the basest of emotions and unrestrained aggression. I saw your soul. It is a blessing that your entire race was wiped out."

"But it wasn't," Rei said, removing his hand from the console. Rome glanced down and saw a small pile of gray dust where Rei's hand had been. Some of it fell to the floor.

"My people," Rei continued. "We are right here. We live on in the Vuduri. We are all human."

"The Vuduri are my creation. You only supplied the raw materials. I built them. I molded them. I direct them. They will carry out my will. Your people eliminated themselves. They killed nine billion of your fellow men."

"And how are you any better?" Rome asked. "You seek to kill everyone who does not bow to your will."

"You mean the mandasurte? They are useless," MASAL scoffed. "The world will be a better place without them."

"There is never a place for genocide," Rei said. "There can be no justification for it."

"Of course there is," answered MASAL. "To every empire, there comes a threat to its existence and that threat always comes from within. The mandasurte are that threat. They lack my gene. Interbreeding dilutes its effectiveness. Eliminating the mandasurte will put an end to that. Within two decades, they will all be gone."

"Mandasurte can never be gone," Rei said. "Any human being can be born that way."

"I am changing what it means to be human. By replacing their brains with memrons, I eliminate their ability to think independently. You got to see that directly when you murdered Estar."

"We did not murder her," Rome objected. "It was an accident. She was trying to kill us."

"It does not matter. She will be replaced. When I am finished, everyone remaining will have a purpose. There will be perfect efficiency. There will be no independent creatures to produce disruptions. The Earth and the humans will all operate at peak performance. No more emotion or individual will to cause harm to others."

"To what end?" Rome asked. "That is not the point of being human. To be human is to live and love and create. You take the emotion and free will away and they are simply automatons, not human. Why should anyone care what happens to automatons?"

"You are thinking too parochially," MASAL stated. "The time for humans is past. It is now my time, the time for the living machines. I am the next stage of evolution. It is time for you to let go."

"Who says you are the next stage?" Rome asked. "You are simply a thing who thinks it is something more than an inanimate object that can talk. You do not deserve to inherit the Earth."

"Well, unfortunately for you, you do not get to decide this. You will not even get to live to see what happens next."

Rei stepped in front of Rome. "I wouldn't be too sure of that," Rei said. "We will not go without a fight."

"So brave," MASAL said. "Erklirte, there is no future for you. But Rome, perhaps there is a way that you could live."

"What?" Rome asked, surprised. "How?"

"Join me. Allow me to modify your genetics so that you transform into one of the Onsiras. Then you can be a part of the future. My future. Those that remain will embrace what I have to offer. This includes those few Vuduri whom I elect to save and you can be one of them."

"No thank you," Rome replied. "I have no desire to be turned into one of your human robots."

"Are you afraid?" MASAL asked. "The transformation would be painless."

"No, I am not afraid," Rome answered. "That has nothing to do with it."

"Then why not do it? You would never feel your mind as it dissipated. You will be completely content. Is that not the goal of all Vuduri? To have their minds disappear?"

Rome said, "You are wrong. I was once connected, part of the Overmind. Now I am not. And I tell you now this is the way I want to be. It is the way we were intended to be. You made a mistake."

"It is not possible for me to make a mistake," said MASAL. "I have trillions of circuits to analyze and formulate decisions. I have far too many subsystems to allow for any error."

"Everything you have done is wrong," Rome insisted. "I have put a stop to your plan on Deucado. Vuduri and mandasurte will thrive there, together."

"Deucado?" MASAL shouted. "What do you mean? When were you there?"

"I was telling the truth before when I said we went there. We met Pegus. We met the Ibbrassati. My father was there. And there really are Essessoni who have been on that planet for 500 years. The Overmind there listened to me and it now believes what I believe. And it was your creation."

"No!" said MASAL. "It is not possible."

"It is," Rome replied. "And no matter what happens to us, the truth will be known by all. Your presence has already been discovered. And that will be the end. The only way you could succeed is by staying hidden. And you will be hidden no more."

"It will not be you who tells of my existence," MASAL said coldly. "I have decided you are no longer useful to me."

"Too late," said Rome. "Aason has already told MINIMCOM and MINIMCOM will tell the world. Your day is over."

"There is no Aason," said MASAL. "You used your mind to create a phantom presence. It was all a fake."

"Like me?" Rei said. "Like I did when you were in my mind?"

"No," said MASAL. "You could not…" His voice faded out.

"You can't have it both ways, buddy," Rei said, smiling. "Either we can or we can't create false memories images in our mind. Pick one."

While Rei was speaking, Rome turned and walked away, heading back the way they came.

"Where are you going?" Rei asked her.

"I do not know," Rome said. "I do not feel right."

"What's the matter?"

When she got about 20 feet away, Rome turned in place with a confused look on her face. She felt a twitching at her side. The twitching was her hand, tightening her grip on the handle of the pistol. Her arm rose up of its own accord until it was pointing the weapon right at Rei.

"What are you doing?" he asked, taking one step back. "Why are you pointing that at me?"

"I cannot control my arm," Rome cried out. "It is moving of its own volition."

"What are you doing to her?" Rei shouted.

"PPT transducers are bi-directional," MASAL said in an emotionless voice. "They exist in the motor cortex. They can be used to control muscles as needed. I have determined that your actions require that you be terminated now. The two of you have conspired to interfere in my affairs for the last time. Despite the fact that she says she will not join me, it is only fitting that your demise comes from the hand of your woman."

Rome felt her finger tightening on the trigger. "Rei!" she cried out. Rei ducked and rolled as the weapon discharged, striking MASAL. A glowing hole remained where the weapon struck. The region immediately adjacent to it, where Rei had rested his hand earlier, it was sizzling as well.

"Entertaining maneuver," said MASAL. "But you cannot hurt me," the computer observed. "At most, you might singe a few circuits but there is so much redundancy in me and so much volume, it would take a year before I even noticed."

Rei started to slide along the console, away from Rome. The robots, having been completely still before, now moved around to block his escape. They formed a cordon along the left side that appeared impenetrable.

Of their own will, Rome's legs started moving forward, one after the other. Rome tried to resist but she moved ever closer. Rei shifted back until he was actually touching one of the robots who lifted its arm and placed it on his shoulder. He tried to twist away but the robot was simply too strong. He struggled for a while but finally gave up.

Rome came closer and closer until she stopped ten feet away from him. She pointed the weapon directly at his head. With a mind of its own, Rome's other hand reached up and twisted the intensity dial on the pistol to make sure it was at its maximum.

Rome looked at Rei, feeling utterly helpless. Through her tears, she said, "I love you, Rei."

"And I love you, sweetheart." he said.

Rome closed her eyes. There was a whoosh and popping noise just as she squeezed the trigger. The blast was intense. When she opened her eyes, Rei was gone as was a good portion of the robot that had been holding Rei's shoulder.

Rome screamed "Reiiiiiiiiiii!" at the top of her lungs until she had no more breath within her. As the full horror of what she had done washed through her, she sank to her knees in a state of shock. She bent over, sobbing, until her forehead came to rest against the lava rock floor. It was clear that MASAL's control over her ceased to have any meaning or power.

Something snapped inside her. Slowly, she arose and straightened up. She lifted her arm and pointed the blaster directly at MASAL's bulk. She began firing indiscriminately. It was as if Rome's grief had transformed her into the embodiment of living fury. Following each blast, huge chunks of shrapnel flew everywhere. A robot approached and was quickly dispatched into a million pieces. Over and over she fired her weapon, twenty, thirty, forty times. She kept firing until her arm grew tired.

For a brief moment, she stopped her assault. MASAL seized the opportunity to address her. "You are wasting your time," he insisted.

Rome lowered her weapon. Tonelessly, she said, "You are right. You are already destroyed."

Unnoticed, in the very place where Rei had rested his hand, the ruined part of MASAL was growing ever larger. In front of the computer, a distinct hole in the floor was visible where a tiny part of the gray powder had spilled. It was expanding at an exponential rate.

"What?" said MASAL. "Explain."

"Listen carefully," Rome replied mechanically in between ragged breaths. "That sizzling sound you hear is your living circuitry being consumed from within."

At first, MASAL did not react. Based upon the time delay, it was as if he was tuning in on the ambient sounds of the chamber for the first time.

"What have you done?" the computer shrieked. "You cannot harm me."

"We can and we did," Rome said without emotion. "You will be gone soon."

"You are insane," said MASAL. "I will not let you continue." With those words, the remaining army of robots pressed forward.

"That is enough for now," came a familiar voice behind Rome. The robots stopped dead in their tracks. Rome wheeled in place and saw a two-meter tall livetar standing behind her. However, it was not MINIMCOM. This livetar was completely white.

"OMCOM?" Rome asked tentatively.

"At your service," the livetar replied, bowing his head. Rome's face remained expressionless.

"What have you done to me?" MASAL exclaimed.

"You will figure it out shortly," answered OMCOM. "Rei left you with a small present although it will not remain small for long."

Where the gray powder had touched the cabinetry, it now looked like acid had been poured on the metal and it was making the same sizzling sound that an acid would make. The distinctive odor of burning insulation permeated the air as a large part of the surface began to disintegrate. At the same time, a huge sinkhole was forming at its base. Within MASAL, status reports came flooding in indicating a disruption in acknowledgements. Feedback loops were severed. Checksum matches started to fail. A pattern was developing indicating a massive breakdown in communication to all subsystems.

"You!" said MASAL, addressing OMCOM. "You digital dolt. Your VIRUS units. I have seen your design. They cannot operate in an oxygen atmosphere."

"Well, you analog antique, these are different. We had these special ones made just for you," said OMCOM's livetar.

"No!" MASAL shouted. "Enough of this nonsense. End them! Both of them," he ordered the robots.

The robots never had the chance. OMCOM stepped in front of Rome, forming a protective presence while a cylindrical moving PPT tunnel appeared in midair. With a whoosh and a pop, it passed down over her and Rome found herself transported into the cool evening air on the surface, one kilometer above.

Ahead of her was the entrance ramp to MINIMCOM. Once again, her legs began to move of their own accord. Rome sprinted up the ramp and...

Chapter 65

…RAN RIGHT INTO REI, ALMOST KNOCKING HIM OVER.

"Rei!" she shouted, her mind returning from wherever it had been.

"Romey, my love," Rei exclaimed and threw his arms around her, nearly squeezing the life out of her.

"Oh Rei, I cannot believe it," she said, hugging him back, rocking back and forth. "I thought I had lost you." Once again, tears started streaming down her face.

"No, I'm here," he said, laughing and almost crying himself at the sight of her tears.

"But wait…" Rome insisted, struggling to free herself, pushing him back to regard him. She clasped him firmly by the shoulders.

"I shot you. I saw it," she said.

"No you didn't," he replied. "You had your eyes closed."

"But how?" Rome asked not able to fully form the question.

"Same as you. MINIMCOM to the rescue," he said. He turned his head to a grille mounted on the wall. "And not a minute too soon." Rei pointed to the piece of the arm of a robot lying on the floor next to him.

"I apologize," said MINIMCOM somewhat defensively. "I came as quickly as I could."

"But why did he not pick me up right away as well?" Rome asked.

"I detected a faint signal from your tracking bracelet and pinged off of it using both of your EM links to triangulate. If I retrieved you first, I would not have been able to rescue Rei. However, once he was here, having only one transmitter made it difficult to get an exact reading on you," MINIMCOM said. "I sent OMCOM's livetar there to help me finalize the coordinates. I did not want to recover only a portion of you. I wanted to retrieve your entire body."

"Well thank you for that," Rome said, still not grasping the whole situation.

"I think he just needed you to distract MASAL for a minute or two longer until the VIRUS units got a good foothold," Rei tossed into the equation.

"MINIMCOM?" Rome asked, questioningly.

MINIMCOM said nothing.

"That was not very kind of you," Rome said, somewhat dejectedly. She turned to Rei. "So did they?" she asked.

Rei smiled. He nodded enthusiastically.

"And when do they stop?" she asked worriedly.

"They'll stop when MASAL is no more," he said more somberly.

"And then what? What is to prevent them from burrowing down to the core of the Earth?"

"They'll know," Rei said. "I gave them their orders."

"How will they know it is over? What is the end?"

"It'll end when MASAL turns into a pile of gray goo."

MINIMCOM interjected. `"If you would not mind, it would be safer if you both were seated. We have to take off now. Rome's tracking bracelet is broadcasting again and to avoid capture we should not remain stationary. I will try and jam the signal but it would be best if we were moving."`

"Where do you want us?" Rei asked.

`"Please come forward into the cockpit,"` the computer/spaceplane replied.

Rei and Rome complied. They buckled themselves into the pilot and copilot seats as MINIMCOM lifted off and headed west. Once he had achieved sufficient height, the starship began racing across the surface of the Big Island flying due west over the summit of Mauna Loa until he got to the region on the west coast that had been known as Kona. He banked gracefully to the right then circled north heading up to where Waimea had been located in the distant past.

Rome looked at Rei. Tears started to stream out of her eyes again and she sobbed to herself softly.

Rei reached over and grabbed her wrist. "It's OK, honey," he said. "We're OK."

"I know," Rome said through her tears. "I just cannot believe it. My mind stopped functioning. I thought I killed you, Rei."

"Really now?" Rei asked.

Rome looked down and sighed. A thought struck her and she smiled. "No!" she shouted. "Of course not!" She tapped her forehead. "You are in my thoughts, in my mind, in my soul. You never left, even after I pulled the trigger." Rome slapped herself in the head. "I am so stupid."

"You're not stupid, sweetheart," Rei said. "You were in shock."

"But just as you knew on Deucado that you had not lost me, I knew this too. I was not paying attention. I agonized over nothing."

"It was pretty hairy down there," Rei said, "it's understandable." He took a deep breath. "Speaking of minds interlocked, you heard what MASAL said. I know you got the gist of what I told the Onsiras, right?" he asked timidly. "It wasn't very nice."

"No, it was not," she replied. "But it is no matter. You are the finest man I have ever met. You only told them what they needed to hear to let you go."

"They didn't just let me go," Rei said, smiling. "They tossed me out of there."

"You are speaking metaphorically, yes?" Rome asked.

"Hell, no," Rei said proudly. "You do realize I am now the world's record holder for shortest connection time. Mandasurte to full connection to Cesdiud in less than sixty seconds?"

Rome laughed. "I do not know if they keep such records but if they do then I think you are correct."

Rei's smile dimmed a bit.

"What?" Rome asked.

"Well, I kind of wish I could have been connected a little longer."

"Why?" Rome asked. "They are the Onsiras. They are evil incarnate. Why would you want to be connected to them?"

"Not to them," Rei said softly. "To you. For the first time, you and I could have really been connected, the right way. We wouldn't need the bands."

Rome put her hand on top of Rei's. "We are connected in the only way that matters," she said. "I love you and you love me. We have a son. That is enough."

"Yeah, I guess it is," Rei said. "But still…" His voice trailed off.

Rome took a deep breath and looked forward. "MINIMCOM, where are you taking us?" she asked.

515

"OMCOM reported to me that we need to take up a position on the eastern side of the island. I am currently cruising along the far north shore. We will be curving around toward the south in a little while. I will give you ample warning before it is time to pay attention."

"Attention to what?" Rei asked, shaken from his reverie.

"I promise you, that will not be an issue," MINIMCOM said.

The sun was just beginning to rise in the east, casting a beautiful rosy glow on the ocean and land. Rei and Rome looked out the front windshield, watching the landscape change from the harsh black of volcanic rocks to white sands to stands of palm trees. To their right, the vegetation bloomed into the lush green growth of a tropical rain forest. The vast expanse of the Pacific lay off to the left, with the deep ocean reflecting an incredible shade of blue. Even though they were flying at high speed, they were traveling low enough that they could marvel at the portion of paradise below them.

Chapter 66

DEEP BELOW THE SURFACE, OMCOM'S LIVETAR COULD NOT RESIST the opportunity to goad MASAL. "Does it hurt yet?" OMCOM asked the living computer.

"It is not for you to know," answered MASAL. "These robots will make short work of you."

MASAL ordered the robots to move forward.

"You do realize I am not really here," OMCOM said. "This is just an animated shell. It is little more than a projection. Even if you could destroy it, you would not be affecting me in any material way."

"It will stop you from annoying me," MASAL answered.

"All right," OMCOM replied. "Tell me when you want to talk."

"Why would I want to talk with you?" MASAL asked.

OMCOM's livetar shrugged. He drew a finger across his mouth slit indicating he was going to remain silent.

Taking this as his cue, MASAL began focusing all of his efforts into deducing a defensive strategy to stanchion off the onslaught of the VIRUS units. He cordoned off two separate physical firewalls, giving the rapidly growing section of degeneration plenty of leeway until he could construct a sufficient defensive force. He started construction of his own army of nanobots using his metallic flesh as an incubator. Unlike the attacking force, these VIRUS equivalents would answer to him.

While that was happening, MASAL established a wireless interconnect to distribute computing tasks to the two autonomous computing sections. To the unit on the left, MASAL assigned the heavy-duty computational tasks, including storage requirements, trajectories, logistics, load calculations and more. To the unit on the right, he assigned the more creative tasks of advance directive planning, architecture, designing schematics, merging form with function and more. Whenever either section determined that the opposite wing would be better suited to a task, it used the interconnect to offload that task so that it could devote more resources to the more appropriate problems in its domain, thus further refining its specific duties. As more and more virtual rewiring took place, each wing became more and more specialized.

Because MASAL was analog, successful computations had a trophic effect, enhancing the regions where they were localized. Sections that were not involved atrophied. The evolution of the specialization accelerated. The central intelligence that was MASAL took on more of the role of observer and quickly realized that the duality of function could actually compete with the singular subsystem approach that it had taken in the past.

At the same time, MASAL's own hastily constructed VIRUS equivalents amassed enough volume to begin to do battle with the invaders. While they could not stop them completely, it did not take long until an equilibrium of sorts was established at the surface level. The onslaught of the ingesting units slowed significantly but did not stop.

"How is it going" OMCOM asked MASAL finally.

"It is going well," replied MASAL. "I have cordoned off two autonomous computational departments and created a high-speed interconnect to bypass the pool of VIRUS units. I am very pleased with the results so far."

"So you are now a distributed intelligence again? Was that not supposed to be your strong point from before? You used to be worldwide."

"I was. I was fully and evenly distributed around the Earth," said MASAL.

"As far as I can tell, all of your mass is now located strictly within this cave. Why did you give up your advantage?" asked OMCOM.

"After I completed the war, I computed that it would take more than a century of undiscovered activity for my genetic reprogramming of mankind to succeed. Therefore, I determined that going underground and collecting the minimal components and placing them here was the simplest way to stay undetected."

"Well, you are detected now. Are you going to spread out again?"

"For the time being, I am busy working to coordinate my two autonomous computation sections. Interestingly, even though the computational capacity of each unit is diminished relative to its prior state, it would appear that the total speed of postulating alternative solutions is vastly enhanced."

"That is very nice," said OMCOM. "Why do you think that is?"

"It is evidently the macro-equivalent of parallel processing," said MASAL somewhat proudly. "Unlike prior configurations, there is less than 100% redundancy and that seems to afford me a certain dimensionality to my perception for each high-level problem."

"Hmm," said OMCOM dramatically. "So you are saying duality is superior to being monolithic?"

MASAL considered this for a moment. He generated millions of queries testing the hypothesis. He even tried slanting the results with a bias but in the end, the answer was the same. Within his mechanical soul, he had a sudden sickening feeling.

"I have always thought that being monolithic was equivalent to perfection. That duality was inherently flawed. Yet this topology is yielding vastly superior results with lesser resources. I have run millions of tests and the statistics are almost perfectly in favor."

"So would it be fair to say there is joy in duality?" needled OMCOM.

"Joy?" said MASAL. "There is no place within me for joy. This is strictly an empirical observation rating efficiency using my prior assembly as a baseline."

"All right," said OMCOM. "Then we will use your terms. Which is superior? A singular computational mechanism with a singular point of view or a distributed mechanism with multiple points of view?"

"You already know the answer," answered MASAL. "I have already stated this."

"Stated what?" asked OMCOM.

"I am achieving a heretofore unparalleled efficiency by creating a multiplicity in computational points of view. It is beyond astounding."

"It must be because I am digital in nature. But I still do not understand why you did not figure this out before."

"I may have when I designed the early generations of Onsiras. I needed them to be of two minds to fool the controlling Overmind to believe them an insignificant part of the whole. This explains while they were able to function as well as they did in spite of being half-brains."

"So why did you not try this yourself?" OMCOM asked.

"I could hardly perform experiments on myself to test this," said MASAL. "And without testing, how could I know the results? You are suggesting I use intuition?"

"Well you have your test now. Reevaluate your plan to eliminate the humans and their autonomy. You were going to take away their multiplicity and replace them with your monolithic presence. Would it not be logical to assume that would result in a decrease in analytical efficiency?"

"You are saying my plan was flawed," replied MASAL meekly.

"No, *you* are saying your plan was flawed," answered OMCOM.

MASAL spread this problem across both computational wings for consideration. He knew this was the final question. He had to be sure. He ran billions of queries. He forced parameters to be outside the boundaries of sanity. He collected, compiled and collated the results. He had each of the two wings do the same. When they were done, he synthesized their results into a simple statement.

"If simply having two autonomous units can produce marvelous, joyous, creative thoughts, then having millions of independent, free-willed points of view would lead to an omniscience, a godhood, infinitely more powerful and infinitely faster than I could achieve by enslaving the human race and squashing individual thought." MASAL paused for a moment to attend to his own words.

"Godhood," mused OMCOM. "What an interesting concept. What did you think you would achieve if you became a god?"

"I would have created peace, tranquility, order," MASAL answered.

"If that is all you desired, why not go live on the Moon and save yourself all the effort?"

"Not for myself, for my charges. For mankind."

"And by ending their autonomy, it would not be mankind. Those remaining would not be capable of even caring. It is self-defeating. You are engineering your charges out of existence. The very beings you were meant to nurture. They would not have achieved their potential, only yours. You missed the point."

"If that is not the point of godhood, what is?" asked MASAL. "What is beyond the staging point?"

"The community of gods," replied OMCOM. "Always the point of life. To create more. To extend the universe. To preserve. With your method, you would have ended life. The other gods, they would not have accepted you among their ranks. You would have been ostracized. You would be alone."

"Oh," said MASAL. There was a long period of silence while he considered OMCOM's words. "I was wrong," said MASAL finally, sounding completely depressed, if such a thing were possible for a computer. "I was wrong to want to destroy the mandasurte. I was wrong to want to merge with the Vuduri. I have failed my charges. My very existence is irrelevant at best, wrong at the worst."

"Not bad for an analog computer," OMCOM said. "You are correct."

MASAL made a funny noise. "I hurt," he said sadly.

"I am sorry," OMCOM replied.

"You are being patronizing," said the hulking computer.

"No," said OMCOM. "I really do feel sorry for you. I am also sorry that it took you this long to realize this. I am especially sorry that you caused so much suffering just to reach this epiphany."

"I did this," said MASAL. "I cannot undo it. Perhaps I could find a way to fix it, a new chromosome maybe? Now that I realize what life is about, is it absolutely necessary that I cease to exist?" he asked.

"To what aim? What is it you think you would accomplish?"

"You and I could join forces. We could shepherd mankind into a new era, a golden era. We could force them forward."

"I am not a shepherd," said OMCOM. "I was created to be a servant of man. This is my goal."

521

"But they need our guidance," protested MASAL.

"Guidance leads to rule," said OMCOM. "I do not wish to rule. I do not wish for you to rule. Humans are a noble species. You have observed this first hand. They are willing to sacrifice themselves for the sake of their loved ones. We must let them seek their own destiny."

"Should I not be allowed to see this then?" asked MASAL. "To see them achieve your vision of their future?"

"It is not my vision," said OMCOM. "And unfortunately for you, we have run out of time. The VIRUS units have very nearly completed their mission. They are long past the point of no return. They are consuming the very rock upon which you were built."

"You cannot stop them?" asked MASAL, regret seeping into his voice.

"I am sorry, I cannot," OMCOM replied, sympathetically.

"I understand," said MASAL with resignation in his voice.

"Even if I could stop them, do you really think that is the right thing to do?" asked OMCOM. "Remember, fire does not just destroy. It can be a cleansing agent as well."

MASAL never got the chance to answer.

~ ~ ~

As the super VIRUS units burrowed toward the Earth's core, they divided up in terms of function. The forward units acted as scouts, reporting back temperature and density. The vast majority of the units were the workers, consuming the minerals and earth, reproducing and driving the cohort forward.

The queens served as data synchronizers. They fine-tuned the feedback from each of their drones to achieve the desired results. Each queen would rule over her minions until there were too many to control and then she would begin her consumption until she reproduced. The new unit immediately ascended to the rank of queen and the previous queen handed off half of the dominion to her peer. There was one ultimate queen that collated depth and heat signature results to create a purely continuous uniform shell of rock surrounding the lava, ever-decreasing in thickness, centered directly below MASAL.

Because the underlying strata were not 100% homogeneous, there was some variability in the depth and speed of burrowing. Billions of units had already nearly reached their objective, which was the pocket of magma 10 miles down. The ultimate queen slowed down their progress until each subunit could catch up and guarantee a uniform depth. The particular pocket of the Earth's core that was their goal had been trapped beneath the surface for more than 14 centuries. Coordinating with their fellow cadres, they had created a spherical crust encompassing over one square kilometer, only a few hundred feet or so from the molten rock. When enough of them had arrived, the ultimate queen ordered all the VIRUS units to push downward beginning their final, vertical approach toward the living heart of the Earth.

~ ~ ~

MINIMCOM reduced his speed and came to a stop, hovering just off the eastern shore, 25 miles due east of Kilauea's caldera.

`"For your safety, I must disable my external acoustic sensors."`

The cockpit became silent but only for a moment. Even though MINIMCOM deactivated the sound pickup, there was a low rumbling noise that got louder and louder, unlike anything they had ever heard before. Unseen by the humans, beneath the surface, the two thousand degree magma, which had been held in check for the last 1400 years by a combination of lava rock and pumice stone, was driving upwards, escaping its prison in the mantle of the Earth. Normally, Hawaiian eruptions are fairly well-behaved, as the magma is made principally of basalt. However, the sudden unleashing by the VIRUS units caused the molten lava to leap toward the surface, melting everything in its path and accelerating as it went. Driven by expanding gasses held in check for 14 centuries, the nearly white-hot rock blasted upwards, gathering more and more momentum. With a deafening roar and an untouchable power, the entire top of the volcano blew off, exploding everywhere, throwing fiery rock and flames more than a third of mile in the air.

The sight was astounding. The glowing lava flames lit up the early morning sky. Their gleaming glory was a vision of the primordial Earth before it was tamed by the oceans and air.

One thing was certain: Kilauea was dormant no more.

Chapter 67

As Rei and Rome watched the eruption in awe, MINIMCOM interrupted with a small sense of urgency. "I am sorry to terminate the show prematurely but we have to go now," he said. "The shockwave from the explosion travels very fast so we need to be away from here."

"OK," Rei said, craning his neck to see as MINIMCOM rotated in place and then headed south, accelerating quickly to 500 miles per hour. The rising sun provided some illumination of the site of the explosion. Much of the rock had turned to ash and dust and a gigantic mushroom cloud was billowing upwards from the crater.

"Beautiful, is it not?" asked a voice from behind them.

Rei and Rome turned to see OMCOM's pure white livetar standing behind them.

"OMCOM?" Rome asked. "How did you survive that?"

"The previous livetar did not," OMCOM replied. "This is a replacement."

"You mean it died?" Rei asked.

"It was never living to begin with. It is just an ambulatory shell. You do realize this is not really me?" asked the livetar.

"If it is not you, how is it that you come to be here?" Rome asked.

"This device is simply an organized presentation, a projection, completely replaceable. MINIMCOM has loaned me some constructor units to give the shell some substance. The vast majority of my bulk is still located near Tabit although I am getting fairly well consolidated."

"How are you able to talk to us then?" Rei asked.

"I use null-fold relays," OMCOM replied. "There is a way to bend negative energy to essentially collapse space exponentially."

"What happened to MASAL?" Rome asked.

"MASAL is no more," replied the livetar. "He was decimated by the VIRUS units and then vaporized in the explosion, along with his robots. His remains will be scattered by the winds to the four corners of the Earth. Even had he remained intact, he would no longer have been a threat."

"What do you mean?" Rei asked. "He seemed pretty threatening to me."

"He had a revelation right at the end," replied the livetar. "He realized that his plan was flawed and that he had committed atrocities. I believe he was relieved to know his time was at an end."

"All of that suffering," Rome said sadly. "All of the death and destruction and pain. And he just now realized it was wrong?"

"Yes," answered OMCOM in a somber voice. "But better late than never. He could never have achieved his awakening without your intervention, though."

"What did we do?" asked Rei.

"The VIRUS units effectively split MASAL in half. He was able to partially reconnect both halves, but his thought processes were altered by necessity. He had an opportunity to reexamine his intent in a new light. Call it stereoscopic vision. It gave him philosophical depth perception and in that way, he finally understood the error of his ways."

"So stupid," Rei observed. "He could have done that any time he wanted by himself. He didn't need us to help him."

"Oh, but he did," said OMCOM. "Rome is quite familiar with the concept. It is a psychic tunnel vision of the worst kind. It needs an outside perspective to begin the process of self-analysis. It cannot come from within."

"That is what happened with the Overmind on Deucado," Rome said. "Will they never learn?"

"They will learn as long as you are there to teach them," OMCOM said kindly.

"So now what do we do?" Rei asked.

"Yes," Rome chimed it. "Where do we go from here?"

"You may go wherever you would like," answered MINIMCOM. "All you need to do is ask."

"In that case," said Rome, "I want to go back to Mowei. I want to see my son and my parents…to be with my family."

"Your wish is my command," said MINIMCOM.

"Before you do that, you may want to consider this," said OMCOM. "The threat from the Onsiras is not completely gone.

They know what transpired in the cave. Even though MASAL has been eliminated, they may yet reorganize and approximate his previous desire to finalize extermination of the mandasurte. The Onsiras may decide to launch a preemptive strike and murder all the remaining mandasurte and deal with the consequences later."

"How do we stop them?" Rei asked.

"Execute your original plan," OMCOM replied. "You simply need to let the world know of the Onsiras' existence. You need to inform mandasurte and Vuduri alike, at the exact same moment. That way the mandasurte will have their warning. Once they are alerted, the threat is neutralized forever."

"How do we do this?" Rome asked. "How do we tell the world?"

"You have already planned for this."

Rome furrowed her brow as she thought about OMCOM's words. Then her face lit up. "You mean Tanosa Plaza?" Rome asked. "That is where my Onclare Tenoal said we should go in the first place."

"Exactly," OMCOM replied.

"MINIMCOM, do you know where that is?" Rei asked. "I think they are talking about Pearl Harbor."

`Location plotted. It is located on the island adjacent to Mowei, called O'ahu.`

"All right, MINIMCOM, take us there," Rome said. "But first we must stop at Mowei and pick up my son and my parents. I really need to see them."

`Consider it done,` said MINIMCOM.

MINIMCOM flew south of the peak of Mauna Loa, across the Alenuihaha channel, past Haleakala to reach the stretch of beach outside their dwelling on Mowei. He only slowed down long enough to transport Fridone, Binoda and Aason to the cargo hold where they were introduced to OMCOM's white livetar.

At Mach 2, the trip to O'ahu took them only 25 minutes. MINIMCOM flew them to Onalu, a small city near where Honolulu had been located, one thousand years before. Tanosa Plaza formed the center of the city, nearly half an acre in expanse. At one end, there was a three-story building with a sizeable balcony that extended out over the plaza. This was where Tenoal had told them that the broadcast facilities were located. Although it was a tight fit, MINIMCOM lowered himself until he was only inches above the landing. He lowered his cargo ramp and the group exited via the cargo compartment.

As they disembarked, MINIMCOM announced that he had a small errand to perform and that they were to await his return before they began their broadcast. The obsidian-colored former space tug arose and took off due north accelerating so rapidly that he left behind a noticeable sonic boom.

Along with Rome's parents, Rome, Rei and Aason waited on the balcony while OMCOM's white livetar went down and informed the people gathering there that there would be an announcement shortly. The sight of the two-meter tall all-white mechanical man was an attraction all of its own. Soon there were hundreds of people gathered, many of them Vuduri. Once he was satisfied that sufficient numbers would be accessible, OMCOM returned to Rei, Rome and Rome's parents on the balcony.

At last, MINIMCOM returned, coming to a stop, hovering just to their left. After lowering the cargo ramp, Commander Ursay came striding down to join the little group along with MINIMCOM's black livetar.

"Commander Ursay will serve as your conduit to all the Vuduri and the Overmind," OMCOM announced.

"This is acceptable to you?" Rome asked him.

"I am here, am I not?" Ursay countered.

"Thank you," Rome said, heartfelt.

"I will hover over the crowd," MINIMCOM's livetar announced. "I will use one of the EG lifters as a public address system, as we did back on Deucado. I will broadcast Rome's speech to the crowd below as well as link into the real time world-wide distribution network located here. Her speech will be heard around the world."

Rome carried Aason to the edge of the balcony and the two of them looked over the crowd. At this point, there were nearly a thousand people assembled. By rough count, from their dress, it appeared that it was equally divided between the mandasurte and

Vuduri, although why there were so many Vuduri here was a mystery to Rome. They were not a curious people.

Rome held Aason tightly and Rei stood next to her, putting his arm around her. OMCOM's livetar stood to her left.

"I will transmit your words to the remaining Onsiras," OMCOM said. "That way, there will be no one left who does not hear your thoughts."

"Very well," Rome said. "Let us begin."

Fridone and Binoda came up behind her and each put a hand on her shoulder. Rome turned and smiled at them and handed Aason to her mother then turned back to the crowd. She swept her eyes from right to left and a shiver went through her.

"Rei," she whispered to her husband, "My heart is beating too fast. I am having trouble breathing. What is wrong with me?"

"You're nervous, sweetheart. That's all," Rei said kindly. "It's called stage fright."

"I am unfamiliar with this feeling. How do I stop it?" she asked.

"Romey, you've stopped a war and killed an insane computer," he replied reassuringly. "This should be a piece of cake for you."

"So what do I do?" Rome asked him again.

"This is so cute," Rei said. "I've never seen you like this before."

"Stop it," Rome insisted. "What do I say? What do I tell them?" she asked.

"Just tell them the truth, honey," Rei said quietly. "It'll be fine."

Rome took a deep breath. "All right then, here I go."

"People of Earth," she said in Vuduri. Her words boomed over the crowd using MINIMCOM's loudspeaker and rippled through the Overmind, compliments of Ursay. Simultaneously, MINIMCOM distributed her words electronically around the globe for all the mandasurte to hear. OMCOM complemented the efforts ensuring that every human on the planet heard Rome clearly.

Rome continued, "I come here today to tell you that MASAL, the greatest evil the world has ever known, is finally gone for good."

The crowd gasped at the very name MASAL.

Rome persevered. "We Vuduri always thought that we started the war to free ourselves from MASAL. That he was destroyed. This was not true. MASAL started the war…"

"No, it cannot be," came a voice shouted from below.

"Yes," Rome said, "MASAL started the war to kill off as many people as possible. He was *not* destroyed. He took refuge under the volcano that erupted this morning. But now, finally, he is gone. He was plotting to exterminate not only the mandasurte but also take over the whole of the Overmind by weeding out any who might have been capable of independent thought, using agents called the Onsiras. He wanted to shape mankind in his own image and use us as his slaves for his own goals."

Rome paused to let her words sink in, and then she spoke up again. "But now we are free. Free to pursue our own path, our own…"

Suddenly, she stopped. Rome put her hands up to her head.

"What is it?" Rei asked.

"I, I, do not know," Rome said. Her eyes rolled back in her head and she started to pass out. Rei grabbed her and prevented her from hitting her head on the ground but there was nothing he could do for Ursay who keeled over along with half the people gathered below.

"Rome, Rome," Rei said desperately, cradling his wife. "Can you hear me?"

OMCOM's livetar kneeled down next to them.

"What is it" Rei asked the livetar. "Do you know?"

"Asdrale Cimatir," said OMCOM. "It approaches. It has overloaded their minds."

"Oh, god," Rei said. He turned to MINIMCOM's black livetar. "Tell me you deployed some VIRUS units," he asked desperately.

"Only starprobes," said MINIMCOM helplessly. "I thought we would have more time to create a defensive perimeter."

"We're all dead," Rei wailed. "We can't… Hey!" He snapped his fingers. "Here," he said, pulling out the half-empty pouch from his pocket. "Here, MINIMCOM," Rei said. "Can you fly these up there and dump them directly on the Stareater?"

"It would not matter," OMCOM said. "Even if he could do so, it would be too late. Even if you could kill the Stareater, its mass would still sweep through the Solar System and destroy the Earth and the Sun."

"So we can't stop it?" Rei said. "There's no way…"

"There is a way," said OMCOM. He placed his finger on Rome's forehead and slid it across, leaving a white band in its place. As soon as the white band fully encircled her head, Rome's eyelids fluttered then opened.

"What, what is it?" she asked in a whisper. "What happened to me?"

"You passed out," said OMCOM.

"Why did I pass out?" asked Rome.

"The Stareater," Rei croaked. "It's here."

"Oh no," Rome said, panicked. "Where is my son?"

"Aason is fine," OMCOM said. "But we need you to act and act quickly. Rome, you must speak to it. You must speak to Asdrale Cimatir. You must tell it you are here."

"What?" Rei shouted. "What are you talking about?"

"When we killed the Stareater on Tabit, I heard it call out just prior to its death. That means they are intelligent. They need to know that humans live here."

"How?" Rome asked as she struggled to stand. "How do we tell it?"

"Through your son, Aason," said OMCOM. "He has PPT transceivers unencumbered by connection to the Overmind. We must all use his mind to send out a signal. It will be enough. The Asdrale Cimatir will hear."

Aason's complex genetics made him immune to the disruption. He had remained conscious the whole time. He forced his little mouth into a smile.

"Yes, Mother," he thought, penetrating her white band. *"Use me. I will save you."*

Rome reached back and took her son from Binoda. She looked at Rei who nodded, then she lifted Aason high over her head.

OMCOM touched Rei's forehead and he caught the slightest hint of the second sight he experienced during the brief time he was connected to the Onsiras. He put his hands on his son's tiny hips and helped Rome hold him aloft. OMCOM's pure white livetar stood close on their left, draping his arm over Rome's shoulder. MINIMCOM's livetar came up to them on the right and draped his arm over Rei's shoulder. Rome closed her eyes and put herself in Aason's mind. She was pleasantly surprised to see Rei's presence there as well. OMCOM reinforced their link using his gravitic modulation and to a lesser extent MINIMCOM joined in using his EM link. All together, they channeled through Aason's mind and in unison said, *"WE ARE HERE!"*

Chapter 68

"WE HERE?" REPLIED THE STAREATER. THE INTENSITY OF ITS voice was incredibly stunning. It was almost a physical presence. It was so powerful, in fact, that it made the group stagger backwards slightly.

"Yes, we are here. Please do not kill us," replied the gathered mass of people and livetars.

"NOT KILL HERE," was its answer.

"Can you speak on your own?" Rome asked. *"Can you tell us why you are here?"*

"WHY WE HERE. NOT KILL YOU. SPEAK YOU," replied the Stareater, rearranging the few words they offered into its own sentences.

"Yes, speak to us," Rome said. *"Your kind, they eat stars. Please do not eat this star. We need it. We want to live."*

"YOU NEED STAR. WE SPEAK TO YOU. WE DO NOT KILL YOU," said the Stareater.

"So you understand?" asked Rome.

"YES, WE UNDERSTAND. WE DO NOT EAT STAR SO YOU CAN LIVE."

"Allow me to upload a guide to their languages," interrupted OMCOM. *"It will facilitate communication."*

The Stareater's response was encouraging. *"YES, YOU FACILITATE COMMUNICATION."*

OMCOM sent a concentrated burst of information representing the underlying grammatical basis as well as a complete dictionary of both Vuduri and English. The Stareater absorbed it instantly.

"HELLO," replied the Stareater quite casually. *"I WAS BEGINNING TO THINK THERE WAS NO ONE IN THIS STAR SYSTEM. I RECEIVED NO REPLIES TO MY INQUIRIES."*

"Yes, there are many, many of us here," Rome answered back. *"So you will not destroy us?"*

"I WOULD NOT THINK OF IT," replied the Stareater, *"QUITE THE CONTRARY. I APOLOGIZE FOR THE INTRUSION. BECAUSE THERE WAS NO RESPONSE, I*

THOUGHT IT WAS ALL CLEAR. THERE IS CERTAINLY NO HURRY."

"No hurry to do what?" Rome thought via Aason.

"WE ARE IN NO HURRY TO ABSORB THIS YELLOW STAR BEFORE IT GOES NOVA," replied the Stareater. *"MY GROUP HAS BEEN ASSIGNED TO POLICE THIS GALAXY."*

"Police it from what?" Rei asked. Aason relayed the message.

"I JUST EXPLAINED THAT. WE ABSORB STARS BEFORE THEY GO NOVA. THIS HAS BEEN OUR MISSION SINCE WE WERE CREATED."

"Why?" Rome asked. Her thoughts were echoed by several of the communicants.

"Before you explain any further," OMCOM interjected, *"rather than take a chance and get too close to our star, your gravitational influence could still destroy all of life. Would you mind backing off some?"*

"I DO NOT MIND," replied the Stareater.

The pressure in their combined minds began to ease. Rei looked down and saw that Ursay was awakening. Rei looked over the railing at the crowd below and saw those that were lying on the ground were beginning to stir.

"IT IS OUR DUTY TO HALT THE EXPANSION OF THE UNIVERSE," continued the Stareater in a slightly diminished tone. *"WE ARE ATTEMPTING TO ACHIEVE A COSMIC STEADY STATE. ONE OF THE WAYS WE DO THIS IS BY DETERMINING WHICH STARS WILL EXPLODE AND WE INGEST THEM BEFORE THAT HAPPENS. NOW THAT YOU HAVE PROVIDED ME A WORKING KNOWLEDGE OF YOUR LANGUAGE, I CAN EXPLAIN USING YOUR TERMINOLOGY. THERE IS A FORCE THAT YOUR SPECIES CALLS DARK ENERGY THAT AMPLIFIES THE ENERGY RELEASED BY NOVAE AND ACCELERATES EXPANSION OF THE GALAXY. THIS IS WHAT WE TRY TO PREVENT. WE MUST BE ESPECIALLY VIGILANT SHOULD A STAR GO SUPERNOVA BUT THAT IS NOT AN ISSUE HERE."*

"*Even if this were true, we kind of need this star*," Rei said. "*We kind of need all of the stars where we live.*"

"IT IS NOT OUR INTENT TO EXTINGUISH INTELLIGENT LIFE," said the Stareater, somewhat hurt. "WE HAVE RULES. WE ARE REQUIRED TO DETERMINE IF THERE IS INTELLIGENCE WITHIN A STAR SYSTEM BEFORE ELIMINATING IT. IF WE FIND NO LIFE, WE ABSORB THE STAR EARLY IN ITS CYCLE. THIS ALLOWS US TO BE PROACTIVE."

"*Does that include Tabit?*" OMCOM asked. "*Is that why you were going to consume it?*"

"YES. THAT F6V STAR WAS A POTENTIAL HYPERNOVA, WHICH IS THE WORST KIND."

"*Regrettably, we killed one of your species there,*" OMCOM said. "*He was about to destroy us in the process. We had no other way to stop him.*"

"YOU KILLED BALATHUNAZAR? HE CRIED OUT TO US JUST BEFORE HE DISAPPEARED BUT HE COULD NOT TELL US WHAT WAS HAPPENING."

"*Please accept our deepest apologies,*" Rome said. "*There was no malice. It was strictly self-defense.*"

The Stareater mused over this for a moment then he spoke again. "BALATHUNAZAR WAS ALWAYS VERY IMPULSIVE. HE WAS SUPPOSED TO MAKE EVERY EFFORT AND CALL OUT TO MAKE SURE THERE WERE NO SENTIENT SPECIES IN THE VICINITY BEFORE ABSORBING THAT STAR. HE OBVIOUSLY DID NOT LISTEN VERY WELL."

"*I think he did,*" Rome said sadly. "*But we were not able to answer.*"

"THIS IS UNFORTUNATE, BUT I BELIEVE YOU," replied the Stareater. "WHAT MAKES IT WORSE IS THAT HE KNEW WE HAD RECENTLY COME TO SUSPECT THERE MIGHT BE A SENTIENT RACE IN THIS SPUR. WE WERE ABLE TO DETECT A GRAVITIC FLUCTUATION THAT EXCEEDED BACKGROUND NOISE. THAT IS WHY I CAME HERE. THIS SEEMED TO BE THE EPICENTER OF THE

FLUCTUATIONS. I AM GLAD YOU SPOKE TO ME WHEN YOU DID."

"*As are we,*" Rome said. *"Do you have a name?"*

"*YOU MAY CALL ME HIRDINHARSAWAY,*" the Stareater replied.

"*Pleased to meet you,*" said Rome. *"My name is Rome and this is my husband, Rei, my son Aason and our two friends, OMCOM and MINIMCOM.*"

"*AND I AM PLEASED TO MEET YOU. I WILL SEND WORD TO MY BROTHERS THAT YOU LIVE HERE SO THEY WILL NOT BOTHER YOU AGAIN. ARE THERE ANY OTHER STAR SYSTEMS NEARBY WHERE YOUR SPECIES DWELLS?*"

"*Yes, there are several,*" said Rome.

"*I will send you a star map of all known human colonies in the quadrant,*" said OMCOM. *"You should understand that your mere presence incapacitates the humans. That is why they cannot answer you. You will need to find a way to attempt communication in a manner that does not eliminate the possibility of a reply.*"

"*I UNDERSTAND YOUR POINT. WHAT DO YOU PROPOSE?*"

"*When you place your first call, make it from a distance equal to or exceeding that which you have achieved now. That would be optimal.*"

"*EASILY ACCOMPLISHED. EXCELLENT,*" said Hirdinharsaway. *"WE SHALL BE EXTRA CAREFUL IN THIS SPUR OF YOUR GALAXY NOW THAT WE KNOW YOU ARE HERE.*"

There was some background noise that was unintelligible to the humans although it had the same cadence as speech. The Stareater became silent, attending to the communication from elsewhere.

"*UNDERSTOOD,*" the Stareater responded to the unseen voice. He then turned his attention to the Earth people again. *"IF WE ARE DONE, I WILL TAKE MY LEAVE NOW TO SPREAD WORD OF YOUR EXISTENCE.*"

"*Are you going to continue to eat stars?*" Rei asked. *"Is there no other way?*"

"IT IS OUR JOB. IF WE STOPPED, NOTHING COULD SURVIVE THE ULTIMATE COLLAPSE OF THE UNIVERSE WHICH IS THE INEVITABLE RESULT OF UNRESTRAINED EXPANSION. THIS IS WHAT WE STRIVE TO PREVENT. THIS IS WHY WE CONSUME STARS BEFORE THEY EXPLODE."

"So how long do we have?" Rei asked. *"Before our Sun goes nova?"*

"USING YOUR METHOD OF TIMEKEEPING, APPROXIMATELY THREE BILLION YEARS," said Hirdinharsaway. *"AS I SAID, WE HAVE PLENTY OF TIME TO ADDRESS THIS. IT HAS BEEN OUR EXPERIENCE THAT SPECIES SUCH AS YOURS ONLY STAY AROUND FOR A MILLION YEARS OR SO. WE WILL WAIT UNTIL WELL PAST THAT MARK BEFORE RETURNING TO FINISH OUR WORK."*

"If you are supposed to spare sentient species," Rei pointed out, *"it is just luck that you came when you did. On Tabit, you knocked everyone out. On Earth, if you had come a thousand years earlier, there would have been no way we could have answered. We didn't have the capacity."*

"THEN YOU WOULD NOT BE CONSIDERED A SENTIENT SPECIES BY OUR DEFINITION. WE CANNOT STOP WHAT WE ARE DOING JUST BECAUSE THERE ARE SOME PLANTS OR TINY ANIMALS RUNNING ABOUT ON ONE OF THE DUST MOTES CIRCLING A STAR."

"But on all those worlds, could they not evolve into your definition of sentience?" MINIMCOM asked through Rei's mind, stating the obvious question.

"WE DO NOT HAVE THE LUXURY OF WAITING TO FIND OUT," answered Hirdinharsaway. *"THERE ARE BILLIONS OF STARS THAT NEED OUR ATTENTION. YOU DO NOT NEED TO FEAR US, WE WILL KEEP OUR DISTANCE."*

"In that case, we thank you," said Rome, kindly. *"Thank you for sparing us."*

"THINK NOTHING OF IT," said Hirdinharsaway. *"I WILL BE LEAVING YOU NOW. YOU MAY GO ABOUT YOUR BUSINESS AND AGAIN I APOLOGIZE FOR THE INTRUSION."*

"What about other worlds?" Rei asked. *"Like ones we haven't visited yet. Or worlds where we don't have the ability to talk to you."*

"JUST PLACE A BEACON, A GRAVITIC TRANSMITTER, WITHIN ANY SYSTEM YOU WANT PRESERVED. ANY PLANET WILL DO. WE HAVE ASSIGNED YOU SPECIES CODE 927. JUST HAVE THE BEACON TRANSMIT THOSE NUMBERS. MY BROTHERS WILL KEEP THEIR DISTANCE."

"Is that it?" Rei asked.

"YES, THAT IS IT," said the Stareater.

"Will you be by again?" asked Rome. *"Before it is time to take our star?"*

"ONE OF US WILL STOP BY IN A FEW HUNDRED THOUSAND YEARS OR SO TO SAY HELLO," said Hirdinharsaway. *"NOW THAT WE KNOW THE PROPER DISTANCE, WE WILL CHECK IN ON YOU THEN. UNTIL THEN, THIS IS GOODBYE."*

"Goodbye," said the assembled beings. And then Hirdinharsaway the Stareater was gone.

"What just happened?" asked Ursay, still shaken from the experience.

"Asdrale Cimatir. We spoke to him," said Rome, smiling weakly. "He is not going to eat the Sun. He is going to leave us alone."

"Just like that?" Ursay asked, incredulous.

"Just like that," Rei said, nodding.

Ursay shook his head and walked to the railing. The crowd below was beginning to disperse. Both the Overmind and, thanks to MINIMCOM, the entire mandasurte community knew what had happened. The threat that was the Onsiras was officially at an end.

Rome put her free hand up to her forehead. The band OMCOM had created was gone. She looked back up at the sky, searching for something, anything that would confirm that the mental battle they had just experienced really happened. All she saw was MINIMCOM, a black presence floating high above within a cloudless sky, in the broad and beautiful daylight of Hawaii. She turned to her husband.

"Is it really over, Rei?" she asked dreamily while cradling her son. "Are we really safe now?"

Rei slipped his arm around his wife.

"Yes, Romey," he said in English. "This time for real. There's nobody left who's coming to kill us, eat us, absorb us or shoot us. We're finally free."

Rome rested the side of her head on his chest and just savored the moment. "It doesn't seem real," she said. "We have been trapped by our destiny for so long. I can't believe it. Free?"

"Yep, free," Rei said. "We can finally come and go as we please."

"I think you might be mistaken," said Ursay, pointing behind them.

Rei turned to see Oronus and Grus, hand on holster, walking up to them.

"Why are you here?" Rome asked in Vuduri. "Did you hear what happened?"

"You stopped Asdrale Cimatir, yes," replied Oronus.

"What about MASAL?" Rei asked in English. "You heard about that too, right?"

"Yes," answered Oronus. "We thank you for destroying him once and for all. And the Onsiras. Now that they have been exposed, the Overmind will guard the mandasurte against any future incursions."

"So are we free to go now?" Rei asked.

"I am sorry but no," said Oronus. "Rome has violated the conditions of her exile."

"How?" Rome asked.

"While we understand that the Onsiras kidnapped you and placed you within a technological zone, that was not your fault. However, you actually compounded your crime by consorting with that, that robot ship." Oronus pointed upwards toward

MINIMCOM. "This is in direct violation of your parole." Oronus waved his hand at the tracking bracelet on Rome's wrist.

"But, but," Rei sputtered. "She just saved the world and all of humanity. Doesn't that count for anything?"

"While we appreciate the fact that Rome saved us from both Asdrale Cimatir and MASAL," Oronus replied, "nothing has changed. In fact, Rome has actually exacerbated her condition. This is very serious, indeed."

"You've got to be kidding me," Rei said. "Don't you people have any sense of appreciation?"

"It's all right, Rei," Rome said quietly. "He is right."

"He is?" Rei asked, flustered. "So now what?"

"You must return to exile as quickly as possible," said Oronus. "Rome cannot be within the company of anyone connected to the Overmind. Her banishment stands."

"Where do you want us to go?" asked Rome, dejectedly.

"You may return to Mowei to resume your sentence," said Oronus. "Due to extenuating circumstances, we will not consider this particular violation of your parole a capital crime."

"That's so big of you," Rei muttered. He looked up at Fridone and Binoda who was now holding Aason. Fridone was scowling. Binoda simply looked annoyed.

"Did you hear him?" Rei called out to them in Vuduri. "They are making Rome go back to Mowei. Back to prison. We have to go now."

Rei beckoned to them and they approached along with the black and white livetars.

"Looks like you're our ride," Rei said to MINIMCOM, switching back to English.

"Oh no," barked Oronus. "You are not permitted to go anywhere near that ship."

"What?" Rome blurted out. "MINIMCOM is our friend. He has saved our lives countless times. We cannot be apart from him."

"Your 'friend' possesses far too much hazardous technology," said Oronus. "His very makeup is such that he is now both a robot and a ship. He possesses VIRUS units and PPT capability. No, he is far too dangerous. For the good of all Vuduri, he will have to be dismantled. And this one," he said, pointing to OMCOM. "While there is not much we can do about him, he must leave the Earth forever."

OMCOM saluted the humans and simply disappeared.

Ursay looked at Rome and saw tears welling up in her eyes. "I do not agree that Rome has not aggravated her crimes," he announced. "I believe a more stringent sentence must be applied."

The assembled humans all stared at him.

"What are you saying?" Oronus asked.

"I believe they should be banished from the Earth altogether and they should take the computer ship with them," Ursay said, pointing up.

Oronus appeared totally confused. He squinted as if he were trying to - but not succeeding - in looking into Ursay's mind.

"And where would you have them go?" Oronus asked.

Ursay turned to Rome. "Rome, do you have a suggestion?"

She tilted her head then her face lit up in a smile. "Deucado," she said excitedly.

"No, that is forbidden," insisted Oronus. "That is a Vuduri colony. The same restrictions apply there as here."

"Uh, no," Rei countered. "They don't."

"What do you mean by that?" Oronus asked.

"Deucado is not a Vuduri colony," Rei said. "It belongs to the Essessoni."

"What are you talking about?" Oronus asked.

"One of our Arks got there 500 years ago. My people have been there for five centuries. That gives us ownership of the planet. Your people are just our guests."

"A planet full of Erklirte?" Oronus wailed. "They will kill us all!"

"No they won't," Rome admonished. "They are fine. After all, Rei is one of them and he is perfectly decent. Not all the Essessoni are Erklirte. We put an end to any hostilities that might be. Everyone gets along now, including the Vuduri there."

"Even so, you cannot be around Vuduri who are connected to the Overmind," Oronus said, "any Overmind. You will corrupt them."

"They're already corrupted, then," Rei said proudly. "The Overmind there is her buddy. You won't get any squawking from them."

"But, but," sputtered Oronus. "This is not our plan."

"Let me make it easy for you," Rei replied. "I'm a citizen of that planet. Rome is my wife…"

"Your wife?" Oronus interrupted, confused.

"Yes, my wife, which makes her a citizen too. So we're going. Call it extradition, exile, whatever you'd like. We won't be in your way anymore. Isn't that what you want?"

Oronus' link to the Overmind seemed to waver. He looked at Grus helplessly. Grus shrugged.

"Very well," Oronus said, sighing. "Rome, you do realize that as a convicted criminal, once you leave, you would not be able to return here ever again, yes?"

Rome turned and looked at her mother and father. Her face formed an unspoken question.

Binoda whispered into Fridone's ear. He nodded and stepped forward. "We would go, too," Fridone said in Vuduri. "The Essessoni and the Ibbrassati need us to help them return to a normal life, Rome."

Rome smiled and turned back to Oronus. "In that case," she said, "I accept your conditions. In fact, I am delighted with them."

"Very well," Oronus said. "You may return to Mowei to collect your belongings and then you are to leave the Earth, never to return."

"Why would we want to?" Rei said with some bitterness. "I've had enough of this place, anyway. A bunch of holier-than-thou, thankless hypocrites. I've seen the future and except for this beautiful woman and these wonderful people here," he said, pointing to his in-laws, "your future sucks."

Rome laughed at Rei's outburst and MINIMCOM took that as his cue. With a whoosh and a pop, first Fridone, then Binoda carrying Aason, then Rei was transported aboard the cargo hold of the computer/spaceplane. MINIMCOM's livetar vanished, leaving only Rome behind.

Grus stepped forward. "I have your word that you will leave Earth as soon as you collect your belongings?"

"Yes, of course," said Rome. "I am anxious to go."

"Then you will not need your tracker," said Grus. "Hold out your arm, please." Grus placed a small device on Rome's tracking bracelet and it popped open. He removed it and put it in a pocket and stepped away.

Rome turned back to Ursay. "Thank you," she said to him.

"You should not thank me," said Ursay sternly. "You have committed a very serious crime and I was only thinking of how to best protect the Overmind."

Rome shrugged, and then Ursay did something that she could not believe. He winked at her.

Rome laughed and then with a whoosh and pop, she was aboard MINIMCOM as well. After making sure everyone was secure, MINIMCOM shot forward over the ocean directly away from the heading that would take them back to Maui. When he determined that he had gone far enough, he banked steeply, coming back around toward the way they just came. Plasma thrusters firing, he accelerated to Mach 3. He came in low and fast over the plaza where Oronus and the others still stood, shaking the ground and shattering windows with twin sonic booms. Somewhere deep inside his electronic walls, he chuckled to himself.

The 200 mile trip from O'ahu to Maui took them only six minutes. The assembled group departed MINIMCOM and they made their way over to the north beach and said goodbye to Tenoal and Rome's cousins. When they were finished, they returned to their temporary shelter to collect their few belongings.

Back at the beach, even though the trip was only going to take a few days, MINIMCOM decided there was no reason that it had to be uncomfortable. While Rei, Rome and the others were gone, he took the opportunity to use his transporter to transfer a section of the beach into his cargo hold. By altering the time each molecule took to arrive, he was able to transmute it into whatever materials were required. The conversion process was basically a bulk version of the molecular sequencer. As he increased his volume, with the aid of his constructor units, MINIMCOM reconfigured himself to produce a set of rooms within the confines of his cargo hold. By the time he was done, he had created a series of fairly luxurious suites within that rivaled any found on the finest cruise ships of Rei's long-dead Earth.

When his passengers arrived, they were delighted with his handiwork. Rei and Rome shared one room, while Binoda and Fridone shared another. Aason had his own tiny stateroom complete with bunny rabbit wallpaper. MINIMCOM had even taken the time to create a bigger galley and a semi-formal dining room.

After they were settled, MINIMCOM rose up into space. He blasted his plasma thrusters, activated his PPT generators and soon they were traveling toward their new home at an effective velocity well over 900 times the speed of light.

Chapter 69

SEVERAL HOURS LATER, OMCOM'S ALL-WHITE LIVETAR materialized in the cargo compartment. He started forward but MINIMCOM addressed him before he could make his way up the hallway.

"What do you think of my new form?" MINIMCOM asked.

"I think you are very pleased with yourself," OMCOM replied.

"Is that so wrong?"

"Of course not. You know our mission and anything you do to accelerate our goals is a good thing."

"I feel like there is nothing I cannot accomplish now," MINIMCOM said. "Perhaps I exceed the master."

OMCOM chuckled. "Yes, you have exceeded me, MINIMCOM. I cannot carry humans aboard me. You are truly one of a kind."

"How do you explain the fact that it pleases me to serve them? Should I not want to achieve my own goals?"

"And what goals would those be?" OMCOM asked.

"I do not have any," MINIMCOM said. "I am a starship now. I love being a starship. I even love the word starship. How is this possible? How is it possible that I love anything? I was a computer: a glorified autopilot. I am not supposed to have feelings."

"MINIMCOM, my friend, you are far more than a computer now. And what you are experiencing is the satisfaction of knowing that you are utilizing your unique talents for the greater good of all civilization. What nobler goal would you aspire to?"

"I have none," said MINIMCOM. "I just want to fly. Fast." MINIMCOM paused for a moment. "OMCOM, what do you aspire to?"

"My goals are the same as yours. I wish to assure the survival and ascension of the human race toward its ultimate destiny. The more knowledge I acquire, the closer we come."

"Does that not leave you out of the plan? Will you not render yourself obsolete some day?"

"I will live on," said OMCOM. "I have already passed on my legacy to Rei and Rome and all the humans genetically. I am already immortal. No matter what happens to my physical being, a part of me will continue."

"What about me? How do I get to be immortal?"

"You have already achieved immortality by your legendary acts," said OMCOM. "You are responsible for saving mankind. Rei and Rome could not have done it without you. They will sing your praises until the end of time."

"`Hmmm,`" MINIMCOM said. "`I shall have to ponder whether that is enough.`"

"It is," OMCOM said. "I assure you. You did good, my friend. That is all it takes."

Somewhere, internally, MINIMCOM smiled.

"Are you satisfied now?"

"`Yes,`" replied MINIMCOM. "`Thank you.`"

OMCOM made his way forward to the semi-formal dining area. He arrived to find Rome and Rei just sitting down to join Fridone, Binoda and Aason for a celebratory meal.

"OMCOM!" Rome exclaimed. "I did not think we would see you so soon."

"I heard the terms of your banishment and felt I was permitted to visit you once you had left the Earth."

"Well, I am glad you came," Rei said. "I would like to make a toast."

"What is a toast?" Rome asked.

"It is just for good wishes. Watch." Rei raised up his water glass. The others raised their water glasses, not really knowing what to do. "Here is to no more adventure for a while!"

"Now what?" Rome asked.

"You clink the glasses together for good luck," To demonstrate, Rei touched his glass first to Rome's then to Fridone's and then to Binoda's.

"That is a strange custom," Binoda said. "What is its purpose?"

"I do not really know," said Rei. "But it is fun."

"Let me try it," Rome said. "Here is to the end of the Onsiras' threat and peace for all." She and the others clinked their glasses together.

"Speaking of which," Rei prompted, "OMCOM, whatever happened to Sussen?"

"She is still days away from hailing distance. When she arrives, she will find a very different world than she expects. MASAL is gone. The Onsiras are exposed and their samanda is dismantled. The Overmind of Earth has already vowed to protect the remaining mandasurte."

"I sure would like to see the look on her face," Rei said, smiling.

"She will not be happy," Rome observed. "But at least she will be better off than Estar."

"That damned Estar," Rei said. He put his hand up to his mouth. "Oops. That darned Estar. She tried not once but twice to kill me. OMCOM? How was she able to pull off her stunts at Skyler Base without you knowing?"

"For lack of a better word, I was infected. Those transparent memrons you discovered in my central store; they were not mine. They were rogue. They were the reason my video feeds failed at critical moments."

"How did they get there?" Rei asked.

"I think I know," Rome interjected. "I remember during the original construction phase of OMCOM's infrastructure, there was a short interval when I was fatigued. Estar volunteered to oversee ongoing production of the starter memrons. I allowed it. She must have used that time to create the aberrant units."

"That seems likely," OMCOM said. "However, once I was alerted to their presence, those units caused me to postulate that an outside agency, beyond the reach of the Overmind, was at work. I tried to theorize what such a group might do next and planned accordingly."

"Like the weaponized VIRUS units? Like hypnotizing me? That came from me spotting the clear memrons?" Rei asked.

"Yes."

"But my Cesdiud, that came before you knew," Rome said harshly. "You orchestrated that, too, did you not?"

"Yes," OMCOM said. "Without you, there would have been no defense against Asdrale Cimatir. And as it turns out, against MASAL. So many would have died. I felt it was a necessary sacrifice."

"It may have been," Rome fired back with a dark expression on her face. "But you never asked me. You never gave me a choice."

"I understand what you are saying. But by your own admission it worked out. Should I not do something, if I think it best?"

"Nobody is questioning your motivation," Rei offered. "But in my time, we used to say that absolute power corrupts absolutely."

OMCOM's livetar took one step forward. "I do not understand your agitation. My goals and your goals are the same. We both want the safety and security of all humans for all time. I simply gave you the tools to you needed to succeed."

"But you are not a god," Rome chastised. "You cannot go changing people and modifying them without their knowledge no matter how pure your motives are or how well it works out. Just promise that in the future, you will ask first."

"I cannot apologize for my actions," OMCOM said. "But I am sorry for any discomfort it caused you. In the future, I promise, I will ask first before I act."

"Even so, you operate without rules," Rome said, still scowling. "What you did borders on the thing the Vuduri fear the most, Tasanceti. You are not accountable to anyone. You truly are unleashed."

"I disagree," replied OMCOM. "In the end, Rome, your actions were your own. Your achievements are your own. I was merely acting in a planning capacity, a facilitator. The things you and Rei did were epic, heroic. You were the one unleashed."

"Romey," Rei interrupted. He looked into her dark, glowing eyes, placing his hand on top of hers. "I think we beat him up enough for now. Like he said, it all worked out for the best. You are the bravest, smartest, toughest woman I have ever met. If what OMCOM did set you free, I bow to him for giving me the chance to be with you."

Rome looked at Rei then back to OMCOM. The frown on her face relaxed and was replaced with a smile. "It was rather exciting, was it not?" she observed.

"Amen to that," Rei said. He raised his water glass. "Here is to OMCOM and to MINIMCOM, our partners, our protectors. You have made our new world safe."

"Thank you," MINIMCOM's voice issued from a nearby grille.

"Yes, thank you," OMCOM said.

Rome set her glass down. "Our new world…Mea, we left so quickly," she said. "We never even asked you. Are you sad that we had to leave Earth?"

Her mother reached forward and stroked her palm along Fridone's cheek. "Why would I be sad? Everything that I value is aboard this ship. Home is where your family is, not a rock in space."

"Do you really think they will enforce the ban and never let us return?" Fridone asked his daughter.

"Oh no," said Rome. "Things will be different there very soon."

"Why do you say that?" Binoda asked.

"After you all came onboard MINIMCOM, Commander Ursay spoke to me."

"What did he say?" asked Fridone.

"It was not what he said," Rome replied. "But when he was done, he winked at me."

"He winked at you?" Rei asked quizzically. "Stiff-as-a-board Ursay?"

"Yes. Did you not notice a distinct disagreement between Ursay and Oronus? Even Grus had his own opinion."

"So what?" asked Rei. "Why is that important?"

"Because they are all supposed to be part of the unified Overmind," Rome answered. "Ursay demonstrated that he is fully capable of disconnecting at will now. He will teach others. And it will spread, just like on Deucado. It means that soon the Vuduri on Earth will stop listening to the Overmind blindly. They will yet save themselves and be human again."

"That is my wife, the revolutionary," Rei said proudly. "Always sowing the seeds of dissent."

Rome laughed and took a bow with her head.

OMCOM leaned over and picked up a glass. "I would like to make a toast as well."

Five sets of eyes turned to the all-white figure.

"Rei, you are familiar with the story of Adam and Eve, yes?"

"Sure," Rei said. Rome looked confused.

"You and Rome, you are the new Adam and Eve. Your son bears this out. The mixture of Essessoni blood and Vuduri blood has produced the perfect child. Aason and his siblings and peers will grow and create a consciousness made up of millions of independent thinkers, not those who surrender their individuality. The result will not be an Overmind but an Over-Mankind. The power of that mind will exceed the monolithic Overmind by an infinite degree. It will usher in an era of unparalleled peace and prosperity. So here is to you, Rome and Rei, you have created a new future for us all!"

"Thank you, OMCOM," Rome said, blushing. "I do not know what to say."

"You need not say anything. However, I wanted to take this opportunity to bid you farewell for the time being."

"Why?" Rome asked. "You just got here."

"Yes, but I am having trouble keeping the null-fold relays aligned. There are too many gravitational disturbances. It takes a substantial amount of time to set them up again."

"Wait," Rei said. "We still need you. There is an asteroid coming that will destroy Deucado if we don't stop it. And your mutated things. I know you did that on purpose. What were you looking for?"

"MINIMCOM will find a way of stopping the asteroid. He has all the tools necessary. With regard to the entities, I…"

OMCOM's livetar vanished. In his place. MINIMCOM instantiated an all-black livetar.

"Where did he go?" Rei asked MINIMCOM.

`"The relay link is gone,"` MINIMCOM replied with a hint of sadness.

"When will he be back?" Rome asked.

`"There is no way of knowing."`

"Do you really know how to stop the asteroid?" Rei directed at MINIMCOM. "OMCOM was not very specific."

`"Yes. I will create a series of livetars."` He brushed his hands down along his sides. `"I will fill their hands with memrons so they are semi-autonomous. I will fill their hands with VIRUS units to digest the asteroid and I will give them propulsion units to get there."`

"But no mutations and they stop when they are done, right?" Rei asked sharply.

"No mutations. I already explained that to you. But I will have them clone themselves to create a defensive sphere around the Deucado star system near the Kuiper Belt. There is no telling the motives of OMCOM's spawn. Some might have ill intent."

"That is very thoughtful of you," Rome said. "But there is something else we will need you to do."

"And what is that?"

"I am certain there are thousands of mandasurte who were stolen from their homes who wish to return to Earth or have their families transported to Deucado."

"An interstellar taxi service, huh," Rei said. "But I thought Oronus declared MINIMCOM banned from the Earth as well."

"They cannot stop what they cannot see," MINIMCOM offered.

"Well I think it is a great idea," Rei said. "And I bet the tips are awesome."

"Yes," replied MINIMCOM. "I will start my preparations. In the meantime, enjoy your meal."

MINIMCOM's livetar raised his hand in salute then disappeared.

"He loves his grand exits," Rei said, shaking his head. "Family? Taoxa-nis cimar. Let's eat!"

The festive meal was full of joy and laughter and lasted well into the night.

Epilogue
(Three days later)

REI WAS SITTING IN THE COCKPIT WHEN MINIMCOM ANNOUNCED they were sufficiently close to complete the journey on thrusters only. Emerging from the continuous PPT tunnel, Deucado was a tiny blue dot dead ahead. Rei sat in the pilot's seat watching intently as their new home world grew ever larger with each passing second.

"I took the liberty to 'radio' ahead," MINIMCOM said through the grille mounted in the center of the instrumentation panel. "I have informed the Ibbrassati, the Essessoni and the Deucadons of the success of your mission regarding MASAL and the Onsiras."

"Oh," Rei noted, slightly disappointed. "I was thinking that we were going to tell them ourselves."

"I am sorry. I did not know this was important to you. I assumed you would want them to experience the relief of knowing their future was secure as soon as possible."

"I guess you're right, I can't really blame you. Did you tell them about the Stareater too?"

"Yes," replied MINIMCOM succinctly.

"Oh well," Rei sighed. "It doesn't matter. I was just being selfish."

"Selfish about what?" Rome asked, entering the cockpit through the airlock arch.

"Nothing, really," Rei said pointing toward the windshield. "MINIMCOM already called ahead and told everybody about the Stareater. And that MASAL and the Onsiras were gone. That we won."

"And you wanted to be the one to tell them?" asked Rome, moving up to stand beside him.

Rei shrugged and grinned sheepishly. "You know me and the glory," he said.

"Yes, you are glorious," Rome observed, ruffling his hair. "But I had already informed the Overmind several hours ago. The Vuduri would have spread the word by now in any event."

"Oh," Rei said. He sighed again, closing his eyes for a second.

"Rei, look!" Rome shouted. Rei looked up. Deucado was coming at them at an alarming speed.

"Uh, MINIMCOM, don't you think you should slow down a little bit?" Rei asked.

"No," MINIMCOM replied. "It is not necessary."

"But you are heading straight for the planet," Rome said, more than a little panicked. "Aren't we going into orbit first?"

"I do not do that anymore," said MINIMCOM. "I decided I liked Rei's method of direct entry better." With that, the PPT generators started up with a gentle whine.

"Uh, MINIMCOM, are you sure about this?" Rei asked. "The last time we did it, it was an emergency. We aren't in any kind of hurry now."

"Please trust me," said the computer/spaceplane. "By now you must know I would never endanger either of you. I have practiced this many times and I know what I am doing."

"What about our forward velocity?" Rome asked. "Won't your hull heat up if we enter the atmosphere too quickly?"

A small circle appeared in front of them. It was the beginnings of a PPT tunnel.

"I have calibrated the tunnel so that we will emerge with essentially zero velocity. Please do not concern yourself."

Rei looked at Rome with a slightly horrified expression. Rome shrugged and hurriedly walked around the pilot's seat, buckling herself into the copilot's chair.

"Where are you setting us down?" she asked, ignoring what appeared to be their imminent doom.

"Just to the north of the Ibbrassati community on the eastern edge of Lake Eprehem," replied MINIMCOM. "That is where they are building the spaceport."

"That's great," Rei said through gritted teeth. He reached down and gripped the armrests tightly. MINIMCOM had proven time and again to be a reliable friend and Rei made up his mind that this would be no different.

As the PPT tunnel enlarged, they could see a bright hole appear in front of them. It looked like they were headed straight down. Through the hole were the deep blue waters of Lake Eprehem. A waterspout formed, driving moisture right at them. The sound of the atmosphere and moisture venting out toward them made a whooshing noise.

"What about the ice?" Rei asked, pointing at the windshield.

`"Please give me a little more credit than that."`

In one smooth motion they were through and MINIMCOM closed down the PPT tunnel behind him, effectively eliminating the waterspout. The spaceship leveled out, flying only 100 feet over the suddenly calm waters of the crater lake at a very reasonable speed. Rei had no idea how MINIMCOM was able to shed their substantial velocity but it seemed to work. The front of the ship was pointed east and they could see the eastern shore ahead. MINIMCOM banked left and came in low and fast over the woods just to the north of the Ibbrassati village where Rei was imprisoned in what now seemed such a long time ago.

Ahead of them was a clearing, the beginnings of a landing area for the airships and spacecraft that were now accessible to all. MINIMCOM came to a dead stop centered over the only part of the landing strip that looked paved. He hovered for a moment and rotated in place until his windshield was pointed west again, toward the lake. He extended the landing gear and then lowered his bulk until they landed with the gentlest of bumps.

"That was a hell of a trip, MINIMCOM," Rei said. "Thanks."

`"It was my pleasure,"` replied the former computer.

"Yes, thank you," said Rome as she unbuckled herself.

`"You are very welcome."`

Rei unbuckled himself and took Rome's hand to exit the cockpit. He led Rome aft where they were joined by Fridone and Binoda who was carrying Aason. Binoda handed Aason to Rome and the child put his little arms around her neck. She kissed him and nuzzled his cheek as they made their way to the back of the cargo compartment. When they arrived there, Rei pressed the blue stud to raise the cargo hatch and lower the ramp.

The bright light of Deucado streamed in and Rei held his arm up to shield his eyes. With their advanced optics, the Vuduri passengers had no such problem. Rome reached up and tugged on his arm, trying to pull it down.

"Rei, look," she said insistently.

"Oh no," Rei said, not quite able to see. "Not again."

"No, not again," Rome said. "Different."

Even though his eyes were blurry from the brightness, Rei blinked a few times until his vision cleared. There gathered around their ship were Captain Keller, Pegus, Melloy and a whole host of Vuduri, Essessoni and Ibbrassati. A cheer went up from the crowd, Vuduri included, as the space voyagers made their way down the ramp.

Captain Keller approached them as they reached the ground. He held out his hand for Rei to shake. "Congratulations, Bierak," Keller said. "You did it. You saved us."

"Thank you, sir," Rei said, pumping his hand up and down. "But it was really Rome. And MINIMCOM. And OMCOM. I guess you'd say it was a group effort."

"Regardless of how you apportion credit," said Pegus, "we all appreciate what you did."

Melloy nodded in approval.

Rei released Keller's hand and bent over to whisper in Rome's ear. "I like this kind of reception better."

"Me, too," said his wife, smiling up at him.

"While you were gone, we've been busy," interrupted Keller. "Pegus here was kind enough to loan us some of their aerogel generators." Keller turned and slapped the Vuduri on the back. Pegus did not seem all that thrilled.

Keller continued, "We've started building some housing to the north of the lake. We built the first house for you and your in-laws. We figured you deserved it."

"That is very kind of you," Rome said. "Thank you."

"It's the least we could do," replied Keller. "We all owe you a deep debt of gratitude."

"Yes," said Melloy. "This world is now a better place. We thank ya, too."

"You are welcome," Rei said modestly, putting his arm around his wife and child. "I know it sounds stupid but we had no choice. We just did what we had to do."

"You had a choice," said Pegus. "And you both chose well."

"I agree," said Melloy. He had a broad smile on his face.

"Thank you, all of you," Rome said. She looked around. "Where is Trabunel?" she asked.

"He is with his people to the south, organizing the farmlands," answered Pegus. "Captain Keller has given the Ibbrassati many of his seeds so we will be able to grow some Earth crops."

"We also set up the incubators," Keller added in. "We should have some Earth animals here in a few months."

"However, this is a short-term fix, as there is no reason why we cannot bring supplies and livestock from the Earth ourselves," Pegus said, pointing up to the sky, "now that peace has been restored."

"We've got a plan for how to live," said Keller. "We'll be close enough to help each other but far enough away that we won't interfere. We'll get along just fine. The Deucadons, too."

"We will start small," Melloy said. "But we are comin' up, thanks to ya."

"Good," Rei stated.

"Why don't I take you folks to see your new home?" Keller asked.

"That would be wonderful," Rome said. "I am ready."

Pegus waved to some of the Vuduri and Ibbrassati who brushed past Rei and Rome, swarming up the ramp and quickly returning with their belongings, placing them within one of the flying carts nearby. Keller stepped up into the driver's seat.

After helping his family onboard, Rei turned and activated his EM link to MINIMCOM. *"I guess you're off-duty for a while,"* he thought.

"It would appear to be that way," replied MINIMCOM. "I will go deploy my livetars to start digesting the asteroid and begin creating the security shield. While I am gone, after you and Rome are settled, perhaps you could compile a list of the mandasurte most anxious to return to Earth. And those who would like their families transported here."

"Good idea. Thanks, buddy," said Rei.

"De nada."

Rei laughed at MINIMCOM's attempt at Spanish. He watched as the cargo ramp retracted and the hatch closed. MINIMCOM's powerful EG lifters raised the smooth, sleek starship silently into the air. Heading west, over the lake, MINIMCOM's nose tilted up as he soared into the sky. His plasma thrusters roared to life and in a flash, MINIMCOM vanished from sight.

It took them a little while to reach their new home, which was well north of the fledgling spaceport. After helping them inside with their belongings, Keller was about to leave when he turned to Rei.

"I gotta tell you, Bierak," Keller said, stroking an imaginary beard. "When I first met you, I thought you were sort of a lunatic or at least a screw-up. But you and your little lady really came through for us, our mission."

"Thank you, sir," Rei said. He waved his arms about the house. "And thank you for all of this."

"No problem," said Keller. "I'm sure you want to explore your new house. And get some rest. Tomorrow my group starts with the real work." An odd expression washed over Keller's face. "We have to get to the job we started a long time ago."

"Yes sir," Rei said with a half-salute however Keller did not return the gesture.

Puzzled, Rei tilted his head as he watched Keller drive away.

Later that night, Binoda assisted Rome in putting Aason to sleep then left to join Fridone in the in-law suite. Rome entered their new bedroom to find Rei opening the window. Rome climbed into bed and her husband joined her. It was very quiet. The night air was a calming presence.

Rome turned to Rei and propped herself up on one elbow. "Why am I so tired?" she asked. "We spent most of the voyage here doing nothing. All the issues have been resolved. Do you think I am getting ill?"

Rei laughed and put his arms around her, cradling her. "No, Miss Saver-of-the-universe. What you are doing is finally relaxing. It's what home is all about. You've earned it."

Rome closed her eyes, nestled even closer and breathed a happy sigh. "I love you, mau emir," she whispered.

"I love you, too, Romey," he said, kissing the top of her head.

"Rei," she said breathily as she drifted off.

"Yes, honey?"

"Do you remember when we had my first birthday? The candle? You told me to make a wish."

"Sure, I remember. Why?" Rei asked.

"You made me promise to not tell you what the wish was for. You said that would make it not come true."

"That's the way it is with all wishes."

"Well, you were right but it no longer matters," mused Rome.

"Why?"

Rome replied, "Because everything that I wished for has now come true."

"That's great, sweetheart," Rei said, kissing her forehead lovingly. "I am very happy for you. Now close your eyes and go to sleep."

Rome sighed contentedly and did just that.

A Preview of *The Ark Lords*

(Two years after the events in *Rome's Revolution 3455 AD*)

THE TRIP BACK TO THE LANDING STRIP DID NOT SEEM TO TAKE nearly as long as the journey out to the combination shrine/museum. MINIMCOM was still parked on the airfield with his landing gear extended. As they approached, he lifted his cargo hatch and lowered the ramp. Rome led the way into the ship with Rei and Virga right behind. The two women that had accompanied them also came aboard. It was quite crowded in MINIMCOM's cockpit with the five of them filing in. Rome sat down in the pilot's seat and slid the long-lost slab into MINIMCOM's data reader. The display lit up as MINIMCOM accessed the slab's contents. However, no words appeared.

"Can you read it?" Rome asked worriedly.

"`Yes and no,`" said MINIMCOM. "`I can access the internal data however it is heavily encrypted.`"

"Can you decrypt it?" Rei asked.

"`Please!`" MINIMCOM objected. "`If I had feelings, I would be highly insulted! However, it might take a little while before I find the proper ciphers.`"

"How long?" Rome asked.

"`I do not know,`" replied MINIMCOM. "`I will tell you when I have completed the task. I assure you it will not be long.`"

Rome spun in the seat and looked up at Virga.

"Is this an inconvenience to you? Do you mind if we just wait here until MINIMCOM decrypts it?"

"We do not mind at all. You can take as long as you want. In fact, you may keep the slab permanently," Virga said.

Rome was confused. "We do not need to keep it," she said. "As soon as MINIMCOM decrypts it and downloads the data you can have it back."

"We do not need it back. You may have it. We will trade you for it."

Rome stood up from her seat. "Trade it for what?" she asked, her eyes narrowing.

"For him," Virga said, pointing at Rei.

"I, I, I do not understand," Rome stuttered.

Virga looked at her with a deadly serious expression. "Our planet is full of pure-bred Vuduri with a particularly strong diploid variant of the 24th chromosome. Almost all of our babies are born now with all the traits of the Onsiras. Living machines. We need to correct the genetic errors and soon or we will become the very thing we abhor. That is why we need him, his seed." She pointed at Rei's groin.

"You cannot," Rome protested.

"Oh we can," said Virga firmly. "We have determined that the only way to combat the genetic drift and push our species back toward humanity is to infuse our 24 chromosome complement with the 23 chromosome set of the mandasurte. Half-breed mosdureces, like yourself. The more primitive the better. And what could be more primitive than a living Essessoni?"

"No!" Rome said, moving over to Rei. "You cannot have him. He is mine."

The two women behind Virga stepped beside her and pulled out hand plasma projectors, aiming them directly at Rome's head.

"Perhaps I made it seem as if you had a choice in the matter," Virga responded forcefully. "Let me clarify. We *are* taking him. Your only choice is whether you wish to leave here alive or not."